The
GETTIN PLACE

BOOKS BY SUSAN STRAIGHT

Aquaboogie
I Been in Sorrow's Kitchen and Licked Out All the Pots
Blacker Than a Thousand Midnights
The Gettin Place
Highwire Moon

The
GETTIN PLACE

Susan Straight

ANCHOR BOOKS
A DIVISION OF RANDOM HOUSE, INC.
New York

FIRST ANCHOR BOOKS EDITION, AUGUST 1997

Copyright © 1996 by Susan Straight

Library of Congress Cataloging-in-Publication Data
Straight, Susan.
        The gettin place / Susan Straight.—1st Anchor Books ed.
        p.   cm.
        1. Afro-American families—Oklahoma—Tulsa—History—20th century—
Fiction.   2 Afro-Americans—Oklahoma—Tulsa—Fiction.   3. Family—
Oklahoma—Tulsa—Fiction.   4. Tulsa (Okla.)—Fiction.   I. Title.
PS3569.T6795G48   1997
813'.54—dc21   97-10888
CIP

ISBN 0-385-48659-6
ISBN-13: 978-0-385-48659-0
Designed by Jill Gogal

www.anchorbooks.com

Printed in the United States of America

10   9   8   7   6   5   4   3   2

To the memory of Alberta Marie Sims: I miss your smile and stories and endless generosity; and the memories of Lanier and Mozelle Sims and Minerva Andrews, all Tulsa people.

I owe thanks to many: Dwayne Sims (as always), Richard Parks and Pat Mulcahy, the Holly Robinson Writer's Workshop, General Sims, Gail and John Watson, Arnold and Evelyn Williams, Clarice and Jesse Lee Collins, Percival Everett, Rob Bauman, Ben Sanchez, Brenda Richardson, and the countless relatives and friends who tell me stories.

All characters and events, aside from major historical figures and incidents, are fictional.

September 1991

PROLOGUE

THE SWEET, BLOOD-LADEN smoke, clinging with the sheen of hair oil and soot, reached into the dark room of his dreaming, and Hosea saw the ruffled-thin mouth of the boy who had hit him with the rifle butt. The wood was meant for his temple, but Hosea had ducked and the shoulder blow had sent him into the dirt road where the pale boy came down hard, full on his flat hand with the heavy boot, grinding, pushing the sharp cinder deep inside his child-soft palm.

Hosea didn't open his eyes. No, he told himself calmly. Not Tulsa. You on your own place. Rio Seco. You smellin somebody's campfire in the riverbottom. Your fireplace been out—feel cool enough in here that you ain't gotta look.

In the small coldhouse he and Salcido had built of river rock forty-one years ago, when Hosea was thirty-five and just married, he slept each night near the fireplace he'd added for himself much later, after his fifth son was born and he'd begun to escape from the night-mingled breaths and baby cries in the main house. No smoked hams or dried chiles or olive jars crowded the hollow spaces in the stone walls now. It was a warm house for him in winter. The plum wood he stacked outside was so hard and seasoned that one thigh-thick burl would burn hard, subside into gray, and often leap back into flame long after midnight, startling him from sleep.

But he heard no heat glistening in the ashes now, and no waves of warmth breathed onto his right side. He felt the pleasant morning cool prickle his face. Not like Oklahoma—that bone-chalking chill on his grandfather's farm, scraped-thin flannel rags around him at night, afraid to move his nose an inch from the mask he'd made of an old shirt.

He blinked, but the film of dawn and dreaming began to cover his irises again, and in the shifting gray he saw smoke rising from burned foundations of houses, wreathing the iron bedsteads that crouched like spiders in the rubble, and he felt the throbbing heat in his shoulder where the boy had poked him again with the rifle to make him walk. He followed the raised hands of the men in line before him, trying to look sideways for his father among the sprawled figures on the ground, some with ashes piled on their charred coats.

Without shuddering, without blinking now, he breathed in the faint smoke drifting from the burning Tulsa dream through the slit of open window above his bed. Hosea closed his mouth, pulled the smell fast into his nostrils, and turned his good-hearing ear, the left one, toward the tiny window. A pair of voices spiraled thin somewhere among the trees on his land.

Propping his hand on the cool stones, he stood quickly, listening, and then he pushed open the heavy door to see the house where his wife, Alma, her grandmother, and the grandchildren were sleeping. In the half-moon's light, the deep turquoise star shape on one of the adobe walls still made him blink; Alma had been talking about painting the house a few months ago. The dark-blue patch looked like a gaping hole. But no smoke rose from the chimney, and no glow lit the windows in the purple night that was almost finished.

It was too early for his two oldest sons to be gathering for coffee, smoking Swisher Sweets while they pried open their eyes. And the other men, the mechanics and rim polishers and talkers, wouldn't come for hours. Behind the trees dangling with chains to lift engines, the huge stone barn across the yard was dim and gray, the metal sliding door still shut.

Hosea rubbed his forehead, feeling the almost morning moisture rising from the nearby riverbottom. It was not yet dawn. The coyotes' whirling messages were long finished, and the crows hadn't started their early arguments. The wafting smell must have been the dream again, the dream of Tulsa burning, the same ashen days he'd been seeing in his sleep for . . . He pressed hard fingertips against the bones of his temples. Seventy years.

He'd seen fires in the riverbottom last summer, and nearly a year

ago, the Rio Seco sky had turned black from the huge Grayglen blaze.
Last month, a cigarette ember flipped by a speeding commuter had
ignited the palm fronds woven into his chain-link fence. Right by the
front gate, where the men parked, the dry fronds had blazed into a
fringed wall of licking red, and everyone had run from the barn with
fire extinguishers and hoses. The fence was charred, bare mesh now.

The voices were so faint that Hosea couldn't make out the direction.
Could be his two middle sons, who usually slept in the trailers near the
olive grove. Hosea wondered if he should walk the fences. He wouldn't
get back to sleep now anyway; he seemed to need less sleep each year.
Sometimes, when the mockingbirds or coyotes woke him, he built up
the fire and sat in the coldhouse staring at the embers until morning.
Sometimes he saw his friend Lanier, who needed less sleep now, too,
since his wife had passed and he'd moved to Treetown. Lanier had been
wanting a small piece of Hosea's or his brother's land to raise a few
pigs.

He tried to see across the shallow ravine to the olive grove, but mist
hung lightly in the branches—not fog that would shroud the whole
city, but airy wet that swirled along only on the wide riverbed, cloaking
the trees. His five acres were covered with trees, and he liked the veiling
mist in winter, the steady, softened drip of rain, and the deep shade in
summer. He looked up into the huge pepper tree, where the chains
swung gently in a breath of wind. Back at the coldhouse, Hosea pulled
his dark-green work jacket and huge key ring from the wooden chair
and then knelt beside the bed, pausing. His wife's grandmother, who
spoke only Spanish, had been trying to describe for him strangers she'd
seen in the hills nearby, and Hosea knew she didn't mean the homeless
Vietnam vets who'd lived in the riverbottom for years now, because
she didn't circle her ear with her tiny brown forefinger. He reached
under the narrow bed for the old .22 rifle.

The older tow truck was parked on the other side of the barn, where
he'd always kept it so that the rumbling start of the engine wouldn't
wake Alma and the kids on a night job. But now Demetrius, his oldest
son, had the newer flatbed tow truck parked at his house, and he took
care of all the night calls. Hosea stopped beside the barn to turn up his
jacket collar, the gun cradled in his bent arm. He remembered the
Proudfoot boys, the ones around Demetrius's age, and how they had
called themselves Midnight Auto Supply. Back then, in the seventies,

Hosea had patrolled the yard and storage lot with the rifle, trying to keep the Proudfoots and their hoodlum friends away from fenders and batteries and Pinto doors.

He let himself smile when he walked down the wide dirt road he'd cleared years ago. About ten Proudfoots lived over there in Olive Gardens back when it was farmworker housing, back when he and Alma had lived there, too. And Demetrius and Octavious, his two oldest, had fought them all, fought every boy in Treetown at one time or another. Now Demetrius had a new house across the riverbottom, and he needed more money. He wanted Hosea to get Arrow Towing on the police rotation, advertise in the Yellow Pages, not with one line but with a picture ad.

But Hosea knew that the cops remembered Octavious from his most famous fight, the one with a deputy's son, in high school. And he knew too many police who hated Oscar, his only brother, who ran a barbecue joint next door to him.

The breeze pushed at his face again, coming off the hill, and he knew a stronger wind would blow all the moisture from the air after the sun came up. He headed left, toward the rear of the five acres where the ancient olive grove slanted up the base of the hill. His wife's grandmother often sat in the old stone olive shed, where the curing vats were, even after the season's olives were sold. Abuela was past ninety, and she slept as lightly as Hosea did, but he knew she hadn't gone to the grove this early because he always heard the creak of the wooden kitchen screen door and then her hesitant shoes on the gravel.

On a small flat clearing before the road reached the trees were two old Airstream trailers, camouflaged silvery in the mist. Julius and Finis, his third and fourth sons, were meant to be guarding the property when they slept here, but they weren't capable of much. Finis had burned up his brain with a drug-soaked cigarette years ago, and Julius only used his brain fully when trying to get some jelly roll. Hosea figured that's who the higher, nervous voice could have been just a few minutes ago: some woman arguing with Julius about what he had or hadn't promised her. Jelly roll. Oscar sang about jelly roll late at night, when most of the women had gone home and only the men sat in his barbecue joint, drinking and thinking about quivering, rubbing thighs.

Hosea couldn't hear voices now, and no music came from the trailer where Finis usually slept. Finis needed music to breathe, and his radio drumbeats usually made Julius leave the woman in his trailer to stalk across the dirt with a pair of Walkman headphones. Finis lost headphones weekly, and people knew that if they came to the tow yard to trade something with Julius, a rim-polishing job or spare car part, they should bring headphones.

Julius must have been sleeping at a woman's. Hosea looked at the two trailers, shuttered tight and ringed all around with eucalyptus that dripped their long, gray leaves onto the curved rooflines.

He leaned against the cool metal walls for a moment. Who the hell knew where Finis was sleeping? The man was over thirty now, and stopped in the head at eighteen, when that chemical smoke had dropped a gauzy red film over his eyes and loosened drumbeats in his skull. But some of these crazy Treetown women still must have let him sleep somewhere.

Hosea held the gun loosely, breathing in the fragrant oil of eucalyptus. The noises must have been coming from Oscar's place. The wide eucalyptus windbreak, beginning with these huge trees, separated his land from Oscar's, along with the six-foot stone wall Hosea had built after the coldhouse. When Hosea walked into the closest gap between the pale trunks as thick around as two men's ringed arms, he thought that maybe the smell had come from there, too. He pushed at the iron-barred gate.

The barbecue joint and attached house were in the front of the property, and way in the back, among more eucalyptus and some wild, abandoned olive, Oscar brewed liquor—hard stuff and the thick brown choc beer he'd learned to make back in Oklahoma. But Oscar only sold it by the glass, inside the house, and he had his own men who watched the place. Hosea paused at the edge of his brother's land, half-hiding behind a tree, scanning the folding chairs and barbecue pit. He'd thought Oscar might have been up and cooking early, sending some strong pig smoke through the breeze and working on extra cases of ribs for the Friday-night crowd.

Back toward the steep hill that bordered their property, the long ridge of rocky land separating them from downtown Rio Seco, was the thick stand of eucalyptus where Oscar made the choc. Hosea stared at the trunks nearly glowing under their mist-garlanded branches. The choc beer used to be murky and dark in the huge glasses his father drank from, back in Tulsa; his father would take him to the tiny house off Greenwood where men sat close at small tables, each pouring a heaped tablespoon of sugar into the quart jars until the beer came frothing to life.

The trunk near his face was as smooth as skin, the shed bark under his shoes crackling long strips. Hosea remembered how strange these trees looked to him when he came to Rio Seco. In Oklahoma, the tree trunks were rough and dark—oak and pecan and sycamore. Then he'd followed Oscar to Los Angeles, where there were only palms, it seemed, among the tiny stucco boxes where he'd rented rooms. Palms that swayed, distant above postage-stamp plots of grass and wavering heat and hard faces. The first time someone had told him about Rio Seco, out in the country to the east, he'd thought that the man, a welder at the assembly plant where Hosea worked, was talking about more palm trees, a scrawny forest of bare trunks in desert sand. But when he came to Treetown and saw the orange groves lush and blooming, the olives and eucalyptus shimmering silver, and the pecans and cottonwoods along the riverbottom, he felt the cords in his neck loosen and he breathed the strange, shaded scents.

Sound traveled thick and caught in the wet mist when it clung like this. He heard the voices again, and the strongest one, when he turned his head and held his lungs closed to let it register, was white. He walked quickly from the trees and back to the trailers, to the road leading down to his storage lot. The only white people who came around this part of Treetown were commuters or dumpers.

The stream of commuter cars that had begun two years ago when all the new developments were built outside the city wasn't yet whining along the street this morning. Every weekday, they tried to avoid downtown freeway congestion by racing down Pepper Avenue, screech-slipping to a stop at the sign on the corner by his place, then accelerating like hundreds of bees to speed down the riverbottom road toward a distant on-ramp that took them to the bridge, toward all the new developments, then farther west, toward Los Angeles.

Hosea stopped at the bare welter where the trail to the olive grove and the wider, tire-packed road to the car-storage lot made a gravel-strewn crossing. He spat morning thick from his throat and listened again. He'd heard his youngest son, Marcus, do perfect white-man voices, playing around on the phone or making his brothers laugh. But Marcus lived downtown.

The dumpers came out at night, broke people who left couches and

concrete and cats along the riverbottom road or on the bench of earth
along his fence because they didn't want to pay the high county dump
fees, and because the law turned its back on trash in Treetown. Or
maybe the voices were white teenagers drinking beer and playing that
chainsaw music in the riverbed. But when he started down the slope
toward the lot, he heard a laugh, a *huh-huh-huh* boy laugh, and then a
muffled scream.

If the short, thickened call had been a wounded owl or even a dog—
but mist-dulled dawn wasn't the time for hunting. No sharp sound rent
the air again, but he thought he heard a faint rustling, a popping.

He ran into the thick stand of pepper trees cresting the slope. On
the faint trail cushioned by leaves and pepper berries, where none of
the kids ever ventured to hide now, he stared ahead, listening for the
direction of the scream. By the time he'd reached his rusted chair, from
where he could see the whole riverbottom laid out in a darkened belt
of cane and cottonwoods, the shots punctured the mist, two rounds
ringing close and small-caliber.

The shots hadn't come from Oscar's place. And the Olive Gardens
low-income apartments, where gunfire frequently pocked the night and
echoed all over Treetown, were blocks eastward across Pepper Avenue.
These shots were near the storage lot. Maybe a Mexican down there
huntin wild pig, Hosea thought. Maybe one a them Vietnam vets gone
wild in the cane. He moved slowly through the trees toward the slope.

The smoke gathered heavier when he descended the slope, and he
saw the glow when he rounded the bend near the huge cottonwood
and ancient Apache truck marking the edge of the storage lot. Crouching
behind the chalky hood of the Apache, he thought, Why some fool
light up a car? He want it, and he think he gon get by the boys, why
he didn't take it? Ain't nobody stole a whole car in a good while, and
who the hell start a fire?

He lifted his head cautiously over the big truck hood, blinking in
the fierce light of the burning car, and heard the sheeting roar of flame.
The frame was barely visible through the leaping tongues of red and
orange. The '78 Ford Granada, the car closest to the gate—that's what
he thought it was. He came around to the road, cutting through the
patchwork of cars, still crouching, and the scrape of metal parts—
someone starting an ignition—shrieked through the fence. Hosea ran
to the wide gate, the .22 raised, but he stopped abruptly, his forehead

tight. The gate was still locked. Fanning the keys with his fingers, he popped the lock. When he swung the gate toward himself, he heard the engine roar, and a sharp, pearly elbow hung from the passenger window of a black Jeep that raised dust as it swung around in the field across the riverbottom road: a male elbow, slightly bulbous above the wide bone. Hosea saw a fringy tail of yellow hair slapping the Jeep's roof, flipping out the open window when the tires spun.

Hosea crouched and looked through the diamond loop of wire his grandfather had taught him to fix on the target. He shot three times while the Jeep fishtailed again and came past him, rounding the road's curve at the hills and heading toward the freeway, leaving only the sound of flames cracking door and roof and bone.

He could smell the people inside the Granada. The scream—had he heard a woman? Pressing his tongue hard to the roof of his mouth, he forced himself near the fire for a moment, slitting his eyes, but even then the heat forced his head down long enough to see a glint of gold in the dirt near the passenger door. He squatted, snatched the necklace, and the flames, too high and thick now to reveal anything in the car, drove him back across the asphalt to the field.

No gas in the tank, he thought, breathing hard. Car been there for years. But the fire gon spread to the other cars, get on them palm fronds and head all up in the trees. Everything dry as hell from the drought. He fingered the gold chain without taking his eyes from the car, shielding his face now from the rippling heat, the glistening smell. No water down here to put it out, he thought, turning to run through his lot and up to the house to call emergency.

When the roaring sound of a powerful engine came from the other way, around the corner from Pepper Avenue and hurtling along his fence line, he froze against the blank space of field, and as the headlights swept up close, he raised the .22 again, looking for the head behind glass. They comin back for me, they goin out, too, he thought. I'ma take one with me this time.

But the wide roof was as black as slate, the white door gleaming, visible now, and the thick wrists behind the police-issue .357 were the last thing he saw before he raised his head, before the bullet tore into his shoulder and threw him into the soft wild oats.

CHAPTER ONE

WHEN THE SCENT of the flowering apricot tree brushing against her bedroom window mixed with the milk-pearled breath of her new grandbaby, Alma would lie half-awake before dawn and dream that Sofelia whispered into her dampened neck.

Her baby girl. Sofelia murmured about the boy she'd fallen in love with, the one who'd taken her away, a boy who buried his long fingers in the thick, wavy hair at her nape that Alma had combed each night and who cradled her head on his chest now.

Her last baby, her only girl, and Alma had always slept beside her, half-dreaming and half-vigilant for the chills or mosquitoes or dreams that might harm her. And when Sofelia had finally asked to sleep in her own bed, it seemed it was only months later that she'd disappeared.

When Alma heard the faint, hoarse cry somewhere outside, distant and short, she nearly wept at the silence trailing behind.

Alma knew her new grandbaby Jalima's breath was regular and warm near her elbow, but every morning when her ears turned empty and her eyes sifted out the dark, the loss she felt made her breastbone into a brittle chalk stripe.

She waited for the stinging to rise into the base of her throat, as it always did, and to distract herself, she whispered, "What you gon cook today?" Was she asking herself? Or Sofelia? Then she heard the metallic reports pinging through the lessening dark, and she thought her own grandmother must have already gotten to the kitchen, settling full, cast-iron pots onto the burners to ring sharp like hammer beats. Alma sat up on the edge of the bed, tracing the line of ache in the long bone over her heart.

The three loud pops sounded like backfires from the old trucks Hosea's friends drove, and she patted the pillows around the bed's edges so the baby couldn't fall, thinking she'd better make extra sausage. She opened her bedroom door, pulling one of Hosea's old shirts around her. He hadn't slept in this room for a long time, since Sofelia, but she liked the smell of his cigarillos and coffee and skin. Then she noticed that Abuela's door was still closed; if her grandmother was up and about, the door was always propped open with a basket of dried rose petals.

Alma started down the white-plastered hallway, trailing her hand along the cool walls even though she knew this glowing tunnel by heart, and at the last bedroom door, her oldest grandson, Kendrick, stood. "Somebody shootin, Gramma," he said, his hands clenched to fists near his sides.

Alma frowned. "You think so?" she asked, peering past him to see his younger brother Jawan, who was only three, still wrapped in blankets. Then she heard an echoing, louder report that seemed closer.

"Shot," Kendrick insisted, following her into the long living room, dark and shadowed. Alma stood looking through the lace panels over the big window, but she saw no one in the gravel yard that sloped down to the fence and front gate and Pepper Avenue. The living room's formal back faced the avenue, and its glass-paned doors led out to the courtyard.

"Go get your papa," Alma told Kendrick. She wondered if Hosea was awake. Kendrick's fingers were long and ginger gold on the lace curtains, all of him longer and taller since he'd turned ten, and she saw him bite his lips. He think his daddy's in trouble again, Alma thought. Julius made plenty of men angry at how easily women followed him home, and sometimes the women were enraged that they couldn't stay in the silver trailer forever.

When Kendrick came back, Alma was still standing there clutching the shirt around her, somehow remembering pot lids clanging roundly onto bubbling and laughter. "He ain't in his house," Kendrick said, and Alma heard shouting, faint through the trees.

She opened the front door, standing on the damp gravel in her bare feet, hearing the distant whine of a helicopter racing toward her. The faint outline in the lightened eastern sky looked like a tiny electric mixer, its handlelike tail stiff, sparks flashing from silver beaters.

An accident on Pepper Avenue, she told herself, seeing the beam knife down onto the riverbottom road and the helicopter begin to circle as if rotating in the grip of a giant hand. She and Kendrick began to run.

When they reached the corner of Pepper and the riverbottom road, she saw skeins of red twirling among the pepper branches: three sirens, sitting atop carelessly parked sheriff's cars, the pulsing lights looking festive and toylike. When she saw Hosea, his boots pointing to the branches, his arm lying outstretched in the sandy edge of the road, his head hidden in the weeds, she began to scream, tearing off the shirt as she ran so that she could hold it over the spongy bloom of blood.

Two of the men whirled around with guns drawn, but she kept running, even when she heard Kendrick cry out and drop to the ground, the light thud of his chest on the roadside like a moth against glass.

When the stiff palm rested against her collarbone, stopping her forward movement, she closed her eyes so she wouldn't see the official face at arm's length from hers. Alma waited, hearing the harsh voices mingle with the spitting radios. An officer moved his shoes on the asphalt: "I thought it was a fuckin gang banger, baggy-ass khakis and big jacket. Shit, it's a fuckin old guy."

"That's his wife," she heard a softer voice call, and she recognized it, the voice she'd been praying for, Salcido's boy, who was a policeman.

"It's okay, son, get up," Tony Salcido said to Kendrick, and then his hands were on her back, helping her forward to Hosea.

His neck was ashen. She crouched in the tall weeds. His mouth was carved tight, and the sound of sirens trailed down Pepper Avenue while she tried to wad the shirt over his bloody shoulder. Another policeman squatted beside her. "He can't be moved, now; you shouldn't do anything till the EMTs get here, ma'am."

The ambulance men kneeled then and lifted Hosea on a stiff board. Alma gasped, and the Salcido boy's hand was at her back again. "He's just injured, Mrs. Thompson; that's how they transport someone injured."

Alma saw the burning car now, the jack-o'-lantern glow of fire through the windows and the fire engine pushing near. Men trained hoses onto the car, which faded to black.

Alma told them she'd heard only the shots. Yes, she and the injured man were married. No, he hadn't been asleep in the house. He had his own place. No, they hadn't argued. He hadn't argued with anyone. No, she didn't know anything about his gun. Or the fire. Alma looked up from the distant jimsonweed where she'd fixed her eyes. She saw smoke lingering over the storage lot, men walking along the fence line, and one figure bent near the smoldering car. He stood and shouted, "Hey, we got two bodies here! Goddamnit, Salcido, call EMT back. This looks like coroner's OT."

Alma's knees loosened like a doll's when she heard him, and she thought, Julius, Finis, somebody done got em from the trailers. God, what them boys did? She felt Kendrick pull away from her, and she knew he was thinking the same thing.

The deputy walked toward Salcido, holding his hand over his mouth, then rubbing his bent-back wrist around his forehead. "Looks like women," he said. "Two women burnt all to hell."

The stairways were dim and steep, the night smell of cement still trapped by shadow, but when Marcus reached the courtyard of his apartment building and glanced back at his window, knowing he'd forgotten something, the wind had begun to clear the mist from the huge arched panes.

He hesitated near the curved wrought-iron railing that lined all the stairways. He'd already been to the gym when it opened at six A.M., walking the two blocks in the darkness. When he'd come back, his red message light flashed, and he'd known it could only be one of his brothers calling that early. Damn sure wasn't a woman. He was fresh out of females since Colette had moved back to Chicago. When he'd pressed the button, his mother's voice was, as always, uncomfortable on the machine. "Marcus? Marcus," she said. That was all she ever said to the empty space before she hung up.

Then he heard his oldest brother, Demetrius, after another beep. "Marcus. Marcus! Shit." His voice was ragged and impatient, as always, and he hung up, too.

Marcus didn't want to call either of them back. He was heading over there now anyway. And walking, goddamnit—he couldn't believe it.

He leaned against the railing for a moment. He'd left Demetrius's navy work shirt on the bed, the one he'd borrowed last week when he'd changed the oil on the Lexus at his father's place, more for show than anything else. "Hell," Marcus said softly, turning toward the court-yard. "I had that bad boy dry-cleaned just so Demetrius wouldn't talk shit, but I'm not carryin it all the way to Treetown."

He smiled at the thought of chemical creases and plastic wrap on the Dickies work shirt. Now Demetrius couldn't say, "Why you bring me back a dirty shirt and make more work for my wife, man?" Demetrius still loved to call Enchantee "my wife" in front of Marcus, even after eight years, because Marcus had loved her first. Marcus rubbed the razored line of his fresh-cut fade, remembering Demetrius dressing to go out, back when Marcus was in junior high and Demetrius was grown. The silky, long-pointed collars lay on the bed like bent wings, and Demetrius would spit from the doorway, "Don't let them grubby fingers touch nothin, boy. Only lady fingers touch them shirts." Marcus would watch the shimmering Qiana patterns stretch across the wide shoulders, feeling his own bony elbows hang from the plain white T-shirts all five boys usually wore. Marcus was the baby boy. That was what their lips popped scornfully all day: "*Ba*-by boy. Sissyfly. Go head on and bawl."

But when you thirty and he's almost forty, ten years ain't hardly nothin, Marcus thought, smiling again. Three negatives. Our favorite way to use em; that's what Brother Lobo used to say. Africans always emphasize.

He walked along the curving cement wall. Brother Lobo's black history class at Rio Seco High had changed his life, altered the way he saw everything from his father's chicken coop to his friends' insults. Lobo had been his idol for years, even after Marcus had come back from college to see him nearly blind at forty-five from glaucoma, barely able to play dominoes at Jackson Park. If Marcus didn't get any class assignments next week at Rio Seco High, where he'd only been teaching for a year, which of his flat-eyed freshmen would even remember him?

It could have been one of his students who stole the Lexus, for all he knew. He crossed the darkened courtyard, where the slow dawn hadn't reached through the three giant palms growing from circles cut in the cement. Las Palmas was the best apartment building in this historic downtown district. Marcus looked at the facade, the arches and gargoyles and hand-painted tile apartment numbers. It was taking him long green, longer than those palm fronds, to pay the rent on number 24 and the lease note on the Lexus, and now here he was walking, just like any wandering Treetown brother. Like his own brother Finis. The rest of them would bust up laughing when they found out about his car.

Leaving the arched entry, he moved his eyes casually up and down the street for patrol cars. A brother strolling this district at dawn was always an intriguing sight for law enforcement, even if he was wearing a J. Crew pullover and chinos, not sagging-to-the-sidewalk khakis. He stopped at the corner, thinking again of Demetrius's shirt. Demetrius talked big yang about Marcus's clothes, his apartment, his car. "My baby bro got him a *sherbert* car—a damn Lexus," Demetrius would laugh, and the men in the barn, working on engines and rims, would laugh, too.

"The ride's maroon," Marcus would say easily, knowing that the mangled pastel word didn't have a damn thing to do with the paint job.

As of yesterday, the ride was history, he thought, just like all this. He passed the museum, the newly renovated opera house, and the new coffee bars and bakeries catering to the crowds growing every month since downtown was no longer "redeveloping" but had become "The Historic Moorish District." The garden district had flowery yards, the Victorian district three-story gingerbread mansions; now the Moorish district had all its buildings and facades restored or newly faked with creamy plaster, red-tiled roofs, grillwork scrolling, and fountains.

The Lexus was history as of last weekend. Somebody else's story now, a quick tale to tell. Yo, man, we plucked this Casper's Lexus, from downtown, and you know that dude in San Bernardino needed him some Lexus parts? He got em now. . . .

The only brother in the building, Marcus thought, and they gotta steal my hooptie. The insurance adjustor sure thought the thieves were brothers. In his halting-hard accent, maybe Boston, the man had said, "Mr. ah, Thompson?"

"Yes," Marcus had said carefully.

"Your Lexus was stolen from outside your residence on Las Palmas Drive?"

"Yes."

The voice shifted, emanating conspiratorial sympathy. "Well, the police found your vehicle stripped, in a lot off Olive Street. Do you know where that is?"

Treetown. Marcus played along with the clucking pity in the voice. "Way down there, huh?" he said, biting off his consonants.

"Not hard to guess some nice young riverbottom gentlemen have, ah, distributed the parts by now. Well, I'll send you the forms, and you'll get them back to me, right?"

"Sure," Marcus said, rounding that *r* hard. "Did they tow the car yet?"

"I'm not sure." The voice turned cautious.

"I'll take care of it. My father runs Arrow Towing. Off Pepper Avenue. *Way* down there by the riverbottom, about as way as it gets."

Marcus turned on California Boulevard, which ran the length of downtown and went all the way north past the university and the airport. He passed mouth after mouth of gated, dark parking caves. The brothers took my hooptie and didn't even check the glove compartment fulla tapes, he thought. Robin Harris. Richard Pryor. What white dude's gon have *Bicentennial Nigger* and some old BarKays and Cameo? No solidarity, man.

He was hoping his brothers wouldn't be at the yard when he asked his father to lend him a car. He needed transportation by Monday. Coming out of the chilled, ghostly corridor of banks and office buildings, Marcus blinked in the glare from the sliver of sun reflecting off the mirrored towers gathered at the corner of California and Pepper Avenue. The city was trying to attract companies to the newly built Los Arbolitos business park, with its spindly, just planted jacarandas and orange trees. Marcus listened to the fountain splashing around the huge concrete sign. A flapping banner advertised office space from one of the towers. The problem with vacancies, according to what Marcus read in the newspaper and heard in downtown conversations, was that although Los Arbolitos was attractive, it was at the edge of "a transitional area." In other words, this section of Pepper Avenue was too damn close to the Westside, and, even worse, to Treetown.

Down there. No, Treetown wasn't south, he thought. Due west. But it felt like down to them. He'd heard newscasters say the same thing about South-Central L.A. "Down in the south-central part of the city today, robbery claimed a life . . ." And in Rio Seco, people in restaurants said, "You're heading down there through Treetown? Yeah, it's a shortcut to the freeway, but . . ."

Marcus waited at a stoplight on Pepper, looking at the blurred territorial edges. A long stretch of vacant lot, barely needled with winter grass among the broken glass and snowy Styrofoam bits, led to the slope of the arroyo that meandered through the city, spilling into the riverbottom not far from his father's place. Marcus and his brothers used to travel up the arroyo every day to find aluminum cans and other boys and fights in the Westside, sometimes even clambering up the banks and venturing downtown. Back then, downtown was half-deserted, but the cops still knew within a few minutes if a knot of Treetown boys walked up Pepper Avenue past a certain point.

He was near that certain point right now, he thought, smiling. It was a small, bare street marked with nothing but a scatter of green foxtails growing around the silver-edged hole where the sign pole had been knocked out by a car. The city had conveniently neglected to replace the sign, which used to read Gray Lane and lead down a long slant to the collection of houses called Gray Hollow, old shacks, really, that used to house citrus workers like his parents. Adjacent to the old houses, the last of which had just been bulldozed last year, was Jackson Park. The city had razed the houses and flattened all the tree-covered lots nearby, then fenced in the park with chain link and only one gate after a shooting that had wounded Brother Lobo and killed a young brother named Louis Wiley. Now some of the men that used to congregate under the pepper trees in the lot, playing dominoes and drinking, gathered in his uncle's barbecue joint.

Marcus crossed the street. The city was just as happy to leave this little lane to natives only, who had to want to get to the Westside this way. Commuters could stay on the avenue and go to work. They didn't need to venture down that slope. He grinned at the thought of his father and brothers watching the steady stream of cars passing their lot, remembering one day when traffic backed up and they sat in the yard laughing at the stoic, panicked faces briefly robbed of motion, almost out of Treetown.

The blue strip mall, a collection of tiny stores segmented like a long caterpillar crawling beside the avenue, was the uneasy outpost in this no-man's land. Marcus knew the businesses, a dry cleaner, a video store, a liquor store, nail salon, and doughnut shop, all depended on the commuters and downtown, and the owners were probably holding their breaths waiting for more commercial development between them and Los Arbolitos.

Marcus always stopped at the Donut Place, where the Cambodian owner, Som, made the best pillowy-soft glazed doughnuts in the city. But not today, he thought. Last week, Som had pushed forward a thin, sullen boy he said was his nephew. "Remember him, Teacha? He come last year from the camp. He go to the school, take your class now, okay? He need to learn so much." The boy had looked away. "He don't want get up one o'clock to make doughnut, he have to go to school, right, Teacha?"

I'm not a teacher today. I'm a walkin brother, Marcus thought. From here to the overpass, the sidewalk along Pepper was edged in another vacant lot. Everything in a long corridor had been torn down back when the city built the freeway, in 1960, the year he was born. His father and uncle said that Westside and Treetown used to merge together in one black neighborhood, and this was where the stores and barbershop and a bar had been. "Used to couldn't tell," his uncle Oscar would always say. "Niggas was niggas. But the Westside was city cats, lot of em worked for the aircraft plants. And Treetown was country. That's what they called us. But they came over here to drink, I'ma tell you that."

The overpass was a block away, as gray and curved as a huge rattler dusty from the hills. The pastel-pink bungalows of the Kozy Komfort Inn were like dollhouses from this distance, all in a straight line among short palms with fanned fronds. You'd expect to see the shimmering blue pool and girls in bikinis, way back in the fifties.

But the pool was filled in, the motel grounds defined by chain link topped with barbed wire. Usher Price sat on a folding chair outside the bungalow at the end that used to be the motel office.

When he saw Marcus, he slid through the propped-open sliding gate, squinting in the faint light under a palm. Marcus slowed his pace; he passed here driving every now and then, but never walking. He didn't know what to expect, what Usher might say or do, since it had been years since he'd seen him. Maybe since a few years out of high school, and Usher had smoked way too many Super Kools, cigarettes dipped in liquid PCP: same thing as his brother Finis.

"Say, man, Marcus? Hella long time," Usher said, close now, his eyes watery with what looked like weak tea, his thick hair combed straight back from his scarred forehead and patted down to a spongy flare at his ears.

"Usher," Marcus said, touching his palm to Usher's hard calluses. "What up?"

"You, man," Usher said, looking past Marcus to the street. "Seen you drivin to your Daddy's place in that Lexus sometimes."

"You see me walkin now," Marcus said, shrugging. "Midnight Auto Supply got my ride."

They both laughed, knowing that the young guys who stole cars now had nothing to do with the old Proudfoot brothers, the ones who'd stolen every vehicle in Treetown back in the seventies. But saying the three words to someone his age from Treetown made Marcus's heart unclench a bit.

"Where you stay now?" Usher fixed his eyes on Marcus's face, and Marcus heard the word float through his forehead. Stay. White people, downtown people, always asked, "Where do you live?" But growing up, he'd always heard the softer word. Where he stay now? She stay with her sister in Olive Gardens. Marcus smiled, knowing that Brother Lobo would love to talk about the origins of the word. Back after slavery, all those brothers drifting from place to place, until "Where you live?" became "Where you stay?" Temporary, fleeting. Where do you rest your head, for this moment?

"I'm stayin downtown, on Las Palmas," he said, and Usher nodded. He knew that for anyone in Treetown, no matter how long he'd been living elsewhere, his home was his father's place. Marcus pulled out a five-dollar bill from his front pocket, the money he'd put there because he'd known that walking would bring him Usher, or someone else from way back. He wondered who else he knew sleeping behind the dusty windows. The Kozy Komfort had gone from a seedy motel to a way station for the men so close to mental deterioration that they got government checks. In a few hours, figures would weave among the palm trunks or sit in the squares of shade cast by each tiny, peaked porch over the rooms.

Behind him, Marcus heard the short blip of a siren, like radar locating his spine, and he held himself perfectly still, the familiar prickle coating his forehead and spreading across his shoulders. That twirl of sound, lassoing him in one circle . . . the patrol cars stopping him and his brothers and friends whenever they'd walked where they weren't welcome with arroyo mud sculpting their shoes. "See some ID? You fit the description . . ."

He and Usher stared at the dirt between them. But the sound was swallowed by the powerful engine moving fast down Pepper. "Big shit goin on in the jungle," Usher finally said. "I seen lights goin past my window in the dark. Fire engines." His eyes were dreamy, sliding about in remembrance. "Like red rockets."

Marcus looked toward the overpass. The wind was picking up now, and he could feel it much stronger here than in the protected slots between buildings downtown. "You seen Finis?" he asked, the same question that rang in his ears each time he heard a siren.

Usher shook his head. "He come up here to hang, but he don't sleep here. Ain't he stayin at y'all place?" Marcus nodded, and Usher went on nervously. "Some dudes from L.A. here now. They always sayin they hate this country-ass place. Judge sent em out."

Touching Usher's palm again lightly, Marcus said, "All right, man, I'll check."

Walking toward the tunnel, he thought that no one in Treetown ever said good-bye. People he knew from the high school or downtown called out "Bye!" or even "Bye-bye!" But once, when he was about ten, he'd turned and said, "Good-bye, Aintielila," to his uncle's wife at the barbecue place, and she'd frowned deeply, her high forehead rippling with lines.

"Don't never say good-bye like that," she told him, "unless you really goin someplace. For good."

In Treetown, people said, "Next time, man," or "Later," or "I'll see you." They said, "All right-then, brothaman," to finish their business. Or, "I'll check, man," drawing the thread already that would lead them to cross each other's paths again.

Marcus breathed lightly in the dank, chill air under the freeway and didn't look at the markings of Treetown and Westside and Agua Dulce and Terracina boys. When he came back out into the stronger light, he felt the wind gusting in steady currents, like it had all day yesterday. A fall wind rushing down from the nearby desert, shredding the remnants of mist that clung to the trees. Everything was stronger in Treetown: the fog rose from the riverbottom and held tight to the many branches. In summer, it felt cooler here, in the dusty shade. And the wind came straight down the desert pass, slicing through the hills and down the corridor of riverbed.

Downtown, the wind was silent, only a vision of dancing litter or struggling pigeons outside your glass. But Treetown was constant rustling and snapping of dead palm fronds from the tall trunks that lined Pepper Avenue, like all the old streets. Marcus looked down the avenue now and saw the pencil-thin trunks swaying together, fronds all blown west like a row of toothbrushes.

Marcus paused, watching the whole landscape shifting, swaying, as if he were underwater. The pepper branches moved like seaweed, and yesterday's vicious gusts had torn new, green leaves and twigs from pecan and carob and ash, piling them with bark and wood in drifts along the roadside like beach debris. While he stood, a plastic bag flew from the freeway overpass down toward him like a jellyfish.

The bag puffed onto the small sign and slithered off again. Marcus faced the back of the sign. He knew the front read CITY LIMITS—RIO SECO—POP. 342,000. But there was nothing facing this way to tell a stranger where he was headed. He better know, Marcus thought. Treetown. An unincorporated, poverty-stricken, high-crime, semirural area west of downtown. Those were all the descriptions the newspaper applied when rare stories about drug arrests or killings in Treetown went longer than a paragraph.

Even though the city had finally annexed Treetown several months before, noting that the several-mile-square area was completely surrounded by districts receiving city services, no one had gotten around to moving the sign. Marcus walked past the breathing, pale bag at his feet. His father and uncle had complained bitterly about the annexation, saying that code workers and all the other "government men" would come around to find everything wrong.

He could see in a long, unbroken line now, walking down the slight slope. The Pepper Avenue bridge used to span the river just past his father's place, and people had crossed the old bridge daily to the citrus groves where they worked. Marcus saw the wisps of mist pushing away from the riverbed and the two large piles of rubble along the treeline. The big flood in 1969, when rain had fallen for two weeks and washed boulders and sand and trees toward the ocean, forty miles away, had torn away the old bridge. No one crossed the river to work now, and most of the groves were gone, with rows of precision housing instead of trees.

Marcus walked along the long block wall built by the city to hide the flattened land and scattered rubble left near the freeway, after the county had razed buildings considered too close to the construction. Millard's Barber Shop, Good Time Liquors, Lonzo's butcher shop. Marcus stared at the webbed graffiti on the pale cinder block. His uncle always said, "Too many men. Too many black faces hangin out right there, that bothered them cops, them government people. They redeveloped that shit best way they knew. Clear it out."

Past the wall, scattered olive trees still sprung from the earth where old groves had been cultivated. The piles of rubble Marcus could see now at the edge of the field were dotted with tiny trees, wild tobacco and pepper and eucalyptus. A deep, rutted path was worn into the field here, leading to the part of Treetown closest to the freeway. He could see the scattered houses maybe a quarter of a mile across the vacant land, see the small wooden spires on Treetown's two churches, West Rio Seco Church of God in Christ and Standing Rock Holy Fellowship of the Lord. Marcus always thought of how big the names were, and how small the stucco buildings where heat and music and perfume floated from the windows when he had stood outside years ago. His mother was Catholic, and she went to the church in Agua Dulce, farther west.

The old Treetown/Agua Dulce school, condemned now and used only for adult education classes, stood past the houses in a field. It was tiny, too, a Spanish-style building sprawling low. The only two-story structures in Treetown were the Olive Gardens low-income apartments. That was where he assumed the police vehicles had headed, since that's where trouble usually happened.

Back when the old citrus housing used to flood, when parts of Treetown were under two feet of water during winter rains, the county had torn down the wood-frame houses and built the stucco boxes of Olive Gardens. Then, during the ten years when the bridge was destroyed, the groves were razed, and the Goodyear Tire plant closed, the men who used to live in the grove workers' housing and the small houses nearby had disappeared. Now mostly women and children peered from the windows Marcus could see in the distance. He knew they had heard the sirens, too. The sky was slowly lightening, but the yellow glow of the high windows floated in the dark like cats' eyes.

Only a single road led into the main part of Treetown now, Grove Avenue, and that was still half a mile away, to the left. But on the right, Marcus saw the dark belt along the freeway where it curved toward downtown, and the old olive-pressing place in the fallow two-acre field closest to the underpass. The ancient wooden shed was marked with silver and black writing, the low stone wall was crumbled, and the tiny stand built of river rock, where someone had sold fruits and vegetables years ago, was marked, too. Wild grapevines grew around the edges of the land, up to the start of the steep Los Olivos Hills that separated Treetown from downtown.

As he was walking slowly along the dirt near the plowed field that began his uncle's land he saw the yellow police tape and two patrol cars turned sideways across the avenue.

He didn't stop. They were far enough away that they probably couldn't see him yet, and his father's place was beyond the tape. He saw no figures out of their cars, strolling or running or staring at him, so he continued casually until he reached the three huge pecan trees in a hard-packed dirt circle. Leaving the road, he went into the swirling dark space under the trees, leaning against one trunk, waiting to see if they would come and question him.

His eyes were closed; he heard hissing leaves and another plastic bag skittering past, but he listened for tires or hard soles approaching. These were the Jungle Brothers' trees. Right here. This was as far as any boy from the Westside or anywhere else could walk into Treetown before Marcus's brothers would confront him to find out if he and his friends were planning to look for Treetown girls or steal riverbottom fruit or find a Treetown fight. And the Thompson boys loved to fight. The Jungle Brothers. Demetrius would stand there, eyes moving from face to face, hands loose at his sides and slightly curled, like he was holding something even though he had only his fists, and he would chant one of Oscar's songs. "Ain't no use to stand there wit you eyes all red, cause I hit you so hard get yo gramma dead."

Marcus was the only one who wouldn't fight. Now he pushed off the pecan trunk and walked toward the stone bridge over the canal. Whatever was going on past the tape, he didn't want to mess with it. He didn't even want to know about it, which little Olive Gardens gang banger had shot somebody. Nobody rolled around in the dust under the trees now, punching each other out. They shot at each other from moving cars. The Jungle Brothers were old men. Even Sissyfly, the baby boy, was thirty.

He'd be out of the cops' sight in a few minutes anyway, and he breathed again, walking along the canal path between the glassy, sliding water in its moss-slick channel and the olive trees, remnants of one of the groves that now stood here and there in silver havens throughout the neighborhood. His great-grandmother's grove was the only one still harvested and watered, and that was where he was headed. The canal path would wind him around behind his uncle's land and his father's place, and he could avoid the red lights and the cops' gaze.

Sissyfly. That's what his brothers had always called him, when he wanted to tag along with them and see the *Superfly* and *Shaft* movies but didn't want to fight in the riverbottom or the groves or at school. His father thought he'd hung out too long with his mother and sister after he'd had meningitis, way back when he was five. "Too much female coddlin," his father said.

But he'd loved his sister, although he didn't understand some of the girl things she did. He'd watched her prance along the pepper-tree roots, carrying an umbrella, her face intent on the fall of air she knew was below her. His brothers barely knew her; she wound around their legs like she was braiding ribbons to their knees, her long hair streaming behind her, and when she had collected candy and laughter, she retreated back to Mama, her face private and closed again.

Even though they rarely talked to her, his brothers fought for her every day, when she went to grade school turning pretty and girls pulled her hair, when she went to junior high turning beautiful and boys came to the yard looking casual, holding their raps just behind their teeth.

Now she only talked to him. She called him every Friday night, from L.A., where she lived some place she wasn't willing to tell him yet. For three months, she had called him, saying she had found his number from information and please don't tell anyone. Not Mama. No. And he had to watch his mother, who still spun around the place in a dreamy circle of longing, waiting for her baby girl to come home.

The canal began to curve at the base of the hills. To his right was the acre field that Mr. Lanier leased from Uncle Oscar, to grow black-eyed peas. Marcus walked to the left, along the chain link topped with barbed wire that ran along the back of his uncle's property. He listened closely for sounds of official voices or fighting; maybe the police had been called out for some leftover drunks at The Blue Q, but he knew Oscar didn't put up with fighting or customers who overstayed their welcome. Oscar and his big guys put them out in a minute.

The wind gusted sharply, tearing skeins of mist from the branches, and the slap of a short siren came at him again, pushing him against the fence. He smelled ashes then, and wondered if the riverbottom had burned like it had last summer. He waited for the sound of tires on the canal road; only official vehicles could enter the path at the gate off Pepper or at the water intake down the river. Someone had seen him. He fit a description.

But he heard car doors slam down on the riverbottom road, and voices there, near the storage lot. After years of listening for his brothers and father, trying to avoid work, he knew where every sound echoed. The cops had to be looking for something among the cars. Instead of heading down the fence and down the slope toward the gate, he crossed the two-plank footbridge he and his brothers always kept over the canal.

Bending to gain footholds on the steep, dry trail they'd worn into the boulder-strewn hillside, he waited until he reached the wide rock where a tobacco tree grew in the cleft made by dripping water long ago. Then he turned, hidden by the yellow tubular blossoms, the decomposed granite rough at his shoulders. Police cars were gathered on the riverbottom road, the gate was open, and he saw no sign of his father or brothers. Suit-jacketed strangers had gathered near a blackened smudge. Marcus frowned. The Granada.

He thought of Finis first, like they all did. From here, he could see the road to the storage lot, the path that led toward the olive grove, but the trailers were hidden by trees. The house and barn were barely visible, patches of stone and plaster through branches. But you could always see the courtyard, the gravel area under the arbor where his mother and great-grandmother usually sat. No one was outside.

The steady voices from the storage lot rose and fell like dogs barking and answering, and he slid down to rest his back against the rock and wait for quiet. No use in moseying down the riverbottom road, and worse to sneak through the back fence at his secret place, looking like a thief. His palms rubbed the sandy remnants of rock near his shoes. He and Finis used to sit here for hours, eating plums and then, later, drinking Uncle Oscar's home brew. Talking about girls and teachers and Daddy always wanting them to work. Marcus closed his eyes, picturing his brother's blurred eyes and weaving head, moving to the music, seeing powerful legs and the burned back of his neck. "Man, that's a walkin brother," people always said, seeing Finis striding loose all the way across the city. "He never get tired. Gotta keep movin."

Pinching quartz grains hard in his fingers, staring at the clear shards, Marcus hoped Finis was sleeping now, his feet buried deep in tangled blankets. He dropped the grains and brushed off his fingers. No one came up here now. The grandkids his mother was raising played computer games; they didn't hike up here in the hills. They weren't wild like the Jungle Brothers.

But not far from his feet, he noticed a few empty bottles and a small paper bag. He pulled them toward him with a stick. Liquor he didn't recognize—the labels said "Southern Comfort" and "Crème de Menthe." Marcus looked inside the bag, pulling away from the seaweed-rank odor. Inside were two small, shriveled objects, burnt red and faintly glittered like ancient stones. And a sliver of something frayed, like a chewed matchstick, giving off the fishy smell. Marcus closed the bag, pushing it beside the thin trunk of the wild tobacco, and he lay his bare skull against the boulder, listening to the slamming of more car doors and new, rough laughter.

Two voices trailed closer to him now, and he knew from all the years he'd spent lying there, listening, that they were going up the sloping path through the olive grove. White male voices, low and punctuated with silence while he heard things being shifted around in his *abuela*'s small olive shed.

"Jackpot, Harley," the first voice said. The clanging sound of an empty can echoed against the rocks. "Here's the gas. I guess the old man set it. Or somebody else on the property. Check it out—still got residue from where he poured it. See, right here where it dripped?"

"Two females, right? In the car? Maybe transients."

The voices began to move away. "Who the hell knows, down here. Anything goes."

Marcus tightened his laced fingers around his head and felt his backbone rub against the rock. Old man? Females? He took in huge silent gusts of the damp air rising from the pebbles underneath him, waiting for the voices to subside. Abuela never kept gasoline in her olive shed. She hated the smell, and never needed fuel. Finis? Would Finis have set a fire? No. . . . Finis couldn't plan anything but where his feet would go in the next block. Marcus pressed his fingers into his forehead, making dents, and the wind brought the acrid smell of burned tires drifting over him.

Alma thought the white oval was a grain of rice clinging to her middle finger, but when she bit nervously at the swollen pad of her fingerprint her teeth pinched hard and she felt skin clinging to her tongue.

Faint, her jaw ringing when she ground her teeth, she dropped into a chair at the kitchen table. Kendrick watched her hands with his huge sand-colored eyes, and she looked away from him, fastening her gaze on the finger. She hadn't cooked rice, or anything else; she'd washed the floor, scrubbed down the sink and stove and table, mechanically, her lids jumping with the sight of Hosea lying on his back, and all the water had bleached the plump oval blister. The skin left uncovered was red, raw, and she turned the glistening mark down to the table. The blood pulsed so close to the not-ready skin. Hosea's white shirt had been plum-dark with blood in the dim light, and she knew Kendrick's lashes were coated with the same dust as hers, kicked up by the deputies' shoes.

She couldn't go to the hospital. Hosea was in the jail ward, Salcido had told her. He was a suspect. The men had told her to wait in the house, and after they'd surrounded the land with yellow tape, they swarmed over the gravel, into the buildings. She had called her sons, dialed the numbers for Demetrius and Marcus, dialed the number of the Proudfoot girl where Octavious was staying, and called out Julius's and Finis's names into the air.

No one was here yet. No one could cross the thick yellow tape trembling in the wind.

Abuela and the two younger grandchildren were in the living room, watching television with the same bland, unmoving faces, not bothered by their incomprehension while morning talk people drank coffee and smiled.

"How he know they females?" Kendrick said suddenly, his chin rising and his eyes fixed on hers.

Alma pressed all her fingers harder against the wooden tabletop. She thought about the bodies she'd seen, her mouth filling with saliva, and she couldn't imagine, didn't want to imagine, what burning would leave.

"He know cause it's his job," she told Kendrick.

He rose quickly, elbows bent like spider legs, and said, "I'ma go wait in my daddy place." He'd already been to the trailers, even though she had told him to stay by her, the police stalking everywhere, squatting and measuring, and now she pushed herself up from the chair and caught his wrist.

"You need to stay here, stay out of trouble," she said. "You don't know who might be runnin around the place, or maybe over next door. You just wait till your uncles come, when they get through."

But Kendrick, who had begun to question her all the time, even refusing to do chores, tore his hand from under the hot oval of wet skin and ran out the kitchen door.

Alma closed her eyes, swaying by the door. She could hear her grandmother move into the kitchen, and she shook her head and moved outside into the warming air.

Stopping under the eaves, she looked at the closed door of the coldhouse, where the policemen had spent a long time. No one went inside Hosea's place except her—not his sons, grandsons, or friends. She didn't want to see what they had done, looking for evidence.

She had never seen so much blood before. When her infant brother died, she was five, and she watched him waste away, turning paler and yellower from diarrhea and fever. She had never slept in a painted house then; they had lived in a car those two years, she and her parents, moving from field to field, and then in barracks housing outside Fresno, picking strawberries, when the baby died.

She hadn't seen her parents die, in the crash of a bus taking migrant pickers to a field. The bus lay in a water-filled ditch for hours in pre-dawn darkness; Alma had been home with her grandmother, sick with a cold. Her parents' faces were thicker, waxy, unnaturally shined in their coffins, the water swelling their pores, but she saw no blood.

And she had never driven a car herself, because she knew how the vehicle would fly from under her fingers and leave the road, heading for the canals and ravines and ditches all around her in Treetown. She saw blood when her sons fought, back then when they came home with black-dried traces like paint under their noses and along their knuckles. But not a red wash spreading as fast as her hands could move.

She pressed her lips together until they burned, but that didn't seal in the panic, and she didn't want any sound to escape and frighten her *abuela* or the babies, so she bit at the raw finger again and again and walked toward the fence. The deputies were gone from here; were they gone from the storage lot, with the women she couldn't imagine? Beyond the palm fronds woven into the chain link, the cars had not begun to speed past. She stared at the gap of charred fence. She had called her sons.

Her job was to keep them all alive. If they were clean, fed, and clothed, if no foul germs or bacteria tainted their plates or water, if their bellies stayed full from food and not distended with gassy air, if she washed the hands and faces and dishes and towels and tables and floors and clothes, her fingers drying in the wind and then stinging from bleach and ammonia, bursting themselves open like fruit until slices of finger pad bled into the white-enameled sink . . .

She hadn't gotten to touch his face with her fingertips before Salcido's son had pulled her away.

The back wall of the house, by her garden, was blue now. She had never lived in a painted house, in all her sixty years. When she had bothered Hosea about the walls, saying she saw mud everywhere, he said, "It keep the water off, if it ever rain around here again. And keep anything else out want to get in. That's all walls supposed to do." He watched her pace the yard, touching plaster. "I don't want to mess with this place. Been here this long—this color—and ain't no need to change."

But Alma looked at the houses in Treetown proper, on the other side of Pepper Avenue. Not Oscar's joint next door—even though it was called The Blue Q, it was more of a dim purple. She saw the lilac of Bertha Williams's wood-frame house, the stucco on Carlita Perry's duplex pink as baby-girl nightgowns, and she studied the rusty-brown paint on the Olive Gardens apartments, where she'd lived when the complex was shacks for citrus workers.

The migrant housing camps where she'd first grown the long fingers with tips blunt and wide as clamshells from all the cotton and cabbage and lemons she'd picked—those shacks and barracks had walls of splintered, oil-darkened brown.

Hosea's hubcaps, nailed to most of the trees, were silver or rusted bronze. The olive trees and gravel paths and barn were dusty, coated with earth, waiting for the rain that hadn't come in six years to wash them brighter. The men laughed when she took the hose and sprayed the barn's walls and the coldhouse, and Hosea watched her, smiling faintly.

She had begun to paint a few things, then. The grandchildren were impatient under her palms; her grandmother was faded and distant and waiting for rain, too. Hosea and the men were occupied with cars. Alma painted two old wrought-iron chairs near Abuela's olive trees, stroking them silver, and then the enclosures for the chickens and rabbits, the large cages that her mother's friend Hurriah had fashioned from bedsprings years ago.

A white woman had come one day as she painted beside the kitchen. Older than her, with too-flushed cheeks melting into a quivering neck, the woman had said she was a historian for the newspaper, researching old adobe houses in the area. Alma had walked with her back to the olive grove, but she hadn't asked any questions, hadn't said anything to Alma while she wrote in a small notebook. She had stared at the bare, tangled wisteria vines covering the long front porch when they got back to the house. Hosea had been with Demetrius on a tow job in Los Angeles, and the few men in the barn only stared at the woman, who walked gingerly on the packed-hard dirt in her short white heels. Alma knew Hosea wouldn't have let the woman wander around as she had, taking pictures of the wisteria and still-wet swatch of paint. Hosea had stopped talking to most white people long ago.

She felt the searing begin again at the base of her throat, the rising sounds. Riverbottom sand had coated the back of his head when they'd lifted him from the field, the dusty pallor in the harsh police lights veiling his forehead. Alma swallowed, choking on heat, hearing footsteps behind her and Marcus's voice call out, "Mama!" even as Demetrius's tow truck rushed heavily over the gravel toward her.

CHAPTER TWO

BY OPENING HIS eyes slightly, Hosea could see the tag around his wrist, the squarish numbers that identified him. He breathed slowly, holding himself immobile even though the pain in his shoulder came in jagged, tearing shocks that trembled all the way inside his forehead. The tag was like the long police badge they'd pinned on him and his mother, all the people in the camp after the army had rounded them up while Tulsa burned, while his father's body burned, while the smoke rose in furrowed breaths from their house and everyone else's. The smoke had stretched out into long, smothering veils when he and his mother had tried to run. His shoulder had hurt, where the boy had smashed it.

He lifted his eyes slowly from the tag, not looking directly at the figure hovering near him. He could hear the breathing, smell the antiseptic wafting from the skin. His shoulder felt as huge as a pillow, hot as an ember, and his blood quivered with heat.

The white dress moved toward him, hanging close, the white hand reaching for his good arm to wrap around it a blood-pressure cuff. He tried to keep himself from shaking noticeably. Staring at the minty wall while the dress rustled around him, he saw all the white clothes his mother had hung on the line that day in 1921, before the men came; he saw all the ghostly shapes swaying in the backyard while the men threw dishes on the floor, while they fired their guns and he hid in the closet with his mother, pressed against her swollen stomach.

"You're awake," the ghost said flatly, and the heavy door clanged.

He had never slept inside a hospital. When his wife had a baby, instead of sitting in the small sterile room with other men, he waited

on the perimeter of the building, pacing, for someone to come and tell
him she and the baby were fine. His son Marcus had been sickly when
he was small, but Hosea had always let Alma walk through the thick
glass doors and sit beside the boy's bed. Hosea had waited in the parking
lot in his truck, welcoming the asphalt-tinged heat instead of the frigid
medicinal air.

In Tulsa, when he was a child, people died in the hospital. People
said white doctors injected poisons into colored blood, gave them other
poisons to drink. They ruined women; they stared with clinical interest
at body parts and eyes and throats, like they did at the exposed organs
of the dead.

Hosea stared at the painted metal mesh covering the window. He
heard voices outside. The gold tooth. He remembered after the burning,
seeing a white man walking downtown with a gold tooth—a nigger
tooth—around his neck. Men sold postcards of bloody and burned
bodies. Who knew how many white people carried those postcards in
their wallets, how many wore glittering molars under suit jackets or lab
coats?

The door clanged again to let a deputy inside the room. Hosea heard
the metal clinking heavily on the belt, and he turned his head to see a
boy, maybe twenty-two, twenty-three. "How you feeling?" the deputy
said, not unkindly, and Hosea nodded slightly, feeling the heat surrounding his eyeballs dip and shift with his movement. "You know
you're gonna have to talk to the homicide detective when he gets here
in a while, right? You aware of what's going on?" The boy's wide red
fingers on his belt came closer.

"You call my wife?" Hosea whispered, and the deputy shook his
head.

"I don't know that," he said. "I guess they're still trying to figure
out what the hell happened."

"That's my land," Hosea said, staring at the wall. "Inside the fence."

"That's your land where those two women got burned up," the
deputy said. "That's all I heard. The homicide guy's on his way."

Homicide. Hosea remembered the gold chain glinting in his hand,
and when the deputy left, he brought his palm up slowly before his
face. He saw the blue-green cinder deep in the center of his palm,
grown inside long ago, the thick man's skin lined and creased to protect

the jagged seed. He reached out his hand to feel the edge of the bedstead, and his eyelids gave him dark again.

The sharp iron rim of his new bed in the front room felt cold against his legs when he dangled his feet. His mother's voice rang through the open front door, and Hosea knew she was leaning against the porch railing, talking to Miss Letitia next door. "Robert call hisself takin me out tonight," she said. "To the Dreamland, see a picture."

"You know you ain't walkin up there, Sophia," Miss Letitia said. "Big as you is? Close to your time."

"Two weeks off," his mother said, and Hosea felt the morning sun on his knuckles. The women kept asking his mother, telling her: your time.

The metal was warming to his legs. He'd slept in the big bed while his father was gone to France, but now he was a little man, his father said. "You done turned six while I was gone?" he'd teased Hosea when he came back. "You ain't even waited for me?"

His mother frowned when she heard "little man," but Hosea always jerked his head from under her fingertips when she said, "He still a baby, Robert."

Hosea heard his father's feet on the porch then, his soft laugh a gravel rush of breath that came up his throat and through his nose. Edging toward the door to see his father's eyes, Hosea held his spit in his throat carefully. Sometimes the pain from his father's arm, where the French bullet had left worm-twisted scars all around his collarbone, would get up into his eyes; the blood would rise up to the white part, like rusty screens covering the shine, and he'd stay with his friends in the choc joint across the street. Even his father's teeth would look darker then, coated with a muddy film.

"You gon dulge me this one time, huh?" his father said, taking the plate with the slice of sweet potato pie, and all Hosea could see was his father's jaw, shining with the sweet oil he rubbed in after he shaved. His father laughed again, long fingers already bent around the coffee cup. "Cause it's the last day a May, or cause it's Monday?"

"Cause my back hurt," his mother murmured. "Y'all can eat your favorite this mornin." Hosea stared at the wedge of pie. His mother usually made eggs, bacon, and biscuits every morning, saying she wanted

to fill up their bird legs. Hosea waited for his father to turn in the
wooden chair and look up.

"Cause your friend comin today, and you look . . ." His mother
stopped. "You in good shape today?"

"Better shape than you." Hosea's mother's dress had lost nearly every
pleat from the push of her belly. "Hell, you sit down here. I'ma get
more coffee."

When his father stood, Hosea saw the long slashes of white, nearly
blue like milk-bottle edges, around the brown of his eyes, and he saw
the corner of his father's grin.

He ran to the bedroom to look in his mother's hand mirror. The
narrow, tilted stare that other boys teased him about, calling him "Chinee
eye, Injun nose, nigger face." His father had his eyes that morning.

"You gon come with us to pick up the wash from Retha's lady?"
his mother asked, emptying the small pan of dishwater into the dirt
yard between houses, and Hosea watched his father stop buttoning.

"Where Fred?" he asked sharply. "Send him—he love to visit with
the white folks." Fred was a distant cousin, a Pullman porter on the
trains. "I ain't in the mood to cross the tracks today."

Hosea sat down on the back two steps, the kitchen behind him,
smelling the hair irons heating up in Miss Letitia's, the sooty-sweet
vapor that rose from her stove all day. Front room, bedroom, kitchen—
all four shotgun houses on their tiny street were the same, each pair of
steps like a tiny tongue leading to the yard. Hosea tied his shoes, hoping
his father would take him to the garage on Greenwood. Greenwood.
The street was lined with brick buildings edged in white-stone icing:
candy stores, groceries, barbershops, chili parlors, and the Dreamland
Theater.

But his mother said, "I guess Hosea can carry it." She set the pan
on a tree stump and pushed the heels of her hands into her back. "But
you know that lady still want to talk to you about the yard job. She
offerin steady money, Robert. And half the time Milton ain't got enough
work at the garage." Hosea's father opened his mouth, but she went
on. "Now your friend Maceo comin up here lookin for work, too.
Maybe he want that yard job." Hosea heard the glitter in her voice.

His father spat into the dirt near the street, grinning, his feet wide.
"Me and Maceo should put on our uniforms and parade down there
to her house—oh, her husband love that, now. Like red to a goddamn

bull." He smiled wider at her. "Don't give me that evil eye. We livin better than the farm. Greenwood got plenty work, got two more cabs need fixin, and that's where I'm steppin now." His shoes raised tiny breaths of dust when he crossed the yard to kiss her, his fingers in a tight row on the back of her neck under her rolled hair. And his father's hand came down looser, cupping Hosea's skull, tickling. "Carry your mama's things," he said. "When me and Maceo come back, we gon take you somewhere, boy." The warmth left Hosea's forehead, and his father said, "Here come trouble. Let me go."

Retha came out of Letitia's back door, saying, "He don't even realize, girl." She looked at them, hair stiffly shined, and said, "Y'all ready? We *been* late, and you know Mrs. Hefferon ain't happy I done spent the night in Greenwood steada up over the damn garage." She blew out her breath. "Monday."

The big brick house had a long driveway, and Hosea saw the curtains tremble when the women clicked the back gate. "She done had a dinner Saturday night, so you know what you lookin at," Retha said softly.

"French lace," Hosea's mother murmured.

"She call herself givin me a dollar less that night, talkin bout that big plate of food she want me to take. All that nasty sauce, I couldn't even eat it." Retha sucked at her teeth, and Hosea saw the back door open.

"Good *morning*," the white woman said, her face slanting down the steps, and Hosea saw her hair, as snowy and nested as goose feathers. He dropped his eyes, remembering what his mother said. Don't be starin in them people faces. They don't like that.

The kitchen floor was as shiny as tears. The woman said to Retha, "I trust you had a nice breakfast, as we've had to get ours." Her voice was as curly as the tendrils of a pea vine, the green strings licking tight around a wire.

Hosea kept his eyes on the heels of his mother's shoes. There was no smell of men in the kitchen, no cigar or leather or sweet oil, but he knew the man who hated red, like a bull, was somewhere in the house. "Your husband hasn't come about the yard," the woman said, and his mother shook her head. "Some people in Tulsa think they're too good for yard work. Or any kind of honest work. That's what Mr. Hefferon says." She waited. Hosea held still. "Well. You've done this before. You do remember the French lace? The table runner, the doilies, these cloths, the napkins. Mr. Hefferon's mother brought them from France."

Hosea stared at the froth in his mother's hands, froth folded into squares. French. Like the bullet, and the shell his father had sent from France, the dull-nosed thing Hosea had held. The metal was engraved with dotted letters, stuttered into the brass: FOR MY LOVE SOPHIA— VERDUN, FRANCE 1918.

"Retha has no patience for fine wash, and she'd ruin them." The woman went to the back window and stretched her neck to look out. Hosea saw the pink skin under her throat, swirled with lines. Then she dropped her chin and looked at his mother again. "Mr. Hefferon's mother will be here tomorrow morning, and I'll need things arranged. She's terrifying. And Retha drives me to distraction." She paused, staring at Hosea's mother. "I'll need those by this evening. They're so thin they shouldn't be long drying."

His mother turned, her fingers in his shoulder like tips of a fork when he forgets to move.

On the sidewalk, she said, "She know that much about em, why she don't wash em herself?"

The French lace looked like foam in the washtub, and his mother's fingers swirled through the bubbles, trailing and turning. When the creamy patterns were flat from the wringer, she hung them on one of the lines stretching from trees, and she began to wash all the white clothes from Miss Letitia's house and theirs. His father's white shirts gaped and turned on the line, and Miss Letitia's towels and cloths and blouses. One of Miss Letitia's beauty smocks and two of his father's T-shirts lay on a clean board in the sun. The rust stains where car parts and sweat and hair irons had touched were sprinkled with lemon juice and salt.

His mother's fingers raked softly through the bowl of beans now, and she dropped a pebble near his foot. "Your daddy loves beans and ham hock," she said. "He and Maceo probably be back in a few hours. Go on, see if Miss Letitia need you. I'ma rest after I put these on the stove. Go on, Hosea."

He didn't run, because that might make her sad that he didn't want to be there with her in the yard, sitting idly under the stiffening, waving white, but in Miss Letitia's doorway, breathing perfume and laughter, he felt his chest racing, hoping for a quarter. And she looked up from the dripping hair under her wrist.

"Didn't I say it was about time somebody come over here and got us some barbecue?" she laughed. "This boy live for Greenwood Avenue and looking for his daddy. Here." She pressed damp money into his hand.

Greenwood was crowded with people doing afternoon errands, and Hosea wove through the sidewalks, heading to the cab garage. The man in the folding chair shook his head when Hosea reached the doorway. "Your daddy out fixin a car, boy. Go on, now, before you get in the way."

Hosea walked back toward the barbecue place Miss Letitia liked best, smelling the way afternoon changed the air, thickened it with sauces and hurrying and exhaust. But inside the restaurant, people were arguing, yelling, gesturing at newspapers. He sat in the corner to wait for the plates, and the men said, "You see this shit? They gon talk about lynchin that boy? He ain't done a damn thing but bump that girl in the elevator. White girl want to make a fuss. White girls love trouble."

A short, light-skinned man near the door had a deep voice. "Tulsa ain't the place for that. They gon find out this time." The bell on the door clanked hard when he went out.

Hosea stared at the faces chewing, talking, the tongues and fingers and elbows close to him. Between the arguments were quiet gashes, not like the usual thread of laugh and murmur that rocked him half-asleep while he waited for Miss Letitia's order. He sat stiff on the stool, hearing the short, spat words. Kill. Hush. Stop. Now.

"Thompson."

The voice was thick with quelled coughing.

"Thompson. You want to wake up and answer some easy questions?"

The man's skin was sallow, grainy, and his black hair was combed straight back into strict grooves from his temples. Hosea kept his eyes on the face for a moment, then looked at the notebook.

"Easy questions. The Granada was on your lot. The gate was locked and you had the key, the gas can was in your shed, and the two women were sitting in the front seat when they got burned up. How'd they die?"

Hosea remembered the voices drifting through his trees. What would he tell this man? Somebody killed them? He'd think Hosea was getting smart. I don't know? He'd think Hosea was getting stupid. That was why Hosea spoke as rarely as possible to strange white people. He thought of Marcus again; Marcus loved talking to strangers, and he had no problem with white ones. He ran his mouth to anyone.

"Thompson. Are you trying to remember how you did it? Were they trespassing? Drunk? Or did one of your boys pick them up? You got a couple of crazy ones living with you, I heard. Let's make this even easier. You're in here cause you brandished your weapon at the peace officers. But I don't know if you're the one who killed the women or if your son did it. Finis. That's the crazy one, right? People tell me he doesn't have much left upstairs. Druggie. Did he like to bring women around when they didn't want to come? Did he pay them to visit and then get pissed?" The man paused, the tiny black hairs on his fingers trembling. "We got a lot of possibilities."

Hosea was afraid to move his shoulder. It still throbbed hot. He fixed his eyes on the notepad. Finis? Who knew what the hell Finis thought, except Marcus. But this detective thought Finis had enough planning left in his brain to kill someone. Two. Hosea tried to picture what the women had looked like before smoke and flame. But strange women never hung around his land.

"Maybe some other crack addicts, right?" the man continued, watching Hosea's eyes. "What do the brothers call them? Strawberries? Nice girls, huh? And after your son got some pussy, he got mad cause he didn't want to compensate them?"

"No" Hosea said softly, his lips dry. If he said nothing yet, if he could just talk to Marcus, they could think whatever they wanted about him. But his forehead was swimming with pain, and when the man's pen rubbed on paper, when he called Hosea's name several times, Hosea kept his eyes closed. He knew the ghostly nurse would return eventually.

The door opened. "Uh, Janice," the man called. "Janice. I think he's fading out." Hosea heard her shoes squeal softly on the floor, and he kept his breathing shallow.

She stayed in the doorway. "Pain medication," she said. "You sleep a lot."

"Either that or he's not speaking to me," the man said sarcastically. "Whatever."

"He's had surgery for the bullet wound, okay, Harley? He's not young."

"He's what, sixty?" the man said, and Hosea heard the notebook rustle. "I haven't even been down there yet to Treetown. I just got the stuff on the phone from Fernández."

"He's seventy-six," the nurse hissed precisely.

"Damn! That's pretty old to be getting crack-head sex in a car. Gotta be the son. One of em. Guess there's a bunch." The man's voice murmured along. "Two crack-head ladies burned up in a '78 Granada. Nice chariot to heaven."

The nurse laughed. "Why do you talk so much, Harley? I thought detectives were supposed to listen, be observant, all that. Every time I see you, you're running off at the mouth. Even to yourself."

"Because people can correct me, or agree, or whatever." Hosea waited. "I can't figure this shit out by myself, right?"

"You finished?" she asked.

"I guess he is," Harley said, tapping the pen as fast as crickets calling. "For now."

Hosea knew that the sharp-smelling fingers would touch him with the blood-pressure cuff, and when the door closed, he turned his head to look at the window going purple with evening.

The dark corners in the house pooled over the floor, and his mother still slept. She had taken in the French lace, dampened it for ironing and layered it in the basket, but she still lay in the bedroom, arm high on her stomach. Miss Letitia had come to say she'd heard there was trouble with a white woman, but she didn't know exactly what. She and her friend were going to do hair for two girls on Detroit Avenue, because tonight was the spring prom for Booker T. Washington High.

Hosea sat in the front room, waiting for his father and Maceo. Maceo had been friends with his father in France, and he'd come last year from Mississippi to visit. He'd brought Hosea a slingshot.

When he heard a car door slam, he ran to the window, wondering if they'd borrowed a cab. But he saw a black car and the goose-feather hair. Retha's lady. She wore a dark coat, and her hands were blinding

white. Gloves. He saw her eyes fix on the house, and his throat clenched
with fear. Trouble. White women made trouble. When he heard another
car door, he ran to the bedroom, closing the door.

The house was sifting darkness now, and he sat on the floor near his
mother's bed, hearing her husks of breath. Knocking came soft on the
front door. "Sophia?" He knew it was Retha's voice, but he knew the
gloves were there on the porch, too, and he covered his ears.

His mother's shoulders rustled on the bed, and she twisted her head.
"Who at the door, Hosea?" she asked faintly.

"The white lady," he whispered, hearing the voices move toward
the back.

"White lady?" She tried to sit up. "Oh! The lace." She raised herself
on the pillows, her hand nearly disappearing in the cleft between her
belly and chest. "Hosea, baby, go on out there and tell her I'll have
Robert bring it up there early in the morning. Tell her early."

He went to the kitchen door, hearing them talk through the cracks.
"Look at these clothes outside! Where is the lace?" the wiry voice said.
"What's wrong with everyone?"

Retha's murmur was dust he couldn't hear. He pressed his cheek
against the wooden door, and his mother said, "Hosea?"

The white woman's face filled the tiny window in the door when
he pulled back, her cheeks as gray and heavy as wrung cloth, her mouth
stretching open when she reached to look inside. She saw him, and he
froze while her face moved, her lips making sucking movements near
the glass when she spoke.

She was angry, pulling the meat from softened ham hocks, but his father
made a fuss about the food, reaching for his favorite pieces, the long
pink splinters that his mother pried from between the narrow bones.
The foot, Hosea thought suddenly. We eatin the toes. The meat between
leg bones. He lifted his pants leg and touched his shin. "You get hurt
runnin around?" his father asked. "That how you got your mama mad?"

His father's eyes were still not red. He gave Maceo a plate, and Maceo
put his hand deep into his pocket, pulling out copper-bright BBs, a
palmful. Hosea clawed his fingers to scoop them from Maceo's broad
hand. "Pretty soon you be old enough for your first gun," Maceo said,
and Hosea closed the cool metal balls into his own hand.

"Don't be angry at the boy," his father told his mother.

"I had to get up and tell her you'd bring it in the mornin," she said. "She was mad by then, cause he wouldn't open the door. I don't know why he actin foolish."

"Daddy," Hosea said. "They was talkin bout killin in the restaurant."

"Who?" his mother said, her voice sliding high. "Who talkin bout that?"

Hosea watched his father's moustache, as thick as a broom's edge, cloak his lips. His father stared at him. "Talking bout killin a pig, probably," he said, standing up. "Come on outside, now. Show Maceo what you can do with that ax."

But they had enough wood already. His father crouched on the ground. "I know you been heard about some people gon kill a boy. But that ain't gon happen, and you ain't gon talk about it in front of your mama. She don't need to worry right now." When he stood, Hosea looked at Maceo, who stared across the street at the choc house.

"Can I come with you?" he asked. "They got candy, too."

His mother spoke from the doorway, and he could see the half-moon of plump under her chin, glistening at her neck. "He need to be in bed."

"Take him off your hands for a minute," his father said, catching Hosea by the side of his face with careless fingers.

They walked through a lot to the house where men went in and out all day and night for a shot. The two sisters who owned the house were thin and red, with fine freckles like sand at their temples, and they grinned at Hosea. "Look who call hisself grown now," one called.

"Give him some a that pecan candy," his father said, and Hosea stared at the pointed hooves of pigsfeet, suspended in cloudy liquid.

The men each dropped a spoonful of sugar into the glasses of choctaw beer, so the thick drink bubbled milky as liquid clouds before they drank it. "I missed this stuff, man, when we was over there," Hosea's father said. "Remember that wine, Maceo? Didn't sit on my teeth. Wash right through me like acid."

Maceo said, "The white folks over there wasn't as tiresome, though. Came back to the same crackers here."

Hosea's father stared at the wood wall, his lips wet under the moustache. He could smell the sweet beer floating down to his face. "I came back to Greenwood, man. Ain't no place like it, I'ma tell you. I met cats from Georgia over there, from Maryland and Mississippi, and nobody had nothin close to Greenwood. Negro Wall Street. Don't have to see no white folks if you don't want to."

Maceo said, "White folks always talkin bout niggers got too many ideas over there."

Hosea knew they were talking about France. The French bullet. The French lace. He wondered if his mother would be angry when she smelled moist smoke on his head. She always bent to smell his hair and tell him where he'd been.

Two men burst inside. "They gatherin up at the courthouse, crowd of white men, say they gon bust that boy loose."

Hosea felt his chest fill with spiderwebs. The other men began to talk louder, arguing, some leaving, but his father put a hand on Hosea's elbow to draw him back down. He didn't know his legs had pushed him up.

The fatter sister said, "Ain't no need to go with them ruffians. They always courtin trouble." She frowned at the door.

But Hosea's father said slowly, "*Court* somethin take a plan. Don't need a plan to find trouble tonight. They kill that boy they got in jail, they might as well kill niggers for breathin." He paused. "Anybody."

"Over a foolish white girl," the sister said. "You take that boy home." She nodded at Hosea.

Hosea's father drank again, and his eyes slanted toward Hosea, then fixed on Maceo. "I ain't lookin for trouble," he said, "but if trouble get lost downtown, and he find me, I'ma have to kick his ass a bit and send him on his way, now."

Maceo stretched his hands on the table. "Trouble got a whole lotta relatives," he said.

Hosea's father stood, pulling Hosea up with him. "Don't he?" he said.

She was ironing the French lace, patting it fast and light, and her face was so wet her hair curled over her forehead like tiny vines. "You done forgot about the Dreamland so quick, huh?" she said, barely looking up.

"Ain't nobody goin to the pictures tonight," Hosea's father said, and her face swiveled up like a sunflower.

"Robert?" she asked. "Hosea?"

He stood in the space between rooms—the kitchen, where the smell of heat and cloth and milk rose from her, and the bedroom, where his father sat on the bed loading the gun he'd brought home from France. Metal and oil and smoke—that was what he smelled from his father's hands. But she thumped down the iron and came to clutch his shoulders. Her stomach against his back was hard and damp, and her fingers held him until the door closed.

He twisted away and went through the kitchen door, smelling the clean nothing of cloth and air. He heard men shouting when he ran out to the street, where he could barely see his father's back crossing the tracks.

Running after them, silent, he could feel the copper balls sliding in his pocket. He stayed behind then, like his father had told him to stay close and yet far from the animal you were hunting. On his grandfather's farm, he'd followed rabbits like this. But his father and Maceo began shifting in a swarm of other dark coats. He knew that the guns tucked into their elbows and palms gleamed blue-black.

After a few blocks, Hosea knew they were downtown, and the mass of men narrowed into a black river, his father's head high above the others. Hosea fixed his eyes on his father's ear, his collar, his forehead.

The white voices from across the street were as hard and as flat as shovels. The white man who hated bulls—was he here? Did he see Hosea's father? Hosea saw the feather hair of the woman, heard her wire words. He watched his father's head bob and move, waiting for a glimpse of his eyes, but the shouting rose up like crows from a field. Then the river of men parted in streams flowing too many ways, and when the gully cleared, he saw his father and Maceo, and a white man angling toward them like a fish. Hosea froze, his back against coarse brick, and he heard the white man, harsh and loud.

"Nigger, what you doin with that gun?" The white man cut in front of Hosea's father.

"I'ma use it, if I have to," his father replied.

"No, you ain't. You givin it to me." The hand shone in the streetlight, reaching for the French gun in his father's fingers.

"Like hell," his father said, the wind roaring from his throat, and the river closed again before Hosea heard the shot that rang out, echoing off the buildings above him.

He pressed himself into the deep doorway, hearing the gunfire pock the dark as loud as hail on a tin roof, louder than the screaming inside his throat. A shadow filled the doorway, and Maceo said, "I see you, boy. Come on."

The gunfire and shattering glass were jagged everywhere, and when Maceo lifted him to his shoulder and began to run down the sidewalk, close to the bricks, Hosea could see dark-humped forms in the street. "My daddy," he said, but the thump of Maceo's shoulder into his chin knocked the words back down his throat.

When they saw a crowd of white men knotting the street, Maceo pulled back into another doorway, and Hosea peered over his coat. A dark man lay writhing on the sidewalk, moaning, and ambulance men were shouting at the crowd to let them through. But they pushed at a solid mass of jeering faces. Hosea saw a huge, pale face floating above the street, and the fat curls that Miss Letitia loved framed the pale skin: Mary Pickford, on a sign above the sidewalk. When Maceo inched around the doorway and into the alley, the bricks scraped Hosea's cheek bloody.

The alley was long, dank, and empty, and Hosea closed his eyes, afraid of the faces that would find them. But Maceo still ran, and Hosea's mother was in the front doorway, screaming his name when he opened his eyes again. Maceo dumped him onto the steps, shouting, "I don't know, Sophia! I'ma wait for him at the corner. Robert gon make it back. Take that boy inside and stay down, on the floor."

His mother's fingers raked Hosea's head, pulling his eyes so close to hers that he felt her eyelashes brush his when she asked him the questions. He understood nothing she said.

The blinding glare of overhead lights hurt him through his eyelids, and the woman's voice blurted short sentences above his arm. The ripping sound of the blood-pressure cuff hurt his face. His whole body was pulsing with heat now, as if the bullet in his shoulder sent traces of powdery fire to circulate everywhere. "Do you . . ." He could hear the beginnings of what the voices said. "Is the . . ."

The cop's voice was harsher. "We've got one white girl, okay? Pamela Sawicky . . ."

Another woman's voice, deeper, developed on the other side of his bed. "Secondary . . ." He felt a needle. "Watch . . ."

They pulled the mattress from the big bed to the floor. His mother's wrists scissored him softly, one over his chest and one behind his back. The black walls held shouts and shots and answers like distant conversation. He looked at the spidery iron bedstead. You a little man now, his father had said; you still my baby till this one come, his mother had said. After a long time, he heard her sleep breath.

When he closed his eyes, he saw the men lying in the street, no faces, just coats and one hand, knuckles down on the black, the fingers curled to receive something from the sky.

When he heard the airplanes, Hosea realized he had slept, because his face was tight to his mother's back and he felt the soft pads of flesh that stretched around even to her spine. The floor was gray with dawn now, and he felt her trembling, the rigid shaking she did after long sobbing. He heard the ragged tear of guns, the airplanes closer, and then a steady sound like a zipper torn across the morning.

It was the sound he and the other boys made with their tongues thumping their mouth roofs to make machine guns in the war. "Mama," he said to her shuddering back.

"What did you see?" She didn't turn around. She whispered it to the room.

"I seen a man try and take Daddy gun. And then people start shootin." Hosea smelled the doorway, dank and close. "And Maceo don't know neither."

"I heard Maceo on the porch. Your daddy must be hidin somewhere till they stop." She was silent, and the airplanes droned past again, the bullets spitting loud. France. They were in the war now.

He stood up, pulled at her shoulders, but she lay on her side still, her eyes closed again. He ran to the front window, and Maceo was outside on the tiny porch, his French gun loose in his hands, his knees bent and crouching. Hosea opened the door, crouching, too, and Maceo turned.

"Get back inside," he told Hosea, looking across the field, and Hosea saw white men surrounding the choc house, saw the flames glowing squares in the windows. He heard trucks rumbling down the street, and over the flat sky, smoke began to join in climbing, billowing drifts.

"Go," Maceo said. "Stay down on the floor. I'm comin now."

He pushed Hosea back to the bedroom and told Hosea's mother, "You and him go back in the kitchen. They lookin for men. Stay down."

Hosea heard the men shouting when they came to the houses. "Home Guard," they yelled. "Send the men out first, then everyone else. Now, dammit. All the men."

He felt as if his chest would burst into flame. He heard the bullets strike the glass in front, and then wood splintered at the door. "Send the men out, goddamnit, or we'll level this damn shack."

Maceo's feet slid across the floor, and Hosea heard him say, "I'm comin out. No gun."

When the door opened, the shots peppered the walls. Hosea's mother gasped and pulled him toward her, backing into the tiny cupboard in the corner where she kept brooms and mops, and they pressed themselves inside as boots scraped the porch steps.

"Ain't a damn thing worth a dollar in here," a man said. "Check the bedroom for a trunk or somethin."

Feet came heavily into the bedroom. Hosea's breath rang in his ears. He felt his mother's belly against his face, and then a tremble began in her thin skin, through her dress. Hosea shivered, and the baby's elbow or foot thumped against his temple, drew a dull line down his jaw.

"Niggers on Detroit Avenue got something worth carrying," another man said. "These niggers ain't got shit. Come on. Get the stink out of here with that."

Their boots sounded near the front door, and Hosea heard a clanging kick. Then he smelled sharp liquid, and smoke.

"They burnin, Mama. They burnin." She was still, and he could hear the glisten of flame gathering in the wood. Then he smelled scorching hair, and his throat closed with risen spit. Maceo. "Mama," he shouted, pulling her out the back door.

The flames were already rising in Miss Letitia's house, and one of the white men dangled her money box from three fingers, turning when he saw Hosea and his mother in the back, among the swaying shirts.

• • •

The thumping of metal on the floor, a soft clang, wakened him. He opened his eyes briefly, expecting the fluorescent glare again and the antiseptic fingers, but the room was dark except for a small light on the wall, and the woman who'd bumped the wastebasket turned her copper-bright face to his every few minutes, expectant and nervous.

"Mr. Thompson?" she whispered, coming closer.

He didn't answer, not recognizing her. Her earrings swayed against her neck. She said softly, "My son Nacho been paintin cars at your place. Nacho?"

He nodded, the movement jarring his eyes. "Can't nobody call you up in here, come see you. What you want Nacho to tell your wife?"

Hosea tasted a slurry of ash at the back of his throat. He tried to swallow. She brought the water cup to his lips, glancing at the camera and the door.

His throat felt as hard as charcoal. "Tell my wife to get Marcus," he whispered. "He the one. He need to find out about them white people. On the place. That white girl. He know her." He closed his eyes to remember the voice, the name. "Sawicky. He know that name. I done heard him say it before."

She frowned and nodded, then turned to lift more water to his mouth. Hosea felt hot with shame at his face lifted, as helpless as a baby bird's.

"You do a burnout for a white dude?" Demetrius shouted at Julius in his mother's kitchen, where they'd all crowded around the old white stove and the wooden table for coffee and tortillas. "Or some sister?"

Julius stood near the door, rolling his eyes. "Man, I ain't done nothin for nobody."

"He never do nothin *for* nobody, like a favor," Octavious said. "But he do anything for money."

"Shut up, man. I wasn't even here," Julius said, stepping out into the morning sun that flooded the yard. Marcus watched him go to the barn, shaking his head.

"Hush," his mother said. "Y'all gon scare the kids, and they been terrified enough as it is. Go on outside. All I know is Mrs. King said your daddy want Marcus to try and find out somethin about white people around here. A girl name Sawicky . . ."

Demetrius turned quickly to Marcus, who sipped the strong Café Bustelo his great-grandmother always made. "Why he think Sissyfly here gon do anything? Just cause he always hangin out with white folks downtown don't mean he know nothin around here no more."

"Three negatives," Marcus said, nodding sagely, just to piss off his brother. "He's serious."

"See? All he do is talk shit," Demetrius shouted. "Look, I'ma go out and find this motherfucker messin with us and kick his ass."

"Demetrius," his mother said. "Go on outside. Now. You upset. All y'all go on over your uncle's. Talk to him and his wife. All them people they get over there drinkin and carryin on—maybe some a them drunk men done got Hosea in trouble over these women." Marcus saw the anger in his mother's stiff-held neck, the skin puckering slightly under her jaw. She had never liked Oscar's wife. She sighed and closed her eyes. "Make me nervous in here, you four, and I don't know who all might come round. Maybe more police, and they don't need to see y'all fightin. Go on."

Demetrius and Octavious dropped down the two kitchen steps into the yard and stalked toward the barn, but Marcus stood outside the doorway watching them. Sawicky. A white girl named Pammy Sawicky must have been in the car. He did know that name, and he remembered that sneering, changeable face from high school. But she sure as hell didn't hang out with brothers. Especially not in Treetown. And why would his father think he knew anything about her now?

He'd looked everywhere last night for Finis, checked the Kozy Komfort and the Taco Bell, looked in on the trailer. With no car, he was glad no one had noticed he was ambulating. His stolen Lexus had already been towed by someone else. But he needed a ride to find his brother. Finis disappeared now and then, but the cops wouldn't understand that.

He looked at his brothers leaning against the stone wall. Julius do a burnout? Sometimes someone told Julius about a car she couldn't keep up payments on; Julius would tow the car somewhere stolen cars were often dumped and then set it on fire. But he damn sure wouldn't burn anything on the place, and how would the two women have gotten into the Granada, anyway?

Julius stared off at Pepper Avenue, fingering his soft goatee tenderly.

Marcus saw him ignore Demetrius's shouts. Women loved that smooth face and never-shaven chin. Julius never had to shave—he'd never had a job because women always took care of him. Women in Treetown, on the Westside, all the way to San Bernardino and San Diego talked about Julius and what he said in bed and what he held inside the baggy Dickies. But Julius had never messed with a white woman.

Demetrius and Octavious gave up on Julius now, putting their coffee cups onto the stone ledges on the barn wall, glancing impatiently at Marcus. Demetrius was taller, six feet, but they both had broad shoulders and skinny legs like their father. Smooth skin, too, nearly hairless. Marcus was the only one who had to shave daily, leaving darkened nicks under his jaw. They all had their father's Indian cheekbones, African-sculpted lips, and their mother's wavy part-Mexican hair, slicked back from their foreheads and woven into single braids ending between their shoulder blades. Finis, even Sofelia as he remembered her. Only Marcus kept his hair so short his skull showed at the temples.

His oldest brothers swung across the dirt area to look at a parked truck, moving as if they were connected by invisible filaments. He knew he could never be that close to them, and suddenly he thought of Enchantee. She can't be that close to Demetrius either, cause he still lives over here, really.

I don't, he thought. Why did his father want him to figure anything out? He was the last one to know what went on at the place. That's what his brothers were mouthing over there, eyes cutting at him, when the screen door creaked closed. His mother stood beside him. "I don't know nothin about this, and Pops don't know nothin about me," he said. "I ain't the one."

"He know you better than you think," she said, looking distractedly down the slope toward the olive grove. "Mrs. King say he look okay. Weak. I guess they had to go all in his shoulder get that bullet out." Her eyebrows shivered in a wince. "Got bars on the windows—can't nobody go see him. Jail."

Marcus didn't want to hurt her with a sarcastic remark about disbelief that his father understood him at all; he couldn't even imagine his father prone, especially not weak and hazy-eyed. He turned the other way to hide his face from her and saw a purple hump near the coldhouse where his father ate and slept.

"Mama? You paint that old smoke oven? When you do that?" he

asked. The stone and adobe-brick oven was shaped like a squat beehive; his father and uncle used to smoke meat inside, and the boys would always pull back curious faces smeared with ash when they searched the dark cave for something they thought their father had hidden from them: forbidden pecans, Christmas gifts, possessions sparking too many fights.

His mother brought her fingers to her temples, her elbows flying out like wings. "Last night," she whispered. "This morning, really, just a few hours ago before the sun come up. I couldn't sleep. I didn't figure no police come around that early. I had been messin with the color, and I wanted to see it."

"Purple?"

"Don't you recall that kinda purple?" She tilted her head and looked at the oven. Marcus saw something between lavender and eggplant, something dusky and cut with maroon. "When I taken you to the ocean that time?" she said.

"No," he said, and Demetrius shouted, "Marcus, come on with your slow ass!" Demetrius had his arms folded now, his jaw high, his large eyes half-hidden under his lids, and Marcus thought, Ain't no damn way I'ma ask him to borrow a hooptie. I ain't askin him for nothin.

He'd borrowed his next-door neighbor Kurt's Cabriolet, just for the morning. Kurt was a chef at a downtown restaurant, and Marcus had worked as a waiter there for most of the summer.

"I'll catch up," he called, and his brothers turned, their backs in blue so dark they turned to shadows as they entered the eucalyptus grove.

"Go on back in, Mama," he said. "We ain't fightin. Not right now. We got things to do."

He followed them over the crushed leaves past the barn, toward the stone wall that separated the properties. Good fences make good neighbors. They taught us that in school. Robert Frost—New England. But this was a high river-rock barricade to keep out the drunks and wanderers. And this old iron gate, where Julius waited for him, was not for neighbors. For two brothers.

His uncle Oscar's place was small and bare in the harsh light when they walked silently toward the purple wood frame. No sign. It was only The Blue Q if you knew how to get down the long, narrow drive past all the trees and people parked or standing and watching for strangers. On Friday and Saturday nights, when the eagle flew and people came to The Blue Q to play, the huge dirt expanse was crowded with cars and laughter and arguments and wreaths of cigarette smoke rising to the trees.

But this early on Sunday, when they peered inside to see their uncle sitting at one of the tables, only the smell of *menudo* and ammonia swirled from the door.

Uncle Oscar looked up like he'd expected them to come, and Marcus took a deep breath of the heavy odor when he sat on one of the folding chairs. Innard meat. Waxy honeycomb tripe for the *menudo*, the recipe his great-grandmother had shown Uncle Oscar's wife years ago, when they'd figured out how to make a little extra money on a Sunday after people had been drinking for two days. And the chitlins that cooked nearly every day in here—their smell gristly and twisting from the huge pots in the back.

Demetrius said something low to his uncle, and Marcus saw the thick brown drink in a mug by his uncle's hand. The homemade stuff. His uncle rarely drank before dark, and Marcus could see the liquor in his eyes, laced with rusty webs, and in the loose shine of his bottom teeth, which he usually kept behind a tight, watching grin.

His uncle looked past the others, straight at him. "You ain't been here in a good while. Been eatin in them downtown places? Cause I know you can't cook. Love to grub, but you can't cook worth a damn."

Marcus held his smile, not sure. His uncle loved to mess with him, more than his brothers, but for years Oscar had handed him tight-rolled hundred-dollar bills to help pay college tuition.

"Been eatin in my neighbor's place," he said casually. "New restaurant."

"Duck à l'orange and that kinda shit?" his uncle said, eyes moving fast from face to face. "Medallions a meat cost fifteen bucks?"

Marcus shook his head. "No. He cooks a lot of Southwest and Asian. Like Thai and California, mixed." He'd play along. But he wouldn't add that Kurt was half Japanese and gay.

Oscar drank from his smudged glass. "All them white cooks in them fancy-ass restaurants trying to cook like somebody from somewhere else cause they ain't got nothin." Marcus frowned, his brothers smiled, and Oscar slammed down the glass. "They ain't got no culture. Don't nobody want to eat turkey and pumpkin pie every day. They gotta borrow some good cookin."

He looked at the ruffle of a chitterling floating in the bowl by his fingers, the meat glistening with reddish Tabasco. "See? They think chitlins is the nastiest thang on earth. Wouldn't touch it. But they eat snails and veal brains and tongue." He paused, and Demetrius looked at Marcus, shrugging slightly. They'd have to be patient.

"I'ma tell you who got class and soul. Much as a white man can. The French," Oscar said. Marcus and the others had heard this before; Oscar had been in France during World War Two.

"They eat chitlins! Damn if they don't! Call it somethin else, but they eat it, too. In that farmhouse where we stayed coupla nights, people gave us tongue and chitlins, and some garlic they roasted and rubbed on the bread. Meat tasted so good we liked to cried." He smiled down at his choc beer. "Then we had to get back to killin people. And when I find out who set Hosea up like this, I'ma kill him."

Demetrius said, "You can't think like that, cause it could be some gang bangers from Olive Gardens. Could be a whole lotta young guys messin with some women over there." He put his arms behind his head like he was stretching casually. "You know I'd be happy to kick some ass right," he started. But Julius interrupted.

"And they'd be happy to come shoot up the place," he said. "I been over there."

"All them foolish women, I bet you have," Octavious muttered.

"And them little bangers wanna be like L.A. Hard."

Marcus said, "I get kids at work like that. I see a lot more kids than you guys. I don't think most of the gang bangers are smart enough to plan somethin out. If somebody wanted Daddy to get shot at, they had to think for a while."

Julius said, "You got Westside Loc Special, over the freeway, and you got these new kids callin theyselves Treetown Posse. Maybe the two girls was messin with the wrong dudes."

Demetrius began to walk around the room, weaving through the chairs and tables still scattered from last night, scuffing up the sawdust rank with spilled beer and ashes and crumbs. Marcus heard Oscar's wife, Lila, come in the back door to the kitchen, and pots moved, silver clanked. Demetrius's voice was slower now. "Look. Don't nobody steal from us."

"Hell, no," Octavious said.

"Sometimes batteries, they do," Julius said.

"I'm talkin about serious stealin." Demetrius folded his arms. "And you know why. Cause when we got started, I went around to the known ones and jammed them up. Remember? I hit up the Proudfoots and them Millers lived in the Gardens, went all the way to the Westside to the thieves. I wasn't havin no Midnight Auto Supply shit on our place. I told em if anything come up missin, I know exactly where I'ma look. And they knew I was kickin ass and takin names." He looked at his uncle. "And ain't nobody tried nothin for a long time, even on the lot. But this fire—the damn gate was locked. And they said he had the key out."

Marcus said, "And somebody put a gas can in Abuela's place."

Julius said, "Nacho say he was talkin about white dudes. You seen any?"

Lila came out then, with her purse on her arm, and she set down a new bottle of Tabasco on the table near Oscar. "I'm goin to the store. Sugar and Tabasco." She looked at them sitting and standing, and Marcus saw the dim, shafting light hit her turquoise-green eyes. His aunt had golden skin marked with lines only at the corners of her eyes and mouth, but those were deep-carved lines, and her mouth was always set hard into her facial bones. The boys used to talk about how Aintielila carried a derringer in her apron pocket, how some people were more scared of her than of Uncle Oscar. But they both had to be fearsome to run a place like The Blue Q for this long. "I told Oscar last night about the white man," she said, and went out the front door.

Oscar splashed thin hot liquid into the bowl. "I went over to see your mama last night, see if she okay, and I heard that paintin boy say what your daddy thought. I came back here, trying to think if I seen white folks for a long spell. Not none, even sellin somethin. Lila set up here all quiet. Then she say some guy come by two, three months ago."

"What he look like?" Octavious asked.

"I don't know. Me and your daddy had gone to French Oaks with Lanier, see about some pigs. He want to put a couple over there on the pea field. Lila say he come up the drive with Fulton Chester. You know, preacher in that holy roller church on the Westside. She go out in the front, and Chester smilin and smooth-talkin, sayin he heard round town I was lookin to sell the place. Talkin bout, 'I know y'all taxes went up when the city decide to annex over here.' Shit, like I'm hurtin. He know damn well how many peoples in here every weekend, cause he used to be in here his own self ten years ago. Now he raisin hell about alcohol and drugs every Sunday.''

"Take a sinner," Julius said.

"Who was the white dude?" Marcus said, impatient.

"He smilin, Lila say. 'Well, I might be interested in acquirin some property in this area.' And Lila tell him she don't know what he talkin about. She can't stand Chester for a minute. Told em she had work to do.''

Marcus stared at the dark liquid left in his uncle's glass, smelling the sweet-bitter ferment mixing with the chitterling broth. "Obvious question ain't answered then," he said.

"If you ask Aintielila, she say they all look alike to her," Octavious said.

"Said he look like any sherbert," Oscar said.

Marcus smiled, knowing what was coming. "Marcus probably see him every day then," Demetrius said.

"Yeah," Marcus said. "Every day." His father and uncle had a specific set of parameters for a sherbert, having to do with affluent men who not only liked sweetened foods and fancy ice cream, but even wanted their buildings and shopping malls to be creamy pastels, their gas stations peachy-stuccoed, and their cars . . . Well, a Lexus fit the description. Along with living in the historic downtown area.

"I can't help you there," Marcus said. "Lots of white guys buyin and sellin land, walkin around downtown, but I don't know them. And look over there by where Demetrius lives now. Everybody always sayin, 'Ask Marcus, he live downtown.' You in that new Rivercrest development, man, must be thousands of houses, fulla white people. And pale furniture.''

Demetrius smiled easily. "Just cause Enchantee wanted to move out there don't mean I changed."

"Oh, we gon start that again?" Marcus said.

Oscar interrupted them. "Hey. Lotta white men buyin land. But two times since that one come, city code guy come out here with the cops. I had to waste gallons of good stuff."

"Damn!" said Julius. "Rock turn it all out?"

Oscar nodded. When police or anyone dangerous came on the property, Oscar or Lila threw an empty tin pail down the unused stone watering trough by the house; the clanging signaled Rock, the watchman in the grove by the choc still, to turn loose the barrels into the remaining orange trees and let the irrigation water run, washing the beer deep into the furrows in a few seconds. Even when trash abounded in the parking lot, the water trough was always empty, and Rock cultivated the soft earth around those orange trees nearly every day, so the liquid would seep inside the crumbly dirt faster.

"Them two walked all around here, talkin unsanitary conditions, fire marshal mention crowdin last year. All that shit." Oscar paused. "Nobody been over there to your place. I axed Hosea while ago."

"Somebody musta been," Demetrius said. "He talkin about white dudes on the lot."

Marcus stood up. "Anybody ask Abuela? Maybe she saw somebody. I know she mad somebody spilled gas in her place."

"You ain't gon eat no chitlins?" Oscar called when Marcus reached the door.

"I ain't hungry," Marcus said, hearing the others walking to the kitchen.

"What you eat—a goddamn bran muffin?"

Marcus walked around the frame house, past the stone trough and the drum barbecues and zinc washtubs, toward the thick trees in the back. Oscar's land was equal to his father's, but bisected by the canal. The pea field Lanier leased was two acres, and trees covered most of the rest. He wound among the peeling trunks, looking at the piles of potpourri under his feet.

He laughed to himself. Crushed bark, dried lavender leaves, pink pepper berries, and papery magenta bougainvillea from the wild vine growing along the chain link in places. He squatted and held up a palmful, scented and light. He'd been in his first year at USC, in Los Angeles, talking to some white girl in her dorm room about their midterm in history, and he'd seen a huge bowl on her dresser. Chips of color and strong smell. "You buy that?" he'd asked, curious. "What is it?"

"Potpourri," she'd said, laughing. "You've never seen that?"

"See it all the time. Never bought it," he'd mumbled, embarrassed. And she'd smiled at him for the rest of the semester, joked with him about finding some free potpourri. He'd left school after that year, and he didn't want to remember that now.

But he'd forgotten himself once, and he'd said the word in front of his brothers. Foolish-sounding word, and he'd never mentioned it again.

All that free perfumed stuff piled into a nearly solid wall along the chain link, where he'd walked along the other side yesterday. Rock wasn't around, and the barrels for the choc beer were hidden in the stone pump shed where the irrigation water was controlled. The twenty orange trees, in a perfect square surrounded by a track of packed earth, were glossy-leaved in the sun. Marcus smelled the damp ground around each tree, saw one leathery citrus peel near his foot, and he threw it into the mesh of hidden fence.

Walking along the wall toward the gate, he tried to think of what his father wanted him to do. So someone was setting up a Thompson— had they expected his father to go out there with a gun, or Julius, or Demetrius? Had they just picked the Granada randomly? Not if they had to climb the fence. Pammy Sawicky had been inside the car . . . He refused to think about that yet.

He skirted the trailers, too bright to look at in the glaring sun, and stood near Abuela's olive shed. The dim, cool interior of the small building, lined with cement curing vats that were dry and chalky now, was empty. Abuela's chair was close to the rabbits and chickens in their curlicued cages nearby, but when he closed his eyes, he could hear the steady scraping of Abuela's rake.

His mother's Mexican grandmother spoke very little English, and she had to be close to a hundred years old. Marcus knew she thought while she swept and raked, that every cool morning and darkening night while she stroked the gravel and swirled into the cement corners, she figured out what she needed to inside her head. She'd told him many times, when he was little and following her around to do the chores she couldn't do—stooping to pick up the tiny piles of debris, bending to carry the heavy water bucket—that she didn't want to talk then, when she raked. She shook her head and put her tiny, bent forefinger to her temple. "*Piensa*," she'd say, nodding gravely. Think.

Her steady strokes echoed slightly up here, where he could see parts of the storage lot. He turned to look at the mountain, cloaked in thin February green. The boulders and tobacco tree where he'd waited yesterday, where he'd hidden for hours as a child, peered over the olive

trees. Marcus looked again at the black smudge of earth where the car
had burned: The Granada and all the evidence were gone now.

He could see parts of the house, too, but no one was outside. The
adobe walls were blistered in places where they faced the hills, he knew,
though he was too far to see the peeling whitewash. The wind and rain
blew down from this way. Because of the long drought, his mother
and father had been able to put off several things they usually did at
this time of year. Gravel. Marcus tried to remember when they went
to pick up truckloads of speckled gray pebbles from Salcido's building-
supply yard. Around Christmas, before the serious rain. They had to
rake it off the trucks and even it out along the paths and driveways and
yards, all of them, raking and patting and stomping.

Constant work, this farm. That's what it was, a car ranch. The low
riders coming to pick a part on the lot, the scufflers coming to find a
car just to get them through a few months, the women sweetly begging
Julius to fix them up with a ride.

Feed the rabbits, the chickens, pick the olives, the apricots, the
avocados and oranges. He'd always hated the constant work, the never-
ending swarm of people trading and arguing and questioning, the
orders—that was one reason he lived downtown. And whenever his
students complained about cutting the grass, and the rich kids smirked,
Marcus would smile and think of the gravel and the whitewash.

He and his brothers would mix burned lime, Liquitex, and sweet
milk in huge pails before the winter rains. They'd slap on the whitewash
mix old Archuleta, who'd built the house, had taught their father to
make, slathering the snowy thickness onto the adobe that sucked it in
like spongy-pored bread.

The fences. The chain link and barbed wire and stone walls always
needed work, too. People cut them, sagged the wire with drunk-spun
cars, and festooned them with impaled cups and cans.

Only the dead cars on the lot needed no maintenance, and that was
where he used to hide. The vehicles were there to be vulturized, fender
by windshield by universal joint, but he would slump inside that old
'78 Granada, silver and rusted-out, because it was closest to the riverbottom and he could read his books, look up to see when the sky began
to lower into the cottonwoods and he needed to get his behind back
up to the house before they came looking for him.

If his father sent Demetrius or Octavious, they'd kick him around just for fun, daring him to hit back, sticking his shoulders with knuckle prods, popping the side of his head with fingertip slaps.

When the wind blew off the hills behind him now, swirling up the soot from the storage lot, he couldn't force himself to imagine the women in the Granada, slumped on that torn maroon seat, might have been alive when they burned. But he couldn't see how they'd gotten inside voluntarily, unless someone was planning to have sex. Lots of places to hide a dead body or two, especially in Treetown, with plenty of vacant lots and places where people dumped trash. But starting the fire meant something else. Someone was insanely angry, but had enough patience and planning to work around a locked gate.

Walking back to the barn, he could hear his brothers. Julius said, "Why you don't believe Felicia give me some? Hey, don't you remember that old song Uncle Oscar used to sing, one a them about the iceman and the handyman? 'Honey, I'm not the best, the best in town. But I'll be the best till the best come round.'" Marcus saw him snapping his fingers.

The other two had their shoulders engulfed in the exposed engine of a '69 Ford truck with gasket troubles. Mr. Slim's truck always had gasket troubles. Marcus stood a few feet away, looking at the intricate arrangement of metal and hoses and wires. It might as well have been a human heart needing surgery for all he knew. Demetrius looked up and rested his elbows on the frame. "What you want me to do with your car?" he asked softly.

Marcus glanced at the Cabriolet, parked near the fence by the street behind a lien-sale Toyota. He hadn't thought they'd noticed.

"I'm talkin about your Lexus got ripped. I'ma go over Layton's and get it for you today. You want it here?" Demetrius looked serious, patient.

Marcus tilted his head, suspicious. "How'd you know?"

"Like Layton wouldn't call me up when he seen your name? You know he got cop rotation."

The police had a list of tow yards they called after accidents and thefts; Demetrius had wanted to be on it for a while, but his father and Octavious didn't want any part of it. Now we got a different kind of cop rotation, Marcus thought. But he was surprised that Demetrius didn't want to play up the stolen Lexus with this audience. "Thanks, man," he said. "But it was leased. I think the dealer get it back."

"All right, then," Demetrius said, lowering his face again to the gaskets.

"Maybe you can look for a hooptie for me," Marcus said casually. "Classes start next week." Demetrius nodded. "I was gon look for Finis again," Marcus added.

Julius turned and said, "I heard he got a lady friend near the Gardens. Find that hard to believe, but somebody told me her name Sharon, or somethin like that."

Marcus turned to head down the slope, where cars sped past the blackened fence now, and he heard his mother talking to Demetrius just as Enchantee's car pulled the turn into the gate so quickly gravel popped the wire.

She got out, carrying Demetrius Junior, and smiled at Marcus. "Hey. Haven't seen you in a while."

Marcus felt warmth rise in his throat, watching her walk to Demetrius and set down his son. She was dressed for work, creased maroon pants and an embroidered vest, and the bones under her arched eyebrows gleamed with gold shadow. Every time he saw her perfect makeup, the wash of color at her cheeks, her lips outlined full with dark red pencil, he remembered what a fool he'd made of himself when they went to the art college downtown, not far from where he lived now.

She'd worn silver under her brows then, in 1979, and shiny gloss on her mouth that he stared at while she talked to him in the arched hallways. He'd followed her for months, theirs the only dark faces in the college, and when they talked, he told her everything: the African connections he'd learned in Brother Lobo's class, the way his father's place wasn't forty acres and a mule but ten acres and five boys to work, how he wanted to work in a museum of historical artifacts all related to black history.

She'd wanted to be a graphic artist, she'd told him, to draw the fashion models for advertising, to make the shadows work on paper. She'd let him press against her in the hallways at night, kissing and talking, talking about the things no one on Pepper Avenue wanted to hear.

She leaned into Demetrius's neck now to tell him something: Along the side of her neck was a tiny rosette of hard-pulled blood, much smaller than the big, splashy marks Demetrius had left on her when he'd marked her for his own back then, when he'd known what to do instead of talking to her brow bones.

"How you feelin?" Enchantee said to Alma, but she kept her head down, searching through her purse for something.

"Worried," Alma said.

"Who were the women?" Enchantee asked.

"Don't nobody know yet," Demetrius said. "All kinda strange women in the Gardens, Julius said."

"You don't have to tell me," Enchantee said, moving away when his mother held out her arms for D'Junior. "I have to get to work."

His mother murmured, "Sofelia don't even know her daddy hurt so bad, and I ain't even seen Finis."

Marcus thought, Friday. Sofelia'll call on Friday, and I'll be able to tell her somethin. Maybe she'll come out here and see Daddy. But when Enchantee moved past him, he smelled her perfume. "Gotta make that money," he said. He couldn't help his voice. "Gotta pay that house note."

"Yeah," she said, meeting his eyes, hard. "I sure do."

"What you gon cook for em tonight?" Alma called, her voice stronger.

"I don't know yet," Enchantee called back, close to her car.

"Why you didn't put a coat on this boy? He gon catch a cold!" Alma finished, and Marcus watched Enchantee back out, waving, smiling bright and false.

They're caused by viruses, okay? Viruses in the air. Nothin to do with a chill or the weather or a coat. Ask the pediatrician. Oh, but Alma'd say, "How you know? You always believe doctors? Sometimes the old way work better." All those rituals she wants Enchantee to learn. The Thompson way is not the only way. No. Uh-uh.

Enchantee muttered all the way up Pepper Avenue. What I'ma cook? Why can't your son cook somethin? He handicapped? No—he's a Thompson. Somebody always cook for him. And Marcus—lookin all hard at me, like he thinks he woulda been better. He's still thinkin that. Talkin about "Gotta make that house note." He don't know—just pays his own rent, his own stuff. But for a house—no, you both gotta work, and work hard.

She turned onto the next street, glad her shift began a little later on Sundays. Give people an extra hour to sleep in before they complain. She thought again of Marcus. He scared her, always quoting statistics about black men and diseases, like Brother Lobo's glaucoma. About pork, and how black children walked earlier than any others. How the system then slowed them down. He knew everything, and almost all of it was scary, so she backed away whenever she could.

When they'd been at the art college, she'd liked listening to Marcus at first. His intensity, the way he didn't look at her ass or chest. But when Olive Gardens got to be too much, when her aunt's daughters and neighbors began to talk about her thinking she was somebody, calling her Miss Thang and laughing at her for spending money on the fat art books, she'd met Demetrius at a party. He was big-shouldered, quiet until they were alone, telling her she was so beautiful that she needed protection.

She did, back then. Other girls were as pretty as she was, but they laughed easier, talked, joked, and gave in. Enchantee didn't. She didn't want to have anything to do with the men in the Gardens, few as they were, or the ones who hung around. She went straight from school to the apartment, and her unflinching gaze and unwavering stride pissed most men off.

Only now she was taking care of Demetrius: the cooking, the house, their son, this job. Too much.

She had begun to hate the whole place, the house and yard, filled with men and cars and children, because the Thompsons thought it was the only place in the world. The fringy chain link was the boundary of a planet. And the way they did everything—the beans on the stove all day, the cussing and fighting and borrowing among the brothers, the kids wild—was the only way. They looked at anything else—her cooking, the way she talked soft to Demetrius Junior and didn't beat him, the way she had everything scheduled down to the minute, like this morning—as laughably wrong.

No, I didn't put no coat on D'Junior this morning, because it's sunny and he complained. And yeah, I told Demetrius I didn't want him or D'Junior hanging around too long, because with all this mess, who knows when the cops are comin back. Or maybe somebody start shootin again: It's too dangerous until they find out what's goin on. But I know they'll stay all day. I'ma go home to my empty house. But it's *my* house.

.   .   .

Sometimes she heard the voices at night, swirling into the ear not buried in the pillow. "Hello? My paper . . ." "Damnit, the carrier . . ." "Once again, dear, someone has stolen . . ."

Their cubicles were divided by thin partitions, which looked like asterisks from a distance; each of the women had pictures of children and birthday cards and Post-its tacked to the fake-burlap covering that formed her wall: These were the things she stared at while the voices droned and her fingers flew across the computer keyboard.

Enchantee typed in another new start from the developments across the river. She knew that zip code. And when a voice complained tremulously, an old woman's voice, that she'd called to start the paper several times since she moved onto 96th Street in Terracina, Enchantee knew before she typed in the address that the word "controlled" would flash in response. Controlled. Too many carriers got taken for money, too many newspapers got stolen, too much danger. The *News* wouldn't start new subscriptions in a controlled area.

She paused, writing down a note for a carrier. Olive Gardens was way past control, she thought. That's why she had to get out of there, because she wasn't about to raise a baby like that. Treetown was getting wild as a whole, too much shooting, and even though Demetrius didn't like having to drive to the yard, he didn't argue too much when she'd looked for months at new houses.

But now, today, with this shooting and burning at his father's place, she was worried about them both. And D'Junior—she hated to take him to her aunt's place. But she didn't want him with strangers.

When she left the carrier's note in his box, she grabbed the "Regional" section that someone had left on a table, and she poked Janine's shoulder on the way back to her cubicle. The supervisors measured how much time you took away from your terminal without even looking at you. They stared at their screens and knew everything you did.

"Break time comin," Janine said. "I'm starvin."

Enchantee turned the pages slowly during the down times when no calls came through. It was slower now, almost lunchtime. The front page of the section showed three men named to committees by the city council. They all had silver hair, wore wire-rimmed glasses and red ties. Red ties with little patterns like ladybugs or diamonds.

Another article with a big photo was about the renovation of the Las

Palmas Hotel in the downtown district. Near Marcus's apartment, she thought; Demetrius had shown her.

Nothing about her father-in-law or the two women for several pages. On page seven, she saw the "Social Newsmakers" column, with a picture of Abigail Smith. Enchantee stopped. Abigail looked nearly the same as when they'd been roommates at the art college, with her light gray eyes eerily vacant in the black-and-white photo.

Abigail Smith, a graduate of Rio Seco High School who also attended California Academy of Arts, has returned to her native city, having been recently hired as a "Food & Travel" writer for the News. She is also a freelance writer for several national magazines. Her fiancé, Bent Carson, will report on music and entertainment for the News. Her parents, Mr. Charles Smith, president of Rio Seco Savings and Loan, and Anne Smith, a well-known local artist, will host a reception to welcome their daughter back to southern California. The affair in their home on Plymouth Hill will feature California cuisine catered by Très Bon Fête.

Janine tapped her now, saying, "Time to grub, lady. What you readin?"

Enchantee pointed to the article. "Two reporters. I saw her fiancé the other day."

Janine peered to where she was touching the print. "Bent? He's named Bent? And they make fun of our names. Come on."

Enchantee carried the newspaper into the cafeteria, and when they had their food, she found it. Page eleven.

TWO BODIES FOUND IN BURNING CAR: MAN SHOT AFTER
THREATENING DEPUTY

Sheriff's deputies responding to a call about gunfire in the Treetown area of Rio Seco found two bodies in a car engulfed by flames at a towing yard. An unidentified man was shot and injured when he aimed a weapon at deputies arriving at the scene. He was taken to a local hospital, where his condition was unknown. The bodies were badly burned, and the Rio Seco County coroner's office will conduct autopsies to identify the victims and ascertain the cause of death.

Pepper Avenue was closed by investigators at the crime scene for nearly five hours, causing a major traffic problem for downtown commuters forced to find alternate routes.

The Treetown area has been plagued with crime and drug problems. Officials said the murders could be gang- or drug-related.

Janine shook her head. "See? If it's a black neighborhood, the whole place gotta be fulla gangs and drugs."

Enchantee picked at her food. "Well, they sure make it look like Demetrius's father did it. And he got shot in the shoulder. He's in bad shape, I think."

In the parking lot when the shift was over, she stood talking for a minute to Janine, and Mary and Teresa, two of the other operators. "You think it's hard now—wait till your baby gets to school and you gotta deal with homework," Teresa told her.

Mary said, "At least mine are grown. But I worry about my grandbabies just as hard."

Enchantee just nodded, wondering whether D'Junior was still at Alma's, wondering what he'd eaten and if he'd slept. She felt her neck loosen. Alma always did make him take a nap. And she knew he'd never get hurt over there from carelessness.

She walked toward her car and saw Abigail Smith's shining mushroom cap of pale hair, that perfect half-moon smile. Abigail was laughing with her fiancé, walking quickly toward the building. Before she even thought about it, Enchantee called, "Abby!"

Abigail squinted at her, and Enchantee knew she wasn't wearing her glasses. She'd hated them in college. "Chani?" Abigail hurried over and hugged her. "It's been, literally, years!" She turned to her fiancé. "Bent, this is Chani; we went to the art college downtown together. Neither of us lasted too long!"

Enchantee smiled. Abigail was wearing stirrup pants and a sweater. For a food writer, she didn't look fat, just soft, her skin kind of thick and cushy over her bones. "I read about you just now," Enchantee said, suddenly shy.

But Abigail laughed easily. "Yeah, we were just going up to tell my aunt how much we liked it. She gets real upset when people don't make a big deal out of her stuff. But listen, what are you doing here? You're working here?"

"Just part-time," Enchantee said, shocked at how easy that sounded, the half-truth.

"And you got married!" Abigail clasped her ring hand. "To who? That one guy who kept following you, with the puppy-dog eyes?"

"No. Somebody else," Enchantee said. "You never saw him. We have a boy."

"Are you still living in . . ." Abigail trailed the words off. "I heard it's getting sort of . . . dangerous there."

"We live in Rivercrest, in a new development," Enchantee said easily. "You probably haven't seen it yet, if you just got back."

"No. I heard it's really nice," Bent offered, smiling wide.

"Listen, give me your number. You have to come and see me, meet my son." Abigail took out a small pad of paper. Enchantee wrote, thinking that it was strange the way she said "my son." Abigail said, "As a matter of fact, getting child care is a bitch. Maybe you know somebody?"

"My son's three. He stays with my aunt or my mother-in-law," Enchantee said. "I'm kind of scared of strangers havin him."

"See?" Abigail turned to Bent. "It's not just me. I want somebody who can come in, somebody trustworthy." She looked at Enchantee. "I've been looking in the papers, but . . ."

"Well, I have to go check on mine," Enchantee said. She hesitated. What could she say? I still remember your green fingernail polish, and how you taught me to pluck my eyebrows? Abby was older than she was, maybe four or five years. Enchantee smiled again and said, "Give me a call."

In the car, she thought, I never went to her house, all that time. And she never came to mine. But now, it's like we're more equal. Maybe.

She could see the palms bending with the wind, leading in corridors down all the streets and avenues. Rio Seco was famous for the palm-lined streets, and when Enchantee had first moved downtown, somewhere she'd never even been shopping, she was sure the skinniest, tallest palms would bend close enough to her room to brush against her window.

Hosea would wake with the slurry still forming in his throat and glance at the mouth of the detective talking to him. Sometimes he saw a mouth as small as a piggy-bank slot, and a pair of blue eyes fringed with pale lashes. He would close his eyes again.

Marbles. He'd always hated eyes like marbles, hated marbles, the way they sat in the dirt like floating eyeballs with detached filaments of blue or green inside.

A man with a gun sat in the truck, staring at the women and children crowded in the flatbed while he sat propped against the cab. Hosea saw white men hanging in the windows of the tall downtown buildings as the truck rolled slowly through the streets. He saw white women and men crowded on the street corners, laughing and waving and shouting at the trucks, and he was afraid to look at his mother beside him. Then, on one street, he saw the charred coats and upturned faces of three men. He pressed his face to the wood slats. The hands were curled under like rabbits', held stiff to the sky. The feet were gone. The flames had eaten the flesh, leaving only stick bones that ended in a straight nub like a hoof. His saliva rose again, flooding his molars with acid, but he swallowed again and again until he felt the sting drop slowly through his chest to his breastbone, where it fanned heat under his ribs.

Sudden bursts of shouting and gunfire were ahead of them, and the parading truck sped up to a fan of white steps. A huge building. "The Convention Hall!" one of the white men hollered. "Hurry up!"

Hosea saw a line of black men marching, with hands high and limp, and white men guarding them with stiff guns slanted at their heads. Two other men ran up to the line of marchers and began to shoot, and one woman in the truck near Hosea's mother screamed, "Dr. Jackson! They shootin Dr. Jackson!"

Two of the men hanging on to the truckbed rails jumped off and ran, and when the truck stopped, the driver ran, too, holding his gun. Hosea saw heaps of dark cloth lying on the street, and he clambered over the wood slats and crouched near the wheel. Hosea moved quickly, bent still, to the front of the truck, and then ran down one of the alleys. He was going to find his father—a coated heap or a marcher.

But at the tall slot of sky he reached in the alley's end, another line of knee-bent men was shuffling past, and when he paused, searching the dust-smeared eyes above moustaches, one man cried, "My hat!"

A boy taller than Hosea, with brown hair as straight and stiff as tiny sticks under his soft cap, snatched the hat and threw it into the street. When he turned to fling it, crying, "Shut up, nigger, and walk," his marble eyes found Hosea's, and he sprang into the alley to push Hosea with his gun. The barrel drooped, too long for him, but he swung the butt around toward Hosea's head.

The flared end of the wooden butt slammed into his shoulder, and the boy's boot clamped down onto his outstretched hand.

When the always cold hands grasped his to apply the blood-pressure cuff, he didn't open his eyes. He always waited until the steps had traced all their paths around his bed before he looked at the hospital window. The square turned a vague gold, then a slatted gray. If he heard the door open, he made sure his eyes were closed, and he didn't open his mouth. The detectives came by now and then, the feather-haired nurse. He had never been so close to so many white hands and faces, had never felt bluish fingers on his wrist.

He looked at the identification tag around his wrist with blurred eyes. The ember throbbing in his shoulder was still hot, and the wreath of heat had not left his head. The dizzying white of the nurse's uniform and her knuckles nearly silver in the artificial light made him weak.

When he found his mother under the grandstands at the fairground, where they had taken many of the prisoners who were women and children, her eyes were darting, unfocused. "Mama," he whispered. "Mama. I'm right here."

But she wasn't looking for him. The shadows blended through the slats of wood when the sky grew dark, and the whole park was full of faces. His mother began to hiss breath through her teeth. She called for Letitia, for Retha, not for him. In the dank cave, Hosea saw two older women coming toward them, bending to hear her whispers, and another woman pulled him away by the elbow. "Come over here, little man," the woman said. Her eyes were milky with film. "Come help me get your mama some water."

He sat with this woman against a fence, watching all the women and kids mill about or lie down in the dark. A few men sat in a knot near one grandstand, talking fiercely, quietly, and when he stood near them, one said, "They want the land, damnit. They want to move the railroad tracks, put up a new station right there."

"White folks go crazy over anything," another said softly.

"No," the first one insisted. "I'm a lawyer. I can see what they're doing. Wait."

He stared toward the grandstand where his mother lay. He knew she was having the baby. He felt the tracing of foot nub against his jaw, the insistent movement against his side in the truck. He listened for her, but in the babble and cry of lips all around him, he could hear only the hollow popping sound the old woman's lips made when she adjusted her mouth as if she was used to smoking a pipe. He dug his hand deep into his pocket and pressed one of the copper balls Maceo had given him hard into the whorls of his fingers.

All night, he lay near his mother, in the smell of blood and salt and crushed straw. She lay on coats, the baby hidden in the dress someone had brought her from the Red Cross. Hosea saw splinters of wood embedded in her loose roll of hair.

A woman came by and said, "Sophia?" Hosea didn't know her face. "That you? What you got in . . . Lord God, you done had that baby? Dr. Jackson, you was gon go to Dr. Jackson this time."

"They killed him," Hosea's mother said, her voice reasonable to Hosea's ears but her skin waxed and stiff.

He lay carefully, not moving, until daylight filtered gray through the roil of smoke and the loose breaths of all the people under the grandstands. He saw white people at the fences then.

They would gesture to a face inside the fairground, and a guard would take the figure outside to the white person, who sometimes led three or four away. Hosea was chilled with fear, racing along his shoulder blades. Did the white people choose who they wanted to shoot now? He stared at the bobbing moon faces gathering outside the fence. And he saw Retha's brown jaw in among them, her eyes finding his, her long dark finger showing him to the white woman.

When Retha bent down to his mother, she said, "Come on with me, Sophia. Only way to get out of here is have somebody speak for you. I been done talked to Mrs. Hefferon all mornin. She said you only done a few jobs for her, and I told her you ain't got nobody else. Come on. Let me help you up."

Hosea held his mother's dusty dress when she walked silently toward the crowd at the gate. He felt the long badge pinned to his shirt, the needle pricking his chest. Police protection, the man shouted. You can only go with an employer. Is this your employer?

His mother stood, wordless, but Retha said, "She do laundry for Mrs. Hefferon. We goin home now."

His mother winced at the words, and when the white woman stared at them from beside her black car, he felt the acid rising again. Clenching his throat, he stopped. She stepped forward. "The French lace," she said, her voice flat. "I'm sure it's burned."

Hosea's mother nodded, her mouth still sealed by a rim of shine between her lips, a sliver of damp Hosea could see when she tightened and then unrolled her mouth.

"I don't know what's wrong with everyone," the woman said. "People shouldn't be agitating niggers to think that . . ." She stopped and put her fingers under her earlobes, pressing hard. "Now, Retha says you want to come and stay with us."

Hosea held his air inside. His mother was silent. The baby was only a slight lump in her dress, under the coat Retha had draped around her.

"Don't you know any other white families?" the woman said, moving her fingers to her temples, and Hosea saw red dents there when she dropped her hands to her sides. "You'll have to crowd in with Retha."

"I don't mind, Mrs. Hefferon," Retha said. "We should get the baby out the air."

"He wouldn't open the door for me," the woman said, fixing her eyes on Hosea's face, and a lacing of heat crawled through his scalp. People passed all around them, raising dust. "I hope he won't cause trouble. He can pick up the yard for today."

Hosea saw his mother's lips work, the shine spreading.

"That lace," the woman whispered. "You have no idea. Mr. Hefferon's mother . . ." Retha put her hand on his mother's back and propelled her toward the car door, and the woman spoke louder. "Don't you want to say thank you, boy? You'll have a place, and a little man's job."

Hosea's mother turned slowly, and she met his eyes. Her skin was smudged with light dust like gold powder, and she wet her lips again. "He don't need to talk just yet," she whispered. "He just a baby."

"He's a little man. He's already looking for trouble," the woman said, the skin under her chin twisting when she held her face higher, waiting, and Hosea brought the copper balls out of his pocket in his clenched fingers, holding them fisted against his leg, imagining them sunk deep into a necklace in the folds of her throat. He blurred his eyes, so that she was only a shape, and passed her to stand by his mother.

"Where'd you get the old gun?" the first detective said as Hosea opened his eyes. The room was nearly gray, like dawn, and the nurse with brown skin stood nearby. Mrs. King. Her name tag bobbed on her chest when she brought him water.

"I can see you're a night owl," the man said. "You can't sleep forever. We got those girls ID'd now. It's been four days, and it's time to wake up. You had two white girls in the Ford Granada. You have an old gun with three shots fired. Either you're up for murder or somebody you know is. We can start with that. Who likes white girls at your place? You like white girls? One of your boys? Who hangs around with white girls? One of them was a city councilman's daughter, so this should be good. You ready?"

Hosea stared at his right hand, the one he could move. This detective was about the age of his oldest son. His irises swam in constant movement. Hosea brought the cinder up to his face. It was a greenish tattoo, deep inside.

His hand was clean, dry. He recalled a pair of dark hands, with long red fingernails, cradling his palm in a washbasin, rubbing with a cloth.

The detective said, "I'll sit here forever. Or until somebody finds your son Finis. Nobody's seen him around your place since that night. You ready?"

Hosea brought the clean palm to his mouth, and with his front teeth worked at the edge of the thick callus near his ring finger. He sawed his teeth back and forth slightly until the flap of hard skin cut loose, then he lay back, chewing the skin softly, slowly.

CHAPTER THREE

MARCUS HEADED FOR Chipotle Chile, Kurt's restaurant, to return the car. He knew Chile would be crowded, but Kurt and his friends Lakin and Javier always had room for him at the table closest to the kitchen, where they sat watching and gossiping when they could. Talkin shit, he thought, opening the door hung with red chile *ristras* and blue corn; that's what they call it at The Blue Q. The two places might as well be in different countries.

That was what he thought most nights when he ate here or in the Japanese place, when he saw a movie at the art theater. He ended up unconsciously translating things into his father's or brothers' words, then stepping back to look at the chasm dividing the phrases and foods and scenes.

He slid past the crowded tables, the flying elbows and shouts of the crowd, and swiveled his knees into the booth near the exposed kitchen. People here liked to watch their food cook.

"Starving by now?" Lakin asked. She was Finnish, a dark-haired, paper-skinned small woman who worked as a prep cook and hung out all night.

"You got it," Marcus said. Kurt was swerving around the kitchen, his wide cheeks coated with sweat.

"Must be making something for an old man," Javier said, grinning. His ridged teeth glowed against coppery skin. He was from New Mexico, and he'd decorated the place with the chiles, indigo corn, and wooden furniture.

"You're the oldest," Lakin said, nodding. "We all compared."

"Thanks," Marcus said, catching their puzzled frowns. But he didn't want to joke around. He settled back, watching people moving their mouths around food and phrases and arguments. His father's voice slid behind his ear: Thirty years old and still workin on your history, huh? Teachin ready-made history, his uncle would add. Somebody else's history.

But when he'd asked for his, for their history, he'd gotten lips held tight around cigarillos and brusque dismissals. All his life, for school and for himself, when he'd questioned them about what they did as children, about how they'd come to own land that touched, they'd turned away, saying, Nothin to do with you, boy.

A hand deposited a plate beside him. Lakin laughed. Kurt had fixed him up quick with fat, spicy pinto beans in a bowl and inky-dark tortillas. Marcus bent his head to the beans, the mist clouding his eyes. He didn't know if it was because he kept picturing his father lying on his back in the hospital bed. But he couldn't help it. Beans, he thought. Same thing everybody's eatin in Treetown. And they munchin on yellow corn tortillas. Not much difference. But it is.

Javier said, "Kurt knows what you like, huh?"

Marcus chewed the beans in their thick red sauce, nodding. He couldn't talk. His head was too full, like a flu swelled there. Bullets. That's what they called beans at home. "We havin bullets again, huh? Surprise—bullets and corn bread." Kurt and Javier and Lakin and him— they all knew each other from here, from movies and downtown architecture and beer, but they didn't really know him.

"Who's movin and shakin tonight?" he murmured when he was done, when he'd drunk a beer and his head felt slightly smaller.

"Oh, we've got some city council guys, we've got a bunch of museum women, we've got opera people," Lakin said, scanning the crowd. They could see almost everything from this back table, but this wasn't a prized location. Obviously, since they were allowed to stay in it frequently. "Some reporters I recognize from the newspaper," she said, dropping her voice. "They've been talking about that double murder down there in Treetown. What a rough place."

Javier shook his head. "See that girl over there?" He inclined his forehead toward a table where four women sat, slumped elegantly over dessert and coffee. "I heard her crying in the bathroom before. I think she knew one of the girls that got killed, because she kept saying to her friends that she had told her to stop. Something like that."

Marcus stared at the woman's face, her eyes pink-rimmed inside mascara, her freckles stark on her forehead. "See over there?" Lakin went on. She loved to categorize people and recognize faces belonging to regular customers. "She's a museum and charity type, she's in here all the time, and that's her new husband, Web something. He's like a developer or something. Big bucks. And he looks younger than *you*, Marcus." She touched him with her elbow, but the teary woman had gotten up and headed for the bathroom again, and she fixed her eyes on Marcus.

"Hey," she said, smiling slightly. "You don't remember me?"

He tried, smiling back. She was wearing a black miniskirt and a big sweater, and her brown hair was thin-curved behind her ears. "Shella Frohling," she said. "We went to school together. I guess you heard about Pammy."

Marcus saw her eyes grow glossy. He nodded, and suddenly he knew his father had heard him use the dead woman's name back then. Watch out, brother, that white girl gon do a Pammy Sawicky on your black ass, the guys would say to each other.

He blinked hard, and said, "Yeah. I remember you. You guys were friends." He stood up. "You want to go outside for some air?"

Her calves, in black tights, were as round as baseballs. Marcus stared at the moving muscles because he didn't want to run the gauntlet of faces.

Pammy Sawicky. In high school, she went Chicano first, wearing Pendleton shirts buttoned at the chin and then falling open to show a ribbed white undershirt. Her lips were dark red, her brows a thin-penciled arch, and her khakis were creased.

Then, sophomore year, she was black. All of a sudden, she hung out near the fenced parking lot with the few Treetown people. She got rides to the Westside, Marcus remembered, and was always hanging from the window of some brother's car. Her thick brown hair was corn-rowed, her scalp glowing pearly between the braids. Marcus watched her. She put her hands on her hips and said, "He ain't none a my man," when someone challenged her.

Marcus followed Shella to the pedestrian mall, where restaurants had set up chairs and tables and hung trees with sparkling white lights. He sat down beside her. "You hung out with Pammy senior year," he said. "I remember." She nodded, turning away to light a cigarette.

Senior year, Pammy went back. "Like nappy hair in a rainstorm," Treetown girls said. It was the football season, and when Pammy, who had still been dating Lee Terry, a Westsider, disappeared from school for a week, Marcus remembered being curious about the lack of her pale, animated face near the fence. When the assembly was called to parade and then elect football's homecoming queens, the dark-haired Treetown and Westside and few Agua Dulce kids sat in one area of bleachers. It was 1978. Four white girls walked, their dresses shimmering, their arms stiff-curled into elbow crooks of football players. One black girl, from the Westside, Leticia Smalls, walked with Jerome Taylor, a fullback. Treetown and Westside cheered. And then Pammy Sawicky came out, in a gold-toned satin dress, her hair straight and turned under at the ends, on the arm of a football player from Southwest High, on the other end of the city. Blond bristly hair, bull neck, straight smile. Her fingernails weren't red, black, and green. They were pink.

"You won homecoming queen senior year," Marcus said to Shella, and she nodded.

"And Pammy got beat up at the game by some girls from Treetown," Shella said. "You helped her out."

"Yeah." Marcus looked at the twinkling tree lights, the passing people still carrying briefcases from work. Pammy had called him a nigger. She'd spat, "Fuck you, nigger. I don't need you."

"Pammy was hanging around downtown a lot," Shella said. "Not around this part, but by the bus station and the bars down on California." She pushed her hair behind her ears tightly. "I heard she was doing a lot of drugs. Speed."

Marcus nodded. Speed was the white drug. Once you went back, you better stay that way. "I never saw her in Treetown," he said. "Never."

Shella nodded. "I know. That's why I can't figure out why she'd have been sitting in a car down there."

Marcus smiled. "Yeah." He remembered one day, after the fight, when Pammy had come up to him in a hallway, no one else around, and said, "Hey. I'm really sorry. About what I said to you." Pammy had paused, her eyes darting behind him, then back to his face. "I mean, you aren't like that. What I mean is, my dad always said there's a lot of different kinds of people. There's niggers, but you aren't one." Then she'd turned and fled back down the hallway.

Marcus stood up, smiling wider, falser, at Shella. "I can't figure that out myself," he said.

Marcus went out to buy a newspaper the next morning, and when he got back inside the apartment, a message had been left on the phone. "Marcus, this is Natalie Larchwood." Marcus smiled. The principal at Rio Seco High.

"Mr. Whalen graciously and conveniently waited until our teachers' meeting this morning to tell me that he might schedule surgery in November and need a leave of absence. Marcus, I'd planned to try and give you a few freshman history classes and some study halls, but in any case, please come by on Friday to discuss a contract. I think this might work out well. Thanks."

Marcus slapped the wall and said, "That'll work out *fine*. Hell, yeah." He made coffee, glancing at the newspaper but not wanting to open it yet. Finally, he sat in front of the big window overlooking the tiled domes of the downtown Moorish-style buildings.

The photos and names on the front page of the city news section stared out at him, and the coffee burned into his throat to meet something rising there.

LIFELONG FRIENDS FOUND BRUTALLY SLAIN

Rio Seco police detectives are working overtime to investigate the deaths of two Rio Seco women whose bodies were found locked in a burning car at a dilapidated towing yard in the western edge of the city, an area known as Treetown.

Pamela Sawicky, 30, and Marissa Kent, 29, were burned beyond recognition, and their distraught families only learned of their whereabouts when coroner's officials obtained dental records to identify the women. Sawicky was the daughter of Rio Seco City Councilman Warren Sawicky. Kent was a Rio Seco native working as a pet groomer in the downtown area.

"Pammy was my pride and joy," the distraught city councilman said yesterday. "She had some problems in the past, but she was turning her life around. She had just moved back home to attend city college. I lost her mother ten years ago, and I am angry and devastated. I want to find out who would commit such a heinous act. The Lord calls it specifically—an eye for an eye."

Sawicky had been arrested twice for misdemeanor drug charges. Kent had never been arrested.

The women were found when police responded to a call about gunfire in the area and found a man with a rifle. Hosea Thompson, 76, brandished the weapon at officers and was shot in the shoulder. He has been treated at Rio Seco County General Hospital, where he is held in the jail ward, but police will not say whether he is the sole suspect in the double homicide. Investigators are seeking another resident of the address for questioning.

Homicide detective Ron Harley said ballistic tests would be run on Thompson's weapon, but that anyone who might have seen the two women on Thursday night should call him at the department. Information about their whereabouts could help police learn how the women died.

Marcus bent his head toward the photos smiling out from the page, his mouth as dry as cardboard. One woman was blond and square-mouthed, like an athlete. Marissa Kent. The other was narrow-eyed, brown-haired, with grainy skin. Pammy Sawicky. He lifted his eyes. He had to find Finis quick. He was the other resident. When the police had assumed the two women were crack-head sisters from Treetown, nobody had been too worried. But now, with everybody in Rio Seco seeing these two faces, all hell would break loose. Marcus hadn't seen Pammy Sawicky since graduation night. But maybe Finis had. He didn't even know her, but if she was doing speed, maybe somehow he'd run into her near the Kozy Komfort. Why would the two women have gotten into the Granada, which hadn't moved in years? Finis wouldn't have had anything to do with it; he'd never be capable of even a short conversation with a white person who didn't know his music. Marcus pulled on jeans and a sweatshirt, breathing hard. Finis had to say where he'd been that night, and since.

He walked quickly toward Pepper Avenue, cussing the fools who'd stolen his car. White people on the land, his father had told Mrs. King. Could somebody have been angry about a repair job or a car they'd bought off the lot? But Marcus had never even seen a white person buy a car from his father. He strode faster, past the closed pink doors of the Kozy Komfort, shut up like a dollhouse, and decided not to take the back way along the canal since that would look strange to the police probably watching the house. Along the roadside after the underpass, he put his hands casually in his pockets. Two cops in an unmarked car were parked beside the last shell of a building on the other side of Pepper, about a quarter of a mile before his father's gate. The walls were a mosaic of graffiti, intricately overlaid colors, and Marcus concentrated on the curving painted shapes instead of the sunglasses and mouths of the men watching him. He nodded at them, hoping they already knew who he was. Which brother. You don't want me, he chanted over and over.

His mother was sweeping nervously near the kitchen steps. The barn and yard were empty. When she saw him, she blinked swimming eyes.

"Demetrius and Octavious went on a tow. Julius holin up at some woman's house on the Westside. Kickstand—that what y'all call him?" Marcus nodded. "He say he ain't workin till this mess cleared up." She paused, pushing the angled broom deep into a corner. "And your daddy won't say nothin to nobody. Them police keep comin, tell me that, ask me about Finis. I been waitin for you to come and look for him."

Marcus looked at her maroon cheeks, flushed and spread wide. He knew his mother wouldn't say anything to the police, but not because she thought Finis had something to hide. He had no interest in white women, and he was unable to kill spiders because it was bad luck. But his mother, like most Treetown women, was terrified of policemen. They'd seen doors bashed in by the battering rams during drug raids, the wrong family prone and stomped on the wrong floor; they'd seen the wrong man shot, the wrong woman shoved into a wall. They'd seen the right ones fall, too, at times, the burglar smacked and cuffed, the drunk fighter held tight by uniformed arms. But he knew his mother's tongue was frozen dry to the roof of her mouth whenever a policeman even nodded at her, even though now and then an officer brought a car or some other small business to the yard.

"A woman called me this mornin, say she read the paper and Finis been stayin with her. SaRonn. She live on Jacaranda, Marcus. She said he ain't there right now, but go see her. Here." She ducked inside the kitchen door, reaching for the wall where keys were hung on hooks. "Take Octavious's car."

Marcus shook his head, smiling, and touched the key ring with the silver eight attached. "Long as you don't tell him."

He eased the cherried '64 Impala onto Pepper Avenue. Avocado-green flake on the outside, red leather tuck and roll on the seats, and black dash. Spoked rims. This was Octavious's baby, his statement to the world. And he didn't like anybody else driving it.

Marcus turned quickly onto Grove Avenue, the narrow ribbon of asphalt edged with sand. After a quarter mile, a few houses appeared on the side, and he turned left on Olive Street. Four even smaller streets radiated off this one, and this was where most of Treetown's houses were lined. Verbena, Lantana, Dracena, and Jacaranda. At the far end of Olive Street was Olive Gardens, a hulking pistachio-green box of stucco.

Marcus went slowly down Jacaranda. The wood-frame houses here were set far back on their big lots, nearly half-acre size, and most had pecan or pepper trees scattered around. Laundry and swings and ropes and punching bags hung from branches. Marcus remembered several of the houses where old ladies had lived when he was younger, the porches curtained with variegated ivy, the windows hidden by untrimmed bushes. But he saw young women on a few of these porches now, watching him.

SaRonn. He didn't recognize that name at all. He hoped she would be looking for him. He was almost to the end of the street, where it curled around in a comma blocked by trees, when he saw a woman wave at him from the yard of a tiny yellow house.

When he stopped carefully near the small rock-lined ditch that passed for a gutter on all the Treetown streets, he heard a loud, hollow smash on the trunk of the car, once, twice, three times. Shit, he thought, they said guys are gettin jacked for car rims. What the hell. Octavious probably don't have a weapon in here. He was reaching forward to open the glove compartment when a heavy female voice said, "Eight, I'ma *kick* yo black ass. You know I'm outta milk, goddamnit."

Marcus let his hand drop from the glove compartment, hoping this woman wouldn't damage his face before she saw it. "Hey," he called. "It's not Eight. It's his brother."

Marcus made sure the voice had moved past the door before he opened it, so the owner of the voice would be separated from him by good, heavy sixties craftsmanship. He swung plenty of metal between them and got out.

Had to be a Proudfoot, he thought, with her slanted-up eyes and broad forehead and the heavy bun of hair, with dangling braids the size of caterpillars over her ears. There were so many Proudfoots in Treetown that he had trouble keeping them straight, and Octavious was living with one.

Not this one, though. Octavious and Belisa Proudfoot had been together three or four years; Belisa was smaller, just as loud, but without the muddiness in her eyes.

"You which brother?" this woman shouted. "I ain't seen your ass before."

"The baby brother," Marcus answered, trying to be pitiful and safe.

"Shit." She folded her arms, feet in slippers wide on the dirt. "He told me he would get me a car, cause mine been broke down, and he ain't done shit. I seen him this mornin with Belisa, and I told him I needed some milk and other stuff for my kids. Nigga said he come back and give me a ride. I ain't seen his ass."

"He's on a tow," Marcus said. He turned to look behind him for the woman named SaRonn, hoping she had a softer voice and fresher eyes.

"Then he don't need his car, do he?" the Proudfoot woman said. "Give me his keys and let me make this run. I'll be right back." Before Marcus could move, she had snatched the keys from his fingers and grabbed the door handle.

Marcus moved closer to her, smelling beer and wood smoke on her clothes, but she shoved him with her shoulder and got into the car. "I can't let you take Octavious's ride, sista," he started, trying to reach into the window, but she started up the car and said, "Get the *fuck* out my way. I said I'll be back."

Marcus saw the plume of dust rise up to his face, and he whispered, "God *damnit*! She's gone wreck Eight's car and he's gon kick *my* ass." He realized that people were watching, and he tried to shrug. "I can't be hittin a woman, though, right?"

A woman smiled at him. "You Marcus? I'm SaRonn." Her cheeks were as dark and gold as the raw honey he'd seen Mr. Lanier collect from near the orange blossoms, and one thumb-print dimple went deep into the left side near her mouth. She wore faded jeans and a white T-shirt, and her hair was cut short over her head except for a crimped fringe of hair at her nape that he saw when she turned to walk into her house.

A small girl was in the doorway, he saw, a miniature SaRonn about two years old. "Come on in," SaRonn called.

There were five of the narrow, long houses on the lot, he saw, all in a row. Each front door was covered by a peak-roofed overhang with a slanted yellow section radiating out, propped on thin pillars of wood painted blue. They looked like the top halves of drooping stars, he thought, following her inside.

Her front room was glossy wood floor, a couch covered in a Mexican blanket, and a big TV playing music videos. Her daughter skated on a small hand towel, shrieking with glee, over the shining floor.

"I just waxed it, and she's on a magic carpet," SaRonn said, sitting on the couch. "I wanted to tell you about Finis. Your brother, right?"

"Yeah," Marcus said, though he couldn't imagine that a woman as pretty as this, as unruffled as this, would be seeing Finis. Well, *seeing* him, but not fooling around. "I guess you can tell me now, before Octavious kills me."

She laughed. "I don't think Bennie's gon wreck his car. She just hates walkin, and you know there's no store around except the liquor store."

"Look like that's where she'd want to go," Marcus said.

SaRonn's eyebrows lifted in warning. "Now, don't start," she said. "She's gon get some beer. But she's gon get some meat and milk and the rest, too. She's got three kids. Her husband was treatin her so bad, beatin on her when they lived in San Bernardino. She left him and came on back here. She stays in the back house, farthest from the street."

Marcus nodded. "And Finis been stayin here?"

She smiled now. "Not like that, okay? He found out I just got cable and this new TV, and he sits where you are, watchin MTV for, like, five and six hours. Then he falls asleep on the floor. Willa pokes him in the ear and he doesn't even move. Huh, Willa?" She looked at her daughter, who nodded.

"You from around here?"

"I remember you," SaRonn said, smiling dimple-deep again. "I was in your sister's class. Sofelia. She ever come back?" Her grin faded.

Marcus shook his head. He fought the urge to tell her that Sofelia called him, that she should call him tonight. He stared at this woman's eyes, the saffron irises rimmed with black.

"Finis been goin to work early in the mornin, with the Mexican guys layin concrete. You know him—all he said was, 'Chain gang, baby.' "

"Sounds like him," Marcus said. "Most people don't even listen to him no more."

But SaRonn shook her head, the wispy tail of hair touching her neck. "I kinda like breakin the code." She stared out the side window. "You know, I danced with Finis at a party once, a house party on Pepper, remember back when it was houses all along there, and stores?" Marcus nodded. "Finis was older, and he was so quiet, but I liked his eyes. You got em, too. Ice-tea eyes." She grinned again, and Marcus stood up, uncomfortable. Her daughter skimmed down the short hallway.

"I better go lookin for him," Marcus said, watching a dust devil spin across the field behind the trees.

SaRonn stood, too. "I was just gon say a few months after that party, his eyes weren't like that anymore. He smoked some wack, huh? That's what I heard."

Marcus nodded. Back then, in the seventies, wack was everywhere. First, angel dust came east from L.A., and when country people found out how easy and cheap it was to make PCP, drug labs came up everywhere in the Rio Seco area and the desert. The easiest way to get an angel dust high was to dip a cigarette, usually a Kool, into liquid PCP. A Super Kool. Some guys smoked a lot of Super Kools; some died of cardiac arrest, some became manic, pointless wanderers, and some were lucky and just appeared mildly retarded.

Finis had smoked only one. At a party, too. Someone had given him a Super Kool, and the kaleidoscope of his brain had shifted permanently.

"But I used to see him walkin, and I remembered how he danced with me. I don't mind hearin him talk about songs," she said softly.

"I'm the only one can usually figure out what he's talkin about," Marcus said, hoping the thumb print would come back. "Now I got a fellow scholar to check with, right?"

"Yeah." She went to the door. "He said he's workin the Alta streets. In Agua Dulce?"

Marcus nodded. "Thanks," he said. "I'll check you later. Cause I'm prayin the Proudfoot come back with Eight's car."

"I'll take care of her," SaRonn said. "You take care of Finis. And yourself."

.   .   .

Marcus walked along the dry water channels back toward Grove Avenue. Some of the older houses along here had little arched bridges over the ditches to their driveways. He stared at one house, one of the ivy-covered porches, remembering when the old lady had died. Clara Mae, his mother had called her, crying, when they went to the wake in her house. Now the ivy was dangling dead stems, and he saw the peeling facial boards. On the right side, three hot-pink lines slanted like war paint. A young girl about fifteen sat on the steps, wearing a cast on her arm. She stared him down, but when he passed the driveway, she looked away.

He hadn't told SaRonn a single lie, he realized, turning the corner and facing the wind. He hadn't thought about himself long enough to compose one while they talked. But he hadn't met anyone from Tree-town for a long time, a woman who didn't already know everything about him and his brothers. The other women looked at him and smiled and lies fell from his mouth like empty sunflower shells. Colette, from Chicago—he told her he hated sushi, even though he loved it, because she made fun of brothers who ate trendy food. He told her he'd gotten his B.A. in four years, instead of seven, and that he'd been working in L.A. before he came to Rio Seco.

Alana, the blond woman he'd met at the sushi restaurant downtown, who smiled and asked if she could sit at his table, believed that he was new to Rio Seco, too. She was from Minneapolis, working at the local arts foundation across the street. She loved hearing that he'd studied art at the wonderful Deglet Noor building downtown.

But after they believed him, he wanted to talk about movies and music and where they should eat. He picked the films carefully, and when the women sat in his apartment, drinking mineral water or a Japanese beer, looking out the large window at the tiled domes and creamy walls holding palm shadows, and he sat carefully beside them, close enough to smell the scent from their necks but far enough away not to make them wary, he never talked about himself again. And they loved it. They told him everything.

But then, in the morning or the next bright day they saw him, their eyes would shift away from how much he knew, how little they'd discovered. And Marcus would get tired of the whole framework. He'd been saddest about Colette, who took him as a challenge, who put her hands behind his neck and said, "If you don't start talking, I'ma strangle you and you can keep all that information to yourself forever." But she had moved back home to go to graduate school.

Marcus strode fast along the long stretch of Grove Avenue lined with empty land, patches of trees, furrows where someone had disked an acre, and far to his right, the leafy, bending tops of the pecan trees in the big run-wild grove along the riverbottom.

SaRonn. He didn't remember her. Back then, at the house parties, there were so many beautiful girls in Treetown that brothers from the Westside, from San Bernardino and L.A. and Pomona, came to check out the weekend gatherings in someone's front room or backyard. Enchantee. Her cousins, the Perry girls, with their gleaming dark skin and baby hair sculpted into waves on their foreheads with sweet oil. The Proudfoots, who, back then, with their braided ear curls and scornful eyes and their pride in slippers and curlers and shapeless T-shirts that only made them look longer and leaner and sexier because they didn't care, always angered Treetown brothers by choosing outside men. And his sister, Sofelia, who would have been the loveliest if she'd stayed around.

He didn't remember her friend, or that house party. But sometime back then, when Rio Seco was growing bigger and more people had moved in from L.A. and other cities, the fights over women or crap games or a forty ounce went from Thompson-style punching and boxing to strangers driving past the crowded porch with guns. Olive Gardens turned crazy, and most of the women were having babies and getting married. Except Enchantee, who he didn't want to think about, and Sofelia, who had disappeared.

"Let me find Finis and just get back to the pad," he said to himself. "And hope Bennie don't wreck Eight's car. I know Finis didn't have no part of this thing with the two women. The cops gotta find out somethin soon. And I don't want no part of hangin around the place until they do."

He looked out at the first houses of Agua Dulce, scattered along the road now, looking like Mexico. Chickens jerking their heads in the dirt yards, plaster walls topped with wrought iron, old stucco houses painted blue and pink and pistachio. He saw the wrappers from Mexican chile candy, the soda bottles from Tijuana. And when he turned up the street that led suddenly steep up the hill, the graffiti read:

JOKER
INDIO
SMILEY
GÜERO
VATOS LOCO DULCE

He had Güero in one class. The name meant "white guy," and the kid was very pale, with thin black hair combed straight back and a soft fringe of moustache. Some kids from Agua Dulce were bused to downtown, and some were bused to another school. Like Treetown, there were no schools here.

He saw Salcido's huge building-supply yard below him once he passed a few streets. The yard ran close to the riverbottom's edge; pale sand, gray gravel, red brick, and block stones rose in piles with wooden buildings behind. His father and Salcido had built many of the stone-and-cement gutters he'd passed today, and they'd built the barn. Salcido's son Rubén was the one who always gave Finis cement work.

Alta Vista Place. He began to climb the steep hill terraced with narrow streets like layers on a cake. Alta Sierra. Alta Loma. And the last one, Alta Linda. Marcus had peered down each street, and finally, he saw the trucks.

Finis was wading in plush, liquefied cement. He didn't see Marcus, who looked at the other three driveways where Rubén was spraying water onto the damp burlap covering the new work. The cement had to wet-cure for several days, and the winds had been fierce and drying. Three days, at least, Marcus thought. Finis gotta be accounted for.

Finis wore knee-high rubber boots and backed away slowly from the smoother like the spongeless mop that he ran across the trembling surface. Over and over Finis did it, pulling the smoother toward him and pushing his ankles through the gray soup. He loved repetitive jobs like this, picking olives and painting and digging and cement work.

"Marcus!" Rubén called, turning toward him. *"¿Qué pasa?"*

"Hey," Rubén's brother Bebos called, too. He was cleaning the truck, which had finished mixing.

But Finis never stopped his movement, still concentrating on the skimming and stepping until he was finished, lifting his boots neatly from the last patch of cement and then making his melting footprints disappear.

He lifted his chin to Marcus, his face as blank as the smooth gray now, his eyes surrounded by a tiny mesh of crosses from all his miles of walking and squinting into the sun. His smile was always private.

"Why you didn't come to the pad all this time?" Marcus said, impatient now. "Daddy got hurt, man. And some bad shit happened over there."

Finis only nodded. "Fire—full alarm, child," he said.

"Yeah," Marcus said. "You done?"

Finis nodded again, judging his work with sweeping eyes. "Rubén!" Marcus called. "He done?"

"Yeah," Rubén said, coming to stand beside them and survey the four driveways all in a row, with their wooden formings still around them. Like four new graves, Marcus thought suddenly, turning away.

"Your brother Tony, he didn't tell you the cops were lookin for Finis?" Marcus asked Rubén.

Rubén frowned, rubbing his jaw and leaving gray dust along his neck. "Tony's been testifyin or somethin, I ain't seen him for a few days, man," he said in his sibilant, clipped Agua Dulce accent. "Why?"

Marcus knew the Salcidos didn't read the paper any more than the Thompsons did. "Some trouble at the yard," he said. "Somebody else's trouble."

Finis walked beside him down the sloping street, and Rubén called, "Negrito! Come by tonight and get your money from Big Pops!"

Finis waved without turning around and sang, low, "Money, money, money, money—MONEY!"

Marcus was silent. The Salcidos called Finis Negrito Indio, Little Black Indian, and Marcus smiled to himself, thinking that with Finis's stoic appearance and his short, secret answers, he looked about like a Hollywood Indian.

They could see the riverbottom laid out in a wide straight swath from up here. The trees and bamboo and vines were still winter-brown mesh, but patched with dark green. The golden, sandy riverbed cut through the center, threaded with only a narrow silver line of water. Marcus felt the memory of the river like twirling in his chest, and he said, "Come on, let's go home by the old trail."

The aspirin-sharp smell of the damp sand around the willows hit him as soon as they left Grove and plunged into the opening where a wide path led to the thickets and cane and the river. Finis followed him on the silent cushion of dirt and new grass.

He remembered all those years following them, Finis and the others, when they went hunting. Marcus was the tracker, and he'd slant off away from them to stare at the decomposing granite boulders on the hills, at the banks of the riverbed where red willow roots glowed under the dappled light. When the boys took their BB guns, and Demetrius his .22 rifle, they'd say, "Ain't no need for you to come, baby boy. You won't shoot, anyway."

He wouldn't. But among the arrowroot and silty mud, he was the one who saw the long-toed print of raccoon, the star-shaped print of possum. Mr. Williams over on Jacaranda would pay ten dollars for a fresh-killed possum if it was warm when you handed it to him. And Marcus's *abuela* made thick, red, spicy stew with rabbit. He'd find the scattered beads of rabbit droppings, and when the boys finally listened, walking his way, he felt sweat fan out along his back under his coat.

But if one handed him a gun, and they saw the rabbit hump through the tumbleweeds and then hunker down like he was invisible, if they saw the possum finally hanging by its tail in a pepper tree, he'd hand back the gun. Or drop it and turn away.

Finis, now treading soft behind him, had loved to hunt, too, loved to hand the meat to their mother. He always sang, even back then, and because he was more than a year older, he'd been to see *Superfly* with the others, even though Marcus had begged to go and had been left home. One night, nearly midnight, Marcus followed Finis, who sang softly of Superfly, the tail ends of words floating back: by and by, no questions why, do or die . . .

The sky was hard and purple, stark with the fall moon, Marcus remembered now, looking at the wind scouring the willows ahead of him. The hunting moon. And the raccoon wasn't afraid of Marcus when he ambled out onto the trail between them. A young one, Marcus thought, that's why he ain't scared. The raccoon's fingers dangled when he stopped to look at Marcus, and then Finis turned. Finis shouted, "Move, Marcus! Lemme shoot! Move!"

But Marcus was frozen, watching the raccoon scurry for the underbrush, and by the time the others got there, Finis was so angry he nearly cried when he told Demetrius about the missed chance. Finis had turned

to Marcus then and said bitterly, "Sissyfly, Marcus, that's you." He
began to sing,

> *Sissyfly*
> *You gonna fuck up by and by*
> *When you lose everybody know why*
> *Only game you know is fuss and cry . . .*

Marcus turned and ran back up the trail so they wouldn't see the
shining snail marks on his cheeks, and hid in the storage lot for hours.

Now he turned to see Finis walking, docile, his eyes focused on the
path. "You only sing somebody else's songs now, my brother," Marcus
said, hard. "Don't make up none a your own."

Finis said nothing. His face, darker than Marcus's from hours in the
sun, was thinner, more than slightly older. Marcus looked at the neat
new braids in Finis's hair. He knew SaRonn had plaited the long thickets
for him.

"Cops probably waitin for us," Marcus said to himself, walking faster.
Along the trail, he saw coyote shit: berry seeds, small bones, and chewed
fur.

When they came out past the pecan grove, at Pepper Avenue where
the rubble from the old flood-destroyed bridge still lay piled along the
edge, he saw the car. One police vehicle was parked near the storage
lot, on the strip of frontage road, and he knew the other one was
probably still on Pepper Avenue.

The two cops near the lot looked up, but they didn't move. No one
was in the barn or the yard. Marcus was about to turn the knob on the
kitchen screen when he heard the hearty voice. The two men came
out from beside the barn, one writing, and Marcus saw that they'd been
looking at tools. They think one of us bashed somebody? he thought
quickly.

"Radio said you were coming," the shorter cop said. His moustache
was thick, a brown shelf over his mouth. He smiled. "Strolling through
the riverbottom, huh?"

Marcus said, "Taking the quiet way," without any hesitation. If he waited and thought, he'd say the wrong thing. His blood rang in his temples.

"Not hiding?" the cop said, feigning surprise.

The other officer looked older, and he was taller, but he was only watching. "We're just looking around," the first one said. "Glad to finally see Finis here. Finis, right?" He stared at Finis, who smiled slightly, his eyes focused on the barn. The man looked at Marcus: "Country boys strolling in the riverbottom. Down in peaceful Treetown. You're Marcus. I've seen Finis here several times, seen all your brothers, but I never met you."

Marcus nodded. "I don't live here now."

"Nope. You live downtown. Teach at Rio Seco." The man smiled. "I went to San Domingo."

Marcus nodded again, feeling like a puppet. San Domingo was out in the valley past French Oaks. Snowy white rancher population. When football teams from the city went there, taunts like "nigger" and "wetback" snaked all through the sidelines, Marcus remembered.

The officer turned, businesslike, to Finis, who stood with his hands loose and his smile fixed tight. "Where you been these last coupla nights? Since the two women got burned up over there?"

Finis said softly, "Not just knee deep, she was totally deep . . ." Marcus took a long breath. Funkadelic lyrics. Finis was talking about SaRonn.

"Come on, bro. Let's make sense."

"You best not be lyin, be denyin, comin from Mississippi, child," Finis whispered. Marcus moved slightly to attract attention.

"He's been staying with a woman over on Jacaranda," Marcus said.

"She vouch for you that night?" the older cop said patiently.

"You best not be jokin, you better be strokin, in Far East Mississippi," Finis said.

"Great," the younger cop said.

Marcus added, "He's been working with Rubén Salcido on cement jobs for four days, starting right at six A.M." He saw them look at each other when they heard Salcido's name.

"You trying to make nice cover stories for him? You been working hard on this?" the younger one asked.

"I was worried about him," Marcus said quickly, before he lost his guts. "I checked it out."

"Worried he killed somebody?"

"No," Marcus said, trying to slow down. "I always worry somebody's gonna hurt him."

The older officer stepped toward Finis and said, "Nobody's gonna hurt him. We're just going to take him downtown to talk to the homicide guy." He turned to his partner. "Salcido's been testifying in that used-car guy's case. If he comes by, we can check."

"What you got in your pockets, bro?" The younger cop reached for Finis's jeans. Finis looked at Marcus, raising his fingers like a blind man touching someone's face.

"Nothing," the cop said. Then, when he stepped back to write something on his notepad, Finis reached deep into his front pocket and brought out a clenched fist. He moved toward Marcus, opening his fingers over Marcus's upturned palm. Marcus couldn't ask, not in front of the cops.

Two teeth, star-ended like molars, and a long white cigarette of a bone. It was bleached, chalky, thin in his hand. "Cherokee people, Cherokee tribe, so proud to live, so proud to die," Finis said softly, flat-toned.

When Finis got into the backseat, Marcus went to the kitchen door. He held the bones tight, but he had no idea what Finis was talking about. I'll put em in his trailer, Marcus thought, and his mother's face appeared above him, streaked with tears, looking out through the window.

Indian bones. All over the riverbottom. Bottles mottled with rainbows in the glass when he found them buried in the sand. Indian people. Shards of dishes. Animal bones. People bones. That finger bone.

Put em in the bunch. They go in the bunch. Except the finger bone. I need that. In my pocket. When I get back.

Cruisin. Just cruisin.

Smiling faces, smiling faces, sometimes, they don't tell the truth.

When I get back.

.   .   .

"I got rules in here, okay? You know I got rules. Cause it's no rules out there. No rules outside this door." Mortrice's mother touched her glistening fingertip to his hairline, his hollow neck, and the knob at the top of his spine. Protection oil, from a special bottle she got at a *botánica* full of candles and herbs and bottles.

When he turned his back to her and bent forward, exposing the knob, he thought, Gardens Gangster Posse Rules. Say they rule all over school. They write it on the wall. Every bulletin board. Wrote it on the chalkboard in marker one day, and can't nobody get it off. Forever.

Back in elementary school and junior high, he'd sat under those bulletin boards, staring at the words. Underneath them, the pockmarked board was blank. There were no rules listed. At home, his mother always whispered about rules. He knew exactly what they were. But in school, during those years, he'd waited nervously for the instruction.

They were simple, once he'd found them out from the homeys. Protect your homeys. Kill for your homeys. Die for your homeys. Now he was going to be a freshman in high school. He was going to be the sergeant at arms. He knew all the rules.

His mother sat at the spider-legged dinette table now, facing him, and Mortrice slumped back on the couch, feeling the dabs of oil gather warmth from his skin.

"My brother Marcus comin to get us this weekend," his mother said. "Mortrice."

She had been saying that all week. Her voice was low and soft as the humming beat he heard all night from the radio beside his bed while he waited. He had to go out in the evenings whether she let him or not. She didn't know why. But she knew he slipped out sometimes. Not through his ground-floor bedroom window, covered with wrought-iron bars. Through the front door, after she had finally slipped into exhaustion. He wouldn't confront her. Not his mother, with the softest voice in the Gardens, with her cheekbones rising like pillows toward her eyes, her hair in a long fat braid down her spine. And now she'd begun to anoint him with the oil at night, before he went to his room. Because she knew.

"I know," she said now. "We movin to Rio Seco cause I know what's gon happen. I can't have you gettin killed off in these streets. That's where you think you live now. I hear when you come back through the door at night, Mortrice. We goin this weekend."

Mortrice had seen the place before, but his mother didn't know that. Whenever she said the words, "Rio Seco," like a chant, he saw a skull in the riverbottom cane. He closed his eyes, felt the springs in the couch. He could hear the music outside, from the cars parked in the courtyard with doors open and Kenwoods blasting DJ Quik. All the men sat outside in their rides, and since it was nearly dark, the women were moving back inside the apartments before the shooting began.

His mother was silent now, staring at the faint black stripes behind the heavy drape she kept pulled over the window. The living and eating room was usually dim with shifting shadows, like a bear's den he'd seen in a schoolbook. They had lived in this apartment all his life, and his mother was in permanent hibernation. But she was so beautiful, so quiet, that Mortrice knew why his father had loved her. She never sat outside with the other women in Soul Gardens, loud-talking and hollering at her kids or the men. Her mouth was nearly always closed, a full, mauve mark even though she never wore lipstick. No makeup, no bows in her hair, even though she did hair for other women. His mother sat inside her lovely den, with fabric shimmering on the walls and beads hanging in the doorways, or she quickly traversed the ten feet of cement to Tiki's next door, where she did hair in Tiki's always crowded front room. She rarely spoke there; only her eyes traveled from mouth to mouth when others laughed or argued.

She talked only to him, mostly at night, like now, and when she did, her voice moved as gentle and soothing as it had back when he slept with her, back when he was three or four, when the shouts and shots outside had frightened him, and he would crawl under her arm to hear about the riverbottom, the tall bamboo that shivered in the wind and the vines hanging like drapes over the tunnels where she and her brother had filed like Indians.

At night, after the harsh street lamps in the project parking lot hissed to glaring life before someone shot them out, she told him about the trees speckled with apricots and lemons, about the wild pigs in the riverbottom, the rabbits racing through the olive grove. Once, in a whisper thick from her throat like she could barely breathe, in a voice he'd never forgotten, she'd told him about her five brothers who could kick anyone's ass.

But she had never taken him to Rio Seco.

When he'd started school and had to be a little man, he'd stopped showing his fear, and she'd stopped talking about the riverbottom and Rio Seco. He hadn't slept in the sheet that smelled of her Jergens and peppermints for many years. At night now, he lay in his own narrow bed listening to the shouts and laughter he knew, that he couldn't be afraid of: Lil Tony, Bam-Bam, P-Dog, and the others his age. And the deeper, slower voices of the older homeys. The Original Gangster few, the ones who weren't dead, who ran the courtyards.

He lay in his own bed, waiting to go outside and do his job, the one everyone knew he did best. He was patient and thorough and silent.

His mother said, "This weekend. Mortrice." All he could do was nod and go into his room to wait until it was time.

Mortrice knew Kenneth was his father. He knew it. He saw Kenneth look at his mother, saw that he nodded to her but never spoke, and even so, he knew Kenneth was the one.

Way back when Mortrice was ten, beginning to defend himself in the courtyards over lunch money and thrown elbows and insults, Kenneth had watched him. One afternoon, when a boy from across the broad avenue had challenged Mortrice on the sidewalk after school, casually, with the left side of his teeth showing in a sneer, Mortrice had glimpsed Kenneth's midnight blue Monte Carlo parked nearby, four heads silhouetted low while the occupants drank Olde English 800 and cooled off. He'd looked at the widening square of perfect teeth, like ten white doors facing him, when the boy taunted him. Then he ducked his head suddenly to slam the grin backward onto the glittering sidewalk. He straddled the writhing chest and clenched the ribs between his knees, slamming the boy's head against the cement. Past the teeth were white egg curves of skull and something inside the soft part that hated him.

Kenneth and the others got out of the Monte Carlo and came slowly across the street, and Mortrice felt them all behind him, silent until the blood ran from the boy's thick curls and trickled down his forehead. "Yo," someone said, and he got off the boy, who stumbled against a chain-link fence and pushed himself upright, walking a jagged line down the street.

"Nigga was talkin shit, huh?" Kenneth said.

Mortrice only nodded, waiting for the breath clotted in his chest to loosen and spread to his closed-off throat.

"You ain't even gotta get a name, lil homey. You cool. Mortrice. I heard your mama say it." Mortrice fixed his eyes on Kenneth's fingertips on the brown bottle. "Mortrice. It got somethin in it like . . . Shit, man, like rigamortis or somethin. Like death." Kenneth turned to the others, and they nodded and smiled, pulling whistled air through their teeth with satisfaction.

Mortrice stared at Kenneth's light cheeks and forehead, as pale as graham crackers, and the sprinkling of freckles. When he got home, he went to the bathroom to study his own skin. Slightly darker. He'd already found three small moles on the inside of his wrist. His mother's face was smooth and flawless, her broad cheekbones tinted magenta under the brown. She had no freckles, no marks anywhere. But now he knew where his marks had come from.

He had seen the way Kenneth squinted at his forehead, his knuckles, that gaze shifting only with each long-blinked pause. And last week, before Mortrice had said anything about what his mother had begun to murmur, Kenneth had taken him to Rio Seco. He had known, somehow. He had known because of their shared blood. Their marks.

Mortrice lay on top of the sheets, fingering the thin scar splitting his right eyebrow where Bam-Bam had hit him three months ago when he finally got beat in. Their posse was still small. Ten homeys had stood around him in a tight knot, kicking and slashing with fists, and though Mortrice's brain told him to curl into a ball, his blood trembled with stiff anger and made him lash back, tangling his fists with theirs. When they were finished, they had laughed at him, still spinning on his back. "Yo, man, break dancin went out long time ago," P-Dog said. Then they helped him up. His ribs were bruised, his face streaming blood, but he was proud of the deep splits all along his knuckles.

Now the scars were pale threads wrapped around his fingers. He hadn't gotten the tattoo on the back of his neck yet. He closed his eyes and clenched his fists. His mother was serious. Two more days and one of the kick-ass brothers would come, probably in a truck, from Rio Seco.

He reached under the pillow for the .25, and the handgun's barrel was still cool even though his head had left a hot dent in the cloth over it. In Kenneth's apartment, Mortrice loved to sit at the glass table and watch his own hands turn and open and clean the guns; he loved the smell of oil and bluing and powder. He would be sergeant at arms. He was the only one with patience enough to read the gun magazines and send away for the kit. He read the instructions every night, and at the glass table, he rubbed the gun parts with the rag that was nearly translucent from oil, so that everything glowed clear and polished around him.

But he couldn't leave her alone. He opened his eyes again and saw the pumpkin color of the sulfur lamps beginning to glow. He heard her open the door, and she stood in the dimming doorway. "I'ma go call," she whispered. "Right now."

She was always alone if she wasn't next door, or with him. She walked only those few feet to Tiki's, like now. Tiki got the groceries. Mortrice's mother cooked, sat in the front room, and went next door to do hair. With the sweet-sheened dollars, she paid for the groceries and hair supplies and his clothes.

In the back of an old textbook from school, Mortrice had three hundred dollars in flattened bills. Kenneth had paid him to take care of the guns. The others liked to ride, to shoot, but when they were finished, they had no idea what to do with the dirty, often jammed weapons.

Mortrice hadn't shot at anything except trees. Yet.

Last week, when he was supposed to go out with the other new homey, Paco, to prove they were down, something happened. No one came to get him from the place where he waited near the Dumpster. He had crouched there, watching the older men string out along the chain link to drink from big bottles, watching the small boys scatter and run like schooling fish until late, watching the women peer outside from triangles pulled in their drapes. When the sky grew cloudy and electric after midnight, he went inside. His mother was asleep on the couch, her neck long and curved to the side like a bird's.

The next night, Kenneth had pulled up to the asphalt just outside the door. He'd sat right there, where Mortrice's mother could see him, and when she'd gone outside, huddling in her doorway, she'd called, "You ain't takin him."

"He comin," Kenneth said casually, his arm dangling from the open window of the Monte Carlo. "Ain't nothin goin on. Just me and him."

Mortrice slid past her, astonished at the empty backseat he could see from the doorway, and she closed her eyes, leaning against the grimy wood frame. Tiki called from next door, "You need to leave that boy alone." She stood with her two daughters in a broad line of crossed arms.

"Shit, I'm old enough to be his daddy," Kenneth called. Mortrice hesitated at the passenger door of the Monte Carlo. "I'm older than his mama. I ain't gon hurt him. Niggas hurt theyselves. Every nigga gotta choose." He had a strange, closed-in look on his face when Mortrice slid onto the seat.

They were alone on the freeway. Mortrice had ridden the freeways for a few months now, from Venice to Lennox, Pomona to Fontana, but this was the longest they'd ever driven. And Mortrice wasn't sure if he'd done something wrong. He hadn't done anything but ride, listening to music and pulling smoke into his lungs and waiting for the metal pieces laid out in perfect order for his fingertips.

Kenneth drove slower, more hesitant tonight. His voice was quicker and angry, though, almost like he was talking to a woman instead of spilling out far more words than Mortrice had heard him say before.

"You know where we goin?" Kenneth barked when Mortrice saw that they had left the unbroken constellation of L.A. lights.

"Whittier?" Mortrice said, unsure, reading a passing sign.

"We goin to the country," Kenneth said, and Mortrice read more signs. Hacienda Heights. Diamond Bar.

"We was drivin last night," Kenneth began again, abruptly, staring ahead at the sparse traffic on the wide lanes. "Shit, I don't remember where we was goin. Some expedition. Lil homey name Paco—you only seen him once. He just showed up last week. He told me, Can you call me Paco? And stutterin and shit. Stay over there in the three hundreds, somebody told me. We was ridin, he was three deep in the back with Bam and Kool, and we hit this bump in the street, man, like a piece a wood or some shit."

Mortrice looked out the window when Kenneth paused. Paco. A small boy with dusty hair and huge eyes that Mortrice had looked away from, because of their fear. He didn't want it. He smelled a strong, green sharpness now, like the odor of heated, packed grass from the school lawnmower. He saw a black mass of shifting shapes far below the slow lane, heard a bellow, and saw stacked bales of hay like huge cinder blocks.

"The shottie go off back there," Kenneth said. "I think Kool had lil homey holdin the shottie, and it went off in his face."

Mortrice turned his eyes toward Kenneth, keeping his breath shallow and even, his mouth closed like his mother's, and the green smell turned brown in his nostrils as he tried not to see the pellets and the blood.

"Shit, I didn't even know this lil nigga, didn't know where he stay or nothin. Kool said some lady got him, not his mama. He don't have no people. Kool and Bam trippin and shit, and lil homey, you know, he went out, like, instant. Face all gone like that. He had it point-blank."

Mortrice kept his gaze on the two dark moles at Kenneth's temple. Marks. My people got marks.

"So we kept goin on the freeway, man, and I seen this water."

He slowed the car, and Mortrice saw that they were coming to a bridge. When they crossed the riverbed, the water was like a narrow sidewalk of silver. The shining was surrounded by pale sand and then tall patches of dark, and the Monte Carlo was off the bridge, heading down an exit ramp.

"We put him down here," Kenneth said, driving slowly, peering at the bushes beside the narrow road along the river. Mortrice saw festoons of bare vines hanging from the trees. He knew that this was his mother's riverbottom, and his breath came harder. He smelled wetness and skunk.

"It was like he was sleepin on his back, cause his boots was all straight up," Kenneth muttered, and the car stopped at a sandy field. "I know you ain't got no fuckin mouth, Mortrice. Like death and shit. I'm just checkin, like, checkin it out. Get out the ride, man."

Mortrice stood on the damp sand, and Kenneth waited, his face immobile through the windshield, like he was listening to one last song on the radio. Then he crunched into the bushes, and Mortrice followed.

"It was real cold out here, man. The country," Kenneth said, low. "It was a tree like this where we went in." Mortrice saw a gnarled trunk, burnt wood glittering like charcoal in the moonlight. Kenneth bent suddenly under a low, reaching branch and moved into the bamboo.

Mortrice held his breath, lowered his head, and pushed through the feathery green. He followed the sound. Raising his head in a clearing, he saw Kenneth standing straight, the bamboo arching over him like a tent. "Like he still sleepin, man. Shit. His arms still folded," Kenneth said, and Mortrice saw a figure lying on its back, hands on his chest. When they took one more step, a blur of ember eyes and long tail leaped from the face, and Mortrice dropped to his knees.

Paco had no face. His flesh was gone, even his eyes, and only the gleaming white skull smiled above his jacket.

. . .

Mortrice knew he had slept. He heard his mother close the front door. She had called Rio Seco. They were coming to take him. He couldn't leave her.

"I bought lil homey them shoes." That was all Kenneth had said in the car, much later. When they flowed through the L.A. streets, never-ending lights and stores and windows, finally stopping at Kenneth's apartment, he had said nothing to Mortrice. He'd popped the trunk, and pointed. Mortrice stared at the shotgun, spattered with black blood. He'd reached inside to pick it up, cradling the heavy barrel, touching the brittle pattern that fell away from his fingers.

His mother opened the bedroom door and stood, watching him. He pretended to turn in sleep, slowly, sliding the .25 into the fold of his sheet, but he didn't put his finger inside the trigger. He lay his whole palm over the small gun and waited.

When Sofelia called, Marcus was pacing in front of the big window, watching people in the courtyard. There was a festival going on down-town that let crowds sample foods at many of the new restaurants. A *tapas* fest, they called it, after the Spanish bar food. It was the first in a series of "new ethnic and regional favorites to kick off fall!"

"Daddy got shot by the cops, by accident," he told Sofelia quickly. "I've been waitin to tell you. He's okay, got hit in the shoulder, and he's in the hospital."

"Bullets," she whispered, so low he could hardly hear. Women's voices crowded behind her.

"You havin trouble?" he asked. "You still want me to come? You gotta let me tell Mama."

"No, no, Marcus, don't tell nobody," she pleaded. "I'll tell you where I am, and you gotta come get me and my son. They gon kill him. I know it."

Marcus held the phone to his ear and saw two women with red hair, nearly wine-dark, cross near the palms. They laughed, swinging small purses. One lived in number 3, he knew. "Sofelia," he said, "I gotta get a truck. You got a lotta stuff?" He couldn't believe their conversation was so everyday, after a blank space of more than ten years.

"No. I ain't bringin hardly nothin but some material."

"Some what?"

"Fabric."

"Okay." Marcus hesitated. He was talking to a woman he didn't know at all. "I guess you don't need much, cause Mama got everything."

"I ain't stayin with Mama," Sofelia said. "I can't."

Before he realized what she'd said, his mind played idly with "stay" again. But then he frowned. "What?"

"Marcus, please," Sofelia's voice pleaded, breaking hoarse. "I'ma tell you where to take me when we get back." He heard her breathe hard. "When you comin? Nothin's workin on him no more."

Marcus watched the figures flash through the arched entryway, and then he looked at his calendar. "Three more days, okay, so I can get a truck." He exhaled softly. "Where you stayin now?"

When he'd hung up, he looked at the address in L.A., somewhere off Imperial. He hadn't been to that neighborhood in a long time, since college. He hadn't left his ordered, comfortable downtown route this much in years. Marcus stepped back from the window, and when he turned off the light, he could see himself rubbing his temples in the dark glass.

Walking through the bustling streets of the festival, he smelled garlic and tomatoes and perfume and beer, but quickly he was in the darkened, empty area of downtown that emanated only brick and cement and traces of exhaust, then the hay scent of vacant lots. When he passed the Kozy Komfort, he saw tiny dark figures moving hurriedly in doorways. I wonder if the cops let Finis go yet, he thought. I hope he go straight home and don't hang out tonight.

He passed the entrance to his uncle's place, just a square cut into the trees, an open gate, but dust still hanging from all the cars. He knew they'd be partying big-time back there tonight. The eagle had flown, and he would be landing at The Blue Q.

Turning at his father's gate, he saw the barn lights, and Kickstand and another man looked up quickly. "I didn't know who the hell that was, sneakin up all pitiful," Kickstand said when Marcus neared the circle of tools.

"Demetrius lend me a truck, I won't be walkin," Marcus said easily.

Kickstand spat sunflower seeds into the dirt. "I'm workin late on this sorry fool's old carburetor." The other man grinned sheepishly, willing to accept Kickstand's abuse as long as it took to fix the ancient Cadillac. "All your brothers gone over your uncle's," Kickstand added. "Somethin come up."

Marcus looked at the lit kitchen window. He didn't want to see his mother; he didn't like lying to her. She wasn't as easy as other women, he thought, shaking his head. And he had a hard time keeping Sofelia's secret.

But she opened the kitchen door and waved at him. He knew she'd have seen him; from where she usually sat at the table, sorting beans or working, she could see everyone who drove onto the place.

She was at the old wooden table now. Marcus hugged her, smelling the burnt brown sugar of her hair. "How's Daddy?" he asked. "They found anything out?"

She shook her head. "I only know what Revia King tell me every night when she get off." She glanced at the old tile clock on the wall. "She don't come by till near eleven. And all she can say is how he feelin, that his infection been goin down. But she don't know nothin about what them police do when they go in there and talk to him."

His mother bent her head to the table and circled her neck with her fingers, a tight collar, rubbing hard. When she looked back up, he saw the gray smudges under her eyes, like shading from a pencil, and his heart twisted inside. If he told her about Sofelia, she would still have his father to worry about, but the two pain creases between her eyes, the ones he swore had cut into her skin when Sofelia hadn't come home and his mother had started squinting hard down the driveway all day, might fade a little.

"You find somethin out about your daddy?" she said, seeing him straighten and prepare to talk. "He wanted me to tell you—he told Revia about a white boy in a black Jeep. He ain't told nobody nothin yet. He say they gon do what they gon do, the police. Like always." She paused, frowning. "But he said, 'Tell Marcus about the Jeep.' Revia was sure."

Marcus thought of Pammy Sawicky, of the kind of white guys who sold speed at the high school and how they got older and sold it from

houses and bars. He remembered one from school—Buddy Louden.
But the rest of Buddy's friends had been Harley riders, guys who didn't
hang out with brothers. He had no idea of how to trace a white guy.

He shook his head. He wasn't going to mention anything to Demetrius
except Pammy Sawicky. He didn't want to set himself up to blow
anything, to sound stupid. "Mama, I'm goin over to Uncle Oscar's to
talk to Demetrius about a truck. Kickstand said somethin came up."

She shrugged. "He called over here and said he wanted to talk to
em. He didn't say why." Standing up, she put two fingers along Marcus's
cheek. "I think he don't want to scare me. But I don't see what worse
could happen."

When he went outside, Marcus stood for a moment looking up at
the hard-edged stars. Only two miles from downtown, less than that,
and you could see the whole night sky here, littered with stars, while
outside his apartment you could see only the diffused glare from streetlights and mirrored buildings and glowing offices.

"*En boca cerrada no entran moscas,*" a musical, birdlike voice said from
the darkened courtyard to his left. His great-grandmother laughed, just
two whiffles of sound, and Marcus walked over to sit beside her in one
of the old wrought-iron chairs under the palm shelter that ran the length
of the U-shaped central area.

Her hands lay on her knees like two golden, curve-legged spiders,
and her eyes were only slits of silver in the dim light. Marcus smiled
and lay his hand over one of hers. Spiders. Ants. Flies. All the words
she had taught him while they picked olives and stirred them in the
curing vats. "Flies don't enter a closed mouth," she had said just now,
since he'd been standing there with his wide open to the sky.

"*Pero* it's night, Abuela," he said. He spoke a strange mixture of the
nouns she'd taught him and other words he'd picked up, but he had
no sense of grammar. He'd taken two years of French at Rio Seco
High, because that was what college prep kids were taking, and he
wanted to be one of them. No one cared about speaking Spanish then.

"*Sí,*" his great-grandmother said. "*Pero en la noche, los murciélagos
vuelan.*"

Marcus nodded. His *abuela* loved anything that flew. She spent hours
watching mockingbirds and jays, sparrows and red-tailed hawks; in the

evenings, she waited for bats and moths to trace paths through the branches.

"Mi pequeño perico," she said. My little parrot, Marcus thought, smiling. That was what she'd always called him, when he listened and repeated. But none of his brothers ever would sit still long enough to learn any of the words or sayings she loved so much. *"Dos gringas, las muertas,"* she said slowly, for him.

"Someone put gas *en tu placa*," Marcus said, thinking. "I forgot." He frowned. "You didn't see anything?" His *abuela* understood more than she could say, like most people who live around other languages but keep theirs.

She shook her head. Then she put one tiny, gnarled hand on the one he'd laid over hers. *"El valiente vive hasta que el cobarde quiere."*

Marcus stood, nodding, but he was tired, and the words thudded dully in his brain without meaning. *Valiente* meant brave, but the rest was a blur. She nodded back, and he left her there, a tiny sparrow herself, with her black mantilla over her silver-sheened forehead and sharp nose, her shining black eyes on him.

He called, "Don't work too hard, man," to Kickstand, who leaned over the Cadillac.

"Shit," Kickstand muttered. Marcus crossed behind the barn and headed slowly to the gate between the properties. He heard only his shoes on the bark and leaves, and his forehead hummed with fatigue. When he entered the eucalyptus and saw a stark, peeled-white trunk nearby with a rust-speckled hubcap nailed to it, he saw his father's face. His father would know exactly what kind of hubcap it was, if someone came to ask. His father knew every inch of this land, and whoever had started the fire had wanted to shoot him, or to get him shot by the cops. Marcus stared at the facets of the hubcap. *Cobarde.* His *abuela's* words shifted for him.

The brave one lives as long as the coward lets him.

He had to be careful walking through the trees on the other side of the wall, the ones around The Blue Q. People took care of business in the trees, sometimes love business, sometimes pharmaceutical business, sometimes old and never finished business.

Marcus never came here on a weekend night. Occasionally, he came in the late afternoon with Brother Lobo, who liked to sit and listen and talk in the confines of walls since the bullet had grazed his arm. But

that was mainly a talking crowd. The weekend crowd was serious—
drinking, eating, loving, and kicking ass for necessity and for sport.

He wound through the trunks, knowing Rock was at watch, as
always, near the choc brew and the orange grove. He knew Jerry and
Joe would be keeping muscled order in the front parking area, the way
Uncle Oscar paid them to. But you never knew who might be in the
trees here.

He heard soft laughter behind one, saw a thick elbow bent out in a
vee where a man leaned into the lips, quiet now. He kept his head
down and walked fast, a wire of heat racing through his groin. When
they were little, he and Finis used to hide here, hoping to catch a
glimpse of passion and flesh.

People milled about in the packed dirt near The Blue Q. Marcus
slowed, checking faces that turned to see where he was coming from,
who he was with. Usher Price's oldest brother, Wheeler, nodded at
him. Most of the men who drank and ate at The Blue Q were in their
thirties and forties, the kind of men L.A. and Rio Seco people called
"country" or "old-time" or "down-home." Even if they were native
Californians, guys like Wheeler and Rock and Jerry were down-home.
But not me, Marcus thought. Demetrius can pull off both, he can go
between here and there and anywhere. But I can't.

At the door, Jerry took his five-dollar cover charge, laughing. "Yeah,
nigga, you know your uncle don't love you for free on no Friday night.
Give up them ducats." Marcus walked past the hand-lettered sign that
had hung by the door for years: NO GUNS, KNIVES, OR ATTITUDES.

The smoke hung blue and heavy, as if ivy grew from the ceiling.
Marcus saw that the tiny stage, just a wooden platform near the wall,
was empty. The jukebox was playing "Float On," and a few couples
danced in the bare space near the wall. He had to smile. If Uncle Oscar
or one of his friends wasn't playing blues, the younger crowd played
The Floaters or Earth, Wind and Fire or old Commodores. And that
was old-time now.

The tables were crowded with people eating Aintielila's greens and
chitlins and Oscar's barbecued ribs and hotlinks. Toward the back, the
service window was open, the permanent menu above it, and Marcus
could see his aunt moving in the kitchen.

He knew his brothers and uncle would be sitting at Oscar's table in
the far rear corner, where he could watch the whole place. Marcus saw

Demetrius's head moving while he talked, saw his brothers' black hair gleaming in braids, except for Finis, whose hair was dusty and pulled into a thick, careless wedge with a rubber band. Finis's head lay on his arms, and Marcus was relieved to see him intact.

Uncle Oscar's face was the only one turned to his, the deep sickles framing his mouth.

"You better paid," he said, one sickle deeper with a half-grin.

"You know it," Marcus said, pulling a folding chair toward the others.

"I ain't servin no sherbert gourmet food," his uncle said.

Demetrius said, "You ain't had to come. You ain't gon want to help out on this now."

Marcus didn't wait, but took a breath of smoke and sauce. "Demetrius. One of the girls in the Granada, Pammy Sawicky, I know she wouldn't come down here with no brother. Some white dude had to bring them onto the place, had to get em inside the gate to make it look like one of us did it."

His brothers all looked at him. "How you know?" Julius asked.

"Cause I knew her in school."

"Back when you was a brother?" Demetrius said, hard.

The others laughed, and Marcus said, "Shut up, damnit. I'm serious. And Daddy seen a white guy. So we gotta put this together."

Uncle Oscar blew smoke from his cigarillo onto the table. "Yeah. We do. But while we doin that, somebody's gotta be standin watch. That's what I'm tryin to get y'all to understand."

"I understand," Octavious said. "But hold up." He turned to Marcus, his green-tinged eyes murky in the dimness. "Why the hell you give my ride up the other day, man? First you take it and don't ax me, then you let somebody take it and don't say shit."

"Oh, man, give Sissyfly a break," Julius said. "She hard. Check her out." Marcus turned, following Julius's nod, and saw Bennie Proudfoot dancing close with a man near the wall, her mouth moving constantly up under his chin, her feet dragging, and her hips shifting hard.

"Who's got her kids?" he said without thinking, and Octavious shook his head.

"SaRonn," Octavious said. "Belisa tired a watchin em. Bennie lookin for love every day." Marcus was surprised; Octavious didn't spit the words.

SaRonn—he remembered the fringe at her neck, her eyes. He looked at Finis, whose eyes stayed close even with the mention of her name. "I don't remember her at all," Marcus said.

"She been gone a few years," Octavious said. "Belisa said she was in L.A."

Marcus thought, So maybe I ain't gotta lie. Not this time. But he looked at Demetrius again, and at his uncle, who said, "When y'all sorry-ass fools tired a talkin about women, let me know. And tell me who gon be watchin."

"I said I would," Demetrius said. "Julius and Finis ain't good for shit in them trailers."

"I see what I need to see," Julius said. Marcus watched him smile, unapologetic. Julius never backed down; he never cared enough about anything but what he wanted for himself.

"How are you gonna stay anywhere but home, with Enchantee waitin on you?" Marcus said. He wanted to say something about the new house, but he didn't.

"Somebody gotta stay near the barn, and somebody need to walk the fences at night," Uncle Oscar said. "With a piece. Cause whoever did it, they gon try it again if this one don't work. Way them cops keepin Hosea look bad, but they gon have to let him go once they do they ballistics."

"How do you know?" Marcus asked, frowning.

"Shit," Uncle Oscar said. "Hosea gun so old they ain't never seen no bullets like that. And your mama said somebody was shootin three, four times. Them women got bullets in em ain't your daddy's. What else they got on Hosea? Ain't nobody seen nothin." He blew smoke again. "But one a y'all better see somethin next time. Better catch somethin, goddamnit."

Marcus looked at the gray smoke floating in a fist, then dissolving. He thought of the ashen wells under his mother's eyes. "Demetrius, man, you gotta let me borrow a truck," he said. "I gotta move somebody, a favor, in three days, and then I'll come out to the place and walk. I'll sleep instead a you, so Enchantee ain't gotta be alone."

Demetrius raised his chin. "I bet you worried about her, huh?"

"Save that shit," Marcus said. "You got a truck?"

Octavious said, "Only truck runnin good right now is Daddy's."

They were all silent. Their father's 1956 Chevy truck, a green so faded it was as pale as shallow water, was in the far corner of the barn.

Kickstand kept it clean and checked; he'd been working on the brake lines when Hosea was shot.

"I don't want to take the truck without askin him," Marcus said, uneasy.

"Can't ax him nothin right now," Demetrius said softly.

"You better go on and take it, if you movin a woman," Oscar said. "You ain't never kept no woman. Look like you need all the help you can get."

The only way Hosea knew that a dry Santa Ana wind was scouring his trees, sanding grit along the cars on the lot, was that a cold spark had passed from the nurse's hand to his. The static in the room jumped blue when she'd plucked at his wrist.

The constant shifting of white shapes in and out of the room left him exhausted from holding himself rigid and watchful. Sometimes faces peered from higher up, from over shoulders, at him. He kept seeing the pale woman on the billboard above the injured man in Tulsa, the razor scallop of her lips where she smiled down at the street.

The cops wore dark jackets, but they flashed pictures near his face, and the photos showed more pale faces, more sharp smiles. "These two women . . ." "Where were you . . ." "Where was your son . . ." "Why was the gate . . ."

He said nothing. "He's playing dead . . ." "Those two women are dead for real, Thompson . . ." "This isn't a game . . ." "Maybe he's senile . . ." "His son's senile from angel dust . . ."

He waited. They would decide, no matter what he said or didn't say. They were the kind of men who moved their mouths and wrote on papers and informed other men of what was already done. If he spoke, he might hurt Finis. That was all he could think about while his head was lined with velvet heat and his mouth was full of prickling coughs that had begun to rise from his chest to lodge in his throat. The smells of the hospital liquids and people and the stale, electric air hung in a web around him that at night grew smaller and smaller, shrinking down to the dome of harsh light around his bed and his body.

He waited for the next metal creak of the door and the next float-and-jerk shape to hover over him.

. . .

One box. That was it. Everything Mortrice had fit inside the box his mother had gotten from Tiki. His jeans and shirts, his cassette player and tapes, his two pairs of sneakers.

The kit stayed inside his pillow, with the .25. His bed was a second-hand frame Tiki had found at a yard sale years ago, and his mother said to leave it. "We gotta go fast," she said, sitting at the dinette table, her upper body calm, her knee bouncing so hard that the table shook. "Just what we can carry."

He could carry the kit. It had finally come in the mail, to Kenneth's place since mail was hard to get inside the Gardens. Mortrice had ordered it from a catalog advertised in a *Guns & Ammo* issue he'd bought at the store. The kit was small enough to fit in a large coat pocket, but the zippered leather case contained all the tools needed to break down and clean the guns.

On the same page with the ad for the kit, he'd seen a course in gunsmithing. Not just cleaning, but altering the barrels, repairing weapons. You could send for that in the mail, too. You could learn it at home. He hadn't told Kenneth about the course when they'd opened the package with the cleaning kit. Kenneth had nodded with pride and said, "You got skills, man, skills and sense. You gon be down, hell, yeah."

The liquid warmth that had filled Mortrice's chest when Kenneth said the words, the fingering feel like a cupped palm at the back of his head, was gone now. He'd only felt that when his mother sat beside his bed at night, telling him stories, telling him how when he was a baby she never let anyone else touch him because he belonged only to her, to no one else in the world. And now he was going out to leave her behind, only for an hour, and give up that tingling rise he'd just begun to recognize.

He had to choose, and Kenneth was waiting in the Monte Carlo.

"Mama, I'll be right back," Mortrice said, straight to her upturned face. He wasn't going to wait for her to fall asleep. No sneaking around tonight. No sense. And he had sense.

He waited for her to answer. But she only stared at him, her eyes moving over his face, his big coat. After a long time, she said, "When?"

"Soon as I'm done." He bit his lip inside his mouth.

"My brother comin in a few hours, Mortrice. He said first thing in the mornin. It's goin on midnight." His mother laid her palms flat on the table. "Ain't no good-byes that work, baby," she whispered. "I know."

"I'll be back soon," he said, and he turned for the door.

They went all the way to Venice, Kenneth driving cool and smooth like he just wanted to see the water flashing dull under the clouds like melted lead. No one was in the back. Mortrice wanted to tell him, to get it over with, but Kenneth's smile when he rocked slightly to the beat from the radio, his head turning slow and easy like a periscope to watch the streets, was too valuable to wipe away with the wrong words. Mortrice leaned back against the seat and dozed to the swaying car and the music.

They pulled up at Kenneth's apartment, a green duplex with a carport cave. Mortrice went up the stairs, hearing Bam-Bam, Tony, and someone else inside.

His name was Capper, an older guy who'd just gotten out of Chino. He nodded to Kenneth and looked at Mortrice. "What up?" he said, his voice slow. "That your boy?"

Mortrice held his breath. The words meant anything. And Kenneth said, "Yo, man, that's him. Lil nigga can break your piece down sweet, specially if it's fuckin up."

They all turned to look at him. Mortrice put his hands in his coat pockets and said, "I didn't bring the kit, man. Not tonight."

But Kenneth only said, "Cool. Capper ain't goin nowhere, huh, fool? You can do it tomorrow."

Mortrice sat on the couch, sweating under the coat collar, waiting to be alone with Kenneth again. I shoulda did it already, he thought. Dudes might stay around all night. And Bam-Bam think I ain't about shit anyway.

Capper and Bam-Bam rolled the weed into fat cigarettes, and when the yellow smoke drifted toward the ceiling, Capper said, "Man, I missed that good chronic. The right shit."

Kenneth drew in the smoke until it filmed his eyes. Mortrice sucked in the burnt-sweet taste and felt it coat his skull with the glistening resin the antidrug people always talked about when they came to school. He watched Kenneth move from room to room, feeling his head sway behind his eyeballs to the music.

When they were in the car again, Mortrice jammed in the back with the other two, and Capper in front with Kenneth, he saw the streetlights passing in long, lemony tails. They stopped at the red light on the street fronting the Gardens, and only a few gold lights shone in windows like broken teeth. Mama waitin for me, he thought, his head warm on the seat, his arm wedged against Tony's, his body hurtling away from the green light in the cushioned, armored boat. "Kenneth," he said, over the music. He heard his throat shouting. "I gotta get out."

"So get out, nigga," Tony said, slamming his shoulder into Mortrice's.

But Kenneth turned and said, "What? You gotta go home? That what you think?"

Mortrice hesitated. The lights hurtled past him on both sides like glowing wires. "Yeah," he said, but Kenneth pulled the car to a stop at a side street off Vermont, behind a row of stores.

"Why you say it like that?" Kenneth said, his face immobile now, hovering over the seat like a burnt-red sun in the neon light reflecting in the car.

"I gotta go to Rio Seco with my moms tomorrow, maybe for . . ." Mortrice paused. "Maybe for a month, man. I don't know. She trippin."

Kenneth smiled, a fingernail crescent with no teeth. "So she trippin. That don't mean you gotta trip."

Mortrice was silent, and Tony said, "Who care about the little mothafucka? Come on, man, let's get with the expedition and shit."

Capper said lazily, his voice floating forward, "This little nigga tryin to front? He think he gon break him off some in Rio Seco? He been marketin some product?"

Mortrice shook his head and realized Capper couldn't see him. "No, man, I ain't doin nothin."

Bam-Bam said, "He ain't sold nothin noway, cause he ain't been around enough."

Kenneth said, "He think he gon be the sergeant at arms and shit. He talkin bout he can take care of everybody. Huh, Mortrice? You ready, huh? Got your shit in the mail."

Mortrice said, "When I get back. I'ma help her out. When I get back, I'ma . . ." His tongue was coated with sand.

Kenneth interrupted him, shouting, "I thought you was *down*."

Capper said, "He goin to Rio Seco. We sent two niggas out to Rio Seco already, man, remember? When they got out Chino, they went out there to them apartments. The Westside." He finally turned his head slightly so that Mortrice could see his profile, his heavy, square cheek wider at the jaw. Prison food, they'd been teasing him about. "Kenneth, man, I thought you was takin care of shit while I was gone. This little nigga think he gon go off on his own and shit. Hey. What his name?"

"Mortrice," Kenneth said, facing the wall beside the car.

"Hey. L.A. already in the house, okay? Already in the country out there, Rio Seco. And ain't no extra room for frontin. If your mama takin you home, and you ain't with the homeys in that posse, I don't want to hear shit."

"No," Kenneth said. "He ain't gon hang with them. He choosin now. He need to stay here. He got shit to do." He turned back to Mortrice, his freckles dark across his forehead. "You choosin a woman. You a homey for *life.*"

"Live for your homeys, die for your homeys," Bam-Bam murmured. The mingled breaths drew water from the windows, and Mortrice closed his eyes.

"Ain't no choice," he said softly, and he thought no one had heard him.

Kenneth said, "Yeah, it is. Mama boy or home boy."

Mortrice waited. For "My boy." For "Man, this your daddy talkin."

"Walk, then, nigga." Kenneth turned and started the car. The others were silent.

"Where?" Mortrice asked. His hand grasped the cold door handle.

Kenneth shrugged, looked out the window at the darkened street they faced. His curls were suffused with red light from the liquor-store sign behind them. "Wherever you goin."

Mortrice pushed open the door. He knew it wasn't right. You got beat in, you got beat out. He heard the music go up loud, but no one said a word. He closed the door, looking only at his hand, and felt himself swivel to walk down the sidewalk, toward the liquor store and the light. The Monte Carlo screeched down the narrow side street, and he lifted his head.

When he reached the corner, waiting at the broad avenue shuttered with black wrought-iron bars and metal shutters, he heard the car behind him again. He was about to turn, but he began to walk. He went past the liquor store, down the next block, and he hadn't heard the engine move with him. He slowed, and the deep-throated cough of the shotgun came from almost a block away.

He didn't turn; his back was a shell. The metal studded his back with tiny embers that burned so hard they pushed him into his face, onto the cement, while the tires far behind screamed in a loose circle and sped the other way.

This shape was white-jacketed, but a man's deep voice said, "They're moving you."

Hosea opened his eyes. Behind the hands grabbing IV poles and screeching parts of his bed, the homicide detective said, "He's takin you down to the other ward. Your whacko kid's out, too. Your ballistics came back, and we've got people that saw some things you didn't. Cause you might not have been around during the shooting part." When Hosea's bed swung around sharply, bringing him closer to the hairs curving like antennae from the mussed head, the man said, "But you were around for something. And if something happens again, we're gonna see it. Don't think we won't."

The air in the hallway reeked of sweat and metal. Hosea heard men's voices. Jail ward. He saw deputies in the doorway of one room, heard shouting. Then swinging doors closed and he was hurtling through icy walls.

He kept his eyes closed then, until all movement had stopped. When it was silent in the new room, he looked up at the television playing on the wall. A pleated drape separated him from a sleep-breathing presence in another bed. And Hosea was cold—so cold, with the rushing hallway air still in his ears, and this new icy-walled room like a refrigerator.

His shoulder ached with a dull pain deep inside the bone, but his skin didn't throb with heat the same way it had for—for how many days? He stared at the television, which held no clues about the date. White women with hair thin and curled stiff, like spiderwebs sprayed bronze, spoke to each other across a coffee table in one of the rooms he always glimpsed when he saw Alma or the grandkids watching evening funny shows.

A white woman came in to check him after a time, this one young, with long dark hair in a braid. She touched each item lightly—the bed, IV, table, him—and said, "The doctor on this floor will stop by soon. You just came from—" She hesitated. "From the other ward. He'll be checking on you."

She stopped, frozen at the sight of the TV screen, and when the exchange was done, she laughed lightly and went back outside.

Hosea looked at the grinning women, their hands bent stiffly around their coffee cups, their backs ramrod straight, their eyes as empty as dry washtubs. Like Mrs. Hefferon, whose eyes had seemed as glassed-blue and blank as returned milk bottles. The woman in the elevator—the one who'd screamed when Dick Rowland stumbled and touched her. Dick Rowland, who shined shoes, who'd laughed in the barbecue place. He'd touched her by accident, his feet throwing him there too close to her arm, and the river of men had wanted to cut pieces of his body and burn him alive. That's what the men said—the mob wanted his flesh for hers.

Hosea shivered in the thin sheets, the ones the pale hands pulled at while he lay burning and stiff. The two white women whose faces had hovered in the detective's hands, over and over—someone would want him, or his sons, or whoever would do, for flesh. Maybe they would burn his land, start the palm fronds and trees on fire. For flesh.

The smell of it. The sweet-terrible smoke, carrying blood, had settled in his head, and the sifting kept bringing back the things he hadn't seen in so long. He reached his hand to his shoulder, covering the dressing where the puckered hole would appear. His father's French bullet hole was a writhing trail of raised skin. His grandfather's brand, where the man had marked him for life like an animal, was a twist of shining scars. Hosea clenched his eyes closed, feeling his skin crackle. Who would come for his flesh?

"I can't do this! This is like a fucking war zone! What the fuck kind of triage is this, when this kid and the others are sitting here for hours, waiting, because we've got people with bigger holes in them?"

The hissing-hoarse whisper came from behind the curtain in the small stall where Mortrice lay. He had seen doctors moving around, seen a nurse who came and cut off his bloody, torn shirt.

"Okay! You've made your point. He wasn't life-threatening. He isn't screaming. No one's in a state of rigor mortis, okay? You're gonna have to get used to life down here or move on, Vangen. Go."

A short, thin man with brown hair reaching back in a deep scallop from his forehead came through the curtain. Mortrice glanced at the face, the hairline, and then he turned his back.

There wasn't anyone to call. His back had been burning like pepper was pushed deep into his muscles, but he knew enough about bullets and scars to be sure he wasn't dying. He was getting more marks. He lay stiff while the doctor picked the shotgun pellets from his flesh. Five. He let his tears soak the coarse sheet under his cheek, remembering the grit from the street rubbing there. He couldn't call his mother. How could he get back home?

He didn't even know where the ambulance had brought him. He knew the name of the hospital—people always talked about it. But he didn't know where he was. He closed his eyes, imagining the coppery pellets holding his skin. Kenneth. Kenneth had told him to walk. Had given him more marks. Scalding water ran from his lashes, and he waited until the doctor was finished to rub the moisture fiercely into his cheeks.

When he was sitting up in the small stall, hearing the fever groans and screams of someone who'd been shot, the cops came.

"Who did you, homey?" The redheaded one started, shaking his head at Mortrice's back patched with white. He was short and square, his shoulders so wide to Mortrice it looked like he had sandbags under his uniform.

"Come on, man," the taller Chicano cop said. "Bangin?"

Mortrice shook his head.

"So you were just walkin, out by yourself for a stroll on Vermont, and somebody you never seen tries to cap you?" The redheaded one leaned against the bed. "Cause you were exercisin?"

"Man, people try to cap guys all the time," the other one said. "But from where you told the doctor you live, and where you were, man, I'd say you got dropped, huh?"

Mortrice stared past them at the drops of blood someone had left on the floor nearby. His? Two black dimes now, waiting for someone to pick them up. He heard the hoarse whispering of the doctor somewhere else.

"Okay, homey," the redheaded cop said, nodding. "Who's gonna take you back to the Gardens?"

Mortrice was still silent. Shit. I can walk. Almost light now, probably. I got some money. Take the bus.

"Let's go," the redheaded cop said, pulling his arm gently to ease him off the bed.

In the back of the patrol car, Mortrice's heart beat more wildly than when the doctor dug into his back. He wore only his big coat, since he'd left the shredded, bloody shirt in the hospital. Kenneth would see him. Someone would see him in this car and he'd be dead for real. He closed his eyes, but he saw Paco's glowing skull against the dark earth, the folded black hands on his chest. He began to choke, coughing and trying not to cry.

"He's cold," the redhead said to the other cop. "Where can we get him somethin?"

Mortrice watched the streets slide past, and the car swerved into a liquor-store parking lot. He watched the redhead go inside, and in the glass storefront, he saw the cop gesturing to a rack of T-shirts. The owner, a Korean man, gestured back a few times, and then the cop laughed. He came out carrying a wad of cloth, throwing it into the backseat.

"Hey," the cop said. "Don't want you freezin, homey."

Mortrice examined the shirt. BUDWEISER. KING OF BEERS. He took off his coat, feeling shamed, and slipped the shirt over his head. His bandages stretched and stung.

"How much?" the Chicano cop asked.

"He was an Oriental," the redheaded cop said. "Too much."

They turned onto Mortrice's street, and after two blocks, he said, "Hey. Drop me now. Uh, please, can you drop me now?" When the car slowed, and the eyes turned back to him, he said quickly, "Thanks. Please." If Kenneth or anyone else saw him . . . even neighbors, who had big mouths . . . if his mother saw him . . .

The redheaded cop draped his arm across the seat so he could look full at Mortrice. "Hey, homey. I hope I'll never see you again in my life. Be careful, okay?"

Mortrice felt the eyes on his like rays for a moment, and he looked away. He scrambled out of the car and onto the sidewalk, dizzy in the gray dawn.

•   •   •

The truck shuddered smoothly in the slow lane, and Marcus caught the glances of drivers in newer cars, cellular phones attached like limpets to their ears. Grim sherberts, his uncle called them in a slow, disdainful growl. Like the grim reaper, he'd say. "They ain't never happy. Drive like they got a sheriff trailin they ass, talkin on the phone, lookin at a magazine, listenin to a damn cassette. I done heard French, Spanish, chantin, everything. They can't just drive. That ain't good enough."

He came up behind a car merging onto the freeway. The bumper sticker on the Toyota van said DRIVER CARRIES NO CASH. SHE'S A MOM. Marcus had to laugh. It sounded like Enchantee complaining this afternoon.

She'd stopped by the barn to pick up Demetrius Junior just when he was getting the truck. She'd been invited to a party downtown, and she wanted Demetrius to come. D'Junior had clambered onto her and held her like a monkey, and Marcus saw her swaying back and forth unconsciously while she talked to the men; her wrists were curved under her son's bottom, her chin resting in his hair. "Demetrius," she'd said. "All I do is go to work, go home and work, and go crazy. And you've been workin around here for days."

"Daddy ain't back yet," was all Demetrius said, not looking up from the oil filter he was examining. "I'm just keepin an eye out."

Enchantee had shifted her son on her hip and said, "Demetrius. Whoever did this, everybody says it's a random thing. You need to stop this vigilante stuff and come home." She lowered her voice. "I know you guys are packin. And you know how I feel about that."

Demetrius stood up and wrapped his arms around her from behind, tickling D'Junior's neck. "Everybody in California's packin. I'm just protectin myself, baby, you know that." He looked over at Marcus. "And Sissyfly here's gon spell me tomorrow, huh?"

"Save the old name," Marcus had said, but Demetrius had already forgotten him.

"Go head on to the party. Chill out with your old roommate—what was her name?"

"Abby," Enchantee said.

"You partyin in my hood?" Marcus said, trying to smile.

"Historic downtown," she said. "I think that's where they live."

"Have a good time." He watched her walk to her car.

Marcus had backed the truck out of the barn, with Kickstand's watchful eyes on the exhaust. "You know you *bet* not do nothin foolish in L.A. and leave no marks on that truck," Kickstand called.

Marcus smiled now, cruising slow through the tracts outside Rio Seco. He'd told them he was going to L.A. because he wanted to make sure they thought the truck could handle that, but though they'd all pressed him about what woman he even knew in L.A., he was silent.

He'd sure as hell drive careful to this Solano Gardens address Sofelia had given him on the phone. He hadn't seen his sister since she was thirteen. He still pictured her trying to wind her thick, wavy hair into a bun, pulling baby hairs down onto her forehead and slicking them with Vaseline into shining, sculpted waves. Her face was a triangle, wide cheekbones and delicate chin, and all the boys in junior high were following her around. Her brothers were supposed to keep an eye on her, to knock back rough hands or older players. No Treetown boy said "Mmm, mmm, mmm, I can't wait to get some a *that* after the dance" about Sofelia, because a Thompson would hear and some ass would be kicked. No Westside boy better cross that pecan-tree marker on Pepper Avenue looking to rap with Sofelia. And she was a spoiled, solitary girl until then, Marcus remembered. She had as many clothes as his mother could make or buy, and her hair was always perfect; he watched her play alone in the yard, though, pirouetting under the trees, talking to herself in the olive grove. She was too young to go anywhere with the oldest boys, and too old to want to follow Finis and Marcus to the riverbottom anymore. She started stopping off at Olive Gardens on the way home from school, to hang out with girls who lived there.

And then, a few months later, she was gone. She had sent her mother a letter saying that she'd met someone and was going away. She said something had changed and that she couldn't come home. She said she would come back someday, but that her mother shouldn't worry. She loved her.

The police shrugged when Alma showed them the letter. Marcus had seen his father stand against the kitchen wall, only watching them, his mouth a grim moon and his jaw leaping with muscle. His mother had cried for several years, and then she'd kept the swimming, glossy tears inside her eyes, and finally, the liquid seemed to have collected in a reservoir that drew plumpness away from her forehead and left the two deep scores between her brows.

Sofelia had a son, he thought. The reason she started callin me, the reason she's comin back to Rio Seco. She'd never mentioned a man's name, but she'd said somebody might kill her son. Bullets. He stared at the dusty expanses between sprawling tracts. We out in the country. I don't even know how old this boy is, but he can't have a Rio Seco problem. He can't be connected to Daddy's place. It's gotta be some random thing that those women were partying in the Granada. With some fool.

A brown Mercedes surged ahead of him from an on-ramp, and Marcus tapped the truck's brake, scowling at the driver already zigzagging through traffic. He'd loved the way the Lexus handled on the freeway, responsive and sleek, a thrill when he'd raced through the desert night just to feel the dark wind slip past his elbow.

"*Bet* not dent this truck," he muttered, and felt clammy sweat on his shoulders. He shook his head, embarrassed to know that even at this age, he was still afraid of his father, of messing up. And from Kickstand's voice and the others' glances, he knew they wouldn't want to be driving the truck too far, either. His father was impressive. Impassive. Demetrius and Octavious laughed about it, Julius and Finis obviously didn't think about it, but Marcus resented his nervous palms and faster heart whenever he approached his father.

"Where you get that pipe cutter, man?" someone would ask Julius, who was in a woman's yard using the ancient tool to sever long pipes into manageable salvage for the iron man.

"At the gettin place," Julius would say, and Marcus would shake his head.

"Do Daddy know you got it?" Demetrius would ask, and Julius would shrug, his eyes veiled.

"Daddy know where every hubcap and engine and hammer is, man, all the time. He gon kick your natural ass if somebody steal that pipe cutter," Marcus would add.

But he thought now that it wasn't often their father had whipped them. Julius had stolen baseball caps and shoes from a store, and he'd gotten the switch—a green plum branch across the legs. But that was Mama, wielding the wood. Finis had run away to the riverbottom. Mama had done that beating, too, Marcus realized. He tightened his hands on the wheel, remembering what his father had said when Marcus had refused to fight a boy in Olive Gardens, a boy who'd blackened his eye and smacked Sofelia so hard in the face her gums were laced with blood.

"I can whup you or life can whup you," his father had said. "Your mama can beat you or life can beat you."

His mother had laid the switch across his legs twice, then cried and said into his neck, "You can't let nobody hurt your sister. Never. You gotta be a little man, Marcus. You nine now."

Sissyfly. Brainiac. Baby boy. He heard all the names, approaching downtown Los Angeles. Julius and Finis had caught the boy, slapping him down until he cried.

The buildings nestled in haze to his right, and the horizon was turning rusty with the tired Monday sun. He looked for the buildings of USC next, working his teeth on the sides of his mouth.

He'd gone to USC that first year, freshman year, fresh outta Treetown on a partial track scholarship with a Westside boy named Tommy Flair. He saw the dorms, remembering the girls with alligators on their shirts, the potpourri, the boys with boat shoes and no socks. The ivy-laced brick walls and stark white modern buildings he and Tommy passed each night when they ran, worried that they wouldn't be fast enough in the spring. The fall crispness burned into their lungs when they sped around the philosophy building and campus security guards tackled them, threw them face down, and kept their necks under thick soles. The third time it happened, Marcus froze his spine, a different guard's splayed fingers pressing his chest into the asphalt; in his mind he heard, I can beat you or life can beat you. He raised up an inch against the whorls of flesh, but Tommy's widened eyes told him to stop.

They came home within a month of each other. Marcus glimpsed the Felix the Cat car dealership he used to see from his dorm window. Tommy had become a cop. Marcus worked for his father, dropping pins from tow chains, forgetting winch cables, refusing to understand spark plugs and timing chains. He went to the art college for a year. Then he took history classes, spreading out the fees, finally getting his teaching credential. Next week I'll get my Treetown and downtown and Cambodian and Guatemalan kids. Give them classical Greek civilization when they're more interested in the barbarians.

He got off on Vermont, heading past block after block of barred storefronts. Furniture, cheap clothing, electronics. Liquor stores everywhere. He passed the Jamaican restaurant where someone had taken him that college year. More storefronts, strip malls, and then he turned on the street Sofelia had named.

Near the housing project, he passed young boys with plaid Pendletons and their khakis switching back and forth in the empty fall of material under their butts. A few older men leaned against the chain-link fence surrounding the complex. I'm a stranger, and a farmer, in this truck, Marcus thought. Eyes followed him when he turned into the court and looked for her door number.

Other doors were open, and music mixed with laughter flowed from apartments and car windows. But Sofelia's door was closed. Then Marcus saw her heart-shaped face, peering out from a slice she'd pulled in her drapes.

He stood by the truck for a moment, waiting for her to come running out. He'd seen the smile bright in the dimness behind the glass. But when the door opened, she hovered inside, her arms moving up and then down like a baby bird's. Marcus stepped through the doorway, and Sofelia's arms went around him as tight as wings, her heart pounding against his ribs.

When she finally pulled away, she bent to pick up the box near her feet. Marcus said, "You in a hurry? You don't want to tell me nothin before we get on the road?"

She dropped the box and hugged him again, murmuring, "I missed you. I—I don't know nothin else to tell. We have to go."

She went into a back bedroom and came out carrying a shopping bag. Behind her was her son. He had her pointed chin and wide forehead, and his skin was flawless mahogany. No acne scars, no stiff hairs. The boy stared at Marcus with his hands tight on a gym bag. His eyes were dark and too glossy, like fresh oil. He went out to the truck, moving stiffly, and Sofelia said, "Mortrice. He been in the bed all day, said he sick. Had his covers all pulled up around him." She shook her head, and Marcus saw the boy throw his box into the back and get in after it, his face contorted when he faced them from where he sat against the cab.

• • •

Newton Place. Brookline Place. Boston Street. Rockport Place.

Enchantee drove slowly up the steep area called Plymouth Hill. It was above historic downtown, a few terraced rows of streets lined with the biggest, oldest mansions in Rio Seco. Not the new-money castles and stucco giants on the outskirts of the city, but the Spanish-style and Tudor-style and Victorian houses built for the first Pilgrims to make it out to wild California back in the old days.

She'd been here before, when her aunt had worked houses around here, picked up by women at the gathering place in Treetown by the old market, one of the buildings the city had razed along Pepper Avenue. Her aunt, Demetrius's mother, many Treetown women had sat on that old wooden bench when they needed money because someone had broken an arm or a man was sick or had disappeared. The Plymouth Hill women needed bodies because someone was graduating or a man was retiring with a huge party.

Enchantee felt her forehead prickle with nervous heat. Abby had said this was a casual get-together for her and Bent, for newspaper people and friends to relax. Even though Enchantee knew she wasn't the kind of newspaper person Abby meant, something in her wanted to see Abby's son, see where she lived now. She remembered vivid fragments from college: Abby's jewel-green Herbal Essence shampoo, her fascination with Enchantee's sketches and drawings, the way she'd painted Enchantee's fingernails and called her Chani. A new girl, an artist. That's what she'd been in the dorm room, down the arched plaster hallways.

When she went through the gate in the high brick wall, surrounded by dark hedges and bloodred roses curving over trellis structures, their blooms like tiny thunderclouds in the dim evening light, she remembered this house. Her aunt had come out of that gate, to the car where Enchantee waited with her cousin Johnnie and Johnnie's boyfriend, and announced, "I ain't workin for her again. Gotta be silent as death in there the whole day, so she can paint. No. Uh-uh. I see her comin, I'ma look the other way." Her aunt had settled herself into a soft heap in the backseat by Enchantee, her hands frosted with ashy, dry skin when she held them up and shook her head.

Abby passed by the open door, a flash of red in the envelope of gold light. Enchantee stood there, not sure what to do. A couple came up behind her. "Hello," the man said. The woman nodded, and Enchantee nodded back. They looked like reporters, with their satchels and rumpled hair and easy smiles, but she wasn't sure until Abby said, "Hey, guys!"

"Chani!" she added, curling her hand around Enchantee's shoulder to draw her into the living room. Enchantee saw people sitting and standing, the wood-paneled room bright, little trays of food on tables and glasses on a bar in the corner.

Abby said, "I'm so glad you came!" Enchantee looked briefly into her face, at the gray eyes framed with golden shadow, and she smiled because it sounded like Abby really meant that. "This is Bent, my, uh, what are we calling each other today, babe?"

The reporter with the comma ponytail shook her hand. Enchantee said softly, "We met, in the parking lot."

His face grew red palms like he'd been slapped, and she saw how easily he was embarrassed. "I, I've met so many people," he started, and Abby interrupted.

"It's okay," she laughed. She said to Enchantee, "He's been over-whelmed by my mother's social shit, and now I'm getting to him." Bent was still flushed, and Enchantee couldn't tell if it was because Abby was telling her everything. "Go on in, tons of people from the paper are here," Abby called behind her when she pulled Bent toward the door to meet someone else.

Enchantee hesitated. She scanned the room, but of course the faces speaking to each other animatedly were only vaguely familiar. A small boy with a cap of pale hair like Abby's came careening through the doorway, running into Enchantee's knees; he looked up at her with sapphire eyes, finding nothing in her face, and pushed her legs away to propel himself through the living room.

"Dylan!" Abby called to him, but he rocketed through the clumps of calves like a pinball, heading into the hallway on the other side.

Enchantee glimpsed a feather-haired woman she'd seen at the newspaper emerging from there, and she watched the collision. The woman's coral, cracked cheeks trembled, and she said, "Young man, I think your mother and the rest of us have had enough of your behavior." She leaned against the wall, her eyes fierce on Abby moving through the guests.

The boy stopped cold and said, "I'm sorry," his voice as high as a bell, and Enchantee smiled, knowing he knew his mother was approaching. She went closer to him. He was only slightly older than D'Junior, she could tell, and suddenly she missed her son, would have rather had his warm hand curled in hers when she moved through these rooms.

"He hasn't had a nap, Aunt Carrie, I'm sorry," Abby said, her voice high, too. She saw Enchantee and smiled. "This is my offspring. My heart." She linked her arms around his neck loosely.

"Where's your mother?" Enchantee sat down on the leather couch beside Abby, who rocked her son slightly. He stared at Enchantee's face.

"She's in Palm Springs, at a concert," Abby said, leaning back, her own eyes nearly closed, and Enchantee recognized that conduction of boy warmth that melted the mother with the child. "That's why I'm having this. It's kind of hard, us being here in her house. We're saving money for our own place."

"Are you Mexican?" Dylan said suddenly, his voice gravelly now. "We didn't have Mexicans in Boston. I didn't saw any. But Bent says I saw some now."

"Dylan," Abby said quietly. "Chani's not Mexican. And Mexican people do live in Boston. You just . . ."

Enchantee saw his eyes flutter and close. "That's okay," she said.

"He doesn't understand colors and shades on people yet," Abby said, bending to lay him down on a blanket she pulled from the couch.

Demetrius Junior does, Enchantee thought. She looked at the huge office, with black windowpanes in diamond patterns, a fireplace, a large wooden desk in the corner, a television, and books on the walls. This room was as big as her aunt's living area.

"Abby?" A woman's hushed voice came from the doorway.

"Connie!" Abby whispered, pulling the blanket in a cocoon over her son. "I'm glad you came. Hi, Web. How's my big sister treating you? Better than she used to treat me?"

Enchantee stood near the wall, watching the two blond sisters hug each other. A man Demetrius's age watched with amusement. His brown hair was combed straight back from his heart-scalloped forehead. "We won't bore you, Web," Enchantee heard Abby say. "If it's not real estate or politics, it's not worth words, right?"

They went down the hallway, and Abby turned back to Enchantee with a curved arm. "Come on," she said. "Mothers just want to have fun."

Mortrice lay in the truckbed, his back starred with pain. He raised himself up when he felt them get on a freeway. His uncle looked like a country-ass nigga. Soft. Had on jeans and a Lakers T-shirt. His mother had said he was a teacher. Nigga can't teach me shit, Mortrice thought, looking at the freeway signs. He turned his head to the wind to see the sign with RIO SECO—54 MILES.

When they'd left downtown and the belts of light past L.A., after they'd passed through three valleys, by his count, he had watched the black mountains ringing the basin like huge faces with sharp noses and parted lips. Huge men on their backs. Bodies like women, sleeping. Or dead.

To his left and right, he saw faint red-gold glows like distant sunsets. But they were lights gathered at the base of the hills. Then long stretches of empty blackness hurtled past.

His mother sat in the cab. He'd watched her move quickly from the doorway to the truck seat, saying nothing, her face fierce and closed, like it was a long journey. He knew he had never seen her leave the apartment. Now her shoulders were pressed against the glass; he turned his head to the side, saw fabric wrinkled near his head.

The river sounded a hollow space under the truck, and he sat up hard, scraping his back on his bag. The silver skein stretched endlessly to the west. And his uncle angled the truck off on the same ramp Kenneth had taken him down. Marcus closed his eyes. He wouldn't see the tree. He would wait until they had turned at least three times.

One. Two. Three. He saw a downtown smaller than L.A., with old, strange buildings full of curves and bells and red tile. The truck stopped in front of an apartment building with as much wrought-iron as the ghetto.

"This where you stay?" Sofelia stared at the Las Palmas building, her mouth closed tight. She'd refused to stop at their parents' place, or anywhere, just yet. She'd asked him to take her, just show her, where he lived.

"Where you gon go?" he asked her softly. "You can stay here."

She shook her head. "I got a place. Tiki's sister got a place, and she's goin to Alabama for a while. She got a sick aunt. I'ma stay there."

"Where?" Marcus pulled away from the curb.

"Olive Gardens."

"Damn, Sofelia, you said you were worried about your son!" Marcus drove slowly. "Olive Gardens got plenty of gangs, too."

"Gotta be better than L.A.," Sofelia said, watching out her window. Marcus wondered what she remembered, but he was afraid to ask. He drove down Pepper Avenue. The boy's head didn't move.

"When you gon see Mama?" Marcus turned on Grove Avenue, and Sofelia lowered her head onto her chest.

"Soon as I can," she whispered.

"I'ma have to tell her," he whispered back, cruising past the darkened streets, glancing down SaRonn's way. "She's been hurtin a long time."

Sofelia shook her head, lifting a shine-tracked face. "No," she said. "I have to tell her. Soon as I can."

Marcus pulled into the parking area of Olive Gardens. The brown stucco boxes were side-by-side like trains pulled into a square. Marcus looked at Sofelia. What could have happened to make her leave, to make her keep her silence for this long? Why the hell would she want to come here instead of home? She sat, frozen, against the door. Marcus touched her index finger, and she folded forward like a closing book.

Her son had gotten out of the truckbed, and he opened the door, cradling his mother's shoulders. "Come on, Mama," he said, the first time Marcus had heard his voice. He pulled her slowly from the seat, and Marcus quickly came around to help him.

They led her to the door and knocked. A heavy, gold-skinned woman with pink rollers as tight as snails on her head opened it. She said, "Come on in, girl. Tiki just called to see was you here."

Sofelia sat on the couch, her face blank, while Marcus and the boy brought in the few boxes and bags. The TV was on, the news was starting, and Marcus looked at his watch. Ten o'clock. He stood awkwardly near Sofelia, and suddenly the woman hollered, "See? They show that Rodney King video damn near every day."

．　　．　　．

Mortrice scanned the ghostly faces hovering in a circle around the brother getting proned out, over and over, LAPD style. He saw mouths open and close, imagined them hollering it out like they did: "Prone out! Prone out now!" Mortrice glanced at the boots, the baton, the faces above spread-wide legs. They beatin him into the set, what it always look like to me. LAPD Posse. Or they beatin him out.

Enchantee was in the kitchen, putting away the glass she'd used and tossing the paper plate with olive pits. The bullet-shaped black olives were sour-salty. Demetrius's great-grandmother made olives that were reddish-brown, like apples.

She'd felt crowded by the backs turning and swerving in each room, by the bright, fleeting smiles and words. She'd barely talked to Abby again, but she'd met a nice woman who worked on the recipe page. Enchantee had told her about Alma's meals that took all day stirring and had no recipes, and the woman had agreed that working mothers should be able to use Noodle Roni without feeling guilty.

Enchantee moved toward the door. "You've got to try these olives while I get your drink," Abby was saying to someone. "I've got Kalamata from Greece, Spanish olives, and these great big fat ones from Northern California. Olives are making a comeback. And I've heard they used to press a great olive oil here in Rio Seco."

Enchantee paused, waiting for people to move, and she saw the two older women sitting on a huge couch near the hallway. When the tide of people deposited her behind them, she leaned against the wall. Nearer to her, the puffs of hair, red and white, looked like two plump, short-tailed birds perched on the couch back. She heard Carrie Smith Donohue say, "Well, I see how angry people are that the sheriff and the police haven't managed to charge anyone in those two awful murders down there in Treetown."

The other woman said, "Two young girls like that. And the council-man was right—that area is completely out of control. I wouldn't drive down there for anything."

"Well, I have," Carrie Smith Donohue said softly, and Enchantee held herself still against the wood paneling to listen. "I've taken a look at some of the buildings down there. You won't believe how old some of them are."

"Well, who would build new houses there?" the other woman said.

"No, I mean some are historic. Some of them are as old and possibly valuable as the adobes in San Diego's Old Town." She paused and took a sip. "Of course, they aren't preserved . . . ," she went on, but her friend turned brightly to her.

"I hadn't been to Old Town in ages, but my daughter-in-law took me last year and it was marvelous. Such cute little restaurants, and a wonderful gift selection in the shops. She bought Christmas presents for everyone."

Enchantee waved at Abby, and Abby hurried over, catching her in the hallway. "Wait! Chani!" She paused, out of breath. "I'm so glad you came. Hey, do you know anyone who could help me out in the afternoons? I still haven't found the right person to watch Dylan—that's pretty obvious, from tonight. And we're starting on this new magazine format."

"You didn't find anybody to come here?" Enchantee looked at Abby's flushed neck and swinging hair.

"I did, but she didn't work out with Dylan. She didn't understand kids. And the hours are so unpredictable."

"I'll ask around," Enchantee said. She watched someone take Abby's elbow; Abby mouthed "Thanks" when the person drew her over to the olive trays. Enchantee walked slowly toward the library.

Peering inside the darkened room, she saw the television flickering and Dylan on the couch, blanket over his head like a hood, calmly sucking his thumb, eyes intent on the screen. "It's that video," he said without looking at her. Enchantee saw the ring of men, the eyes bulging in the dark face when it rose momentarily. She dropped her gaze to the small face floating like a moon against the couch, and let out a shuddering breath.

The doctor talked of physical therapy for his shoulder, of a sling, of movement and medication. Hosea had closed his eyes for a long time. The medicinal air seemed to rest behind his eyeballs, aching and cold.

When he opened them, hearing the man behind the partition whuffle, from laughter or pain Hosea didn't know, it was night. The room was dim and grainy. The images he'd seen so many times on the television were grainy, too. Shifting, violent, jerky, darker night. A boot was raised now, the knee bent. Hosea felt the grit rubbed into his palms, his neck, felt his cheekbone ground into the cinders. A white woman's face abruptly filled the screen. Hosea felt the medicinal stench sear his throat when he tried to breathe.

"Serves the nigger right for not stopping," the thickened voice said from behind the drape. "He didn't obey the officers of the law." Hosea turned away from the sound, and he saw the telephone inches from his head.

Marcus waited to turn onto Pepper Avenue when Enchantee's car passed, her amber face small in the window. He followed her through the gate of his father's place, catching her arm when she got out of her car.

They went straight to the living room, where Kendrick, Jaman, and D'Junior were lying on a blanket watching a movie. They were laughing and kicking each other. Enchantee bent down to pick up D'Junior, and Marcus's mother came out from the bedroom down the hall.

"Who's that?" she called. "Demetrius?"

"Marcus," he called.

Her face was lifted high, her eyes wide. "Your daddy called, from the hospital. They lettin him out. Go find Demetrius, he walkin round here somewhere. You two go and get your daddy. I'm makin up the room." She ran to Marcus and hugged him, pushing him with her chest toward the kitchen. "Go on and hurry. They lettin him out. He said come on."

Her voice burbled and rang bright; he could hear it when he walked past the closed-tight coldhouse to stand at the road leading to the storage lot. "Demetrius!" he shouted. "Marcus!"

That was how they identified themselves, whose holler ricocheted from tree trunks.

"Demetrius," he yelled again, and then he listened. No stick thocking tree trunks, no whistling, no answering call.

A hissing spark flared in the pepper trees between the road and the bluff overlooking the riverbed, and Demetrius strode from the low branches. He drew hard on his cigarillo, his other hand curled loose over the gun in his waistband, and Marcus thought, He was watchin where Daddy always watch. From that chair. He look like a bigger man. But he's gon get this land, he's the one like Daddy. Same ways.

"You didn't holler," Marcus said.

"I knew where you was, fool," Demetrius said. "Where you always stand and holler. Too lazy to walk around and look." He took a deep drag on the cigarillo and blew smoke into the ferny leaves.

"Enchantee gon love you walkin around with a piece, Mr. Vigilante," Marcus said. "Whoever did this ain't fool enough to come back." He stared at Demetrius's broad, brick-flushed cheekbones in the light shining slanted from the barn. He thought, I ain't the one look like Daddy, or think like him. But I'ma be the one find out who did it.

"Always bringin up Enchantee," Demetrius said, cocking his head, his eyes narrow slants. "You think I don't love Enchantee? I don't listen to her? You ain't never been married, man, okay? We hear each other, me and her. I work my ass off to pay for that house she wants." He turned and then spun back. "You know what, Marcus? I ain't gon call you baby boy. But I'ma tell you this. You better do a twelve-step program and get over her. That's what they call it, right? Downtown people. You need to find twelve other women and get done with it. Cause I had my twelve other women before I met Enchantee. And she was it. No question. You ain't seen me fool around, ain't seen me question myself. Get yourself right, man, and don't keep sweatin me."

When he began to walk toward the barn, Marcus said, "Daddy called from the hospital. We have to go get him. Come on."

Demetrius said nothing when Marcus got into their father's truck and started the engine. He went into the barn, to put away the gun, Marcus knew, and came out to sit in the cab.

Marcus kept the hot quiet lodged in his throat when he drove.

When they got to the lobby, harshly bright against the night, Marcus watched Demetrius put his hands in his pockets, the oil-veined fingers hidden. He stared at his brother for a long moment, at the work shirt and creased boots; Demetrius hated talking to official-type white people, like those behind the information desk, as much as their father did. Marcus glanced at his own jeans and T-shirt—moving-Sofelia clothes. But he stood close to the desk and smiled. "We're looking for Mr.

Hosea Thompson, please," he said, smiling just wide enough to be friendly. Not scary, not country.

The door to their father's room was open slightly, and Marcus pushed it slow, peering around to see him sitting stiff on the side of the bed. His father looked up as if blind. "Daddy?" Marcus whispered, and Demetrius echoed.

Their father's head trembled and shuddered, and he moved his eyes to their faces. "Let's go," he murmured hoarsely.

He was wearing his hospital gown and dark-blue work pants. But his feet were bare. Marcus saw only a pulled-shut partition on the other side of the darkened room. No nurse, no one discharging his father, giving instructions or pushing a waiting wheelchair.

Demetrius went to the closet and found the boots. He and Marcus each bent to a foot, and Hosea was silent. Marcus looked up to see his father's face, sculpted harsh in the tiny light over the sink. His eyes were nearly hidden by his cheekbones. Three etched Xs marked the skin at the outer corners, and a straight-carved crease dropped the length of his face. His father's nose was curved as hard as a bird's. They each dropped a boot, and took an elbow to help him from the bed.

"You just decided you leavin, right?" Marcus whispered when his father leaned on them heavily for a moment, then drew himself away.

"Who the hell else supposed to decide?" his father said. "Better be me or God."

Demetrius said, "Come on, then," his voice gruff and nervous. They went out the door, the chortling snore from behind the curtain never letting up, and Hosea began to walk straighter, steadier, when they reached the elevator.

In that glaring light, Marcus saw his father sway. His hand, when he grabbed it, was as hard and callused as a turtle shell. Marcus saw that his father's flesh had melted away, his cheekbones full and taut, as if curved shields had been slid under the skin. He looked past to Demetrius, with the same wide, sharp bones he had, they all had. And in the shining steel doors, he saw himself, blurry, looking exactly the same.

CHAPTER FOUR

PAZ WAITED FOR the angel moths to hover near her few late flowers, the tiny chamomile daisies and nearly spent marigolds she'd loved when she was a child in Mexico. The air was glittering now from the wind's wash. Paz knew it was almost too late for the darting, pale angel moths that had come all summer. But for some unaccountable reason, she still expected to see them—the comforting movement like stitchings of lace around the blooms while she sat perfectly still in her chair near the garden.

It wasn't hard for her to sit, silent and patient. She was ninety years old. Abuela. No one spoke her name, Paz, except in Agua Dulce, when she went to Salcido's place to have his great-uncle Feliciano read the newspaper to her now and then.

Palomas de la luz, doves of the light. She waited for the moths, but since they weren't here yet, she swept down the cement under the veranda's overhanging palm fronds. They were newly green, just lapped there by her dreamy-eyed, hollow-faced great-grandson. The one who always showed her the bones held startlingly clean in his palm.

All morning, she usually swept. All afternoon, she watered and plucked and harvested. And in the evening, especially this late, nearly ten o'clock, she sat and listened for the owls. She moved the broom along the chair legs, pushing the debris from the wind into a pile. She had been born to sweep, it seemed, since that was all she remembered doing in Mexico.

In the small town past Ensenada, where she could see the turquoise sea through the olive trees, she had never had a mother or father. She had been given to the family who ran the olive grove and the roadside

stand; she swept each room in the house of the daily dust that swirled
up from the fields around Maneadero, and she swept the yard bare and
clean. She washed all the clothes and hung them to dry; she washed all
the dishes and stacked them to dry; she lay down when the man who
owned her slapped her near her eye; she grew a baby who swirled under
her loose dress while she swept and circled and swept until a passing
family absorbed her like a flock of birds and carried her north to the
citrus groves in Rio Seco.

She wanted to see the barn owl tonight. Paz left the broom standing
and pulled her black sweater around her closely, her black scarf tucked
into her collar and held tight at her throat. She moved down the road
her granddaughter's husband had packed so hard with all his tires. He
was in the hospital, and she had lit candles in her bedroom and prayed
to the Virgin of Guadalupe that he would leave there with his body
intact.

Why she wanted to see the ghostly face of the huge barn owl she
wasn't certain. The owl lived in the cottonwood near the field of cars,
but at this time of night, it hovered and called near her olive place.
Maybe it was talking to her rabbits, just reminding them that in the
real world, they wouldn't be safe behind curlicued metal.

She passed the silver trailers. Her preening, cold-eyed great-grandson's
windows were dark, and only a dim light like a candle shone in her
dreamy-eyed one's curving capsule. She felt herself float down the path,
a wraith, a night moth drawn to the square of moonlight and the owl's
face when he would rest in the open window of her tiny place.

But Paz stopped to see the rabbits, their eyes glowing dully red in
the light, their cages glimmering with the copper paint Alma had applied.
She touched one of the old mattresses' intricate whorls. She remembered
when her daughter, Elva, had loved a man from an island. *Muy negro*,
the man, with oceans in his walk. Hurriah, his name was, and Paz had
mistrusted him until she'd watched him sweep their tiny migrant-shack
yard like a Mexican. He loved beans like a Mexican, raked fancy designs
into the dirt while she smiled. They lost one baby, kept one, and then
the island man and her daughter had gone wide-eyed, she was sure,
into muddy ditch water on a bus full of rough-handed pickers headed
for a winter cabbage field.

Paz hurried into the small stone shed to pick up her pole and push
open the wooden shutters that closed over the only window, high up,

facing the southeast. In the gaps between her olive trees and Oscar's eucalyptus, she could see the edging haze around the moon. She sat in her chair, holding the stick to prop her hands, and waited.

The Mexican women in Agua Dulce had birds in cages—parakeets, canaries, doves. But Paz had the mockingbirds in the mornings, the sparrows and wild parrots and crows, the jays shrieking for sunflower seeds. In the evenings, when the other women draped towels over their cages and the rustlings died down, Paz watched the bats dart into the dusk, and the angel moths that were somewhere between bird and insect came to drink from her flowers. But her favorite were the owls, with their shadowing wingspan and the silence with which they pumped their wings and passed over her, with their cautious and comforting calls. And the barn owl, snow-white face outlined in a dainty dark circle, came to peruse the olive place each night, she knew, though she could rarely stay awake long enough to see the face appear suddenly in the window.

Paz felt her back curl into patience, but she heard sounds. Not bird rustlings or the rabbits' faint thrum. She closed her eyes. She heard a snipping noise, electric, almost as sharp as the cries emitted by the bats. The plink of wire—that was how the bats sounded. But when these metallic clicks were silent, she heard brush moving and feet dragging nearby. She stayed on the chair, as hunched and dark as a starling, she thought, drawing her scarf down to her brows.

The dragging and footsteps came closer, to the far side of the stone shed where a path ran behind it, along the stone wall, and then voices said something in harsh, boy English.

A different voice said something faster, in rounder words. Paz kept her eyes fixed on the window, holding the stick tight. She heard, "Look, Betty-Bill!" A stark white face leaped into the open space, the makeup fiercely perfect. Paz saw arched dark eyebrows and a red mouth that gaped open. Then the face flopped forward and disappeared, a trail of red hair spilling over the sill for a moment before it slipped back out.

"Shit!" she heard, and laughing. Then the footsteps, maybe three or four sets of shoes, went farther down the path.

She waited until the noises were fainter. How could she run down the road toward the house without the voices seeing her? She stood, close to the rock wall, and peered out the doorway. They could be heading to her dreamy-eyed great-grandson's trailer; their voices were white, their laughter crackling with small bones.

Paz slipped out the doorway and across the road, to the trees on the other side of the property. No one would see a starling in the dark.

Marcus waited impatiently at the red light on California and Pepper, hearing his father's thickened breathing. He stared at the onyx-shined windows on the Los Arbolitos business park a few blocks away, afraid to speak. Then Demetrius said, "Damn! A patrol parade goin our way."

Blurs of red and blue came up behind them as fast as UFOs in the dark, swerving around to race down Pepper Avenue. Marcus waited until the street was dark again before he pulled out. "Go slow," his father rasped, and Marcus went slow, watching the rearview.

He cruised under the freeway overpass, and they were all silent, straining to see where the lights would be clustered.

Three were at the gate of Oscar's place, and more were somewhere inside his father's place, because he could see snatches of neon flickering in the trees. "Go! Go!" Demetrius shouted, leaning forward to grip the truck dash.

"No!" Marcus shouted back, slowing the truck. "No. We fly up in there, we might get shot. No."

"Marcus, drive!" Demetrius turned his face from the implacable flashing, his forehead twisted.

"Daddy, they didn't let you out, huh?" Marcus had tried to keep his shoulder from touching his father's. He'd seen his father wince in pain when he moved the arm. "They lookin for you?"

"For what? To pay a goddamn bill? I ain't asked to go in there," Hosea said, his voice graveled. "They was fixin to let me go. Don't nobody want me. Come on. I want to know what the hell goin on now."

Marcus kept the truck barely moving. "Who's home?" he asked softly. "Mama, Abuela, the kids, maybe Enchantee. Finis and Julius?"

"Shit, just drive!" Demetrius shouted, slamming his palms on the dash.

"Listen!" Marcus pulled the truck onto the sandy shoulder near the three pecan trees. Jungle Brother territory. He shook his head, watching two small cars slowly pass. "Daddy already got shot findin out what the hell was goin on once. Demetrius—go back downtown, turn slow and cool like you ain't in no hurry, go back there and get on the freeway. Take Daddy to your crib. I'll go find out what's goin on. Check on Mama and them."

"You crazy," Demetrius said, but Marcus was already out of the truck, waiting for his father's voice. He turned to see his father's eyes dark as glinting rainwater in the oil pans.

"Don't get hurt," his father said.

"I ain't screwin up," Marcus called softly.

He walked casually along the shoulder toward Oscar's fence line, keeping his head up, hearing the truck turn and fade, and he was almost surprised that Demetrius had listened to him. The pulsing lights felt like thrown ropes, drawing him in. I better not screw up, he thought. I can't go around the back like last time. Get my ass fired up. Can't go through Oscar's place in the trees. Gotta go heads up. Smile. What's the problem, Officer?

But no officers were in sight when he reached the open gate to his uncle's. The radios spit and cackled, and it was all he could do to walk past the cars, the broad, shining cars that had scared the shit out of him all his life. The laughing voices above him and his brothers as they lay on the downtown sidewalks, voices saying, "You sure you didn't liberate nothin in the store, boy? Look at those liberated haircuts on that one. You were just sight-seein?"

He continued the casual stride toward the burned web of chain link at his father's driveway. Through the black diamonds, he saw two parked patrol cars near the barn, one cop standing near the lit doorway writing in a pad. Marcus walked a few steps up the low slope, calling, "Excuse me, Officer, uh, is it . . ."

"Stop there, okay? ID. See some ID."

The officer frisked him lightly while he held his hands palm down before him. "Wallet's in the right one," Marcus murmured, and the deputy pulled it from his pocket.

"Why you walkin, bro?" the cop asked, slicing a flashlight across his driver's license. The beam showed a thick brown moustache, a strong chin round like the end of a bat. "Marcus."

"Friend dropped me off at my dad's here," Marcus said, his voice clear but not too precise. A bro voice. "I live downtown. I teach at Rio Seco."

The man nodded, peering hard into Marcus's face for a moment, like he was making a decision. "Where's your car?"

Marcus made himself smile. "Got stolen last week. I'm on foot."

The officer's shoulders slanted downward a little, and he shook his head. "Downtown's gettin like a used-car showroom."

Marcus felt brave enough. "What's wrong here? Somebody steal one of my dad's cars?"

The man gave him a hard glance. "Your dad's the one they were lookin at for the two women. He's in the hospital, right?" Marcus nodded. "Now we got another woman back in there recently deceased, and a guy in a trailer who thinks this is fuckin *Batman* and he's the Riddler."

Marcus kept his face blank and calm. "Did you guys talk to my mother?"

"Investigator's in the house talkin to your mom. Alma, right?" He consulted his pad. "And some older lady. She only speaks Spanish, though."

Marcus breathed in and stretched his lungs. "The guy in the trailer's probably my brother. I can talk to him."

The officer worked his tongue into his jawline. "He's alone in the trailer. No friends. And you're cruisin up now by yourself. Your friend vouch for where you been?"

Marcus let the pounding in his chest increase. "It was my oldest brother. We were gettin my dad out of the hospital."

"You said it was your friend."

"I meant my brother."

"Shit. Come on, right here. Don't run or do anything stupid."

Marcus walked in front of the hard shoes, hearing more cars with static-filled radios pull into the driveway. The officer called behind them, "Takin this guy for questioning. She's back here."

The belt behind him jingled like Christmas bells. Marcus moved down the faint trail leading from the barn to the trailers, hearing voices from the eucalyptus windbreak. He came into the clearing and saw Finis, head down so all Marcus glimpsed was blurred braids and bony shoulders like wings under the white T-shirt. "That your brother?" the voice behind him asked. "Or another friend?"

"My brother," Marcus said. Finis slumped against the trailer wall, another cop beside him.

"Ask him what the hell's goin on," the first one said.

"Finis," Marcus said. "What up?"

Finis raised his face, his eyes empty on Marcus's. He glanced at the two uniformed men and their roving narrow beams. "Flashlight," he sang softly. "Spotlight. Neon light. Stoplight."

"Come on, man," Marcus whispered. "Were you sleepin?"

"I love music, any kind of music," Finis sang.

"See that shit?" the second officer said. "Guy's pissin me off."

"He was listening to his headphones," Marcus said. "You never see him without em. He's always alone in here unless one of us comes back." He turned back to Finis. "You hear anybody? They say it's a woman back here."

"The mothership," Finis said, shaking his head.

"What? What the hell is she?" The officer's voice was rising above the approaching talk of more men.

Marcus paused. To talk to Finis, you had to know Parliament/Funkadelic, the Supremes, and everything in between, and he was sure these guys didn't. "He was in his trailer, listening to headphones, and once he's like that and locked in, he can't hear anything." He closed his eyes, imagining Finis's silver Airstream slanting into the sky, rising up with his brother inside and cruising off to safer places. But this had always been as safe as they could keep him.

"Come here," the first cop said suddenly, grabbing Marcus's arm and leading him toward Oscar's place, into the glowing lavender trunks of eucalyptus. The vertical shafts of pale bark and the crazy-slanting beams from the flashlights made Marcus dizzy for a moment. Then he saw two men crouched around a prone form in the thickest gathering of trees, just at the stone wall. "You guys got another white girl dead down here. Your brother's a fuckin mental case who thinks it's a joke. Look at her."

Marcus stared down at the angular face so stark under thick makeup, the open, dark-red mouth, the hard knees like tiny plates under stockings. The two men on their haunches laughed. One of them pointed to the woman's breasts under the tight bodysuit. One full cone, strangely stiff for a woman lying on her back, pressed at the fabric. But the other had slid between her ribs and her arm.

"She's not a woman. She's a damn he/she. A guy."

.　　.　　.

The four faces floated and bobbed in the small room like uncooked pancakes arranged in a skillet. In Finis's forehead, all the snatches of songs he remembered from school and church and radios and cassettes and dances and jump-roping girls swirled in an ordered chaos, waiting their turn.

"So, Finis. What up with the dead people, huh? What up with that?"

He saw the smiles around the false-black words.

"Tell us the story, bro. What's been goin down over there? Story time."

Once upon a time right *now*.

"Why the hell do you have all those bones in your trailer?"

Dem bones gon rise again.

"What'd you smoke—angel dust?"

Angel baby, my angel baby.

"Okay. Your brother—what's his name?—Marcus—he told us you think different from the rest of the world. But you can fuckin well talk, cause you got a tongue. Come on. Who's the gentleman that thought he was a lady?"

Who's that lady?

"Somebody cracked *her* skull big time and then stuck her fuckin wig back on her head."

Put on your wig, woman, we goin out to shake and finger-pop.

"So you're in your spacious abode chillin out, groovin to some tunes, and you didn't hear a damn thing? We're expected to believe that shit? Not a damn thing?"

It's your thang. Do what you wanna do. I can't tell you who to sock it to.

"Fuck it. If you can't talk, you can't walk. Take him on back."

Marcus zipped his jacket while he walked down the stairs. Leather— not pleather, the vinyl stuff people used to laugh about when he was in high school. He squinted at the sun poking fingers into the courtyard, and when a dark figure in a huge black coat stepped beside him at the archway, he jumped back so hard his shoulder hit the plaster.

"Hey," the boy murmured.

Mortrice. Marcus trembled hard and let the fear dissipate. "You got a good memory for addresses," he said as the boy fell into step beside him.

"Streets in L.A. a lot harder," the boy said, looking away, and Marcus thought he wanted it to have a double meaning.

"You walked?"

"You walkin."

"Yeah. My hooptie got stolen, and I haven't been able to get another car yet." They headed down Las Palmas, toward historic downtown, passing restaurants and antique stores and the ancient brick storefronts painted over with soap and medicine ads from the early 1900s. "These old buildings are about the only ones to survive the ugly sixties," Marcus said into the silence.

"Funkytown," Mortrice murmured, his voice low again.

"What?"

"Funkytown. You know—dudes that wanna be artists and shit. These kinda restaurants and shops—they think they funky. I seen places like this in L.A. Like Echo Park and Venice."

Marcus laughed. "Yeah. Funkytown is my home. So you just cruisin along for geography?"

"Mama said go to school and get registered. With you." Mortrice stared straight ahead. "I didn't know you ain't had no ride."

"So," Marcus said, swinging his leather satchel. "So. What kind of car should a brother from Funkytown drive? Cause I'ma have to buy somethin quick. I gotta help your mama out, undoubtedly. And I gotta find out who's been dumpin bodies on my dad's place."

"Bodies?" Mortrice snapped his head around. "Dead bodies?"

"Hard to dump live ones." Marcus felt his forehead pound with a headache. He needed more coffee.

"A lil nigga, shot up in the face?" Mortrice kept his hands jammed into the huge coat's pockets.

"What the hell are you talkin about?" Marcus said. "What you know about bodies?"

"Nothin," Mortrice said, voice blank. "I just got here, man. In your truck."

"My daddy's truck," Marcus said. "Two white women. Bodies." He swallowed hard, hearing himself. "And a white dude thought he was a woman, I guess."

"Damn," Mortrice said, his voice lighter. "I ain't seen no white face yet. Till I got to Funkytown."

"This ain't funny," Marcus said. "I'm serious." They stopped at the light across from the high school. "How's Sofelia? Your mom? Why didn't she come with you? I coulda picked you both up."

Mortrice stared at the school, the sprawling Spanish-style buildings and students gathered in clumps on the lawn, cars jamming the street and parking lot.

"Mama don't go out the house," he said.

Marcus frowned. "Nowhere?"

Mortrice shook his head. "Never."

"How long did you guys live in Solano Gardens?" Marcus pictured the bleak buildings and towel-size plots of dead grass.

"Forever," Mortrice said, walking across the street. "This where I gotta go?" Marcus saw his lips working nervously, his shoulders stiffen wider.

"I'ma help you out. The district lines are pretty strange."

Mortrice's eyes were darting at the groups of students. Two white girls waved and said, "Hey, Mr. Thompson!" Mortrice said softly, "What niggas go here? From the Gardens?"

Marcus said, "You mean what young brothers and sisters attend this school? Like I said, the city played games with districts way back when. Treetown had an ancient school, built when my mother worked the groves. City condemned it in the seventies, and now it's only for adult-ed classes. They cut Treetown and the Westside in half. Half here, half at Linda Vista High. We've got everybody here—rich white kids from historic downtown, the ones with stubborn parents who want to support public education." He saw Mortrice not paying any attention to him. "We've got white kids from several areas. And you from Treetown."

"Treetown serious country, right?" Mortrice had stopped on the sidewalk.

Marcus nodded. "Yup."

Mortrice said. "My—this dude I know—I knew him in . . ." He paused. "He said that's a buncha bullshit. California. Everybody talkin about we got all colors here and it's cool. He said that's bullshit."

"Where's he from?"

"L.A." Mortrice closed his face like a hand had passed hard over his skin. He waited for Marcus to head up the steps.

"I was one of the first brothers from Treetown to come here," Marcus said, stopping near the administration building. "Okay? You'll be a new—" He looked at Mortrice, the smooth, dark skin and Sofelia's huge, liquid eyes. "What's your last name? Your daddy's last name?"

"Who give a fuck?" Mortrice said. "My last name Thompson."

When Marcus had filled out most of the papers, telling the admin staff that his sister was ill and housebound, he took Mortrice to the door of his first class. English. Mortrice glanced back at him, eyes half-lidded and hard, but Marcus saw the nervous stitch at his lips. "I got you after lunch, right? History?"

Marcus shook his head. "You got world history. Mr. Whalen," he said. Mortrice sucked in the skin under his mouth and then shrugged, turning away. Marcus watched him walk stiff-legged down the corridor, and he headed for the teachers' lounge.

Sterile coffee, stale fund-raiser candy on the table, and the bitter smell of his friend Judy's plants rushed at him when he opened the door. He saw the open newspaper near the coffee, but he didn't want to look. Another homicide victim was found . . . Several teachers were looking at assignments and bitching about students. Marcus took out a textbook: *Ancient History*. He didn't see Judy, who taught English, or Val, who did math. Skimming the opening pages, Marcus found the words blurring into ant lines. He took a scrap of paper and wrote down his rent, utilities, gym fees, restaurants. Clothes. He slanted his hand over the numbers in case anyone nosy drifted behind him. He'd saved up for the down payment to lease the Lexus, and damn, he missed that ride. The speed, the power when he drove to Palm Springs just to see the blank, dark desert hurtling past.

"You already working?" He heard Judy's voice. She touched his shoulder and sat down, her dark hair lying in neat feathered wings along her head. "Partying at your friend's restaurant again?"

"Not last night," Marcus said. He and Judy were the same age, but she'd been teaching English for five years already, and she liked to tease him about handling the work.

"I need some caffeine before I think about my lovelies' reaction to *The Scarlet Letter* this morning." Judy sighed.

Lovely. That's what one cop had said last night, before he'd spit into the trees. She looks lovely now, huh? Shit. What makes a guy do that?

Dress like that? Marcus thought. Or kill like that? Which bothered the cop more?

What's makin a guy bring em here and knock em off? another cop had said while Marcus was being led away. He'd seen Finis's erased eyes, and he'd tried to explain about the music. But the white guy his father had described—the black Jeep—Pammy Sawicky, the changeable girl—he hadn't been able to collect any of those scattered fragments until he was safe on his own couch. He knew Finis hadn't done anything. But if someone was killing, or dumping, women on the place, maybe his father or his uncle hadn't told him or anyone else about an angry customer or even someone from way back who wanted trouble.

He clenched his eyes shut, then stared at the tiny numbers he'd written. Judy sat back down with her cup, saying, "What's so funny?"

Marcus took a breath. "What kinda car can you see me driving?"

"No Lexus this time?"

"Something different."

Judy smiled. "Okay. How about a Miata?"

Val sat down nearby. "Uh-oh," he said. "I heard red sportscars like Miatas are cops' favorite for speeding tickets."

The grainy video images from the TV, the lifting face and boots, shifted inside him, but Marcus stared at the wall covered with memos about meetings and committees and discipline, and Val and Judy stood up when the general exodus began. Three of the older teachers, men who'd been somber and slightly lined when Marcus was a senior, passed behind him. Cottrell said, "Off to the wars. For those of us who aren't PC, Ph.D.'s, or afflicted with PMS. If we were, we could be teaching gender studies at the university."

Whalen said, "And our health care would be a hell of a lot better."

Val, watching them, said, "Jealousy is an evil breakfast."

Cottrell said, with what passed for a smile, "I've never heard that one."

"I made it up," Val said.

Marcus drew soft lines on his forehead, hoping his headache would diffuse itself a little. He wondered what Mortrice would do in Whalen's class. He knew from Val and Judy that Whalen called kids like Mortrice

PDPs when he spoke softly to his friends in the lounge. Whalen thought it was their private joke. Pupils of the Darker Persuasion.

Well, we had a hell of a good time in my classroom last year, Marcus thought, standing up. Even my PMCs. Pupils who are Melanin Challenged. Everybody's got a history.

He smiled, remembering when he used to come home every day repeating all those profound lines of wisdom from Brother Lobo's class. His father would listen, fingers never still, palms filled with the plush mixture of oil and saffron dust when he finished changing a tire. "You want some black history?" his father would say in that voice, half-whisper and half-smoke. "You last hired, first fired. Been that way all the time. Go get me that hubcap. No—the '62 Chevy. That one."

Marcus walked into his classroom, seeing the faces lined up, swaying and bobbing like five funky conga lines. "Let's boogie," he said at his desk, and a white kid with surfer-straggled hair that he remembered from last year said, "Yeah, ancient history with Mr. Thompson. Boogie back to the seventies, man."

Within days, Marcus had resorted to the book. He listened to their voices, looked at the faces, but he couldn't concentrate, and his distraction was obvious to the students. "I heard this brother's class was cool, man, but he got us readin out the damn book like everybody else," one boy complained outside the door, and Marcus rested his head in his hands.

Last year, the classes had gone best when he made everything up. Work in music they liked, movies. Let them talk about clothes and history, about their own families. They loved to talk. Nobody ever listened to kids.

But he couldn't stop thinking about his father, about Finis, about the red hair skeined over the eucalyptus leaves. While they sat, mostly silent and hunched over the pages, he stared uneasily at the book. "Greek, Indian, Chinese, and Hellenistic Civilizations." "Changes in the Barbarian World." He remembered Whalen's class, when he was a new student at this mostly white school. "Marcus, did you see *Roots* last night on TV? Do you Treetown fellows know your roots?" Whalen had smirked, going on to the two other Treetown kids in the room. Usher Price and Freddy Prince.

He didn't. He couldn't put anything together, even now, about his father's life. Back then, after Whalen's class, he'd asked his father in the barn about his history. The high windows near the roof laid striped shadows on the dirt, and the array of tools glistened like weapons. "Daddy," Marcus had begun, and his father's hands never stopped tightening the bolts on the air compressor. His uncle was sharpening a knife on the grinding stone at the doorway. "I have to write a history paper. When did you come here, to Rio Seco? Why you left Oklahoma?"

They'd both glanced up at him, not at each other, and his father spat into the fine-pounded dust. "Hell. California farthest I could get from Tulsa 'thout freezin and look for work. Ocean east or ocean west. Wasn't goin east."

"Why they want to know that?" Oscar had snapped. "They ain't teachin no history I know."

"For a paper," Marcus repeated doggedly. "When did you guys come?"

"Long time ago," his father said harshly. "History. Shit. History ain't gon repeat over here, okay? My history ain't got a damn thang to do with what you suppose to be learnin."

"We come from free people? Or slaves?" Marcus held his breath.

After a long silence, his father said, "Who axin you that?"

"School they talkin about family history. Cause of that show *Roots*."

The long fingers flared and then clenched around the wrench. Marcus saw Demetrius and Octavious drive up in the low rider they'd worked on all year, and he swallowed quickly. "They didn't have slaves in Oklahoma, right?"

"Indians did," his father said.

Marcus frowned. The shining chrome grille edged closer. "Were your people Indians? Or slaves?"

"Hard people," his father said, glancing up now.

"Were they free?" Marcus whispered.

"I don't know what you want to call it," his father said, standing up.

"Do you know?" Marcus shouted. "I gotta write somethin."

"So lie," Oscar interrupted. "White folks all come on the *Mayflower*, right? That's what they writin. We come to California cause we wanted to be in the movies. That's why people say they come here, right?"

Real helpful, Marcus had thought, waiting, expecting Oscar to keep talking, but all he heard was the rasp of the knife and the sliding whisper of metal.

"What Sissyfly buggin you about now?" Demetrius said, slamming the car door.

His father shrugged slightly, taking another wrench from the wall shelf. Marcus said, "We talked about *Roots* at school."

"Shee-it," Demetrius said. "I rather see *Shaft* any day."

"He at a white school," Octavious said. "Sherberts everywhere."

"Like I got a choice, when they closed Treetown," Marcus said.

"Hell, go get your GED at the adult school," Demetrius said.

"I don't want no GED."

"You want to see sherberts all day," Demetrius said. "Downtown." He shook his head.

Marcus paged ahead aimlessly in the textbook, glancing at the nodding heads and moving pencils and drifting eyes. "The Dominance of the West"—huge section. "Africa and Oceania from 1850 to 1945" got twenty-two pages toward the end.

"You didn't find any African roots?" Whalen had asked him, eyebrows jumping like nervous fingers. Marcus had gotten a D on the paper. He'd asked his mother questions, but she'd had no idea where she'd been born since they were always in a car then, on the move. All she'd said was, "We worked all day, baby. Half the night, sometimes. Everything was brown, everywhere we went."

Pammy Sawicky had sat near him. She'd gotten a C minus, because her essay wasn't complete either. "Your grandfather was born in Poland?" Whalen said loudly, looking over her paper. "And that's all you know?"

Everyone had taken that opportunity for Polack jokes, and Pammy, who was in her black incarnation then, had tried to weave her chin side-to-side like an angry sister. Whalen had hated Pammy's clothes and voice, and it showed whenever he spoke to her.

He doesn't even remember me, Marcus thought now. Doesn't recall anyone's name longer than a year, he claims. I wonder if he recognized Pammy's name in the article. When she died. Shit. Back to that. Her history, Daddy's past. And the redhead. What the hell do they have to do with each other? Finis damn sure wasn't going to be able to figure it out.

. . .

Alma lay in the dawn-gray bedroom, Jawan and the baby grandgirl'
beside her in a damp puzzle of limbs. This time, she knew she'd heard
her *abuela* clinking the coffeepot onto the stove.

No shooting, no police, no other sounds. How could there be, after
last week? She closed her eyes, listening to the puffing soft breaths. Finis
taken away by the police, Marcus trying to talk them out of it with his
schoolteacher smile. When he came back inside, alone, he'd slammed
a kitchen chair to the floor in frustration, shouting, "It's *language*! It's
always about what they hear and what they see!"

She couldn't make herself move, couldn't untangle herself from the
tiny fingers curled into her nightgown, the small foot alongside her
spine. She had made this room ready for Hosea, with extra pillows on
the bed and his small radio from the empty, ash-smelling coldhouse.

But he was at Demetrius's house, across the river, where the lemon
and orange groves used to cover the slopes in dark-green patchwork.

She saw her grandmother's figure pause in the doorway. Alma felt
her eyes swim with hot tears, child's tears. She smelled the coffee, the
way it used to waft through Olive Gardens when she woke.

The women's voices would follow the coffee steam through the long
block of connected wooden shacks and down the dirt yard, where they
collected water in the pearl-tinged shadows while the men knocked
clots of yesterday's grove mud from their boots before they headed to
the trucks.

Alma used to watch their mouths, the women from Texas and Oklahoma and Mississippi, while they bent at the single tap under the huge
chinaberry tree. Her mother and father were already gone in the narrow
boxes, side by side. And her *abuela* rarely spoke, leaving early for the
groves, so Alma would follow the other women and listen to learn what
she was supposed to do to keep a man someday. Because that's what
they did—feed the men and wash the men's clothes and pluck the
chicken for the men, clean the rabbits, argue and complain and speak
nearly every word about the men.

She followed them all day. You sorted through the beans by single,
dangled bulb light, pinching out pebbles and twigs, all the while sucking
your teeth and saying, "Like he gon come home for lunch anyway—

you know he spend the whole time gamblin with them fools from Florida."

Measured the fine-powdered red pepper into your palm, cupping your hand as curvy as a pigeon's breast before you flung the mound into a huge pot with only a violent fanning of your fingers, sending a chili cloud to float on trembling water, saying, "He think I ain't watchin him, he dead wrong."

Rinsed the flat collard leaves over and over, rubbing gently at the filmy sheen that sheds water and flicking away a coiled cutworm with your thumbnail, hearing Ocie Mae call, "Come over here, Alma baby, and I'ma do somethin with that hair. Your gramma gone to work already. Give me that pot. That all you and Paz gon eat? I'ma put a ham hock in there right now."

When she met Hosea, she was not twenty, and he was much older, but she wasn't afraid. He sat near her on the truck, helped her at the packing house when she sorted lemons by size into the crates, and he ate her food with quiet wonder. He listened to her murmurs in their narrow bed, moving his hands in answer.

The babies came year after year, and the women down the line of doors came to help Abuela when the pains reached sharp-nailed fingers around from her spine to her heavy belly. Hosea drove her to the hospital in Rio Seco that first time, and after a few hours, the doctors whose faces glowed gray under the tubes of light told her it was false. They told her to go home. And once she was in the tiny back room, the narrow bed, the baby began again; when she screamed, the women came running through the yard, pulling Demetrius's head from her with sliding fingers careful against his skull.

The rituals, the navel string and fingernails and first curls of hair, the first pieces of sweet potato and green bean chewed to tonguing softness before she pulled them from her own mouth and pushed them carefully onto the shiny, waiting gums. Alma had always craved the absolute order, after the shacks and cars and tents they'd lived in when she and her parents and grandmother were migrant pickers; she was dizzy with the joy of repeating the same gestures and strokings and wiping of folded skin and clenched baby fists and dishes and her own table. Her own plot of yard, where she pulled tomatoes to slice and salt for Hosea.

When Archuleta had died and left them the big adobe house, after Hosea had built the stone barn and walls and tended the trees, she hadn't known she was pregnant again. She hadn't stopped nursing Julius, and she hadn't felt anything move. Her first baby girl had slid from her early and curled purple, eyes sealed.

Alma picked up her stirring, frowning grandgirl now, clasping the bobbing warmth to her shoulder, and went to the kitchen for a bottle.

With the baby slumped comfortable against her stomach, sucking and twirling her fingers in Alma's gown, she stared at the chair Marcus had righted and sat in last week. She had watched the rosette on the back of his hand while he talked.

His hand was square-fingered and wide-palmed now, but when it still had the chain of dimples across the back, a needle had been planted in the baby plumpness, and the sunken scar had never faded. Whenever Hosea said, "He ain't sickly no more, he need to stop all that readin and do some work," Alma had glanced at the vivid mark and said, "Leave him be."

He'd had meningitis, and the doctor with the robin's-egg eyes repeated impatiently, "His navel and the wind have nothing to do with it." But she kept crying. In the hospital room with the smell of medicinal death, she thought of all the bacteria and TB germs and whooping coughs and tainted dust floating with the dust down Pepper Avenue to coat her screens and floors. The wild dogs in the riverbottom, the rusty nails in the yard, flying splinters when they chopped wood, the white men in uniform and in general who stared at them, her boys, with clenched disdain and rigid anger when they laughed in the park, who drained the city pool on Fridays as soon as her sons and the other Treetown and Agua Dulce boys had splashed during their allotted time.

She'd lowered her eyes from the doctor's gaze to stare at Marcus, his fist as tiny as a walnut, the needle held in with stark, white tape. She'd already been slightly plump with someone else, but she hadn't yet known there was another curling set of bones inside her when she prayed to God, fingers tight on metal crib slats, that she would give up any part of her body for this son. Anything He chose: her right hand or left, her hair or teeth, her womb.

He was walking, staggered and joyful, when Sofelia was born. Alma had done everything perfectly. Cautious, worshipful with her baby girl. Ocie Mae, her ancient cheeks as dark and as long as eggplant, had helped Alma for weeks.

And Sofelia was gone. As if that had been what she'd prayed away, what she'd promised to let go.

Finis was slumped somewhere in the police station, and imagining that made Alma's throat quiver. Mr. Wiggles—she'd heard his friends call the wandering men like Finis strange names, words from their music that sounded like foreign incantations to her. Her quilt-gaited son, the one with nothing but secret rhythms in his head, was locked up.

A man wearing women's clothing had been stretched under a sheet, Marcus had said. "And I don't know how I'm supposed to figure any of this shit out. Daddy think I ain't about nothin anyway."

"Your Daddy think more than you ever know," Alma had said absently.

Hosea was across the river now, his hair still smelling of hospital fear, his shoulder raw with bullet tracings, his chest far from hers. That first night, when the officers had roamed the property, they'd laughed at Hosea's bed in the coldhouse. She'd heard them joke about "what they call married down here." They understood nothing about living with someone for forty years.

"The old man never said a fucking thing to the investigators," Alma had heard one of the uniformed men say last week. They'd been gathered in the yard, watching Finis in the backseat. "They were kickin him loose because some girl downtown said she saw the victims get in a black Jeep with a Caucasian. But the old guy wouldn't say shit. And his son only says things that don't mean shit." She watched from the darkened window. The officer raised his index finger and pointed it at the backseat of his car. "Hey, you—out of the gene pool!" he called, and the other men laughed when he'd jerked the finger up like a firing gun.

The baby's lashes flagged. Her fingers cradling the heavy head, Alma stared out the same window at the light falling through the trees, trying not to think about those same germs and dusts and bacteria floating into Hosea's body, about those same men with impatient eyes and batons. What could she do now?

She walked to the barn, nudging Julius with her foot, and he shuddered in the old easy chair where he'd slept. "You, Julius. The one go round makin these babies with crazy Mamas don't keep em. Take this pretty one." She lay the baby in his arms, and he slumped further into the chair.

Kendrick was rolled in a blanket beside his father, sleeping, oblivious like a child even when he woke scowling like a man.

Alma went to the veranda, where her wooden chest held all the paints. "The old guy," they'd kept calling him. Hosea. She couldn't see him or tend to him long over there at Demetrius's house, and Enchantee was gone to work all day. But Demetrius had told her, "He can't come back till we find out what the hell's goin on."

She knew he could see the back wall, the blue one, from across the river. She'd been to the house to look at his shoulder, at the raw, pearly skin that made her throat swell. She'd stood on the second floor, where the gathered trees of their place were visible.

Alma took the purple paint and walked to the back wall and garden, studying the window frames of her own bedroom. She knew Hosea would only see a chip of blue, a chip of his place, like a small piece of broken shell. But she painted the frames and sills for herself, too, for the back-and-forth motion and repetition and the ritual she'd begun when she'd chosen the colors.

From his rusted chair in the pepper trees along the ridge, he'd always looked over the riverbottom to see these houses laid out along the hills and narrow flatland like a huge, endlessly complicated game of dominoes. The white houses were just that close, end to end, and the streets branched off from a main line in tight formation.

Hosea sat on the daybed in the guest bedroom, slanted to see out this second-story window into the harsh western sky, where the sun glared onto the stucco walls, no branches to filter its strength. No mature trees here, just broom handles stuck into the ground in the postage-stamp front yards.

The last chance for real rain this year had passed, he knew. He'd told Alma more growers, like the Hungarian on this side of the river, were going to sell out. The irrigation rates went up with each year of drought. Grow nothin but roofs over here now, he thought. Here and everywhere else.

All he could see was a warren of block walls around backyards, walls like cells in a honeycomb. You didn't like your neighbor around here, you had no choice but to see his face. Hear him pissing and coughing, since the bathroom windows were only a few feet apart.

Hosea had been coughing almost constantly since he'd come here, and once, in this upstairs bedroom, he'd raised his head from a strangled bout of trying to clear what felt like cotton candy from his lungs to see someone staring from the corresponding window an arm's length away. Hosea kept leaning into the screen, trying to pull fresh air into his chest. Maybe that would loosen the clotting. The face floated away quickly, glasses flashing brilliant.

Demetrius lived here. Hosea remembered the first time he and Alma had come to see the house, last year. "Only way we'll ever get ahead is to buy a new house like this, and maybe sell it in a few years," Demetrius's wife had said. "I'm trying to fix it up real nice."

He looked around then at the pale-blue kitchen, the apricot-colored living room, the four bedrooms. The master bedroom was big, with a walk-in closet and separate bathroom, and these other ones were cubicles. Not like the big rooms at his place. Enchantee had told him, "A lot of people in this development don't have kids. They use these rooms for exercise or storage. I met three people on our street like that."

He wondered who lived in the house next door. Hosea leaned his head against the wall, feeling the wash of heat rise again in his skull. His shoulder sent only mild rays of pain through him when he moved; this fever and coughing were something else, he knew. Stabbing aches pushed behind his breastbone when he breathed or coughed.

Alma had come yesterday morning, with Demetrius, and when she'd heard him coughing, she'd said, "You caught some germ in there, Hosea, in that hospital room. Listen to you." She'd made tea with honey, chile peppers, and garlic, and after he'd drunk it, his chest had swelled, burned, and he'd thought his lungs were cleansing themselves. She'd stayed a few hours, sitting in the dining room with him. He'd said, "You like this kitchen, huh?"

"Easy to keep it clean," Alma had said, wiping down the counters, moving like a plump, spinning dancer around the room.

"You think we should get you one a these sherbert houses, huh?"

"I like them kitchen. And three bathrooms." She'd frowned at him. "But what would I do with you, stubborn old man? You ain't slept a bit since you left your coldhouse. I'd have to build you somethin in the backyard."

Hosea shook his head, holding down the laugh that hurt his chest. "Not in this little play yard."

Demetrius had come in from the garage, and Hosea'd said to him, "Your driveway ain't no bigger than a thumbnail. How you gonna work on that Chevy in your garage?"

"Can't work on cars around here," Demetrius had said, grinning, his big arms folded. "Against the rules. Can't hang clothes on a line. All that shit. Enchantee read the covenants, somethin like that."

"That's why you need to stay here a while," Alma had said, sitting down at the table, touching his shoulder. The bandage was fresh; she'd just looked at his wound. "Nothin for you to worry about over here."

"You need to check the canal intake, irrigate the oranges," Hosea began, and Demetrius had nodded.

"Nothin to fix over here at my crib, Daddy," Demetrius had said. "Nothin to drive or argue about. Just relax and let your shoulder heal up."

But even with his forehead glistening over from the heat suffusing his skull again, he knew they were leaving something out. He'd asked that first night why the police cars were there, what was going on. All Demetrius had said was, "They were just walkin around the place again, talkin about clues and investigation. Just messin with us. See? You don't need to be bothered with all that shit."

But Alma had been silent, her scarred fingers touching the placemats.

When he got up from the daybed, his ribs hurt like he'd been kicked. He walked slowly through the doorway, stopping at the wooden railing that edged the carpet here along the open hallway, where the doors faced nothing but air and white. He gripped the railing. He'd only been inside a two-story house once before. Tulsa. And the stairs up to the apartment over the garage, where he and his mother had stayed with Retha.

He saw his grandson's open bedroom door. Inside, he could smell the faint odor of grass and dirt and boy. The bright bedspread was rumpled, the toys piled in a wooden box in the corner. Hosea knelt on the small bed and looked out this window. He could see across the riverbottom to the hill, to the car roofs of his storage lot glinting in the afternoon sun. The dark mound of trees. Then a shard of blue, like Milk of Magnesia glass, above the fence.

His vision spun, and he put both palms on the wall for support. Black began to rise watery behind his eyes, and he thought, "I'ma just rest here. Just for a minute." He felt himself curl on the bed, his good ear down on the pillow, a tiny metal truck under his forearm.

When he woke, his breathing mottled and shallow, the room was black. He lifted his good ear, but the dark house was silent. Hosea steadied himself, feeling the noises inside his chest, and slid his feet across the floor. He began to cough violently at the door, and when he bent over, his fist at his heart, he felt a small hand holding him up.

His daughter-in-law had come down the open hallway, and he saw dim light from her doorway. She said, "Come on. Stay in here if you want, and I'll bring you your plate."

She led him back to the boy's bed, and he sat, dazed. Enchantee brought him more of Alma's tea and a plate of macaroni and cheese with peas and ham. She knelt on the floor, looking up into his face. Hosea could hardly swallow the food, and he tried to drink the hot liquid that again burned and expanded inside him.

"D'Junior's sleepin with me," Enchantee whispered. "Demetrius is out on a tow job in San Bernardino. He and Octavious have been workin hard. Even Julius is helpin Kickstand out in the barn. Don't worry. You can sleep right here. It's one o'clock. I'll be gone early with D'Junior, and you just rest until somebody comes. I'll leave some grits on the stove for your breakfast."

Her lilting whisper pushed him back onto the boy's pillow. The fast-sweet words were like Retha's when he was frightened in the garage apartment by his mother's sobbing mixed with the baby's wrenching cries. Retha would kneel beside him, where he slept on a pallet, and murmur until he slept.

When he heard the crows screaming and angry, the shrieks hurling over the roofs in spirals, he thought he was home. From their circling, repeated assaults, he knew a hawk or other predator had taken one of them or their intended prey. Hosea opened his eyes, expecting to see the small coldhouse window and the crows' shadows.

The comforter with elephants and tigers was tangled around his feet, the window blinds were drawn tight, and he couldn't breathe. He gasped and tried to push himself up, his throat rattling, burbling in panic.

The dizzying hallway led to carpeted stairs hanging in space, slats with air between each one. He put his bare foot down on the first step and felt breath brush his ankle. Stopping, gripping the slick wooden rail, he lowered himself onto the staircase, trying to breathe. Like Tulsa. Like the stairs outside the garage, the wrought-iron steps where he'd felt the feathery woman's eyes hard on his spine every time he ascended. Her voice would call out, "You, boy!" in a rising shriek, and Hosea would stop, frozen, while she yelled about the grass or trash or a grimy fingerprint he'd left on the door.

Hosea waited for a long time, breathing shallow curls of air, staring at his touching anklebones. His shoes. He had to get his shoes if he wanted to walk home. Just across the river. He had to get back to his place.

He pulled himself up by the banister and backed up the two steps, going crouched into the guest bedroom where his boots lay near the single chair. He tried to lace them with shaking fingers, but his fingertips were numb with cold, and he kept panting in small breaths.

Demetrius had a phone in his bedroom. He took all the night tow calls now. Hosea crept along the hallway near the wall, and he sat down on the wide, neatly made bed. He dialed his number, and one of the grandkids answered. "Arrow Towing."

"Who that?"

"Grampa? It's Kendrick."

"Where your gramma?" Hosea's voice was choked with the thistles in his chest.

"She gone to get Finis. They let him out. Her and Demetrius. Eight and my daddy gone on a job. Ain't nobody here." His grandson paused, the childish voice lowering. "I'm suppose to say, 'If you stuck by the road, give me the address. Somebody comin.' "

"Okay, boy," Hosea whispered. "Okay."

He had walked from farther than here a hundred times before. He had walked from the groves way out past the Hungarian's land when the truck had broken down—he and the other men, laughing, carrying their jackets and bags in the hot evening dusk, joking that if they'd brought their guns, they could shoot dinner on the way home through the riverbottom.

His gun. His grandfather's gun. The policeman who'd shot him had taken the old rifle. It was probably still in their hands. He hadn't done anything wrong, or they wouldn't have been ready to let him go. He could get Demetrius to go down there for the gun.

He rubbed his forehead and tried to stand, leaning on his son's night table. He heard voices outside again, next door, and he held himself up at the wall near this window. Honeycomb yards and glass-cage windows everywhere.

Hosea stared at the nearby windows, all shuttered with blinds. Silver. The man next door had silver glasses, silver hair. Silver belt buckle flashing.

He closed his eyes and began to feel his way down the floating stairs, hearing his grandfather's voice on the farm outside Tulsa. "The silvery ones, like Retha's lady, I know they scary. They old, and got more hate stored up. They know what they know."

"You hella lot older than next door," he tried to whisper to himself, lowering his feet carefully. But the sense of falling down those stairs, the hot webs in his head, and the talons inside made him feel frightened and as dizzy-young as 1921.

He walked along the tile floor, his stomach swaying empty. Hunger was a thumb against his spine, then a cabbage hard and swelling in his belly. He'd felt that many times—it was as familiar as his hairline.

But this was the other one, the fearful swell and lurch that had begun then, that day in 1921. Nailed fingers scrabbled upward into his diaphragm, talons reaching behind his lungs to clench his heart with fear when he walked beside his mother to that black car and metal-feathered head.

Inside the garage, he ṣaw Demetrius's primer-rough '56 Chevy, a shad-owed hulk. No engine yet. No fixin here. Covenants. No colored can own property in any of the areas east of . . . Treetown. Not downtown. Not Grayglen or Plymouth Hill.

He stepped out of the garage, trying to force clean, outside air into himself. But his lungs pushed it back out. No coughing. Walk. Walk.

No fixing. No hanging clothes. No walking. No people. He walked around the corner at the end of the long street and then down the only road that led out, facing the riverbottom. Behind the walls, no houses were visible—just a multitude of chimneys rising like periscopes.

Maybe soot clotted his lungs, he thought, feeling sweat trickle down his cheeks and neck. That 1921 soot, somehow freed by the burning car to swirl thick poison through his system. He moved his shoulder. Maybe lead from the bullet had triggered a reaction. His fever ached on his skin, and he staggered. Drunk. No. When I get to my place, get Oscar to bring me some choc. Clear out my system. Then I be drunk.

At the light pole on the corner, he steadied himself. A few cars passed, windows mirrored by the sun. He crossed the street and began trudging through the sandy, vacant fields that led to the levee.

He had come this way before; after he'd left Los Angeles, he'd been dropped off beside the road several miles back, and he'd tramped through the groves looking for work. Cleaning canals, picking, anything. His stomach hard and empty, he'd slept in a grove, and someone had told him about Treetown. He remembered the name, and he'd walked this way, reaching the sandy bank where he had to clamber up and over.

He stumbled, sweat blinding him, and then he put his hands out to pull himself up. Like a baby. Crawlin baby.

At the top, he paused, crouched with palms on the ground, racking pains in his chest. The riverbottom. First time he'd seen it, he'd felt his heart pound. Not like the wide, steep-banked Arkansas River through Tulsa, where he'd searched the tangled roots of trees in the water's edge for his father's body. And the arms and legs, stacked, braided like rot-soaked wood where they'd caught on the blackened, wet tree limbs.

This water was shallow and gold, trembling its way down the sandy, bleached channel like it couldn't hide anything. And the channel wasn't a deep, forested, hidden place where men could wait with guns. There were thickets of bamboo and eucalyptus and cottonwood, and willows along the water whose roots were red hair waving in the water.

But here, where he knelt on the bank, he could see for miles, the trail of shine snaking through its valley below the hills. He saw all the way to Orange County. He lifted his eyes, and he could see his trees.

The beauty of his hill, with the foxtails and wild oats gone to tawny gold, the lowering purple sky, the eucalyptus twisting like feathers. Not Oklahoma. His land. Every new gopher hole a tiny mountain. Every hubcap where he nailed it. Every tree watered. Every vehicle worth cash. The path from here to there, the one Finis used to call the Indian path.

Hosea heard a car door slam, heard someone shouting. He didn't look back. Probably security patrol in a place like this. He ain't runnin in here, Hosea thought, trying to rise. He can't shoot me. Leave me here. No place to hide bodies. Ain't deep enough.

He stood and felt a slide of black drop over his eyes.

Marcus didn't panic when he saw his father fall. He ran hard up the dirt bank and knelt to feel his father's pulse at the neck. His father's face was glossy with sweat, and his neck was as hot and dark as heated cast iron. Marcus heard the rattle of breath in his chest.

He slid down the other side of the bank and took off his shirt to dip it in the narrow stream that had branched off the river and flowed along the levee. Hunting—he remembered Julius getting hit in the head with a low branch, falling unconscious, and how they'd wet his face and tried to wake him.

He patted his father's face with the soaking shirt, smelling the river water mix with sweat, but his father's eyes didn't open. Rising, he curled his back and slid his hands under his father's shirt until they met. He lifted him so they were hug-dancing, and then he lay his father on his body lengthwise and began to slide down the levee.

Digging in his heels, he pulled them down the short bank. His father trembled and stirred at the jarring of Marcus's feet on the bottom. "Daddy," Marcus whispered. "I got you. Come on."

Trying not to wrench his father's bandaged shoulder, Marcus draped the other arm around him and lifted the feet a few inches off the ground to carry him to the truck.

CHAPTER FIVE

HE BOUGHT THE newspaper on the way home from work. Before he could call the hospital and find out if his father was still in Intensive Care for the eighth day, before he could call Sofelia and ask if she was ready to venture outside, before he could call his mother and find out where Finis had hidden himself, his phone rang.

"Marcus? Do you think you could drive me to the show, brothaman?" Lobo's voice was tentative. "I don't want to disappoint the faithful. My friend Darnell can't give me a ride."

Marcus rubbed his eyes before he spoke. "I just got here, man," he began.

"I know you got a lot going on," Lobo said. "But the music might ease your mind." He paused. Marcus knew he hated having to ask people for rides, hated the way independence had been snatched from his irises.

"You got it," Marcus said.

In his father's truck, he opened the newspaper. On the bottom of the "Regional News" front page was a short article with no photo.

THIRD BODY FOUND AT TREETOWN YARD

Homicide detectives are investigating the circumstances surrounding the death of a man found at a towing yard where two Rio Seco women were killed in early September. Those deaths are still unsolved, and authorities are not certain whether the man found last week was somehow involved. His identity has not been released, pending notification of relatives, and police officials would not comment further on their investigation.

Marcus leaned back against the seat. The police had let Finis go after six days; he'd been going to explain everything to his father when he'd found his father stumbling in the riverbottom. Now Finis had disappeared, his father was fighting for his life in the hospital, and the police were walking the place nearly every day, crouching in the leaves, searching the outbuildings, frightening his mother into raw-lipped silence. They'd begun asking a lot of questions about The Blue Q, since the man had been found just over the wall.

He started up the truck just as Kurt came down the sidewalk carrying a few bags from downtown shops. Kurt leaned into the passenger window, his black-needled hair gleaming, and said, "Oh, the Cabriolet just didn't sound as loud and macho as this, right?"

"Give me a break," Marcus said easily. He looked at the tiny silver hoop in Kurt's ear, thinking that he never worried about lying or not lying with Kurt or Lakin or his downtown acquaintances. They always kept the conversation comic and sarcastic, skimming quick. Marcus said, "This is my father's truck. Matter of fact, my moms sent you this." He reached down to the bag on the floor and pulled out the jar of olives and the packet of olive tamales. His mother and Abuela had been shaping the tamales and folding them into corn husks for days, as if by cooking they could drive the devils away with fragrant steam.

Kurt's face crumpled strangely, and he said, "The woman's never met me."

"Hey," Marcus said, frowning. "You lent me your ride. And all my mom ever gives anybody is food."

Kurt took the packet, his mouth working. "My mother never gives me a fucking thing," he said, turning quickly and going under the archway.

Marcus drove down Las Palmas through the historic district and then turned into the older, shabbier residential area on the northern edge. Nothing historic about these small wood-frame houses and stucco apartment blocks. Stopping at a light, he checked the street signs. Back in the early seventies, Brother Lobo and a Chicano guy named León had rented an old two-story house here, painted men and women with huge Afros and *Raza* headbands along the outside of the top floor and lettered CONSCIOUS CAFE AND GALLERY on the door.

They'd displayed black and brown art, served soul food and *frijoles*, held poetry readings and small concerts and youth-group meetings.

Marcus remembered Julius letting him tag along a few times. Julius had been looking for half-conscious girls, of course, but Marcus had stood in awe of the double-naturals crowding the small rooms like storm clouds, of the pictures of tribal warriors and Mexican saints. And the music—jazz and El Chicano, War and Gil Scott-Heron.

The building code people shut them down after a year, and the owner razed the place.

But Brother Lobo, with his too-fine hair making his natural fall toward his shoulders by the end of the day, with his walnut skin and face long and narrow, began teaching black history at the high school when Marcus was a junior; for two years, Marcus had followed the man like a mosquito, sucking up words, venturing contributions to Lobo's ongoing list of things Africa transferred to America.

Bandannas. Okra. Drums—tribal and funkafied. Oral traditions. "Even TV," Brother Lobo would say in class. "Transplanted Africans that we are, we love television over books. Okay. We prefer storytelling from mouths. But that's no good, damnit, because those are somebody else's stories, and we're sitting on our butts entranced. No. Uh-uh. Choose the greater oral storyteller—music."

Marcus smiled, pulling into the narrow driveway. Lobo's apartment was a converted garage behind a large, old house. Marcus paused, thinking of his father when he touched the dashboard and saw the pack of Swisher Sweets under the ashtray. He'd finally gotten up the courage in Lobo's class to say, "My father stays in his own house. Not in ours. He eats out there, sits by his own fire."

Brother Lobo had smiled and nodded. "That's common for men in the motherland."

"All the Jungle Brothers in y'all crib, man, your daddy probably can't breathe from the funk," a loudmouth Westside boy had said, and when Marcus had turned on him, the boy had sneered, "Shut up, man, you the baby boy. Can't throw down for nothin. I heard."

"My brothers," Lobo had said, standing between them, and Marcus was ashamed at his relief. "Let's use words."

He stood in the doorway now, waiting. His sight was so vague that he couldn't walk without assistance. Marcus crossed the dusty lawn. When he'd graduated, Lobo had brought him here for the first time, saying, "Now I don't have to give your grades. Now what you think and say is yours."

"That doesn't sound like your car," Lobo said, walking beside Marcus with his sleeve always in contact for guidance. He didn't want people taking his arm. Not yet.

"My daddy's truck," Marcus said, opening the door. He placed the albums carefully on the seat.

Heading up California toward the southern rim of the city, he saw the university floating in the hills like a flock of seagulls—white buildings with sharp wings and flat roofs, built in the seventies.

Brother Lobo said conversationally, "You know I have less than a year before complete darkness."

"I know," Marcus said,

"Or blackness." He'd told Marcus that glaucoma ruined black people's eyesight far more often than others'. He was only forty-five, but the disease had washed through his vision as quickly as a rising tide. Squinting hard with the eye that could see something held very close, Lobo leaned forward so that his nose nearly touched the radio. "Does it work?"

"Yeah," Marcus said, driving slowly. Brother Lobo would recite all the statistics and diseases and killers that targeted dark skin; Marcus remembered talking to Enchantee in college, trying to impress her with his knowledge, and she'd turned to him with brows leaping together. "I don't want to know!" she'd whispered vehemently. "Why are you telling me this?"

"Got to have music," Lobo said, shifting the radio tuner to the right. He tried to joke about living for the oral tradition now, curling a wry grin around his big teeth.

"It's Deep Funk Friday here at the University of Rio Seco," said the midwestern voice Marcus had expected. "We're in our last half hour now, and the funk's fierce and furious on 107.9. Right, Stone?"

"Right, Bobcat. And you know what we get into now. Nothing but soundtracks, blasts from the past." Marcus pictured the blond goatee and glasses on Winston.

"Here they go," Lobo said, puffing out a laugh.

"Themes from *Shaft, Coffy,* and *Superfly.* Enjoy." The dramatic splash before Isaac Hayes echoed from the radio.

The truck roared up the slight incline lined with fast-food restaurants and newer hotels. Marcus had to laugh, too. "Every week I listen, and I know I can't hear this stuff anywhere else, but damn, it feels funny.

What they say between the songs, their voices—like they're making fun of it, but they like it. Hell, I don't know."

Lobo surprised him. "I don't know myself." He turned toward Marcus. "Marcus. Your uncle's place is a favorite resting spot for me. You know that. And I usually go early in the afternoon, not because I don't like to hear your uncle play the blues, but because . . . well, for the distinct pockets of talk I can hear before serious drinking. For the dominoes. And for your aunt's food. You know she never looks at any of us in there. But last week, I was in the corner alone, waiting for Floyd King to show, and I heard a white man come talk to your aunt. She was in the kitchen, and he was in the doorway. He had a brother with him, a brother's voice went first, and then the white man was asking her about prices on the place. Selling the land. Her voice went high, like I haven't heard it, and she told them to leave her alone. 'I told you before, go on outta here,' is what she said."

Marcus stared at Lobo's fingers splayed for support on the dashboard, like delicate starfish. "Uncle Oscar wasn't there?" Lobo shook his head and motioned toward the buildings. "I wanted you to bring me here for another reason, aside from your company. Come on."

The strains of "Superfly" were drifting from the speakers when they opened the door to the radio station. Marcus grinned at himself in the reflection from the window. Sissyfly—you gonna mess up by and by. Not this time. I'ma handle everything.

Then Winston's voice said, "Well, it's about time for the man who brings us the best in soulful women. We've got our signature farewell, right, Bobcat?"

"For all you students out there cramming hard, working on those killer papers, here's our cryptic message to you: 'There Ain't No Chicken in Harlem.'"

Marcus helped Brother Lobo stack his song picks, and the student named Bob, plump and pale with a shadowy brown beard, came out smiling. "You like that?" he asked, grinning. "Hey, I'm gonna rush back to my place and catch your show, man. Nobody picks Aretha cuts like you."

The blond one came out, and Brother Lobo went inside. The blond one said, "He is the Man. The Eminence."

Lobo's voice in the mike was soft and steady, as always, the way Marcus heard it every week on his headphones at the gym before he went out to eat. He'd driven here a few times, but never stayed to watch.

"I'm your brother," Lobo said, staring into the porous metal. "But these are the True Queens. The true queens of black music, their reign spanning the decades. We'll start, as always, with Bessie."

He said the same thing every week because, as he'd told Marcus, it wasn't his show. It was theirs. Now he turned to Marcus and said, "You know, originally I wanted to call the show Ebony Queens, but that was too limiting. Look."

He nodded toward the array of album covers. "I can't see them, but I know them." The faces, all shades of nutmeg and black and sand. "Which one's Billie?"

Marcus handed him the album, Billie Holiday heavily made up, her skin like ancient ivory piano keys. "Your aunt looks like her, doesn't she?" Lobo asked.

"Yeah, I guess," Marcus said, thinking of his aunt's somber wide mouth and high forehead, her thin, oiled hair always in a bun.

"Let me know when we get close to five," Lobo said, turning back to the microphone.

After "St. Louis Blues," Lobo queued up Sarah, Ella, Billie, and Clara. "Almost five," Marcus told him, and Lobo said, "We'll need Dinah."

"Yeah," Marcus said. "When I'm listening, you always say the same thing after five. A request."

"Pick up the other phone when I do, and be quiet," Lobo said when it rang.

Both phones lit up red, and Lobo said, "Okay."

Marcus heard Lobo say, "True Queens, KURS."

"Can you play some Dinah for me?" a voice said. " 'Backwater Blues' and 'Salty Dog Blues,' like you do?"

It was Aintielila. Her voice was flat, unemotional. Marcus couldn't imagine how her face looked right now. She always hovered in the kitchen serving food, shooting diagonal glances at anyone who bothered her.

"How you doing tonight?" Brother Lobo asked her.

"Livin'," she said.

"Working like always?"

"Where I always am. Ain't no change. You gon play them songs for me?"

"Ain't no change," Lobo said, and she hung up.

Marcus stared at Lobo, whose eyes roamed the console. "Every week, same time," Lobo said. "She never says who she is. Almost a year, and she calls every time like I won't play them this week if she doesn't ask."

"She's making pies for the weekend crowd now," Marcus said.

"Last week I finally got up the nerve to ask her where she worked," Lobo said. "She said, 'In this kitchen. I got the radio on here. Don't nobody come in here mess with me. And it feel like a real kitchen, in a real house, when you play them songs.' Then she hung up."

Marcus pictured his aunt rolling crusts for peach cobbler in the summer after he'd walked over with the baskets of fruit. Pecan pies when he carried over the shelled nuts. Lobo turned to the microphone and said, "This is Dinah, going out to the queen of the kitchen."

Marcus had always thought that was just Brother Lobo being fancy. When Lobo recited the names and played the songs, Marcus leaned against the wall to close his eyes and sift through the images of all the women sliding like spilled cards through his brain.

Nina and Carmen and Esther. Marcus saw his aunt, Enchantee, Sa-Ronn's face. SaRonn's outlined lips and long column of neck. Maybe Finis was hiding out at her house. His mother had said she hadn't seen him, and she was worried.

When Lobo said, "Lena," Marcus tried to imagine what his father was thinking, in the intensive care ward. They'd only been allowed to glimpse him, inside the forest of IVs and vines of tubes. Only his mother had sat beside the bed a short time, whispering close to his father's ear the way Marcus hadn't seen in years. Marcus remembered someone bringing up Lena Horne's beauty, years ago when he was little, and his father saying, "First time I seen Alma, she looked better than Lena. Looked better in a work dress and her hair all braided than any woman I ever seen."

His father had double pneumonia, infection raging through his lungs and chest. Why had he started walking, out there at Demetrius's place? Marcus felt his father's weight slung across his chest; he'd only been

able to carry his father inside the emergency room with Demetrius's
help.

Demetrius would be looking for him now, needing help again with
the tow jobs. And Sofelia . . . Marcus watched Mortrice at school, the
carved-hard glances that said, "Don't come near me yet." He'd stopped
at Sofelia's door twice, but when he asked if she'd come see Mama,
she shook her head, her mouth pulling in her lips, her nostrils wide
with frightened breath.

"Aretha," Lobo recited, playing "I Never Loved a Man (the Way I
Love You)."

Marcus felt an ache in his groin and up his backbone. Some woman
had sung this to Julius once in his trailer, sung it higher but just as
serious. Marcus had never seen her face, but his own neck had burned
where he stood in the pepper trees, listening to them laugh and then
call out. He'd been fifteen or so, and the next day he'd stepped carefully
through the trailer, looking at the ghost smiles left red on a glass, at
one earring on the floor.

The homicide investigators had ransacked both Julius's and Finis's
trailers several times, along with the coldhouse, looking for traces like
that. Marcus was sure Julius was with some sister somewhere. No short
supply of beds to conceal him. He heard the churchlike fervor in Aretha's
voice, remembered the passion in the woman's throat slipping out the
trailer window. Who the hell would ever sing to him like that?

That was what he and Lobo would end up talking about in the truck
on the way home: why something always seemed missing to the women,
why neither of them could give up enough of what the women seemed
to want. "But that's all right," Brother Lobo always said.

He felt the pulsing wires of headache begin. Natalie and Chaka—
he knew from listening each week that Lobo would end with the same
two queens: They were the youngest.

"Pack'd My Bags" and then "Keepin a Light." Lobo's voice was still
steady and calm, but Marcus stood up, his shoulders leaping with the
chill he felt inside.

"These are for all the true queens keeping their lights shining in the
window. Too many brothers have packed their bags and moved on.
Traveling light. Rambling. This is for all the sisters waiting on someone.
Good night," Lobo said.

. . .

The two houses behind SaRonn's were dark, but her window shone dim and soft behind fabric she'd pinned over the glass. Marcus knocked, and she answered right away, calling, "Who that?"

"Marcus," he said. "Finis brother."

"I remember," she said, opening the door. "Come on—it's bath time."

He followed her down the small hallway into the bathroom, where she perched on the edge of the tub where her daughter was scooping bubbles into empty margarine containers.

"Can't leave em for a minute when they're in the bath," she said, looking up at him. Her baby hairs were sculpted with shining oil to frame her face.

"You were waitin for Finis?" he asked.

SaRonn nodded, looking down at her daughter, who held out her arms to be picked up from the water. "Come here, burrito baby," SaRonn said, rolling her into a large towel and carrying her, squirming, into the single bedroom.

Marcus stayed in the doorway, watching Willa roll on the India-print bedspread, screaming with laughter. SaRonn's arms were rounded and strong when she picked the long bundle up again. "I see how you lookin at me," she said. "You tryin to figure out if I have a thing for Finis, right? You one a those dudes that thinks no one can be friends."

"Not hardly," Marcus said, trying to lean cool against the frame. "I ain't said nothin."

"Yeah," SaRonn said, smiling wide. "You didn't have to. Look—you know why I like your brother? Not just memory lane, okay? I like sittin in the living room listenin to music with somebody who ain't starin at my chest. We just chill out and listen to the words. Finis just got a new Sly and the Family Stone cassette. Your brother Julius found it for him at some flea market."

"Julius?" Marcus said, and frowned.

"Yeah," she said, gently drying Willa's hair. "Julius bought him a bunch of tapes this week, I guess cause his place got messed up by the cops." She looked up sharply at him again. "Finis took his Walkman and the tapes and left four days ago."

"Where'd he go?" Marcus shook his head at his own impatient words.

She took a long time answering, picking up her daughter and tucking the glistening crown under her own neck. Finally, she said, "A song, you know. I'm tryin to think. I never heard it. Like a blues song or somethin. He said, 'Whichaway do the bloodred river run? Run from my window to the risin sun. Dumper say, Loader sent me plenty cement and clay. Bloodred river risin six foot a day.' "

Marcus whistled. "Sure as hell ain't Funkadelic."

SaRonn shook her head. "I don't know what it is. But he looked so sad, and he walked down that way." She nodded toward Agua Dulce. "Away from y'all place."

He drove to The Blue Q, glancing at the driveway of his father's place and seeing the flatbed tow truck there. Demetrius was around, he thought, keeping an eye on the fences.

He'd left SaRonn quickly so he wouldn't look at her chest, or her neck, or any other part of her body. He didn't want her thinking he was like anyone else. But he also wanted to ask his uncle about the lyrics before he forgot them. With Finis, every word meant something important.

A man leaned toward the truck as soon as the tires crossed the fence line at The Blue Q. "Hosea?" he said, and then his face drew back in surprise. He was a friend of Rock's, older and gruff. "You drivin this one, boy? How's your daddy?"

"Intensive Care," Marcus said. "Uncle Oscar checkin everybody out?" The man nodded and let him park.

Marcus could see by the cars that the place was full, and he knew he probably wouldn't be able to corner his uncle. After he paid Jerry, he stepped inside the moist smoke and saw the tables circled with faces, the stage lit with one dangling, yellow-shaded bulb.

His uncle sat on a folding chair with his guitar and a jackknife, looking at the crowd. His seamed cheeks sparkled with sweat, and his head was wreathed with eerie golden smoke. Behind him was Eddie Lee, with another guitar, and a man they called Texas Jimmy, with a set of drums.

Oscar met Marcus's eyes, and he lifted his chin a few inches. Marcus saw Aintielila leaning forward on her elbows for a moment at the serving window. Then her face disappeared into the kitchen, and Oscar said suddenly, "All right. Got fellas in here from Missippi, from Georgia. Oklahoma. Eddie Lee here, you know he one a them horse trainers they send outta Tennessee. And you know by his name where this other fool from. But every man in here know what I'm talking bout when I'm talkin bout these evil women."

A few men shouted from the back of the room, and one woman hollered, "Evil is as evil do!"

Marcus leaned against the wall, feeling the heat laced with barbecue spice and tangled with perfume. The guitar lay, strings up, flat across Oscar's lap, and he bent over it like he always did. His uncle slid the jackknife down the strings, making a sharp moan, and Eddie Lee picked a stair step of notes. Texas Jimmy started a beat, and Oscar said, "Somebody told me they wanted old-time. All right. This man—I'ma call him Lonnie, now."

He sang,

Lonnie love his Treetown women
But he don't like they evil ways
He love them old Westside women
But can't stand they mean and evil ways
They can fuss and steal and fight
Damn near six out every seven days

A woman shouted, "Oh—and y'all niggas don't?"

Another woman said, "He know what he talkin bout." Marcus smiled, thinking he hadn't been in The Blue Q this time on a Friday for years. Old-timey music and arguments.

His woman love her corn whiskey
And she drink that old homemade brew
Them women love that corn whiskey
And they drink the best homemade brew   *(You know that)*
Get as drunk as they can be
Fight till Lonnie step between em two

People were dancing in the small area beside the stage, women's shoulders dipping and rising to the beat. Marcus saw Floyd King, Lanier, and a few other men at a back table. His uncle moved the knife again and the strings moaned with menace.

You know he got another gal
She live down on Deep Olive Street
I mean he love another gal
Live down on Deep Olive Street
She been done killed two men
He ain't lookin to be number three

Marcus laughed, feeling the rough wood against his shoulders. His father used to joke with Oscar about "Deep" Treetown. They talked about somewhere in Oklahoma called Deep Greenwood. "Every place got a Deep in it, if you know where it is," Oscar would always say.

Lonnie say he got another gal
She stay over on Pablo Street
Say he got another gal
Way over on Pablo Street
That pretty woman fight so bad
The cops don't want to drive that beat

She can make a Magnum talk
And she keep a good long knife
She can make a big old Magnum talk
And she sharpen up that old long knife
Way that woman kill her men
Graveyard can't hold one more life

Oscar ran the blade hard down the strings and ended with a scream of steel. "You better watch out for that graveyard love," he said in a deep voice, and then he smiled.

Marcus looked out over the faces, mostly Treetown and Westside people, but some unfamiliar ones from around the county. If they come in here, they're country. The words are from the old days, the old Treetown. Now it's Olive Gardens bangers bumpin electronic music from their speakers and shootin from movin vehicles.

He thought of the lyrics SaRonn had recited, and knew if he didn't write them down now, after hearing all these songs, he'd lose them. He moved around the back of the room, cutting through chairs and tables, to the kitchen. "Aintie," he called, pushing open the door.

She was whirling slowly from plate to plate, ladling out greens and black-eyed peas. The back door to the kitchen was open, and Marcus glimpsed a figure outside tending the smoking barbecue drums. His aunt methodically finished the plates and pushed them onto the shelf, where a pair of hands took them right away.

"What you need?" she asked, moving toward him slowly. "Your daddy okay?"

Marcus nodded. Her long cheeks were smooth and gleaming with moisture, the deep curves around her mouth like brackets. "You got a piece of paper?" he asked, and she nodded toward the counter. He tore off two pieces of scrap, took a short pencil, and turned back to her. "Aintie," he said, "somebody told me a white man was back here botherin you about sellin this place."

Her brows and lashes dropped like dark slashes across her face, and then she turned back to her pot, her elbows jabbing hard in the space. "Who told you?"

"Somebody seen him here. Why is he buggin you? He know you?" Marcus kept his voice soft. He watched her spare wrists turn.

"Your uncle don't need to worry about no white man," his aunt said, turning to him finally, her face drawn square and fierce now. "You know he don't. It was just somebody tryin to sell somethin."

Marcus hesitated. Lobo had said he was trying to buy. He saw Rock come inside with a washtub full of huge, curved racks of ribs. The bones lay like shallow cradles, dark sauce seared into them. "Here," his aunt said. "Take you some ribs and go set down out there. Go on. Don't worry about nothin right now."

He carried the plate and paper to one of the back tables near the door, where customers mostly ate or watched. He sat down and bent over the paper, trying to remember the right words. Red River. Cement and clay. Blood.

"Look at him. Can't even stop actin like a teacher long enough to eat some soul food," a voice said above him.

He raised his face and saw Bennie Proudfoot and her sister, the one who'd taken Octavious's car. But their brother was talking, Bantam, they called him. He was built like a rooster, and had a mouth as big as one.

"Why you even come if you gon grade papers?" Bantam said, half a smile working his cheek.

"I'm not gradin papers," Marcus said impatiently. "Okay?"

"Nigga don't know how to party," Bantam said, and they moved along to the kitchen window for their food.

Marcus looked down at the scrawl of writing, looked at his uncle muttering something low into the microphone that made the dancers laugh, and he picked up his plate to go outside.

He didn't want to look at the women, the ones who didn't want to hear anything he could think up. They wanted casual raps and sweet talk that murmured out from practiced throats. He went back into the kitchen and said, "I'm goin out this way, Aintie. Thanks for the plate."

She glanced up and nodded, and he went out back past the silent drums breathing black veils.

When he parked on the street near his apartment, he knew someone was watching him. He clutched the plate, checked for the slip of paper with the lyrics in his pocket, and walked, listening for the car door.

"Marcus," the quiet voice said. "We gotta talk."

Tony Salcido fell into step beside him. Salcido wasn't in uniform: He wore jeans and a multicolored sweater. "You want some of my uncle's ribs? No pressure," Marcus said, grinning, holding out the plate.

Salcido smiled, too. He was one of the few nonblack men who ever felt comfortable inside The Blue Q. He was a Salcido, and any Salcido went way back with Thompson blood and land, down to the river-rock walls and the Salcido trucks always getting fixed in the Thompson barn.

"No," Salcido said. "Let's walk down to that Chile restaurant."

They were silent until they'd found a seat near the front. Marcus glanced at Kurt's head bobbing behind the opening to the kitchen, but he didn't see Lakin or Javier.

Salcido dipped blue corn chips into the salsa and said, "Theirs isn't as good as my mom's, but it's better than some."

"Nothing's as good as your mom's. Or mine," Marcus said. "But if we were just chillin, we'd both be at their houses doing it. Eating free." He ordered two Coronas with lime.

Salcido said, "Nobody's seen Finis. He hasn't shown up to work with Rubén, nothing." Marcus nodded. Salcido went on. "Your *abuelita*, she don't really know what's going on at your place, but she told my uncle Feliciano something about this sound she heard, like electric chirping, far as I can get it out of my uncle. And she saw the body, I mean, the face, of the dead guy. The cross-dresser. Somebody had to have been carrying him to where he got dumped, from what she says."

"What did the investigators say when you told them?" Marcus said, leaning forward. "Chirping?"

Salcido shook his head. "The main guy, Harley, he thinks that sounds crazy. He—it's hard for me to talk to him, to bring him something like this, from Treetown or Agua Dulce, you know? Cause I'm the only one. They think . . . well, I always gotta watch myself. They think everybody wants favors."

"You know Finis is hiding cause he's scared," Marcus said. He chewed the gritty blue corn, thinking of the tamales his mother and grandmother were still making. The soft dough and shredded meat and olives. He hoped Finis had grabbed a great big packet of them to take wherever he'd gone.

"The county supervisor's on a rampage, because of his daughter," Salcido said, glancing around the crowded restaurant. The usual well-dressed crowd, Marcus thought. Done with plays, movies, opera, galleries. Drinking Mexican beer, wearing Indian jewelry. Salcido looked back at Marcus. "You know power types hang around here," he said, hushed. "The supervisor and the city council are talking about the department's percentage of unsolved homicides, about Treetown and Agua Dulce being lawless, all that. You know if it's a drive-by in the Gardens or Dulce, and no one gets caught—"

"That's different," Marcus put in.

"Yeah. Harley's gonna be over at your father's place and your uncle's."

"The Blue Q?" Marcus frowned.

"The last body was dumped right next to the wall, you know, like maybe somebody over there threw him over. Hell, I don't know. But Harley's thorough, man. You better stay over there, since your dad's still sick and your mom's on her own. Demetrius and Octavious never were too good at conversations with law enforcement. Just like Rubén." Salcido let out a rueful breath. "My brother still don't like talking to me."

"I know. Cause we know too much shit, too much of what people do to get by." Marcus looked out the window at the women passing, their earrings flashing, and he remembered Shella telling him about Pammy Sawicky. If he was going to help out, he had to find out who she was hanging around with when she died.

"Stay over there with your mom, and check the fences," Tony Salcido said. "Somebody's gotta be breaching your fences. Or doing this from inside."

He told his mother he'd be there whenever he wasn't at school, until his father came home. Demetrius left to take his son home, Octavious and Julius went to The Blue Q, and Marcus ate his plate of ribs while sitting in his father's house.

The coldhouse. He sat on the wooden chair in the doorway, scraping meat from the flat bones with his teeth. I'm country now, he thought. Still burpin Corona from the Chile, and now nobody there would recognize me. Two miles away. Hell, Kurt would love these ribs, if he tried em.

When the bones lay on the plate, he looked down at the bare tangle. Daddy would say what he always said: "Good thing we ain't got no dog, cause he'd cry you give him them bones. Not a scrap."

His father had always laughed at how much the boys had eaten. And he'd never wanted a vicious junkyard dog. "Somebody come over the fence to steal somethin, I want to stop him, not pick his mangled ass up off my land," his father used to say. "People know what we got over here."

"We got Demetrius and Octavious to kick they ass later," the boys would say. His father had the gun he kept under the bed. Marcus reached underneath his father's single bed, covered with a thick Mexican blanket, but, of course, the gun was gone. Still at the police station.

Demetrius had offered him a gun before he left, pulling him aside in the kitchen, but Marcus had shaken his head. "What you gon do? Tell em you a teacher armed with homework and make em run like hell?" Demetrius had said.

"I'm just gon walk," he told himself now, leaving the small stone house. He looked at the closed-up barn. Kickstand was tired of working with cops coming around, he'd told Alma. He'd be back in a week. Let everybody cry about their transmissions and brakes for a few days.

Marcus walked around the too silent place. His mother, his *abuela*, and the kids were locked up tight inside. Marcus headed over to the trailers, which were both locked up, too. He touched the pearly, silver sides, wondering where Finis had gone, wondering what SaRonn was doing now.

He headed to the storage lot, walking down the slope and noticing someone had bought the old Apache truck. The corner looked bare without the rounded hulk of hood. Usually people bought stuff from the front, where they kept the lien sale cars near the barn. Those were newer, in better shape. Marcus stared at the accordion-fronted Toyota Celica and the old Ford station wagon with the side completely caved in. He remembered those accidents. Nobody from Treetown would touch it.

His feet sank in the loose, sandy channel, where the arroyo filtered down through the lowest part of the property, before he climbed again to the olive groves. Abuela was asleep. He hadn't been able to ask her what she saw, and he probably wouldn't understand enough of it, anyway, if she told him. Her olive house was locked tight, too. He walked through the shimmering trees flipping their newest leaves in the breeze like tiny silvery fish, and he stopped here for a long time, remembering that sensation of being underwater when he lay under these trees. When he was in trouble and couldn't leave to walk along the canals or hide in the riverbottom along the red threads of willow roots, he would lie in the farthest corner of the olive grove, looking up into the sun to imagine that the dappled surface overhead was the water.

Once he'd wet his arms with saliva and rolled in the sandy silt of the arroyo, where flakes of mica were thick, and then he'd lain here, right here under the tree where he crouched now. The sun had shown him sparkling metallic scales on his skin, and he'd held his arms and legs close and wriggled like a fish, moving slowly through the leaves and dirt but staring up at the rippling watery aura above.

His father had said, "Boy, what the hell you think you doin?" The rasping, smoky voice had hit him like a stone, and he'd struggled to stand up. His arms were coated with dust, brown and dull, and his skin had prickled under the tight coating. "You can't say?" his father had growled. "I'ma tell you somethin, Marcus. You ain't actin right, most of the time. You think about yourself, what you want to do, what you ain't happy about. Your own little world all the time, sulkin and hidin. You live here, on this place, with a lotta people. You better join the real world pretty soon, boy. Cause don't nobody survive alone."

His father's voice had been hot and low, his hands as black as starlings dangled from his sleeves.

Marcus was eight at the time. He had walked slowly to the fence, picking up the hoe and chopping at the weeds around the olive trees, loosening the earth.

He walked along the fence now, listening, peering at the hills, but he didn't see or hear anything.

CHAPTER SIX

IN THE DEEP umber heat of the October days, Paz stayed in the doorway of the olive house until long after dark, smelling how the warmth worked rosy fragrance into the green olives above her. Those days and the now cool nights by the light of this harvest moon were readying the fruit.

Paz walked to the far edge of the property to look over the riverbottom. The milky trumpet flowers of high jimsonweed were closed into long white fingers, stark in the hard sapphire light. The dead sunflowers hung like prickly cotton balls from thin stems.

She remembered the fall they'd picked cotton out in the desert, she and her daughter and the island man, who talked about all the kinds of cotton he'd seen. Paz had raised the dust between rows with her tiny feet, watched it settle on her arms, thinking that if she could only collect it each night she'd worked in someone's field, she would have enough dirt to grow her own food.

She walked in the feathery spaces between her olive trees each evening, the branches loaded with small green ovals that dipped toward her. The olives began to shade golden, then blush a soft winy-red on one side. It was nearly time. Her granddaughter, Alma, was spending all her days at the hospital, watching over Hosea. The great-grandsons stalked through the leaves and gravel like hollow-eyed children who wouldn't stop playing hide-and-seek even though they were exhausted. Paz kept seeing the startled, chalky face where she'd expected the owl, and she carried her thick walking stick.

When she came near the chain link facing the hills, she saw a narrow tendril of smoke rising from behind the boulders where her great-grandboys had used to hide. Paz studied the stones, hearing nothing. The jagged edges of the smoke turned blue, and she knew it was a cigarette, not a fire. When she went back to the olive house, she peered around the doorway and eventually saw a boy who looked Indian, like a sun-darkened Mayan with pulled-tight eyes and wide lips. The boy clambered silently down the hillside and over the canal footbridge. He peered into the fence, and Alma spoke around the stone wall.

"*Al nopal lo van a ver sólo cuando tiene tunas,*" she said, thinking he wanted the olives, that he might be checking their ripeness. The prickly pear has company only when it bears fruit—he stood near a *nopal* with its flat spiny leaves now, staring uncomprehendingly at her. Paz squinted at his brown skin, his glossy black hair, and then he ran down the canal road, disappearing around the corner of the hills, leaving behind the scent of menthol and ashes.

She began to pick the olives the next day. The twenty-four trees had been planted during mission times, and their trunks were 130 years old, thick and low-branched so she could reach the fruit dangling close to her. Finis had picked the higher olives, standing on the wooden ladder, his fingers gentle and patient, never dropping, but sliding the olives into the felt-lined bucket and climbing down to roll them softly into their boxes.

She missed the slight bobbing of his head, like a dove, and the way his silence was soft and companionable. She missed Hosea, too, who usually came in the afternoons to pick rapidly, his silence sharper and distracted. Paz reached for an olive, thinking, I am ninety-seven. He is seventy-six.

When she visited Agua Dulce and the youngest Salcido children asked how she and their old *tío* Feliciano could still get up to greet each dawn, Paz glanced at Feliciano's hands, always shaving wood from a saint's face. She thought of Archuleta, those years he had hired her to pick the olives, how old and curved he had been. Hosea's hands were always slick with grease from engine parts, black on both sides. And even though Paz's back hurt like a cradle of fire each noon and into the night, even though she couldn't bend farther than a slant, her wrists and fingers were as strong as wire.

"We wake up because we have work to do," she always told the children. "You must always have work, if you want to stay alive."

The next morning, when she went after dawn and warm tortillas and coffee to the grove, two boxes were already filled and waiting by the olive house doorway. Paz frowned at the neat mounds of olives, the right ones, tinted properly and not too green.

The Indian boy? she thought, seeing no one in the grove, no one near the fence. But he hadn't understood her. Why would he climb the fence to do this?

She couldn't move the boxes inside, so she made several trips to take olives into the cement curing vats on the wide-board floor. For days, she stirred the briny liquid she and Alma had made, watching the olives cure softly. The canned olives, with their oxidized black flesh and tinny, rubber taste, were the work of huge factories and laziness. She remembered the smoky haze and ripe smell hanging over the town of Maneadero during the season, the way the oil had drifted into hair and wood and had even coated the dust to clinging velvet.

Every morning, the two boxes were full again, in the same place. Paz looked up into the branches, seeing that the picker had used care in selecting the olives, the way she always did. Each tree needed to be harvested many times, to catch the olives at their peak of flavor.

She was afraid, somehow, to sleep in the olive house and wait for the person before light. When night fell, she remembered the harsh-planed, pale mask of face that had bobbed in the window that night, the dead mouth. Her ankles and heels were cold. When she'd worked in the big curing sheds in Maneadero, stirring, sorting, stirring, her bones and the balls of her feet used to ache from the bitter cold toward the end of the season. She wasn't allowed to stop, to step outside the cavern. Here, she could sit in her chair and feel the sun in the morning.

She made herself rise at five, when the night still drifted. Holding her walking stick, in case the Indian boy was disturbed, in case a spirit was picking her olives, Paz walked toward the grove.

In the shallow, sandy ravine that cut through the land, she paused, looking up to see a lantern burning in the trees. She could hear the ladder creak, see the branches tremble. Humming sifted through the leaves.

Finis stepped carefully down the ladder, holding the bucket. He froze when he saw her, and then he grinned.

"Grandma's hands," he sang, and she understood him.

Into her palms, he placed two stones—black, glittering and round, with perfect white rings looped on their bellies.

Marcus slept in his father's coldhouse, the fall night warm and feathery against his face. At daylight, he heard his *abuela*'s shoes pinch the gravel, and he stared at the gray-stone walls his father had built; stone houses were usually rough-cemented and then plastered inside. There were a few stone houses on the southern side of the city. But his father and old Pablo Salcido had built these walls with large flat stones laid horizontally for natural shelves along all but the wall behind the bed. Marcus remembered when the ledges held crowded jars of olives and jams and dried fruit in packets; now, his father had a few jars of pomegranate jelly, a pack of Swisher Sweets. His mother must have straightened everything after the deputies had left, he thought. He saw pieces of metal, nuts and bolts and odd nails, on the low ledges, near where his father sat in the chair each afternoon fixing something.

The weather was still too hot, according to his mother, and she fretted over her trees and flowers. "Get Demetrius to take you over to the hospital and check on him, Mama," Marcus told her, sitting at the table with the hot tortillas his *abuela* slid from her black griddle onto the plate. He laid scrambled eggs down the center and salsa in a jagged vein.

"Okay, but who's gonna water?" his mother asked, folding her arms. "Not this one, thinks he's too grown to do anything but play stupid TV games."

Kendrick, Julius's oldest son, dropped his head to the side and rolled his eyes. "Nintendo," he said.

"Maybe you can make him do chores," his mother said, leaving to dress.

His *abuela* took the baby girl, Jalima, with her to the olive house, and Marcus told Kendrick and Jawan to help him with the buckets and hoses. They poured water slowly into the irrigation furrows nearest the house, around the roses, which weren't on canal water. Marcus heard his *abuela* whistle, as sharp and high as a mockingbird, and they went to find her holding pails full of rabbit pellets.

He had to laugh when Kendrick said, "Shit," under his breath, remembering how many times he'd hated the long trek to the garden carrying fertilizer.

"That's what it is, dude," he told Kendrick. They hoed it into the circles around each rose. Then the boys went inside and Marcus turned on the canal irrigation for the orange trees, watching the water arc from the cement and shine in ribbons down the five rows.

His mother came back in the afternoon, eyes swollen and filmy, and she only said, "He been in there too long. Only get more dangerous germs through them tubes and in that air. He go in and out . . . " She broke off and went into her bedroom.

The homicide detective came the next day with the officer Marcus had seen the night they'd found the body, the one with the brown moustache as wide as a thumb under his nose. Harley, the detective, was balding, with black hair combed straight back, and a blue sport shirt that showed arms with black hairs, too, hairs looking nearly groomed in their regularity.

He sat in the coldhouse door on Marcus's father's chair. Marcus sat in a folding chair from the barn, and the cop walked around in arcs.

"You're a teacher," Harley began. Marcus nodded. "You spent the night here. But you live downtown. Look: Let's talk like two intelligent people. We've got three bodies on this place. Obviously, your dad didn't kill the guy, whether or not he had anything to do with the two women."

Marcus wanted to talk; he wanted to say that Pammy Sawicky wouldn't have gotten into a car with a Treetown brother, but he knew that would wreck this friendly-fake intimacy the detective was setting up. He wanted Marcus to listen.

"I'm gonna tell you a few things, okay? The autopsy report on the guy says he was bludgeoned repeatedly, back of the head. Anger. Somebody was viciously angry." Harley paused, looking at the kitchen door for a moment. "The two women in the car—one was shot before she asphyxiated. The other wasn't. They both burned after that." He let that image sink in. "Doesn't even seem like the same killer, huh?"

"I'm not an expert," Marcus said, keeping his voice even.

Harley nodded. "We questioned your brother Finis, obviously. Pretty useless exercise. Now I understand you don't know where he is?" He folded his hands and hung them between his wide-spread knees.

"Maybe he went to visit some friends," Marcus said, hearing the words and wanting to wince. He lifted his shoulders. "He's probably scared shitless."

"No doubt," Harley said.

"How in the hell would he have a friend? Who could talk to him?" the cop muttered, walking past them.

"Well, and you're no doubt hanging out here, hoping he shows up," Harley said, nice and friendly. "You let us know. We're gonna keep an eye out, too, okay? We don't have a murder weapon for either of these. But your father's gun wasn't the one used on the woman. You got a gun, Marcus?"

"Nope." Marcus felt the sweat tingle in his scalp.

"Your brothers do." Harley stood up. "Right?"

Marcus stood up, too, pushing his hands into his pockets. "Finis doesn't."

"Yeah, okay," Harley said. "Well, we'll probably see you. Right?"

Marcus left the silence floating in the doorway.

Enchantee brought the newspaper the next day when she got off work, and Marcus sat across from her at the kitchen table to read it. She shook her head, paging through a magazine, D'Junior snuggling into her neck. "I can't believe somebody would do this," she murmured. "Took them a long time to figure out who he was."

TREETOWN MURDER VICTIM WAS LOS ANGELES MAN

After nearly two weeks of frustrating investigative efforts, homicide detectives have discovered the identity of a man found dead at a towing yard in Treetown. Jean-Luc Bessier, a French national who had lived in Los Angeles for two years, was killed by an unknown assailant soon after arriving in Rio Seco for a modeling job, according to family members finally reached in France. He had spoken to relatives about traveling to Rio Seco to shoot photos for an album cover. Bessier, who was found dressed in women's clothing, had no friends in the area.

Investigators have yet to uncover a motive, or even a murder weapon, in the killing, and they appeal to the public for information about Bessier's whereabouts in the hours before his death. He apparently boarded a bus in Los Angeles on Friday evening for the hour-long ride to Rio Seco, and investigators hope to learn about his movements following the ride. Anyone with information should call Detective John Harley at 293–5684.

"Damn," Marcus said.

"Hush," Enchantee said over D'Junior's head. She caught her lip in her teeth. "I don't want his daddy talkin about it, either."

"What you readin?" Marcus said. He took the magazine when she pushed it across the table. "Real estate? You just bought a house."

"We looked at these for so long, it's a habit for me to pick them up now," Enchantee said, watching D'Junior run toward the living room to see Kendrick and Jawan. "And I saw what they're doin up the way from us in there, too."

"Where?" Marcus saw her finger on the page—"Cottonwood Canyon Ranch Estates." The advertisement was a full page of rolling hills and oaks and a lake, with a map below showing the land above Demetrius and Enchantee's development.

"Ours is Rivercrest," Enchantee said. "I guess right above us is gonna be another development, and then way up there by the hills is that one. There's a few houses up there already."

"But nothing here yet," Marcus said, looking at the picture of the elaborate stucco gate with a logo and landscaping, and empty country behind. He read the text aloud. "Two-acre estate lots—peaceful tranquility, beautiful views, private lake, new schools, and mature trees await the discriminating buyer. Highly desirable area is fast developing." He saw the prices. "A hundred and fifty to two hundred seventy-five thousand dollars!"

Enchantee shook her head, smiling. "We didn't pay that, okay?"

"I know you didn't," Marcus said. He put the magazine aside, looking at the way her lipstick was faded soft. "Long day, huh?"

"Yeah," she said. "It's hard when Demetrius has to do everything over here. And I have to do everything over there." But she smiled. "I'm glad you're helping Alma out."

"Demetrius doesn't have to hang out at night, cause I'm walkin the fences," he said. "Serious. And look at this—" He nodded toward the newspaper article. "Whatever happened, whatever's been goin on, it's gotta have stopped now. It's been a while. Keep Demetrius home. Tell him how lucky he is." Marcus got up and went to check on the boys, who were wrestling in front of the television, their thin arms and legs tangled and immobile, like snakes. He turned back to the kitchen doorway.

"Hey, remember when that land used to be Diamondback Hills? Everybody was afraid to go up there, said they had nests of rattlers in the rocks."

Enchantee was rubbing her neck. "Not anymore," she said. "Come on, Demetrius Junior. We have to buy some food."

"You guys can eat here," Marcus said. "Mama won't mind."

"I will," Enchantee said, and then she sighed. "I mean, she's always got enough mouths to feed." She reached up and touched the carnations in a brown glass bottle that was covered with an iridescent rainbow sheen.

Finis had found the bottle years ago, in the riverbottom. Marcus went back outside to walk around the trailers once more before dark.

Two men with cameras came to the locked front gate in the evening. Octavious had just brought in an abandoned Hyundai, and he was talking to a couple of guys who were looking for an engine for a Ford pickup. Marcus went outside to dump the trash for his mother at the cans near the fence, and he saw the news van and the bright lights.

"Excuse me!" the reporter shouted.

Marcus stared at the big camera trailing wires.

"Can we come in and talk to some of the residents here? Do you live here?" the man said, grinning.

"No," Marcus said. He knew what his father would say, what Demetrius would do. Walk away. But he had to know. "What's this about?"

"We've gotten reports that three people have been killed here in the last two months, and that the police have been unable to solve the murders. Do you know anything about it?"

"No," Marcus said, turning to leave.

"I'm Phil Cottrell, Channel Seven's Inland Valley bureau. This is legit, man, come on!" The guy's voice went rougher, and Marcus saw Octavious and the others staring down the driveway.

"Go inside and close it up," Marcus told Octavious. "News guy. I'm goin in the house, and I'll be back."

The house was quiet and dark. Everyone was sleeping, even Kendrick, who'd argued to stay up and watch a movie. Marcus heard the barn's metal door clang shut.

When the van left, he went back outside and tapped on the door. "Eight, man, it's me," he called. Inside, Octavious and the men sat on crates and chairs, discussing engines.

"I got a friend with a rebuilt one for you," Octavious said. "Let me go over to the Westside and get it. You can have it Wednesday. But if you want Kickstand put it in, be about another week. He—uh, he takin a break."

One of the men said, "I know that fool ain't got in trouble again." Kickstand was known for fighting, too, and he'd done time for assault.

"No, man, he's just chillin at home for a week," Octavious said, glancing at Marcus. "Cool?"

"I'll bring the dinero Wednesday," the man said, and he left with his friend. At the gate, he called, "What them white dudes want?"

Octavious shrugged. He turned to Marcus and said, "This shit ain't fuckin up the business. No way, man. Bad enough Kickstand nervous about all these cops. Ain't no way we can let no TV people around. What the *fuck* is somebody tryin to do?" He threw an oil can hard against the stones.

"I don't know," Marcus said. He went to the far corner of the barn, past the three cars in varying states of repair, to the small walled-off bathroom his father and Demetrius had built long ago. It held a shower, sink, and toilet. Marcus threw water on his face and looked into the wavery mirror that he'd always thought, when he was younger, would turn his face into a dream. "You gon carry a piece?" he asked himself softly. "You gon find some tracks?"

Back in the doorway, Octavious was crouched on the ground, staring at the bare chain link where the fire had been. The long stretch adjoining the gate was like a window out onto Pepper Avenue, where cars still raced past. "We're gonna need big money when Daddy get out the hospital," Octavious said. "Big money for the bill."

Marcus hadn't thought of that. "But he got shot by the cops . . . "

"And then y'all took him out without the doctor lettin him go. And

he got worse on his own. We probably gotta pay everything," Octavious
said. "Come on."

He locked up the barn and they walked along the boundaries of the
land, silent for a long time. Marcus watched himself following slightly
behind Octavious, studying his brother's thick braid. "You ain't drinkin
tonight?" he said finally, when they'd reached the trailers. The silver
walls were still blind and quiet. "No eight ball?"

"I knew I was gon walk with you," Octavious said. "I don't drink
that eight ball hardly ever no more. Just some of Uncle Oscar's stuff
on the weekends. When I'm kickin it."

"You think Finis is okay?" Marcus looked at the dusty trailer.

Octavious shrugged. "I hope he ain't got picked up for vagrancy
somewhere. Walkin around with no ID—that's enough if he went
across the river."

They walked toward the olive grove, then down the edges of the
storage lot, stopping at the trampled ashes where the Granada had been.
Octavious turned to him and said, "You gon take this or not?"

He held out a handgun. Marcus picked it up. A Ruger .9-millimeter,
a heavy, wide gun in his hand. "If you gonna be walkin, you better
take it. I'ma get me another one," Octavious said.

Marcus handed it back. "Shit, y'all used to talk about me cause I
couldn't shoot rabbits. What made you think I can shoot a man?"

"Marcus," his brother said, with more patience than Marcus had
expected, more than he'd ever heard before. "If somebody's trespassin,
with all this shit goin on, he ain't doin nothin to you or nobody else but
harm. Okay? And you shoot him, he's on your property, it's justifiable.
Especially now."

Marcus shook his head and hooked his fingers around the fence,
peering out through this gate. The palm fronds were newly green, thrust
down through the chain link like a thousand spears to hide and guard
the lot. "Why's Mama payin Nacho to paint these green?" he said. He
could see the droplets from the airless sprayer Nacho had used.

Octavious put the gun back into his holster, dropping his shirt down
over it. "I don't know," he said. "Maybe she think it's good luck.
Come on."

It was like hunting again, walking silently for a long time, just his
thoughts and footsteps meshing like gears, and Marcus didn't mind the
circuit through the trees and past the cars and down toward Pepper

Avenue. Before he left, Octavious stood in front of the coldhouse, offering Marcus the gun one more time.

"You sleepin here again?" Marcus nodded. "Ain't no hesitation on my part, man. If I see the dude fuckin with us, I'ma kill him. I'ma get this over with so when Daddy get out, it's done. Like nothin happened. Just work, like always."

When Marcus turned away from the gun, Octavious said, "Don't mess up and get yourself killed, Sissyfly." He grabbed the back of Marcus's neck and shook him slightly before pushing him away.

The next day after he'd joked with the students and avoided the teachers' lounge, after he'd stopped by Kurt's for *carnitas* not quite as good as Abuela's but accompanied by a laughing discussion of Spike Lee and John Sayles, he went to his apartment and stood in front of the antique trunk he'd bought when he first moved downtown. He'd moved the two glass bottles Finis had given him long ago. Dark blue—Milk of Magnesia. People in Treetown sometimes hung them on trees to ward off bad spirits. Marcus held them for a minute. Finis was fleeing bad spirits, maybe in the riverbottom, maybe in a Kozy Komfort room in another city, where he'd be a vague silhouette with nobody like SaRonn to remember his eyes.

SaRonn. Marcus rubbed his temples. In many ways, it had been safer, easier, all these years to gaze at Enchantee and attach his resentment to Demetrius, keeping true heat out of reach, flirting with Colette and the others with a dry, powdery remove. SaRonn. The sound and smell of her was way too complicated. He took some clothes from the trunk and replaced the bottles.

When he got to the dark coldhouse, he lit the glaring Coleman lantern his father used during the night. Sitting on the bed, he looked over the papers from the world history classes. Textbook questions. Having the students work in groups meant less work, the older teachers always said. Marcus graded the answers quickly and then walked over to the kitchen door to look at the disintegrating wall near the steps.

His mother had been hollering yesterday, her voice cracking loud for the first time since all the trouble had begun. Jawan, playing there, had chipped away adobe and plaster under the starry patch of blue paint.

When Alma had seen the hole, widened like a sore, she'd yelled at the boy until he'd dropped the slabs of plaster and fled to the trees.

"And y'all boys keep sayin you gon mix up the adobe and plaster this hole up, but you never do!" she'd shouted, turning to Marcus and Julius and Octavious, near the barn. "All y'all got time for cars, every day got time for cars, but don't none a you got time to help me out with this house! It's meltin away, look at it! Y'all damn lucky it ain't rained for years!"

She'd slammed the back door, and Marcus had found Jawan hiding behind a pepper trunk. "Man, I used to hide here, too," Marcus had told the tear-tracked face. "Don't mess with Gramma's house. You wait till you old enough to slap that plaster on. Maybe we'll do it next week, huh?" Jawan had nodded.

He decided to walk along the wall between his father's place and The Blue Q, to jump the fence in his old spot and cross the canal to the hill, where he could look down on the place and watch. Truthfully, he wanted to look across the riverbottom, too, and over the lights of the city, so that he could connect the pieces of what had happened and think about Finis. In the riverbottom—that's where he thought Finis must be, and all the homeless men living in cane shelters and cottonwood groves might not listen to Finis's language.

The air along the wall swirled gray and cooler, and he kicked at the leaves to unearth the scent of menthol. He passed behind the dark, closed olive house and then, at the corner of the fence where the land was divided, he pushed his toe into the heap of tangled leaves and branches to leap up and over the barbed wire.

But the fence sagged when he pushed against it, the chain link loose and weak, and he nearly fell backward. All this time we've been walkin the fences, nobody's checked the wire here, he thought. Daddy'd be hollerin as loud as Mama about the house.

He poked at the gap along the pole, seeing where the wires had been cut, and he wondered how long ago someone had done that. Even Julius, who was always trying to sneak past his brothers or a waiting woman at the barn, wouldn't cut fences. And nobody but Abuela ever came back here anymore, now that Marcus didn't wander the canal roads.

He looked at the glittering teeth atop the stone wall. For the last ten feet, his father and Salcido had embedded broken glass in the top like they did in Mexico, to keep out intruders.

Marcus pulled gently at the fence and climbed carefully over the barbed wire, jumping down onto the path. He'd walk along the canal before he went up the hill. The sliding water was so black that he could see stars reflected like floating bits of cotton.

Since the drought had intensified, the water was fat and placid near the tops of the banks. Marcus headed toward the bend where the canal curved around the hill, so he could watch the storage lot and the riverbottom road. Where the water turned right in a loop that reflected sudden silver from the lone streetlamp, he heard voices from around the hill.

"Fuck you, man, I'm the one with the fuckin nine. If we see anybody, I'm the one fuckin shootin."

"Shit, you can't hit nothin from further'n two feet. I shot better'nat when I was a kid. In Texas . . . "

"Fuck Texas. You're in Cali now, man," the first voice said.

Marcus spun around and ran, light-footed on the sand like when he was hiding from his brothers, but he heard the murmurs, closer. Ahead of him was only the fence, which he couldn't jump in time, and the steep hillside over the plank bridge. He saw the cement cover of the canal's water intake, where the rush hit the metal grate to keep out trash and the water was sucked into his father's irrigation system. He dropped himself over the side and felt his body float backward, hard, under the cement. He had to catch the metal ring just before the overhang with his right hand or there'd be nothing to hold on to in the slick, mossy channel before the grate. This was where kids died when they swam in the summer and didn't pay attention, where they got crushed against the grate by a sudden rush of water when farmers needed more.

His fingers slid down the cement edge and curled around the metal ring, and he felt the knock of his shoulder against the canal's side. He had a few inches between his chin and the surface, and he ran his left hand up over the underside of the cement, trying to find something else to hold, to balance the current against him. He found a rough chunk of concrete and latched his fingers onto that.

"You've been fuckin up all along, Sketch, man."

"Fuck you, man. You're tweaked. This is your third day up, shit, you can't even think right."

"You pick the girl, Sketch. You the one like her hair." A new voice.

Marcus kept his eyes wide. He couldn't tell if the two voices were white or black; something was slightly off. And the third was clipped and odd, like Spanish.

"How the fuck was I supposed to know her dad was rich?" the first voice said, and he saw the sneakered feet pass to his right on the path.

"Fuck rich," the clipped voice said.

"He's right. We should fuck some rich girl."

The clipped voice said, "That why you get in trouble last time."

The nervous voice said, "Bodie's right, Sketch. You fucked up large."

"Don't call me Bodie."

"If we see any of these guys, the ones Bodie said live here . . . " The nervous voice paused. "Man, it looks like Texas down here. Shit. The woods and all."

"Yeah—you're still a country boy. You been here what—a year? Cali crystal's got you tweaked. This ain't fuckin Texas." Sketch began to rap. "I'm a Nigga-wit-a-Attitude, and I got the . . . "

The clipped, somehow familiar voice said, "You can only say it if you are black, man."

"You're the closest, Bodie," Sketch taunted. "Got some jungle blood in you."

Marcus felt his chest melting cold from the water pushing against him; his feet moved along the grassy-slick bottom like a cartoon runner. He breathed the green, dank air, and the three sets of feet moved far enough past him that he could see shoes, hear them crunch along the fence line. He listened hard in the liquid silence.

"I climb a tree," said Bodie. "I sleep in a tree. In my country, shit, sleep in a tree so a tiger won't get your ass. You don't know shit."

But the other two were bent over a bag they'd set on the path. Marcus saw thin white elbows pumping like leaping bones, but the cement overhang cut off his sight above the figures' waists. "Here," Sketch said, muffled, and Marcus hunched his shoulders, trying to hear. "I forgot it was in the fuckin Jeep all this time until—you know, he called. He was pissed as hell. I told him the dude was a extra job, shit, like a freebie."

"Only free cause Tweak, he get too horny," Bodie said.

Marcus glimpsed a figure running to the fence corner where he'd come over, throwing something in a soft arc into the trees, and when the figure turned, Marcus thought he saw black gloves and pale arms, as if the hands had been cut off. "We're done, man, that's it," the voice called, coming back closer.

"You're too fuckin loud, Sketch, you're gonna get us killed!"

"You got the gauge and Sketch got the nine," Sketch sang, disappearing. Only their feet showed again, and Marcus felt his neck cramping with the effort to hold himself upright. He prayed nothing would float down the canal, no wood or raccoons or trash to hit him in the face, knock him under.

"You aren't fuckin Vanilla Ice," the nervous one said.

"I'm fuckin cooler than Vanilla Ice," Sketch said.

"I'm tired of your fuckin nine," Nervous said. "You shoot now and we're gonna get busted. Plus, that's what you shot the chick with. Didn't he tell you get rid of it?"

Marcus heard a foot slide across the sand, crushing grit, and then a small splash in the water ten feet ahead of him.

"Fucker was a cheap gun," Sketch said. "You think I'm jumpin in cause I miss my nine? I'll get me another one."

"Bye-bye," Bodie said.

"Only a fuckin Jap would say bye-bye," Sketch said. "Come on."

"Only a fuckin American would be so stupid," the voice named Bodie said softly, just near Marcus's hand, and he closed his eyes, afraid the face would drop down over the cement to see where the gun had gone. He hadn't felt it bump him.

But the feet joined the others running back down the path, around the curve. After a few more minutes he felt a wire of pain running across his knuckles, shooting down his wrist as if the metal ring were electrified. "Shit," he whispered. "Shit."

The gun would be clanking against the metal grate behind him by now, or maybe even sliding through. Marcus forced his foot, toe first, to the side of the cement channel and jammed his shoe sideways in a deep crack. Lucky we in Treetown, he thought, where the canals are in worse shape. He brought the left hand down and reached past the metal ring to a chink taken out of the bank by rushing water. Dirt was crumbling underneath, and he sank his fingers into it, pulling hard.

He crawled up onto the path, lying with his cheek on the sand, staring at the lip of trembling water below him. The place he'd always been afraid of, where he'd just been, the shallow cave where the water rose to liquefy breath.

He rested a moment on his hands and knees, seeing himself coated with sand like a piece of Shake 'n Bake chicken he'd glimpsed at a white school friend's house. He shook his head and rose up, walking fast toward the fence.

It was like facing the curve of a huge wave, looking up at the flare of wire at the top. Marcus held the chain link so he wouldn't fall backward, and the fence gapped open again, right at the pole. He pulled hard now, at the snipped line, and the space was wide enough for him to slide in.

Crouching down, he examined the loose leaves and debris on the ground here. What'd they throw in?

He walked carefully along the wall, and after a few more feet he saw it resting on a heap of pepper berries and bougainvillea flowers. A tire iron. Damn.

He bent close, keeping his balance. The black metal was dull with dried blood, and a clump of synthetic hair, as red as licorice, clung to the handle. Marcus felt his head drain, as if the water had penetrated his forehead, and he made himself fall backward, away from the long, shiny strands curving over the black.

CHAPTER
SEVEN

MORTRICE FIRED THE .25 four times into the field, aiming for the white piece of wood planted in the furrows. He felt a sting of pain in the webbing between his first finger and thumb, and he lowered the gun to see the blood welling up in shiny rivulets, dripping down his wrist.

"What's wrong, man?" Chris asked anxiously from where he stood near Mortrice and B-Real.

Mortrice crouched, put down the gun, and examined his hand. "Baby shavin on me," he murmured. He knew from his magazines and the gunsmithing book that his handgun was cheaply made. He knew a thin sliver of the slug had been scraped off and had flown backward to embed itself in his hand. Gunpowder had drifted into his skin, too, and he saw the blood cleaning a path for itself. "I need me a better gun," he said softly.

"You need you a nine, cuddy," Chris said, and Mortrice stood up, looking at the two faces. "Lemme see yours."

He handed Chris the gun. Chris called him "cuddy," for cousin. Chris's mother was Zefi Perry, who lived a few doors away from his mother in Olive Gardens. Chris said Zefi was sisters with someone named Enchantee, who was married to a Thompson. He said his father was gone, but that his mother had been with Julius Thompson for a while. That made them cousins.

In L.A., to call someone "cuz" meant he was blue. Crips. To call someone "blood" meant he was red. Bloods. To mess up and call someone the wrong one meant you were dead or he was dead. Mortrice had been mostly silent for these weeks in the new apartment, listening for the new codes and rules. He saw who went to school, who didn't, what they drove, what they wore, how they looked at him. He read his magazines at night, taking out the .25 and staring.at it in his hand, wondering when he would need to use it.

But so far, when the boys around him had found out he was from L.A., they'd breathed only admiration and curiosity. B-Real and Chris had brought him out here, to the riverbottom far north of the city, to shoot his gun. They wanted to shoot it, too.

"Go on, man," Mortrice told Chris. "Might cut you."

"I don't care," Chris said. He held the gun out the way Mortrice had, steadying his arm, and fired at the wooden marker. Mortrice waited to see if the gun had flung a sliver into Chris's face, into his eye, but the same blood appeared in the same place on his hand.

"Like a tattoo and shit," B-Real said, his voice frightened. Mortrice knew he was afraid of guns; he was a rapper, only interested in words. "Do it hurt?"

"It ain't about nothin," Chris said, handing B-Real the gun. B-Real handed it back, and Chris and Mortrice laughed.

When they were driving back to Rio Seco, Chris said, "There your peoples' place, right there." He pointed to a row of fencing off the road; above the fence, covered with palm fronds, all Mortrice could see were towering trees. The car turned the corner and sped past, and he glimpsed a dirt yard through a gap in the fencing.

"Who people?" Mortrice said. He'd been looking for the tree in the riverbottom, the tree where Kenneth had left Paco's sleeping form, and the word "people" was a code he didn't understand.

"All them Thompsons, man," B-Real said.

"Your uncle is Marcus, right, the teacher?" Chris added. "So they your peoples. Don't your mama go over there?"

Mortrice thought about his mother's complete inertia on the couch in this new apartment, the way she asked him the date every day, the way he'd had to go to the store with Chris and B-Real for the few things they'd eaten. "She said she waitin for the right day to do somethin," Mortrice said slowly. "She said she the only one know."

"Where your daddy?" B-Real asked.

"Wherever he wanna be," Mortrice said.

Chris wasn't paying attention. "Check out the black Jeep," he said, nodding toward the vehicle they were approaching. Mortrice could hear Eazy-E beats drifting from the Jeep's windows, but when Chris sped up and swerved around to pass the Jeep, he saw ghostly faces under the dark, knit caps. "Don't that look like a white boy from school?" Chris said.

B-Real shrugged, and Mortrice turned to stare at the pale discs floating in the Jeep's windshield. Then Chris turned hard onto Grove Avenue, into Treetown.

"My name is B-Real, but on the mike I'm Dyno-Steel, always got the cold lyrics, make the females see my skill," B-Real sang next to him, but Mortrice was staring at the blood darkened thick on his hand.

"My home is Treetown and it's crazy loc down, real brothas cruise here, not wannabes and clowns," Chris shouted.

Hosea had slid in and out of the watery awareness of dim lights and blinkings and tubes like vines draped around him, choking him with thick stems reaching under the sheets.

He saw the vines cloaking the riverbank outside Tulsa, the tree trunks he scraped when he fought through the brush looking for the bodies. The bodies the white people had heaped onto trucks that night and dumped outside the city, everyone said. Bone tangles in pits; swelled fingers in the river. People whispered.

He'd left the garage apartment, the exposed stairs and moving eyes. He'd walked miles to the river, avoiding the ash-heaped graveyard of Greenwood. He'd stalked through the thick growth, touching the water, looking for his father.

When he swam up from the swelling currents of vague heat and swathing sheets and sand in his lungs, he met Alma's eyes. She watched him from ash-ringed hollows, reaching out to touch his arms with fingers warm and dry.

"Come on, Hosea," she whispered. "Come on back now."

He had been looking for his father. The pit of space in his stomach vibrated with the loss when he knew where he was. He closed his eyes, opened them. Close. Open. His skin hurt like a too tight sheath.

He had found a body in the water.

On the way to Texas from Oklahoma, when he was sixteen and his stepfather's hard-swung blow to his ear had left a ringing hollow in his head, he'd walked across the Red River and found a body in a rushing creek. A black man's features, whorls of black hair left near the ears, but the skin stripped by the rushing icy water to a pallor like a ghostly newborn lying in the tree roots' embrace.

The gunshot wound in his forehead was as round as a navel.

Alma stroked Hosea's cheek, brushed her lips across his lifted hand. "You comin back," she said. "I'm right here."

Hosea had struggled to pull the body from the rushing water. He'd had his knife and his grandfather's gun. He'd worked for one day to cut the branches and clasp the thickened, cold arm. Then he'd jabbed at the icy earth to make a hole. He'd shot a wild dog snarling at the body with his grandfather's gun.

He wanted the gun back now. He stared at the tubes, then at his wife. She said, "You been out of Intensive Care. I been waitin right here for you."

He struggled to move his legs in the current of white sheets.

Alma gave him hot lemon juice with honey, garlic, and ground chile. She handed him a blanket where he sat in the big leather chair. They both looked out the lace curtains to the fence and over it, across Pepper Avenue to the hills of Agua Dulce turning salmon in the afternoon sun. She said, "You think you gon eat somethin?"

"Eat anything you cook after bein in there," he said. "Eat anything you cook any day."

He was weak, but the blurring had receded from his eyes. His skin looked somehow softer and yet stretched tighter over his face. He slept there after a while, the same way he did in his doorway now and then, and Alma sat in the kitchen with Abuela, knowing that she would keep her thoughts trained on what he would eat and not what he would have to learn.

Ground meat, rice, broth. Abuela began shaping the meatballs for *sopa de albóndigas*. Alma glanced outside at the grandsons playing near the barn, where the boys worked. She was waiting for Marcus.

His father had asked for him. He came, wearing shorts and a T-shirt, breathless. "I went to the gym after work," he said. "Demetrius said Daddy came home."

"He's sleep right now," Alma said. "Let him be for a minute." Marcus glanced into the living room and came back to the table. Alma said, "He asked for you."

"I got somethin to ask him, too," Marcus said, staring at the piles of meatballs. He grabbed a tortilla from the covered basket on the stove and spread apricot jam on it. But he sat back down without eating, holding the rolled tortilla loosely.

He'd come into the kitchen the night before, stumbling against the wall so hard that a plate had fallen and shattered. Alma had come from the bedroom to tell him that his father was better, and she'd seen Marcus leaning against the wall, his eyes closed, his chest moving hard. His clothes were wet, but when she'd asked him what was wrong, he'd shaken his head and gone into the bathroom. He'd gone back out to the coldhouse without speaking.

Now he stared out the kitchen window at the barn. Abuela said something low in Spanish. *"Quien más mira menos ve."* Alma remembered her grandmother telling her that when she used to watch the men in the yards, laughing and talking to women. "The more one looks, the less one sees."

"You're too quiet," Alma said to Marcus. "You always have plenty to say. Or plenty to ask."

Marcus blew out a breath and buried his head in his palms. "Yeah. That's what you and Daddy always say. All talk and no action."

Alma tried to smile. "When you were little, you always asked questions, asked the boys about car parts and bugs, soda cans, everything. And then you were five, already correctin them." She made her voice small in imitation. "Uh-uh, that ain't a Junebug. It's a fig beetle. You said get you a cup—that's a glass."

"No wonder they hated me from the get."

"You just bothered them," Alma said. She watched her youngest son's clean hands, his short hair and gleaming exercise shorts. For all his classifying of words, he had never learned how to put on a tire or work on an engine or do anything the other boys did. She'd been so proud of his books and his chattering, his papers marked with stars and then As, his college diploma. Children couldn't stop fighting or trying to better each other, even when they weren't children anymore.

"You know what Daddy told me one time?" Marcus said suddenly, searching through the rice for bits of stone or stick. "He said, 'It's a lotta men make things, or fix things or sell things. But you want to talk about things. That's how you gon make your livin. Talkin.' I never forgot that. And now all I can do is tell him this shit. Talk. I don't know what I'm supposed to do. All talk and no action."

His father stood in the doorway. Alma smiled to see him leaning in the plastered alcove there between the two rooms to greet the statue that had been there since old Archuleta had built the house. "Hey, lady," Hosea said, "I'm back." He looked at Marcus. "Talk."

Damnit, Marcus was thirty years old, and he couldn't speak for a long moment. Where the hell did he start? His father was scary in the parallel gashes of his eyes and the gaunt-sharp cheekbones, in the absolute stillness of his head and shoulders while only his pupils followed your lips that tried to explain.

Marcus stood up, pacing around the kitchen. "Okay. You went down to the lot cause you heard shootin that night, and you saw the car on fire. You saw a black Jeep with a white dude in it, right?"

His father nodded. "Blond ponytail or something, flyin out the window."

"So you shot at the Jeep?"

"Three shots."

"Then the cops came and you turned around. They shot you. Which way did the Jeep go?" Alma and Abuela kept their heads down, he saw, their fingers moving.

"East along the river, toward the freeway." His father moved slowly to the kitchen door, peering out the glass. He straightened and said, "Let's take this outside."

Marcus knew his father didn't like his mother hearing any of this; Marcus didn't want her to hear about the tire iron, but he didn't want his brothers to know yet, either. All night, all today, he'd prayed no one would go back along the wall and find it. He'd been trying to weigh the choices about who to tell. "Daddy," he said, holding his father's arm. "Come in the living room first. Okay?"

He led his father back to the red leather chair, and then he crouched beside it, speaking low. "So the Jeep went toward the freeway. The girls in the burned car were white chicks I knew in high school. I heard from a friend of one that she was hangin out downtown. And I knew she didn't like brothers." He paused. "So the detectives questioned you big-time."

"I couldn't tell em nothin." Hosea stared at the hills, darkened to magenta.

"No. Neither could Finis. But then, that night we came and got you, remember all the flashin lights?" Hosea nodded. "A guy dressed like a girl got his head bashed in somewhere, and the body got dumped near the wall. Past the trailers."

"Goddamnit," his father said, the force dipping his head. He swung his face around to Marcus. "Somebody's . . ."

Marcus held up his hand. "Yeah. Listen. The cops pulled in Finis, sweated him hard, and when they let him go, he went off and hid somewhere. We haven't looked for him, because we been walkin the fences. And nothin happened for a week, until the paper runs a story sayin no clues yet, no murder weapons." Marcus rocked back on his heels, glancing to the kitchen. He heard the door slam, heavy boots on the tile floor. Leaning forward, he said, "I was walkin last night by the canal, and I heard three guys. I hid in the intake . . ."

"Water runnin?" Hosea frowned.

"Yeah. I could hear them talkin about the Jeep, and that this was like a job for somebody. The cross-dressin guy was extra. And one of em kept talkin about Texas." Marcus rubbed his eyes. "Shootin in Texas. Trees. Like he's from there." .

His father's head jerked back toward the window, and he lifted his chin. "Texas." Marcus heard something choked in his father's throat. "He mention me by name?"

"Huh? You? You been in Texas?"

His father didn't look at him. "Then what?"

Marcus frowned. "Then one threw a tire iron over the fence, behind the olive shed. They argued about this gun, a nine-millimeter somebody shot the girls with. Threw it in the canal, and it probably stuck on the grate."

Demetrius stood in the doorway, arms folded. "Which gate?"

"Hold up, D," Marcus said. "So I went and found the tire iron, behind the olive house. Didn't touch it. It's got blood and long red hair on it. Her hair." He saw the stark-chiseled features and cherry mouth. "His blood."

"On the place?" Demetrius said, his voice rising. "Where?"

"Wait, damnit," Marcus said, louder. He kept his eyes on his father. "These three guys—maybe somebody paid them. Maybe the two girls got killed for drugs. One guy said, 'The dude was extra.' That last guy—dumped like he coulda got it fightin at The Blue Q. So this murder weapon—now it's planted here. But who the hell's gonna believe that happened, that I was in the canal? Sounds like a story I made up—to get Finis off the hook. That's what this cop Harley's gonna think. Do we go to him or what?"

"Shit," Demetrius said, drawing out the word to a prolonged sneer like he always did. "I'ma find out who settin us up and take his ass *out*. He ain't fuckin up this family."

Marcus waited for his father to speak, but his father was still staring out at the hills. The houses in Agua Dulce were a collage of tiny pastel squares on the slopes. Marcus said, "Demetrius, man, you take him out, or these three dudes, you go down for murder. Or one of us shoot whoever trespass next, and we go down. Whoever's plannin all this can't be comin around. Those guys were young—two white boys and one I can't figure. Somebody wants us in jail, then he don't care if we all kill each other off."

Demetrius said, "What—you gon call the cops and let em take you downtown? Cause you know that's where you goin. And you'll screw up your job. You got a good gig, Marcus. You can't lose it."

"A good gig?" Marcus looked at Demetrius's eyes; his brother turned and slammed his palm against the plaster.

Hosea turned to them and spoke softly. "We gon call Salcido's son."

"He came by my crib and told me what was goin on, Daddy," Marcus said. "He's in a rough spot, you know."

"Call him," his father said. "We're close enough to blood. And if them three voices you heard done got rid of the weapons, they finished. We need the other one paid em. Ax Salcido what to do. Ax him about the gun in the canal."

Una mosca en la leche. A fly in the milk. That's what Salcido told Paz his great-nephew was in the sheriff's department. If he arrested Agua Dulce men, people hissed, "Tío Taco!" at him. But downtown, he still looked like a wetback.

Paz watched the men in uniforms hop down awkwardly into the dry canal. She sat in her chair outside the olive house, in the sun. Her bones softened in the warmth, her huge knuckles glowed and her spine loosened. The men talked loudly to each other, pacing down the channel so that only their heads bobbed like coconuts. She stood and walked over to the fence, hiding behind an olive trunk, looking down the canal.

They had to stop the water to search for the gun; that's what the nephew said, according to Salcido. Her *perico* great-grandson had seen someone throw the gun into the water, and his great-nephew had told these men where to look.

She saw the water grass lying limp and brown after a day of dry heat; at the grate, where two men bent, the thatch of trash and grasses was solid, as wide as a sea turtle caught and splayed on the metal. The men reached into the turtle's belly with gloved hands and shook their heads. They threw stones and hangers and fish skeletons into the channel, and then one drew out the black gun, holding it aloft daintily like a piece of desiccated fruit.

Detective Harley and the younger cop with the moustache like a frayed, thick broom were waiting at his father's place when he got there. Marcus put down his school papers carefully in his mother's kitchen, where his mother sat at the table watching him. "Let me go help these guys out," Marcus said casually, turning his face away fast.

"Come on downtown, so we can write this whole thing down at a comfortable table," Harley said easily, walking toward Marcus.

"So you're saying I'm a suspect now?" Marcus asked, leaning against the adobe wall by the door, covering the star with his back. "All I did was tell you what I saw."

The moustache hiding the mouth said, "Pretty funny, pretty coincidental, that you strolled on up right after we found Bessier, huh?"

But Harley was obviously the one in charge. "We're not worried about that, McCartin. Come on, Marcus. Let's get all this out on paper, so you can assist me with the whole sequence, okay?"

Marcus stared at his smiling insistence, at the ridges of dark hair over Harley's eyes and on his knuckles when he extended his hand.

He sat numb in the back of the unmarked car, staring at the dashboard.

In the station, he walked erect behind them, and he sat in the chair Harley pulled out for him in the square, windowless room.

Harley sat across from him, pen poised over notebook paper, but McCartin leaned in the corner behind him, only a floating bend of elbow visible when Marcus glanced left. "Okay," Marcus said. "It's gonna be kinda long."

Harley smiled. "It's already been long, a long story. Go ahead."

Marcus told him the whole sequence of events, beginning with what his father had said about the black Jeep and the ponytail, ending with the clipped fence and the figures near the canal. He mentioned nothing about The Blue Q, but he left nothing out that had happened on his father's place.

Harley wrote steadily, and then he was silent. Marcus didn't sit back, didn't want to see the thick elbow hovering near him; he stared at the table edge.

McCartin spoke from behind him: "Like somebody's gonna carry around a bloody tire iron all the time and just now remember—Hey, that's right, I have to get on down to Treetown and drop this off? Not very professional, huh, if, like you said, it's supposed to be a *job*."

Marcus was quiet, watching the table tremble slightly under the weight of Harley's pencil when he erased something and wrote again.

"These white guys *walk* all the way to Jung—to Treetown, and no home boys notice them and jam them up?" McCartin waited. "And what kind of nicknames are those supposed to be? Bodie? Come on. No, man, that doesn't sound very professional to me. Sounds more like a psycho amateur job, okay? Like your nutcase brother Finis. Hell, he sat there talking about Mississippi and motherships. Finis must have paid you guys a visit—hey, even if you didn't *see* him personally, he must have dropped the weapon off there, right? He come around for anything else lately?"

Marcus kept his eyes focused on the shaking table. There's a worm in the ground—he only comes around when he wants to get down. "Nobody's seen him since . . ."

"Since he sat where your ass is parked," McCartin said.

Harley stood up abruptly and said, "Okay, McCartin, thanks for keeping Mr. Thompson company. I'm a slow writer. Can you get us some coffee right now? Appreciate it."

The elbow swung within a few inches of Marcus's head, and the door behind him shut hard.

Harley sat on the edge of the table, stretching his arms over his head briefly, and then he pulled out the chair to straddle it, facing Marcus. The notebook lay open near his hands. "Okay. Your father was the only one anywhere near the scene when the two girls were killed in the car. All your brothers have women for alibis." He grinned. "Pretty funny, huh? Demetrius and, uh, Octavious were at home." He looked at the notebook. "Julius was with a woman in Olive Gardens. She's not a great talker, but plenty of other women saw him, too. And Finis was supposedly, according to your mother, with this woman named SaRonn. Lives in a little place down there in Treetown. Real close to your father's place." He grinned again. "Now you, you're the only brother living downtown, working downtown, and no woman's spoken up for you."

"Very funny," Marcus said, breathing hard. "I was at a restaurant until about ten, and then I went home to grade papers. I didn't even have a car—mine was stolen the week before."

Harley pulled his face back in surprise. "Oh—you think I'm accusing you of participating in something?" He shook his head. "Nope. I'm not. Look, obviously your father didn't kill Bessier, since he was in the hospital. And I don't think he had anything to do with the women. I don't. But I can't help thinking that Finis has the kind of derangement necessary to pull off stunts like this." His voice had grown harder. "And I think you'd cover up for him. Hey—you knew Pammy Sawicky, didn't you?"

Marcus looked at Harley's reasonable brown eyes. "Yeah, I knew who she was in high school."

"You guys graduated the same year," Harley said. "Not too many Treetown home boys at Rio Seco High then, right?"

"I'm not a home boy," Marcus said. "Okay?"

"I'm just saying, Finis didn't go to Rio Seco. His was the last class to stay at the school in Treetown, and then I guess he dropped out. So maybe he never got to meet white girls, like you did. You go out with any white girls downtown now?"

"You're stepping way off," Marcus said, folding his fingers tightly in front of him. "We're about done, right?" He tried to keep his flooding heart from rising into his voice.

Harley stood up abruptly. "Yeah. Just about. I've got three dead people and some story about guys named Sketch and Tweak and Bodie. You don't even know what race the Bodie guy is. And he talks about the jungle, according to your tale. Maybe Bodie's somebody's nickname for Finis."

"He doesn't have any nicknames," Marcus said.

"Maybe you don't know everything about him. You've been downtown a long time. Maybe you don't know Treetown like you used to, Marcus." Harley went by him to open the door.

Paz watched the water run back along its course, dredging up the strawdry grass and carrying it in small rafts to gather again on the cleaned grate. From her chair, moved near the fence, she could see that the canal banks were in some disrepair. Long ago, Indian and black men, like her granddaughter's husband, had waded into the trembling water to clear weeds and choking vines, to clean and patch the channels. Then they would catch fish and pile them in baskets along the banks.

She sat near the water for days, sometimes thinking of the black gun and the etched, floating face, sometimes seeing the fairy moths dart near the canal and the bats dip sharply to the surface. No rain, for the seventh season. In Mexico, only the olive trees and cactus would survive. People's ribs would show like ripples, and babies' skulls would hang far too large on their twiglike necks.

But here, in California, the water crept along in regulated ribbons, even though the clouds had gathered and then parted as if God breathed down heavily to watch the land.

She stared across the riverbottom at the ridge of hills circling this valley. The river wound from the mountains, shielding lowlands from the desert, stretching through each valley until the flat land near the ocean opened up like a fan. She knew this because she'd worked nearly every field in every plain all along the coast. The rivers forked like lightning when they felt the pull of the sea.

In that ridge of hills, when the land below had been strawberry fields owned by Japanese, she and the others had had work for months. In the early spring, the months just passed; between planting and harvest, they weeded. The ground would be black and wet, the green weeds springing up and holding tenaciously to the furrows. When they pulled, the roots clung to balls of soil.

During the evenings, she and some others would walk up into the oak-studded hills looking for wild onions and garlic, the men with guns in case they saw rabbits or birds. And after the heavy rains, shallow pools would appear among the oaks and rolling slopes of new grass. The pools were wide enough to attract ducks and herons, and after the men shot once and hoped to hit their meal for the night, the women wandered down to the now silent edges of the pools. Paz would squat and study the lilting, fringed movement in the water, lit clear by the low sun. Tiny *camarones*, shrimp with curved backs and lacy legs, danced in the shallows like fairy ghosts. She was entranced, staring for so long that the others had to call her from further down the slopes.

When her daughter was born, she had taken her to see the fairies every spring. "Where do they go when the water is gone?" her daughter had asked, and Paz thought for a long time.

"They spin hard webs around themselves and hide in the earth until spring comes again," she said. "Or they die and their spirits must float down with the drops."

Then, in the 1930s, the rain fell for two weeks without stopping. When the skies had cleared, those in the migrant camp had ventured out of their shacks to see the dead chickens floating in brown muck and the cars mired up to their windows. Paz looked across the riverbottom churning wide, and saw a lake.

A true lake, stretching wide enough to show blue nestled at the base of the hills for months. Reeds grew along its edge, animals built their homes nearby, and people rowed across the water. A woman older than Paz told her that she had seen the lake twice before. She was an Indian from one of the *rancherías* south of Agua Dulce, one who worked in the rich houses downtown, and she spoke Spanish. *"Espíritu,"* she told Paz. *"Lago Espíritu."*

The lake drained itself into the river after a few years, and Paz had only seen it once since then, in 1969 when the river tore out the Pepper Avenue bridge and tumbled boulders all along the course. Espíritu Lake was smaller that time, and it had evaporated more quickly. More people were breathing its moisture, Paz thought.

She looked at the hills, brittle gold now. Spring had been only a moist drag of tongue across the land, a few coughs, and summer had beat down like steady, molten copper. She settled against the walls of the olive house, in the shade. She'd watched the tree bark and the birds and she'd smelled the ground. This winter would bring heavy silver frost, and then rain.

CHAPTER EIGHT

FUNKYTOWN. THAT'S WHERE he had to go after school today, because he couldn't find any way to talk to his Uncle Marcus at school. He couldn't just casually walk up after ancient history and tell his uncle that his mother wanted something. The date. She knew the date, and she needed a ride.

Mortrice hung with B-Real and Chris at lunch. B-Real helped him classify everyone by their clothes and music and words and cars. It was easy when you knew the rules. The codes.

All the white kids, who'd seemed a floating and faceless mass that swarmed around him like swerving headlights the first weeks, had their own categories. Goths wore black clothes, had bottle-black hair and skin as pale as mayonnaise. Tweakers were high on speed, wore dirty clothes, and had faces full of sores. Caspers were rich, with thick sweaters and teeth like white fences.

Brainiacs were mostly white, but a few brothers and Chicano kids joined their tight knots at lunch. B-Real said they were practicing for a Model United Nations, so they kept calling themselves by countries.

The brothers were either Jocks, scattered Brainiacs, or Worlds.

Worlds came in all colors. Whatever their hair, they wore dreadlocks, and wire-rimmed glasses, beads, berets. They listened to reggae and other off-beat music. Mortrice thought that B-Real, in his soul, wanted to be a World.

But he was from Olive Gardens. And Worlds got their asses kicked in the Gardens.

Mortrice sat in his last class, English, studying the heads in front of

him. He looked down at his hand. He was tattooed now, the cut from
the metal sliver etched dark from the gunpowder he'd rubbed in while
it healed. On the plump, meaty backhand side, in the cleft of webbing,
was where girls tattooed their man's initials and a heart or cross surrounded by teardrops if he was doing time.

I got a better one, he thought.

And he knew what he would do if Chris and B-Real took him to
the guy they said could get him a gun. The guy who knew a dealer
who'd sell him a nine. He had a name picked out for them, and a place
for their marks.

He went to Funkytown on foot, telling Chris he didn't need a ride, so
no one would see him talking to his uncle. He walked through the
fancy area of hotels and big buildings, then circled back around to the
restaurants in the narrow doorways, the shops with incense and vases
and bread. B-Real like this place, he thought. I don't really know what
go on in the brother's head. He think he could put him on a beret and
be cool over here. He don't know shit.

He knew his uncle had had a meeting after school, and he waited
near the archway trying to look casual, hoping he wouldn't see any
5–0 patrol cruising. When his uncle stepped past the thick concrete
doorway, he was careful to say, "It's Mortrice, right here, it's me."

His uncle had swung around like an opening door, smashing backward
against the cement. "Damn, don't be sneakin up on people!" he said.

Mortrice held himself still. "Ain't nobody sneakin. I was just standin
here." He watched his uncle move slowly up the stairs. "Why you all
nervous?"

"Life is a nervous proposition, okay?" Marcus said, more like himself.

In the apartment, definitely decorated World, Mortrice didn't sit
on the black leather couch. He touched the brass candlesticks on the
windowsill and said, "I only came cause Mama say next Saturday. That's
the day. She need you take her somewhere."

Marcus looked surprised; Mortrice had thought he'd know what she
was talking about. "She say where?" he asked, and Mortrice shook his
head, smelling incense.

"Just say can you pick her up after lunch."

"Yeah," his uncle said, sitting on the couch, rubbing his forehead. "Tell her yeah."

"What you drivin?" Mortrice said, leaning against the wall. "That old truck?"

"Only till my dad's shoulder moves better, stops hurtin him."

Mortrice hesitated. "You nervous cause a them bodies?"

Marcus looked up. "What are you talkin about?" he said, hard.

"You told me." Mortrice looked at his uncle's murky, tired eyes.

"I forgot," Marcus said. "Yeah. I mean, no, I'm not sure what the hell's goin on." He frowned at Mortrice. "Why? You know somethin?"

Mortrice shook his head, moving for the door. "I just axed, okay? I heard at school the dude dress like a woman was wearin makeup. This dude, I heard him say that fit his band he was startin. The Humma-nequins. Somethin like that."

His uncle was still frowning, eyes squinting and forehead crumpled like he was hurting, so Mortrice said, "Don't forget, she said Saturday." He ran down the narrow steps and through the arches that felt like tunnels.

At the Gardens, he went into the apartment to check on his mother. She was sitting at the table in the one small room, smoking. She'd begun smoking when they'd moved here, and she sat there holding the cigarettes tightly, watching the ashes grow like caterpillars, staring at the shiny purple fabric she'd hung over the curtains already on the window.

After a while, he told her, "I gotta go see this friend. From school. He gotta give me somethin I need."

She nodded, her eyes moving fast. They were clear and glossy, since she slept for hours, and her braid was always neat. But her hands never stopped tapping and shaking and curling around the embers.

He went four doors down to where Chris lived. The guy who knew the guy—he was supposed to meet them there today. Julius. He had been with Chris's mama, and he was going to hang out today. Chris said they could get him to take them to the guy with the guns.

"What up?" he said to Chris.

"Ain't nothin but a party," Chris said, rolling his eyes toward the apartment behind him. "Shit. Too many people in there all the time."

Mortrice followed him inside. A large, soft-faced woman sat in a kitchen chair, in the same position as his mother, but this woman was sorting through black-eyed peas, and her legs filled the chair with flowered rolls. She glanced up at them, and then shook her head.

Two women sat on the couch, dark and full-faced like the older one, but their bodies were angular and knuckled. One held a crying baby, and the other talked on the phone. Two small girls trailed in and out of the bedroom carrying pillows, and another girl about ten snatched the pillows back and disappeared.

Mortrice followed Chris on his circling motions through the living room, back out to the narrow strip of concrete fronting the apartments, inside again to ask, "Mama! Julius comin by or not?"

The pretty woman, her eyes tilted up and mouth lined with brown, was saying into the phone, "Niggaplease. You know you lyin."

"Mama!"

Chris's mother put her fingers over the phone and said, "Who in the hell know but him? Okay?"

After a dizzying hour of motion, Chris had interrupted his mother enough times that she'd hung up and hollered at him, "I wasn't lookin for that fool Julius to come by! I was tryin to talk to somebody else! Get out my *face*, boy!"

Mortrice heard a car pull up to the walkway, though, and he turned casually so that he wouldn't seem too eager to meet the man. A woman got out, her face full-cheeked and her eyes tilted high, too, but her skin light copper and her hair in a bun. She held a small boy who cried big, stuttering sobs. "I wanna go home now!" he said.

"Shit," Chris muttered beside Mortrice. "My auntie and some more noise."

Enchantee looked at the boys hovering in the doorway like slumping, broken-backed dolls wearing the wrong clothes. Her cousin Zefi's boy Chris and another little Gardens gangster. She went inside, D'Junior burying his face in her already wet neck, and her aunt said, "Oh, no. Uh-uh. They rippin and runnin enough in there without another one."

Enchantee tightened her jaw. "You see I just got off work. I came by to visit. I ain't leavin him here. He don't believe me, neither." She set D'Junior down and pushed him away from her legs. "Go! Go play with your cousins!" He stumbled toward her, eyes splashing fresh, and she pushed harder. "Do I look like I'm playin?" she shouted. "Go on!"

He turned, wailing, and the girls herded him toward the back room. Enchantee could hear the ten-year-old, Stevie, say, "Don't pay no tention to her. They get like that."

Enchantee went past her aunt to the tiny kitchen for a glass of water. She hated doing that, showing them all that she wasn't spoiling him by being too kind. Sign of weakness: Can't have that. Whenever she held D'Junior and talked to him softly, trying to explain something like why she had to go to work, or why the girls didn't like to share, her aunt and cousins rolled their eyes and tipped their heads to the side scornfully.

"Makin him *weak*," her cousins would say.

"He do it cause he better," her aunt would say. "Cause you told him to or he get his ass beat. Ain't no need to tell him nothin. Put that boy down."

Because that's the way Auntie was raised, and they were raised, and that was the only way, Enchantee thought. The kitchen was a slot barely wide enough for one person, but every dish was clean and the floor smelled of ammonia. The bathroom was another slot, and the bedroom was exactly the square size of the living room. Every room was clean, from the curtains to the walls. Aunt Zepherine's worst insult, which she uttered often at Olive Gardens, was, "She keep a nasty house."

Enchantee turned to look out the door. Each woman had her own little square of grass to share with the upstairs neighbor. Upstairs people had railings for hanging wash, but downstairs people had to use the chain-link fence. She could see the clothes, like flags, strung all along the boundaries of the complex, see the shadows of the two boys like sentries.

Her aunt glanced up. "What you want?" And that don't mean she can't stand me, Enchantee thought. She glanced at DeeDee and Zefi, expressionless on the couch.

"Two worst things ruin a week," she said, sitting at the tiny dinette table. "Sick kid and a sick truck."

"What he got?"

"Just a cold." Enchantee reached for the black-eyed peas, leaning forward to listen for D'Junior. She heard no screaming from the bedroom.

"He all right," her aunt said. "What you want, now?"

"I wanted to ask you about Mrs. Smith, live on Plymouth Hill. You said you hated her house."

"Huh? Why you want to know about that house?" Her aunt got up to dump the peas into a pot.

Enchantee watched the people gesture wildly on a soap. "Her daughter Abby, the one I went to school with, she has a boy same age as D'Junior. She wants them to play together this week. Play date." She smiled and went on. "She needs somebody to watch him, help her out. An assistant. She works for the paper."

"She wants a maid," Zefi said from the couch.

"No, they got somebody to clean," Enchantee said, irritated. "And she's payin seven bucks an hour. Cash. Demetrius said the differential went out on the big truck, so we need the money. He's been workin on it for days. And you know his daddy got them big hospital bills comin."

Her aunt was silent for a time. "Mrs. Smith—she didn't want to see you while you was there. She was a artist, she always said. Painted flowers from her yard. Always talkin about she was sensitive for noises and smells, so her kids had to be somewhere else and I had to tippytoe around." She paused, her dimples pooling when she closed her mouth. Then she said, "The toilets had to have blue water, smelled like it went straight in my eyes. And flowers all over. All them smells was too sharp, made my head hurt."

Enchantee watched her aunt get down a bag of potato chips. Like magic, the bedroom door opened and the girls came out, hearing the crackling plastic. Her aunt poured the chips into a big bowl and set it on the table. "Y'all know better," Enchantee said to the reaching hands. "One handful, and don't make a mess. You, too, boy." Her aunt was strangely silent.

Enchantee ate a few chips, hearing the girls laugh and D'Junior say, "I'm a rabbit—look!"

"It was the things she said," her aunt said, harsh, her arms folding tight under her full chest. "She thought she was perfect. When I told her I couldn't come no more, I heard her talkin on the phone in the kitchen. Talkin bout I was so fat and probably rather sit home and get welfare."

Enchantee bit the inside of her lip. She and Janine had talked about that at work, how when you stood in the grocery checkout line, people

automatically looked at how you paid for your food. Glancing. Especially
if you had kids with you.

Her aunt said, "Look. I had me a figure when I came out here to
California. I was seventeen. Your mama had passed, and they sent me
out here with you. You was three." She stopped, looking up at the
low ceiling. Zefi and DeeDee had gone outside to talk to someone in
a car. Enchantee stared at her aunt's glowing neck, the fold like a
necklace. "All the women in them houses downtown figured I already
had a kid, I wasn't nothin. The men seen you and thought I might as
well have some more. When they daddy came round, wasn't no good
to say no." Her aunt stopped. "And then she talk about I'm so fat. She
didn't know me for shit."

Enchantee stared down at the gold flecks in the Formica table. She
remembered hearing men at The Blue Q talk about her aunt, about
"all that good jelly shakin on them bones." She couldn't say anything.

Her aunt walked into the bedroom, turning to say, "Go on and work
for her daughter. You think you ain't me anyway. So you probably be
fine." Her laughter huffed from her chest, and Enchantee felt her face
flush hot.

In the car, D'Junior said, "I see a motorcycle, Mama."

"Mm-hmm." Enchantee felt them fall into the chant-and-response
of late afternoon. She stared at the cars on Pepper Avenue, racing along
the riverbottom. She hadn't seen Demetrius or the flatbed truck in his
father's yard.

"I see a bumpdragon," he said.

"A what?" Enchantee frowned.

D'Junior pointed to a Volkswagen in the distance. "Daddy tell me."

"Whatever."

"I got a present," he sang. "Stevie gave it to me."

"Yeah?" she murmured, seeing the stream of cars on the freeway
entrance.

"She said it was for boys. Not girls."

Enchantee went up the ramp and wedged the car into the slow lane,
thinking they could eat pork chops and rice. Yeah. And the last of the
apricots from Alma. "What is it?" she said absently.

"See?" D'Junior uncurled his fingers, and a shining copper-nosed bullet lay long in his small palm.

"What are you doin with that!" Enchantee shouted, snatching the bullet, the car swerving. She righted the steering, clenching her hand around the heavy thing.

"It's mine!" he shouted back. "Stevie find it in the yard! She said it's for boys!"

Enchantee stopped listening, even when he cried and screamed. She drove with one hand, refusing to open the other, seeing the bullets in the yard where they'd lived in Treetown. She'd found one herself, when Demetrius had still been touching her pregnant belly, and she'd told him they had to move. The constant sounds of shots that had just begun, then, from the Gardens, were like thudding cantaloupes against her windows. She'd seen the shells in the street; she'd seen the bullet in his heart, in her baby's heart.

Blindly, she drove into Rivercrest. Demetrius had always had a gun, but she had never actually seen it. He kept it in his truck, or when he walked his father's property. When she pulled into the driveway, seeing him lying underneath the flatbed on the street, Demetrius Junior stopped crying.

"Mama! See Madison and Morgan? They ridin bikes!"

Enchantee dropped the bullet into her pocket. She watched him run into the open garage and take out his Big Wheel, and she wiped his wet face with her sleeve, walking out to the street with him.

"Be right back," she called to Demetrius's boots.

Across the street, Janny, the twin girls' mother, was standing in her driveway wearing what Enchantee thought was the uniform of stay-home mothers in the development: jeans, boots, a V-necked pastel T-shirt, and lines of blue drawn inside her lower eyelids.

But Enchantee liked Janny, because she always made fun of the fertility drugs she'd taken when she got desperate for kids, of the way the twins liked each other more than her, of the uselessness of trying to keep the house clean.

"Hey," Janny called. "We need a guy for racing purposes!" She smiled at D'Junior charging forward on the Big Wheel. Enchantee put her hand into her pocket and felt the bullet wedged tight into the lining. She smiled.

•   •   •

Marcus rubbed his eyes hard when he parked at Donut Place. It was Monday morning, and he'd been grading papers all weekend. He needed two soft glazed, some yeasty layers of fat and sugar, before class.

Som's wife, Phally, came out from the back, where Marcus knew they spent much of their time with their small son. Marcus always heard him playing behind the thin wall dividing the shop from the back. "Oh, Mista Teacha!" Phally said. "I look for you."

"Marcus," he reminded her, but she always shook her head, her licorice-dark eyes wide.

"In my country, teacha get respect from every people," she said. "Not like here. My husband nephew, he never study, he stay out from school."

"Then I hope he's smart," Marcus said. Som came from the back, his eyes bleary but opening when he saw Marcus.

"I hope I see you," Som said, coming around the counter to propel Marcus toward the back. "Come, come back here, because my nephew, he get me in trouble at the school and I don't do nothing. You have to tell them they don't know about this. This is from my country." Som's voice rose and fell softly, as always, the cadences strange and faintly Spanish to Marcus even though he knew Cambodian wasn't close.

The nephew stood in the crowded back room, his thin chest rising hard under a black T-shirt, his forehead sheened with sweat. His skin was dark, his hair waving black and his eyes long and tilted. He looked blankly at Marcus, and his uncle grabbed his arm and spoke angrily in Cambodian. Som turned to Marcus. "He just come home, just now, he stay out all night and my wife, she scare where he go."

"Hey, Samana," Marcus said. "I've seen you in Mr. Whalen's class, right?" He smelled gasoline, acrid and sharp, on the boy's shirt. "You run out of gas?"

"Yeah," Samana said, smiling slight and thin. "You run out of dough-nuts?"

His uncle interrupted with another stream of Cambodian, and Samana said, "Okay! They call me into the office and the school cop guy, he want me to tell about my uncle. About my skin."

Marcus saw the long, purple stripes on the side of Samana's neck when he turned to show them. They were hickey bruises like they had to have been applied by a girl with precision lips and teeth, Marcus thought, but then Samana showed Marcus his inner arms, also lined with oblong marks. He turned and raised his shirt when his uncle poked him, and the stripes radiated from his spine like branches.

"The police, they come to arrest me," Som said. "They say I have to go to jail, me or my wife."

"They think you beat him up," Marcus said. "That's what it looks like. A hell of a belt, or a stick."

"No, no," Som said, shaking his head. "He take the bad wind, he have fever from the bad wind."

The boy looked bored, leaning against the TV now. "It's like you get sick, and you have to get the shit out."

His uncle's face darkened, and he pushed the boy hard enough to jar his elbow from the wood-grain top. "See? No respect. But I don't go to jail."

Marcus felt his throat grow warm, remembering all the beatings he'd seen his friends get, with switches still running sap. "How'd you do that to him?" he said casually.

Som pulled a dime from his pocket, and took a jar of mentholatum from a shelf. He squatted, applied a shiny smear to his inner arm, and scraped hard with the dime. The serrated edges pulled red trails in his skin. "This take out the bad wind. You do it good. The headache go, fever go. You finish." He looked up at Marcus.

His nephew said, "It only work if you're Cambodian," smiling at Marcus. But his eyes, as black as the empty screen, darker than any brother's Marcus knew, were not amused. Marcus frowned—something about the voice was echoing in his head.

"Why didn't you tell them at school it was just a cure?" Marcus said to him while his uncle went back to the front of the shop. Marcus folded his arms.

"I don't like tell Cambodian stories," Samana said, sitting down on the couch and leaning his head far back. Marcus stared at a long, fresh scratch just along the boy's jawline, under the bone. It was hidden when he snapped his head back down.

"You tired, huh? Staying out all night partying?" Marcus said, turning for the doorway.

"Yeah," Samana said, his voice flatter than his uncle's, without as much lilt. "American style."

Marcus heard the siren when he took the box of doughnuts from Som, and they both stared through the plate-glass window at the patrol car speeding past, heading toward Treetown. "Always trouble down there," Som said. "So early the morning."

Marcus rubbed his razor cut again. "Trouble out west," he murmured, to Som's frown. "Thanks for the doughnuts. I'll pull Samana out of class tomorrow and make him tell his story at the office."

Near the window, Marcus saw the garlanded shrine in the corner. Phally knelt to put three fresh doughnut holes and a steaming cup of coffee at the feet of the Buddha, between the gently smoking sticks of incense. Som called, "I do that cure on you, if you get a bad wind, okay?"

"Only works on Cambodians," Marcus said.

"No! Work on the skin," Som called.

Marcus started across the parking lot, thinking, Treetown got their own remedies. Uncle Oscar tell you a drink of his choc cure any bacteria or virus. That alcohol knock the sickness and you out cold.

After work, he went to the gym. He'd been hoping to see Tony Salcido in the Palmas Deli or maybe Kurt's place, but now that he saw the familiar stride on the StairMaster, Salcido's eyes slid away quickly.

Marcus changed from his school clothes in the locker room. Salcido wasn't going to talk to him. He hadn't come by Marcus's apartment or his father's place since Marcus had told him about the weapons. After Harley's questioning, Marcus had stayed inside his apartment for days, going over and over the story, knowing how concocted it sounded to the detectives. Harley had waited for him in the school parking lot one day and said quietly, "We did the ballistics, Marcus. The nine fired the bullet into your friend from the old days. Pammy Sawicky. But it's a stolen weapon, and no fingerprints, right? They all got scoured off by the trash and water movement. Pretty convenient. And the tire iron was wiped nice and clean. So thanks for the find, but any time you decide to let us in on the rest, you let me know. I'm still figuring we'll have to make that other find, right? The person we discussed? You'll keep in touch, and so will I, right?"

He didn't want to talk to Salcido about the killings. He wanted to ask if Rubén had seen any traces of Finis. Marcus had finally ventured back out to the riverbottom, trying to walk casually down the paths past homeless guys with elaborate shelters in the cane. Many of them had been burned out two years past, when a series of fires had swept through the cane and trees, but now the brush was thick with summer, and Marcus saw hammocks, beds, bamboo furniture. He didn't see his brother.

Usher hadn't seen Finis at the Kozy Komfort. And SaRonn hadn't been home when he stopped by her house. Marcus walked behind Salcido, knowing that too many law enforcement guys worked out at this gym for Salcido to be friendly there. Not since I'm a Thompson. From Treetown. Shit.

Salcido stared at the TV screen, and Marcus went to the last machine in the row. A short, soft-bodied woman with blond hair in a smooth cap around her forehead smiled at him when he stepped up. He smiled back, thinking she looked like someone he'd seen, but then he concentrated on the flashing numbers.

"Didn't you go to the art college?" the woman said. "In— "

"In 1982," Marcus said. "Just for a year."

"I remember you. You went out with my roommate. Enchantee."

"Yeah," Marcus said, looking down at the red bars pulsing and blinking.

"I'm Abby," she said. "You don't remember?"

"Marcus," he said. "Yeah, I do. But I don't know if Enchantee would want me to tell you."

"What?" She laughed, leaning closer. "Come on. She and I just got to be friends again."

Marcus grinned. "She told me you helped her with her makeup or something."

Abby threw back her head to laugh, and her pale neck was laced with lavender veins. "She's still so beautiful," she said, her eyes glinting. "And she never notices anyone looking at her."

"Yeah," Marcus said again.

"Well, what are you doing now?"

"Teaching history at Rio Seco High."

"Oh, I loved that place. But I started skipping class, and my mother sent me to private school. I kicked around a lot before I went to the art college. I'm the food and travel writer for the newspaper now. We're doing that new weekly magazine."

"Yeah, I like that," Marcus said. "You gave my buddy's place a good review. Chipotle Chile."

"I *love* that place!" she said. "They're doing a great job."

Stepping off, her hair sticking together in tiny spears over her forehead, she said, "Come by sometime, because my fiancé and I are always having people over. We get bored in quiet old Rio Seco—we were in Boston before. But downtown's really trying harder. Chani and I are taking our kids to the Streetscape thing next week, you know, the art market and concert evening."

"Chani?" Marcus asked.

"Oh, she used to go by that in school." She toweled her face. "Hey, here's Bent right now."

A thin-shouldered man with a blond ponytail put his arm on her shoulders. "This is Marcus," Abby said. "We went to the art college, with Chani. Bent's writing about music for the paper."

"Nice to meet you," Bent said, and Marcus nodded.

"You like any particular kind of music?" Marcus asked.

"Well, jazz, blues, classical, Stones," Bent said. "I'm not too much into metal or New Age. Hey, I'm over thirty and I admit it." He smiled. "But I love rap."

"You like women singers, you should listen to the university station on Thursday nights. My friend does a hell of a show."

Bent nodded eagerly. "Cool. Hey, I hope we see you sometime, so we can talk songs."

Abby added, "Come on by. We're trying to get a salon going! Like the old days. Chani's got my number."

Marcus saw Salcido watching him when the couple left. Salcido stepped off his machine, too, and lifted his chin for farewell.

It was still early when he looked into the Chipotle Chile, but Javier saw him and unlocked the glass-paned door.

"Hey, I'm not even beggin for food today," Marcus said to Kurt, who sat in the corner booth with Javier and another man. "Just wanted to tell you congrats for the good pub in the paper."

But Kurt didn't smile. He was reading a letter on the table. Javier said, "They cremate the box, too? That's crazy."

"Who?" Marcus asked, sitting next to the unfamiliar man.

"Bessier. Jean-Luc Bessier." Kurt looked at Marcus's frown. "The guy that got killed a few weeks ago down in Treetown. It was in the paper. Back page," he said bitterly.

Javier said, "His family doesn't want to pay for his body to go back to France. That's where he's from."

Kurt folded his arms and leaned against the wall. "No front page fucking headlines for a dead faggot. No one cares. No one wants him. No services. I don't even know the fucking guy."

"Marcus, this is Ernesto, he works at the coroner's office taking pictures," Javier said. The guy nodded at Marcus. "He told us no one's claiming the body."

"We're gonna get some money together to cremate him. Have a service on the ocean," Ernesto said.

"Faggot funeral," Kurt said, closing his eyes.

"Fucking stop it," Javier said. "Quit whining. We need to get the money together. I'm gonna put out a jar in here for people who know."

Marcus watched Javier write out a sign for the big jar. "Funeral expenses for a friend," he read. He saw the chiseled face and swerve of red hair, and he closed his eyes, too. He couldn't say anything. He didn't want to imagine what the face looked like now, where the long red hair was.

"I've had to do this too many times already," Ernesto said. "But usually it's AIDS. I'm so tired of people dying."

"Me, too," Marcus said at the same time Kurt did. When they looked at him, he pulled out his wallet. "Here's the first donation, " he said, dropping a twenty into the jar and heading out the door, thinking of how the dead man's eyelashes had been thick as fans above his startled eyes.

Whenever he walked, he felt a corresponding stride or swinging pair of eyes. Twice now, Mortrice had startled him by stepping out from the darkness to talk. And when he drove to Treetown, he always felt a pair of headlights as persistent as trailing gnats.

He pulled his father's truck into the space near the barn, and Kickstand's face appeared from behind the hood of an old Cadillac. "You still foolin people, drivin your daddy's truck?" Kickstand said. "Makin em think you somebody got sense?"

"Everybody over at Uncle Oscar's?" Marcus said.

"He got a ton of chitlins over there, gettin ready for all them Texas and Oklahoma people celebrate Juneteenth," Kickstand said. "I'm from Texas. And nary one a you Treetown niggas probably bring me no chitlins back."

"Oh, man, I'll try not to forget you," Marcus said, grinning. "Except I ain't got no sense."

He tried the kitchen door, since, for the first time, his mother had begun to lock it. Getting out his key, he saw that all the windows closed. No one was inside, and he studied the row of keys on the wall pegs. He picked the single key attached to a polished green stone.

In the late afternoon light, hundreds of gold strings looked hung from the trees near Finis's trailer. Inside, the air was close and already dark. Marcus opened the window near the table and let in a dusty glow that touched the bones, stones, and glass covering every surface except the small bed.

He didn't want to disturb the order Finis had carefully arranged here, the bones in several piles that he could identify as small animal teeth, cow vertebrae, and long, thin extremities. The stones were random to Marcus. He stared at four jagged glass shards as big as his palm. They were brown, but iridescent with mottled purple, gold, and magenta swirls.

He remembered the day Finis had found them in the baked-hard ground across the river, up in the Diamondback Hills, not too far up because the boys were afraid of the tangled snakes people said writhed in dens among the boulders.

Marcus looked at the rounded pebbles edging the dusty sink. Marcus touched the line of green stones connected like a caterpillar near the faucet, and locked the door carefully.

He didn't look at the leaves near the wall when he walked the few feet to his uncle's. The police had trampled them thoroughly. Marcus saw the wrought-iron gate, locked, too, and he wedged his tennis shoes into the stones to climb over.

The men were gathered in the back dirt area behind the kitchen, where white five-gallon pails of chitterlings sat between chairs and several metal washtubs full of water. Marcus looked first for his father, who was sitting motionless, his left hand clamped around his elbow; when the shoulder hurt, Marcus had seen, his father held himself like that.

"This downtown fool probably done forgot how to clean chitlins," Uncle Oscar said, looking up, and Marcus's father lifted one side of a grin around a cigarillo.

Demetrius said, "You want to eat em, you got to clean em."

Marcus picked up a short, sharp knife on the counter inside the open back door and sat down on the folding chair between Demetrius and Octavious. Julius was inside, talking to his aunt.

Marcus began scraping the shit off the pale intestines, pushing hard. "You know somebody told us once he use a power drill with a wire brush to do this?" he said.

"Old man out there past the Gardens," Demetrius said. "Gaskins."

"Any way you do it, it's gon be work," Oscar said. "I seen men stretch em out across the yard, they was so long before they cut em. I seen women pick at em with they fingers, gettin the stuff off. I gotta have me the right knife."

Then they were silent. Marcus watched the lumpy, grayish-white leavings, as thick as cottage cheese, drop from his blade. His uncle did fifty pounds a week, and everyone in Treetown and on the Westside came here for the chitlins and sauce. Marcus turned the tough, sliding meat over and began on the other side. He waited. It was all they talked about now, when they were gathered like this.

"Po-lice got mad when I told em ain't no white women been over here," Oscar said, his knuckles laced with shine. "I told em don't nobody round here have no interest in a white girl. They didn't like that."

"They think some drunk dude came over from here and tried to get some white stuff in the parkin lot," Demetrius said. "And when she wouldn't give him none, he killed her. Put her and her friend in the Granada."

"The fence been cut both places and mended," Marcus's father said. "Been rolled back and fixed." He looked at Marcus.

"How the hell that explain the fuckin dude?" Octavious said. He shook his head and picked up his bottle of beer.

Marcus was quiet, dropping the chitlin into the washtub and closing his fingers around another. He thought of Bessier's mother, getting the phone call from America, and hanging up.

"Julius," Demetrius shouted into the doorway. "I still think somebody pissed off at you."

Julius leaned out, both hands bent backward around the door frame like a kid. "I ain't messed with no white girl. You crazy? I got enough trouble with the sistas around here."

"And they men," Octavious said.

"Only women get real mad at that fool," Oscar said. "And ain't no woman did that."

Demetrius spoke softer now. "Okay. I'm thinkin all the time, and I'm—Maybe one of the other garages is mad cause I been askin around about the city contract." The others stared at him. "I was lookin to raise us up, man. I asked a couple people how to get one."

Only two garages in the city had the police contracts—Rotella and Layton. They got all the abandoned or illegally parked vehicles, and they made big money on storage fees and lien sales. Like the Lexus, Marcus thought. "You and Layton are cool," he said. "Y'all been tight since school."

"I know," Demetrius said. "But maybe Rotella, or even somebody else that wants it, too."

"No," Hosea said finally. "Somebody wants us in jail. Me, or one a you."

"Cops?" Octavious said, frowning. "Ain't none of us been throwin down for a long time. They used to hate my ass, but . . ."

Oscar interrupted him. "Don't no cop want you like that. If he did, he just pull you over and kick your sorry black ass. Ain't you seen that boy on TV enough times now? Beat the shit out of him. If po-lice wanted you, they just stomp you. Stomp you out this world."

"Like nobody else in California speedin," Marcus said, thinking of all the times he'd been driving eighty in the Lexus through the desert and had seen the white headlights hurtling toward him in his rearview. He'd seen cars racing out there, exotic cars going faster than a hundred.

"I bet the brother was talkin shit to his homeys in the car, had the sounds on too loud, and he didn't even know they was followin him," Julius said from the doorway. "Remember that happened to Tiny D, back in the day, and they kicked his ass."

"Remember Sarita's cousin, the football player got killed in that place by Long Beach? Signal Hill," Marcus said. "Said he hung himself. Didn't like brothers drivin through there."

"Remember when they brought that batter-ram and knocked down them two houses on Grove?" Demetrius said. "Two old ladies lived there, and the police wrecked them cribs. Wrong house."

"That one dude got shot tryin to come out the door," Octavious said. "Drug raid on the wrong house, too. Remember, in eighty-five?"

Demetrius said, in a strange, tangled voice, "Enchantee's mama got killed for wrong." Marcus and the others stared at him, his face down tight to his work with the knife, stretching the gristly tissue. "Her mama was nineteen, ridin with her brother. Judge down there in Georgia took away his license for a year after this white lady run into *him*. And he was drivin anyway, so when the cops tried to stop him, he kept goin. They ran him off the road. Killed em both. Enchantee was three. They lived in this little cabin, she said. Two rooms. And her aunt brought her out here."

He threw the cleaned intestine into the washtub. "All y'all are here, ain't nobody watchin the place. Kickstand only one over there." Marcus watched Demetrius stand up and walk to the stone trough to wash his hands. "I'ma go keep a eye on things," he said, and he headed back toward the trees.

"Julius, get out here and do some work," Octavious called, but Aintielila came to the doorway.

"He done gone out the front," she said. "You should know."

Marcus's father said, hoarse and soft, "Everybody got one lazy fool. One child won't work."

Marcus and Octavious were smiling, but Aintielila said, "Less they ain't got no child at all." Marcus watched her turn in the doorway and disappear back inside.

He scraped the white stuff like sodden cotton, thinking about what Brother Lobo had told him. The white man who kept coming to bother Aintielila, the way she called to ask for the songs. No one but Uncle Oscar really knew her at all, and in the crowd and smoke of The Blue Q, she kept her face an impassive shell around her eyes. And Texas— why had his father acted so strange when he'd heard "Texas"?

Marcus was surprised when Octavious spoke up again. "Maybe somebody really wants Finis," he said. "Made it look like he did it. Scared him off."

Oscar slung more meat into the washtub and stood up. He was thin and short, his fingers surprisingly long and flecked with white now. "Finis don't exist," he said, pushing his cap far back on his forehead. "He don't exist for no white man. Finis a shadow man."

"What you mean?" Marcus began, but Oscar said, "Hold up."

He went inside and came back with mayonnaise jars filled with swaying dark rust liquid. Putting the jars down on a stump, he pulled sugar packets from his pocket and emptied one into each jar. The choc beer frothed and rose, and he brought one to each man.

Marcus drank the thick, sour-sweet choc, smelling faintly of molasses and yeast. "Best lunch I got," Oscar said.

Marcus's father was silent after he drank his. Marcus watched him stare out toward the trees, wondering what he saw.

"Shadow man," Oscar began again. "Me and Hosea don't exist, neither."

"You gon spell it out?" Marcus said, impatient.

"I ain't got no Social Security card," Oscar said. "You ain't neither," he added, nodding toward Hosea, who shook his head. "Shit, I ain't never looked for no government to give me money. After I seen my friend Lanier come out the service with half his toes gone, and they ain't gave him nothin." Oscar paused, downing his beer. "Hell, *I'm* Social Security. Me. I got this place to sell if I need money. Live in a trailer. Lanier bring us meat when he owe us. I don't need nobody."

"Ain't good to need nobody," Hosea said, still looking at the trees where Demetrius had disappeared. "Ain't good to have your name on all them papers."

"Papers?" Octavious said, and Marcus watched their fingers clenching across the knuckles when they scraped.

Aintielila came to the doorway. "Octavious. Go next door—y'all got a tow call," she said, and then she disappeared again.

"All them papers the government want your name on," Oscar said. "Got a paper for every move you make, so they can watch you. Hell, you don't exist neither, Eight. Kickstand, Julius, none a you. Just Mr. Teacher here."

After Octavious left, Marcus thought in the silence about all the Treetown men who worked different jobs for cash: mechanic, tree trimmer, concrete, odd jobs, and hauling. Like his brothers and Usher and the Proudfoots. After high school, they had ceased to appear on official papers.

He remembered when the census takers had come around, and the city of Rio Seco had published population numbers. Treetown laughed. A white man at the door? Nobody lived there, nobody employed or seeking work. Nobody here but us mice. Except welfare women, who had stacks of paper with their names and everything else about their lives.

"Only reason the government want your name on some paper is so they can get they money," Oscar said, grasping another chitlin. "We got annexed down here, what, last year? No sidewalks, no streetlights, still got septic tanks, and the city want taxes. Shit. Go down there to them nice new government buildings near where you live, boy. They want licenses for everything you do. Mechanic, roofing, sellin liquor. All they want is more money. Say, 'You need a license to prove you know what you doin. Doin good work for the damn citizens.' "

Oscar paused to spit onto the dirt. "If I don't do good work, a nigga can come back here and kick my ass. He can kick Eight's ass, he don't like the way y'all towed his car. He can tell people don't come to us. Or he can go downtown to them fancy offices and complain on paper. You got a white auto shop, somebody complain at the city, the shop boss shrug and say to his buddy down there at city hall, "Oh, well."

"Liquor license is different," Marcus said.

"No, it ain't," his uncle said. "Drinkin—they don't care what you sellin. Shit, them sherberts downtown by you drinkin every day. They just don't like what we drinkin, what cup we use, and do we eat pigsfeet steada—what that Spanish shackin food you told me about?"

"*Tapas*," Marcus said, grinning.

"Yeah," his uncle muttered. "Shit."

"What's this got to do with the guy who got killed, the girls?" Marcus said, feeling his cheeks fall back into place. His father and uncle were silent, drinking from the jars. Marcus remembered the three figures by the canal, all disjointed moving parts, shoes and the black cap, black gloves, an elbow as white and bent as a straw.

"All this time," he said, his voice impatient, "you been tellin me to figure out why some white guy with a ponytail was drivin a Jeep, messin with these girls. You shot at him, Daddy, but you won't tell me nothin. You never have." He took a breath, looking at his father's half-closed

eyes. "I mean, did a white guy used to own this land? Did you or—"
He glanced at the doorway. "Did you guys or Aintielila have any trouble
with a white owner a long time ago? Did you have some trouble in
Oklahoma or somewhere? Or Texas?" He waited in the sharp silence.

His father finished the choc beer and finally spoke. "Nothin but
trouble in Oklahoma. But that don't have nothin to do with California.
I came here lookin for work, I had met Salcido on the road. First, I
didn't want to ax nobody for nothin. I slept in the pecan grove down
there by the river, was a whole bunch of us there. Mostly Indians. I
cleaned the canals with the Indians for a while, and then I got some
work in the groves. Met up with Salcido and started layin stone." He
paused, staring at the empty jar. "No white man ever owned nothin
on this side a Pepper Avenue. Never. Just Archuleta. It was Indians
here first, all along the river. Then Spanish came from New Mexico,
and white came from Boston or around there. The whites liked the
weather, that's what Archuleta used to say, but they didn't like the
Spanish or the Indians. Hated adobe and stone. They built downtown,
only wood, like Boston. Plymouth Hill. That was bankers, lawyers,
doctors. They had people to clean and cook. Across the river was the
farmers, and they had people to work the groves. But wasn't nothin
but Spanish in Agua Dulce, and Archuleta on this hillside. I started
workin for him, buildin the barn, workin the trees when he was too
old. And never had no papers."

"Ain't nobody lookin for me or your daddy, no matter what you
think we done before," Oscar said, meeting Marcus's eyes with his red-
rimmed ones. "We ain't never been in California. We ain't never got
paid nothin but cash. Ain't never paid nobody else nothin but cash.
Demetrius take care of Arrow Towing, right?"

Marcus's father nodded slowly. "My name ain't even on the land.
Your mama's name on the papers from Archuleta. 1957. Archuleta
knew he was dyin, and he ain't had no people. He sold the land to her
and Lila for hardly nothin. They names on the papers." He closed his
eyes. "Only one would want me is a ghost," he whispered. "And wasn't
no ghost I seen in the Jeep."

Marcus opened his mouth again, but Oscar said, "See? We ain't here.
So who could be wantin payback for somethin we don't know about?
We ain't here." Marcus watched their mouths close tight around their
cigarillos, and they swallowed smoke.

• • •

At the darkened house across the rock-lined gutter, where two pink slashes were painted on the facial boards near the roof, Mortrice watched Chris talk to the girl wearing the arm cast. She laughed and shook her head, and Chris snaked his shoulders around to do a dance step for her.

B-Real sat in the front seat of his mother's old Nova. Mortrice sat in the back. B-Real said, "Man, I don't know why Chris want to talk to that girl. He been thinkin she was fine since we was babies. And all she do is work for the rock man."

They watched when two men approached the porch and leaned close to speak to the girl. Chris stood in the porch shadows. The men bent forward as if they were touching the cast, then twirled suddenly and dipped their hands into their pockets.

"He ain't gon front you no more," the girl called when the men were about to jump across the stone channel. "Y'all done had enough. He gon be lookin for you."

"We gotta go," Mortrice said, keeping his voice hard. He was the one now. He was from L.A. He was giving orders. "Honk him, man."

Chris bounded off the porch when he heard the horn, and he got into the passenger door. "She done loved me all her life," he said. "She just don't know it yet."

"Come on, fool," Mortrice said. "The dude suppose to be waitin."

They had driven around for an hour, waiting for the man named Julius to show this time. All the way east to where cows still roamed a lush field near the riverbottom, and Mortrice had smelled the night again, the chuffed, chewed grass. You didn't see them cows? Kenneth had said. Don't nobody care about nothin way out here. Don't nobody care about no dead nigga out here in Rio damn Seco.

B-Real drove back up Olive Street to the Gardens, and before they'd even entered the parking lot, Chris said, "There go Julius right there."

He was a thin man with a thick braid touching his spine, and when he turned to see the car, Mortrice saw his broad cheekbones and black goatee. "Yo, Chris," Julius said, peering into the car. "You lookin for me?"

"Why you dog me out last time, man?" Chris whined. Mortrice said nothing. No use to bring up the past. Go on and do what you gotta do now, Kenneth had said. Mortrice winced, trying to stop the voice from echoing in his skull.

Julius slid in beside Mortrice, and Mortrice kept his eyes straight ahead. "Get on California and go all the way toward Hillgrove," Julius told B-Real. "You little fools is sweatin, y'all so anxious. What you need a piece for? You ain't got nothin to steal."

Chris turned halfway around. "Fools from the Westside and way over in San Bernardino keep comin into the Gardens, tryin to sweat us," he said. "You gotta be strapped. Huh, Mortrice? Everybody in L.A. strapped."

Mortrice felt the eyes turn to him. "Mortrice? What kinda name that?" Julius said, laughing.

"Name my mama give me," Mortrice said, hard. "You sayin she wrong?"

"I don't even know the lady," Julius said. "And I would if she lived in the Gardens, okay? I know all the ladies in Treetown and the Westside. Plenty in San Bernardino, too. What's your mama's name?"

Mortrice pictured the sapphire flashes beating muted at the window when he'd left with B-Real a few hours ago, the TV screen blaring at his mother while she sat smoking, staring at the purple fabric draped over the curtained window. "Sofelia," he whispered. "Her name Sofelia."

He waited for the man to say something stupid about the name, but he heard only a hiss of breath through nostrils. "You been livin in L.A.?" Julius finally said, his voice higher. "Long time?"

"All my life," Mortrice said, frowning. "But my mama from here."

"Man, your mama's my baby sister," Julius said, slapping his thighs nervously. Mortrice stared at him. "Who brought you to Rio Seco?"

"Dude name Marcus," Mortrice said. "My uncle."

"Oh, shit!" Julius said, shaking his head. "Oh, shit." He looked out the window and said suddenly, "Lookahere, lookahere. You gotta turn left, my man, and go down this street. Yeah."

Mortrice saw a row of Spanish-style houses, all on long dirt lots. He saw dogs leaping at fences and campers parked in driveways, white and Mexican kids playing outside. "So you my nephew," Julius said, staring at him. "Cool. Cause Zach don't like no strangers at his crib. I'm about the only brotha he know. And we go way back to Juvenile Hall, long time ago. But Hillgrove people keep to theyselves. Yeah, yeah, right here, lil man."

Nephew. Maybe Julius lived at the fenced place Chris had shown him that night. Your people. That's what he'd said. Mortrice kept his mouth closed. He wanted to concentrate on the gun right now.

They walked down a long dirt driveway toward a small stucco box of a house, the same light tan as the earth here. "Zach can see you comin, now," Julius said. "Mr. Zachary," he called softly. "Call off your Rottweilers, okay, cause it's only Julius."

Mortrice felt his heart knocking at his chest. They needed this redhaired man who stepped outside his door slowly. They needed more toast if they wanted to protect themselves from the glaring, hooded eyes watching them through car windows everywhere they went. From guys like Bam-Bam who were getting sent out to the country when they got in trouble. From everyone.

Zach grinned slowly and nodded toward the door. Julius led the three boys inside, where they stood awkwardly in the small front room. Mortrice could smell marijuana smoke in the curly red hair that passed him. Zach leaned against the wall, folding his arms high on his chest, just under his grin. He had a red beard as crinkly as a scouring pad taped to his chin.

"No hickeys, man?" Zach said to Julius, and they both laughed. Mortrice kept his face expressionless, not looking at Chris or B-Real.

Julius turned to them and said, "Me and Zach, at the Hall, we was the ladies' men. Shit, I'm too old to get marks on me, man. Hey—this is my nephew, Zach. Mortrice."

Mortrice nodded. "I didn't see this guy before," Zach said, his voice more guarded.

"My sister Sofelia's kid," Julius said, staring at Mortrice. "Yeah." Chris and B-Real shifted their feet, uncomfortable, but Mortrice met the bottle-green eyes under the red brows.

"What you need?" Zach said, quiet now.

"These lil men feel that the world has gotten to be a dangerous place, man, and they feel the need for protection," Julius said.

Mortrice waited, thinking that Julius was the kind who talked just to hear the words flow like insects swarming around his face. One of those southern-sounding country guys, spinning too many slow words around females. The older men in L.A. were like that, some of them.

"Use a rubber," Zach said. Mortrice worked the inside of his cheek between his teeth. Then Zach smiled. "That's what Julius shoulda done all those times." The smile faded. "You sure, Julius? I don't need no fuckups." Julius nodded.

Zach led them from the front room to a back bedroom. Mortrice saw a woman's clothes on a chair. The bedroom was tiny, the plaster walls veined with cracks.

Mortrice stood behind him when he touched the dark wood arching over a little cave built into the wall, one of those holding a plaster saint with her palms limp, as if she were dropping money on the ground. Zach pulled at a carved panel under her, and a door swung open to reveal a smaller cave with two shelves. Mortrice didn't let himself lean forward. Zach was watching him, he knew. The top shelf held six guns. The bottom held a foil-wrapped brick of something and several baggies of weed, and more guns.

"Man, this guy owed me big-time. He brought me all these forties from the highway patrol," Zach said.

"That what them big-ass things is?" Julius said casually. Mortrice looked at the barrels and grips; the .40s looked awkward to him, like heavy muscle and chicken bone.

"Say property of CHP right on em," Zach said. "Got em from the manufacturer, cause they never been fired." He stared hard at Mortrice, then pulled a gun from the top shelf. His eyes were the color of mustard, and his reddish beard swung like a sponge when he turned suddenly, holding what Mortrice recognized as a Ruger .9. Mortrice felt B-Real shift behind him, but he didn't move. "This what you want?" Zach said, quiet.

Mortrice reached out for the gun, felt the cool, squared-off length and metal weight. "All you little perpies want nines," Zach said, his eyes holding Mortrice's. "Me, personally, I like this one." He bent suddenly and pulled out a huge semiautomatic from a holster under his shirt. "The Desert Eagle," he said, pointing it at Mortrice's mouth. "Forty-four. My new favorite."

Mortrice shifted his eyes to the thick black barrel, the bluing reflecting the lightbulb like a hot, silver eye. The metal spur lapped over the pale fingers.

"Them Israel soldiers like em," Mortrice said. "Mercenaries."

Zach slid the gun back under his shirt. "Yeah. Mercenaries." His beard shifted, stiff. "Who's got the dinero? I know Julius don't have it, cause he spends all his on the ladies."

"Nothin better to waste ducats on," Julius said. He glanced idly into the hidden shelf. "You get this hash from that place?"

"The best, direct from Afghanistan," Zach said. "My brother, downtown, he gets some, too. He says downtown freaks only want speed and Ecstasy. Rich assholes don't like to smoke." He turned suddenly to Mortrice again. "A hundred. Nephew." He worked his fingers until he saw the money. "My brother, he just found out this year he's got a son. Big as you. He never knew he stuck his dick in the wrong place."

Mortrice pulled the bills from his pocket, hearing B-Real and Chris breathing hard behind him. Kenneth's money, he thought. My money. He'd worked for it, cleaning the guns, touching the scabs of dried blood on the shottie.

"All right then, man," Julius said to Zach, moving out of the bedroom now that Mortrice had stuck the gun into his pants behind his loose T-shirt. Mortrice looked at Chris and B-Real now; their mouths were tight.

"Hey, Nephew," Zach said, close to Mortrice's skull. "You got the same cool blood as your uncle, right? No mouthin off."

"Right," Mortrice said, feeling the ridge of metal along his spine.

Chris and B-Real spoke up when the car had turned back onto California toward downtown. B-Real said, "Man, you just stuck it down there, didn't even check to see if it was loaded."

"Shit, man, lemme see it," Chris said.

"Shut up, both y'all," Julius said. "Why the man gon give you bullets? And you ain't seein shit in the car. Five-O everywhere, fool." He turned to Mortrice. "Take me to see your mama, boy. I can't believe this. Can't believe Marcus wouldn't tell Mama. They always talk about I'm hard-hearted, and he the one. Know who Mama been waitin for."

The tattoo, Mortrice was thinking, their voices flying past him. Mama always put that oil on me before. She ain't put none on since we came here. I need the tattoo. He looked down at the darkened web between finger and thumb. The tattoo only for us, he thought. For protection. Keep everybody off us, less we gotta get on them. He remembered two Chicano guys he had seen at school, with words inked on the slick, bumpy inside of their lips and letters across their knuckles and teardrops beside their eyes.

The light was off when B-Real pulled into the parking lot. Mortrice stared at the darkened window. "This where we stay," he murmured to Julius, who followed him to the door. He opened it and saw the empty chair, the cold ashes in a plate.

Sofelia had said, "Take me to Aintielila, okay? Please, Marcus?"

He drove the few blocks there, while she shivered and wrapped her arms tight, fingertips yellow where she dug her hands into her skin.

"I can't hide this no more," Marcus told her when he pulled into The Blue Q parking lot. "I can't do this to Mama."

"You won't have to," she said, her eyes closed. "This is the day. I tried to remember. And Mama don't want me."

"What?" Marcus began, but she shook her head and tried to pry open the door handle, still shaking. She fell from the truck into the dirt, half on her side, and bottles of shampoo and conditioner fell from the bag she held.

"Sofelia!" Marcus shouted, running around the truck to help her up. "What the hell are you talkin about?"

She kept her eyes trembling tight, the lids jumping as if lightning played behind them. "I can't look at all that sky," she whispered. "Big pieces of sky."

Marcus led her around the back, to the kitchen, and he called, "Aintielila!" He hoped his aunt wasn't carrying her pistol in her apron pocket, hoped she didn't think he was the white man. "It's Marcus! And Sofelia?"

"Who?" his aunt said, moving to the doorway. "Lord have mercy!"

She ran forward and hugged Sofelia, held her in the embrace Marcus couldn't ever manage with a woman. Her neck was a perfect cradle for Sofelia's head.

Marcus carried the bag inside after them. Sofelia sat on a wooden chair near the huge sink and whispered, "Aintie. Can you help me?"

His aunt took the bottles without asking questions and propped Sofelia's neck over the sink on a big towel. Marcus hesitated, and his aunt glared at him and shook her head.

He went into the darkened front area, cavernous with chairs lined at the walls. Walking slowly around the room, he dropped to his knees and crawled along baseboards until he came to the kitchen window where food was handed through. Crouching underneath the shelf, he could hear their voices.

"Aintie," Sofelia murmured. "You washed my hair, and combed the shiny stuff in it. Back then. What you put in my hair?"

"Brillantine," his aunt said softly. "Shine it up nice."

"Then you combed it all out and made a braid over my forehead. Cause I was goin to the concert with Tiki. Mama said I couldn't."

"She did," his aunt said. "She worried about you."

Sofelia was quiet. Then Marcus heard her say, "Did you miss me, Aintie?"

"Yeah, baby. We all missed you."

"I know Mama missed me. But she hate me now."

"No."

"She think I'm dead."

"She think you in love."

Sofelia was silent. "I love my son." Another long pause, and Marcus heard water swishing in the sink.

"I seen the riverbottom on TV, on the news. They was talkin about some fires, and I seen the trees. I remembered."

They waited. "I went to the concert. I got on the bus. Tiki had moved to L.A., and she told me L.A. was better, more parties than out here in the country. She came to the station. She said my hair was pretty, and I said you did it."

"Uh-huh."

"We was outside, in a big stadium, and people was all around us. Funk Festival. Me and Tiki and her friends was dancin. Then some boys sat with us in the stadium. One boy sat with me. He said I was so pretty, he never seen nobody from L.A. so pretty. He told me, 'Come on, I buy you a soda. Tell your friend you be right back.' He took me to a place under the stadium, and threw me on the ground."

Marcus clenched his eyes shut, holding his knees.

The cold milk flooded like a jellyfish down Alma's chest. She had been working in the orange trees for hours, hoeing in rabbit leavings. The baby girl, Jalima, was crawling now, and Alma had only shrugged when her pink overalls turned brown from the knees down.

Julius had bought new clothes for Jalima last week. He was good about that, with all three children, working odd jobs and bringing them what they needed. Clothes, toys, the video games Kendrick loved. He just didn't want to take care of them, Alma thought, looking at her dirty hands. Nobody wants to take care of kids. You don't get no breaks. Them girls Julius fool around with, they too busy drinkin and smokin. And he too busy runnin around. She moved along the floors now, snatching shoes and socks and trucks and paper.

Clutter. Alma wouldn't allow it, not after all those years of traveling in the station wagon whose floorboards were ankle deep in debris and socks and foil and torn flannel. She'd hated sleeping in that tangled cocoon. She swept the wood floors quickly now, throwing the boys' things into their room.

But standing in the room that smelled like sweat and sticks and orange peels, looking at the beds, she felt a sharp slant of sadness inside her belly. They were slipping away from her, all the grandchildren. She was happy that the baby was crawling, of course, but now the tiny hands pushed at her to get down. The harder Alma held her, wanting to kiss the shell-like ears and feel the velvet inner arms crooking around her neck, the more the baby squirmed for her new independence.

Alma leaned against the wall, holding the broom. The baby still slept with her at night, but Hosea slept on the other side now and then. She had felt his thumbs in the hollows of her cheeks, his forefingers framing her temples, and his lips against her neck.

He was back in the coldhouse most of the time now, he and the boys walking, walking, their faces loosened now and then when they laughed at something Kickstand said. Alma sighed and went into the kitchen to cut crinkle-edged circles of yellow squash, laced inside with seeds like fairy necklaces.

Sofelia had called herself a fairy for years, tiptoeing around the tree roots to surprise her brothers, carrying an old parasol and wearing tulle skirts that Alma had made for her. Alma closed her eyes and lay down the knife.

The harder she tried to hold on, to Sofelia, to these last children, the more they pulled away. Especially the boys. Because after they'd finished her chewed-for-them meat and green beans, after they'd learned to drink from straws and comb their own hair and button their flies and twirl a steering wheel with one hand, how could she protect them? She hadn't protected Sofelia, or Finis, and now she couldn't even see them.

Their shoes and boot soles and tires had crunched relentlessly down the gravel and turned suddenly silent on the asphalt of Pepper Avenue.

She heard heavy footsteps outside the kitchen door now, saw Julius's face in the doorway. "What you want now?" she asked.

"Mama," he said. "Sofelia livin out here. In the Gardens."

Alma looked at the yellow coins of squash floating under her fingers. "What you mean, livin here?"

In her third son's eyes, she saw the triumph of a jealous child when he spoke. "Marcus brought her out here. To the Gardens. Swear to God."

She dried her hands absently and went outside. The afternoon light was playful and gleaming in the trees. She started down the driveway, and Julius caught up with her. "Mama, let me drive you. Come on." She began to walk toward Grove Avenue, and when she'd reached the corner, Julius slowed beside her in the Volkswagen from the yard.

"She ain't home," Julius said when she got in awkwardly, holding herself tight in the small seat. "Her son showed me where."

"Son?"

"He bout fourteen, fifteen," Julius said, squinting through the dusty windshield.

Alma tried to add the years in her mind, but she couldn't. She couldn't think at all, couldn't see the face she thought she should. The one turning under the parasol, elfin and blinking.

She stared at the passing houses. Ocie Mae Williams, Zenia Smith, Concha's old house. Some empty, some with children. Julius pulled across the bare dirt before the parking lot of Olive Gardens.

Nothing but women, girls, and babies. Not like the families when these big buildings were small shacks and people sat outside peeling oranges and building fires. These women smiled at Julius, holding babies and hanging clothes and sipping from cans.

Alma stood in front of the closed, grimy door. No one was there. Julius said, "The boy gone, too."

"She live here?" Alma asked again. "Here?"

"Mama," Julius said, fingers at her elbow. "Come on. Let's go over Marcus's place downtown."

He drove back down Olive, back down Grove, and when he turned on Pepper, passing Oscar's place, Alma saw Hosea's truck. The one Marcus was driving. "Look," she said, pointing.

• • •

"When you comb, it loosen up my brain," Sofelia whispered. Marcus heard his aunt's feet moving on the floor. "I never let nobody touch my hair since that day. I did it myself. Nobody never touched me after that. Except my son." She paused. "That boy kept me down there a long time. He slapped me and I had blood in my mouth. He laid on me whole buncha times. It was dark, had chairs and tables down there, all around me. Just a little space. He had some cigarettes." She paused. "He said, 'You need a Spanish fly. Make you treat me better.' He put it in my mouth. And I don't remember nothin for a long time."

"Oh, baby," Lila said, her voice twisted with sobs.

"Then when I could see somethin outside my head again, not all the dreams, I was in a alley. It was cold, like night. I didn't have no pants on. Mama said they was too tight. I had my shirt, and in my pocket was Tiki number. I had to crawl, like I was a baby. I thought I was a baby goin long the fences at home. But some lady in a car seen me, and she didn't know me. She looked at Tiki's number and take me where Tiki stayed."

"Your friend was lookin for you?" Lila said, tears in her words.

"She say it been more than a week."

Marcus felt the moisture running down his collar, felt a ball of rage at the back of his skull. We woulda killed him. The Jungle Brothers. Country-ass niggas. We woulda killed his big-city ass.

"I couldn't think about nothin for so long. I slept in Tiki bed. I didn't know where I was. She told me how I did, how I acted, long time ago. I didn't know anything. Then I knew I was havin a baby. I knew I wasn't no crawlin baby in the dirt. Me and Tiki was thirteen. All that time the boy was on me, slappin me, I could hear drums over us from the concert. I wanted to hear some music."

"Why you didn't call us?" Aintielila said. Marcus edged out from under the window and walked toward the doorway, wiping his face with his shirt. "Why you didn't come home?"

"I thought Mama and Daddy be so mad. I use to hear the boys say they kill anybody mess with me. I thought they kill the baby."

"What?" Aintielila said. Marcus watched them now, Sofelia sitting straight in the chair, her long hair wet and gleaming strings over her shoulders.

"Tiki said maybe they kill him, I heard her one night. But I didn't remember nothin for a long time. After the baby come. I couldn't come out Tiki's room, I stayed there forever. They taken the baby out so he could walk after a while, but I stayed in there."

Marcus said, "Sofelia? You okay?"

Her eyes were blank on him. Aintielila combed steadily, her face impassive now. And they heard a loud car pull into the yard.

"Your uncle out with your daddy," Lila said. "Go on, see who that is." Her mouth tightened, her eyes glanced out the open door.

Marcus went around the corner and saw his mother and Julius running toward him, around the stone trough. His mother grabbed him by the elbows, her head just under his chin, and she slapped him across the face hard enough to jar his teeth.

When she saw her daughter sitting empty-eyed in the chair, her hair streaming like black lava down her arms, Alma stopped a few feet short of touching her. She stared at the amber skin, the mouth open. Sofelia's face dropped forward like a wilting flower, and Alma turned to see Lila watching her.

Instead of the waiting love and relief she'd always expected to bloom inside her, she felt a surge of anger as dark as oil in her lungs. "You got her?" she whispered harshly to Lila, who stood with her hard face and the belly that hadn't known children. How could Lila, who only knew men and laughter and drinking, have her baby girl? But when she turned back to Sofelia, not seeing Lila shake her head, she heard the distance of her daughter's small voice saying, "I'm sorry. I'm sorry, Mama."

Sofelia still didn't leap up to embrace her. Alma bent down and took her daughter's stiff neck onto her shoulder, put her arms around her, and Sofelia sat as wooden and unbending as a grown boy.

"Mama," Marcus began, but Alma turned, feeling the dark liquid spread from her chest to her belly.

"No," she said. "Nary one a you never felt pains for no child, and I can't believe you could do me this way. Keep her from me. No." She pulled Sofelia up and said, "We goin home now."

But as soon as they left the doorway, Sofelia shrank under her mother's touch, fading away. "I can't," she whispered. "I'm sorry."

Marcus stepped forward and lifted her into his arms. Alma saw him stagger a minute and then right himself, walking down the dirt parking lot toward the street. Alma turned to her sister-in-law and said, "Never. I never forget." She saw Lila bite her lips until pearls of red showed.

"I think she come cause she know about when I . . . ," Lila began, but Alma turned away before she could hear the rest. She followed her children down the tree-lined drive.

Julius took her arm when they walked along the outside fence, traffic hurtling past them. Alma stared at Sofelia's hair waving over her brother's arm. When they neared the gate, she saw the van and the men with cameras.

"Excuse me! Excuse me!" a man in a suit shouted. "Is this young woman injured? Do you need an ambulance?"

Alma stared at the van: CHANNEL 7 NEWS. The man pushed a microphone near Marcus, who swatted it away with his shoulder and kept walking, turning into the gate that Julius swung open. Alma moved quickly past the man shouting at her and bent her head to make it up the slight incline to her kitchen, where she thought she knew what to do. The voices faded when she reached the blue starfish beside the open door.

CHAPTER NINE

MARCUS SLIPPED OUT the kitchen door as soon as he laid Sofelia on the couch. He knew anything he said to his mother would only make her angrier; he hadn't seen her face flushed and swollen like this, like brick dust was rising underneath her skin, since Julius had told her one of his girlfriends gave Finis the Super Kool.

The bright, bluish camera lights were gathered like miniature helicopter search beams outside the gate. Julius and Kickstand were swinging the gate closed, ignoring the questions of the reporter whose face glowed like chalk.

Marcus wasn't going back to The Blue Q for the truck. He headed along the path to the olive trees, jumping the fence where the tire iron had lain, and then he jogged along the canal road. The moon glowed neon in the slick-flowing water, and the floating weeds were black islands. Marcus was cold down his neck even while he ran, hoping no one was armed and cruising along here tonight. He smelled the water that had run into the earth behind his uncle's place where he'd irrigated the orange trees.

When he came around the curve to the bare field where Lanier wanted to keep his pigs, Marcus slowed, out of breath. The StairMaster don't have nothin to do with runnin, he thought, walking fast toward the three trees. He paused, head down, and when he looked up, he saw flickering lights in the old olive-oil processing place, the wooden building where they'd pressed and bottled long ago.

He stared at two figures crossing by the edge of the field, near the banks leading up to the freeway. Guys carrying water jugs and bedding rolls. Homeless men must be camping out in the old building now.

Marcus reached Pepper Avenue and glanced down the street toward the knot of lights still outside his father's place, a distant constellation. Going back to his apartment was a long walk. He sprinted across the avenue and clambered over the rubble left from the freeway, the piles of dirt and concrete growing wild tobacco and sunflowers and olive seedlings. On the other side was the trail Olive Gardens people walked to get to downtown by foot. Marcus shook his head, thinking of how effectively the city had blocked off everything they hated about Treetown. Only the one road in and out. Go all the way through Agua Dulce if you want a big grocery store. Shop at the SaveMart where the Iranian guys Tasered anybody they thought was trying to steal.

He knew where he was going now. Clusters of young men stood around a few houses, staring at him when he passed the street nearest the Gardens. Marcus nodded and kept going until he saw the droopy-starred eaves over SaRonn's door.

"Who that?" she called after he knocked.

"Marcus."

"I ain't seen him," she said through the curtain, and then he saw her face against the screen.

"I was lookin for you," he said, and her slow smile crinkled the skin around her eyes.

He sat on the couch, watching Willa pour pinto beans from one pan into another, then arrange them in a muffin tin. "That keeps her busy for hours," SaRonn said, sitting on the floor near the girl. "Why you lookin for me?"

Marcus looked at her wide silver hoops, the silver bracelet, her white T-shirt and black jeans. SaRonn's forehead glowed wide under the short arc of hair. Start tellin the truth, he thought. Cause she ain't studyin you anyway. She likes Finis.

"I came by a couple times to see if you heard from him," Marcus said slowly. "But I came for your opinion tonight."

"You walkin?" she frowned, and he nodded.

He told her the whole story about Sofelia, beginning with the first surprising phone call and ending with Sofelia's hair still drying in the sink. He only said that Sofelia had talked a long time with his aunt

THE
GETTIN PLACE
237

about why she'd disappeared, that they'd cried, and then he told SaRonn about his mother.

She was quiet for a long time, only the sound of spattering beans against plastic and tin breaking the silence. Willa studied him after his long outburst.

"You gotta give me some time to think about this one," SaRonn said, standing up. "You askin me if you wrong?"

Marcus followed her to the kitchen. "Yeah. I guess I am."

She leaned against the ancient white stove, as gleaming clean as his mother's, and Marcus felt a fingering ache at his ribs when he thought of his mother's face. "I don't know," SaRonn said, turning to the tiny counter. "You want some ice tea?"

They sat on the couch and drank the tea while Willa's measuring grew slower and she eventually leaned her head against SaRonn's knees. "Come on, baby," she said, carrying the girl down the short hallway. "Say night-night." Willa's hand lifted in a solemn wave behind her mother's back.

Marcus closed his eyes and felt the fatigue sift through his head. He slouched further down on the blanket-covered couch. Maybe he'd stay away from his parents' place for a while, since he only kept screwing up. The gettin place. I'm only gettin trouble.

He didn't know he'd slept until he heard SaRonn click on the TV. He sat up with a start. "What time is it?" he asked.

"Near bout eleven," she said, sitting on the other end of the couch. "You sure were tired."

"I still gotta walk home, unless you got a hooptie for rent," he said, rubbing his eyes.

"Bennie got some old car back there now, but the battery's dead," SaRonn said, turning to the news.

"Octavious ain't fixed it?" Marcus asked, grinning at her.

"Marcus," SaRonn said. "Look."

He saw himself on TV, his face gaunt and craggy in the camera lights, Sofelia limp in his arms. Julius and his mother were next, holding their hands up against the lights and hurrying into the yard. But the voice speaking was the anchorwoman's.

"Dramatic footage of a Rio Seco crime scene later in the program," she said. "First, this news."

"What's goin on, Marcus?" SaRonn said, drawing away from him. "You in trouble, too?" Her hands went to the fringed hair at her nape.

"I don't know what's goin on," he said. "I went out the back way. Sofelia—she can't handle bein outside or somethin, I mean, her son told me she stays inside all the time. When everything broke loose at The Blue Q, she just went limp."

"Agoraphobic," SaRonn whispered. "I read about it." She stared at the screen, too.

"I don't know why those newsmen were there," Marcus said, his throat closing, imagining the teachers and students watching his face like this was *Cops*.

Then the anchorwoman said, "Out in Rio Seco, police report a startling rise in the murder rate this year. As of this week, twenty-four people have been killed in the city. Two men were robbed and shot last week, and another man was killed in a drive-by shooting earlier this month. And, most alarming, three people have been found dead at this run-down towing yard on the edge of the city. Our Inland Valley correspondent, Jim Skelton, is on the scene."

The man Marcus had seen appeared again, looking earnest and holding his microphone outside the locked gate on Pepper Avenue. "Christine, this property has been the scene of *three* murders in the past few months. We were alerted to the unsolved crimes during a press conference held earlier today by the father of one of the victims, Rio Seco City Councilman Ray Sawicky. His daughter, Pamela, was found burned to death in a car in this towing yard in early September."

The screen shifted to show men in suits lined near a podium, and the city councilman spoke into the thicket of microphones. "It has been over a month since my only daughter was found slain," Sawicky said, his jaw trembling. "And police have yet to find her killer. In our council meeting today, I brought up this city's high number of unsolved crimes because something has got to be done. If our police force is understaffed, let's address that. If the police chief is willing to let certain areas of this city, like Treetown and Agua Dulce and Terracina, go completely out of control, let's address *him*. Someone has got to clean up the criminal element and criminal attitudes in certain places. Brutal, unsolved crimes send only one message: You can get away with murder in Rio Seco." His eyes blinked furiously behind his glasses.

The reporter said, "Local real-estate developer Web Matheson, who announced today that he would consider running for the congressional seat to be vacated next term by retiring congressman Jim Parker, added to this tough on crime message."

Marcus saw a man he thought he recognized from the restaurant. Combed-back brown hair and a wide mouth, smooth stride to the podium. "Crime in our area hurts socially, economically, and emotionally," he said. "I think we need to pledge to clean up this city, and do whatever it takes. My heart goes out to Ray Sawicky and all the families of crime victims. We need strong leadership to be tough on crime."

"What the hell?" Marcus said, staring at the face not much older than his. Then he saw his own squinting eyes. "Me again?" The earlier footage reappeared.

"This evening, Channel Seven News tried to gain information about the scene of those three unsolved homicides. This towing yard in the area known locally as Treetown, an area of modest old homes and increasing gang violence, is where the bodies were found. None of the residents here would speak to us, and when we inquired about how this young woman"—pausing for the picture of Marcus carrying Sofelia—"was apparently injured, residents were uncooperative."

"I look like a thug," Marcus said.

"You look like America's Most Wanted," SaRonn said.

"Homicide detectives are still working on both cases. On September third, Pamela Sawicky and Marissa Kent were found burned to death in a car here. And on September twelfth, Jean-Luc Bessier was found bludgeoned to death. Police appeal to the public for help in solving these murders. In Rio Seco, this is Jim Skelton."

The blond woman appeared again. "Thanks, Jim. Southland residents got some sunshine today after the morning haze . . ."

"They make it look like we got a serial killer livin in the barn," Marcus said. "Shit. I hope Mama and Daddy didn't see it."

SaRonn shivered and dropped her face in her hands. "I'm scared as hell. For Finis and you. All y'all."

Marcus pictured the teachers' lounge tomorrow. "Damn! I know everybody at work saw me lookin like that. Like a criminal."

SaRonn tried to smile. "You'll look like a teacher tomorrow, huh? Glasses and blazer."

Marcus stared at the reddish swirl in the bottom of his iced tea, not sure if she was making fun of him. "You put cinnamon in here?" She nodded. "And when you walk, I hear these faint jingle bells. Like Christmas." She pulled back the ankle of her jeans, and he saw the silver chain with clusters of tiny bells.

"I get these and spices and tea in L.A., at this Indian store," she said.

Marcus looked at her berry-lined lips. "Let's go check out some spices this weekend," he said. "I can rent us a car."

"Willa . . ." she began.

"Willa need a car seat," he said.

SaRonn smiled. "You can't walk home tonight." When she stood up, he knew his groin would swirl and tighten. She pointed to the armchair. "Extra blanket right there. Couch is nice and soft. See you in the morning." She turned back, though, and came toward him again. "Marcus. When you were sleepin, I thought about it. You were wrong. About your mama. Real wrong."

Marcus watched her throat vibrate, her earrings shiver.

"You never had kids," she said. "But I'ma tell you—Willa is my life. I ain't never felt even close to what I feel for her, for a man. No man. Nobody, not even my mama. What I mean is, if she was gone and somebody knew somethin and didn't tell me—I think you were wrong. Ain't no way to describe the hole that had to be in your mama's *side*, in her body, about Sofelia."

Marcus hesitated. "I didn't want to mess up with my sister," he said. "I did what she asked me."

SaRonn slanted her head sharply. "I'm just tellin what you asked *me*, okay?" she said. "And that man on TV, the one lost his daughter? I don't know nothin about him, but he got a big hole, too."

Marcus nodded, and she disappeared into the hallway.

Alma watched her daughter sit huddled in a blanket on the couch, the hair dry now and rising around her face like webs spun from underneath. There was nothing to say. She leaned back, too, keeping her arm an inch from the blanket though it was as hard as anything she'd ever done.

Hosea came in awhile later, squinting and lowering himself to his knee. "That you, Sofelia?" he said, his voice hoarse, and she only dropped her face into her lap.

Alma shook her head in the dark, seeing his face all angles in the light through the lace curtains. "Julius tryin to find the boy," Hosea said, and then he went back outside.

Alma thought about how hard Hosea had been on all of them, how distant from Sofelia. But that was his way. And she had held this baby so tight, tied her to her back when she walked the long path to downtown, performed every ritual with infinite care. The narrow chest had only just begun to mound when she had disappeared. A son? Where was the man with the pillow-muscled arms, the one Sofelia had whispered about to her when she dreamed?

She was afraid to speak, then, afraid the words might drive Sofelia into another room. Alma closed her eyes and only listened to the breathing beside her.

Hosea sat in the barn with his two oldest sons. Demetrius said, "She look like Finis, almost, around the eyes. Maybe somebody gave her somethin bad to smoke."

Hosea shook his head. He thought of all the smoke-filled eyes he saw moving through Treetown. The gaunt women with pilled, hard hair and eyes surrounded by circles black as tires. The men in the Kozy Komfort, the men like Finis who walked and walked like gears had been set in strange motion by chemicals. "I don't understand y'all," he said. "The dope. People in my day got drunk, they was alcoholic, yeah, and they messed up. But they wasn't like you young people. Some of em was lost. Yeah. But they wasn't ghosts." He buried his head in his palms. "Look like your mama's baby girl lost."

"Marcus had to carry her?" Octavious said. "That's what Julius told me. And he said some news van was here, too. Tryin to ax questions about the shit been goin on."

Hosea lifted his face to stare at the locked gate. The shit—that's how they'd been referring to everything. They couldn't say the bodies or the murders. It was like the violence and uncertainty were mixed in a fog permeating the trees. The shit.

"Where they go?" he asked.

Demetrius shrugged. "Julius said he sent em away. Said they stood out there a while and gave up."

"Ain't nothin happened here tonight nobody know about," Hosea said.

"I know," Demetrius said, pacing inside the barn doorway. "Unless this is some new shit we ain't found out about yet."

Marcus was vaguely awake, feeling sun on his neck. Bodhi? he thought, dreaming images trying to coalesce. They called him Bodhi. Like Bodhisattva? The Buddha? Words from the art history class at the college so long ago came in useless procession. Indian art. Stupas. He'd tried to impress Enchantee in the arched hallways. The familiar voice by the canal. Bye-bye. Bodhi. He blinked, feeling tiny tweezers lift his eyelashes.

Willa's fingers gripped the hairs. She tried to examine his eyeballs until he sat up slowly. Then she ran. He heard the faint jingling and saw a tiny anklet around her chubby brown leg.

In the kitchen, the jingling was sweeter, louder. SaRonn put something she called cardamom in his tea, and he sat at the small table near the stove.

"Tell me the truth about what happened to Sofelia," she said, her voice muted and small. "I thought about her all night."

Marcus tasted the pungent, sweet tea. He said to himself, Tell the truth. It ain't so bad.

"I can't tell you that," he said, looking at her downturned lips, her fingers working her rings.

"A man did that to her," she said. "Some men want to do that— turn you inside out and shake you till ain't a damn thang left inside. And you walkin round like a empty pecan. Nothin but dust inside. No," she said. "Uh-uh. It didn't work on me."

"Can we start over?" Marcus said. "Ask me anything else."

"Okay." She stood with hands on her hips near the stove. "Who's your most beautiful woman, the woman you always wanted?"

"Chaka Khan," he said without hesitation.

SaRonn bent over with laughter. "All that hair, that big old mouth."

"Hey," Marcus said. "I told you the truth." He went outside, surprised at how easily it had come out, talking to her. The truth. When she watched him clean the battery on the old primer-gray Nova behind her house, he told her he was so lousy at fixing cars he'd saved a bruised thumbnail as a trophy when he was fifteen.

"A thumbnail?" she asked.

"I was workin on a low rider with Demetrius, banged it up. But I banged out this dent in the wheel well, too. Only time I ever did somethin right. My thumbnail was purple, took forever growin out, and I didn't cut it off cause it reminded me."

She shook her head in silent laughter, and he started the Nova. "I'ma take this to work, okay? I'll be back."

When he'd changed quickly at the apartment, he drove to school, thinking he'd go straight to class. But Cottrell and Val drifted toward him in the parking lot, Val calling, "Hey, is everything okay? I saw . . ."

Marcus hesitated near the Nova, seeing Cottrell's frown when he neared the car. Then the principal, Natalie Larchwood, got out of her green Lexus and raised her palm toward him. "Marcus," she said. "I'd like to talk to you. I got a call from a parent whose son saw . . ." Her spiky silver hair glinted in the sun.

"I didn't know he lived down there," Cottrell murmured to her. "Hard to keep a decent auto in your driveway when you . . ."

Marcus got back into the car. He said, "I'm taking a personal day, okay?" to Natalie Larchwood's concerned face. "Sorry for the short notice." He drove out of the lot.

The brand-new Western Auto Mall was just past Agua Dulce, in a huge swath of land along the freeway. A few tiny frame houses and rabbit hutches still crouched among the trunks of the signs and billboards. Marcus walked around the car lots for nearly an hour until his head had cleared of the images of his own twisted face above Sofelia's and the shock lines in the foreheads at work. Then he rented a Camry from a guy who frequented Kurt's restaurant.

At SaRonn's door, he said, "Let's go to L.A. today. I need some spices right now." She bit her lip and then nodded, smiling.

When they were on the freeway, passing all the new developments crowning the hillsides and moving in red-tiled tongues along the slopes, she asked him if he'd ever wanted to move away from Rio Seco. To leave home.

"I lived in L.A. for a year," he said.

"Yeah, I heard you went to USC." She glanced back at Willa, who was fingering a doll's hair in her car seat.

"I got scared," Marcus said. "L.A. scared me. I mean, I loved the movies and the food, all the things to do. But I was scared of L.A. brothers, L.A. women, and LAPD."

"I was an L.A. woman for a couple of years, too," she said. "After my mama died. Diabetes. And my dad was a drinker. He moved back to Georgia long time ago. So I moved to Echo Park and worked in a thrift store. I wasn't scary at all."

"I didn't know you. I knew these women who wanted money."

"Oh, please. Not all of us want money. Besides," she said, grinning, "you coulda looked at some of those white girls at USC if you didn't want to worry about money."

"I see this question. Yeah, I been out with a coupla white girls. Not in L.A. In Rio Seco."

"They don't look like Chaka Khan."

"Neither do you."

"We ain't goin out."

"That's why we talkin like this. Instead of about movies and music and the weather."

"Okay."

"Okay."

When they approached the skyline, hidden by summer smog, he thought of the day he'd picked up Sofelia, not long ago. And he looked in the direction of USC, and the Coliseum, imagining himself there running on the track, and Sofelia . . .

He wouldn't picture it. He drove toward Echo Park, the opposite way, thinking of all the girls and women who came here on a bus or with a friend, whose arms were taken by men with steel fingers and intentions of shaking them out, like SaRonn had described. He turned to her.

"Somebody turn you inside out when you was here?" he asked.

She shook her head, looking out the window at the pastel buildings, the lake. "No. In Treetown. Home." She pointed to an exit. "Turn off here. Hey, Willa girl, wake up." She glanced at Marcus again. "No questions for now, okay?"

"Okay."

The car soon filled with the scents of curry and coriander and the sounds of Willa playing with a string of wooden beads. Marcus followed

SaRonn's directions to Salvadoran stores on Sunset Boulevard, to Indian stores somewhere off National, and to a hair salon in South-Central where SaRonn bought a special conditioner and a facial tonic and visited with the owner, a tall elegant woman named Trudy. Marcus looked at all the storefronts; they weren't far from where Sofelia had lived, but he didn't want to say anything to SaRonn. Sofelia's face, her words, floated in his head all day. If neither he nor his aunt ever told anyone, Sofelia could choose for herself what to say. He thought of his brothers, knowing that their anger and rage would never let them look at Mortrice with anything but hatred. And his father—Marcus couldn't imagine what would lie behind his father's impassive gaze, those still planes of his face.

Driving back to Rio Seco, both SaRonn and Willa slept in the lowering dark. Marcus sped east, watching the darker purple shadow of the earth rise to meet the bright turquoise evening. Chocolate city, he thought, but he didn't want to wake her to see if she remembered the Parliament song. Finis did. And the vanilla suburbs. But L.A. wasn't set up like that anymore. More like marble-fudge ice cream, with darker swirls and blended territories.

He saw a car pulled over on the shoulder, a CHP officer writing a ticket while standing behind the vehicle, and the high black boots gleamed in the light from the siren.

Drivin careful, all the way home, Marcus thought, a tremor of fear down his back like he felt every time he saw a policeman.

The freeway median went from just-watered oleander and ivy to bare dirt stripes when he neared Rio Seco. The new houses were as bright as bleached backbones along the dark earth. The marble in the swirl, except for Demetrius and some others. Over the river.

He wouldn't look at his father's place. At SaRonn's, when he nudged her awake, he saw Willa's eyes open. SaRonn stumbled, sleepy, to the door, carrying bags and Willa, and he called from the open window, "Who was your most beautiful man?"

"Finis," she said, and Marcus drove away.

Archuleta had taught him to make the square box baskets from arrowroot stems collected in the riverbottom, then smoked hard and cured with coffee. Hosea pulled out a bundle of the darkened sticks and began to weave soft leather cord around the ends to join corners. Salcido was bringing the meat to trade today.

He had to do small movements like this, or his shoulder stiffened inside, as if tendons were pulling against bone. Hosea glanced at his oldest son's boy, the one they called D'Junior, hammering tree roots nearby. "Watch them fingers," he called. "You only get ten."

He examined the tightness of the woven leather. Agua Dulce men had always bought or made baskets like these to carry fighting cocks. The city was constantly arresting men for cockfighting, and Hosea thought about Oscar's comparisons. They eat snails, but chitlins make em sick, Oscar would say. They go to bullfights in Spain, they eat veal and lamb. Babies. But over there in Dulce, down here, we vicious and against the law. Ain't that about a twist?

Salcido pulled up near the barn and handed the huge black *birria* pot to Paz, who smiled. The goat stew inside was rich with tendons and bones and melting-soft flesh. And the large roasting pan he gave Hosea held another goat, one that had been rubbed with spices, wrapped with burlap smeared with spiced paste, and cooked in an earthen pit on Salcido's land for more than a day. "Goddamn," Salcido said, clapping Hosea on the back. "It's too hot for this time a year."

Hosea said, "Watch out for the wasps. Even they been grumpy." He brought out the stick boxes from the barn and loaded them onto Salcido's old Chevy truck. Then he and Demetrius brought the keg Oscar had filled with choc beer and the gallon wine jugs of amber, homemade whiskey.

They sat inside the barn for shade, Hosea and Demetrius, Salcido and his son Rubén. The younger men each drank a shot glass of whiskey and wandered off to the storage lot to look at an old Catalina someone had half-customized before getting thrown in jail. Salcido and Hosea drank a quart jar of beer after the whiskey.

"*Pinchi* heat," Salcido said. "Split half the fruit off my trees. And we're gonna freeze our asses in two months, huh?"

"Look like we are," Hosea said. Salcido's thick throat was ringed by lines filled with red-brick dust when he drank.

"*Pinchi güeros*," Salcido said. "Goddamn yuppies at that new auto mall keep complaining about the smell, and now the code people keep coming into Dulce, man. Zoning change—they want the goats and sheep and chickens out." He took another drink, and this time Hosea knew he was nervous.

"Your brother was born to make *cerveza*, huh?" Salcido said, softer now. "Remember O'Brien?" Salcido grinned, and Hosea did remember. The big citrus grower from Boston with his red-bloomed face, purple veins lacing his cheeks. When he and Salcido had done some work years ago for O'Brien, old man Archuleta had laughed.

"He should grow potatoes or make whiskey," Archuleta used to growl. "You can't do what you ain't born to do. He's losing money."

"I wasn't born to grow no olives," Hosea thought, but he must have said it, because Salcido shook his head.

"Shit, you learned from the best," Salcido said. "And nobody grows hubcaps like you, man." He was nearly drunk now, his wide hands around the jar, his knuckles laced with dust. "We built this damn barn with my goddamn stones. See, the *gabacho*, he hates Agua Dulce. Mexicans, Spanish, us goddamn bean eaters. They hate *frijoles*, and . . ." He squinted. "What's that your wife was always cooking? The black man's *frijoles*, the ones your *hermano* used to grow here?"

"Them black-eye peas?" Hosea asked. He tried to figure out what Salcido was getting at.

"Yeah! They're beans, too, right, they make you fart. See, the *gabacho* doesn't like us farting, man. I hear them calling Dulce Beanertown. Remember O'Brien used to brag about Boston? Beantown? Shit. Now you got all these *gabachos* from L.A. and Orange County moving here, they don't want dust kicking up from my yard, they don't like the heavy equipment. Them assholes across the river complain about my dust, too. No dirt for them. No goats." Salcido leaned forward in the chair. "I think they want half of Dulce for more car dealers."

They walked toward the storage lot, and Hosea said finally, "Sherberts. That's what Oscar call em. Shoppin malls and houses." He was tired of talking, even to Salcido.

Salcido stopped at a gap in the trees and pointed toward the west. "Look, the whole city's growing like fucking anthills. We got too many people. What—four hundred thousand or something?"

"Got some of us when they annexed," Hosea said.

"Rubén!" Salcido called. "You don't need no more *ranflas*! You got three cars you ain't finished yet!" Their sons headed up from the storage lot, but Hosea wasn't listening.

He looked at the hills beside them, the Los Olivos, and then the Diamondbacks, and the wishbone curve of the huge ranges behind them. The Santa Catarina Mountains, rising from the desert, embracing like arms that didn't quite meet, leaving space between their reaching foothills where the freeway poured through like dripping oil.

In the late afternoon, he packed the last crates of olive jars into the truck and told Octavious to take them to the small market in Agua Dulce. The harvest was over. Paz had cured a good crop, and now she moved through the trees, studying, pinching branches here and there.

Hosea took his grandson D'Junior up the path, moving his shoulder cautiously, stretching the sheet of muscles under his collarbone. When he sat down, the boy squatted near his feet to stare at his fingers. "How many fingers you get?" the boy asked. "This not a good finger."

"Ain't no finger," Hosea said, seeing where the boy touched hesitantly. "Thumb."

His left thumb was missing half the nail. The tip had been cut off, leaving a flat, dark-rough scar like a pruned branch. Wood had done it. When he was working in the Texas thicket, in the prison camp deep inside dark forest, and the guards rode the white horses, watching the men work through the night with only the fires from the burning stumps they'd just cleared, an ax had taken the thumb's end. It lay in the firelight pulsing red as a nipple in the dirt. His thumb bled maroon pools that quickly turned to black.

"I got two thumbs," the boy said. "I'm three. My mama be here in half-in-a-while."

"Yeah," Hosea said. "You watch that hammer, hear?" The boy pounded small sticks into the ground with the wooden mallet Hosea had carved long ago for Kendrick, his first grandson.

Except now Mortrice was the oldest. That name. His baby girl, his youngest, and she'd had the first child. Hosea had watched the boy's uneasy movements and darting eyes. The boy acted afraid of even the trees.

Hosea leaned back in the hard chair. They were in the stand of trees overlooking the riverbed. His chair was bronze now. Over the heavy scales of chapped rust, while he was in the hospital facing IV tree trunks,

Alma had come here and sprayed her paint until the wrought iron glowed.

He watched the cottonwood leaves turn and shimmer like sequins in the breeze. From here, he could see all the way to the Hungarian's land in the hills across the river. He knew the Hungarian was expecting a winter freeze on his twenty acres. But right now, the air still pushed down the hills, dry and hot.

Oscar had come to him yesterday in the barn and said, "Fire. I got a feelin about it. That's what I'm lookin for. Cause that's how they got people out in the old days."

Hosea had stared at his younger brother, the baby born while Tulsa still smoldered. "You seen anybody burned out?"

"Shit," Oscar said. "Seen somebody torch a hotel cause the owner behind on payments. Seen niggers flyin out like pigeons." He paused. "Hot as hell all summer, all fall. All these trees. Them fires in the riverbottom coupla years ago, remember? That big fire in Grayglen last year? Just take a match. And a reason."

He listened to the faint clopping of the mallet. The eucalyptus between here and Oscar's had been planted a hundred years ago, to protect the house and olives and apricots from the heated or freezing winds beginning in the desert and gaining strength in the foothills. These trees would flare in minutes, especially after seven years of drought.

Hosea stood up and walked to the edge of the steep slope, looking at the riverbottom road, remembering the burning smell, the black Jeep, the feel of the bullet knocking him backward like a red fist. He wanted his grandfather's rifle back, the gun he'd carried like a third arm. He knew he'd hit the bumper of the black Jeep. But neither the cops nor the Thompsons could search the city for bullet holes that had to have been fixed by now.

The police still had the gun. Every time they'd come to the place, over and over after the television report and another article in the newspaper, they'd asked more questions about Finis and Hosea's business and Oscar. "Maybe whoever killed the queen and dumped him here knocked off your son, too, for payback," one cop had said. "Maybe your son's burned up somewhere, too. Maybe somebody's already solved this. But these politicians and reporters don't know that, okay? We get pressure, you get pressure."

"Ain't no Negro in his right mind ever hire somebody to kill two white girls like that," Oscar had said last night. "I'm lookin for fire. And I'ma kill the man I see holdin the match. Gon be justifiable homicide. Cause if his ass is over my property line, I'ma bring him on. Self-defense. That's what this is now."

Why a white man would want to burn him out, why he'd want the land, was a mystery. They just drove through it, as quick as they could, on their way somewhere else. Hosea watched their moonglow faces bobbing behind glass right now when the cars jammed up at the corner and along the road; he saw their nervous movements and car phones and mouths singing along with the radios. Air-conditioning. Move right along to the freeway on-ramp. In fact, he didn't like seeing them all the time now through the charred gap in the fence near the barn. But Red Man's boy hadn't brought green palm fronds yet to slip through the links.

"Need to find your daddy," he said to his grandson, lifting him up even though his shoulder was stabbed with pain for a long moment. The small hand, gritty with dirt, rubbed against his shirt.

"Don't be wipin your paws on me," Hosea said.

"You already dirty," the boy said, grinning. "Mama get mad when I'm *so* dirty."

"She used to it by now," Hosea said, walking toward the barn. He felt the tired ache in every joint and tendon now, the walking and waiting each night that held each muscle too tight in the dark.

Flowers and food ruled the Smith house, Enchantee found quickly, leaving little time for Dylan or cleaning.

Mr. Smith spent his time at the bank or the golf course, and Mrs. Smith spent hers in the garden. She did that more than she painted now, Enchantee saw, because she was rarely in the second-floor studio where vases and brushes and papers were arranged on tables.

When Enchantee arrived at two, after picking up D'Junior from Alma, she had to pass Mr. Smith in the huge garden. A series of outdoor rooms, Mrs. Smith said to someone on the phone while Enchantee stirred macaroni in the big house. The big house—that always cracked her up. Abby and Bent lived with Dylan in the two-bedroom guest house past the pool.

Mrs. Smith always smiled at Enchantee, but she'd murmured in the dining room, "If you need time to work, Abigail, you should send the boy to day care. Having someone come here to play is ridiculous unless she cleans, too."

Enchantee kept her face bent to the blocks skidding across the wood floor in the living room when Dylan pushed; she kept her hand on D'Junior's sneakered foot. She knew it was the extra boy, her boy, getting on Mrs. Smith's nerves. She heard Mrs. Smith go back out through the French doors.

Enchantee looked at Dylan, his fierce and private gray eyes. "Did your mother like Dylan's daddy?" she'd asked Abby, because she could tell from the way Abby talked that Bent wasn't the boy's father.

Abby laughed. "Hey, I'd turned thirty-two and thought I'd better have a baby, okay? I got it in my head that I'd run out of time and suitable guys. So I went to a sperm bank, and Mom about fainted. Of course, as soon as I had Dylan, I met Bent." She held her palm up, apricot-tipped fingernails waving. "I'm impulsive. She's always hated that, too."

"Well, my aunt hates everything about me," Enchantee said softly. "Says I spoil this boy, and I got myself too big a house, says I think I'm . . ." She stopped, realizing that she wasn't with Janine.

"What?" Abby leaned on her cookbook, chin in hand.

"I'm great or something," Enchantee finished lamely. Scared-a-you, her aunt always mimicked. But Abby wouldn't understand that. She think she some*body*, her cousins would add.

Abby pushed a piece of paper over the cookbook. "My mother doesn't think this is hard work. But here's my plan to bring the newspaper into the nineties, make it more cosmopolitan now that Rio Seco's a big city. Something different each month: one month all Asian food, sushi places and Thai. Reviewing . . . Hey, Dylan, don't do that!"

Enchantee grabbed his hand when he pulled petals off a tiny rose bouquet. "Your grandma won't like that," she told him, and the two boys ran to the dining room, where they liked to hide in the forest of chair legs.

"Listen," Abby said, her voice serious. "I really have to get to work on the computer in a few minutes. A month of 'New Wine Country' cuisine. A month of Mexican food. A month of 'Murder Mystery Theater' type places. It's going to be hard work, and I was hoping that on two or three nights a week you could give Dylan dinner and put him to bed."

"I don't know," Enchantee said, stepping into the doorway to see the boys crouched like blinking cave animals under the table. "D'Junior has to go to bed early."

"Well, maybe you could take him home and come on back, just until about nine or so."

"Two nights a week is all I can handle," Enchantee said while the boys lay on their backs like overturned beetles, shaking their legs.

"You would save my life," Abby said, staring at her daily planner. "A bunch of fund-raisers for Connie's husband, Web. Shit. My life. All planned out. That's why I'm glad I have Dylan."

While Abby was working in the guest house, Enchantee made peanut-butter sandwiches and more macaroni. "I want to eat dinner," Dylan repeated, and Enchantee marveled at the broken-record voice like D'Junior's, the one implanted in all three-year-olds.

Abby came in when they were nearly finished, followed by her mother. "Connie's got two women to serve for the party," Mrs. Smith said. "And Chani?" She turned and smiled. "Will you be here to help out with Dylan?"

Abby said, "The first fundraiser for Web. He's going to run for Congress or something."

"I guess so," Enchantee said slowly, thinking of the extra money.

Abby touched her arm. "I appreciate it. It's a big deal because my aunt's also celebrating this new historical series in the paper, and you know how she is when Dylan runs around."

"Mama," D'Junior said. "Can we go see Daddy now?" He lifted his face like the center of a sunflower to her, and she picked him up.

"We're going home now," she said to them all.

Enchantee slept like she was drugged, and Demetrius ran his tongue along her neck to wake her. "Hey, stranger," he said. "Give me somethin sweet to help me get through the day."

He hovered over her, his lips brushing back and forth on her forehead like she was a child, but his fingers held her hips tight enough to leave dimples, and she buried her face in his neck and rocked with him.

He pushed his fingers through the hair near her neck. "I like it in the mornin. Makes me don't mind so much workin all day, walkin with Daddy at night."

"Yeah," she said, sitting up. "You call talkin about women with Kickstand and them workin."

He smiled. "You call talkin about men with Janine workin. And that white girl, Abby—whatever y'all talk about."

She smiled back. "We don't talk about you."

"Cause I always leave you speechless," he whispered.

The phones were fairly quiet, and Enchantee nearly fell asleep in her cubicle. At lunch, she got coffee and spoke to Miriam, the nice woman she'd met at Abby's who did the recipe column. When Enchantee set her tray next to Janine's, Janine raised her eyebrows. "You talkin to fourth floor now?"

"She's nice," Enchantee said, glancing at today's newspaper. She read Abby's review of a restaurant in Palm Springs, read about a boy wounded in a drive-by on the Westside. Janine leaned over and said, "You see this dude praisin Ice Cube? Says this shit is genius. Give me a damn headache when them boys listen to it in my yard."

Enchantee saw Bent's name. The operators made sport of matching faces to bylines. The written voices never sounded like their owners, according to Janine. "This one's blond," Enchantee said. "I've seen him. He's okay."

"He sure like weird music. Rap, blues, and then he write about the orchestra playin in that fancy place downtown," Teresa said, sitting down.

Janine frowned. "He like all them other white dudes—hear some little fool rap about 'I'ma shoot that nigga balls off' and then call it art."

"He's really nice to his fiancée," Enchantee said. "He's good to her son."

"Oh, yeah—you workin over there, too?" Teresa said. "Them house notes killin you, huh?"

Janine touched Enchantee's neck. "Look at them teeth marks. Demetrius must be makin up for when you gone."

Enchantee laughed.

• • •

At the garden party, she watched Abby and Bent moving as a pair when they talked to the guests along the tables spread with food. She felt Dylan poke her in the thigh. "How long is half-in-a-while?" the boy said, his lashes invisible in the harsh patio lights.

"D'Junior says it, right?" she asked. She missed him. Abby had called to say her mother thought it would be less distracting if Enchantee came alone.

"He says he see his daddy in half-in-a-while," Dylan said.

"I guess he know how long it is," she answered, distracted, watching people move through the gardens and patio. Two Mexican women were replenishing food trays: olives and cheeses and crackers, roast beef, ham.

"Catered by American-Style Boring, Inc.," Abby said into Enchantee's ear. "Mother wouldn't let me near the food, or I'd have livened it up."

"Your aunt likes it," Enchantee said, watching Carrie Smith Donohue in a red-white-and-blue dress of tiny stars on silk. She filled her plate, talking to a wide-smiling man.

Abby nodded at him. "Check out Web Matheson—politician extraordinaire. He better learn to live on this buffet crap." She pointed to three men nearby, laughing at something Web had turned to say to them. "Some of Bent's reporter friends. Every waking moment for Web is working the room."

Dylan tugged at Enchantee's hand later, saying he wanted to watch a video. Enchantee was dozing on the library couch beside him when she heard Carrie Smith Donohue's high, impatient voice in the hallway.

"No, no, the value of this site is that it's *Spanish*."

"What?" A man's voice had laughter in it. "You don't have enough Spanish in Agua Dulce and on the Westside? Seems like everybody's complaining how many people are from Mexico. I mean, I'm new . . ."

"That's *Mexican*. Of course there's no value in that. But newcomers like yourself aren't aware of Rio Seco's noble Spanish heritage. This man Joaquín Archuleta came from New Mexico, and his forebears from Spain. He grew olives, made wine in the Spanish tradition. Do you know there are old grapevines on a fence in this god-awful place?"

"So what are you saying?" The laughing voice was Bent, Enchantee realized.

"This city was the Moorish Rose of the Valley back in the early nineteen hundreds. Rio Seco was noted for beauty and architecture, and Spanish culture—well, we didn't know how valuable it was, and we lost it. We should make every effort to regain it now. Oh, all this time I thought I'd left the photos in the library and they were in my bag." The voices faded back down the hallway.

Enchantee smiled, still drowsy on the warm leather imprint under her body. Carrie Smith Donohue was one of those old women you didn't want to argue with, like the teachers who'd criticize your handwriting and shoes, too. She'd kick Bent's butt in a minute if he didn't listen. She looked over at Dylan, engrossed in *The Sword and the Stone*. Dylan didn't like to cuddle, she thought, watching him hold himself separate, hunched on the couch. "You want some snacks?" she asked. He nodded without looking at her.

She went down the hallway toward the bright staccato voices near the French doors. Web Matheson said, "Bloated bureaucratic agencies are . . ." Abby said, "I really think Thai food is . . ."

In the kitchen, one of the Mexican women fired off rapid Spanish and handed her a tray of desserts. People always spoke Spanish to her. She put the tray outside and grabbed some chips and cheese for Dylan. In the hallway again, she saw that the door to the formal dining room was halfway open, and she heard the high, thin voice becoming agitated.

"Whoever this woman is, she won't sell it now, you said. The place has blue paint all over it, a desecration. When I was there taking photographs, I saw a wizened Mexican woman. But the name on the deed is a colored name. Delilah or something. And the men are all colored."

"No," Web's voice said, and she could hear the grin. "They're African-American, Carrie. With all that's gone on over there in Treetown, I'm surprised they aren't all in jail. But be patient. I've got a friend, an African-American gentleman, who knows they've got illegal activities, and he's working on something now. So hold off on the article."

Enchantee heard the other door to the dining room open and close. In the library, she handed the food to Dylan, and sitting on the couch, she said softly to herself, "Delilah? Oscar's wife, Lila? But the building is sort of purple, even if it's The Blue Q. Who'd want to buy a juke joint?"

"Ssshhh!" Dylan said, hunching forward even more. "I don't want to talk right now."

Standing at the sink, Alma pushed at the pecan husk with her thumb, watching it fall away as easily as a veil from a skull. By this time of lingering fall heat, everyone on the place usually ate and rested on the veranda.

But Sofelia wouldn't leave Alma's bedroom. She sat in the nest of sheets, staring out the same window where the apricot blossoms had brought Alma dreams of her daughter's contentment. The green leaves were turning yellow now, and Sofelia's eyes were blank. Smoke from her cigarettes twined around the white walls like gray vines, then left behind bitter traces.

Sofelia's son, Mortrice, skulked onto the veranda late, only after everyone was gone. He avoided the men working on cars in the barn, and he seldom ate Alma's food. She tried to study his face under the black baseball cap, but he wouldn't meet her eyes, darting into the kitchen like a frightened lizard and moving along the walls to speak to his mother for a few minutes. Alma would come into the room with a bowl of rice, and the boy would scurry back outside. By the time she went out to the yard, he'd be gone. "Took off down Pepper," Demetrius would say. "Hangin out with them Gardens boys. Took Kendrick with him, too."

"Kendrick?" Alma frowned at Julius, who sat on a crate eating the last pomegranates, his fingers stained crimson.

Julius shrugged. "I can't tell him nothin."

Alma felt her head ring with anger. "You don't even *try*. He goin on thirteen. He ain't gon listen to a woman. He need to hear his daddy tell him what he can't do."

In the kitchen again, she looked over the bills. Hosea and Demetrius did everything they could in cash, because they hated checkbooks and banks. Alma paid the utilities and the bill for the Yellow Pages advertisement. She paid the monthly installment on Hosea's hospital bill. She closed her eyes at the silence in her bedroom.

Lila had come to the kitchen door last week, tall and cool. She'd leaned against the wall and said, "I know you angry about it. But I think she come to me that day cause . . . cause she were afraid you wouldn't understand. No, no—don't be like that. I mean to say, she was just figurin . . ."

Alma wouldn't look at her sister-in-law, that taut body and face and the satisfied eyes. All the years she'd gone to The Blue Q with Hosea, her belly swelled and then deflated, her skin stretched with silvery webs, her head tired from late-night feedings, she'd watched Lila. Lila who never came by to cradle the babies, to exclaim over their ears and toes, Lila who always stayed cool and aloof in the kitchen as if Treetown women were far too country for her, Lila who never wanted anyone at the stove with her. When Sofelia was a walking toddler, the boys had taken her over to The Blue Q many times to play in the stone water trough. When she was eleven or twelve, she had gone over there and asked Lila to do her hair, and Alma had held her hurt and her words inside. Lila don't have no one's hair to comb, she'd thought.

"How I ain't gon understand my own child? My own girl?" Alma said. "How you gon understand when you ain't never had one? Too cold and evil to grow a baby. Too *pretty* to worry about no baby. Yeah. All the rest of us was just cows, huh? Why she talk to you?" Her voice was rising, and she tamped it back down like sand in a cup. Like the grandgirl baby's hand patting sand into a cup now, near Abuela's feet. Outside. She watched Lila's wide, straight back cross the yard.

In the evenings, the bright lights still shone like glaring stars over the barn doorway, and she kept the kitchen door open to see the boys leaning into the hoods. Hosea sat with Lanier or Red Man, talking about trucks. And when Mortrice, his black T-shirt and cap hiding all but his face, brought his shadow to the doorway, Alma said, "I got somethin for you. You sit right there. Now." Kendrick was a smaller silhouette behind him. "You, too, boy."

She reached for the key attached to the polished stone. "I want you sleepin here," she said sternly to Mortrice. "On this place. Not runnin around outside. You go sleep in your uncle Finis trailer. Don't mess with his rocks and things. But since he gone somewhere—" She paused to steady her voice again. "Since he ain't here right now, you keep yourself in there at night. And you"—she turned to Kendrick—"you got a bed."

Enchantee stepped into the doorway as soon as they'd left, and she handed Alma a basket of strawberries, saying, "They had these left over from the party at the Smiths."

Alma leaned on the edge of the sink, the bulbous red fruit and the sickly-sweet smell making her weak. She hated strawberries. Whenever she saw them, she saw herself bent like a monkey, walking with knuckles brushing the earth, plucking the swollen fruit as red as bloody thumbs and seeded like the nose of the white man who watched them and counted the flats.

The rows stretched out forever before her back then, the fruit pooled underneath, and her mother and father gone. She and Abuela crouched, and the acid, tart smell rose all around them. When Abuela tried to push a strawberry into Alma's mouth, she gagged.

"Alma?" Enchantee said. "You okay? How's Sofelia?"

Alma splashed cold water on her face and dried it with the dish towel, the comforting scent of damp cotton cleaning her forehead. "The same," she said. "She don't talk. She ate some tortillas. Smoked them cigarettes."

Enchantee said nervously, "I have to tell you somethin." Alma sat down and listened. She remembered the name from the banker husband's front page obituary, mentioning that his widow was the first female member of the Wednesday Club, taking his place in the group that met downtown to discuss city matters.

When Enchantee told her what Carrie Smith Donohue had said about photos, Alma thought an older woman had come in August or so, saying she was from the city, asking Alma where the property ended. Alma hadn't seen a camera.

"She said somebody was tryin to buy Lila's place." Enchantee frowned. "I thought The Blue Q was Mr. Thompson's. Oscar Thompson."

"It's his place. But the land is in Lila name," Alma said, the clicking of her tongue harsh on her sister-in-law's name. "What she say about Lila?"

"Somebody tried to buy her land. And somethin illegal over there."

"All that liquor," Alma said. "All that liquor and all what go on in that parkin lot. She make all that money on people too lazy to cook, people gettin drunk and messin with each other."

Enchantee looked embarrassed, and Alma lowered her eyes. "I didn't know you had a problem with it. I know you don't go over there," Enchantee said.

"I don't go over there," Alma said, standing up. "And if she get in trouble for that liquor, she got it comin. Cause she ain't never cared for nobody but herself." Alma glanced at the strawberries on the drainboard. "Take them with you." Seeing Enchantee's stricken face, she added, "Thanks, baby, for thinkin of me. But I'm fine."

"Ain't nobody gon bust Uncle Oscar," Demetrius said. "He been making that choc and hard stuff since before I was born, and he and Rock know how to work it. He don't sell to strangers, definitely not no white dude. Hell, the city don't care if Treetown get drunk."

Enchantee was silent in her own kitchen. D'Junior was asleep. He'd said, "Did that boy ax about me?"

"Dylan?" He'd nodded. Enchantee told him, "Dylan wasn't in a very good mood. He wanted to watch TV."

"Sometime I like him and sometime I don't," D'Junior had said, sleepy.

"Same with everybody," Enchantee had whispered, kissing him.

She looked at Demetrius's tired face, his hair touched with dust and fingers grained with oil and dirt. "You want to take a bath? We both been workin all day."

"I can handle that," he said. But he was staring at the wall, his eyes unfocused. "Marcus ain't been comin around." He rubbed his eyes and stood up. "I think Eight's walking with Daddy tonight."

"Demetrius," she said. "You're done for the night, okay? With that house. This is your house." She took his hand.

Hosea leaned heavily against the eucalyptus trunk near the trailers. His shoulder was aching again in thin twitches, and his eyes felt scoured with coarse sand from staring past the bark hanging in ribbonlike shreds.

The place was quiet. Demetrius was angry that the custom low-rider jobs for him and Kickstand and the painter Nacho had disappeared for now; Treetown and Westside men didn't want to hang around and look for hubcaps or universal joints with cops constantly cruising up the drive.

Hosea hadn't seen Marcus since Sofelia had come home. He breathed heavily. He'd thought his youngest son, the one who knew how some white people thought, at least, the one who'd always planned everything out cold and calculated, would have been able to figure this one. But now, each night, walking the property, Hosea remembered men hunting men in the Texas thickets, in the black trees, and there had been no figuring that. No boundaries. The Texas voice Marcus had described brought back the howling voices spiraled through the charred stumps.

He walked alone tonight, carrying Demetrius's new shotgun, keeping his fences comfortably close to his shoulder. His father had told him many times, "You gotta know the boundaries if you want to survive, boy. I ain't lyin. Learn them lines."

He'd learned the invisible guidelines in Tulsa: the foundation of his house, the alley, the corner of Greenwood, and then the whole heart of the lively street where people knew his father. The clotheslines and back door to Miss Letitia's. Hosea turned away now from the sight of smoking, faint, concrete outlines and blackened poles, of the bones arranged in stiff piles.

The boundaries of his grandfather's farm had been too wide at first. All he could smell was singed hair on the pigs, and he remembered his father's voice saying, "I ain't cut out for farmin. I'd rather work on cars. All day. I'ma teach the boy to work on cars, he always have a trade."

But his father was dead. Hosea had plowed at his grandfather's, plowed miles of straight lines and turned for another row. His mother and the baby had gone with the man she'd married, the musician, ivory-gray face and sharp hat pulled low. Eventually, Hosea knew the fences, the walls, the well, and the barn.

When he'd left the farm at sixteen, his stepfather's deafening blow clapped inside his ear, he didn't look behind him at the rusty-gold stone walls or the pasture where the white mule widened her black nostrils.

He'd gotten lost in the trees in Texas. The only way he'd escaped was by swinging the ax at a man. He'd become a shadow then, as insubstantial as night smoke.

He remembered the fires consuming the stumps in the Texas forest, the trunks he'd cut and dragged. The white men on horses, watching. Then down below, always, bent backs. The dogs. Big Boss Man—you ain't so big, you just tall, thass all. Whenever Oscar sang the Jimmy

Reed song in The Blue Q, Hosea saw the height added by horses weaving among the trees.

He'd listened to Oscar's slow voice, full of bitterness when he sang. Boss man. Oscar had shot a white man—boss man or policeman or stranger, Hosea had never known. The night he'd come to Rio Seco, looking for a place to stay, he'd put a bullet in a green eye. "He wasn't gentlemanly with Lila," Oscar had said, hoarse and breathless, wary-eyed with the brother he barely knew. Lila's eye was fist-swollen, and blood had dried in a black swath like a sash along her dress.

Alma had nursed her, but Lila had held herself silent and distant. Now, Hosea thought, now that Sofelia had gone to her aunt first and sat mute in Alma's bedroom, his wife wouldn't speak to his brother's wife. She said Lila was dealing secretly with white people about her land.

Shadow men. Hosea had told Marcus no one even knew he and Oscar lived here. They were invisible. He leaned against the tree, studying the hanging folds of creamy skin above his head. He'd never known if he'd killed the young guard, if the ax blow thudding as soft as wet burlap had split the skull or only knocked him out. All through the thicket, in the Texas creek beds where he'd crouched and slept on his haunches and killed birds for quick-charred flesh, where he'd shit and held his belly and cried and turned his hearing ear for dogs, he'd felt that blow in his wrist and hadn't known.

Maybe the man's kin had found where Hosea lived; maybe the voice Marcus had heard by the canal was paid by the kin. Maybe Hosea wasn't a shadow now. The dark gold ponytail had flipped like a thin scarf onto the Jeep's roof. No one but Thompsons and cops knew what Marcus had heard; Thompsons hadn't told anyone, and the cops didn't believe the damn story anyway. Texas. A ghost. Or the ghost's child? Boss men? Sherberts? Drug addicts?

He heard bark loosen and fall, hollow against the eucalyptus leaves, and then he heard feet treading, cautious, inching over the shreds of dried tree skin. The steps paused, moved, paused again, and Hosea waited.

He saw no pale face. Nothing. Then a bulky black form appeared from behind a tree trunk, and when the shotgun leaped in Hosea's hand, the boy's eyes shone bright and he said, "Hey, uh—Grampa."

Sofelia's boy. Hosea's blood felt thin, draining from his neck and back. "Where you suppose to be?" he said, his voice hurting him.

The boy looked at Finis's trailer. "She give me the key."

"Who?" The boy was silent, staring at the gun. "Your gramma?" The boy nodded. "Well, shit, you only what—fourteen? What the hell you doin walkin around?" The mouth still didn't open, and Hosea turned to leave. "You shoulda been sleep. Stay wherever you suppose to stay, damnit."

He walked along the fence near the olive grove, the shotgun too heavy in his arms. He knew the old gun. He wondered where all his sons were. Where was Finis? He'd taught them all to shoot, but he'd told them to fight with their fists. They'd never shot anything but food. "Shoot what you gon eat," he'd said, over and over. And he'd only shot food, too.

Sofelia didn't speak; her son didn't speak. Why had they come here, come home, now? Was the boy trying to sell something on his land? Hosea frowned, staring at the cool slippage of canal beyond the wire.

Whoever came with hands holding matches and gasoline and guns, whoever floated onto his place for payback or money, he'd have to send metal cracking through those bones.

Mortrice kept the kit in the oversized pocket of his big jacket. Since his mother left the apartment that day, and his uncle Julius had come to tell him she was at the house in the trees, Mortrice had worried about where to keep the guns and the kit. The apartment was still empty, and he had a key, so he spent some time there with Chris and B-Real and another boy, Teddy, who said he wanted to be down with them. They watched TV in the dark apartment and looked at the guns. They'd been out in B-Real's car several times, cruising down different streets and looking at graffiti.

Rio Seco was easier to figure out than L.A., Mortrice thought. It was smaller, and divided nice and clean. Treetown. The Westside, where Westside Loc Special thought they were the shit. Agua Dulce was Mexican guys. Hillgrove was where Zach lived—rough white dudes and bikers. Funkytown—his uncle Marcus. And farther up the hill, Moneytown.

Just like school, everybody had their uniforms. Their houses were like clothes. Everybody had territories and eyes looking out to watch and see who cruised through the lines.

He sat in the trailer now, alone, the .9 on the tiny table in front of him. He had to clean it, because Chris had taken it out and practiced shooting cans in the hills. Fool thought he didn't have to take care of a gun. Mortrice had stared for a long time at the arrangement of stones and bottles and bones on the small Formica table. His grandmother— the word felt strange—she had said not to move anything. She said Finis was gone somewhere.

Mortrice counted rows of ten green stones. Ten clear rosy sharp ones. Ten shards of blue glass, and ten of a swirly purplish one. But the bones chilled him.

There was a hand laid out in the center of the table. Couldn't be anything else, Mortrice knew. The tiny end fingerbones were as small as matches, and the longer ones, only three of them, were as straight as cigarettes. The hand was splayed in the center of the colors, chalky and glowing. Every time Mortrice thought about moving the bones, he saw Paco's skull, the same color. Wasn't nothin wrong with his fingers. Just his face.

He spread newspaper on the bed and broke down the .9, examining each part. He began to clean the barrel with the strong-smelling solvent in his kit, pushing the long-handled brush through the channel over and over.

Nobody had sweated them yet, not face to face, but somebody had shot at the Gardens parking lot three times this month. Chris said he and Teddy had been talking shit at school. But they didn't know who wanted to shoot yet. Yet.

Mortrice swabbed out the solvent, pushing cotton cloth through the barrel several times. Then he lightly oiled each part.

All B-Real liked was the name. He'd sprayed it on the freeway overpass and all over the Gardens. But it was Mortrice's idea. His name. He was the one.

AK-1. In L.A., you could read the graffiti like stories.

meant these Crips were Blood Killers and working for money.

$$^W/_S \text{ XVII } ^P/_N$$

meant Westside, the street number, and *por vida*. For life.

Anybody Killer. He'd written it on paper in the apartment, in the dark, before he'd shown it to anyone. No colors. Just black. No Crips. No Bloods.

$$_T \text{AK-1} ^O_G$$

Olive Gardens. Original Gangster. That's what Kenneth was. Now it was him.

He was 1. Chris wrote AK-2, B-Real AK-3, and Teddy AK-4.

"Look. You could see yourself up there," he'd told them. "On the wall." They stared at the black paint on the block walls around the complex. Every time we add a digit, we change the set name. Everybody somebody.

He heard light footsteps on the dirt outside the trailer, and he froze, pulling a sheet of newspaper over the disassembled gun and the kit. "Yo, man," someone said at the window. "Mortrice."

It was Kendrick. "What you want?" Mortrice said, holding the flimsy door partly open.

"Man, what you doin out here?" Kendrick said, his nostrils flaring. "You gettin high?"

"Shut up," Mortrice said. "I ain't gettin high."

"I smell it," Kendrick said, leaning into the space. "Smell like gasoline and glue and shit. What is it?"

"It ain't nothin," Mortrice said, angry. "I ain't gettin high. Go back to your *bedroom*."

Kendrick pulled his face back like a turtle. "I ain't no baby," he said, but when Mortrice closed the door, the footsteps eventually faded.

Mortrice carefully put the .9 back together. Chris had said, "I ain't done nothin, man, all I did was shoot it."

"Yeah," Mortrice had said. "And every time you shoot, fool, you get gunpowder and residue and shit in there. You gotta take care a your piece. Or it ain't gon take care a you."

He slid the .9 under the pillow and lay back, staring at the curved, close ceiling. When he had to walk between the old house and the trailer, he felt as vulnerable as a roach, scuttling through all these damn trees, dangling branches like spiderwebs in his face. And then open space all around here, until he got to the trailer. The silver walls felt narrow and flimsy, like a spent shell casing.

This was his mother's place, the land she'd whispered stories about. Home. All these leaves and hard faces and dirt. In the apartment, he was surrounded not just with the walls at his elbow to protect him, but the other rooms all around and then the walls around the parking lot. He thought again of their writing on the walls, as thin and slanted as chain link. AK-1.

Kendrick was a wannabe. He was only twelve. But he'd seen the apartment, and the other guys, and he wanted to be down. Mortrice thought about the special gun Teddy was making in the apartment. Teddy had learned how in juvenile placement, he'd said. He'd been taking apart a tape recorder and an ink pen when Mortrice left.

Teddy wanted money. He was always selling shit, stolen stuff. Mortrice had fifty dollars in his sock, fifty dollars his grandfather had given him yesterday.

The scary-looking old man, with his sandpaper voice and slanted cheeks, had surprised Mortrice when he'd slipped away from the house. Mortrice had been passing the small stone shed when the voice called him from the doorway. "Come over here, boy."

Mortrice stared at the lifted-high chin and the half-closed eyes; the man sat on a wooden crate, but he seemed to be looking down at Mortrice. "You think you grown peoples?" Mortrice shrugged, thinking about that word. Peoples. My peoples. "You fourteen?"

Mortrice nodded.

"You my oldest grandson, I guess. Your mama ain't well. You doin okay?" Mortrice had shrugged again. The old man reached into his pocket and pulled out five tens. "Here. You might need you some shoes or clothes. Some snacks. You can't get you a paper job till you sixteen, but you want to work in the barn, Demetrius pay you." The man nodded, dismissing him, and Mortrice had walked quickly on the path through the trees, the shifting dark that scared him. No stark edges or fences or cement to tell your way.

He closed his eyes, his hand partway under the pillow to touch the edge of the piece.

CHAPTER TEN

EACH PLATE MARCUS served was elaborately arranged with herbs or decorative leaves along the rim; the sauces pooled around the meat like brilliant suns, and the blue-corn tortillas were stacked like indigo moons.

Marcus tried everything Kurt cooked. He savored the *carnitas* and the four different salsas. But though he didn't tell Kurt, since the entree had been one of the most popular at Chipotle Chile after Abby Smith mentioned it in her influential restaurant review, the olive tamales were never close to being as smoky or rich as his mother's.

When he was doing something mindless like sorting silverware, he could hear the clattering oil in his mother's pan; oil only sounded that comfortable in old cast iron on a hot stove, with people hanging around waiting for the spicy *chorizo* and slabs of red snapper in his mother's kitchen, on a Friday night like this one, Aretha on the radio. He'd catch himself staring at the lovely plates, the broiled salmon with cilantro Kurt made because everyone loved the healthful oils. He would feel a pain behind his lungs when he paused at the counter, seeing the same blue-flowered plates his mother had gotten years ago from a rich Plymouth Hill woman. If the men ate outside, they got the tin plates or old speckleware, but those twelve dishes his mother washed carefully after each meal.

Marcus took his break outside, walking down the pedestrian mall in the warm evening light, his throat full with the tautness in his mother's face when she'd slapped him, with Sofelia's voice a flat ribbon winding hurt around the chair legs where he crouched.

On the old white stove, his mother and his *abuela* always made fish tacos. Fried food is bad for us, he thought and smiled to himself. But he remembered the fish man's van coming down Pepper Avenue. Three dollars' worth of red snapper turned into twenty or more tacos—the thin pink strips into fat golden commas, corn tortillas oiled and warm, Abuela's sauce of tomato, onion, chiles, and vinegar. Not much food, but we fatten it up.

He wheeled around and walked back to the restaurant, passing all the outdoor tables along the walkway. He'd held himself rigid all last week at school, waiting for someone else to mention his thuggish guest appearance on TV. But Natalie Larchwood had only mentioned a special-needs student when she'd called him into the office yesterday, even though her eyes had studied him carefully and her fingers had constantly rearranged the flowers on her desk. Maybe everyone had forgotten the news after a day or two—like always.

Inside Chile, the noise was deafening, and Kurt signaled him. "Get some air?" Lakin called near the kitchen. "Cause there's no breathing now."

As long as he kept his mind on the bright patter and the work, he liked it. Bullshitting with Kurt and Javier and Lakin, and music, movies, particular customers. While he was dishing salsa into bowls or putting out tiny bouquets, he could still hang comfortable. Not like when he tried to work with his father or Demetrius, towing stalled cars or digging a trench. He'd always dropped gravel on someone's back or caved in irrigation pipes. Here, he could listen to Kurt talk about Pauline Kael or Oprah, and he could take five orders for *cerveza* and *chile rellenos*.

He hadn't been to his father's place for days, and he didn't know how to talk to his mother. He watched Kurt dicing green chiles, rocking the blade without looking up at Marcus, when Kurt brought up the ashes. "Bessier had a snake tattoo on his thigh; Ernesto said when the coroner saw it, the old man acted all disgusted and told faggot jokes." Kurt paused, glancing up. "Hey, it's not safe to make ethnic or racist jokes anymore, but faggot jokes are just fine with most people, right?"

"Hey, you know," Marcus began, but Kurt bent his head again.

"I'm not talking about you. So after he was ashes, we didn't have enough money for a plane or anything to scatter them. I kept thinking about the snake, about this guy's life, so I took Javier and Ernesto up to the top of Diamondback. You know where that is, huh?"

Marcus nodded. "My brothers used to take me hunting up there."

"Well, it's a lot different now. We had a hard time even getting up there, because of all the development. Cottonwood Canyon Ranch stuff. Anyway, we hiked up the back trail and went over the top. I figured he could look down on the whole city, you know? There's that spring up there, you know, the one that leaks down into a gully and makes an oasis?" Marcus nodded again. "We put his ashes in there, floated them down the little bit of water."

"You didn't see any rattlers?" Marcus asked.

Kurt only smiled. "We weren't scared of snakes."

After he finished stacking dishes and sweeping the floors at Chile, he sat in his apartment thinking of ashes. Pammy Sawicky and her friend were ashes, too. His father always swept the ashes from his little fireplace in the coldhouse and scattered them into the soil for his mother's roses. Marcus's head ached: Trying to sift all the images, he kept hearing his uncle's phrase—shadow men. His father, his uncles, his brothers: no paper traces.

Bessier was a shadow man. Maybe that's why Marcus kept seeing the face, the beauty some people hated enough to avoid even a glimpse.

Someone knocked hard on the door. Marcus blew out the candle he'd lit, calling, "Who is it?"

"Detective Harley," the low voice came. "I need to speak with you, Marcus."

His beard shadow was like black pepper strewn along his jaw. Harley wore a brown coat and tie, and he paced around the living room. Marcus stayed by the closed door, working hard to keep the tremors he felt from visibly shaking him.

"You know, after that first time when you and Finis came walking up out of the riverbottom, I admired you for your loyalty," Harley began, folding his arms. Marcus tried to look into his face, but the old Treetown fear of cops kept weighing heavy on his lids. Harley's fingers were etched with tiny black wires of hair.

"I did. I don't have any brothers. You got four brothers over there, on your dad's place. You're the only one with no stake over there, but you worried about Finis. So all this time, since the city councilman's starting to threaten to hire somebody to find out who killed his daughter, and all this time, when I've had someone keeping an eye on you when you head down to the river and to Finis's girlfriend's and to the Gardens, where everybody's an expert at hiding, I was hoping you'd worry enough about old Finis to take care of him. And we could just ask him a few more questions. But now I think we might have found your brother before you did."

"Finis?" Marcus felt his tongue, as dry and thick as jerky.

"Come on with me," Harley said.

On the street, Marcus felt a stronger tremor slice down his neck. He didn't want to get in the car with McCartin, with the thick wrists and hidden mouth. "I want to take my car," he said at the curb. "I ain't ridin with you."

"Fuck it, Marcus," Harley said. "It's you and me in the front seat, going to see if my fucking tenth body of the year is your brother, okay? Are you coming or not?"

Marcus smelled cigar smoke and Armor All in Harley's car. He stared at the freeway overpass ahead, and Harley said conversationally, "Look at all this new graffiti. Why can't you guys get kids to write out all their fantasies on paper, in school?" He glanced over at Marcus.

Marcus couldn't think. "Does my mother know?"

"About Finis?" Harley stopped the car. "Does she?"

Marcus blinked in confusion, seeing police cars and lights to the right at the pink cottages of the Kozy Komfort, the chain-link gate wide open. Harley pulled into the parking lot, where the men usually sat outside on a warm night like this, and Marcus saw all the doors closed tight on each tiny stucco facade, like a little girl had shut down the dollhouse.

The door to the farthest cottage near the overpass was open, and officers were milling around. Harley walked just behind Marcus, his shoulder inches away, and one of the men said, "This guy gonna ID?"

"Maybe," Harley said. "Marcus, watch your step. You gotta be ready, now."

Marcus kept his eyes on the ceiling when he entered the tiny room. He saw the low plaster above him, as small and square as a handkerchief. When he dropped his eyes slowly, the grimy wall showed a mist of blood like red smoke.

A thin brother lay on his back near the wall, his chest bare, his face tattered into something beyond recognition. The bones held only garish red pieces of a man, and blood lay bright on his chest like dripped candle wax. Marcus wheeled around to face the corner, where he brought up the food he'd eaten at the restaurant; he felt his own skull wedged into the sharp angle.

"Here." Harley handed him a packet of moistened towelettes, like at a restaurant. "I keep these handy. I don't know if your brother was a killer or not, but somebody used a blunt weapon on this guy, like the tire iron on the—uh—the gentleman dressed like a lady." Harley's fingers pulled at Marcus's elbow. "Did somebody pay Finis back like this?"

Marcus forced himself to look at the face again, the ear hanging loose like a copper amulet. He said, "Why you think it's Finis?"

"The guy has a braid, he's around thirty, he has no ID. This place is a haven for smoke brains like your brother." Harley's voice seemed far away, like a transistor radio deejay. Marcus looked around the tiny room, the hotplate and bed and door to the toilet. "No radio or Walkman, no tapes or anything?" he asked. "If it's Finis, he has music."

"Coulda been stolen," Harley said. "You're gonna have to look at him."

Marcus looked past the swimming red face and down to the bare arms. He bent and lifted the curled fingers, ducking his head and holding his breath at the metallic scent of blood. No puckered sunburst of paler skin above the elbow, where Finis's bad reaction to a vaccine always drew his mother's rueful touch. Marcus gently laid the hand back on the gritty floor. He looked at the chest, down toward the ribs, where Finis had a complicated series of markings given to him by a crazed rooster in someone's backyard in Agua Dulce. Then he saw the long, stitched shine of an old stab wound on this stomach, and he shook his head.

"Great," the same cop said in the same disgusted tone. "We got one fatal shooting at the Gardens and this one, all in one night. And nobody knows nothing." He spat out the door.

Marcus walked out the door and stood near the fence, breathing in the hot dust raised by tires. Harley spoke beside him. "That's how the back of Bessier's head looked. McCartin told me you saw his face. Somebody was that angry with Bessier—like somebody was pissed at this guy. I'm thinking maybe his guy body in that dress pissed somebody off. His—her face, you know? And this guy, with a braid like Finis—his face made somebody mad, too. Right?" Marcus was silent. Harley went on. "Now Pammy and Marissa—well, Marissa was burning, probably, and Pammy got shot with that gun you kindly directed us to in the canal. I guess you can't imagine her fear, right, when the flames were licking up high?"

"Why you sweatin me about it all the time?" Marcus said softly, keeping his mouth close to the dust-coated fence.

"Like I told you, Mr. Sawicky is still broken up about it. He has friends in the department, since he's been a city councilman all these years. Yeah, he was encouraged to hear about the gun, but then, the ballistics and no fingerprints didn't add up to much. He did tell us she had some pretty disreputable friends, some unsavory kinda guys." Harley paused and leaned against the fence to face Marcus. "I'm just saying I hope nobody gets that mad at Finis. I really thought that was him, in there, that somebody was going outside the law. I mean, maybe he'd actually be safer, safer to himself and others, if he was in custody. Nobody could do a Kozy Komfort on him, right? Think about it, Marcus."

Marcus walked away, standing beside Harley's car. Another shadow man, beyond the glaring doorway. Nobody knew him but his mother. No papers, no traces. He shivered uncontrollably now near the car window, seeing himself distorted in the glass.

He called in sick to Kurt's, since even the thought of the salsas and meats brought acid to his throat. The whole weekend, he kept the phone off the hook, the shades down, and he listened to his old tapes. Ohio Players, Rufus, Mandrill. Funkadelic. He saw Finis, liquid shoulders moving steady when he walked, chin poking to his own beat. He read the scribbled blues lyrics SaRonn had recalled, trying to decipher the bloodred river and clay. He listened to Brother Lobo's show, his eyes welling hot while he walked furiously around the living room, touching his wood figures from Haiti and India and Lesotho. Shadow men. The dead teenager in the Olive Gardens parking lot and the dead brother in the Kozy Komfort—they'd each gotten two paragraphs in the newspaper. Page eleven. No witnesses. No suspects. In the brother's case, no one had even identified the body.

Jungletown. That's what the cops called it. Fights and drunks and deaths *down there*. "Only good nigger is a dead nigger," Uncle Oscar used to say, grinning evil. "What I always heard."

But the three people found on his father's place were white. He looked at Pammy Sawicky's yearbook photo, the sharp nose with a circle of bone at the end, the pearlescent forehead. The All-American smile. No more costume changes.

He tried to picture how beautiful Sofelia would have been in this row of senior photos: her glowing cheekbones raised high, her big molasses eyes, her hair as dark as a scarf. SaRonn had said it was a hole in your body, to lose a child. He couldn't know. Pammy's father and the other girl's parents had huge chunks missing, and Bessier's parents, even though they hadn't even wanted his bones, had to be missing the feel of theirs. The hollow Sofelia spot at his mother's ribs wasn't full now, and if Finis was never found, or found like the brother in the motel room, she would lose heart muscle, too.

When he had to eat, he decided to get sushi. The knocking came while he was looking at the menu he kept in a basket near the phone. Marcus stared at the dark wood floor, not moving. Harley—with more questions?

"Marcus," Demetrius shouted. "Come on, man."

Demetrius sat on the couch, his dark-blue work clothes banded with oil at the thighs. "I ain't seen you in hella long," he said.

"I been workin at Chipotle Chile," Marcus said. "Seem like all I do is mess up and make things worse at the place. Mama probably still mad."

Demetrius shrugged and rubbed his jaw; his fingernails were outlined in black. "She just finishin up the pecans, you know. Sofelia still sittin in the bed, smokin."

Marcus shook his head. "Come on. I was goin for some food."

"Naw, man, I probably don't want nothin you fixin to eat," Demetrius said.

"You ain't seen my car," Marcus said.

Demetrius laughed when they stood next to the faded sky-blue VW Bug. "Oh, man," he said, slamming the hood. "This is you?"

Marcus grinned. "Hey, I couldn't make up my mind, so I bought this just for the duration." He pointed to the turquoise Cadillac convertible Kurt had just bought. "This is a Funkytown car."

"Funkytown?"

"That's what Sofelia's son calls this neighborhood. I was tryin to figure out the proper vehicle for a Funkytown brotha like myself. People got their costume, their uniform, and their vehicle. Lifestyle choices."

"Shut up, man," Demetrius said. "Where you takin me?"

In the Japanese restaurant on Las Palmas, Demetrius sat uncomfortably while the woman made up the fresh sushi. There was a long line, and Marcus sat down at the small table with two Kirin beers. Demetrius took a sip and grimaced. "Man, I'll take Uncle Oscar's choc any day," he said. But then he leaned forward. "That's what I came to talk to you about. Somethin Enchantee told me."

Marcus said, "I gotta tell you about somethin first," he said. "You see the dude killed in the Kozy Komfort?"

"Same night one a them Proudfoot boys got it in the Gardens," Demetrius said, his fingers hard on his jaw again. "One a Bantam's boys. Lorenzo. They say he was just gettin back to the parkin lot and some dude pull up in a car and ask him 'Where you from?' And Lorenzo said, 'You talkin to me?' And the other kid opened fire."

Marcus pictured all the Gardens doors closing tight like clenched eyelids. Hear no evil, see no evil. Like the Kozy Komfort doors. He told Demetrius about Harley, about the brother with the scar and no face. "They said they thought it was Finis," he said.

Demetrius was silent, looking at the label on the beer bottle. Marcus got up to get his order. Futomaki, with egg and spinach. He offered one of the colorful rolls to Demetrius, who shook his head. "The brotha wasn't nobody we knew," Demetrius finally said. "I'da heard."

"That's hard," Marcus said. "He was somebody's brother."

"Hey, man, I cain't be carin about everybody," Demetrius said, his voice edging harder. "He was at the Kozy Komfort. Brothas make choices. I learned long time ago: Who you run with, that's who you gon fall with."

Marcus got up to get soy sauce and extra wasabi. He saw people lingering by the counter, waiting for their take-out orders, saw them glancing hurriedly at him and Demetrius. The people eating at other tables avoided his eyes when he walked back across the small room. Jungletown. Demetrius's grimy uniform, his thick braid, his harsh voice. Funkytown. Quiet conversation about movies. Dockers. Him. But not tonight.

"Come on, D," he said, making his voice light. "Try some a this.

You always puttin Tabasco on everything." He handed Demetrius a pinch of rice smeared with the green Japanese horseradish.

"I ain't Oriental, okay?" Demetrius said, low. "I can't eat this fish stuff. Probably don't taste like nothin."

"This is just rice. Try it." Marcus watched Demetrius' eyes water and a flush of maroon crawl across his nose.

"Damn! That green shit go in your nose, man, not in your throat." Marcus laughed. Demetrius drank some beer. "Tabasco, man. Salsa. The nigga in me like Tabasco and the Mescan in me like salsa, okay?" Marcus had to laugh loud in the low burble of talk around them.

Back in the apartment, he gave Demetrius a Miller. "Where you get the Bug?" Demetrius asked.

"Layton. That's somethin else I been wantin to tell you."

"I know—Layton got all them guys restorin V-Dubs now."

Marcus shook his head. "No. You said maybe somebody was mad at you for tryin to get the city contract, the cop rotation."

Demetrius leaned back on the couch. "I shouldn't have bragged to nobody. I said we were goin twenty-four hours now, gettin all the paperwork. Rotella—I know he probably got mad."

Marcus said, "I asked Layton straight up if somebody was mad cause you wanted in on that deep pocket. He said you and him go way back. And he said Rotella was a damn junkyard dog." Marcus smiled, remembering Layton's wry face. "Said he gets everything from the cops and sells it fast as he can. But he said . . ." Marcus hesitated, watching Demetrius lean forward and hold the beer. "He said Rotella ain't worried about you and Daddy and Eight. Said Arrow Towing is small-time. Not like he was doggin you. He just said Rotella and him got the whole city, and with all the commuters, the new people, there was too much work."

Demetrius was quiet for a while, finishing the beer and fanning his fingers behind his neck. Then he said, "Well, I sure can't make no moves now. What I gotta tell you is about somethin illegal. And I ain't doin none a that. I know Julius do sometimes, but not so me and Eight find out."

He told Marcus about what Enchantee had heard—The Blue Q, the name on the land, and something illegal. "You said you recognize this Web Matheson dude from somewhere."

"I swear I've seen his face somewhere besides Chile. Like a long time ago." Marcus thought about the recent news photos of aspiring politicians, but he shook his head. "You said they talked about blue *paint*?"

Demetrius stood up. "Think about it. That's what you supposed to be good at—thinkin. Cause you sure as hell ain't good for nothin else."

"Nice hangin with you, too, my brother." Marcus grinned. "You sure you ain't hungry?"

"Man, I ate neckbones and rice at Mama's. And now I gotta go home and eat whatever Enchantee cooked, so she won't get mad." He stretched at the door, big-knuckled fists frozen for a moment in the air. "I gotta keep two women happy. And you ain't got a one hidin round here. Nowhere." Demetrius stuck his tongue in the corner of his mouth and raised his eyebrows. "My brother."

By the next Friday, after dealing with sullen students in the stuffy classroom where the heating system wanted to kick in for late fall even though the sun was still working overtime, Marcus only wanted to finish his shift at Chile and then sit at a quiet corner table to write down the things he could remember. The strange splinter of dried fish, the salted plums he'd found on the hillside behind his father's. The blues song Finis had given SaRonn for him. He wouldn't think about her neck or her tinkling bracelets, he told himself, walking toward the school parking lot.

Rival car stereos were blasting rap and metal while students stood around talking. Marcus glanced up and saw Mortrice, wearing the big jacket, standing with several other boys and a white man with a blond ponytail.

When the man looked up from his notebook, Marcus saw that it was Bent, the guy he'd met in the gym. Mortrice was shrugging, face impassive. His friend Chris said loudly, "Why you wanna know?"

"I'm doing a series for the paper on the history of rap," Bent said easily. "One part is who listens to rap. I saw you all talking here, I heard the beats, and I figured you for experts."

Marcus grinned at the smooth, cajoling voice he used with them—like a teacher. He stopped to listen. Mortrice, Chris, a boy Marcus knew went by B-Real, and two white kids he didn't know stood near the fence. One of the kids had blond stubble and a spindly braid tail; the other had brown hair in awkward wings over his forehead.

"B-Real the expert," Chris said. Marcus watched Mortrice turn away, his arms folded.

"What do you listen to?" Bent said, his pen waiting.

B-Real said, "I listen to the real thing. Stuff you can't find, cause it's not on the radio. It's in the car and in the street." He glanced at the two white kids. "You better ask them. They think they're experts. That's all they play."

"You guys are buddies?" Bent asked, but Mortrice and his friends were leaving. They didn't see Marcus.

"We got class together," the blond kid said, grinning.

"You guys like rap, huh?" Bent said, writing fast.

"NWA, DJ Quik, all them guys," the blond kid said, rocking slightly. "It's *real*, homes. Real life. Gats and cappin and rollin. If you got the right attitude."

"Josh and William, right?" Bent said, looking up. He saw Marcus then. "Hey, thanks, guys. I might be back looking for you again." Raising his hand, he smiled wide. "Marcus, right? You teach here?"

"Yeah. I'm on my way to my second gig," Marcus said. "I work at Chipotle Chile, too."

"Whoa, Abby's favorite place." Bent put his small notebook away. "I figured I'd find some rap fans here."

"Plenty of them," Marcus said, walking with him toward the street. "Not just Treetown kids. All those Plymouth Hill and downtown kids listen to it."

"Treetown," Bent said thoughtfully. "That's a fascinating area." He seemed to be waiting, Marcus thought.

"Yeah," he said. He didn't know Bent; he hated trying to explain Treetown to strangers.

"You walking?" Bent asked, surprised. "You live around here?"

"Downtown," Marcus said. He was uneasy, but maybe all reporters were nosy.

"Well, let me give you a ride to the restaurant," Bent said, gesturing to a black Montero. "That place is great. Abby says they're going to expand next door and put in a real nice bar."

In the front seat, Marcus saw the newspaper, and he flipped through the city section. Carrie Smith Donohue—he frowned at the name on a column. That's who Enchantee had heard. "Historic Deglet Noor Building Nearly a Lost Treasure," the headline read. He recognized the arched facade and fanciful towers of a building he'd walked past near the art college.

The local arts community rescued this architectural jewel from the wrecker's ball. The completely renovated building now contains galleries and studios. The Deglet Noor is part of Rio Seco's Moorish-Spanish heritage, named for a lovely locally grown date. The building is a lively example of what should not be overlooked in the city's rapid growth and expansion.

"That's Abby's aunt," Bent said, glancing over. "Damn, she kicks ass."

She sure didn't sound like someone who'd want Uncle Oscar's, Marcus thought, looking at her small photo. A stiff-curled helmet of pale hair, a wide mouth with soft, down-turned edges.

On the opposite page he saw a photo of Web Matheson. "I've gotta get some gas real quick," Bent said, pulling into the self-serve station. Marcus nodded, reading.

Local developer Web Matheson has purchased a 500-acre tract of land in the far western portion of the city. The area was once known as Miller Ranch. Matheson has said his company will develop the tract with housing and commercial use.

When Bent started the engine, Marcus saw the primer-gray Nova he'd driven from SaRonn's. Bennie Proudfoot and Julius stared at him for a moment, and then Bent turned toward the restaurant.

"This big series on rap is hard as hell to write," Bent said. "I'm trying to connect rap and blues, go all the way back to African styles of music and communication, you know?"

Marcus blinked, then looked at Bent's laptop computer on the seat. "Big is right."

Bent nodded. "And Abby's acting really strange, I guess cause she's working hard, too. Snapping at me, and I'm the guy, so I'm always wrong, you know? Selfish, unappreciative. Take your pick."

Marcus had to grin. "Sounds like my aunt's favorite line against guys, from an old song. She used to say, 'You men make me so tired—you got a mouthful a gimme and a handful a much-obliged.'"

Bent turned to him quickly. "She likes the blues?"

"My uncle sings the blues," Marcus said. Then he saw the excitement on Bent's face.

"You mean around the house?"

"No, he's got a little place," Marcus said slowly. "He sings on weekends."

"Where?"

"Other side of the freeway," Marcus said.

"Treetown?" Bent parked in front of Chile. "I'd love to do a story on that area, and I'd love to meet your uncle. The blues—nobody listens to the blues anymore. College kids."

Marcus saw Bennie and the Proudfoots, all the bodies in The Blue Q on a Friday night. Blues, funk, oldies. Treetown. No easy explanation for someone who hadn't lived there.

"If you have the time, man . . ." Bent said.

"Maybe sometime," Marcus said, opening the car door, picturing Bent's face at The Blue Q and how Uncle Oscar would look at him.

"What's your uncle's name?" Bent's voice was carefully casual now.

"Oscar Thompson," Marcus said, heading for the kitchen. "Thanks."

In the apartment that night, Marcus wrote Finis's lyrics in order, as far as he could remember. Somebody listened to the blues. To everything. "Whichaway do the bloodred river run?" SaRonn had said. "Loader sent me plenty cement and clay."

Blue paint. That's what he couldn't stop thinking about, whenever he tried to put things together. And not in that context—when he thought of the paint, he saw his mother, smelled her food, felt her fingers across his face. The blue starfish of paint by the kitchen door. The gaping hole in the adobe near the steps.

He slammed his palm onto the paper. He had to find Nacho.

. . .

"Con paciencia y salivita, un elefante se coge a una hormiguita," Paz whispered to the girl, her great-great-granddaughter, who sat splay-legged in the dust near the olive house, watching the tiny ants racing to find water.

"With patience and a bit of spittle, the elephant picks up the ant so little," Alma whispered, too, and then laughed. The baby girl slid her chubby hand into Alma's, pointing at the rabbits.

Paz squinted at the shimmering gray settling over the trees. This late smog and heat were trapped in the olive and eucalyptus leaves, with no wind to stir them free. Even the wasps hadn't settled down yet. But she knew when the sky suddenly lifted like a giant spiderweb pulled from the earth, when it turned dark blue, that ice would follow this winter.

That one time she and her daughter had gone to work fields far north, and they'd been caught in a freeze of crusted ice and snow, she'd known why people always dreaded winter everywhere else. Salcido had told her about the snow and cold in his village in New Mexico, trying to survive when the earth was barren and the animals haggard or fallen.

Paz walked down the slope with Alma and the baby, breathing hard in the buzzing-hot air. She knew Alma would go into the kitchen and pour lemonade for all of them, and then take a glass floating with pearls of pulp to Sofelia, whose skin glistened gray and ashen.

"La sangre sin fuego hierve," Paz murmured at the vision of the too-bright eyes glowing huge. The blood boils without flame.

Nearing the house, Alma said, "Look at that! What do they think they doin?"

Pails and buckets clattered hollow, and Paz saw two men setting ladders against the walls. Her *perico* grandson, smiling, leaning down to check the adobe his father had mixed in a small pit near the house.

"Azul," Paz whispered, seeing the bright spatters like drops of sky.

Marcus heard his mother go into the kitchen. He was near the barn, showing Nacho how to mix the lime, sweet milk, and Liquitex with the blue Nacho had been stirring. "Start over there, brothaman," Marcus told him, pointing to the long stretch of wall facing Pepper Avenue. The back of the house, he thought. Back to the city.

Marcus and his father squatted at the hole near the kitchen. "Lucky it been so dry, or the wet woulda worked this even deeper," his father said. "Why you so hot to paint right now?"

The truth, Marcus thought. "Wanted to do something nice for Mama, since I messed up with Sofelia."

"That wasn't your fault," his father said, eyes down on the mix of sand, straw, clay, and water he'd shoveled into a bucket.

"The tellin part was," Marcus said. "I can do this, okay?"

His father stood. "So hot, I think I'ma form some bricks since I got this adobe mixed up. Paz told your mama she think we gon have a freeze and a wet winter. Don't seem like it to me, but I can always use some bricks."

Marcus slathered the thick adobe mix on the hole, pushing it in hard, tamping it down with a trowel. The coarse wet rubbed against his fingers, and he remembered doing this when he was young, after a long, rainy winter.

He shaped the last layer with his palms, trying to match the bumped curve of bricks. The bricks were nearly a foot wide, the walls of the house like a formidable barrier against the heat and noise of outside. Marcus saw the adobe paling, drying fast. He went to the hose for a drink, and his father called, "Bring me some a that water."

He threw water into the pit, where his father had mixed the adobe with his long, bare feet. Marcus smiled, remembering how they'd laughed at their father back when he showed them how to do this, how they'd slung mud at each other when they were kids. "Y'all got Oklahoma Indian in you," his father used to say. "But you look like California Indians now."

His father poured the slushy mud into a wooden form for bricks. Marcus helped him smooth off the top with a piece of wood, packing the adobe down into the squares. "Old Archuleta and I used to do this," his father said absently. "Used to sell the bricks now and then. But Salcido made it his living. He had the clay right there, and the sand, since he was close to the riverbottom. Had that big yard to keep all his materials."

"I used to love goin there when we were kids," Marcus said, staring at the bits of straw like odd whiskers in the bricks. "Used to slide down that big hill of gravel. We always hid in the boulders, too."

"He hauled them rocks from everywhere," his father said. "That building yard made a lotta houses. Cement and sand and stones."

Marcus frowned, hearing Finis's words. He shook his head and said, "I'ma start by the kitchen."

He could see his mother and his *abuela*, vague shadows through the screen door, when he slathered on the thickened blue coating. But he didn't know what to say, where to start, so he worked in silence until all but the new adobe patch was covered. Even though the mud looked light and dry already, he knew it was moist far inside and had to breathe for a while.

When they were finished outside his *abuela's* room, he turned the corner. His mother had painted this section weeks ago, the blue slightly faded now. He walked near his mother's window, where smoke wafted from the screen like steam from a grate.

"We gotta give this part another coat," he called to Nacho. "Mix up some more."

Marcus watched the dark, blue wet go over the old, porous coat. Inside the dim screen, his face against the smoke, he saw Sofelia's eyes glittering. His mother stood in the doorway now, her square shape hovering there.

"Only two women in the world I'd kill for, Sofelia," Marcus said. "Same two women since I was little. You or Mama. Demetrius tried to teach me to fight, and the only time I could get mad enough was when somebody messed with you. Like that boy from the Westside— whoever he was, me and Finis kicked his ass after he followed you home and scared you. Remember?"

He paused, hearing nothing but breathing and the lapping of the brush. He couldn't say what he'd heard. He hadn't thought enough about this, hadn't planned for the screen and the stillness.

"I was wrong, all those weeks when you called me and said not to tell Mama. Cause she was hurtin. But you were hurtin, too, and I didn't know what I was supposed to do. So tell me, Sofelia. If I need to kick somebody's ass, if me and Demetrius need to kill somebody, just tell me. Because I'm worried about Mortrice."

Sofelia drew in her breath sharply, a rasp like a lit match. Marcus glanced inside and saw no flame, just the floating white bone of cigarette. "The boy don't know us, he's from L.A., and he's hangin at the Gardens with the wrong kids. I ain't his daddy. But if he don't have a daddy around, I can try. Kinda late. He told me once, somethin about his daddy said . . ."

"No," Sofelia whispered, "he don't know his daddy."

"He tried to say his daddy told him somethin," Marcus said.

"No he didn't."

"Sofelia," Marcus said, thinking of the words in The Blue Q, the flat chill in her throat. "Tell him his daddy's dead. Tell him that so somebody else can try. I'll drive you around like before. I'll do whatever you want me to. Come on."

"Don't push her so hard," his mother's voice came, from the doorway. "She ain't well. She got a fever."

"I know," Marcus said, moving so that his shadow fell across the room in the late afternoon light. "I'm gone." He took the bucket and headed for the end of the wall, the farthest corner of the house where you could see through the frayed palm fronds and out to the red sun dropping into purple oblivion.

Early the next morning, before anyone but Abuela was up, Alma sat on the couch listening to the mingled breathings of those still sleeping. Kendrick, Jawan, the baby girl, Sofelia. She imagined she could hear Hosea's rasping throat, Julius's snores. And instead of Finis's tangled night cries, she imagined she could hear the boy. Mortrice. He slept in the trailer, she hoped, his warm breath gathering on the curved metal sides.

Sofelia would move. She would decide, talk, her eyes would cool and slant again with laughter. Alma would have to wait. Marcus had done his best. Lila—she didn't know why she couldn't think of her sister-in-law without a hard ache along her jaw, but she knew Marcus wasn't the one she should hold responsible.

Stepping outside, walking all the way to the coldhouse, she turned to look at her house. The sea-green blue, the cool shoal of shallow water dipping into the gravel, shimmering behind the wisteria, reflected in the hubcaps on the tree near her fingers. She heard Hosea call, "Who out there?" When he opened his door, she held out her arms so he could see.

. . .

The wasps hovered everywhere, in the dangling branches, under the eaves of the house, and when Mortrice walked from the trailer to see his mother, he hunched over. He spent nearly all his time at the apartment, hanging out with the AK crew, driving for hours around Rio Seco and even into San Bernardino. Once, he'd taken them all the way to L.A. Chris and B-Real and Teddy and Lawrence, whose brother had laid on the pavement for two hours while his mother screamed at police to let her hold her boy and they held back the residents with yellow tape. Crime scene. Random. But Mortrice knew the shooter had asked the question: "Where you from?"

On the freeway to L.A., the others had been impressed with his knowledge of the different routes, of all the areas and their nicknames. He'd told them they could cruise a few places, but they couldn't flash or instigate. Mortrice was still thinking of Kenneth, of the Monte Carlo and Capper and all the rest of them, what they might do if someone saw his face. And AK didn't have enough firepower yet to cruise hard. They had to get more money and go back to Zach.

He stepped inside the kitchen, ducking away from the wasp floating effortlessly in the eaves like he was watching a movie in the red tile. His mother was sitting at the table, drinking coffee, her face thin and translucent. Mortrice stopped at the threshold, shocked.

"Where you been?" she asked, like she always had.

"Hangin with my friends," he answered, like he always had.

"Mortrice," she said, her voice as low as a hum. "You ain't axed me about your—daddy."

Mortrice saw Kenneth's face, the eyes, the measurement in each glance. "I ain't had to," he said. "I know."

She frowned, her brows jerking tight. "What you know?"

"I know who he is," he said.

"Who?" she whispered, like she was blowing out a candle. "Who?"

Mortrice folded his arms and looked at the tile floor. "I know."

Sofelia stared at him until he looked back at her. "Then you know he dead, right? He dead and gone." She squinted at him, like this was a test in school.

Mortrice didn't move. "He ain't never said nothin to me," he said finally. "But I knew. I could tell."

"Oh, baby," Sofelia said. "All you gotta know is he dead. He wasn't never nothin, and he ain't nothin now. You always been mine. Only mine. Okay?"

Mortrice stared beyond her at the statue of a woman in a hole in the wall. He saw Kenneth's smile, heard the *shuck-shuck* of the shotgun, and felt the marks on his back tingle like tiny blisters that were just popping.

Marcus wasn't sure where he was going. Something illegal at The Blue Q. He thought of his uncle's choc beer, bittersweet and as thick as molasses, coating and swaying in the stomach. "Like a meal," people said. "I know niggas back in the Depression lived on that choc. Didn't eat nothin, but that took em through."

He drove slowly around downtown, looking at the new microbrewery, the champagne brunch sign on the Las Palmas Hotel, at Charlie's and the Shamrock and the funky new Moosehead Lounge. He wondered if Bent liked the white blues band advertised there.

He drove through the Westside, seeing the many liquor stores and only two bars, since they always lost their licenses and got shut down. Jimmy D's and the High Roller.

Down through Agua Dulce, he saw all the restaurants and bars along 52nd Street, or Little Michoacán. *"Menudo* Served *Diaramente—Carnitas Estilo* Michoacán." *Birrería*—the place where Rubén Salcido took them after cement jobs for *birria* and Tecate.

On Grove Avenue, he cruised along the riverbottom, and then turned into his father's gate. Twelve men sitting at a polished bar, their vodka in silvery circles of glass, their beer in foreign bottles, he thought. And here we got about a dozen dudes dangling malt-liquor forties from their fingers, holding Miller cans like baby bottles. What's the difference?

"Hey," he called to Demetrius and Kickstand and the others, but he headed for the adobe patch near the stairs to see if it was dry. Squatting down to rub his palm across the warm mud, he saw his hand disappear. The same color. He smiled, remembering that day he'd been coloring in school, seeing a nutty reddish-brown slant across the page near his hand. He'd asked the teacher, "What's this color?" She'd read the label, frowning.

"Burnt siena," she'd said.

Marcus had seen his mother's eye-high cheeks in the color, his *abuela's* burnt back of the neck. His father was much darker. Marcus had studied all the crayons, asking the teacher to read the colors. "Flesh," she'd read patiently from the crayon the color of Band-Aids and old gum.

Marcus and Demetrius squatted in the shade near the barn, and Hosea thought about how his oldest son and youngest were getting along better these days. Marcus hadn't even come around much before, and Demetrius was always ready to poke holes in his baby brother, as if his every word was a nuisance.

Hosea sat in his chair, fiddling with an air filter. Seemed like he and Oscar never had that chance. Oscar had been a baby, in that cave above the black-iron stairway at Mrs. Hefferon's. And Hosea had seen Oscar only a few times until he was almost thirteen. Then came the ringing blow to his ear, the long walk to Texas. And in Los Angeles, they were grown men with skin as hard as bark.

Friends. They were more like friends than brothers, even though they'd seen each other every day now for over thirty years, since Oscar had come here. Something different, not like his sons with their easy punching and harsh words and fierce rivalry.

He looked down at the air filter. Oscar had asked him a strange question yesterday. "Who y'all leavin the land to?" Oscar had sat right here, and stared out at the trees.

Hosea had been silent for a long time. Oscar had no children. Hosea had never really known where he'd found Lila, but she didn't have any either. He'd looked at the blue walls so bright and strange to his eyes. "I ain't thought about it," he said.

"You ain't got no will?" Oscar said. "Shit, I ain't. But Lila do."

"Tell the truth, I ain't wanted to think about it," Hosea had said, finally. "All them names. Don't want no fightin."

"Better than the government fightin over every speck a dust," Oscar had said. "Goddamn people want every pebble you ever walked on."

Hosea heard the loud phone ring, and Alma came outside. "Demetrius, you got a job. Downtown. Red Miata on Second Avenue and Columbus."

Demetrius said, "Come on, Marcus. We goin to your part a town, you might as well come. Probably one a your homeys. Sherbert car."

"Shut up," Marcus said. "Don't even start." Hosea watched them get into the big flatbed tow truck and head out to the street, their mouths still moving fast through the windshield.

The guy was waiting in front of one of the office buildings on Columbus, leaning against his red Miata, his tie loosened and jacket off. "Hey," he waved, seeing the flatbed. "Thanks for coming so quickly."

Demetrius maneuvered the tow truck into place in front of the car, saying, "He must be used to Triple A. Guess you can keep him company up here, since you speak his lingo."

Marcus got out and shook the guy's hand. "Jerry Paulsen," he said. "Found you guys in the Yellow Pages. I just moved out here from L.A."

"Housing's a lot cheaper, huh?" Marcus said. He watched Demetrius start to incline the flatbed, the loud vibrating roar of the hydraulics over their voices.

"No kidding," Paulsen shouted. "I live in Cottonwood Canyon."

Demetrius attached the chains and began to pull the Miata up the ramp. Then the flatbed slowly returned to level, and Marcus gestured for Paulsen to get into the cab.

He was uncomfortable, his briefcase on his lap, his jacket over that. "What's wrong with the car?" Demetrius asked.

Paulsen shrugged, his shoulder against Marcus's. "I don't know. Wouldn't start up at all. It's not a dead battery. Maybe the ignition." They were headed down Pepper Avenue now. "Uh, I don't even have a garage here yet, I mean, no mechanics that I've used. Maybe you guys know somebody?"

"Yeah, but it's almost five," Demetrius said. "I'll give you coupla names for tomorrow morning."

Paulsen leaned his head back. "I've gotta get home fast, because it's my wife's birthday. Shit. I guess I'll call a cab from your place, huh?"

Demetrius pulled into the gate and roared up the incline. The place was crowded with cars now, and he motioned Kickstand to move a Toyota truck out of the way near the barn. Paulsen felt frozen against Marcus's sleeve, and Marcus knew what he felt seeing all the dark faces and the loud laughing and beer bottles.

Paulsen stood uncertainly beside the truck when they got out. "Hey," Marcus said. "Don't worry. My brother'll write you up a bill in the barn. Come on in the house and use the phone." Paulsen carried his briefcase like it was full of rocks.

"Shit!" Marcus heard from the barn. "Gotdamn motherfuckers is back!" He turned to see Demetrius stumble from the alcove where he kept paperwork. He was clutching his shoulder. "Fuckin wasps again!" he shouted.

Paulsen's face was as pale and stiff as the meringue Lakin liked to whip. Marcus felt panic thrum through him, and he said, "D, come inside and get some a that bakin-soda paste. Kendrick already got stung this morning."

Paulsen went up the steps as Marcus held open the screen. "Mama," Marcus called. "Mr. Paulsen's gonna call a cab. And Demetrius needs some paste. They just got him."

His mother was standing at the stove, stirring something in a pot. She turned and smiled at Paulsen. "The phone right there," she said. She took the list of taxi companies from the shelf where she kept all her paperwork. "Yellow Cab come right away, most of the time."

Demetrius had stripped off his shirt, and he was grimacing at the welt growing on his shoulder. Marcus saw his stomach, ridged and wide, above his belt. "And you don't even work out," he said.

"Shut up, fool," Demetrius said. "Get out there and take care of the car." He sat down at the table next to Paulsen, who was dialing, his hand shaking. Marcus saw the shallow tin pan filled with white, grainy paste, and Demetrius reached in with his fingers.

Near the barn, he saw a bunch of men sitting or standing near the Toyota truck that said ANTUAN'S LANDSCAPING on the cab door. Near them was the hulking old Apache truck, the one somebody had bought off the storage lot. Its blunt turtle-nose grille was facing a few more men. And he saw Enchantee's car pull up and park near the fence.

"Hey," she called, holding D'Junior's hand. "Abby's fiancé, Bent, told me he knows who your uncle is." Her face was full and smiling.

"Uncle Oscar?" Marcus said, twirling, trying to keep everything straight. He needed to get the Miata off the truck, in case they got another call, and he didn't want to admit that he couldn't remember what to do first. Shit. He didn't want to mess up. All the guys watching. Kickstand called out, "Yo, Marcus, them shorts tighter than panty hose, ain't they? Brothaman?"

"Fuck you," Marcus said easily, seeing Paulsen's face hovering above the steps. He came down slowly, the briefcase welded to his fingers.

"Think I'll wait out here," Paulsen said.

"Here's a chair," Marcus said, motioning to one in the shade near the barn, farther away from all the men. "Demetrius is in there gettin baking soda on a wasp sting," he told Enchantee.

She rolled her eyes. "Like we never heard of Bactine?" she said. "That stupid paste always falls off in chunks anyway." She and her son went into the kitchen, and Marcus took a deep breath and turned toward the red Miata sitting atop the truck like a ladybug on a rollerskate.

"Nigga, put some black pepper in that radiator, plug that leak up," someone said to Kickstand, who was looking at the Toyota truck.

"That stuff gotta go somewhere once it get into your leak," Kickstand said irritably. "Then that shit gon migrate all into your engine and mess up the flow." Marcus smiled. Kickstand hated it when amateurs suggested remedies.

He didn't know where his brothers were. He saw two huge men near the Apache with Nacho. "Yo, you seen Eight or Julius?" he called, and Nacho shook his head.

"These guys are lookin for a paint job on the Apache," Nacho said when Marcus came closer. "Nate and Calvin Cook, man."

"Hey," Marcus said, recognizing the massive ebony faces. They both played for the Rams. "You guys are into old trucks?"

"Nate is," Calvin said. "Cause he need somethin of his own. His wife havin another baby. Ain't that right, Nate?" He nudged his brother hard, and Marcus saw the muscled shoulders collide like pillows.

The young brother Marcus recognized was Darnell Tucker, who trimmed trees for his father now and then. He stepped from around the Toyota. "My wife's havin number three, too," he said, shaking his head. "You got two boys, right?"

Nate said, "This one's a boy, too. She already know. I'ma name him Larkin. After the man taught us to play ball."

"With a name like that, he gon have to be tough," Kickstand called.

Nate laughed. "Either he be like his mama—so fine everybody gotta love him. Or he be like me—and ain't nobody bother him."

Darnell said, "I got two girls already. Even if this is another one, it's the last. I'ma get it done. Three's plenty."

Marcus laughed. "You gon get the cut? You gon tamper with your apparatus at your age?"

Calvin said, "That ain't right, man, shootin blanks. Ain't natural."

"I don't start shootin blanks, I'll be shootin myself," Darnell said. "Or shootin some possums to feed my tribe."

The boy Kendrick came out to tell Marcus that Demetrius said quit messin around. He had traces of the baking soda paste on his arm and neck, and he picked at the dried stuff around the edges. "You supposed to leave it on," Marcus said, trying to sound hard.

"I'ma get my mama come over here and smoke out them wasps for you," Calvin said, peering up at the high eaves of the barn. "She like to go fishin with those eggs."

"We haven't had time to spray," Marcus said. "Too much goin on around here."

Darnell nodded, serious. "They never found out who killed those people? Man, it's been over a year and they never found out who shot my homey Birdman. Louis Wiley." He leaned against the wall, his eyes distant.

"Yeah, my mama keep his little girl, Hollie," Nate said. "Her and Louis's pops, Roscoe, stay together. Birdman's little girl is real smart."

"I'm fixin to bring your pops some palm fronds for that burned-out part of the fence," Darnell said, turning to Marcus. "I keep forgettin."

"Shit," Marcus said, seeing another car pull in. The ancient Buick pulled around slowly and turned its trunk toward the men. Paulsen had started, nearly standing, when he heard the tires, and now he walked toward Marcus anxiously.

"I think I'll go inside and call again," he said.

Marcus watched a thin man about forty get out of the Buick and walk nervously toward him. "What can I do for you, man?" he asked the brother, whose mouth was working around an unlit cigarette.

"Hey, bro, I need to see Julius, man, I got somethin he wanted," the man said, his eyes scanning the other faces as quick as windshield wipers. Kickstand had gone into the barn. Marcus looked at the Buick.

"The car?" he asked.

"No, man," the guy said, taking his arm and pulling him toward the trunk. "Julius wanted this VCR for his lady, and he said he needed these rims, too." Marcus peered down at the stuff in the trunk. Julius always needed something to impress a woman, and he specialized in rims.

"Where'd you get this stuff?" Marcus asked, looking back at the Miata. He needed to get out of here.

"Where I was supposed to get it," the man said impatiently. "Where Julius axed me to get it. Come on. He owe me fifty bucks. You got it or not?"

"Hold up," Marcus said, seeing Paulsen stand, forlorn, near the door. He went to the house. "They comin?"

Paulsen nodded, his face sheened with sweat. "You want some water?" Marcus asked. "Some lemonade?"

"Water's fine," Paulsen said, trying to smile.

Marcus stepped inside the kitchen. Demetrius was patting fresh paste on his shoulder; the first coat had already dried in the heat and D'Junior was picking up the pale shards that had fallen onto the floor when Demetrius moved. Marcus remembered playing with the cracked edges of paste covering his own stings and bites.

"Demetrius always take stings worst," his mother said from the stove.

"They make Bactine because it has an anesthetic," Enchantee said impatiently.

"D," Marcus said. "A guy outside got parts for Julius, he need fifty bucks."

"Naw, I ain't givin Julius shit," Demetrius said. "Not him."

His mother turned and said, "Here." She held out money from her apron pocket. "Julius pay me back."

Marcus went outside and handed the money to the man, who put the VCR into his arms quickly, his eyes still darting to the barn. He stacked the rims on the ground and slammed the trunk.

Marcus was carrying the VCR to the barn, where he figured Julius could find it, when he heard the sirens looping around the gate and the tires hard on the gravel. "Police," a voice shouted while the doors began to slam. "Let's all stop and slowly get prone. Come on!"

"Oh, my God," Paulsen's voice came, a threading cry.

"Gotdamn," Kickstand said. "Now what?"

Breathing in the iron smell of hot gravel, Marcus heard the steps come close to his face. "What'd you just purchase, bro?" the officer said.

"I don't know," Marcus said, and he felt the man fasten handcuffs around his wrists and then pull him slowly up to his knees. His throat closed with fear, and the sun was hot on the back of his neck.

"You just bought stolen goods, bro," the cop said. "Quite a pattern here. You guys can use stolen stuff, huh? Reselling it from here?"

"No!" Marcus said, standing now, facing the blond moustache and eyebrows like frayed, thick rope. "I didn't . . ."

"You asked the guy where it came from," the cop said. Other policemen were talking to the men near the barn, and Marcus felt the cop propel him toward the kitchen door. "Everybody just stay in place, okay? Don't go running off."

"Shit, whatta we got here? Drugs? Look at all this!" another cop said, turning from the doorway. "Hey, you guys, we got some cooking going on in here."

Marcus heard his mother and Enchantee screaming, and they stumbled down the steps, their arms held by one man, until they faced him. D'Junior slipped past the dark pants legs, hollering, "Mama! Mama!"

Marcus closed his eyes. "What are you, the supply guy?" he heard.

Paulsen's voice was as high and fast as helium. "No! I'm just waiting for a cab! My car . . ."

"What the fuck did you do, Marcus!" Demetrius shouted, his shoulders slamming the door frame when a cop pushed him outside.

"Marcus bought some things way too cheap," the blond cop said. "And from what you guys are cooking up in there, you should have money to spare, right? Selling lots of rock? I can't believe you're cooking the shit with kids in there."

"That's baking soda!" Demetrius shouted. "I got stung by a wasp!"

The cops laughed. "Whoa. You never heard of Bactine?"

"Damn, test the shit," Marcus cried, afraid tears would burst forth and shame him.

"Nate and Calvin Cook?" another cop was saying. "What are you guys doing mixed up in this?"

"Hey," the blond cop shouted. "Call Child Protective for the kids."

D'Junior was screaming as high-pitched as a whistle.

Marcus felt the handcuffs begin to shave at his wrist bones, and he let himself go limp and blind.

CHAPTER ELEVEN

HOSEA WAS WALKING back toward the stone wall from Oscar's when he heard the hollow hum of insects overhead. He'd gone to his brother's for a drink of choc beer and to escape the wasps hanging in the doorway of the coldhouse. But now he heard faint screaming over the wall, like a child was getting whipped for something he'd done wrong. The rattling blades of a helicopter separated themselves from the sullen branches above him.

A wire of cold pulled along his back, and even in the trees, he felt exposed like a rabbit, the way he always did when he heard the chopping whine in the sky. The planes in Tulsa, raining machine-gun fire and dropping gasoline bombs, had swooped in great dips over them. This helicopter now began the tethered twirl on a fixed target. He reached the high wall, squinting at the heavy, vibrating whorls pushing down hard on his land.

The eucalyptus were thick at the windbreak. Hosea pushed his boot into a crevice between stones, and he heard a woman's crying screams. Alma. He scrabbled for a handhold on the wall, fingertips scraping the mortar, and when his head reached the top, he held himself there.

He was close to Pepper Avenue, the corner near the parking area, and he could see the knot of policemen and the scattering of his family. Marcus was bent like a rocker under the cuffs, Demetrius was being led to a car. Enchantee was holding her boy tight, back to a uniformed man. And Alma was leaning against a patrol car, crying, her dress front dark with tears and sweat.

Hosea's wrists tensed to hold his body there. His throat was as close and dry as wood. If he ran toward her, toward the commotion of voices and shouting, one of these rookies might shoot him.

A young policeman with a face flushed in streaks appeared near the barn. "If we got stolen property and drug sales, don't we gotta search the whole damn place?" he asked someone. "Inventory all these vehicles, everything?"

"Just where you wanted to spend November," another voice said. "Jungletown. Shit."

Hosea dropped lightly to the ground and began to run, his ankles aching, toward Oscar's. His skull felt hollow, the whapping blades paining him. The sight of Alma's face twisted like childbirth pains filled him with rage. He was going to need bail money. And then he and Oscar were going to kill someone.

The red car sat there in her line of vision like a grotesque, swollen strawberry. Alma sat in the backseat of the patrol car, trembling even though the metal intensified the heat, and she closed her eyes to the red blur.

"She was in the kitchen, though," the cop nearest the window said. "I mean, the old lady was asleep, obviously she didn't know. She doesn't even speak English. But this woman was right there, at the stove."

"Hey, I've seen grandmas selling crack," another voice said. "The snitch said stolen property, he didn't mention drugs. Half the time these hype informants are wrong. But something's weird here. We gotta test the stuff and finish up in the house, so take her and the other two younger females."

"Look at the street out there. This is blocking all the rush-hour traffic." Alma heard faint gloating. "That's what they get for trying the shortcut through Treetown, huh?"

All his life, he'd avoided this place. The smell, the envelope of possessions, the shunting orders and knowing glances. When Marcus gave his Las Palmas address, the looks narrowed down. "Why you buying stolen goods on Pepper Avenue? You don't live there?"

Marcus shook his head. "I didn't know . . ."

"Come on. We got a tape of your little transaction, okay? It's pretty clear."

About twenty dark faces bobbed and clustered and turned when Marcus came into the overcrowded large room; he kept his glance sweeping and vague, and he sat against the wall, tasting thin bile. A face detached and floated toward him. Dokio, a friend of Demetrius's, who'd been in and out of jail for years. "Marcus? Baby boy? What the hell *you* doin in here, man?" Dokio's arms were big, the skin stretched in golden webs on his biceps when Marcus turned his head slowly.

"Stolen property," he answered, low. "I got set up."

"Shit, I guess you did," Dokio said, squatting beside him. "You the last Thompson I think I see in here."

Marcus buried his head in his arms, the acid burning his throat. "I guess I fucked up," he said, staring fiercely at his own skin until the moisture receded behind his eyes. "I fucked up big-time," he said louder, raising his head.

"Shit, everybody fuck up once," Dokio said, staring at the wall. "Or three or four times. I got a fuckin parole violation."

For two days, Marcus stared at his wrists, the dark marks. He watched the other men lie on thin pads spread on the floor, watched them argue and take each other's food. All my life, he kept thinking, I stayed outta here. I don't have a damn thing to do with this.

Arraignment within forty-eight hours. The orange jumpsuit bagged at his waist. The thick iron links tightened it up. Dokio was two behind. The iron circles at his wrists, the jangling, shuffling links at his ankles. Chain gang. His head rang with the jangle.

The judge with shaggy cotton hair and wire glasses. Santa without the beard. The lawyer he'd met once. The district attorney saying, "We've got the transaction on tape, your honor. The property was thoroughly searched and inventoried, and no further stolen goods were found. But people move them out so fast. That's what we're trying to discourage here. Mr. Thompson here bought a VCR stolen from a residence in Woodhaven earlier in the day. We want to send a message about that."

"Not guilty," Marcus said. He tried to remember the mock trials students conducted at the high school. Walking, shuffling again, he realized his job was gone. Had to be. His picture snapped in a flash at the front gate, he remembered. His record. His history. His period of employment in the Rio Seco Unified School District was undoubtedly over, as soon as the newspaper was delivered to the school-board office.

He slept sitting up, a few minutes here and there. My history. The history of the shit. Ever since the shit started. Julius was probably buying plenty of things, since he only cared about what a VCR could get him in terms of ass. Uncle Oscar's place. Daddy's place. This was the illegal sale, the one Enchantee had overheard.

He couldn't concentrate in the ratcheting noise and anger of the cell. He stayed motionless. If I hadn't bought the stuff, Julius would have. I messed up, but he would have messed up, too. Shit.

Hosea and Demetrius drove slowly toward Olive Gardens. The house behind them was as quiet at a sickroom, with Alma and Sofelia and the grandchildren sleeping heavily, crying out now and then. The barn and yard were deserted.

Once the policemen had tested the baking soda and found nothing, once they had searched the house and found nothing, once they had opened every car hood and checked every vehicle and found nothing, they had let everyone but Marcus go home. The whole day. That was how long Alma and the others had sat in windowless rooms, fearful and confused.

His youngest son had called, voice rough. Receiving stolen goods. Trial to come. "*Fuckin* Julius!" Hosea and Demetrius had to come up with bail money, and now, after the hospital bills and slow business and bail bondsman, there were no savings left.

Hosea saw Demetrius staring into the dark yards, saw his jaw pulsing. Demetrius had clutched his wife and son like they were refugees, and then his wife had cussed out Julius like an Olive Gardens woman who'd been cheated. "My cousin said he's hidin out with some bitch in the four hundreds," she'd said.

"Look for my son," Sofelia had whispered. "He gotta be over there. He got a key."

Hosea saw the ancient walnut trees looming dark near Ocie Mae Williams's old house, and then the straggly olive trees at the entrance to the apartments. The cardboard and boxcar-siding shacks had given way to these shoeboxes.

"Enchantee said her cousin told her four thirty-four," Demetrius told him grimly, driving through the narrow parking area.

Hosea nodded. He saw three boys with blue Dickies work pants, just like his, but no shirts, no name tags, no belts. Their white boxers puffed out from the hip-low waistbands, pillowy over their nonexistent butts. His grandson wasn't among them.

They glared at the car, and Hosea glared back. These boys had nothing to fight over. Three rooms in each apartment, with walls thin enough to dimple with holes if you leaned knuckles against the plaster. Furniture from McDermott's on time, falling apart before you'd paid for it. A three-foot cement walkway leading to someone else's asphalt. A parking lot.

That's what they were painting, he saw, looking at the walls and even doors of the complex. Marking the boundaries like dogs leaving scent. That's why they kept driving past houses, shooting at windows and porches and other cars. Other boys.

They couldn't hit shit. Couldn't hit a cow in an open field, much less a rabbit angling across a wash.

No land. They had carpet full of dirt and roaches, cement marked with cigarette ash and piss, and asphalt painted with faint stripes. Property of the government.

But I'ma kill somebody over dirt and rocks and bricks that's mine, he thought. When I find out who, and how, I ain't gon miss.

It was dark when they released him. Marcus stood waiting for his things, bare-handed, the voices pricking his back like thorns. Then he was outside, standing on the sidewalk between the tall government buildings showing only the odd lit windows. The narrow chasm of street led between the courthouse, city hall, the police department, the administrative and law and redevelopment buildings, where no one walked at night. He thought bitterly of the brothers he'd seen cruising in this part of downtown, carrying nothing, carrying paper bags, bare-chested, glaring, smiling, their strides advertising where they'd been. Marcus lived ten blocks from here. He wasn't walking.

On the low, grimy wall near the phone booth, he stared at the shiny black material of his work-out shorts. The gym. He didn't even want to show his face there, the face he knew had been in the newspaper.

And school? The restaurant? He spat into the dirt littered with cigarette butts.

Octavious pulled up in the Impala and silently drove him to the apartment. Marcus saw the arched windows as black as onyx, his VW like a misplaced bird egg at the sidewalk. A Funkytown brother. A Treetown nigger. "Eight," he said. "Trade me hoopties, just for tonight. I need to do somethin."

Octavious nodded and handed him the keys. "Get somethin good to eat, man," was all he said before he roared away in the VW.

Marcus stood in the archway, not wanting to go upstairs and hear the messages he knew waited inside the answering machine. He turned abruptly and got back into the Impala.

On the freeway to the desert, Octavious's powerful engine kicked in, and Marcus pushed the speedometer up to eighty-five, ninety. He felt, rather than saw, the soft, hot blackness whipping past. The brittle bushes were puffs of smoke against the dark. The asphalt was a rough tongue.

"Come on!" he shouted. "I'm speeding!" He felt the sick ricochet of his head when he turned it for a moment. Driving too fast—a man's thing. An American thing. Come on. You guys do it, too. You drive erratic. You're pissed at your wife, the wind's kicking up in the night, and you're heading to a bar even in your uniform. Come on and kick my ass, man. You know you want to. You know it. Look at everyone driving here. I've seen guys in Porsches and Lamborghinis do a hundred and ten on this stretch. Everybody's flying. But I'm flying too high right now. Come on.

He saw the scattered, sparse lights of desert towns, and he passed the few star bursts of real cities. Past Palm Desert, past the Indian reservations, nearing the mountains with flanks as bare and dark as melting skin.

When SaRonn came to the door, he said, "You think Bennie Proudfoot's gon try and car jack me again?"

She glanced past him at Eight's Impala and grinned. "I think she's got a man over there. Maybe a nice one."

She gave him tea with cardamom, curried rice with slivers of ham, and then she pulled his lips to her collarbone. "I ain't havin no more kids," she murmured. "Not yet, okay?"

"Okay," he said into her neck. "I'll be good."

"I'll be good, I wish I could," she whispered. "Remember that old song?"

"Yeah," he said, finding her lips. He didn't want to talk about music.

In a while, he heard faint gunfire coming from Olive Gardens, like stones thrown into deep water. SaRonn said, "There they go again."

Marcus got up, putting on his shorts, and sat on the couch. He didn't want Willa to see him in her mother's bed. Those serious eyes. He rubbed his forehead and dialed the telephone. He could get his messages from here.

"Marcus? This is Natalie Larchwood calling." He gripped the phone. "I saw the newspaper, I mean, I saw what happened. I think you should know that I've already heard from two members of the school board, and from the superintendent." Her voice paused. "Marcus, I'm sure that something else is going on. Please call me as soon as possible, so we can resolve this."

"Marcus? Yo, man, this is Kurt. I wondered why you didn't show for work, and now I know. Hey, don't worry. Lakin's cousin's filling in for you. Call me, man."

"Mr. Thompson?" The voice was faintly familiar, the tongue hard on the consonants. "Good morning. I am go, maybe two, three time, but you never home. Mr. Som talk with you. I hope you be home, because you have by the door something for thanks. Okay. Bye-bye."

Bye-bye. It was like the voice by the canal. Marcus hung up the phone. Bye-bye. Bodhi? Cambodian?

He found his shirt near the couch, and when he slipped it over his head, SaRonn stood in the doorway. "You running away?" she said, arms folded over her breasts. Her India-print pajama bottoms touched the floor, and she looked like she was rising from a pool of water.

"I'm walking out to the car, and I'm going to my place for a minute. I think I'll be bringing back something Cambodian." He kissed her, and she grinned from a corner of her mouth.

Marcus paused near the Impala, seeing a man walking toward him, calling out, "Eight, man, gimme a ride!"

When he neared, Marcus saw Larry Cotton. "I got Eight's car," he said.

"The baby Jungle Brother," Larry said, glancing at the light in Sa-Ronn's window, opening his mouth wide, and giving Marcus a theatrical wink. "You knockin boots with SaRonn, man?" he said, getting into the car.

Marcus hated the tomcat smugness in Cotton's voice. "No," he said.

Cotton slumped down in the seat. "Take me by the Gardens, man, okay?" He lit a cigarette and said, "Yeah, I had that bitch for three years, man, and she had a fuckin mouth on her. She was pregnant, and she didn't want to stay at the house. We was livin over there on Acacia. Man, one time I chained her ass to the toilet cause she wouldn't do what I said. I busted her in the mouth and locked her up. She thought she was somethin."

Marcus swerved the Impala nearly into the stone-lined ditch along Olive. He threw the gear and said, "What the fuck did you say?"

Cotton grinned. "Hey, man, lemme just tell you this. When you gettin a piece a that, stop for a minute and run your finger up in there. She make this noise like a cat, and then she cry."

Marcus swung and hit Cotton in the mouth, the cigarette ember arcing onto the floor. He reached for the throat, feeling the sandpaper bumps along the jaw and the moving lump of Adam's apple under his thumbs. The car door wrenched open, and he and Cotton fell halfway out. Marcus saw the gutter filled with sand, saw coins fall out into the sand, and they both tumbled against the rocks.

Cotton stood up and shouted, "You sorry-ass motherfucker! You ain't your brother! I'll kick your ass!"

"Come on," Marcus said. He waited, panting, his knee throbbing where he'd hit it on the door frame. He held his fists loose, like he'd watched Demetrius do all those years at the three trees. Come on.

Cotton charged him, head bent, and Marcus ducked but felt his eyebrow split open. He wrenched Cotton's shoulders around and threw him onto the rocks. Cotton slid up the stone wall like a crab and crouched. Marcus felt the blood run warm and stinging into his eye. "Come on," he said.

"Shit," Cotton said, scrambling up the short wall to the street. His mouth was a dark gash, and he spat. "The bitch don't mean shit to me. And your sorry ass don't, neither." He walked along the ditch toward the Gardens, not looking back.

Marcus reached into the car, picking up the smoldering cigarette from the floorboards and dropping it into the sand. Only a small black ash mark remained. He sat on the edge of the door frame, his head in his hands, one eye staring at the ember that breathed dully.

Demetrius was knocking on the door of 434, but a woman answered and shook her head. Hosea worked the cigarillo in his mouth. Got two sons gone, he thought. Finis hidin, cause a somethin that ain't his fault, and Julius tryin to hide cause a something is.

They drove around to the other side, where Sofelia's place had been. Demetrius knocked, and the boy Mortrice looked out the window.

When Hosea walked in behind Demetrius, he saw two other boys on the couch watching television, and Julius sitting with a beer at the dinette table, his mouth open. "Daddy," he started, but Demetrius lurched past and punched his brother in the mouth, knocking him off the spindly chair.

Demetrius straddled Julius on the floor, slamming his shoulders into the linoleum. "All that time, nigga, all that time me and Eight was workin so hard, never takin nothin, never buyin nothin! Tryin to build up the business! And you don't give a shit for nobody but your dick!"

Hosea pulled Demetrius up by his armpits. His sons were finished. Julius lay flat, as if he were relaxed even with blood dribbling from the corner of his mouth, as if he'd expected it and was relieved that it was over. In his eyes, Hosea saw that he really didn't care, that if a few punches were his punishment, he'd be back in the trailer soon. Still not changed; still skimming along on his own private tide. Already, he was only interested in his part of the story.

"How y'all know I was here?" he asked, hands relaxed on the floor.

Hosea kicked him. "Sofelia sent us to look for her boy. Get up."

Julius staggered a bit. "Sofelia talkin? Shit, I didn't know that."

Hosea stared at his third son. "Who was sellin you the stolen stuff?"

"Some dude," Julius said, shrugging. "I don't know. He ain't from round here. From L.A. or somethin."

Hosea watched the boys' faces; they were trying to look bored. One looked like a Proudfoot. Mortrice sat on the couch, staring at the television as if no one else were in the room.

"Do better than that," Hosea said. "What he look like? Who he talkin about?"

Julius sat back down, his tongue flicking at his darkening blood. "Dude was about forty, real skinny, a hype. Had a green streak in one eye. Said he stayed on the Westside." Demetrius swore and paced around the room. Julius looked up. "Hey. He said somethin about church, said whatever you do, the Lord forgive you, brother, if you confess your sins. Said his own brother know the Lord and always tellin him that."

Hosea heard someone at the open door. "Demetrius?" Marcus leaned against the door frame, his left eyebrow leaking blood that had dried like a question mark around his cheek. "Fuckin Julius!" Marcus said, and staggered past him to slam Julius back onto the floor. "You cost me my damn job, nigga! Fucked up my name!"

Marcus had hit his brother in the mouth before Hosea could move, but when Hosea bent to stop him, Marcus wrenched himself up, holding his knuckles. Demetrius leaned against the wall, his eyes hard on them both.

"That's enough," Hosea said. Marcus spun toward the doorway, looking out, and then came back inside.

"I was drivin home and I saw the flatbed," he said. He looked at Julius. "You the one been fuckin everybody up! You messin up the whole place."

Julius spat blood onto the floor. "Shit, Sissyfly, *you* the one hangin out in the black Jeep with that ponytail sherbert. You the one."

Hosea looked at Marcus's face. "Where you get that cut?" he asked slowly. "Jail?" Marcus shook his head, silent. "You just get released?"

"Eight took me by SaRonn's. The one know Finis," Marcus said, after a long time.

"Who the hell the dude in the Jeep?" Demetrius said.

"It ain't a Jeep, it's a Montero," Marcus said. "Guy write for the paper."

"What he want? He ax you about the place?" Hosea stared at each face, at his sons' blood, at the younger boys' darting eyes.

"He was askin these guys about music," Marcus said, lifting his chin toward the grandson.

Hosea wanted to lean his head back and take a long breath, but he kept his face still, imagining that his skin was bark. Like he'd learned to do in Texas, when the guards taunted him to make him run. Bark covering any softness. He had to go home, to the coldhouse, to think.

He glanced at the boy Mortrice. "Come on," he said. "Your mama want to see you. She worried."

The boy worked his lips. "I heard they was cops all over there," he said, low. "I don't want no trouble."

"Bet your young ass don't," Julius muttered, and Hosea was dry-mouthed with anger, looking at all of them.

"Ain't your trouble," he spat out. "Ain't gon be no more trouble. Come on." The boy stood up, and Julius began to rise, but when Hosea nodded at Demetrius, his oldest son bent to stop him. "Don't nobody want to see you right now," Hosea told his third son. "You got plenty places you care about more than mine. You best to find one."

The boy Mortrice murmured something low to the others on the couch and walked to the door, his jeans sagging, his back curved, as vulnerable as a bird's white breast under the T-shirt.

"I said I was sorry, man. Marcus fucked up, too, he probably ain't figured it out yet. Hey, if the Lord forgive me, why can't y'all?" Hosea heard the smile in Julius's voice.

"The Lord the wrong one to call," he said to himself, knowing who he and Oscar would be waiting for now. "Especially when you ain't livin the word you spreadin."

"Lila tell me the preacher been here twice while I'm gone," Oscar said, sitting inside The Blue Q with dusty light fingering through the windows. "After that body turn up near the wall. She said he must got somebody watchin for my truck. And he set up in here talkin bout, 'All that crime go on next door, and all the carryin on here, you must be fearful sometime. Maybe you consider sellin the property and move somewhere safer.' " Oscar slammed his fist down onto the table, and the glasses skidded a few inches. "That fool come in here for years, and didn't never see Lila working in the back. He the kind so busy drinkin and chasin tail he never notice her. Or he know she carry that derringer in her apron, and she bout as scared as I am. Shit."

Hosea rubbed a finger into the scarred wood surface. "We gon wait for him now." He thought of Marcus, sitting in a cell. "We gon find out the chain right now. Who wantin what."

They had Octavious drive Oscar's truck over to Jacaranda Avenue, his hat pulled low, and Hosea stayed in the coldhouse while Demetrius drove his truck over there, too. He'd wait for Oscar's whistle.

But the preacher came to Alma. Hosea came up from the coldhouse and saw the black Lexus with personalized plates saying GODLORD parked near the barn. He walked toward the kitchen, looking idly at the shining car, and realized that the voice coming through the screen, melodious and chest-rich, was preaching.

He hadn't had enough time to think, he realized. He wanted to kill this man, not talk to him. But when he found himself walking toward the old tow truck, where a handgun was in the toolbox, he stopped. What would Alma be saying? Would she be crying? Hosea stepped up to the kitchen door.

"Hosea," she said. She was standing near the stove, her back to the white enamel, and the man was leaning against the table, his hat in his hand. Gentleman. His round dark face was glowing with sweat, his brown suit was tight, and his fingernails were edged in crescent moons.

"Good afternoon," Chester said. "Thompson, uh, Hosea Thompson?" He stuck out his hand. "Never had the pleasure. I've met your wife, here, you know, I've come by here before and talked to her about purchasing this property. My church is looking to buy some land, relocate from our present facilities. You heard of my church, right? Holy Christ the Redeemer."

Church? Hosea bit down hard on his cigarillo to taste tobacco instead of burnt anger. "This property? And next door?" he managed to say.

Chester's face opened wider, his smile growing, and he folded his hands in front of him. "Well, now, people are well aware of how I feel about the business going on over there, next door to you all. A woman own that property, too. And I'll tell you the truth—I know what go on over there because I've seen it firsthand, I've lived it. And I want to guide souls the other way soon, with you all's help. These killings here—sign of sin, you could say. Sin comin right over the wall from that place. I think you could realize the possibilities for renewal, renewal in this community, if the alcohol and temptation next door didn't exist. A place of worship could be beneficial for Treetown, my brother. I'm presently located on the Westside, you know, but I have a party who's interested in helping to finance a purchase, to pay a fair price for Miz Thompson's land here."

Hosea took a deep draw on the cigarillo again. "Come on out to the office," he said. "Show you somethin."

"Ma'am," Chester said, dipping his hat toward Alma, who watched Hosea's face. "I thank you for your time." Hosea knew he was relieved to be dealing with a man.

Hosea kept beside the gleaming shoes to the barn, where paperwork was still strewn on the wooden table and workbench from the police searches. Demetrius had had to prove each car was theirs. Tools and car parts were scattered about. The ceiling of Hosea's barn seemed far away when he glanced up, the thick stone walls slanting upward into dim shadows. "Got two cars in here for work," he said to Chester, who looked at the Toyota and Apache trucks. "Business ain't been so good lately, cause we done had all this trouble."

Chester said smoothly, "I've read about these recent troubles in the newspaper, yes."

"Yeah." Hosea chewed on the cigarillo again, waiting. "Well, if my wife sold, she'd want to be with her sister-in-law, the one own land next door. You ain't spoken to her yet?"

Chester nodded. "Yes, I've spoken to her, too, but she don't seem too interested in selling."

"Come on over there, maybe we talk to her together," Hosea said. Chester's eyes searched the barn walls, and he started toward his Lexus. "No," Hosea said, reaching for his arm. "We can walk."

"Uh, I think we might as well drive," Chester began.

Hosea didn't want to touch him. "Suit yourself," he said. He didn't want the man to get away.

The Lexus smelled of sharp aftershave and air freshener. Chester swung out onto Pepper, jerking the wheel, and accelerated ahead of a car that had just turned the corner. He swerved into Oscar's gate.

When they crossed the parking lot, Hosea saw that Oscar had two men sitting in a car, watching the yard. He nodded at Jerry, and took Chester around the back. He glanced at Chester's face. The thin moustache was like a rim of chocolate pudding over his mouth, and his finger and thumb were playing with the tuft of hair under his bottom lip. Hosea couldn't tell if the man was expectant or nervous or scared.

"Lila," Hosea called. "It's Hosea." She came to the back door, her eyes hard on them both, her hands hidden in her wet towel.

"Uh-huh," she said. "You wantin to talk about the land?"

Hosea looked at her, not sure what Oscar had told her. He nodded, and she came past them, to the table outside where they cleaned chitterlings. Rubbing her hands with the towel, she waited nervously while they sat.

"Miz Thompson," Chester began. "I been spoken to you and the other Miz Thompson before, about the man who's interested in the property."

"What his name?" Lila said, her eyes on her hands.

"Mr. Matheson," Chester said.

"Why you comin to ax and not him?" Hosea said, trying to keep his voice even, casual.

Chester smiled. "You know, I been taking classes for my real estate license, and Mr. Matheson suggested that maybe I can try to handle some inquiries for him in the Treetown area. He's a busy man. And I know the area a little bit."

"Your church on the Westside," Lila said. "Mr. Matheson ain't gon help you build no new church here. Be too much to clear all this land and start new."

"You right," Chester said, looking embarrassed. "I'm not sure what Mr. Matheson's plans are for this property. But he's very interested. You already know that."

"How much is he talkin?" Lila said, letting out her breath. Hosea watched the pudding rim twitch above Chester's lip.

"Five acres, each one," he said, his fingers moving on the table. "The market rate for Treetown, he say that's about a hundred and fifty thousand dollars. Maybe a hundred and seventy."

Oscar was standing there suddenly, in the doorway, close by, his chitterling knife dripping pig matter and dirty water. "Chester," he said. "You think that's a fair price?"

The man's face was gray under the sheen. "Maybe."

Oscar wiped the knife on a towel. "Well," he said slowly, looking at Hosea. "Lila here say she maybe tired of all this work. Cookin all these chitlins every week. You want some chitlins, Chester? Don't recall you use to eat em or not when you was in here. That was years ago."

Chester held himself stiff, away from the table. "I try to eat healthy food," he said. "I ain't so young now."

Oscar and Hosea laughed, and Lila got up and went back into the kitchen. "You what—fifty?" Oscar said. "Shit, I'm a hella lot older than you."

"I'm seventy-six, boy," Hosea said. "I been on my land since before you was chasin your first piece a tail."

Chester stood up. "I thought you all wanted to talk business this time."

Oscar waved the knife toward him. "We all older than you, and maybe we tired a workin so hard. Come on back and see the property line."

"Miz Thompson the one own the land, right?" Chester said, not moving, staring hopefully at the kitchen doorway.

"Uh-huh," Oscar said. He tilted the chitterling knife, dry now, toward Chester's stomach. "She done authorized me speak for her, okay? Let's walk the property line, so you can see what we talkin about."

He stalked ahead of them, his brown suit patterned with tiny black wires running vertically down his back. Oscar said, "So he talkin about a hundred grand." He laughed.

Hosea said, "What he want the land for? Time you tell the truth."

Chester turned his face so a quarter showed. "I don't know, man," he said. "I'm serious. He said he might cut me in on some land for my church if I help him out with acquiring some land around here."

"What he done bought?" Oscar said. The eucalyptus trunks glowed lavender in the deep shade.

"He bought all across the street. All along Pepper Avenue, up to the freeway overpass. An old lady used to own it."

"Miz Tolbert," Hosea said. "She used to have the beauty salon and the market and her son had a auto-body shop."

"Yeah, well, I don't remember that," Chester said.

"I do," Hosea said, watching the man's heels grow dusty and grins of pale grit show on his pants. "Redevelopment bought up the land for the freeway, and they told her she had to move. Then the freeway went in half a mile up, and she had empty buildings covered with graffiti."

They were near the still now, and Rock nodded at them. He sat on a chair near the groves, whose leaves were dim with summer heat and haze. He'd brought a small camper in, Hosea saw, which meant he was guarding the back end day and night.

Oscar stopped, waiting until Chester turned to face him. "You used to drink this stuff all the time," Oscar said. "Not the choc. I recall correct, you liked the hard stuff. Came in here snufflin it up and snufflin up skirts, near bout every weekend back then."

"Every man has the capacity for change," Chester said, his hands spread wide. "And that has nothing to do with the sale of your land."

"Shit, yeah, it do," Oscar said. "You gon drink a taste, and you gon answer some more questions." Oscar nodded to Rock, who went behind a huge eucalyptus trunk. Rock put his head out and nodded back.

Prodding Chester with the knife, Oscar looked at Hosea. They stepped into the center of the grove, where the air was as quiet as a cathedral and the shadows and sunlight fell like ribbons.

The barrels were here, right next to the irrigation furrow and the intake from the canal supply. Rock lifted one tight lid, and Hosea could smell the liquor. Moonshine. Corn and sugar and water and time. When the clear, hard stuff was taken from the top and put in quart jars, the murky thick choc beer was left at the base of the barrel. Oscar added molasses and a touch of cane syrup, because California drinkers liked their choc faintly sweet.

Hosea never drank the hard liquor, the silvery liquid that made his neck tingle and eyes swim even when he smelled it, like now. Oscar dipped out a cupful and held it out to Chester. "On the house," he said. "Or we can flavor it up with some blood."

Chester drank the cupful, his eyes meshed with red and his forehead darkened, a thick line creasing hard. He closed his eyes and staggered, leaning against a tree.

"Who kill them two girls on my land?" Hosea said. "You know somebody done that?"

Chester shook his head. "I ain't heard nothing about that," he gasped. "That's crazy."

"Who kill the drag queen?" Oscar said.

Chester shook his head again. "No, man, I don't know nothing about no killings. I—" He stopped, his mouth open like a spout.

"I'ma start cuttin where your chitlins is," Oscar said, sidling up closer. He pressed the knife edge on the white shirt, making a pucker.

"I told my brother to sell that stolen stuff to you," Chester said. "He's a hype. Matheson want you to look bad."

"Your brother," Hosea said. He pictured Marcus, facing down drunks and gangsters in jail. "Tell your brother he ain't gon testify, or you lose your balls. Hog maws."

"He ain't gon testify," Chester gasped. "I'ma send him back to L.A."

"L.A. That's where you from," Oscar said. "You don't know shit about no land. Matheson plannin to burn us out?"

"No," Chester said. "Nobody ain't said nothing about that. I don't know. Shit. Come on, man."

Rock dipped another cupful, and Oscar poured it into Chester's mouth, spilling plenty on the neck and suit front. "Now I'ma tell you somethin," Oscar said, dipping the knife. "Somethin you shoulda known, cause it take a sinner to know sin. I make so *got*damn much money I can buy whatever I want. You sorry-ass motherfucker. I just bought seven acres out in French Oaks for my friend. To keep his pigs. I don't need to sell this place. I need to buy some more pigs. And that's where I'm fixin to take you right now. Cause after I cut you out some healthy chitlins, I'ma dump you off at the pigs." Oscar paused, grinning. "Oh, you from L.A.—that's right. You don't know nothin bout pigs."

Hosea stared at Chester's shapeless mouth, at the ring of fat around his neck. He said, "Pigs eat anything they can chew. If it's too hard, like bones, they stomp it in the mud a while. When they done, won't nobody find nary a chip. Nothin."

"I'ma tell my brother not to testify!" Chester shouted. "I'ma tell Matheson you ain't interested! Okay? I don't know nothin else! Come on, brother. Please." He shuddered against the tree's skin.

"You sure as hell ain't my brother," Oscar said. He flicked the knife tip into the shirt front, like he was coring an apple, and a bright drop of crimson grew on the white. Then he drew the blade back and said, "Who killed them people and dumped em over there?"

Chester whispered, "I don't know nothin about that. I ain't lyin."

"Move," Oscar said, and the man stumbled ahead of them through the trees, his sweat whiskey-harsh.

When they neared the yard, Oscar said, "Follow us, Rock, we droppin somethin off."

He and Hosea got into the backseat of the Lexus, and Oscar told Chester, "Drive to the man house."

"I don't know where he live," Chester stuttered.

Oscar laughed. "Course you don't, nigga, cause he ain't gon cut you in on shit. You think that white man gon let you in on some profit?"

Hosea said, "Drive to his office. He must got a office downtown."

The Lexus went onto Pepper, under the freeway, and into the new Los Arbolitos complex. Hosea saw the turquoise-tinted glass and the spindly olive trees. Marcus didn't live far from here. His son was holed up in his apartment, trying to forget that he'd spent a week in jail and probably lost his job. Hosea was full of racing blood and anger, and when the preacher bent his head over the wheel, his freshly cut nape plump, Hosea took the knife from Oscar and drew a shallow line across the brown. The blood didn't hold a stripe, but melted immediately into the sweat. Hosea felt his stomach roll; he wasn't like Oscar. "Case you don't understand," he said, to keep the rising tamped down. "You a message, even if he don't never know. Tell him ain't nobody sellin one damn stone."

"Come on," Oscar said, putting the knife into his pocket. He nodded to Rock, idling in the old Malibu.

Chester walked ahead of them, attracting stares from women coming out the glass doors. "Which floor?" Oscar asked softly. Chester nodded at the door at the end of the long lobby hall. Hosea looked at his brother, who smiled and raised his eyebrows. They let Chester open the door with the painted letters: WEB MATHESON AND PETER "THE DANE" JASPERSON—SOUTHLAND REALTY. A startled woman at the desk frowned at the three of them.

Before Chester could open his mouth, Oscar said, "Good day, uh, ma'am. We was just takin a load a garbage to the dump, comin up from down in Treetown, and we stumbled across this juntlemon, Mr. Chester. He need some hep with his car, cause look like he been drinkin and maybe got hisself in some trouble. He ax us can we brang him here, say you his friends and y'all hep him out. Sorry to disturb, ma'am." Oscar backed away, nodding and bending slightly at the waist, and Hosea stayed near the door. Chester was swaying on his feet, his breath soaked, and just when Hosea turned, he saw a tall young man come out into the office carrying a sheaf of papers. The heart-shaped hairline he'd seen in the paper. Matheson.

He didn't even glance at the two men in the doorway. He frowned at Chester and said, "Oh, my God. What the hell . . ."

Oscar and Hosea strode down the hallway and into the parking lot. "Them olive trees get too much water," Hosea said, looking at the planters. "But they still gon make a little crop. And all these people gon complain about the mess."

"You want a drink?" Oscar asked in the car. "All that talkin made me thirsty." He took out the knife. "I still got chitlins to clean."

Hosea grinned. "You shoulda made him eat a few."

He sat with Alma in the living room, where they could see the sun sinking like a wine-soaked orange into the dark smog. "I can't even sleep no more for worryin," Alma said.

Hosea stared at the houses of Agua Dulce, at the river, one silver hairpin far to the west. "I think me and Oscar took care of it," he said. "Don't worry now."

He had never asked his brother about how he'd lived with Ford Wilson, the man who'd married their mother. He'd seen Ford beat Oscar, seen him draw bleeding welts in Oscar's skin during the short time they were at his grandfather's farm outside Tulsa. And when Hosea had leaped at Wilson, he'd received the deaf-making blow to his ear.

But later things had made Oscar hard, too. Dangerous. When Alma first met Oscar, when she'd first seen him at the new Blue Q singing and serving liquor, Hosea had asked her, "Some women like dangerous men. Think that's the only kind to have."

Alma had looked at him, those long eyes and the wide mouth, the curving neck in the neon light. "You think you dangerous?" she'd whispered.

Sometimes he'd had to fight or bluff when they lived in Olive Gardens, with the rough men wandering in drunk circles. But he thought about how it looked now: It was worse. People weren't meant for stucco squares. Like roaches. That's how the sherberts thought of them. Chase them out, put up a wall. What the hell could Matheson be planning to do with this land? No white people would buy houses right up next to Treetown and Olive Gardens. They only drove through here because it saved them a few miles.

Matheson would have smelled nigger whiskey and nigger blood on Chester today. But Hosea didn't think it was over. Back in the Depression, people tried to kill the bankers who foreclosed on their land. Men sang, "There's a lotta greedy men—Some rob you with a six gun— Some with a fountain pen."

This land was paid in full. Nobody could steal it with a pen. He looked at Alma, her face rosy in the sunset light. "The boy in the trailer?"

"No," she said, smiling. "He sat in there with Sofelia so long, talkin bout somethin, till he fell sleep right on the floor. He musta been up late before."

"Bet he was." Hosea touched her knuckles, swollen as big as acorns. "Marcus out now. But don't ax me about your third son."

She shook her head. Turning back to the window, her voice wavering, she said, "Maybe I can get them grandboys to help me clean out under them rabbit cages tomorrow. The trees need fertilizin after all this heat. Abuela back so bad, she can't hardly bend over."

Hosea nodded, closing his eyes, fatigue washing down from his temples. "Ain't none of us movin so smooth no more."

CHAPTER TWELVE

MARCUS STAYED INSIDE his apartment for days, watching the cut through his brow swell and fester yellow. The cuts on his knuckles, from his brother's teeth, turned as black and scribbled as pen marks.

The box of doughnuts Som had left near the door was translucent with grease. Marcus ate the hard doughnuts, drank coffee, and slept. He didn't answer the phone. When someone pounded on the door, he didn't move. He stared at his face, misshapen and under-grayed with ash.

"Marcus?" Natalie Larchwood's voice rang thin on the machine. "Marcus, as you know, the board has terminated your contract, but I need to speak with you. Please call me."

"Marcus?" His mother's soft murmur came next. "Your daddy want to see you."

"Marcus?" Kurt sounded harried. "Come on to work, man, we need you. I see your Bug's back, and I hear someone walking in there."

He wasn't going anywhere with his face and his head and his heart infected like this. He could see the stares at the restaurant, at the admin building, and at the barn.

And he wasn't going to SaRonn's. Because he'd already said he wouldn't lie, and he didn't want to start now.

He ran out of food. When he'd taped a bandage over the cut, now a receding lump and a wide black line, he stepped out into the turquoise evening. At the archway, a bulky figure waited.

Mortrice said, "Why you ain't at school?"

"Cause I don't work there anymore," Marcus said. "You always just start right up, huh? No 'Hey, how ya doin?'"

"I see you ain't doin all right," Mortrice said. "Your face tagged up. I heard your brothers talk about you probably wouldn't come around no more."

Marcus was surprised. "You been stayin over at the place?"

"Sometimes." Mortrice got into the Bug with him.

"You need to quit hangin around my building lookin all suspicious," Marcus said. "Gon get your butt hauled in. Ain't hot enough for that big-ass jacket. Man, we wanted to show off we were buffed, wear something for the ladies, when I was your age. How'd you guys get into the camping look?"

Mortrice shrugged. "I seen brothas wearin them Patagonia jackets in a video. Boots. Dudes wear this stuff walkin round here in Funkytown." He frowned. "That old man teachin history class—he sit there and look like he gon die any minute. Show us movies."

Marcus shook his head. "Whalen. Looked like that when I was in his class."

"I ain't sittin in there," Mortrice said.

"Yeah, you are," Marcus said. He drove down Pepper, seeing the blue strip mall, and he remembered the voice. Bye-bye. "Let's get some doughnuts."

The shop was empty of customers, and Marcus called out, "Som?"

Samana came from behind the curtain, his dark face sullen, his black hair cut short enough that he looked like a monk. "Can I help you?" he said without glancing up.

"It's me, Samana," Marcus said, and the boy's face was startled. "Where's your uncle?"

"He get rob, yesterday," Samana said, his voice bored. "After he give the money, the guy hit him. Like you—the eye." Samana studied Marcus's face. "You get rob, too?"

"No." When Samana was around his uncle, his voice sounded very American. But when he was around Americans, he sounded foreign again. "Who robbed him? They catch the guy?"

Samana shook his head. Mortrice was silent, his arms folded. Marcus said, "How's school?"

Samana shrugged. "Same. Boring."

Marcus was uncomfortable asking questions, even more with Mortrice standing there. He didn't want Mortrice involved. "So, you been hangin out with anybody?"

Samana's eyes were onyx. "Why I hang out? I have to work."

"Nobody in a black Jeep?"

"If I have money for a Jeep, I don't stand here all day, right?" Samana folded his arms, too. "You don't work at school now. Why you care?"

Marcus felt a flush at his neck. "I was just askin. Thought maybe you made some friends, had a nickname and all."

Samana said, "Shit. People say 'Semana,' like Spanish for week. Then call me Week-boy. Say 'Semen-a,' they call me Sperm. Shit. Nobody pronounce right. *Sa*-mana." Then he unfolded his arms. "Who care? What you want? Glazed?"

In the car, Mortrice asked, "Why you grill him?"

"Just worried about him," Marcus said. "Just wonderin."

Mortrice looked out the window at the Kozy Komfort. "Old sprung fools always hangin out there."

"They aren't as old as you think," Marcus said, seeing Usher Price on his folding chair.

His father and uncle sat near the barn, watching the Bug shudder up the incline. Marcus got out, and Mortrice headed toward the trailers. "Ain't seen you yet," Uncle Oscar said. "You fightin in jail?"

Marcus spat. "Cut myself shavin."

"Shavin your eyebrows now? Don't tell me sherberts doin that."

"Sit down," his father said. "You got set up."

When his father had told him about Fulton Chester and the brother who'd sold him the VCR, Marcus stared at the blue walls of the house. The adobe patch was only slightly rougher, less formed, than the rest of the wall near the kitchen door.

A setup, to make them look bad. Marcus told his father about the Cambodian voice he thought he'd heard near the canal. "But how could that be connected? Maybe they were random drug hits, cause I know one of the girls was into speed," he said.

"It ain't over," Oscar said. "It ain't never over."

"Hell," Marcus said. "It ain't like I know, like I been hangin around here for years, figurin out all the scams people like to run in Treetown. I was elsewhere, okay?" He heard his voice rising, and he stopped, looking down at the gravel. "I'm thinkin the bodies don't have nothin to do with the stolen goods. It's just people fuckin up in Treetown cause they think nobody cares."

"I sure as hell care," Oscar said. "Chester know he can't pull no more shit like he did. I know the man understand that."

Marcus watched his father twist a piece of baling wire around a pipe. Where you get that pipe cutter? he thought. At the gettin place. "You more worried about the land than you are about me. My name's fucked up, my job."

His father shook his head. "You both the same. This place and your name tied together. Whether you like it or not. Remember it or not."

Marcus stood up, putting his hands on the stone barn wall, glimpsing the pliers and wrench tucked into a crease between rocks. When he turned, his mother was walking up the drive with the mail. "Marcus!" She embraced him tightly. "Who marked up your face?"

"Nobody," he said, and she frowned.

"You get that in jail? My only one never been to jail," she said angrily. "I wanted to go down there and hit somebody myself." She sat down, rubbing her hair away from her eyes. "My boys fallin apart. If Julius was gon mess up and hurt somebody, why he didn't get his own self in trouble? Not you. Not Finis." She rested her forehead on the heel of her hand. "I got my girl back, and now I done lost two more."

Marcus looked at the barn, at the chains draped over branches. They'd swung from his father's tires, from ropes and chains, all of them. Family came first. No room for individual fuckups. If I screwed up, they'd cut me off, too. I gotta figure this out.

"Hosea," his mother was saying now, holding something. "You got a letter from Tulsa."

To Hosea Thompson,

Mrs. Geneva Bolton ask me write you when she pass. You have some thing here. Mrs. Bolton service on Friday at Simmons Grove cemetary. I taken care of her the last ten year.

Clara Roberts

"Who's this?" Marcus said, glancing over his father's arm to read the letter.

"My father's cousin Fred," Hosea said slowly. "Distant cousin. He was a Pullman porter. This was his wife."

"Funeral?" Oscar said, looking at the barn. "You goin?"

Hosea slid the paper into his pocket, standing up. "I gotta go down to the lot, see about that steerin wheel for that Impala."

Oscar stood up, too, moving his hat nervously on his head. "Ain't nothin I need to see back there." He looked into the eucalyptus trees and spat. "I keep a eye out for you here, if you goin. But ain't nothin gon happen. Chester know better."

"Oscar," Hosea said to his brother's back. "Where Mama buried?"

He watched Oscar turn slowly, his face settling hard under the pushed-back brim. Finally Oscar said, "I don't know. He kept beatin on her, beatin on me worse cause you defy him. He was gon take us to Chicago, I heard him say. I left, man. I was—eleven, twelve. Hell, I don't know." He paused. "I never seen her again."

Hosea watched him walk, unwavering, into the trees. Marcus said, "Your mother?"

Hosea turned to the always questioning face, his last son, who never sat easy and talked about rims or rain, who came out with a prickly, frowning request every time. "I said I was goin to the lot. I be back."

The road to the lot was dusty and warm. He knew damn well there was still a steering wheel on the '64 Impala a drunken Westside boy had wrecked, because Demetrius had given the boy four hundred dollars for the end-smashed vehicle since he knew every low rider restoring an Impala would be begging for the parts.

Hosea stared at the pleated metal on the back of the car, and he walked around the rest of the lot slowly, feeling the sun's glare off the baking hoods and trunks: the nondescript Pintos and Gremlins and Dusters, and old Fords and Chevys and the few valuable parts, like the ones from the Impala, that Octavious and Demetrius had been guarding lately, still uneasy about the trouble.

He leaned against the hood of the Gremlin closest to the acrid dark earth where the Granada had burned. Staring at his locked gate, looking past the wire to the riverbottom, he could see a homeless man trudging along the cane down past the field. The man was carrying a discarded wicker chair toward the narrow path leading into the tangled cotton-woods and few pecan trees where an encampment had grown this summer. From his chair higher up, Hosea had seen the tent material in red and green flashes among the trees.

He closed his eyes to the sun. The tent someone had finally lifted for his mother, on the ash-muddied ground where the house had burned, was dirty white canvas, like the others squatting like dirty hens on bare lots around Greenwood. His mother had huddled in the damp corner with Oscar, a baby whose constant shriveled cry from cold and anger threaded like dripping strings of laundry through the tent. Hosea watched his mother's face, the copper gone sallow and smudged with mud and soot from cooking over a fire, her hairline a rumpled cloud of escaped hair, her hands shaking and mouth slack.

He wasn't a man. He was the reason the feather-haired white woman had made them leave the room over the garage, Retha's room. He wouldn't go into the big house and dust, he wouldn't crouch in the fireplace and sweep out the ashes, he wouldn't rub the tires on the black car while she stood a few feet away and glared, arms folded under her puffy bosom and trembling neck and knitting teeth.

He wasn't a man. His mother had no man to help build a shack of scrap wood like the others, to find bricks all the way in other cities when Tulsa wouldn't sell building material to colored, to keep away the white men who tried to buy the plots of earth with no structures on them. His father . . . Maceo . . . ashes and stolen-away bones and not a trace.

The man named Ford Wilson saw her when he came to sell whiskey to the two sisters who were running the choc house from a boxcar salvage shack. He stopped when he saw Hosea's mother near the fire in the yard, and he came around all the time then. "People gotta drink, baby," Hosea heard him say. "And they gotta pay."

His mother took him to Geneva Bolton's house that spring, when Ford Wilson wanted her to go somewhere with him. She wouldn't leave the baby, but she took him to the old white frame house Fred Bolton had built himself before the riot, one of the few houses untouched by the burning.

The Tulsa land was gone. His father's land. His mother had to let it go, to one of the hatted men who told her she had to build or she had to leave.

Hosea touched the flaming hood of the cars he passed when he walked back through the lot. His crop. He knew every wheel and door and dashboard knob on his land. Every gopher hole and orange tree and oil drum. He hadn't been back to Tulsa since his grandfather's body was frozen in the far field, and Hosea had watched the box lowered into the red clay at Simmons Grove cemetery. Where they were burying Geneva Bolton, the last person he'd known there. Where his father's stone-carved name hovered over nothing, all alone, inside the last plot of earth he'd ever owned.

Marcus was inside the kitchen, eating a plate of beans and rice, when Hosea stepped inside. "You gon drive me," he told his son. "My shoulder still ain't right."

"Uh-uh," Marcus said, looking up at him. "Get Demetrius to do it. He know what he's doin, everywhere he go." His voice was as sullen as a teenager who'd been denied. He denied his perfect record, Hosea thought. "I ain't up for facin Oklahoma cops," Marcus went on.

Hosea said, "So you mad cause you got arrested. You held out a long time, Marcus, longer than most. But it's part of the zip code, boy, and it's over."

"You say it like it's a badge," Marcus said, his voice tight.

Hosea shook his head. "Ain't a badge less you want it like that."

"Like what, then?"

"Like a scar." Hosea waited, hearing Alma and Sofelia coming back toward the kitchen. "Maybe a scar ain't your fault—a rock somebody threw. But you can't be shamed of it forever. Can't hide it. I need somebody to drive."

"Feel like hidin my face," Marcus said, stalking around the kitchen in a rooster circle. "I'm on TV, I'm in the paper, lookin like every worst stereotype." He looked at Hosea. "You never saw your mother again?"

Hosea touched the thick adobe doorway and turned away. Marcus said, "Hell, I ain't got a job. I'll drive if you talk. If you start talkin. You can't be a shadow man."

Alma said behind him, "Y'all goin, then?"

Sofelia, washing pomegranates in the sink, said suddenly, "Tulsa? Oklahoma? Where Uncle and Aintie—" She glanced at her mother and bit her lip. "Where y'all from?" Her neck was flushed with crimson like the fruit. "Can you take Mortrice and show him? He ain't never been nowhere."

"He got school," Alma began.

Marcus rubbed his eyes. "He can take a few days off. It's history, right? More history than he's learnin in class. More than anybody ever told me."

Hosea looked at the address on the letter, not wanting to meet their eyes. "I ain't said—" He stopped. He'd never told them anything about Tulsa because his grandfather had never wanted to tell him about Texas. "Too much salt make you bitter," he used to say when Hosea asked. "Harden up your heart."

"We probably miss the funeral," Hosea said finally. "We can leave tomorrow."

They took a 1989 Nissan Sentra from the lien-sale lot. Hosea told Demetrius to charge him. Mortrice was sullen, silent, in the backseat while Marcus drove. Before dawn, he aimed for the faint glow in the eastern desert. If he held up and Hosea took over now and then, they could drive straight through. Marcus drove into the sun, under the sun, away from the sun.

Mortrice slept through Arizona. Nothin to see but sand and rocks. Look like a alien planet in the movies, he thought. Cowboys and Indians.

When he woke, seeing darkness cloud the car windows, they were stopping for food. He sat across the small table from his uncle and grandfather, trying not to look right at them. His grandfather's face was like a voodoo mask he'd seen in a book—all slanted eyes and cheekbones and mouth. And Marcus—he was as soft and brown as the grandmother, except his mouth.

I don't look like neither of em. I look like my daddy. I guess I look like a dead man.

He ate his french fries with his eyes fixed on the pepper shaker.

In the dark backseat, he thought, I could be drivin. They don't know. I done drove Chris's ride all the way to L.A. He watched the play of light on his hands. He felt naked without his piece and his kit. He'd left them with Chris, with threats about what would happen if he messed either of them up. Teddy was still working on his special gun, the one to give them their marks. Mortrice knew Chris and the others were scared it would hurt. Everything hurt. Especially marks.

In his history class, where the old man showed films whenever he could and the flickering sound of the projector put everyone to sleep, he and Chris talked about the guns. They needed another one, since Arthell from the next building wanted to be down with AK. AK-6.

A white kid had overheard them talking, Mortrice knew, because he'd asked Mortrice after class one day, "You got a piece?"

The kid had yellow hair cut real short all over his head, like bits of thread held up by static electricity. He kept running his palm over his head. Mortrice recognized him—he used to have a ponytail.

"What you care?" Mortrice had answered, walking away. He knew the kid would ask him again. He'd seen who he ran with. Wiggers. Two other white boys and the Japanese kid. The one from the doughnut store. All with short hair now, all with big jackets and listening to Ice Cube.

But if AK needed money, they could always turn a piece around, sell it to the white boys. They had money. They'd pay extra. But they'd have to take care of their own guns. Mortrice only took care of his homeys. His blood.

"When you see Oklahoma, maybe you see why we always been country out here," his mother had whispered to him. "Country in our blood, I guess. In yours, too. You just don't know it yet."

When he slept in the trailer, in the eerie scent of damp stones and porous bone, he didn't hear a damn thing but birds and scurrying animals. The kind of animals who'd been seeking Paco's blood, their teeth on his face. In the country.

After the flat, pale yellows and greens of the Texas Panhandle and western Oklahoma, Marcus saw the red clay earth begin to show itself in furrows and gullies. He drove through the early afternoon toward Tulsa. His father said, "That's how the ground gon look in the cemetery where they just buried her yesterday. Red scar."

"So she kept you for a while?" Marcus said. "Your mother was movin around?"

Now his father nodded. "My father was dead. Died in the riot."

Mortrice spoke from the back, where they'd thought he was asleep again. "He kill somebody?"

Hosea sucked his teeth at the boy. "Maybe. Somebody kill him." He paused, staring out the window. "Look, now we comin up on it."

When they began to see the names of the expressways—Creek, Osage, Choctaw—Marcus knew his father was lost. He was murmuring, "Didn't have none a these last time," and looking at the address on the letter. "She live on Garrison, but I don't remember that bein in Greenwood. Get off here and I think I know the way."

They passed blocks of dingy brick warehouses rimmed with black iron, and paralleling the freeway, they came to an underpass. "Turn," his father said suddenly, and emerging from the underpass, Marcus saw miles of open space. Grass, flat, hazy fall air, and deep, wide pits like flood basins. "Look like a park," he said. "Big park, but no bike trails or anything."

His father said, "Stop here for a minute." He got out of the car, his shape frail against the empty landscape. "Goddamnit," he whispered when Marcus stood beside him. "This was Greenwood. The whole damn place gone."

The small frame houses and the brick buildings, all the stores and pharmacies and cleaners and restaurants that had been built back up after the burning and the years of tents and mud wallows and no materials and city ordinances, all were vanished. Hosea stared at the freeway behind them, at the place where he thought Fred Bolton's house had been. Fred standing in the front yard, boasting, "They fought a damn war, man! Soldiers, machine guns, gas bombs! I couldn't get back in on the train for three damn *days*, them white folks was so scared niggas would come in from Muskogee and help out. And everything back. The black Wall Street back, man."

In this vague, hanging air between the few scattered trees, he saw no outlines of ash, no houses. Nothing but undulating, overgrown green.

Hosea couldn't stop the trembling in his back. It was a chill, from the early evening. He got back into the car, and they went north, toward a cluster of houses. Marcus asked at a gas station where Garrison was, and in the grid of streets here, in North Tulsa, where Hosea thought white families used to live, they found the tiny brick house.

The woman named Clara Roberts opened the front door. Inside, the small room was as dark as a cave until she turned on a lamp.

Hosea watched her bring a sheaf of papers into the room. She was broad and sturdy, her shoulders as soft as Alma's under the dress and coat. "I was just fixin to go home," she said. "Didn't have no idea when y'all gon come."

Hosea sat on the couch, and she lowered herself slowly onto a chair. "I taken care of Miz Bolton, help her do her shoppin and cookin and all. She ain't had no children, you know." The woman settled herself and sighed. "I ain't sure which one worse. Don't have no children, ain't nobody to take care of you. But I got my grandbabies now, cause ain't nobody takin care of them. Seem like you can't win."

The papers held a typed list with items and his name. Clock, wardrobe, letters, and pictures. Hosea saw the tired smudges around the woman's eyes. "We gon go get a hotel," he said. "We come back in the mornin and get everything settle. You look like you need some rest."

She nodded. Marcus said, "I'll carry the paper, Daddy." They stood up, Mortrice silently looking at the knickknacks and cabinets and brocaded furniture. "Lotta things," Hosea said.

"Lord, I know," Clara Roberts said. "She left me most the furniture, and clothes and all. But my place so small, I don't know where I'ma put em."

"Somebody comin to pick you up?" Marcus said politely.

"I was just fixin to call my son," she said.

"We can take you," Marcus said. "We have plenty of room."

She locked the small house, and Mortrice looked down the row of homes. "Look like California," he said, the first time he'd spoken.

Mrs. Roberts shook her head wearily. "Feel like California, with this late heat we havin and all this shootin."

"Shootin?" Hosea said.

She winced. "Got these boys call theyselves Crips and Bloods runnin the streets, came back from L.A. to stay with their peoples cause they got in trouble or somethin. Nothin but trouble over by me."

They drove her to an apartment complex not far away, a seventies-looking brown stucco building that said NORTH LANCASTER ARMS. Hosea saw kids playing in the parking lot and clothes hanging from balconies. "Look like trouble just waitin," she said.

• • •

Mortrice stared at the markings on the walls. "Gangster Loc Posse."
"Rollin Crip Mob." He slumped back in the seat beside his grandfather
so that only his eyes were window level.

Ain't no difference, except them brick buildings, he thought. Everything the same, wherever you go. They just talk all soft. But they all
want to be L.A. hard. Look at them brothas hangin by that one car.

He narrowed his eyes, concentrating on the wide, light-skinned man
in a tank-top undershirt, his khakis low, his hands gesturing wide.
Capper. It looked like Capper. He felt his throat closing up, and he
breathed harder. Capper must got peoples here. He must had to run.
Mortrice saw hollow-eyed women dangling over a few balconies, calling
down to men in the parking lot. Sprung. Everywhere was the same.

The old woman got out of the front seat slow and painful, Mortrice
saw. She said, "Lord, it's a crime the way they done taken over. But
you didn't come all this way to hear me complain." She leaned toward
his grandfather. "I'll see you at the house around ten, all right? Take
you down to the cemetery. She gonna have a nice stone. She had a
policy."

Marcus slept deeply on the bed nearest the bathroom. Hosea felt he
couldn't breathe in the small motel room, with the two wide beds and
small table near the window. His grandson stretched out on the other
bed, watching jerky images of women bending over and shaking their
butts, of boys with sunglasses and baggy pants like his pulling guns from
jackets and shooting from car windows.

Hosea sat in the chair. The whole damn place gone. All of it. Expressways and turnpikes curving and twisting everywhere like stiff gray rivers
oblivious to all in their paths. Like the Rio Seco freeway, so long ago.
About the same time, he thought. Cut right through the stores and fish
market and barbershops between Treetown and the Westside.

Urban renewal. Negro removal.

The landscape on the television was dark and pitted, smoldering fires
in trash cans and brown faces ringed around the flames. He glanced at
his grandson; the flickering movements reflected in his wide eyes made
his face come alive in the small room.

• • •

Marcus woke with the sound of trucks idling in the parking lot. His father was asleep in the other bed; Mortrice was rolled into a blanket on the floor beside the television, still silently on above his back.

Clara Roberts was already in the house when they arrived. She had begun clearing things from the crowded kitchen, which smelled like opened medicine and old people. "Can I help you with some of these?" Marcus said, and she smiled, a rosy smudge of lipstick on one tooth.

She was one of those always coiffed, always made-up, wide-waisted middle-aged women who did the work, he thought. A church sister. One of the women like Bertha Williams, his mother's friend, who made invisible rounds to old people's homes and church auditoriums and cemeteries and grocery stores, taking care of everyone. And they were always tired, the opaque hose and thick-soled shoes moving slow and steady.

"She left the house to the church," Mrs. Roberts said.

Marcus's father picked up a box of dishes. "Which one?"

"Well, you know she were a member of Mt. Zion, way back when they burned it to the ground in the riot." Marcus frowned, thinking that they kept mentioning this riot, which must have been in one small neighborhood since he'd never heard or read anything about it. "Then they rebuilt that church, and when they cleared out Greenwood, them two old churches bout the only things left. They down there like islands. The university own lotta that land now."

They stacked boxes on the tiny back porch, since Mrs. Roberts said they'd be stolen from the front if she didn't watch. She moved through the small rooms like a boat through treacherous waters. "You know, Mr. Bolton hated this house," she called to his father. "Hated every brick."

"They tore down the white house over there in Greenwood?" Hosea asked.

She nodded. "Some a them houses was just shacks. But some was real nice, like the Boltons'. The city said everything had to go, said about the expressway and some other project. But after they put in the expressway, they ain't done much else."

When they sat down to rest, Marcus brought his father and Clara

Roberts cans of soda. Mortrice was hanging out in the front doorway, staring at the street. "Your daddy died in the riot?" Mrs. Roberts said.

Hosea nodded. "My uncle died then, too," she said. "Long time before I was born. My grandma had ten children, and he was about thirteen. She use to tell me bout that day. They woke up and heard them planes flyin over, like the war had come over here, and then she was tryin to get the kids dress so they could get away. He run back in the house for somethin, and one a them planes dropped a bomb. Dynamite, I heard. The house went up in fire, and the machine guns was shootin, and they all run. She never found nothin but ashes. Bout five other people in that buildin, too, cause they had roomers."

Marcus leaned against the wall, not believing what he heard. "This was a riot? And planes were dropping bombs?"

Hosea nodded. "1921. Burned up Greenwood."

"And you never mentioned it?" Marcus stared at his father, who kept his eyes on the shelf of knickknacks.

Mrs. Roberts pushed herself up from the couch. "Yeah. They said nobody never knew about how many people got killed. White people killed, too, cause the colored was shootin em to protect they homes. But so many colored died like my uncle, and they never found the bodies. My grandma said she seen three men run out a burnin house, and the white men shot two and threw em back in the fire. Said you didn't know what was in them ashes next day. Nor who." She paused. "They didn't low no funerals. They was cartin up bodies and throwin em in the river."

"Goddamn," Marcus whispered. "How come I never read anything about this?" He tried to imagine the planes, the people running. He'd seen pictures of the Watts riots, but that was stores in flames and people carrying TVs and helmeted men.

"I bet you ain't," his father said, rising, too. "Come on. She need some help."

"She left you this wardrobe, cause your mama always admired it," Clara Roberts said, pausing in front of an ornate, curved-glass cupboard filled with figurines and glass. She reached inside and pulled out a few plates. "These are from slavery days. She told me her grandma had em, and your mama liked the pattern. They yours, too."

Marcus looked at the plates in his father's hands. The tiny flowers surrounded a blank center crackled with veins of brown. "You keep the wardrobe," his father said. "I can't haul it. You keep it, or sell it and keep the money."

She nodded. "It's old. Mrs. Bolton's mama had it." She pushed forward another box. "This the box I was lookin for yesterday."

His father pulled out a bright gold-toned bullet, larger than anything Marcus had ever seen. Mortrice came forward and said, "That a shell?"

Marcus was amazed to see his father's eyes gleam narrow gashes of tears when he nodded. The shell was engraved with flowers and words that Marcus couldn't read in his father's trembling hands. "How she find this?" his father whispered.

Mrs. Roberts shrugged. "Said your mama give it to her sometime after the riot."

Marcus watched his father lay it carefully in the box and close the top. "I look at the rest later," he said, blinking hard. "That a gun in the bedroom?"

They glimpsed the long barrel through the open door. Clara Roberts nodded, and Hosea went into the tiny back bedroom and brought it out. "Mr. Bolton, that belong to him," she said. "Miz Bolton keep his things in that room. I ain't sure who get em."

Marcus took the rifle, feeling the heavy barrel and the wooden stock. He squinted at the year engraved in the metal. "1886?" he said. "That old?"

Mortrice held out his hand for the gun, and Hosea said, "That's an old buffalo gun. I remember my daddy sayin Mr. Bolton got it from his grandpa. Creek Indian. They used to hunt buffalo with that." He watched Mortrice handle the gun. "I had my grandpa's gun, too. Cops still got it."

Mortrice said, "What caliber this gun?"

"What you know about caliber, boy?" Hosea laughed. "Read it."

"Look like fifty-six," the boy said.

Marcus said, "You better put it away before you find out it's got some ancient bullets in it." Mrs. Roberts had gone back into the kitchen, and now she came out with a handful of flowers in a jar.

"We better go on to the cemetery," she said. "You know, I'ma give y'all the key and let you take these. Cause my grandson runnin a fever today, and I want to check on him. Maybe y'all drop me off?"

When they were getting in the car, Mortrice said, "I need to go to the rest room, ma'am. I'm sorry."

She gave him the house key, and he disappeared inside for a few minutes. When he came back out, he said, "Thanks."

Hosea was closing the trunk, where he'd put the box with the shell and the clock and the other things. Marcus asked him, "That shell was yours?"

"My father's," his father said. "How she get it?"

Mrs. Roberts said, "Miz Bolton told me your mama come by after the riot. She had you, that new baby, and that shell. That was all. Then she come back later with a ring, from a sharp-lookin fella, ax the Boltons keep you for a while. Come back after a month, said you goin to your granddaddy place down there in Simmons Grove, cause a blood tie and all. Miz Bolton was so sad, but you know, her husband didn't never like kids anyway. And your mama axed her keep the shell. You know what else in that box?"

Marcus started the engine. "I saw some newspapers."

"All the paper stories about the riot, Miz Bolton saved em. You know," the woman said, looking toward downtown, "if you went over there right now, to the library and the museum, you wouldn't never find them stories. They tore em out all the copies. Like it never happened." She paused. "You can't tear out the truth."

They drove in silence toward her apartment. In the parking lot, she turned to Marcus's father. "You know your way down there to the Simmons Grove cemetery? So different down there now. I remember we use to go there for vegetables. Country—I mean they had those picnics and mules." She had a strange look on her face.

His father nodded absently, staring out the window at the car next to them. "Only ten miles, but it was country."

She stared at him sadly, Marcus thought. "It ain't Simmons Grove now. It's south Tulsa. You see when you get down there."

Marcus heard the two words everyone used to describe Treetown. Down there. Some things were the same, he was thinking, and his father frowned, getting out of the car.

"Got a baby in here," his father was saying.

The baby's brown face was purple with rage around the ears and eyes, and the tiny fists batted around the screams circling him. Hosea bent to the open car window, smelling the angry pee dampening the car seat the infant was strapped into and the sour odor of the carpet.

Clara Roberts was beside him, her face contorted with anger, too, and she reached inside to snap the buckles loose and take the baby into her arms. "Girl next door to us," she whispered, her eyes glassy. "She done left him out here again while she talkin in the parkin lot. Lookin for that dope man."

Hosea stared at the baby, still screaming and stiff, like his nerves had gone rigid. Clara Roberts turned away as if embarrassed and stalked toward the building, the cries winding behind her like rasping smoke.

In the car, Marcus was talking, but Hosea didn't hear him. Oscar, a baby, screaming in the tent. The woman who'd lost a day-old baby in a shoebox during the riot and roamed the streets searching for him. Hosea walking all that winter, looking for a tiny skeleton, for larger skeletons, for ashes and bones.

"Daddy," Marcus said. "You okay?"

He looked at his son's face. A man. But all the babies in Alma's arms, crying or fussing or looking hungry, had driven him to the coldhouse. Not that he didn't love them, but they terrified him. Those glistening, gaping mouths; those toothpick bones. Fit in a shoebox.

He was old when he'd married Alma, when they had the babies. And still they'd frightened him, until their arms grew to size and they smiled when they wanted something.

"Go on down this street," he finally whispered. "South. All the way down."

But past the blocks of restaurants, pawn shops, stores, and car lots that he'd expected, he didn't see the open fields that separated Tulsa from the old Simmons Grove, the city from the black farms. He saw wood-stucco apartments and condominiums lining both sides of the street, and he grew dizzy, confused again, thinking that the baby's piercing screams had made him forget where he was headed. The complexes had big signs. WOODSIDE. TIMBERCAST. WILLOW GROVE. COTTONWOOD.

"Check out the names," Marcus said. "Just like California."

Sherbert names. Hosea waited for the thick woods, but he saw brick walls, wide, sloping roofs, and wrought-iron gates.

"Check out the money," Mortrice said from the back. "Like L.A. big-time."

The homes were palatial, with columns and gray stone and huge garages. Hosea was staring at the largest of the homes, a group gathered behind an arched gate with gold letters that said SOUTHAMPTON ESTATES, when Marcus said, "Daddy—is that the cemetery?"

On the other side of the street, facing the brick wall and towering roofs, he saw the tiny piece of land hemmed in by forest and a chain-link fence. A small sign said, SIMMONS GROVE CEMETERY—EST. 1876.

They got out and approached the fence. Hosea remembered Mrs. Roberts saying, in the kitchen, that few people came out here anymore, that a man had had to put up the fence to guard against kids who'd been vandalizing the cemetery. These rich kids? he thought, glancing behind him at the roofs. He saw beer bottles glinting in the grass near headstones, and a rabbit leaped away toward the back, where the vines and scrub leaned hard against the fence.

Marcus and Mortrice followed him. Marcus read aloud, "Mendoza Aloysius Breedlove. Born 1834. Died 1894. He was a slave!"

Hosea heard the excitement in his voice, and he turned. "He was a Creek slave, and a Creek freedman. He knew my granddaddy." He pointed. "There."

His grandfather's grave, his father's, his grandmother's, whom he'd never known. They lay all in a row, the crude hand-carved stones like chipped teeth. Hosea stared at the coarse, mossy rock. They'd never had enough money for good headstones.

POMPEY AURELIUS THOMPSON. B. 1855. D. 1938. "Your grandfather was a slave, too," Marcus murmured. "I figured, but you never told us for sure."

ROBERT THOMPSON. B. 1897. D. 1921. Nothing was buried there. Nothing but memory. Hosea's eyes stung like a child's, prickling hot. "He died in the riot," Marcus said, and Hosea couldn't stop himself.

"Stop talkin," he said, harsh. "You can talk later. I tell you later. Let the dead rest." Hosea felt his eyes travel over sandpaper when he looked away from his son's hollow cheeks, his lips pulled in tight.

MONETA THOMPSON. B. 1862. D. 1897. With his father crying and still slick. Hosea had children now. He saw what he couldn't imagine back then, when his grandfather had said, "She died givin life."

He walked abruptly to the closer part of the cemetery, away from the huge oak and these older markers with their uneven scrawls and age-darkened edges.

On the far right, the red clay was mounded, hard crust nearly pink. No stone yet—only the flowers, still fresh, and he added the jar to the gathering. Next to Mrs. Bolton was a marble marker with precise carvings. FREDRICK JAMES BOLTON. B. 1889. D. 1970. BELOVED HUSBAND.

Sitting on the stump of the felled oak, he looked at the clay. He had to start somewhere. He never said the right words to this too tender-hearted son. "Marcus," he said, and he saw the grandson Mortrice hovering near enough to hear, too. Marcus kept his face to the forest. A question, Hosea thought. One like his. "You thought of dyin yet, Marcus?"

His son said, "Who doesn't?" His teeth shut, stubborn.

Hosea said, "Old as I am, you see people goin and you wonder when your time up. My time came close as that bullet." He fingered his shoulder. "Talk to a preacher, Chester or any preacher, he tell you about pearly gates of heaven and rest, sweet bye and bye." Hosea stared at the pinkish clay, then at the small, leaning Thompson stones.

"I can't *see* it," he said, his voice catching harsh. "I can't see nothin. What—clouds and people walkin round? All them pictures they shown us when we was little—lambs and grass and white robes. Who? All them white folks from Tulsa was sure they was goin through them gates. Don't tell em they wasn't. What I'ma do around them? My daddy laughin and playin with em?"

Hosea stared at his son now, at the short mesh of hair over the vulnerable temples. "I don't see nothin," he said. "No hell. But I remember you comin home from college one week talkin about karma and some shit. Reincarnation. Comin back again, but you better do good or you come back worse—a fly or a dog. I can't picture that directly neither, but . . ." He stopped when Marcus looked up, his lips parting.

"You were listenin?" Marcus said.

"Wasn't nothin to do *but* listen. You talked all day. Never shut up. Hindu and Buddha and all of it."

"I had world religions class."

"I heard about it." Hosea watched the grandson squat near a stone.

Marcus said, "The people at the doughnut shop are Cambodian. Buddhist. That's how they believe." He stared at Hosea. "What *do* you see?"

Hosea shook his head. "I might could see people floatin above the sky, but in the dark. Watchin. But so many of em, like crowds of clothes hung up movin in the wind." He stopped, thinking of the Dog Star, remembering what his grandfather had told him about that star. And he couldn't go back that far again.

Marcus's eyes were swerving from him to the gravestones. Hosea stood up and said, "You can read them newspapers, about the riot. I don't know what they say. My daddy got killed that night. They burned down the house, and most of Greenwood. Me and my mama went to where they sent us. Then it was like the woman said. I came to the Boltons, I went to the farm. You heard your uncle. Man name Ford Wilson was beatin on her, beatin on Oscar real bad. I stepped in, and I got it, but I made it worse. I took off for two years, and when I come back, Oscar was gone. They was all gone except my grandfather. We farmed for a while, and then he passed. I come out to California."

Marcus looked away, at the trees, and Hosea looked that way, too, seeing the tangled vines he'd hacked through. His grandson was wandering along the sagging fence line, and Hosea saw a gap torn in the wire. A place where boys wandered in to drink and piss on the dead. Hosea ducked through, scraping his leg on a wild rose. He stood in the woods, hearing a nearby roar and hum.

This was where he'd come through. Come home.

Oscar's note was hidden in the earth-pearled flask under the smoke-house, where they'd agreed on. "Mama take me Fred's," the scrawl read. But Oscar had run away the first night, and he'd never come back. He had belt-buckle scars like Chinese writing on his back, and knife welts like lodged bullets.

"Where you goin?" Marcus said behind him.

"Damn, these things got stickers," Mortrice said.

"This ain't landscapin," Hosea said. "Watch yourself."

When his sons had begun to walk, he'd watched the fights and transgressions, but he'd vowed never to beat them. His throat would close in fear of his own fists, and he didn't touch them at all. Instead, he was perpetually intimidating, keeping his eyes stone or spark, lips held still, arms folded.

No hugs, no knuckles against resting cheeks. No holding hands. But he could watch Alma do all that, and he could sit in his chair, knowing they wouldn't run. And they hadn't, except for Marcus, who hadn't gone far, although downtown was worlds away.

"You kept wantin to know," Hosea blurted out. "I told you. My history all bad. You hear any more, it ain't gon be no better." Before Marcus could answer, or ask, he turned to hear the rushing hum, closer now, and when he pushed his foot through a stack of berry vines, he touched wire again. Another fence. Peering past the narrow-trunked scrub oaks, he saw the expressway down a steep slope.

Toward the north, he saw where the asphalt now ran over the river. Hosea's eyes stung from heat and drifting exhaust, from the stream of cars heading home. "Let's go," he said, seeing them come knee-deep in brush beside him.

When they went to the woman's apartment to thank her, Mortrice stayed in the motel room. He told them he was tired. But he didn't want to see the one who could be Capper and the other eyes in the parking lot. The hands in the jackets. Maybe Capper had killed Kenneth, and had to come out here to start over. New territory. No place was different. That's why he needed more toast. Harder toast. The buffalo gun was the biggest he'd ever seen, the barrel heavy and long enough to hold real power.

He opened the box and examined the shell. Some flowers and names. 1918. Like all those years on the graves today. Long ago and far away, in another galaxy. The old plates looked dirty and cracked.

He glimpsed newspapers folded neatly, as yellow as mustard, they were so old. Taking one out carefully, he saw a photo of smoke rising from buildings and men with their hands up marching in lines. Dark men. "Race Riot," the headline read.

Mortrice stared at the photos for a while. When you were in a building on fire, even a piece wouldn't help. He remembered the stories some of the men who hung around Soul Gardens told about the riot in 1965. The cops, the National Guard. Mortrice had seen blank spaces where people said nothing had ever been built again after it had burned.

But if you had a gun, you could stop the fire before it started.

The moon was as bright as a sunlit coin, hanging in the slash of window framing the southwest sky when Hosea woke at three A.M. He sat up in the bed nearest the glare of light.

Hosea parted the curtains further, seeing the full light. He remembered the nights working in the fields, the hard silver glare on the crops he picked. Even in California, he would wake on his own land and work in the edging light. Sometimes his sons did, too. Especially Demetrius, who'd picked oranges more than the others. Never Marcus.

Hosea looked over. Marcus was sleeping near the wall. The grandson was gone.

He peered out the window. The car was gone.

The only place to sit and wait was the hard chair at the small table, where he lit matches and dropped them into the ashtray. He smoked a whole cigarillo, thinking about the vast spaces of Greenwood, empty, about Simmons Grove houses cleared for rubbish, and only the detritus buried underground, still breathing beneath the huge garages. Trash, pottery. Animal bones. Human bones, if they were in the wrong place.

When the Nissan pulled slowly into the parking space, lights off, tires creaking over grit, Hosea put out the cigarillo. His grandson opened the door as quietly as he could.

"Bet not be no drugs in that car," Hosea said. "I'll take your young ass to jail myself."

The boy smiled tightly. "Just had to get me a soda," he said.

Hosea stared him down. "The machine been bangin down soda cans all night."

But the boy stared back, his eyebrows like frost. "I don't like none a them kind."

"I don't see no damn bottle in your hand. Your eyes is shinin."

"I drank it already," the boy said. "I like to drive."

"Get in the damn bed," Hosea said. "You ain't drivin tomorrow."

The boy loaded the box into the trunk with the suitcases early in the morning. Hosea didn't see any signs that he was higher, or lower, than he'd been before. The boy slept hard in the backseat, and Hosea thought maybe he'd gone to see a girl in Clara Roberts's building.

Marcus drove silently for hours through the reddish fields and pale haze. Hosea knew he was still thinking about yesterday. When they crossed into Texas, the panhandle soil faded to rose and then sand; Hosea felt cold air massing. Toward evening, when they stopped for food, Marcus slumped over the steering wheel and said, "You tripped on Texas when I told you about the voice by the canal. Texas means something. You gon tell me now, or wait till one of us gets fucked up again?" Hosea leaned his head back and tasted the dust on his teeth. His son's voice was hard. "Shit, let's go south right now and find out."

"Nothin to find." Hosea tasted ice on the moving air current. He looked for the Dog Star. Sirius. "I went to Texas lookin for work. Lookin for a place my grandpa tell me about."

"What happened?"

"To him?" Hosea stared through the windshield at the cold glitter of the stars, heightened by the coming ice. "What happen to him he ain't wanted to tell me, no more than I want to tell you."

After a long time, Marcus said, "That was his gun, your grandpa's gun, you shot at the Jeep."

Hosea remembered the first time he'd felt the wooden stock. "Cause of this—I lost his gun," he said softly. "You right." He leaned back in the seat again, hearing the highway traffic from this parking lot. "He said his daddy name Augustus Thompson. The name he got in South Carolina. He was from Africa. Said his mama name Persephone. She was born there, where they was. He was the only son. Pompey what the owner call him. The daddy can't name him.

"His daddy hardly never speak. Only whisper to him at night. Never in the day. Only whisper in the dark, inside they place.

"One morning the master say he hear the army comin, and he make em walk. They got a few wagons and walk across South Carolina, walk all the way to Georgia. My grandfather eight, nine. They start buildin, clearin land to farm, and then the master hear the army comin there, too. They start walkin again, in winter. Walkin to Texas.

"They was near the border, and the mama feet was bleedin and swole, from the snow. She said she couldn't walk no more. The master didn't put nobody on the wagons, cause they materials was on there. She lay down in the road, say she can't go no more. The master said he hate a nigger what moan and cry and give up. Augustus go to try and pick her up, and the master come up behind and shoot her in the head.

"Augustus, he stop, he want to reach for the gun, my grandfather say he can see that in his hand. He ain't said nothin. Then the master point the gun, say, 'Can't trust you noway.' Shoot the daddy, too. Swing that barrel round at my grandfather. Say, 'May's well clean out the bad blood. You the only one left with it. No-good nigger bloodline.' But then he poke him and say, 'Walk, goddamn you.'

"Pompey never say nothin again. They walk in the snow, walk to Texas, and the master say build a big house cause they stayin. A man teach Pompey how to cut stone, and they cut limestone blocks for a big house. If they don't work, he chain em to a tree and starve em. They farm cotton. Pompey was eleven, twelve, he think.

"They was so far out they didn't know they was supposed to be free. Some soldiers come through in 1868, and the man chase em off. He tell all the slaves come in the big yard, he gon tell em somethin. About thirty, forty people. He stand up there and say they supposed to be free, ain't nothin he can do about it. And they start movin around, talkin, some get to laughin, he bring out his shotgun and start shootin. Holler a free nigger ain't no use in the world. He shoot for a long time, and Pompey fall under some bodies. He can feel blood all in his clothes. In his ears. He don't move for a day and a night. Then, before the sun come up, he crawl out from the dead people and start runnin.

"His clothes like leather. He went in the creek, and leave a trail a red behind him for hours. He was a wild boy for two, three years. He ate pig. He could see the pigs breathin steam in winter, hidin up in the creek banks, and he kill em with a knife. He lived in the woods and on the creeks till he meet some people goin to Oklahoma. Indian Territory. And he go with a family to Simmons Grove."

Hosea lifted his head and looked at Marcus now. "When did he tell you all that?" Marcus whispered.

"After I come back."

"From Texas?"

"I ain't never told him where I been," Hosea said slowly, remembering the fire, his grandfather's seamed, impassive face. "Told him I been walkin, and he didn't ax nothin else. We was workin in the field one day, and this white woman come out there in a car, with a notebook. Work for the WPA. Said since my grandfather been a slave, could he talk to her; she ax him real sharp, like she gon get mad if he don't."

"The Slave Narratives," Marcus said. "The book's in the library." When Hosea was silent, Marcus said, "You never wanted to tell us any history."

"I taught you how to build a fire. Fix a car. You ain't wanted to know that." Marcus shrugged. "I ain't beat you. I ain't talked to you much."

"What did your grandfather tell her?"

"You can go to the library. Read it." Hosea opened the car door and went outside. "Best wake that boy up if he gon eat."

"You ain't told me about your part of Texas," Marcus said over the hood of the car. "What I need to know."

Hosea could smell the red dust coating the car roof. No more. He touched the dull powder they'd taken with them. "When we on my place. My piece a ground. Then I tell you what I can."

Mortrice lay in the backseat, his head against the door, the cool air fingering his neck. He could see the long barrel of the shotgun the white man would have been swinging around when he leveled the crowd of people in the yard. He imagined the buffalo gun across his own legs, his fingers traveling over the stock carved with swirls and curving designs. Boo-yaa. If the African had been strapped with the necessity, he could have stopped all that shit before the boo-yaa.

When the shooting got too wild back at Soul Gardens, when the night rippled with explosions outside the doors and windows, the mamas used to say, "No. Uh-uh. I'm tired a this. Tired a bein scared all the time. I'ma send his young ass away. I got people in Fresno. Georgia. Tulsa. Greenville. Rio Seco. I'ma send him out there to the country where it ain't so much trouble. Ain't all this killin."

Like the boo-yaa hadn't already happened there. Wherever. Over and over. The olden days. The new days. All the same.

In New Mexico, Hosea watched the full moon, suddenly veiled by black lace. Thunder sounded across the sky, but only scattered raindrops fell hard on the car roof like tap-dancing beetles.

Archuleta had come from here, from a small mountain town where all the houses were adobe and the men carved *santeros* like old Feliciano Salcido. Hosea had hitched a ride with a man from Greenwood named Walker, and the car had broken down near here. The mechanics spoke Spanish, handing Hosea black coffee and cold tortillas in the gathering snow around his feet. A young man hanging around the garage, black hair as thick as paintbrushes over his ears, heard where they were going.

"California?" he had asked, his voice lilted and quick. "I give you a

few dollars if you leave me by Rio Seco, no? My *tío*, my uncle, he's
there."

Marcus drove silent and fast, the radio buzzing static for company.
He done heard that story over and over from Salcido, Hosea thought.
That's a story everybody know.

He and Walker had taken Teodoro Salcido to Agua Dulce, to the
small adobe house on the hillside where they gave Hosea chili and rice
and a thick mud-walled room for sleep. "Come on back, you want
trabajo," Salcido said. "Always work here. Not much money, but you
can find food, no?"

When Hosea had reached Los Angeles, there was nowhere to grow
anything among the palms and cement. But Rio Seco had dizzying
rows of lemon trees, rich, furrowed earth along the river.

His piece of land. When Marcus crossed the border into California,
hurtling them through the jagged moonscape of desert, Hosea said,
"Nobody bet not left no more bodies in them trees." He watched the
mountains rise in the pale dirt like crusted burnt sugar. Lava. He asked
suddenly, "Who you think I'ma leave the land to?"

"Huh?" Marcus turned his head. "Why you say that?"

"You think I'ma leave it to Finis."

"Finis?" Marcus gripped the wheel. "He'll never have any money."

"Yeah," Hosea said, staring at the twisted ridges of sand. "But people
take him in, feed him. Somebody takin care of him right now. A woman
can't go round like that." He paused. "I'm leavin it to Sofelia. After
me and your mama and Paz all pass. Sofelia."

Marcus was silent. "Then the land gon be his someday," he said
finally, tossing a grin toward the backseat. "What you think he's gon
grow?"

Hosea glanced back at the boy, whose eyes were closed. "Long as
he grow old, I don't care what he do with it."

Mortrice heard them talking. He kept his eyes shut for a long time.
Grow more than old cars and bones, he thought. Grow me some . . . .
shit, I don't know.

They talkin bout bodies in the trees. A body with no face? He felt
traces of cold along his shoulders. All them trees on that place. You

could grow chronic, or sell whatever you wanted, in them trees. Nobody would see.

He opened his eyes in time to watch the moon sliding down the windshield. The highway was molten lead, the telephone wires sagging like trashed cassette ribbons. He tried to see the signs, to tell where they were now, but each sign whipped past in less than a moment, too fast to read, and the bullet holes let through slanted needles of light.

CHAPTER THIRTEEN

IT MUST NOT BE AGAIN

Such a district as the old Niggertown must never be allowed in Tulsa again.
Such a district is a cesspool of iniquity and sin, of filth and corruption. In this
old Niggertown were a lot of bad niggers, and a bad nigger is about the
lowest thing that walks on two feet. There were four elements here: booze,
dope, bad niggers, and guns. Give a bad nigger some booze and a gun, and
he thinks he can shoot up the world ...

Marcus put down the *Tulsa Tribune* dated June 1, 1921. He'd tried to
laugh the first time he read the words. Hell, they were almost funny.
"Niggertown," he said aloud on the couch, sun streaming through the
window onto his candlesticks, Nigerian juju music on his stereo. He'd
read all the clippings, with varying accounts of the dead, with the blame
placed on the black residents of Greenwood who were shot, burned,
rounded up by the military, and placed in temporary concentration
camps, made to wear badges and then clean up the charred ruins.

But he kept coming back to this ornately printed editorial on ochre
paper, because of the words. Niggertown. Bad niggers.

His father had lost his father. Clara Roberts's grandmother had lost
her son. No one had ever agreed on how many had disappeared. These
clippings had disappeared from all the libraries. Marcus thought of the
ashes, remembered sitting on the hillside smelling the Granada burn,
not knowing his father's blood was soaking into the wild oats. What
had his father smelled? What had triggered his memories?

Niggertown. Treetown. It wasn't printed now. It was coded.

He stared at his father. The pencil sketch Nacho had drawn hung on the wall, showing the plates of knee angling through cloth, the slant of cheekbone bent toward the sticks in his hands.

Grief counseling? When a student at the high school had been killed in a car accident, the crisis counseling team had worked the campus for a week; the students wailed and talked, built a memorial, held a special assembly.

"In this old Niggertown," he whispered, sliding the box under the table. "Bad niggers don't get memorials. They don't get grief."

He put on the black jeans and Chipotle Chile T-shirt he wore to work. Two hours before his shift. He headed downstairs into the empty courtyard, glad his neighbors were all at work. He didn't know what glances meant now.

He wanted to check the public library for books about Tulsa history and the WPA *Slave Narratives*. Inside the stuffy, not renovated building, he passed the homeless men sleeping at tables, their bags near their feet. In the card catalog under Tulsa, he found only "Oil Boom," "Land Rush," and "Architecture." Marcus bent to finger book spines. Scottsboro. Civil rights. *Slave Narratives*.

The index at the back listed names of informants. Marcus touched them slowly. Pompey Thompson. "Pompey Thompson, age unknown, lived in a dilapidated stone house outside Tulsa. He was uncommunicative, and his memory seemed quite poor."

Marcus turned the pages to his great-grandfather's statement. "We walked to Texas from South Carolina. We didn't know we was free till somebody come and told us. Then we wasn't really free." The sliver of paragraph was buried between long reminiscences.

Marcus slid the book back into its gap. The library was usually his favorite place, where he was at ease with the pages and quiet instead of ringing metal and auto parts and loud voices. But the faces spun before him: the pale, shivering, fading-away mama, Oscar a baby, Bessier and Finis and the bloody shadow man and Pompey and his father. He couldn't breathe in here.

Near the exit, a shelf displayed a sign saying RIO SECO AUTHORS. A familiar face—Carrie Smith Donohue, the elderly woman from the newspaper. Marcus picked up her book with shaking fingers. *History and Heritage in Rio Seco, the Spanish Rose of the Valley.* He smiled slightly at her lipsticked mouth on the back photo. 1955. Before my time, he thought, but maybe my apartment building's in there. Better than reading about bad niggers all night.

Across from the library, he neared the bus station. This two-block section of downtown was seedy and run-down. The city council was arguing about moving the bus station elsewhere so the building could be turned into a railway museum to bring in tourist dollars instead of panhandling palms. "Hey, bro," someone whispered from the alley he was passing. "Hey, you want some white ass?"

Marcus glanced into the narrow passage. Two painfully thin white women leaned against the grimy wall, their feet in dirty sneakers angled wide on the old bricks. "Want to try some white pussy?" the blonde rasped. Her cheeks were dotted with maroon sores, and her wrist bones stuck out like miniature skulls when she tried to tuck her hair behind her ears and smile. Speed kills. That's what the white kids at Rio Seco High used to joke about. The black kids would say, "Man, brothers smoke crack and get all ghostly, but that speed turn them white folks past a ghost. Skeleton."

Pammy Sawicky had been hanging around here, he thought suddenly. That's what Shella had said. Pammy had been speeding, trying to stop, probably looking like those women. So anyone could have picked her up in any alley. But the other one—Marissa—hadn't been into drugs. Maybe Marissa had just been caught up in a drug deal or the wrong alley with Pammy. "Did you know two girls—Pammy Sawicky and Marissa Kent?" he asked the blond woman, and her face lengthened and softened like taffy.

"Fuck you!" she shouted, backing away. "You talkin about them girls got killed by niggers down there? You tryin to scare me? Fuck you, *bro*!"

Marcus walked casually past the next building. Don't run. Don't look bad.

When he neared the restaurant and his heart had slowed, he had to grin. Some white ass—try some. That's supposed to be a big attraction to me, huh? Even with the T-shirt, library book, and glasses, I must look like one desperate country fool. He saw his shadow in Chile's glass pane. Like any bad jungle brother.

. . .

The lunch hours were wild. Marcus was glad for Kurt's distraction; he
didn't have to be clever while he rushed around with bowls of salsa
and blue-corn tortillas. He was still thinking about her offer. Try some.
Like it was certain he'd never slept with a white woman.

He had—with Alana, but after the sushi and Kirin beer and sake,
Marcus remembered only awkward sensations from the dark: her hair
strange and soft like spiderwebs, her lips small and chapped. Nothing
else—not seeing her body, not what they'd done. Some time long
before dawn, he'd sat on the couch, head throbbing, and she'd come
out fully dressed, smiling, to leave. He kept thinking of that little smile.
He'd heard white women joke at college—Is is true, what they say
about black men?—and he had no idea if, with him, it had been true
or not true. What did the grin mean? He couldn't talk past cordial
comments when he saw Alana again downtown. "I'm into Indian food
this month." she'd say. "Try this spicy one." He wondered what adjec-
tive he rated. She'd tried some black you know what. Like Pammy.

Shit. He didn't want to think about that again. Think something
good. He set down an order of chile rellenos. Spicy. Indian. SaRonn,
with her cardamom tea and sandalwood-scented collarbone. He remembered every detail about that night with her, the fight with Larry Cotton,
the smell of the rock-lined ditch.

Web Matheson and two other men came in when lunch was nearly
over, but Kurt said beside Marcus, "The suits are back again. I'm not
chasing anybody out if they got big money." Marcus seated them in
the new bar area, trying not to stare, but he remembered the square,
constantly moving mouth. "We'll be a few deciding," the gray-haired
man said.

Kurt went over to their table, and Marcus nodded at him. He went
to the phone in the hallway between the bar and restaurant. "SaRonn?"

"Yeah."

"Remember me?"

"Mmm-hmm. You think I forgot?"

"No. I, uh, I don't know. I went on a little trip." He watched the
three men lean close together over their drinks.

SaRonn laughed, a low, metallic tinkle like her anklet. "You were
trippin? Now wait a minute, I ain't mad, I was waitin patiently for you

to come by and explain what is goin on in your head. But trippin—
now you sound like any other . . ."

"Treetown fool."

"Yeah."

"Nigga, please. That's next?"

"Not from me," she said, and then he heard crying. "Marcus, I gotta
go. I got a problem here."

Marcus listened hard. "Willa?"

"No, no, somebody else." He heard SaRonn say, "Get the hell off
my porch, boy!" and the crying turned to angry shouts. "I gotta go,"
she said, mouth close to the receiver again, and she hung up.

Marcus leaned against the wall, wondering if the Proudfoot kids were
fighting. He'd go by there tonight. Closing his eyes, he thought of the
curve of her stomach above the flowing pants.

"Half this county is a damn wasteland," a voice said. "A hellhole. Not
like Orange County. You see the freeway covered with tumbleweeds out
here?"

Web Matheson answered the older man with a grin. "That's what
I've been talking about. Driving ranges. Hey, golf is the next big sport,
and you take all that acreage we bought, you grade it and seed it, pay
some Mexican to cut the grass. Then you've got a driving range, you
can hold the land, make it profitable instead of wasted space till you
get the permits and builders." Web took a long drink. "I'm telling
you—it's a no-brainer."

Marcus heard the words echo in his head. No-brainer. Web Matheson—just outside the kitchen door after selling something to Marcus's
mother. A no-brainer. Matheson and another young man, years ago,
laughing in the yard. "I'm telling you—the Jungletown market is wide
open. It's a no-brainer."

Putting on his waiter face, he sauntered out from the hallway. "Can
I get you anything else, guys?"

Matheson said, "Uh, yeah, three more *cervezas*, huh?" He didn't shift
his glance to Marcus.

Marcus was getting the beers on the tray, Kurt laughing about the
day's crowds, when Bent came inside and poked his head into the bar
area. "Hey, Web," Marcus heard, and Matheson said something low.
Bent laughed, clapping his palm on Web's shoulder, and their hands
met in a clumsy high five. Then Bent came toward the kitchen. "Marcus!

Abby saw you through the window. I've been looking for you at the gym."

Marcus nodded. The gym was one place he hadn't wanted to show his face. "We're closing up, man."

"I'll wait for you."

Marcus remembered Julius shouting from the floor—"You the one, man, with the ponytail sherbert in the Jeep." Bent's face was serious now. "Okay," he said, and called to Kurt, "I'm gone, okay?" He walked to the bar and set the beers on the table.

"The place is called the Diamondbacks—way too scary," the younger, blond man was saying. "And Las Flores is too Mexican."

"People love that English tone to a name," Matheson said. "It gives a tract prestige. Hunter's Ridge, Hampton Estates, Fox Hollow Ranch."

"Actually, I've been hearing a lot of French stuff lately," the older man said. "Provence, Jardin—stuff like that."

"How many units per acre?" Matheson asked. Marcus turned for the front door, where Bent waited. Matheson's brother-in-law. The ponytail his father kept mentioning.

"Cool," Bent said outside. "I got something in the car for you."

Marcus stared at the just-washed black hood of the Montero parked down the pedestrian mall. "Yeah?"

Bent's voice rose with excitement. "Listen, your uncle, I don't know if you know who he is. You're lucky, man, he's gotta be a live wire. My dad and his brother are zombies—they go to work, go to the golf course."

"Just like Abby's brother-in-law, huh?" Marcus said. "Web, right?"

"Yeah," Bent said. "He's okay, except he and Abby's dad think what I do is pretty worthless." He stopped suddenly, staring at an antique-store window. "Abby and I want our own house, but we need to make big money on a book contract or something, cause real estate is sky-high out here." He paused. "Sometimes I wish I had more of somebody like Web in me, the money-making instinct. But guys like Web are so single-minded. Narrow-minded. They'd never go to an NWA concert and learn something."

Neither would I, Marcus thought, following him cautiously to the car. "What about Vanilla Ice?" Marcus heard the voice by the canal. Vanilla with the nine.

"You kidding?" Bent grinned. "I make fun of him. I cover serious rap, the real stuff from the hood." He opened the Montero's passenger door. "But the blues—that's my favorite. Get in and check this out."

Marcus left the door open and slid half onto the seat, his head dizzy with phrases and images, the library book in his hand. He saw Bent reach into the glove compartment, and he tensed. But Bent pulled out a CD, and then Marcus heard his uncle's rasping, guttural voice.

I'm the one know how to handle this knife
You don't watch yoself, you gon hand me yo life ...

"Oscar Jacknife Thompson," Bent said. "He recorded a few sides and then disappeared. He plays guitar Hawaiian-style, on his lap sometimes, with the jackknife pressed on the strings."

Marcus listened to the scratchy recording. "Yeah. That's him." But who was Bent?

"Man, I'd really love to meet him. Do you think he'd mind if I came to his place and listened? If I came with you?"

Your guide, huh? Marcus thought. His father and uncle were probably already suspicious after what Julius had said. The Montero. The rapping voice. His uncle would probably expect Bent to be packing. But Marcus didn't see that—he didn't know what he saw yet.

Bent grinned, nervous, not murderous. "Abby always talks about how great it'd be to have a blues club downtown, you know? Serve ribs and catfish."

"I'll ask my uncle," Marcus said finally. "And I'll give you a call."

"You're walking again?" Bent said eagerly. "I'll give you a ride."

"That's okay," Marcus said, getting out of the Montero. "I need the exercise."

Mortrice took the bottle of gin from Chris. Teddy was testing his gun, the one he'd been working on forever, bending over a piece of newspaper to study the ink dripping from the needle. Mortrice drank deeply, the peppery burn prickling down through his chest. Teddy had told them when his mother wanted to get tore-up drunk, she bought gin.

Mortrice took the blunt from B-Real, whose eyes were flickering like a broken TV. Mortrice knew B-Real didn't want to be down far enough for the pain, for the work. B-Real was a World. He like to talk, to sing, to smoke. He didn't like pain. But he always brought the chronic, and he rolled the weed into the big cigar-sized blunts better than anyone. B-Real and Chris and Mortrice hung tight in history class. The old white teacher dozed, as frozen as a statue during videos, and the white boy who'd given them this weed always wanted to talk.

He wanted Mortrice. "I heard you from L.A.," he'd said in his birdy-high voice. "You from South-Central."

Mortrice had shrugged. Teaching geography wasn't his job. "So?"

"So I got all the dope tapes, man, all the rappers from South-Central," the boy had said eagerly, his wine-bottle-green eyes moving around the hall. "From Compton, too. Eazy-E, bro, that's the shit."

Mortrice had shrugged again and moved on. B-Real had already gotten the chronic from this kid, and Mortrice wanted to think about the night, about the new gun. The buffalo gun. He'd been looking at the gunsmithing book, trying to figure out how to make the bullets, but he knew he'd have to go back to Zach. Zach would know a gunsmith who could make them perfect.

Mortrice inhaled hard, holding the smoke curled down inside. They had the two .9s, the .25, and he had the buffalo gun, with carving along the wood and the barrel longer than an arm. When Chris took the blunt, Teddy came close to him with the special gun. "You the one," Teddy said, and Mortrice felt dizzy. The one. One. He heard B-Real's choked voice saying, "I gotta go, man." The hollow click of the apartment door came just as Mortrice pulled down his bottom lip as far as it could go, two fingers resting hard on his chin.

"You know what it look like, like a girl down there," Teddy said.

"Shut up," Chris said, and Mortrice narrowed his eyes at Teddy, trying to feel the venom shine in his irises. Like Kenneth.

"You number one, man," Teddy said softly then. The cassette engine, whirring free of the case, made a high, drunken whine. Mortrice closed his eyes. The paper clip, straightened by Teddy to its full length and sharpened into a needle, jabbed forward from the pen's plastic sheath, carrying the ink. He tasted his blood, salty, ringing copper behind his teeth.

. . .

Marcus walked casually up the slope of Lowell Street. All the Plymouth Hill streets were named for Massachusetts cities; Marcus had been on tow jobs with Demetrius up here. Enchantee had said Abby lived on Concord. But he didn't want Bent to see him. And Lowell was the small street ending in an ancient granite retaining wall right up against the Los Olivos Hills.

The narrow path led up around the side of the rock wall and through rounded boulders to the hills. Marcus stepped up the dry, crumbled trail easily, not running, and meandered up the hillside. Just findin a rock and some solitude, do a little readin, he told the eyes. Some thinkin.

They had never meandered around here when they were growing up. No one from Treetown came past the first steep hill near his father's place, because the rocky trails and brush weren't that good for hunting. And on the other side, this side, you'd be the hunted if you came down off that granite wall.

Marcus and Finis and Usher had a place on the trail where they could see downtown laid out before them. Marcus climbed around the largest hill, the grass dry and rubbing to a shimmery sound, until he saw the slight valley where the four paths met. He took the one farthest west, climbing again, hearing the skittery rustle of lizards and the hollow wind. Where the path began to curve around toward Treetown, a hollow cave was worn into a huge boulder. Marcus squatted to examine the old ashes and beer cans before he sat on the smooth rock.

This is where they'd always stopped, he and his brothers. Plymouth Hill was a long slope dark with magnolia, jacaranda, and maple, high windows peering through, pools like distant chips of turquoise. He and the others would sit here, throwing rocks at bushes and lizards, eating pecans and nectarines and beef jerky. Looking. Descending any lower, toward the walls, would slightly widen that unseen eye, arch the brow, and bring cruising patrol cars.

Downtown, the avenues were laid out as straight as tines in an Afro comb, raking perfect through the city. He could see cars leaving the high school parking lot in a snaking trail of metal. Plenty of black Blazers and Jeeps and four-wheel drives there, too, he thought. Bent got a Montero. Everybody wants that rugged profile. Who's packin, missin a tire iron?

On the other side of the ridge of hills, one of those trails led in a circle and paralleled the river road, ending at the canal. Maybe Sketch and his friends had walked down that one, but Marcus thought they'd probably parked the black vehicle on the sandy shoulder of the riverbottom road and walked along the canal road a short way.

Indians had made these trails a century ago when they lived here along the riverbottom. In some flat boulders, depressions were left where people had ground acorns with pestle stones. Finis had always left bits of colored glass in the deep holes.

Marcus remembered the book in his satchel. Had Carrie Smith Donohue put Indians in her history? He looked at her picture again. Underneath it, the text read: "Mrs. Carrie Smith Donohue began her research into local history after the passing of her husband, a noted Rio Seco banker. With her talent for photography and her keen interest in historical sites, she has produced a valuable volume."

Leafing through the book, Marcus saw the titles. "Moorish Architectural Influences." "Historic Adobe Casas of the Valley." One photo showed a low-slung adobe ranch house fronted with a dusty wooden fence. "The Raymond Miller Adobe was part of a large tract of ranchland acquired by the Illinois native when he married María de Jesús Martínez, whose father was an original Spanish land grantee. The thousand-acre homestead featured an adobe structure built in 1879, containing three bedrooms, a large living area, and an outdoor kitchen. Unfortunately, María died shortly after the marriage."

He turned the page and saw his father's house. "The Archuleta Adobe," he read. The house was dusty beige, too, and he could see faint outlines of his father's hubcaps on the trees nearby.

In 1842, several families came from near the Santa Fe, New Mexico, area to Rio Seco's valley on the Old Spanish Trail. They were direct descendants of ancestors from Granada, Spain. Lorenzo Belarde, Hipólito Jaramillo, Feliciano Salcido, and Joaquín Archuleta settled in the area along the riverbottom, and in exchange for protecting land across the river from marauding bands of Indians, each man was deeded acreage fronting the river by Don Teodoro Banderas.

The New Mexicans held themselves aloof from the city, refusing to work in the groves like the Indians and Mexicans. They built adobe structures and began to farm their small acreage, growing wine grapes, olives, and fruits. The riverbottom area was subject to flooding, however, and in a disastrous January of downpours, most of the adobe homes were washed away in 1875.

The only adobe to survive was Joaquín Archuleta's home, built somewhere around 1845. The three-bedroom home had a fine *sala*, the formal room for entertaining, and a large kitchen. Several outbuildings were also architecturally significant—a stone barn probably built in 1880 or so with riverbottom rock, and a springhouse for storage.

Unfortunately, after the flood the neighboring community was mostly composed of migrant Mexican and black laborers, and the area once considered the gateway to the city because of the lovely stone bridge is now a squalid eyesore. Apparently, Archuleta never married, and sadly, the house passed from family ownership. Presently, a towing yard is situated on the grounds, the sweeping vistas cluttered with junked cars and rusting hubcaps.

Marcus closed the book, the blood pounding behind his eyes.

The sun was lowering, and the mountain range to the east was dusty mauve along the horizon over the city. He walked quickly through the scattered boulders to the descent where he could see Treetown and the riverbottom and the Diamondbacks across the water. The canal was below him, and his father's place. No-brainer. The Jungletown market. The vacuum cleaner—was it still hiding in his mother's closet?

Web Matheson had been to their historic house one day, when Marcus was about fourteen. Matheson was probably twenty, wearing those tight Angel Flight pants like his salesman friend. That big newspaper smile, those fence-perfect teeth, the All-American grin.

His mother had been cooking fish while Marcus did homework at the kitchen table. She answered the front door, where no one but strangers knocked.

"We're happy you agreed yesterday to a home demonstration of the Silver King, ma'am, because, believe me, it'll change the way you clean." His mother was silent, and Marcus heard something being dragged on the hardwood floor. "This machine is so powerful, ma'am, that with the attachments . . ."

Marcus moved into the archway near the plaster saint, peering out at the men. Web Matheson stood to the side, mostly watching. The older one stood very close to his mother, saying, "Even though this is the most powerful vacuum around, it only works if you use it, right? If you really care about clean."

"Here, Web, show the lady how this machine even sterilizes couch cushions." Web twisted an attachment with a flourish and pushed it into the cushion next to her; the puffy slab shrank, the mouth sucking it flat, and then the suction tore off and the cushion slowly revived. "Pretty strong, huh?"

"Baseboards, windowsills—these are places only really conscientious house-keepers worry about," Web said, glancing at his partner. "They harbor dirt and germs. I mean, some women don't care . . ."

The other man said, "I think a housewife like yourself can appreciate how Silver King could aid your children's health. Would you be talking payments?"

"Over the extended life of the machine," Web said, moving closer, "costs are minimal compared to other models. When you add up the years, you'll realize that your basic store model just isn't worth it."

Marcus went to turn off the spattering fish; when he got back, his mother was frowning over a contract in her lap and the men were in the doorway, Web's polyester pants and Qiana shirt giving off a sheen in the sunlight.

Marcus stood by the kitchen window. "Hey, I didn't think the product would do shit down here," the older one said. "It's not like they worry about dirt, right? Look around."

Web laughed and said, "This sure isn't Orange County, Trevor. I told you the Jungletown market was wide open. No-brainer."

Marcus found his mother in her bedroom, counting money from her dresser. She didn't look at him. "Your father ain't gotta know," she said. "Three hundred dollars down. Two more payments. All them attachments cost . . ."

"Damn!"

"Watch your mouth," she said, her voice stronger. But his father had known it was too much even if he didn't know how much. He was angry; he knew where it had come from.

And his mother ended up using the broom every day anyway—the vacuum had too many parts to assemble, and it followed her around like a short, barrel-bellied spaceman, Marcus thought, making her holler and flinch when it bumped into corners and table legs.

He crossed the canal bridge, staring down at the black, trembling surface under the concrete where he'd hidden that night. Just feet and hands and voices. If they'd seen him and shot him, he'd have been just another Treetown brother who'd somehow messed up.

The shadows were thick under the trees, and he went past the empty olive house and all the way around the grove along the fence, looking through to see the newly wet furrows and the desert-dry corners when he went around to the riverbottom roadside. The storage lot, colors deeper in the growing darkness, the faded hoods and doors richer. The gate was locked. He walked along the rising embankment where the green-painted fronds hid the tree trunks behind them, turned the last corner where cars where skidding to California roll stops before speeding past him and everyone else.

She was sweeping the day's dirt into a pile inside the kitchen, her angled broom flicking like a snake's tongue into corners and under tables and around chair legs, the husking sound he remembered from hot childhood afternoons when he lay on the wood floor in the dark front room, trying to stay cool.

"Hey, Mama," he said, and her face rose up to smile.

"Look who must be hungry, and he work at a restaurant," she said. She propped the broom against the wall.

"You still got that vacuum cost more than a car?"

"Oh, I guess so," she said, smiling, at the stove. "Taught me a lesson. Don't let em in the house, like your daddy always said. Next ones came was sellin bury sites. Me and Ocie Mae was sittin up in here. She told them, 'Shoot, I got three sick grandkids and a pile a laundry, boy. You sell me a site, I might jump on in *now*. Take my rest.'"

Marcus laughed. Then he leaned against the refrigerator. "Those two guys? One of them is the one tryin to buy the land, I guess."

She handed him a small bowl of beans and rice, then swept around his feet while he ate. "All this is about money?" she finally said.

"What else?" He paused. "I don't know, not yet. I'm lookin for Daddy."

"Don't forget your book bag," she said when he got up. "You should sit up with him tonight. He say it's gon freeze."

Sirius. The trembling Dog Star. Hosea's grandfather had told him that, on the farm in Simmons Grove where they stood in the icy, bare-turned field. "The master say, 'Look up there, nigger. Tremble just like your lip when you see me and know your nigger-dog hand been stealin somethin a mine.'" His grandfather had paused. "He ruint that star for me. And I won't gon tell you. But now I done told you the rest, and I'm sorry I talk at all. I am."

Hosea had watched the hard stars appearing tonight. He knew what the pulsing glisten meant, the perfectly still air, the way Paz had pointed to birds and bark.

He stood near the Meyer lemons near the coldhouse. The trees were heavy with purple buds, creamy blossoms, thumbnail fruit and ripe, fist-big lemons. Always like that in December, and lemons froze at thirty degrees if they were ripening. Hosea cradled one fruit with his palm, knowing the sizes by heart after years of picking in the groves, with the sizing ring he had to slide onto questionable lemons. Across the river—where the Hungarian would be watching his own grove tonight, fixing the wind machines he'd invented to blow the freeze away from the trees. He wouldn't have one for Hosea till morning, he'd said.

He saw his son, breath white against the dark branches, fingers around a book. He knew what Marcus wanted, but his head was aching and tired from working on an engine all day and now preparing to stay up all night. He knew his voice was grim. "Less you plannin to burn that, it ain't gon help me."

Marcus had expected it, he saw. His son only nodded and showed him the title, then the back photo. "You ain't had enough history yet?" Hosea said.

"She's the newspaper writer, and this place is in here," Marcus said.

He told Hosea about the description of the Archuleta adobe while they stacked wood against the coldhouse wall. Hosea looked at his son's glasses, the clear lenses his son wore because he liked to look that way. "You don't help me move two a them smudge pots, these old trees are history."

Marcus followed him toward the corner of the property, where the old smudge pots were lined like upright toy soldiers with round bases and stovepipe hats. "You can't use those anymore," Marcus said.

"Shit," Hosea said. "What they gon do—put me in jail? Again?"

They dragged the rusty pots toward the lemon trees, and Hosea filled them with oil from the barn. "Ain't gon light em till midnight or so," he told Marcus, heading back to the coldhouse. "Come in here."

Inside, he lit the fat pine splinters under the lemon wood Red Man Tucker had brought him. Then he poured two Mason jars of choc. From a small cup, he dropped in the sugar. He never had ants inside because he did like his grandfather said the Indians did: He threw some outside for them each day. "I know you fixin to ax me all them questions," Hosea said to his son, handing him one jar. "But I got a few for you."

Alma felt Sofelia's fingers gentle in her hair, working in the conditioner. Drapes of warmth fell over her forehead. Sofelia stroked all the strands back from her hairline, smoothing, whispering, "Leave it in a while, Mama. I'ma check on Mortrice. He ain't right."

Alma watched her daughter walk slowly from the kitchen. Sofelia still rarely spoke, but she moved now. She went next door to make pies with Lila sometimes, and Alma was silent. Sofelia's skin wasn't hot now, not thin as parchment and barely holding in her blood.

Mortrice was the one feverish tonight. He'd come sneaking in long after dark, trying to pass right through the kitchen and into the bedroom where Sofelia rested. Alma had gone in to see him lying on the bed, his skin puffed as a swollen belly under his bottom lip. "He must got a toothache," Sofelia said. "And feel him—burnin up."

The boy's eyes were closed, his forehead swimming with sweat, and the swelling went all the way to his chin. He refused drink or food, and Sofelia lay, watching him.

Alma went from room to room. The baby girl slept now in Abuela's room, and her first words were Spanish. *"Arroz,"* she said, pointing to her rice, *"luna,"* gazing up to the moon. Alma felt the damp, cool forehead, and glanced at her sleeping grandmother.

In the boys' room, she laid palms on them, too. So many years she'd been touching skin, checking for dangerous heat, that she knew she couldn't sleep or even sit down until she had made this journey through each room, each night. All the fevers and fears were webbed together with the tendons in her palms until she couldn't stop herself from touching even Sofelia, a grown woman, a woman grown away from her. When she went back to that doorway, Sofelia lay sleeping. And Mortrice was gone.

He crouched on the other side of the coldhouse, his mouth glowing like a burning coal. He'd been going to the trailer, but he'd heard

Marcus's voice, and he'd slipped around the back of the stone walls to the dirt below the small window. He could smell beer and fire; his mouth tasted only coppery blood and green-sweet smoke. Dizzy, he slid onto the cool earth and closed his eyes, listening to their voices.

"Who the ponytail in the black Montero?" Hosea looked at his son, the gold wire of his glasses burning crimson now in the firelight.

"A reporter for the paper. Lives with the woman Enchantee's working for."

"Downtown. You think you a sherbert?"

"Why we gotta do this again?" His son tightened his mouth.

"He your friend." Hosea waited. "He from Texas? He the one you heard?"

Marcus shook his head. "He's from Boston. But I don't know who the hell I heard—I can't recall the voice much, okay? I was tryin to keep from drownin." He finished the choc. "This dude knows about Oscar."

Hosea put down his jar. "Know what about him?"

"Knows Oscar was a blues singer. Jackknife. Played me a song. He said Oscar disappeared . . ."

"How he know all that?"

"From a book, probably." Marcus put down his jar, too. "From the newspaper. Like I know about Tulsa now."

Hosea stared at the fire. "You know what you read. That's all." He saw the way the lemon oil burned fierce. "It was a war. National Guard, airplanes with machine guns. Bombs. They put us in a camp for days. At the fairground. We slept in pigpens and horse stalls and under the bleachers. Where Oscar was born."

"Just like Jesus, huh?" Marcus tried to smile. "I only know what you tell me, Daddy."

Daddy. His daddy. "I didn't see him get shot," Hosea said slowly. "My daddy. I lost him downtown, and his friend carry me home. Then the Home Guard, they had broke into all the hardware stores. They taken guns and ammunition, clothes, everything. They came into Greenwood callin theyselves protectin. They killed the men and looted the houses and burned em down to cover what they done. They taken us downtown.

"I went lookin for his body. My daddy. I seen bodies all over, burnt up and shot. I looked in all the creeks, in the river. I never found nothin from him. My mother had Oscar under them bleachers. It wasn't like no Jesus. It was like hell."

Hosea closed his eyes, remembering the smell of blood so different from any other, the smell of burning in his clothes. Marcus whispered, "Oscar was hard from the start."

Hosea felt the blows to his head. "My mama's husband beat the shit outta Oscar. I stepped in one time, down there on the farm, and the man bust my eardrum. He told me walk, or he kill me.

"I had my gun—the gun the cops taken—and I pointed it at him. My mama was cryin in the corner, tellin me don't do it. I seen she was like a spirit, not a person no more. She was floatin away all the time. I went out in the yard, and I couldn't find Oscar. So I started walkin.

"I walked to Texas, cause my grandfather said he was from Texas. I knew somebody down there might have work. Police caught me up on vagrant and taken me and the others off somebody's porch and down into the woods somewhere. Say we had to work off our sentences.

"We slept in cages. In the trees. They was like horse carts, up on wheels, and they had a hole in the floor for the bathroom. In the morning, the guards throw you out the cage and you couldn't hardly walk. If you run, they shoot you in the back and lay you out under the cage for two days so we gotta shit on your body. Then we gotta dig a hole for you.

"They had white horses, and they taken us to the place we was clearin. Them horses breathin on your back. Poke you with the shotgun. We had to cut the trees, burn the stumps. They was gon build somethin there, the county sheriff was gon build it, cause he come out sometime and tell us we had to work faster or he line us up and shoot us all. Sometime he take one face he didn't like and shoot him for a show. Sometime the guard set the dogs out on somebody just to see will they run or climb a tree.

"I climbed a tree. I stayed up there for three hours, and then they laughed and told me to come down.

"Next day, I was workin all the way at the edge of the trees, and I waited for the one to get off his horse and pee. Sometime they pee on you. I seen he was gon do that, and I hit him in the head with the ax. Two, three times—like hittin a pig. I taken off into the creek and work my way down. Sleepin in the day, walk in the water at night. I didn't know what county, nothin. Just walk down the water and eat berries. It was late spring. Two years I been in the cage.

"I eaten squirrels and birds. Half-cooked em. I got sick as a dog in the water. I come to a town, I had to skirt around and find where I was. All I could think about was my gun. I wanted my gun back. I found some people in a mill camp, and one man taken me in his truck to the town where I been arrested. I couldn't give him nothin. He say he want to help any colored brother he can. I found the house, and I tore up them porch boards for my gun.

"I walked back on the Red River and the Arkansas. I seen bodies even though I wasn't lookin no more. Niggers get killed by whites, by niggers. Sometime just bones. I come up that creek by the cemetery to the farm.

"My mama was gone with her husband. Oscar had been gone. He left me a note. I didn't see him until we was grown, in L.A., where he was singin at a club. And then he come out here after . . ." Hosea looked at Marcus. "I let him tell you."

"He killed someone," Marcus said. "You both did. You think somebody's wantin payback now."

"I might killed the guard. Might not. But he was a white man. After that, I didn't never need my name nowhere. No papers on me."

Marcus was quiet for a long time. Hosea thought he heard an animal scratching in the dirt outside the coldhouse. The choc warmed his back, the fire his front, and the banked embers leapt back into yellow. His grandfather had taught him to build a good night fire. And never use paper. Never let paper capture you.

Marcus heard the palm fronds shift slightly outside, and a possum or raccoon padding away on the gravel. "You hear somethin?" he asked.

His father's eyes were shimmering red, fixed on the fireplace, and he didn't answer until after the hesitant crunch of small stones had faded away. "You wouldn't shoot nothin," he said hoarsely. "Finis used to tell me—you didn't even want to kill no possum to eat or sell." Marcus felt his heart beat, childish and quick; his forehead was still swirling with images of burning stumps and guards and bones. "I was aimin for the tires on the Jeep. Next time, I'm aimin for the head. What you gon do?"

Marcus hesitated, and his father's voice was as harsh as a claw. "You gon talk. Ax questions. I didn't want you to know none a this. Make you bitter."

"Better than ignorant."

"There you go. Every nigger in Treetown come from somewhere else back in the days, and they got somethin they ain't said. If they said it, maybe they ain't said the whole thing."

"You're losin me," Marcus said. "You said the whole thing?"

"Yeah." Marcus saw his father stand up, and he felt fatigue wash through his eyes like watery ink. "Be out there in a hour to light up them smudge pots. You comin?"

"I'ma go talk to someone." Marcus didn't smile. "I'll be back."

Mortrice lay in the closed-tight trailer, his mouth as hot and square as a charcoal briquet flaking into ash in someone's trash-can barbecue at the Gardens. His grandfather was right. No traces. AK was only inside. Only AK knew their territory. Their land. Treetown and the Gardens was theirs. Fools would find out.

His grandfather's face was all hard slashes. Eyes, cheeks, mouth. He kept it to himself. Maybe they were the same blood. He and the old man.

His mother's land. This would be his mother's territory. Her trees. Whoever was trying to fuck it up, Mortrice wouldn't hesitate. Not like Marcus. His uncle was soft. Mortrice touched the barrel of the buffalo gun beside him on the bed. He needed lead, casings, and the form to make bullets. Fifty-six caliber. I got the *cinco*-six. His grandfather was waiting for something. Someone. Mortrice could wait, too.

Marcus hunched his shoulders inside the jacket. The ice was sifting down through the night. White things suddenly glowed as if they wanted to attract crystals in the moonlight. Marcus faced the chalky disc of bone, risen now. Paper squares plastered by the wind to the chain-link fence were as white as gull feathers. The headlights on Pepper Avenue were blinding. Across the vacant fields toward SaRonn's house, even the tiny rocks reflected near his feet.

He heard voices when he reached the tiny front porch, and he remembered the shouting when they'd spoken on the phone. She'd had trouble. Larry Cotton? He listened for a moment, and made himself knock and call out, "SaRonn!"

"Who is it?" Her voice was muffled, cautious, near the doorjamb.

"Marcus."

She opened the door only halfway, leaning out to see him. "Hey," she said in a low voice.

"You still havin trouble?" He tried to peer past her, but she wedged her body in tight to the space, nodding. "SaRonn, I—" He didn't know if he should tell her about Larry Cotton. Then she'd know what he knew . . . would she?

"I saw Larry Cotton that night," he began, and she nodded again.

"I heard his voice out there," she whispered. "You think I wouldn't hear him? I saw you guys in the ditch."

Marcus looked at her forehead, shining when she glanced down the dark street, and he could smell her skin. "Hey," he said, pushing forward slightly, partly to get closer to the scent and partly because he wanted to see what the trouble was, the sobbing that didn't sound like Willa's baby cries. What he'd do was another thing, but he pushed until SaRonn's breath was warm on his neck and he could see over her head.

A young girl with an arm cast was in the hallway, peering at him, her face contorted with crying, her mouth bright with blood and her shirt torn. Marcus felt ten fingertips push him back, digging in hard like they had when he lay on top of her and she held him there by his collarbone. He stumbled backward off the two steps.

"It's not him, Malinda," SaRonn said into the room behind her. Then she turned a stone-hard face on Marcus and said, "Last thing I need is a man shovin on me right now, okay? I gotta go. No—" She bit her lip. "It ain't you. I gotta go." She closed the door, and Marcus walked quickly back through the fields toward Pepper Avenue, his chest hot with anger.

CHAPTER FOURTEEN

IN THE COMPLETE silence of the frozen dawn, Marcus started up his father's old truck. The steering wheel was like carved ice. The eucalyptus and pepper branches hung, unmoving, as if they were in shock.

After midnight, he'd sat up with his father watching the two smudge pots glow angry red and breathe heavy black that drifted through the lemon trees. They'd built their own small fire in the trees and stayed close to the warmth, silent all the rest of the darkness.

His father left the house now and got into the passenger side. Marcus drove along the riverbottom and got onto the freeway to cross the bridge. "I drove this when you were in the hospital and people thought I was you pullin up. They were disappointed when they saw me," Marcus said finally.

Hosea looked at him. "They was just surprised."

Like SaRonn last night, Marcus thought. What the hell was going on over there? Was somebody messing with her place, too? He thought of Finis. Maybe Finis had somehow gotten SaRonn in trouble; maybe Larry Cotton was trying to come back. Marcus looked at the rinds of frost clinging to the riverbottom trees below them. His brain felt slow, opaque with confusion, and when his father handed him the cup of coffee he'd brought from the kitchen, Marcus touched the hard-scarred nub that ended his father's thumb.

• • •

His shoulder, in this cold, wouldn't move well. Hosea imagined the scars inside his muscle contracting, chilling hard like citrus rind. He was glad his son was quiet.

On Cottonwood Canyon Ranch road, Hosea saw that the old two lanes had been widened. A planter striped the middle of four lanes with sprinklers and rocks and landscaping. Takin up water, he thought, just so when you stop at the light, you can look at flowers. While you waitin. You gotta experience somethin. Shit—it's a damn road, you there to drive. And up there, on the hills, they just bedrooms, and you there to sleep. Not have a goddamn hotel with a Jacuzzi and wet bar and couch like Demetrius tell me.

"Turn right here," he said suddenly at the signal light marked Morita Road.

"Been a long time," Marcus said, peering at the narrow asphalt lane.

The groves along the first few miles were dead, the leaves curled as pale as sand, the trees like thousands of dust clouds rising from the earth. Hosea stared at the baked-hard ground underneath, the milkweed purple and clogging the rows. "I guess the sons don't want this O'Brien land," he said.

Morita had been the Japanese farmer who grew lemons and strawberries. Alma and her grandmother had picked the berries, but the Moritas picked alongside them, packing the berries and running the fruit stand. During the war, the family had been sent to a camp in Arizona, where Morita and his wife had died. O'Brien owned the adjacent acreage, and when Hosea had been among the pickers on his grove, he heard O'Brien telling people, "I got the Morita place for a song. A song."

The trees turned green immediately after a chain-link fence, and dead crows littered the roadside. "He's still shootin," Marcus said. "So he called you about the big fan, huh? All this time, you guys only see each other once a year, and you're still buddies. Only white guy you ever talk to."

"He ain't white. He's Hungarian," Hosea said, looking at the fruit. "He done ate what he had to. Like me."

At the wrought-iron gate, the Hungarian appeared in his khaki coveralls, his face smeared with oil, like war paint. Hosea shook the dark-coated hand. "My friend," the Hungarian said. "You would like a drink to heat your inside?"

In his red wooden barn, cluttered with machinery, he handed them each a shot glass of the plum brandy he made every year. Hosea felt the purple fire trace down his chest and pool in his belly. The Hungarian laughed at Marcus. "You are old," he said. "But the baby, eh? And you don't work any land. Look at your hands."

"He live downtown," Hosea said, seeing Marcus roll his eyes.

"No land," the Hungarian said. "Who will work your place? The oldest? Because you are ancient. Like me. Tough old meat."

Hosea said, "The two oldest always work the cars. I don't know who gon work the trees. I got grandsons don't know shit but play TV games."

"Like O'Brien's boys. They are selling it all." The Hungarian walked over to the two wind-machine engines. "They grow houses. And they buy citrus from fucking Florida."

"Those engines runnin on your California oranges?" Marcus asked, and they all grinned. Marcus remembered the gasahol the Hungarian made from oranges; one day he'd poured the fuel into an old Buick to demonstrate, and the car wouldn't cut off. He'd killed the ignition, pulled out the battery, and they'd finally stuffed rags in the tailpipe.

They'd come at Christmas every year before the bridge went out in the flood; they'd brought chitlins and pecans, and the Hungarian's young wife, whom he'd had sent over from the old country, had silently handed them a tray of pastries. Heavy cream-filled tarts, grained and laced with brandy, poppy seeds crunching in prune filling. Hosea could smell the boiling sugar wafting from the house now.

After the bridge was gone, and they had to take the freeway, they'd come less often. "You and your brothers would come with your guns," the Hungarian said to Marcus now. "The oldest, he had rabbits tied to his belt. You were thirsty. I said to give me rabbits, and I cooked them on the fire. You, you didn't touch that." The Hungarian's dark, raisin-small eyes disappeared with his grin. "I told you that when I was a boy like you, in the war, we watched from the buildings to see when a horse fell dead in the street. We fought each other for the meat. Pull hot chunks and run upstairs. You threw up."

"That's me," Marcus said, his voice resigned. "Always a sissy."

"Downtown," the Hungarian mused. "Now we are all taken in from the city, from the people downtown. How is it?"

"Annexed," Marcus said.

"The water bills go up, the drought is seven years already, and they want farmers out, I see that easy," the Hungarian said, turning to his machines.

The large fans could circulate the air in a small grove, enough to keep frost from settling onto leaves and fruit. Marcus strained to push them on the dolly and up the plywood ramp into the truck.

Then the Hungarian led them to the bare high spot near an old cement holding tank. A folding chair looked out over the slope here, across the smoky dead trees and the riverbottom. "You paint your house blue," the Hungarian said, and Hosea nodded, seeing his place a floating sliver like broken glass, his storage lot a faded baby quilt. Marcus squatted to stare out at the view, and the Hungarian said, "Downtown. That glass tower? Matheson. Real estate. He came last month, he asks if I'm interested in selling now. He wants the whole acreage, not just O'Brien land. He points at the tower and says his office is there. Like I care how big it is." The Hungarian spat onto the gritty base of the tank.

"I told him I might sell. I ask him what are his plans, you know, like friendly. He couldn't choose his orange from a tree or even peel it, that kind. He couldn't cut up a goddamn chicken freeze from the market. He starts to talk about a bridge. They will rebuild the bridge. The city wants to connect all the land now. He says he lives up that way." The Hungarian pointed toward the Diamondback Hills, where the cleft of dark green trees spilled down the ravine. "Then I know he's an asshole. My wife gives him a pastry, and he says, 'These are great! Where can you get these?' I tell him my wife makes them. He laughs and says, 'My wife hasn't figured out how to turn on the new stove burners yet.' I smile at him. Jackass."

Marcus waited until the silence was broken by sparrows rustling in the trees nearby. "So they want to rebuild the bridge. Probably widen Pepper Avenue for the commuters."

Hosea saw downtown's pale old buildings like sand castles, and the Los Arbolitos towers turquoise now in the risen sun. "What he say about you sellin?" he asked the Hungarian.

The man shrugged his narrow, stooped shoulders. "I say I'm not ready to go, and he laughs. He says he just built a custom place up there." He gestured toward the Diamondbacks. "He says it isn't going anywhere. He leaves his card."

Hosea knew the address. He knew that Fulton Chester's whiskey smell and sweat stink had evaporated from the real-estate office, but the expensive aftershave and acid white wine that clung to suits were more dangerous. "You think he wants this place here bad enough to burn it?"

The Hungarian frowned. "What? He didn't sound like a hurry."

Marcus turned to scan the developments. "I wonder how many bones they found when they built all that."

The Hungarian laughed as loud as a TV Santa Claus. "You haven't seen all they have built up there? Their own lakes to go with the apartments. No land. But they can look at water from a pump. And the golf course takes water. But that is not a farm. Look at the names— they want to be Italy there, or England. But not Hungary." He spat again, starting down the hill.

Hosea followed him, the thin cold biting at his neck. The winter sun was as pale and fat as butter. This freeze might last for days, and the air was as sharp as razors between the grove rows still locked in walls of shadow.

The flags began after a quarter mile west on Cottonwood Canyon Ranch Boulevard. COTTONWOOD CANYON RANCH—A MASTER-PLANNED COMMUNITY BY SOUTHLAND HOMES. Each wooden sign was spaced in a strip of greenery along the miles of plastered wall.

MORE ROOM FOR SPOT AND WHISKERS TO ROAM. FOUR-ACRE GATED COMMUNITY PARK. MOUNTAINS, BEACHES, HIKING AND BIKING NEARBY. CUSTOM-BUILT FOR SWING SETS AND SMILES. The last sign, before a huge entry with fountains and palms, read A SPECIAL PLACE TO LIVE YOUR LIFESTYLE.

More signs lined the main street leading into the development. Marcus drove slowly. MARQUESSA—LUXURY APARTMENT LIVING. The arrow pointed to a terra-cotta cluster of buildings. TUSCANY HILLS—ELEGANT GONDOMINIUM COMMUNITY. Beige walls and balconies.

"Fancier than Demetrius's area," Hosea said.

"The houses get bigger as we go up," Marcus said. Now wrought-iron gates were set into the walls at the entrances to Caravaggio, Palazzo, and Venetia. "A golf-course community," Marcus read aloud. "Built around a Jack Nicklaus course or something."

Hosea saw the end of the paved road and then the largest homes, scattered on the Diamondbacks. The steep slopes had been cut and graded; flood channels were draped like cement necklaces on the bare embankments, and tiny feather-duster trees were set in rows along the raw dirt.

"Custom sites, acre estates, and view lots for sale," Marcus read aloud. "This must be it, up here. Where he lives."

View lot. Hosea looked at the closest deck, white wood and wrapped with glass cloudy from the morning cold. White people always wanted to view something. On TV, they were always standing on decks and balconies and patios holding drinks, viewing lights.

He didn't want to get out of the truck. The walls and embankments and concrete channels were like valleys enclosing the street, and he wasn't sure if the people in the gate booths weren't watching, calling already. Sundown town? How could you tell if this was sundown town?

After he'd come to Rio Seco and started working the canals and the citrus, moving around to pick fruit sometimes with other people from Olive Gardens, the longtimers like Lanier and Ocie Mae told him about the small places throughout the county where whites from Oklahoma and Texas and Georgia had settled, where the sheriff or police chief was from Tulsa or Dallas, where dark faces better not be glimpsed after sunset. He and all the others knew those names: Manzanita, Campbell, Durant, Mill Station. Lantana—they called themselves Lan-Klan-a.

But here, where he could move his head out the window and study the saddle between the tallest boulder-veined Diamondbacks, where the welt of spring-fed trees was swallowed by red tile, this was past a sundown town. The walls and gates and winding streets, all leading to this one avenue, too new to know.

"Matheson could be over there in Hampton Hunter Royal Windsor Crest Ridge," Marcus said, turning the truck around.

"What the hell you talkin about?"

Marcus grinned. "The English part. I heard him talk about it in the restaurant. Hey, I was tryin to surveil the man best a sissy like me can."

Hosea had to grin back. Then he looked all the way to Grayglen, still charred in patches from the huge wildfire in those hills more than a year ago. "They can see everything from up here. Everything all laid out." What did Matheson see? Sundown was on the other side of the mountains. He was viewing his towers; they'd reflect the sunset in pink and yellow. When Marcus began to drive back out of the torturous loops toward Cottonwood Canyone Ranch Boulevard, Hosea could see Agua Dulce like scattered broken-spaced tiles of color, and then Treetown like a patch of moss on a stone. And his place, huddled into the side of the low Los Olivos, the pepper and eucalyptus like permanent puffs of smoke.

Driving back across the river, he said, "I took Demetrius and Octavious up there to the Diamondbacks when I taught em to shoot. What was they—bout like Sofelia's boy?"

"Mortrice?"

"Him and Kendrick size."

"I don't know. I was little."

Hosea stared at the hills, burnished gold from drought. "I ain't taught you to shoot or hunt. Demetrius taken you."

"I guess he did a bad job teachin me to shoot," Marcus said, his voice bitter. "I ain't killed anything yet."

"That ain't so bad," Hosea murmured. "Let's get some breakfast."

The kitchen was filled with the aroma of coffee and tortillas and eggs. "I heard your truck," Alma told Hosea, setting down his plate. She brushed the back of his neck, and her hand stayed on his skin. "You got a chill."

Hosea passed the flickering tiny candle by the statue. Sofelia was sitting up on the couch, her eyes shining like oil in the dim light. Alma drew the curtains, and Hosea went toward the bathroom.

He pushed open the door and saw his grandson's back in the stark white room. The brown skin was welted with holes and scars. The scars had keloided into gleaming raised shapes like pumpkin seeds. The boy turned from the toilet, and his mouth was closed tight. He held a t-shirt.

"Who did this to you?" Hosea said, grabbing the thin shoulder.

"My daddy," the boy said, and pulling away, trying to put on the shirt.

Hosea followed him into the living room, snatching the cloth up to show the back to Sofelia. "Who did this to him?" he whispered to his daughter.

She took in a shuddering breath. "I ain't seen that."

"His daddy do that?" Hosea stared at her, her brows like Alma's, her hair rubbed into a halo from sleep. Like when she was a baby.

"His daddy dead," she whispered back, watching her boy stalk into the kitchen.

"How?"

She kept her eyes on the archway. "He killed himself."

Hosea stared at her. The baby girl—she'd looked like a small dancing doll when he used to watch her lonely circles around the yard. She and Alma moved in tandem now, mostly silent, their necks bent the same.

Moving into the kitchen, Hosea stood next to the boy again where he ate a tortilla standing near the door. "Who shot you?" he said.

The boy's eyes met his. "Some dude I don't know."

Marcus said, "When did somebody shoot you?"

"Long time ago," the boy answered. "I gotta go."

Hosea saw his hand grab the elbow. "You been in L.A. all your life," he said, and then he stopped for a moment, seeing the fields and the arroyos, the mica-flecked dust rising from his sons' footsteps. "You need to learn how to hunt. How to shoot. I'ma get you and Kendrick startin-out guns. BB guns. You two can start patrollin the fences, and I'ma take you up in the hills behind the canal. Find you some squirrels."

"He don't need no gun," Sofelia said from the doorway. "I brought him here cause he was bangin."

"Bangin?" Hosea said, frowning.

"I ain't bangin," the boy said, folding his arms. "Look at me." He glanced at Marcus, then at Hosea. "I don't need no gun. I be keepin a eye on things in the trailer. I could hear everything out there. Ain't nobody been out there."

"Finis just lost his way," Alma said. "He comin back from wherever he got away to."

Marcus stepped forward, and Sofelia called out, "Who did that to you, baby?"

Mortrice said, "Somebody else's peoples," and he wrenched the door open and dropped down the steps without looking back at them.

The letters were secret, slick and hidden. Only if you down you can taste em, Mortrice thought. Not like Westside Loc Special or Los Dementes, with their neck and forearm tattoos; not like the *vatos* with AGUA DULCE in square-edged letters over each eyebrow.

At school, he slid his tongue across the letters. AK-1. You the one.

Chris was all the way down. Teddy, too. But B-Real, although he'd hang in the apartment with them, was always out in the music building with three X-World brothas. MC Brains, DJ Knowledge, and Dr. Forehead, they called themselves. Gone Worlds.

Chris was hollering about his girl again. He was ready. The rock man she worked for had beaten her up. Malinda. Mortrice watched silently. He watched the Olive Gardens girls silently, too. They wanted manicures, gold, hairdressers. They wanted ducats. He didn't feel anything. Chris shouted, "Man, I been loved that girl since I was five and shit. He wanna fight, he can fight me. He wanna pow-pow, bang-bang, come on! He want me!"

"He got you," Teddy said. He'd stolen the car. They couldn't drive B-Real's new Volkswagen van. World van. Shit.

They waited till afternoon in the apartment, smoking the weed the white kid kept handing to Mortrice after history class, making a big deal like they were homeys. Tight.

Mortrice stared at the TV screen. It was almost time. The fool named Vernon would be at the rock house in the late afternoon, when he always checked the money. Rodney King was getting his ass kicked again. Mortrice watched the boots. He remembered seeing a man stomped to death in Soul Gardens. It took a long time. The boots sounded like mallets.

In the car, cruising, Teddy driving, he stared at the line of cars ahead of them on Pepper Avenue. They'd gone all around through the Westside to come down this way, not from the Gardens. He saw the marks on the overpass, on the wall. Their marks. In L.A., it was B-Killer, Blood Killer. He stared at the line Chris had painted:

$$\mathsf{\underset{\mathsf{T}}{\mathsf{T}}ANYBODY\ KILLA\ \$\overset{o}{_G}.}$$

Treetown. All those trees on his grandfather's place. His peoples. He was getting used to sleeping in the trailer, imagining it was ammunition hurtling through the dark. He knew his mother would jam him up again about the scars. The marks. He'd tell her he didn't see shit. That's what everyone else always said, in the Gardens.

Nobody would see them now. The cars slowed with traffic. Chris held the .9 Mortrice had the .25. He didn't like the little, cheap piece anymore, the way it felt like a toy. He was going to see Zach next week, about the bullets for the .56. The buffalo gun. The *cinco*-six, for next year. For the nine-deuce comin.

His uncle, the one named Julius, wasn't around anymore. Not since that night when the other two tried to stomp him. More shit about the land. All the bodies. Mortrice lay in the trailer sometimes, waiting to hear footsteps, someone dumping a body. Or looking for one. But he was ready, if the leaves crunched outside. And if he shot someone, the someone trying to mess with his grandfather, he'd be cool. They'd be trespassing. On his mama's land.

Teddy finally made it to Grove and turned. "If I pull the trigga, I could be her nigga," Chris sang softly. Mortrice saw the rock house with pink under the roof; he saw the fool's black Jeep Cherokee. A little mailman Jeep was behind it.

Beating someone to death was long and red. Shoot from a car, at the porch where the fool was standing, trying to figure out where Malinda was, and all you saw was the shadow crumple like a puppet with the hands jerked out. No raw meat. No close range. Pulled along like strings from the front, or the back, which way he turned. Like the puppet show someone put on at the Gardens when he was a kid. You couldn't even see the strings. Teddy raced around the corner and down toward Agua Dulce. Chris leaned back with the vapors leaking from the .9, looking back at Mortrice with all that puppy love in his eyes, leaking out to pool above his cheeks.

"She mine now," he whispered.

When Alma peered out the big living-room window, she could see bare outlines of palm fronds tossing like feathers in the strong, sudden wind. This moving air would blow the freeze away and bring moisture, she hoped, after all the years of dry.

The predawn light was only cement-gray at the edges. All night, she'd heard sounds. Palm fronds falling to the asphalt with stunning cracks like gunshots. Wind mouthing as hard as the loose old window frames. Jawan calling out. Hosea walking on the gravel. He and Oscar were sitting up again with the fans, in the trees. For days, they'd slept only in the afternoons.

Hosea was even more silent and blurry-edged than when he'd first come back from the hospital, and she knew it wasn't only his shoulder. It was his face, drifting into loose thought whenever she saw him near the fire, staring at the embers. When she brought him a plate of food, she asked him, "Hosea, you feelin some pain, somethin still in your chest?" he raised his eyes from the coals like he didn't know her.

"Nothin to talk of," he said, and he picked up a few more pecans. "Too much talkin what give me this headache I got now."

Alma looked at the boxes of tiger-striped pecans in the kitchen now. With a long freeze like this, as long as she'd worked hard enough in the fall, they would get through. The tiny green apples, whose juice on your chin was thick and milky as liquid chalk, were picked. The walnut trees were bare, and the pecans curing near all the fireplaces. In the old days, this was when they'd kill a pig, when the meat would be sweet and smoky. But since Lanier had just put a few pigs on Oscar's land, they'd have to wait.

She looked at the shelf where the mail usually collected. Since that boy had been shot and two bullets had pierced the mail Jeep, service had been cut off all week. The freeze had settled like a cupped hand over Treetown, and people were irritable and gray-faced. Oscar and Hosea trudged back and forth from the barn to their groves. But with this wind, the ice might be over. The trouble . . .

She went outside in the bluing dark and pushed open his coldhouse door. The nuts and cured olives and pomegranate jelly lined the rock shelves, glinting in the vague light. Ashes still murmured at the center of his fireplace. Alma sat on the wooden chair to wait.

Take my mind beyond the trees. Finis heard the song while he walked along the canal road. The wind was swirling around him, dropping leaves and dust veils onto the slow water. Marcus loved walkin here. Me and baby brother used to run together. He couldn't go to Marcus's place. Downtown. Cops were comin into Treetown. Everywhere. Finis had seen them when he left the Kozy Komfort. Usher had the old tapes. Finis needed some new songs. It was lonely down at the shack, among the rocks and stones. No bones. No songs.

Slippin into darkness. He loped along the canal path behind The Blue Q. The blues is all right. Hey, hey. At the fence, he searched for the spot where he'd always climbed over. The wire was reinforced now, with barbed wire on top, and he snagged his leg on the splinters of metal. The blood ran warm and slipping down his calf. Finis touched the small hole and brought his finger to his lips.

He moved through the trees to the silver cocoons nestled into the leaves. Darkness. The metal gleamed as dull as knife flashes through the trunks. No music came from Julius's windows, and he stopped, frowning. Silent night. Holy night. All is calm. All is bright.

Stepping up the metal rung at his door, he fumbled with the key attached to the polished stone. Mama had one. I'll always love my mama. He pushed the teeth into the hole, and the door swung outward with a burst of wind, knocking him onto the carpet of rustling leaves.

A face he'd never seen before was crouched over a small eyehole pointed at his forehead.

Lookin at the devil. Starin at his gun. Fingers start shakin. I begin to run.

He stumbled into the shaggy eucalyptus and ran along the stone wall toward the canal, the wind flinging dirt into his eyes.

He'd lit the smudge pots every night after he'd started the wind machines. Damn the law. Smudge was illegal. All that smog ain't. All them people drivin from Cottonwood Canyon to L.A. makin exhaust. I make my own damn smoke. Come and cuff me.

He and Oscar and Marcus sat near the Reine Dulce trees, in the rusty glow from the pots and the small fire they'd built. When the wind came up, they had to tamp out the coals and douse the pots. But in the darkness, the wind was scouring away the ice.

He listened to his brother and son argue. "You ain't sayin nothin," Oscar had prodded.

"He ain't said nothin all week," Marcus had said, avoiding Hosea's eyes.

But he'd finished with talking. Everyone else could talk. Hosea turned up the Mason jar and the choc dregs fell down his throat, the bittersweet thickness coating the raw place where words had scratched like a rasp all that night he'd told the stories to his son. No more stories. He swallowed the residue of the beer that clung to his teeth, shifting all those words back down his throat, dropping each memory and sentence along the hole in the starlike vertebrae he'd seen along creek banks, sliding them down to rest in his back, silent, sheathed.

"The principal called me and said after New Year's, she might have substitute work," Marcus said. "She told me she'd called around downtown and found out the charges got dropped, that she believes it was a setup. And I was always nervous around her. Man, I need the money."

Oscar sucked his teeth. "You can't get your full-time gig back? Hell, I thought once you had a govment job, you could keep it till your head fell off and finally somebody realize your ass is all they got left in the chair."

"Yeah, right," Marcus said.

"Who pay you? The county? City, county, state, U.S., they all the same. Don't nobody really work. That's why I don't vote for none of it."

"You could vote for a brother."

Oscar's eyes narrowed to sunflower seeds. "Shit. He might be black when you vote, but bip, bap, boom, he turn into a white man. Hosea know." Oscar took a long swallow.

Hosea saw his son's face harden in the shadows. "Like me, huh?" Marcus's voice was angry.

"I ain't said that." Oscar paused. "So you want to bring this ponytail sherbert to the club. See me. And what if he the one? He bet not be foolish enough to try no shit. He might got you friendly, but . . ."

Marcus interrupted. "He ain't the one. I hung out with him a coupla times at Chile. He's a writer, okay? He just wants a story."

"He hella damn interested in me and The Q all of a sudden. He ain't axed about you and your place, Hosea?" Hosea shook his head. He and Oscar had talked about the reporter. The black Montero, the brother-in-law. Oscar said, "See, Marcus done hung around downtown so long, maybe he can't read em. But he ain't met the kind we used to see, right? They still out there—they just look different than back in the day."

Marcus said, "Fuck it, then. Just shoot the guy now, right?"

Oscar grinned. "I ain't said that either. Just bring him on."

They heard the police helicopter whining quickly toward Treetown, the fast drone and then slower chopping. The blue beam knifed through Hosea's trees, probing, touching Oscar's and Marcus's faces to stark bone for a moment. Maybe someone was coming about the smudge pots, Hosea thought; not moving. He felt calm creeping back up his spine. Let em come. I'm tired of this shit. I'ma do what I want on my own damn place.

Oscar said something he couldn't hear in the racket of blades, and then the helicopter moved off suddenly across Pepper, hovering over Grove and then Olive Gardens. They stood and walked to the clearing, where they could see the searchlight sweeping like a pendulum. "Plenty of black fools in Treetown, too," Oscar said. "Always givin the police a paycheck."

Shots pinged in the distance, and Hosea tried to shrug off the chill in his shoulders. The blue beam was fixed now, circling. Above the helicopter, he saw Sirius, the Dog Star, risen. His grandfather had seen Sirius nearly every day at this time. The dawn hadn't belonged to him in Texas, he'd told Hosea, and then, when things got worse, not even the moments before sunrise.

CHAPTER FIFTEEN

"STARCHILD. THAT'S THE dude with the sunglasses, man, hung out with your uncle Julius? Old dude, live with his mama. Brain all fucked up from drinkin. Starchild *flew* back and hit the wall like the wind was blowin him, Mortrice. I ain't lyin. Shit. I was layin there all gaffled up in the parkin lot—that's where they put us. Hog-facedown. Starchild come round the corner, try and zip up his pants. Po-lice was hollerin and then boo-yaa." Chris rubbed his wristbones where the handcuffs had left purple dents. "You lucky you was out at your peoples, man, in the woods."

Chris and Teddy and Lorenzo had been splayed out on the asphalt for hours, but eventually they'd been let go. No guns, no drugs. Mortrice had them in the trailer. And last night, whoever the gaunt-faced man had been, the one trying to get into the trailer, his eyes wild and hair braided like a kid did it, he hadn't been a cop. The fool had run when he saw the .9. Mortrice got into the backseat of the car.

"Boo-yaa," Chris said again, staring at the yellow police tape around the rock house. They turned the corner and stopped at the place where Malinda stayed now.

But when they knocked on the plywood in the doorway, and the woman slid it aside, she was older than Malinda. Short hair, baggy pants, long silver earrings. Chris said, "Yo, Malinda in there?" and the woman's face grew as hard as wood.

"Do you little fools see this?" she said, pulling open the makeshift door. "Do you?" She pointed to the blue splinters as long as spears littering the yard. "That's my door. Cause the cops were lookin for

little *fools* like you and big fools like some other people. You got all of
us raided!"

Mortrice heard someone call, "SaRonn?" The woman still blocked
the doorway and she shouted, "Like Malinda gon trade one hoodlum
for another?" Then he heard crying, and she said, "Look what you
done got me—that's what she does now when somebody knocks,
okay?" The woman moved aside, pointing at a little girl huddled in the
corner of the room. "Look at the cuts on her leg! That's from where
they busted the door down! Get out my face." She pushed the plywood
back into place, and Mortrice heard a hook slide into an eye.

Marcus walked into Natalie Larchwood's office, nodding at the secretary,
his fingers touching the tight, twisted eyebrow before he realized it.

"Marcus," she said, her huge round glasses making her blue eyes
look like jewels in clear puddles. "I hoped you'd be patient until now.
A new year, right? Look, I had faith in you, I knew the arrest had to
be a mistake, and Val and Judy both came in to tell me how much the
students would miss out on with you gone."

He wasn't sure she was finished, as usual. But she looked down at
her desk as if sometimes the tumbling sheets of words surprised her,
too, and Marcus ventured, "I missed this place, too."

"Well. The board thinks . . ." She stopped. "Look, I know you're
a good teacher. Mr. Whalen's out for surgery, for at least two weeks,
and after that, I think we can find more sub work." She shook her
head so vehemently that her short steel hair bristled. "Whether anyone
else likes it or not, I want you back."

"Thanks," Marcus said, and she lowered her eyes to her paperwork.

"You've got Whalen's classes for two weeks?" Val sat down next to
Marcus in the teachers' lounge. Marcus sipped his coffee, keeping his
eyes only on his papers until he heard their voices.

"He's out for surgery, but no one knows what kind," Judy said
cheerfully.

Val leaned closer, lifting his brows. "Hey, when you keep the specifics
unclear, and you're his age, and your face always looks that grim, must
be prostate."

"That's awful," Judy said.

"That's awful cold," Marcus said.

Val stood up. "Hey, this is Sonia Martínez. She—uh, she got your classes." Marcus nodded at the woman Judy's age, with a fall of black hair. "Sonia loved our little motivational seminar last week, huh?" Marcus could tell Val wanted everyone to be comfortable. "These kids are just *bombarded* by MTV and materialistic imagery!" he chirped in a singsong imitation. "Let's help them channel their *tremendous* energy into positive, empowering outlets!"

"You're hard, man." Marcus smiled.

"But that guy doesn't have to sit here all day with sleepy kids," Sonia said, quiet.

"He's off to another seminar. We're off to kids who really *tremendously* want to sleep because they were up all night partying in much better clothing than I'm wearing," Val said, waving.

Marcus walked to Whalen's classroom. First Period. Honors History. Kids the others called Brainiacs, dressed in black Goth clothes or Guess. They were working independently on research papers about the Cold War, according to the thin folder Natalie Larchwood had given him. "You know Herb doesn't leave much of a lesson plan for subs. Pretty much standard procedure in his classroom." Marcus nodded to a few students he'd had in world history last year. Standard. Read the book. Answer the questions. Just like Mortrice had said. He felt useless, looking at the bent heads working or napping or writing love letters. These students didn't need anything special. Maybe Mortrice's class would.

At lunch, he stayed in the room, reading the newspaper. He was surprised to see a photo of the overpass near the Kozy Komfort, and under that, an article with Bent Carson's byline.

TREETOWN SUFFERING: MURDERS DOUBLE CITY'S ANNUAL RATE

Approaching the small, recently annexed area of Rio Seco called Treetown, commuters and residents alike can see numerous graffiti markings on the overpass of the 42 freeway; some of the markings are names, others resemble telephone poles. But all signal the entry into one of the city's most troubled areas.

Treetown, an area plagued by poverty, drugs, and recent gang violence, has been the scene of six homicides this year. For the community, which has approximately 1,000 residents, this translates into a murder rate more than double that of the city at large.

Most recently, Vernon Howard, 21, was killed in a drive-by shooting on

Olive Street two weeks ago. Homicide investigators have no leads in the shooting, which also saw stray bullets puncture a parked U.S. Mail Jeep. Mail delivery to the beleaguered area was halted for ten days, an unprecedented action by the Postal Service, but a spokesman said that the safety of letter carriers could not be compromised. Some elderly residents missed government checks.

In the past few months, Lorenzo Proudfoot, 16, was shot and killed in the parking lot of Olive Gardens, a low-income apartment complex that has been the site of much recent gunfire. And a still-unidentified John Doe was bludgeoned to death at a run-down motel on the edge of the area.

The most puzzling and gruesome murders took place in September, involving three nonresidents of the area. Pamela Sawicky and Marissa Kent, both downtown residents, were found dead in a burning car at a Treetown towing yard. Despite intensive and ongoing investigation, no suspects have been arrested. And at the same address, a French national was bludgeoned to death. He, too, was a nonresident.

The towing yard was also the site of a drug raid that netted stolen property. Drugs have been a persistent problem in the mostly black community. The few streets are lined with modest homes and junked cars, no sidewalks or streetlights, and some unkempt yards. Longtime residents shake their heads over this new wave of violence stalking their area.

Marcus laid down the newspaper. A whole lot of bad niggers in that old Niggertown. He was one of them. Stolen property. Drug raid. And what the hell was Bent doing covering this? He was arts and music, he'd said. Not crime. Crime was some guy with a long name. Marcus looked at the story accompanying Bent's. Rick Kolavic—that was him. His story was under another photo—this one of several young men lying facedown and anonymous in the Olive Gardens parking lot.

TREETOWN MAN KILLED DURING GANG SWEEP

Rio Seco police conducted a dawn raid in areas of Treetown over the weekend, searching for suspected gang members, parole violators, drugs, and weapons, in an effort to stem rising crime in the small enclave between the 42 Freeway and the river. Five men were taken into custody at various locations, for parole violations and outstanding traffic warrants. The police action was praised by Ray Sawicky and other members of the City Council, who had recommended cleaning up the community in ways ranging from police sweeps to aggressive enforcement of city housing codes at many run-down residences.

While police were canvasing the crime-ridden Olive Gardens apartment complex, a man identified as Fredrick Prince stepped out from behind a building in what officers characterized as a threatening stance. Prince, who had served time in jail for drunk driving, ignored police orders to lie down and instead reached for his waistband, causing officers to fire. He was found to be carrying only a cigarette lighter; apparently, Prince had been urinating against the building when the raid began, and was fastening his pants. He was pronounced dead at the scene. The two officers who fired their weapons will be placed on administrative leave until the shooting has been reviewed.

Marcus saw the hovering blue trails they'd watched the other night. That was what had been going on. He'd gone home, and he hadn't been back to his father's place. Fredrick Prince? The students began to file in, and he was still puzzling over the name when he turned on the video Whalen had left for today.

The Depression. Marcus stood in the back, looking at his nephew's shoulders, rigid under the huge black jacket he never took off. He'd only nodded when Mortrice had come in, not wanting to put him off. American history. This was a nearly remedial-level class. Marcus recognized more faces when he circled the room. Samana—Som's nephew, without any bruises. The two white kids who liked rap, with baggy jeans and T-shirts, their hair shaved except for braided tails from the crowns. Josh and William? The kids from Agua Dulce—Araceli, Stella, Maria, Bebos, and Frankie Ortíz, he read from the roll in the window light. Mortrice and Chris and the kid who liked to be called B-Real. B-Real's burgeoning Afro was what brought back the name for him.

Starchild. Fredrick Prince. One of Finis and Julius's friends who'd been left behind twice and ended up in Marcus's history class.

He and the others from Treetown, walking up Pepper Avenue and under the new freeway and through downtown to the high school in the winter dark. Crowding into one or two cars with dragging mufflers, or a truck. And Whalen sitting at this desk, or one like it, his bland, round face and light-brown crewcut, looking out over them after Christmas break. "Well," he'd said. "A bunch of mushrooms seem to have sprung up in my classroom. A forest of mushrooms from Treetown. Heh, heh."

Marcus had stared at the heads in front of him, his ears hot. The downtown kids had trails of long hair in thin rivulets along their spines or flowing as thick as lava to their shoulders—but through the falls of hair falling uniformly from pale scarlike parts down the centers of their skulls, Whalen saw eyes and quirks and names.

Under Usher's cloud of hair as soft as dandelion puffs, or Bennie's too light hair that already drooped limp into wide drifts, under Starchild's most impressive natural, big as Sugarfoot's of the Ohio Players, he saw nothing. Like the school nurse, who sprayed her table with antiseptic before you were at the door, and then wiped furiously.

"Can you fit through the door, sir?" Whalen would call to Starchild.

Starchild stopped coming. So did Usher and Bennie and most of the others. They said nothing; no confrontation, that was the Treetown way. Silence. Marcus used to stare into the tiny mirror at home, combing out his thick, wavy, too straight stuff. From his Mexican blood. Poking his forefinger hard at his skull, he saw his natural extend only to the first knuckle.

The video droned on, the heads before him bobbing and weaving in sleep or whispers. Marcus wedged his back squarely against the wall, feeling the bulletin boards behind his neck, and he felt tears flooding the spaces under his eyes and behind his nose. He swallowed over and over, squinting, until his face felt like it would melt.

He met Bent at the restaurant that night. "I didn't know you were covering Treetown," Marcus began quickly at the back table. "So that's why you want to see The Blue Q, huh, to write about crime and shit?"

Bent frowned, but he didn't look away. "Hey, you've been stalling me on the visit to the hood, and I happened to be hanging out with Rick Kolavic that day when he got the call. Since I'm interested in the area, I did that sidebar. I used to cover city stuff in Boston sometimes."

"Yeah?" Marcus pressed his knuckles hard over his lip, waiting until he could think.

But Bent went on. "You didn't tell me you got arrested for stolen goods. That must have felt fucked-up. I heard the charges got dropped."

Marcus was silent. What the hell did you say to that? Bent said, "So, were you just there to pick up a car? All Rick said was he recognized your face."

So Bent didn't know anything about his father's place. Marcus nodded.

"Yeah. But you want to check out the place next to it. The Blue Q. My uncle said cool. This weekend."

"Great." Bent finished his beer. "Hey, maybe we can cruise around the area before, you know, so I could get a better feel for the community."

"So you can see some more murders?" Marcus said, standing up.

Bent's face didn't soften. "Look, man, that story was just something the editor asked me to do. I'm not an asshole, okay? I can see that Treetown isn't just projects. That's what I'm talking about. I want to see the good parts, too. The parts that fascinate me, from the South, how they got transplanted. Like the blues."

"You'll see the blues," Marcus said. "I gotta get to work."

"We're gonna do something else today," Marcus told Mortrice's class. The faces angled up to his, wary and squinted. "Oh, you want to keep sleepin. I know. But I'm kinda bored, guys. I like history. We're gonna start a new project while I'm here."

"We got a book," Bebos said.

"We're supposed to read," B-Real said.

"We're gonna talk," Marcus said. "And we're gonna write. Start somethin fresh for the new year."

"For the nine-deuce," Chris muttered.

"I like that, cause we'll get to language, too," Marcus said, and they groaned. "Get into groups of three or four, get out some paper. I want you to write down what you think people in the distant future might find important as American history if they looked back to 1992. Let's get it on."

They worked on the assignment until the weekend, because Marcus went from group to group, talking about everything from music to clothes to newspapers. He kept thinking of Bent's story, what Rio Seco read about Treetown. By Friday night, he sat in his apartment reading the papers.

Mortrice had worked with B-Real, Chris, and a Proudfoot kid. Their paper, penned elaborately, read:

What the future people probly won't know unless the hood tell them is it was a war in the 90s. The war of the cops and brothers. Every time a

brother turn around it's a police in his face. Or like Rodney King, stomping
him. What we would say is this was a big battle and everybody armed. But
most people now don't know this any way. So do that make it history?

There was turfs and battlegrounds and positions in every city, but nobody
pay attention. There was soldiers and generals on both sides, too. History is
right now, if you think about it.

Marcus stared at the open doorway, watching the downtown lights
sparkle. He wondered what Mortrice had seen in L.A., in his Gardens.
What had Sofelia witnessed? He stared at the lined paper. Soldiers.

Another group, with Samana and the two braided white kids and a
blond girl from downtown, had written in blocky capital letters,

If life's a bitch and then you die, what could people tell somebody from
the future. Who would care. What we could say is as soon as something
was cool it wasn't cool no more. Music like rap was cool, and then it was in
commercials. Clothes were cool, and then old people would wear them so
hell no. And the best times people had was when they were high, and they
can't record that, so how will anybody from the future know what was best.
Floating is best. You can't write tweaking.

History is a bunch of people did stuff and then they died. We do stuff and
then we die. So why should it be different then.

They had a point. They don't care; why should future teenagers care?
He thought it was interesting that they wrote about drugs. They could
tell he wanted them to think for themselves, and he could tell that they
might not be afraid to write what they wanted. Maybe they'd actually
get something done.

Bent and Abby were drinking murky-green liquid from tiny glasses in
the bar at Chile when he came in. Abby waved brightly and said, "Have
a good time, babe! *Esquire*'s gonna love it!"

Marcus didn't say anything. They drove his Bug since he didn't want
anyone to damage the Montero in The Blue Q parking lot, where
people played craps and came to blows between vehicles. Bent rubbed

two fingers into the corners of his mouth and said, "Abby loves those weird drinks. Grappa, Pernod. And she shouldn't be drinking at all, but she says they're medicinal."

"Why can't she drink?" Marcus looked at the afternoon light on the overpass, smudging the graffiti.

"She's pregnant," Bent said. "Web's wife's pregnant, too. Maybe it's a competition thing. But we're really gonna have to save money for a place now."

Marcus glanced at him. "So you're lookin for some exotic Treetown stories to sell, huh? Or maybe you can poke around and sell some info?"

"Like what?" Bent said. "Drug information? What are you talking about?"

"Shit, I don't know," Marcus said, tired. "You want to see Treetown. Here it is."

He cruised down Grove, not turning on SaRonn's street since it dead-ended, but he looked at her house. Something was different. Maybe she had a man putting in a new door. He sped up and stared at old Mrs. Price's yard, where clothespins perched on the empty wires like tiny sparrows. "Some of these places look like the Delta," Bent murmured. "But your uncle's from Oklahoma, right?"

Marcus nodded. "Tulsa." But he fell silent again, watching the yards. Yeah, people had made their yards like home. If home was Mississippi or Georgia, and the people had come to work the lemon groves, they kept home inside their fences. Pigs, chickens. Blue bottles hung from chinaberry trees. They'd moved from place to place, but they'd carried what they thought of as home. Africa. Even Africa. Pompey's father was from Africa. And once, when he'd seen Alma and Abuela raking and sweeping the dirt and gravel in the Thompson lot, Brother Lobo had told Marcus that dirt yards were African. Grass was considered unclean. Bugs proliferated in grass, and damp and germs. Hard dirt could be swept clean and decorated.

Bent was staring intently at a tiny store in a stone building. Two older men sat in the shade of the pepper tree nearby, playing dominoes, and three young women in bike shorts and bra tops came out of the dusty screen door carrying grocery bags. They walked across the street to Olive Gardens. Bent said, "So this is . . . ," and an old Buick Electra drifted across the vacant lot and in front of the VW.

"Learn how to drive, Westside," Marcus leaned out the window to say.

Snooter King stopped alongside the Bug and grinned. "Shoot, nigga, I drive Treetown rules," he drawled.

Marcus shook his head. Why use signals and caution when you expect to get pulled over anyway? "I ain't drivin like that, fool."

"I bet your downtown ass ain't," Snooter said, "bringin your mama to the 502." He leaned forward to see the passenger seat, and his face closed up as smooth as an empty palm.

"You tryin to think and motorvate at the same time?" Marcus said quickly. He knew Bent was listening hard, even though the pen was still.

"Lookin for that Feets woman, the one with big *mantequilla*." Marcus thought, Bennie. Her butt. I don't want to attempt translation here. Snooter said, "I heard she was headin to The Q, but she was supposed to be cookin some necks and bullets for me." Marcus nodded. "Later, Sissy." Snooter pulled away.

Bent was nodding coolly. "I've been to the South, to New York, and L.A., but most of that lost me. Foreign language."

Marcus looked at the swaying trees in the cold evening wind. This was Treetown. Tiny place. Tiny history. People stopped moving. They got Mississippi and Rio Seco and nowhere to go now.

"Sissy's not rude?" Bent asked.

"Depends on who you are," Marcus said, rubbing his forehead, thinking of Finis. "This little store's the 502. California code for drunk driving. Like if you buy liquor here and try to make it home, your ass is sure to get stopped."

He got out of the car. He wanted a soda and some watermelon-chili candy, things he could only get here. Bent was beside him, and Marcus knew he was hoping the old men would talk. Marcus knew they would.

"That one of them Thompson boys?" Mr. Gaskins said. "Y'all ain't brang me no possums for months." His fingers, the skin taut and old-man shined around the nails, held his dominos tight.

"No, sir," Marcus said. For years, he thought. "Been a long time since any of us went huntin."

"Oh, you the baby boy," Mr. Gaskins said, peering up harder. "You ain't never brang none noway."

"No, sir," Marcus said again, heading for the doorway, thinking,

Most I can catch is those three negatives. All I'm trained for. Bent laughed softly beside him.

"Possums, huh? A man I met down in Mississippi told me that was the best meat he ever ate," Bent said, and Marcus looked at him. He couldn't see any sarcasm in Bent's smile. But he didn't want to do this now; he didn't like being a tour guide.

Shawnette, the girl behind the tiny counter, was in one of his classes. "Hi, Mr. Thompson," she said shyly. Marcus got a tamarind soda out of the cooler. "You drive a VW, like B-Real?"

"That's your heart, huh?" Marcus teased her.

Bent said, "This soda looks like something Abby would love to try." He grabbed three. On the way back to the car, Mr. Gaskins looked up again.

"Fittin to rain," he called. "You bet not stay out too long."

Marcus smelled the ozone mixing with the sharp scent of pepper berries: he paused near the car, his chest suddenly flooded with warmth, remembering all the times his mother had sent him here for eggs or *chorizo*, remembering the old men teasing him and the run back along the drainage ditches.

Bent was staring across the street at Olive Gardens. "That's where we'd find the real rappers," he said to Marcus. "The real thing." He pointed to a ring of tiny, flickering lights in the parking lot. "What's that?"

Marcus looked at the people standing near the candles. He'd heard from someone that a shrine for Starchild was in the parking lot. "I don't know," he said, getting into the car.

Bent took a swallow of his soda. "So, what do people drink over at The Blue Q?" Marcus could hear the nervousness in his voice; he knew Bent heard the bitterness in his. He thought of Starchild, who'd gotten drunk at The Blue Q.

"Drink whatever you want, man," he said, approaching his uncle's place, seeing the taillights disappear down the narrow road into the trees. They glowed like intoxicated eyes, blinking between the trunks. Shit—he felt stupid bringing Bent here, having his uncle suspicious as hell, his father probably sitting in the back staring at this ponytail. "I don't come here, man, I told you," he added, half-angry now. "Not at night."

Bent didn't notice what he said. He was moving his head rapidly to take in the cars parked in the dirt lot, the people laughing near the door, the neon sign proclaiming MILLER HIGH LIFE. Marcus saw the tiny notebook still in his hand. "I'd be cool," he said, nodding toward it. "Especially with people all suspicious of—" He wanted to say white folks, but that wasn't fair. "Of anybody might be law enforcement. Since the raid."

At the door, Joe lifted his chin at Marcus. "Two, huh, Sissy?" he said, holding out his hand.

"You countin good tonight, man," Marcus said, his ears warm, and inside, where the smell of ribs and smoke and beer hit them like a moist tongue along the neck, he said to forestall Bent's question, "Let's eat."

He was heading to the window in the back, but Bent touched his arm. "There he is," Bent said. "Do those guys play, too?"

Marcus saw his father sitting in the back corner with Oscar and Mr. Lanier. "They don't play at all," he said, trying not to smile. "Come on—you better get you a plate before it starts." At the tiny counter, instead of Aintielila, Bennie Proudfoot was ladling out portions of greens.

"A plate? Is that a whole meal?" Bent was whispering.

"It's a plate," Marcus said. Bennie pushed plates across the counter to waiting hands. "You workin?" Marcus asked her.

She folded her arms. "Do it look like I'm playin?"

"You cooked?"

"Do it look like I'm partyin?" She rubbed two fingers hard into her sweating hairline. "Your sister be comin to make pies, but she ain't came all week. She takin Starchild pretty hard, I guess. Everybody mad."

"Starchild?" Bent murmured. "Like in Funkadelic?"

Bennie trained her gaze on him, and Marcus quickly said, "Give us two plates—ribs, greens, rice and beans, huh?" She looked at him hard.

Bent handed her a twenty, saying, "I'll get both of those, please."

Sitting down, Marcus tried to think of how to do this the whole goddamn night. Nobody had jammed them up in the parking lot, at least. "Hey, boy," he heard his uncle say. "Ain't you thirsty?"

His uncle's strong fingers set down two glasses. His gleamed black with choc, and Bent's was a Miller. "You the one want to hear some music?"

"I'm honored to see you," Bent said, and his voice was truly soft and respectful. "I'm a huge fan."

Oscar nodded. He looked at Marcus. "Drank up, boy. You lookin peaked." Marcus glanced at his father, watching him with his face as dark and hollowed as a mask. Oscar clamped his chitlin-tough fingers onto Marcus's shoulder. "Y'all listen good, huh?"

Oscar and the two musicians went up onto the tiny stage, and the jukebox playing Denise LaSalle went off.

"I'ma play a few song for a—for the ears should be workin," Oscar said into the microphone. "Y'all drank up, so you can hear me right. I'ma tell you the truth now."

"What's that you've got?" Bent whispered, leaning forward to look at Marcus's drink.

Marcus stared at Bent's small notebook, next to his glass, at the smooth fingers as pale as cigarettes lying beside the paper. Uncle Oscar only poured choc for voices he'd listened to and hands he'd studied for grease at the knuckles and pillowy calluses on the palms. Men from Muskogee and Idabel, he used to tell Marcus; men from the Westside and San Bernardino. Not from Boston. Not from downtown.

"Strong as blood," Marcus murmured, and the guitar screamed under the knife.

"Some Muddy Water," Oscar said. "Listen. For them think they slick." "I am ready for you, I hope you ready for me . . ."

Marcus heard snatches of the song while he swallowed hard, "I'm smokin dynamite, I hope some downtown sherbert start a fight . . ."

The guitar pulsed and then roared, the knife sliding wild down the strings; the harmonica trembled behind it.

"Whoa," Bent whispered when the song began to fade. "This is amazing. But isn't it some screwball wanting to fight?"

Marcus didn't look at Bent. Yeah, he thought. But Oscar thinks he's sendin you a message. You and whoever else.

His uncle smiled viciously at the crowd and whispered, "Bet not mistake me now. Cause I don't play." He strummed hard again. "I'm a *man*—you know how that go? I spell M-A-N. Not no landless boy. Uh-uh."

"Landless?" Bent whispered, writing on the pad. Marcus heard someone call his name from near the doorway.

SaRonn curled her fingers toward him. "I'll be right back," Marcus told Bent, not waiting for an answer.

He followed her out into the parking lot, ignoring Joe's called "Y'all be good now, huh?" She wore a tank top that clung to her back, the faded jeans he'd seen before, and in the cold night air, she shrugged her jacket back on before she turned.

"Bennie called and told me you were here," she said.

"I thought you wanted me off your doorstep and outta your face."

She stopped to pry a stone from her shoe. "Listen—I was takin care of a girl who'd been beaten up." Then she took his hand and walked toward the trees near his father's stone wall. "I don't want anybody to hear us."

She leaned against one of the smooth trunks lit cold and lavender in the moonlight, holding both hands out like a carved goddess with offerings. A black stone lay in each palm; when Marcus took them, they were heated and smooth. Each had a perfect white ring in the center, a blank eye.

"Finis left them the other night. Said give them to you, cause he's scared to come by your place. Cops. Cops everywhere the other night. He said he's slippin into darkness. Lonely. Said you would know the rocks." She watched his face.

Marcus touched the iris, raised like a blister inside the circle. "Finis know all the rocks," he said. "Not me. I just know the songs."

SaRonn shook her head. "He's lookin for you, I know it." She pushed both of his hands, with the rocks, into his pockets. "So is Larry. The police broke down my door in the raid, and I have to get a new one," she said, tilting her head back against the bark and closing her eyes. Her tea-gold face was as bright as a coin in the stark winter light.

"Why'd they bust your door down?" Marcus asked, trying to keep his hands from going around her waist.

"Cause Larry used my address last time he got picked up for fighting in Olive Gardens." SaRonn paused, eyes still closed. "After he saw you that night, he came over to Bennie's and talked shit."

Marcus touched her chin, and her eyes flew open. He slid his hands onto the bark skin behind her. "About me? Cause I didn't kick his ass? I'm the wrong brother," he said, trying to keep his voice light.

"About me." SaRonn pulled his face closer to hers, her fingers cool on his cheeks. "You more worried about him than me?" She didn't wait for an answer. "What are we supposed to do while you brothers get yourselves together? Go through your changes? Marcus. Do you think about me? Do you want to come back or not?"

"I think about you all the time," he said, and he couldn't breathe.

The trees—where he'd watched—the velvet bark and smell of meaty smoke and laughter. He was afraid to touch her; his palms pressed hard on the moist, breathing bark.

"Now you more worried about the tree than me," she whispered. "We can trade. Okay." She pushed herself against his side, moving him by his ribs until his back was to the trunk and he propped himself with legs wide. "Now you gonna have to get a handful of me. Right here."

Her breasts just filled his fingers, and he kissed her until he could taste cloves and cinnamon. Her behind, in the jeans, overflowed his hands and moved against his wrists. Marcus pulled her closer and moved his own hips, and he felt dizzy with the throb of warmth along the front of his body and the chill at his back. The rustling branches overhead and the faint music behind them, the press of her skin, dropped a roar like cupped hands over his ears.

"You gon leave your friend in there?" she asked softly.

"Damn," Marcus said, his mouth cold when the breeze pushed against them.

He led her back inside, where Bent sat stiffly, drinking from the same bottle. Oscar was just carrying his guitar off the platform while people were shouting, "Oh, man, don't be so lazy, Oscar! Get on back up there!"

Inclining his head toward Marcus and Bent, his eyes narrow crescents in the smoke, Oscar said, "Come on back."

Bent said, "Hey, you missed a great show, Marcus."

"Yeah," Marcus said. "It wasn't for me. This is SaRonn. Bent."

At the long back table, Marcus's father raised his chin and eyebrows an inch in greeting. "You gon try some pigsfeet?" Oscar was asking Bent. "You ain't never ate chitlins, right?" Marcus felt SaRonn tremble with silent laughter, but Bent nodded, to their surprise.

"Yeah, sure, they have something like that in France," Bent said. "I'd love some." Oscar nodded to Marcus, and he went back to the kitchen window.

Aintielila stood there now, frowning so hard her black-drawn brows wavered. "Who the hell you brought in here?" she whispered.

Marcus was surprised by the breathy anger he heard. "This dude writes for the paper," he said. "He's Web Matheson's brother-in-law, and Uncle Oscar's gon grill him, I think. He want some chitlins." She slammed a bowl onto the small counter and turned her flowered shoulders away from him.

Oscar was saying, "When I was in France, they ate truffles—now, that's a damn fungus they get pigs to root out the ground. And people think chitlins is nasty. What you been told, that's what you see. Right?"

Marcus watched Bent pour Tabasco onto the chitlins and take a big bite. "Hey," Bent said after a minute. "My fiancée has me eating snails and drinking these nasty European liqueurs when we eat out. I'd rather have this and a beer any day."

Marcus held in his laughter. Bent was cooler than he'd thought. But Oscar started now. "Lanier here, he know pigs," Oscar said. "He had a hundred pigs over there across the freeway before, but the city chased him out cause they wanted that land. Changed the zoning."

Mr. Lanier nodded, his grimy khaki knees poking out from the end seat. "Them pigs ate good, too. Red Man Tucker give me a load a avocados once, and I'm seriest as a heart attack—them hogs eat the meat and spit out the pits like a natchal man."

Oscar was watching Bent, and Marcus saw his father staring over folded arms. "Lanier puttin pigs on that pea field near the freeway," Oscar said. "You know it, right, cause your brother-in-law, he wantin to buy it for some reason. And here you show up, all interest."

Before Bent could answer, Lanier said mournfully, "Them fools sleep in the old packin house, they hungry. You see em in there like haints. But any fool mess with my hogs, he get a ass fulla lead."

"Ain't that right?" Oscar said. "Me and him—we got shotguns, and man right here had one, nice one, but it's gone now." Marcus's father didn't move. "You got a gun, Bent?"

"Nope," Bent said, pushing away the bowl. "Pretty quiet downtown."

"That's right," Oscar said. "So all you interested in is me."

Bent leaned forward, and Marcus touched SaRonn's hand. "Yeah," Bent said. "The blues. The blues—it's history, right? The truest form of music we've got. I wondered . . ." He sat back, looking embarrassed. "Since you're still so great, why'd you quit touring and recording?"

Oscar drank a long swallow of choc, and Marcus glimpsed Aintielila pushing open the kitchen door to gesture at him. Oscar's voice deepened when he stood up. "When I sang 'My daddy died before I was born,' you think that's anybody's song. History ain't shit. Ax Marcus." He went toward the kitchen.

Marcus nodded at his father and stood up, too. "Hey, Bent, it's been a long night. Come on."

When they stepped into the parking lot, Bent let out a breath. "Damn, he sure was cryptic. Pigs. History." He grinned at Marcus. "Can't wait to come back, man. Was that quiet guy a musician, too? With the big hands?"

"Nope," Marcus said, seeing his father's knuckles big as walnuts. "Mechanic."

"Baby boy," a voice said from near the stone trough, and Marcus turned. Larry Cotton stepped out and fanned his fingers wide in mock surprise. "Look like you think you the shit. Hangin out with SaRonn, bringin this dude down here. I seen you nosyin around the Gardens after they popped Starchild." He stared at Bent. "You lookin for excitement, man?"

Marcus watched Cotton move toward the three of them. He gon snatch SaRonn or fuck with Bent, he thought. But he was standing in the rising dust near the pecan trunks, seeing the taunting face, remembering this time what he was supposed to say. "Let's start with I'ma kick your ass," he told Cotton. "And we can end with you all fucked up."

When he stepped forward, knowing Cotton expected him to throw a blow toward the face, he let his shoulder drop down like he remembered Demetrius showing him, like they did in football practice. He rammed Cotton like the tackling sled Demetrius had kept in the yard, throwing his back into the stone trough, and when Cotton fell, he grabbed Marcus and brought him down, too. Something fell with a clang into the trough, and Marcus felt his ribs slam against the rock edge. Then he was rolling away from Cotton, crouching and waiting for the blows. But he saw five red toenails slide near him in the window-lit dust, and he heard Aintielila say, "I'll shoot your evil mouth full, you don't get off my place."

She was pointing her derringer at Larry Cotton, who was crouched, too, rising now to edge past the trough. Marcus heard the music loud from inside, the slamming of more car doors, and he saw his uncle coming fast now. Cotton walked quick and defiant down the road toward the gate.

Marcus didn't know what he expected SaRonn to do, but she only bit her lip and stared into the trees. His aunt said, "Baby, take Marcus's guest on, now. I gotta patch him up."

His cheekbone was burning, and his ribs felt like a stick was lodged between bones. Bent said, "Hey, Marcus, I'm sorry if . . ."

"Not your fault," he said. "SaRonn, his ride's downtown."

"I'll be back," she said.

His aunt smeared salve on the abrasion near his eye, and then she fixed her long, narrow eyes on his. "Don't be bringin no white man from downtown round here again," she said, and left him in the kitchen, staring at the shuttered serving window.

His uncle came in from the back door, the smell of rain hitting the trampled dust outside. He saw the door to their living area creaking part open, and he said, "She didn't like seein that face when she look out in the club."

Marcus leaned against the sink. "Cause he's Matheson's relative?"

"Cause of how he look, too," Oscar said. He stared at the big pot on the counter. "White man and his son wanted to buy Lila's place in Idabel. Back there in Oklahoma. Lil joint she had with her aunt. See, Lila mama was gone. She worked the streets, and look like the daddy been as pale as your friend there."

Marcus shook his head. "Everybody lost their family back then, too."

"Shit," Oscar said. "You don't know shit. I used to sing at they place, when I come through there. Came back one night after the show cause I want to see Lila, and the young one had her in the back. Talkin bout 'You so pretty, I'm so pretty, and you rather be with ugly niggers like Thompson. I make you match ugly.'

"He been done . . . hurt her, you know. Scar her up inside, why she can't have babies. I didn't know then. What I seen, he had hit her, and then he start to shavin her eyebrows." His uncle cocked his neck like he was shrugging off a hand. "I bust in there and got my knife, but when he turn for me, Lila go in a drawer and get a thirty-eight. Shot him in the eye."

Marcus held his breath. "But I thought you . . ."

"We had to get outta there. I taken the shot for my name."

"But it ain't your story," Aintielila said from the doorway. She stalked into the kitchen, grabbing a rag and wiping the counter with furious strokes. "Talkin all out your damn place. This one bring trouble over here, and you run your mouth." Marcus looked away. Her mouth was tightly closed now, her eyes on the wall. She thought they were pitying her. He remembered Sofelia's hair, like flowing ink over her shoulder, her voice meant only for her aunt. She must have told Sofelia the story sometime. When he turned to go out the back, he saw that under the black paint of his aunt's brows, shallow crevices marked her skin.

He heard his VW coming up the road, and he walked out to meet SaRonn, his hands shaking, his lungs burning against the pain in his side.

The shadows were stark in the Las Palmas courtyard, and SaRonn paused, gazing back out at the archways. "Like blue shells," she said. "I always liked these buildings. Always wanted to sit at one a those little round iron tables and have coffee. Like Spain. Like I wasn't here in Rio Seco."

"You downtown." Marcus whispered, holding her around the shoulders. "Some people gon talk about you anyway."

She stopped suddenly, sitting down at the cement bench set into the thick wall. The soft rain splintered off the railings. She shivered a little, huddled around herself. "Before we get inside, I want to tell you one thing. The other one is for inside." Marcus sat down close beside her, smelling her sweet hairdress and the faint scent rising from her neck.

"When you called, when you came by, and I couldn't talk?" she said. "The girl I'm keepin, Malinda, was hurt real bad. Her boyfriend was dealin, and beatin the hell out of her. She knew about me and Bennie, and she came to stay. But somebody shot him, her boyfriend. The mail and all that stopped, then we got the raid. I think it was this boy named Chris, from the Gardens. Zefi Perry's boy. I saw him, and a boy I've never seen. Dark, thin, and I don't know his face, don't recognize any people in his face." She was silent. Marcus tried to picture all the boys hanging out in the Gardens. But he kept seeing his aunt's face with blood on it, seeing her eyebrows red.

His cheekbone throbbed like lit matches were dragging across it, and he said, "I'm cold, and I'm tired a waitin. Come on upstairs."

And when she stood in the dim living room, touching the figurines with drawing-down fingertips, brushing the books with her thumb, he knew he was going to stop lying without even thinking about it. because she could go between two places, three, or ten, without squinting at either one. His artwork, his books, his building. The fog-shrouded trees and hard laughter and Sissyfly. She dropped her jacket onto the couch, and Marcus ran his fingers up from her shoulders to the nape of her neck to touch the soft fringe of curls. SaRonn closed her eyes and let her head fall back. He ran his lips under her soft curve of her jaw, tasting smoke and salt and butterscotch.

"Candy?" he murmured, and SaRonn laughed.

"Willa had some candy and then she kissed me right there," she whispered. "Hey." She stood very still in the doorway of the bedroom. "I heard you and Larry out in the street. The first fight. I know what he told you. All of it. He tried to tell Finis the same thing—the only other guy who's been in my house since I came back. Marcus—I heard you guys."

"Yeah," he said, backing away from her to lean hard against the wall. "What you want me to say?" I ain't lyin, he thought.

"Nothin. I want you to listen." Her collarbone rose like wings when she sighed hard. "All Larry owns is the days he screwed up for me. The months. He owns every hour of that past shit. The man does not own any physical or mental part of me. Okay? It's all mine to give or take back. And I know how Thompson men are—you guys think about fightin all the time."

"Not me," Marcus said, fitting his fingers around her ribs, his thumbs at the edge of her breasts. "I'm a sissy. All I think about is love."

"So why you runnin away?" he said when she began to dress in the wavering weak light.

"Cause Willa's at Bennie's, and she's never woke up in a strange house yet," she said. "Hey, I want to stay till morning because I want to see if you can cook." She smiled and moved to the living room, calling, "It tells a lot about a man if he can cook. I know that now. I see it."

"I'm not cookin at two in the mornin," Marcus grumbled, sitting beside her to tie his shoes.

SaRonn touched the scrape on his face. "I don't know if you can cook, but I see you don't back down." She let her face fall serious. "Can you put in a new front door and paint it blue?"

"Oh, baby," Marcus said. "Blue is my specialty."

CHAPTER SIXTEEN

PAZ HAD WATCHED the purple clouds race in from the desert and split along the hills to dissipate like threads of dye in the wind; for these seven years, the winds had unraveled the moisture and the water had hidden elsewhere. But now she saw the sparrows under the wisteria; she'd unearthed a lizard curled stiff and cold under one of her olive buckets, his eyes sealed for winter sleep. The freeze had reached up to the top tier of the sky to break the water from the wrong circular trails.

The boy was in the hills. The boy with the Indian face and uncomprehending eyes. He was sleeping in a cave up on the slope, coming in the night or early morning to get water from the spigot near her olive shed. She'd seen him; he stared at her for long minutes, but when she told him the rain was coming, when she asked him if the freeze wasn't reaching his bones, he only climbed back over the fence, impassive, his hands in a pair of huge leather gloves like the citrus pickers used to wear. Once he dropped a *saladito*, the salted plums she'd loved as a child, and once a frayed sliver of smoked fish. *"Mi hijo,"* she'd called. "The rain." But he didn't look back from the steep trail up the hill in the dark.

Hosea had sat near her in the olive shed for a few hours after he'd cleaned out the gully running through the land. She had told him about the rain, and he'd nodded, clearing the sticks and brush and a loose car fender from the end of the shallow ravine. But she hadn't been able to show him the boy.

Paz waited for the clouds to meet in an unbroken quilt. She sat under the wisteria and drank coffee. The pecans were sweet now after resting near the fires of fall; she cracked them open and held the nuts like plump, praying brown hands while the first fat drops began to fall.

From under the eaves, Hosea watched the water run off each red tile like a curtain of glass beads, tapping the gravel to echo in a hundred rhythms. Good thing we patched that adobe, he thought. House hold up good now. "Let's go!" he called to Demetrius. "Lady said it's three or four of em stuck."

Hosea drove the old tow truck behind his sons in the newer flatbed. The rain fell in driving sheets along the riverbottom road. All the years Hosea had lived here, he'd seen the flats of downtown receive only shimmers of misty rain. But along the hills, the clouds snagged on boulder-strewn slopes and eucalyptus windbreaks, dropping torrents of water to fill the irrigation furrows and deep-cut gashes in the mountains. The Hungarian would be happy about the water bill now.

Under the freeway bridge, the water rolled brown, carrying trash and branches over the sandy channel. "Be wider and rougher than that soon," he murmured to himself. Demetrius headed down Cottonwood Canyon Ranch, where the water ran thick and red with construction runoff. Hosea saw the knot of cars ahead, at the intersection where Web Matheson's development began. Two women gestured frantically toward the huge, swirling whirlpool.

While the three of them maneuvered the cars from the water, the cold gritty current to their knees, the women moaned. "I'm so glad my husband bought me the cell phone. Oh, my God, what a nightmare. Why the hell aren't the drains working?"

The runoff was so heavy from all the new asphalt and parking lots and driveways that when it got to the cement channels, which rushed the water much faster than the old curving ditches, the drains were overwhelmed. Hollows used to flood, Hosea thought, but all that standin water seeped into the dirt. Trees pull it in between the rows. He looked up when a woman said, "And up there where the golf course community is? There's, like, a whole lake forming. Swear to God."

Hosea put on his straw cowboy hat and walked through the steady rain to his gully. The gravel was scoured away in places on his roads, collecting in the shallow wash under the roiling water risen to the tires of the first tier of cars. He'd always put the worst-looking vehicles here, not only because of the flooding, but for strangers. If he and the boys wanted to show someone a car, they knew what make he wanted, they knew to take him along the third row where the valuable cars slid in and out frequently.

The water flung itself at the sandy earth, washing away the black stain where the Granada had been because now the gully had risen to slip over the two corrugated-iron pipes that took the creek under the riverbottom road. The dark, fine soot swirled over the boundary of his property and onto the asphalt in a rippling ribbon, growing wider and wider. Hosea watched the base of the palm fronds in the chain link grow red with wet. He looked through the narrow space between the gates to see the cars slowing through the water, and then the first one hesitated and stopped. The city would come and put up a sign, and the commuters would have to go back through downtown.

They done forgot we always get cut off, he thought, walking back toward the road to the house. He glanced up through the water running from his hat brim, looking at the olive groves disappeared to gray nothing in the clouds. Them newcomers, they mad now cause they gotta go back around. But he knew that these two weeks of steady rain had filled the arroyo cutting through the whole city, from Grayglen to the Westside, rushing the water to the river. Olive Gardens would be inundated, like always, Grove Avenue covered with three feet of water, and Treetown isolated. Since his first winter here, no one from the county had ever cared to replace the ancient ditches built by the Indians. People who lived down here stayed inside; they had to put up with the water.

But this was city land now. Only trucks or four-wheel drive vehicles would be able to navigate the runoff. Maybe a Jeep. He saw the silver eucalyptus leaves blend into the rain like a solid, shimmering wall. Couldn't nobody start even a spark right now. But it wouldn't rain forever.

"Man, it's been raining for-fucking-ever," one of the white kids said in the classroom doorway.

"Watch your mouth," Marcus said from the desk. "Just cause we try to relax in here doesn't mean I'm not sitting in this seat, okay?"

When they faced him, moisture wrecking their gelled spikes and sparkling in their braids, he said, "We've got about two more weeks together. That's it." He didn't want to add that Natalie Larchwood had said if Whalen didn't make up his mind about coming back, he might get a tarnished handshake. "So we're gonna do a big project. We're gonna write our own histories. Start with your birthday. Write what you know today. And then go home and ask your parents or grandparents, whoever you live with, about what happened before your birthday."

"Who gives a shit—" The blond boy named Josh colored sallow-pink. "Who cares what happened before then?"

"Before the momentous occasion of your birth? Lots of things happened. It's all history, okay? Then you can recall what you think is important after your birthday. Do what you can, and get started. Look, I'm sitting here with a notebook, too, okay? Because I haven't done this like I should have before." He looked at Mortrice, who was staring at him like this assignment was a personal affront. "Come up here if you got a question. Mortrice?"

Mortrice leaned on his hands near Marcus's blank paper. "Why we gotta do somethin stupid like this?"

Marcus whispered, "Because history isn't always in books."

The boy's face was thin and hard. "So if you don't know it, you gotta lie. Like they do in books."

Marcus touched the boy's fingers with a pencil. "Look, I'm writin all the parts before you were born. I'm doin this for you, okay? You just take care of after you got into the world. You better know that part."

"I know I'm tired of this rain," Josh said.

"You're gonna be tired of it for a while," Marcus told him. They couldn't remember this much rain, of course, because they were too young. And over the next days, whenever he mentioned that it used to rain like this all winter when he was walking to school, they rolled their eyes like they did when he mentioned Earth, Wind and Fire or mood rings or eight tracks, anything from the history he said he was writing while he worked on theirs.

"The seventies, man—disco sucks," one said.

"That's why all the rappers are stealing samples from Funkadelic and the Ohio Players, right?" Marcus said. "Just write." He took roll and looked at the essays from the morning honors class. Every day, he had them do the reading or multiple-choice test Whalen had left, and then they wrote for fifteen minutes. He'd been grading papers, making new assignments, and then rushing to the restaurant for his shift. He'd get home after ten and fall into bed, exhausted.

He hadn't seen SaRonn since that night after The Blue Q, since Treetown was cut off by flooding. Bent had come by the restaurant, but Marcus had mentioned only the rising water. He hadn't seen anyone. He sat at the desk, telling the students he was writing his history, and he thought about Finis, about the music from then. He was working his way back to Tulsa. To Texas. But he didn't read that part to them.

Every day, two students were supposed to read what they'd found out from their families. They called it ancient history. But they always made him go first. He sat in the circle after they'd rearranged the chairs, and Marcus held a sheaf of papers, even though he was making most of this part up. "I'll start, so you can laugh like always. Man, my older brothers went to the Rio Showcase. It was over there on California Avenue downtown. Now it's gone. They went to see *Shaft*, *Coffy*, *Cotton Comes to Harlem*. And I wanted to see *Superfly* big time, but I was too little."

"You coulda got in," Bebos said. "With a adult."

"Back then nobody would take you in to an R movie," Marcus said. They all laughed and rolled their eyes.

"Man, I seen everything," Bebos said. "*Robocop*, *Terminator*, *Predator*. We all go. We take my nephews, man, they love it."

"*Lethal Weapon*," B-Real said. "Least there's a brother in that one."

"He only a sidekick, man," Mortrice mumbled.

"It doesn't matter what color they are if the movie's good," Sharon said. She swung her red spiraled curls from her shoulder. "If they have good acting."

"If they have good shooting," Bebos said.

"Mortrice is right, though. Those movies back in the seventies, they were the first time we'd seen black people populating whole movies," Marcus said. "Things are different now."

He was surprised when Mortrice slumped back and spoke louder. "It ain't about are they nig—are they black or white, man, it's all about the cappin. How they die. The gats, man, what the firepower."

"Yeah," Bebos said. "You gotta have action."

Marcus paused. "So would these action heroes be your heroes? Would you listen to them if they came for an assembly in the gym?" They shrugged. "I remember my black history teacher, right across this quad, showing us pictures of Martin Luther King, Jr. and Malcolm X."

"Man, you still here, you didn't go nowhere," Bebos said.

"There's nothing wrong with being a teacher," Sharon said.

"You been here forever," B-Real said. "I want to go to New York. Be somebody."

"Guys? Can I talk?" Marcus said, exasperated. "I lived in L.A. for a year." He didn't even want to address the equation of teacher equals nobody. "So Malcolm X was standing in a window, holding a gun, ready for action."

"Like what?" Josh asked.

"Lot worse now," Chris said. "Now you gotta worry about bangers and cops."

"I ain't in the mood to hear about the cops, man, about Rodney King," the white kid named William said. "My uncle was a cop. I'm tired of seeing that trial on TV all the time."

"Guys, guys, we're losing it. Hold up." Marcus stood. "So what if, let's say, Arnold Schwarzenegger or Riddick Bowe, the boxer, came here? What would you ask an action hero like that?" They shrugged, and Marcus called on his nephew. "Mortrice?"

"Say, so you can punch, nigga. A nine still take you out." Mortrice wouldn't meet his eyes. The class laughed, and Marcus folded his arms to hold in his words.

"Too late for anyone else to read," Josh said when the bell rang. "Cool."

The next week, Marcus called them from the roll. "Time to read ancient histories, man. Bebos and Chris."

B-Real said, "I'm glad I didn't have to read mine till this month. My history's black, and it's February now. Appropriate for the time."

"Yeah, we can have some discussions for black history month about lots of things," Marcus said. "Language—most of America's slang words start on the streets, right, with black kids."

"And style—everybody steals our style," B-Real said. "Like—"

Marcus knew B-Real wanted to name classmates, but they knew

Marcus didn't play—no conflict or personal stuff inside this room. They were usually truthful, but restrained. "Oreos?" Marcus asked.

"And wiggers," Chris muttered.

Marcus waited, but no one seemed to take offense. "Oreos—some people claim that's me. And wiggers—white kids who want to be black, right?" He wanted them to read, though. "So since it's black history month, but we've got all colors in here and not much time, we'll go with that old cliché: When you mix all the shades, you get black."

Chris said sullenly, "I hate black history. It always end up with, yeah, your people used to be slaves. Boom. I ain't in the mood to hear that mess."

Marcus was silent, the faces blurring in front of him. He saw the headstones, his father's father, his own father. "I ain't readin," Chris said, and Marcus let it go.

Bebos read slowly. "My dad and mom were born in Michoacán, Mexico. They came to Agua Dulce to work in the orange groves. They were already married when my mom was fifteen." The girls in the class shook their heads and laughed. "They lived on Alta Vista Street. My dad said back then, Mexicans couldn't go into downtown. In the summer, they could only go in the city pool on Friday, before it got clean. He told me in Spanish."

"That's fine," Marcus said. "What else?"

"They had five kids. I was the last one."

"I bet your mom was glad," Araceli said.

"Shut up," Bebos said.

"Chris?" Marcus asked again, but the boy shook his head. They filed out quickly, complaining again about the rain. Marcus stayed in his chair for a few minutes, holding their smudged-soft papers, thinking of Enchantee, who was raised by her aunt, Chris's grandmother, who obviously didn't like to talk about history. His mother, who was raised by her *abuela*. His Aintielila, who would never talk about her history.

Sharon had stopped at the desk. "You know who had a real sad life?" she said. "That Oriental kid, he told me one time his whole family got killed. He doesn't come to school any more."

Early the next morning, Marcus drove to the doughnut shop. In the lone line of electric blue storefronts, only Som's window was lit in the wet gloom. Som's wife, Phally, came behind the counter. "Teacher!" she said, smiling.

"Something's missing," Marcus frowned, turning around. He noticed the empty corner where the shrine, the incense and flowers and doughnut holes, had been.

"I move, behind here," she said, pointing to the garlanded shelter near boxes of napkins and cups behind the counter. "You know, this man named Smith, he work in the blue tower, he come in all the time to buy doughnut and complain about my religion. He say, 'I like your doughnut, but I don't like that incense crap. You take it out, you are in America now, you pray to God.'" Phally smiled. "I tell him my religion from my grandfather, from my heart. Not from my country."

"You're Buddhist, right?"

She nodded. "You know, the Christian people, sometime they very cruel. The Buddhist, you do the good thing, they add up." She faced the shrine. "I move it because I don't want nobody bother. Those crazy guy, from over there—" She pointed toward the Kozy Komfort. "They come in for cigarette, try to steal something."

Som came out, his face weary, but he smiled when he saw Marcus. "Oh! Teacher! I don't see you for a long time."

"Been running," Marcus said while Som put glazed doughnuts in a bag. "I don't want to tell you like this, but Samana's not coming to school."

He was surprised by the resignation on Som's face; he'd expected anger. "He doesn't stay here. He eat here, he come in and take five dollar. But I cannot tie him. I cannot even rub for the bad wind. The police would come, right?" Som leaned his elbows on the counter and Marcus saw a smear of shine under his nose, smelled menthol.

"You got a cold?" he asked, propping himself on the counter, too.

"Oh! In my country, this is the good smell. Bring the good feeling." Som rubbed his upper lip nervously. "Samana, he come for salt fish when he hungry. He take food in a bag."

"Where's he going?"

Som shrugged. Then he said, "He is not a boy. He is a man. My wife, she is angry. But she know this."

Marcus took out a paper from his bag. "Look. He's missing a lot in my class, anyway. This is what we're doing. He can write his own history."

"Business slow because Pepper closed from flood," Som said, deepening the lines over his eyes. "But we like the rain, bring good luck for our new year. We are plant the rice now, in my country." He paused. "You come to Cambodian New Year with us, okay? Samana come there, to see his grandmother. And we have lot of food for you."

"I never turn down food," Marcus said, taking the bag.

"I tell them about the bad wind, how I get trouble at the school and you talk for me," Som was saying. Marcus was seated, cross-legged, on the floor around the large blanket. A serving dish of eight silver-stacked tiers was near him, and people sat in a square all around the edges of the material.

The woman Som had just introduced him to smiled and nodded, folding her palms in a sharp point. She lifted her head and said, "Teacher very important for us. My daughter, she get trouble last year for Cambodian New Year. She and her friend throw water on some boy and get trouble."

Som turned to Marcus. "That is good luck, to throw water on the New Year."

"One of her teacher tell not to get her trouble," the woman said, and she took the lid off the first tier.

Rice, steak with green salad, vegetables, lobster, shrimp in a garlicky sauce. Marcus ate everything given to him, and he watched the people bend gracefully over their plates.

The apartment complex was in a run-down area bordering the Westside. Children ran everywhere in the courtyard, and women in sarongs crowded the balcony. "Everyone almost Cambodian," Som had said. He'd been waiting for Marcus's car. "Some Mexican, too. We share the dirt." He grinned and pointed to an old fountain in the center, where vegetables were growing.

A shrine in the corner of the front room gave off light incense smoke. People bowed with palms clasped rigid, incense sticks protruding from their middle fingers. A line of black-and-white photos was arranged in the shrine. Marcus saw an old woman in the corner near the smoke, sitting on a folding chair, her feet in blue booties. "My wife mother," Som said, near Marcus's ear. "She cannot see."

"How old is she?" Marcus asked. Her tiny face was blank.

"Not so old. She blind because she see too much bad thing. Some old lady, they see thing in Cambodia, and then they blind." Som shrugged, biting his wide lip. "I want you to come because you try help with my nephew. He never see a teacher in Cambodia, I know, because Pol Pot."

That name again, like a chant in the room. "Pole-po," it sounded like.

"Was Pol Pot kill all. Kill teacher, doctor, lawyer. Kill all day. In my country, teacher very respect. Here, no respect. I see teacher not get nothing here."

"They sure don't get no money," Marcus heard behind him, and Samana stood in the apartment doorway, a sullen grin on his dark face. He moved to the blanket and helped himself quickly and efficiently to the food.

"Don't be rude to teacher," Som said.

"Teacher talk all the time, just talk," Samana said, rising from his squat. "You don't make no money doing that job, man, so you must love to talk."

"You tryin to sound like my dad?" Marcus said, and Samana's face went even darker. He bent to speak to the old woman, and then he turned.

"I just came for some food," he said, and he walked out the door.

Som said, "I sorry, Mr. Thompson. You see?" He pointed to a photo of a young woman. "His mother. Pol Pot kill. Kill all. I don't even know who her son, but my wife mother, she see him in the camp. We take him. But his—his mad, that not his fault. The fault Pol Pot!" Som's voice had risen, and people were looking at him. "And Pol Pot not learn that in Cambodia! Learn in French, go to the France to learn for kill!"

"Hey, maybe you want to sit down," Marcus said, holding Som's elbow. Phally put her arm around Som's waist and led him to the blanket. By the time Marcus got to the balcony, Samana was gone.

His uncle sat at the desk, saying, "Today's Friday, you got a group assignment, and I want some new groups this time. Sit with different people. Araceli, Sharon, you're with Tramaine. Josh, William, you're with Chris and Mortrice." He went on while everybody shuffled around the room.

"What up, loc?" Mortrice saw the two white boys sitting next to him and Chris. They wore baggy khakis and plaid shirts; their hair was shaved at temple and nape, and red and streaked-straw hair was pulled into tiny braids stretched tight across their skulls. Like baby wigs, Mortrice thought. Lookin stupid.

"Answer the following questions about the ancient Romans," Josh said. "Did they smoke chronic every day? Hell, no." He grinned at Mortrice, his fingers plowing the stubble hair. Always moving around jerky, even when he tried to give them weed in the parking lot. Always sketchin. B-Real said the white kids called it that, when they did all that speed. Like this one. They weren't all there.

"I heard you got the gats, loc," the sucked-in mouth said, though he was bent over his paper writing something. "I heard around."

"So?" Mortrice folded his arms.

The boy's face flattened out, brightened, and his fingers parted the static bristle again. "So, see, we could trade. You got em, right? You the one."

"Mortrice the one," Chris said.

But Mortrice shrugged and looked at his paper. "Look," Josh said. "I'll get you some good shit, some excellent chronic, some crystal crank if you want. My—the dude I know, he got whatever you need. For free. Cause we can trade, okay? For the gats."

They met the next week, in the parking lot after school. Mortrice leaned against the chain link with Chris, the cold wind blowing palm fronds across the asphalt like witch brooms flying solo. Colder here than in L.A., he thought. The country get cold to the bone.

He'd been freezing in the trailer at night, but Kendrick was the one crazy wild because his grandma wouldn't even let him into his father's trailer. "You ain't your daddy," she said. "And you ain't gon be him— you ain't old enough to understand half a that."

"You raised him!" Kendrick shouted.

"Some parts a people you can't raise up!" she would say. "All y'all boys sleepin in here." The trailers were shuttered and locked as tight as silver turtles, and in the living room, the TV blared on about the rain. The saggy-jawed newsman said, "Finally, this rain is supposed to end. We have been a Southland under siege for weeks."

The sky was as gray as lead today, but the air was dry. Lead. He'd gotten the lead for the bullets from Zach, when he got the guns. No trading with Josh. Cash, so he could pay the gunsmith.

They were waiting for B-Real, who had scraped together enough to buy a foolish-looking VW bus and paint it red, gold, and green. Jamaican colors, he said. World shit, Mortrice thought.

Josh was pacing, nervous, along the fence. "We can take my ride," he said. "Come on, bro, we got the money. We got some jobs to take care of, loc. Jobs."

The bus coughed into the lot. B-Real drove silently, and Mortrice thought, He ain't never really down for none a this.

Teddy had the guns at the motel. He'd stolen a car the week before and stripped the parts for a Westside brother. They took the cash to Zach, who said, "Don't fuck up. In any way," before he handed them the bag. Three of the CHP pieces, and the materials from the gunsmith.

B-Real pulled up at the Super 8 Motel near the bus station, talking fast and nervous now. "The owner's Indian, check him out. Patel. Where we get the videos—that dude's Korean. Park. And the dude at the shoe store, the one trippin the other day, tellin us to get out? Ibrahim Somethin—he's a Muslim, I saw the Koran on his counter. See—the whole world is out here in California, and don't nobody want to get friendly. Everybody gotta be One World, man. One World."

"One world a hurt," Mortrice said. "Everybody in a world a hurt cause they be trustin people. Shit. Only thing they trust is cash money. You can forget the red and yellow, man. Green."

"Yo, man, I likes that," Josh said. "I likes that. Me and Bill's out for green. We got some jobs."

The Indian man watched them pull into the parking lot. "Stay here," Mortrice said. Inside the room, Teddy lay watching cable TV; the bag was under the bed. "Cash money?" Teddy murmured sleepily. "They got it?"

Mortrice put the bag in the van and said, "Start drivin around." That was how Kenneth had done everything. Always on the move, drivin careful, keepin mobile. Kept his gun in the ankle holster sometimes, sitting in the backseat of the Monte Carlo with his knee propped against the door, his fingers casual near his shinbone.

"Check em out," the blond one said to his friend. Mortrice only handed them two. "They got bullets?"

"Shit," Chris spoke up. "Get your own bullets, get your own bodies."

"Cool, man, we already did some bodies," Josh said, sounding proud, glancing at Mortrice.

"You ain't capped nobody," Chris said.

"Hell, yeah," Josh said. "And we got a job comin up for my buddy here. He likes pyro shit, huh?" The other boy looked out the window, not answering. "Burn up some trash by the freeway. Like a fuckin Dumpster for people."

"Shut up, man," the other boy said. When B-Real turned into the school lot, the two white boys jumped down from the van, the guns in their jackets. Mortrice felt the money in his coat. Bodies. Burning? He watched them head for their car, trying to remember what he'd heard.

"Man, y'all crazy," Chris said, loping along the canal road with Mortrice and Teddy. "It's Friday night. We should be out trying to get some. Find a party."

"Shit, nigga, yo girl Malinda don't want none a you," Teddy said.

Mortrice walked quickly. They always stayed in the apartment; it looked like the woman was never coming back from Georgia. But he was taking them to the trailer tonight; he wanted to try and make the bullets for the buffalo gun.

His grandfather had said something about his first gun, for his birthday, about letting him walk the fences. Mortrice wanted to see what his grandfather considered strapped.

"Let me break you off some," Chris sang, fingering the .9. "For the nine-deuce."

"You see that wigger in class talkin bout nine-deuce," Teddy said. They climbed the fence carefully where it melted into branches; Mortrice had told Teddy to bring wire cutters for a few barbed-wire points.

"Trees always smell like Vicks," Mortrice said. The trailer lay like a bomb in the drift of leaves. Their feet crunched in the scent, and their breaths ghosted white in front of them. But once they stood behind Mortrice at the flimsy door, he looked at the bones glowing on the table like white graffiti, and he didn't want them inside.

"Wait for me out here, man," he said, and he closed the door before they could complain. He breathed hard, and then took out the things from the gunsmith. Lead, the iron container to melt the lead, the forms for the bullets. The problem would be the brass casings, but he wanted to work with the lead first. He moved the bones, biting his lip, trying not to touch them. Poke them with the barrel of the shotgun.

The blue teardrops of gas flame melted the lead slowly, and the heavy smell rose, dizzying, into the dark space. Mortrice thought he smelled smoke outside. Chronic. They'd lit a blunt. He turned off the burner and examined the molten gray, pouring some into the form for the .56 caliber. Then he heard a hoarse shout.

"Who the hell that? Speak, goddamnit!"

Mortrice stumbled out of the trailer into the leaves. "Hey," he shouted. "It's me. Mortrice. Uh—Grampa."

Hosea stepped out from the trees, the shotgun barrel slanting down. "I smell smoke. What you doin sneakin round? Who these boys?"

"My cousin," Mortrice stuttered.

Hosea looked at Chris. "Ain't no cousin, and I don't know him."

"You know me, Mr. T," Chris said, smiling wide. "Zefi Perry my mama. Julius used to be with her."

"Julius ain't nowhere no more," Hosea spat. He stared at Teddy.

"I ain't nobody, man," Teddy mumbled. "I'm like—a mercenary and shit."

Mortrice stepped forward. "You was talkin bout givin me a gun, have me walk the fences. They was gon help out."

His grandfather's face was closed and distant, dark against the beige tree trunk. "This is grown-folk business," he said, nodding toward the main house. "Y'all get inside and watch TV or somethin."

Mortrice blurted out, "I heard some guys talkin about burnin."

"Where?"

"At school."

Hosea began to walk away. "This ain't kid trouble. Get goin."

Mortrice stared at his back. My land, he thought. My mama's place. Shit, this my trouble.

Chris muttered, "Get goin, like this a chain gang."

Mortrice shouted to his grandfather, "I gotta get my stuff in the trailer. Before we come in." He turned to the others. "Fuck that. I ain't no baby."

•   •   •

After midnight. Time to walk. Walkin in rhythm.

Finis had come to see Usher. Usher knew most of the songs. Finis was slippin into darkness. He wanted to talk to his brothers. He'd sat in Usher's tiny room, listening to Anita Baker. Usher was lonely. He was cryin the blues. Finis fingered the stones in his pockets. He'd thought Marcus would come to see him. Maybe Marcus had ignored the stones.

Usher glanced up and began to follow him out the door. "You steppin already?"

Finis swung around the back of the motel to the narrow alley between the rooms and the heavy chain-link fence. Suddenly three dark, wide figures were jogging quickly toward him. Finis ducked into the shoulder-wide space between Usher's room and the next one. He heard Usher call out, "What the fuck you want, Jap?"

"I ain't Jap, mothafucka! Ca-mere! Ca-mere!" The voice was strange. Then Finis heard the wet explosion of a bullet hitting flesh. The *whoomp* of breaking glass and gasp of flame. He pressed the back of his skull harder against the wall. The shoes flew past him again and he heard the tinkle and then sucking of fire two more times.

Finis ran back toward Usher, who lay facedown on the narrow asphalt. The flames were shaking from the windows of Usher's cottage. Finis ran around the corner and saw three men blazing like comets, hurling themselves at the locked front gate like arcing embers. He leaped onto the wire at the end and began to run through the field behind the Kozy Komfort. Far ahead of him, he saw the three bulky figures running toward the freeway, then into the old flood-control tunnel. He turned and headed toward downtown, stumbling in the dirt, seeing the fire play like red lace over the Kozy Komfort Inn sign lifted above the tiny cottages glowing like paper lanterns.

Mortrice and the others were creeping along the high stone wall toward the canal road. "Cold as a freezer," Chris complained.

"Let's go back to the Gardens, fool," Teddy said.

Mortrice was listening for his uncles, for his grandfather. They'd been talking in the trees most of the time, walking together. He put his hand on one of the round stones to steady himself, and he heard distant gunshots.

Then they heard a deep-voiced shout, on the other side of the wall, and the blast of a shotgun. Mortrice began to run; they were near the fence, near the place they'd jumped over. He pressed himself up to the wire, but Teddy and Chris bumped his back hard when they heard shuffling, running shoes in the sand.

"Shit, Sketch, they're shootin—we can't burn the other place tonight," a huffing voice panted. Mortrice lifted his face at the others. The boy call himself Tweak.

They huddled, frozen, in the fingering eucalyptus branches. "I'm a wigger wit an attitude," Sketch sang, his voice scaling high, disappearing, and Mortrice squatted to see three of them slanting across the hill over the canal, cutting around boulders and disappearing.

"They gettin paid for somethin," Chris said. "They wasn't storyin."

"They the ones burnin," Mortrice said. "Fire money."

"Marcus!" A ragged voice called him from the archway at the street. "Marcus!" Finis showed his face in the courtyard light, as haggard and thin as *abuela*'s.

Marcus ran down the stairs and Finis grabbed his arm, pulled him into the shadows near the bench. "Usher, man. They burnt him. Listen."

Marcus heard sirens rolling through downtown. "Stall out, Finis. Sit down. What happened?"

But Finis flattened himself against the cement, closing his eyes so that his face was an empty mask. "Shinin star for you to see, what your life can truly be," he whispered. "Usher." His voice went higher, like Usher's breathy tone. "What the fuck you want, Jap?" Marcus nodded, knowing he was imitating. Then Finis clipped his words, nearly sing-song. "I ain't Jap! Ca-mere! Ca-mere!" Finis opened his eyes. "Boo-yaa." He pointed to his breastbone. "They dropped the bomb on them. Fire, man. Two Sir Noses. Way D'Void of Funk."

Marcus frowned. Two white men. "And a Asian dude?"

"Ca-mere! Ca-mere!" Finis shook his head.

"Where you stayin, man, where you been all this time?" Marcus said, smelling the dust like cement on his brother's jacket.

But Finis dropped his eyes and moved toward the archway. "When the cops get you, you can't be lyin, be denyin. Comin from Missipi."

Marcus tried to think. "I ain't tellin nobody. Finis!"

"Somebody's watchin right now," Finis said. Marcus grabbed his arm and pulled him to the VW at the curb.

"I'ma give you a ride somewhere, so you ain't walkin," Marcus said, and to his surprise, Finis got into the car.

"Agua Dulce, man," Finis said. "Negrito Indio."

Marcus saw more fire engines racing down Pepper Avenue. He went the back way to Agua Dulce. Finis was silent, his lips moving. Past a tiny blue house where chickens were huddled in a cage near the porch, Finis turned the handle suddenly and spilled out of the car. He ran into the narrow alley and disappeared around a corner.

Harley knocked on the door the next morning, and Marcus was ready. He'd rehearsed. What to leave out, what to leave in, how to explain it in non-lyric terms. He didn't know what anyone else had seen. He'd called his mother, who said his father and the others had patrolled all night without seeing anything. But Rock had shot at someone running behind The Blue Q; he hadn't seen anything but shadows.

"Marcus. Got a minute? A few minutes?" Harley sat on the couch, looking at the books and piles of paper near his feet. "Studying?"

Marcus sat in the chair near the wall. "All the time."

"So you know about the fire, right?" Marcus nodded. "And you know somebody at the motel saw your brother Finis before the fire, saw him running after the fire, and saw him coming this way?"

"Yeah. He came here scared, told me he saw two white guys and an Asian guy throw firebombs into the motel. One guy shot Usher Price in the chest."

Harley nodded, writing and looking at his notes. "Firebombs, huh? I don't know. What it looks like right now is explosions caused by a drug lab." He glanced up at Marcus, his jaw a rough mauve from shaving. "And you're right about the gunshot wound. But this witness saw three guys running toward Treetown. White guys and an Oriental heading straight to Treetown? They'd kinda stand out, right? Whereas your brother ran downtown here. Unless he had a room at the Las Palmas, he was trying to hide out with you."

Marcus shook his head, trying to stay calm. "Nope. He tried to run from me, too, cause I wanted him to stay here. But he was scared shitless. He saw it, but he didn't do it."

"Got terrible luck with location, your brother, huh?" Harley jabbed his forefinger at his notepad. "Bodies droppin all around him, and he's just one unlucky asshole, huh? Let's see. The two women. The cross-dresser. Maybe the John Doe at the Kozy Komfort. And now two more burned guys and a shot guy. The shot guy being the one your brother was hanging out with right before he got it." He stared at Marcus, who kept his mouth closed. "Oh, you think we moved on from the women and the flashy model-man? You think homicide forgets about bodies after they're underground, right? We don't forget names. You can't bury a name. They just hang around on my notes and piss the fucking hell out of me every day, okay? Where'd Finis go?"

"Agua Dulce."

"Yeah, right. Two white guys run into Treetown to hide, and a black guy runs into Agua Dulce. Shit, Marcus."

"Like black and brown ain't close?" Marcus stared back. "My mom's half-Mexican."

"And you got family in Agua Dulce, where I can ask around about Finis?"

"No. Just Treetown. And nobody's seen him except me."

"I'm getting tired of hanging out in Treetown, okay? It's nothing but overtime for me." Harley stood up, his fingers tight on his notepad. "Too much killing," he said, his voice softer. "Don't you even care? Or you're strictly downtown now."

"Lotta history in Treetown," Marcus said. "Lotta killing in history."

"What are you talking about now?"

"You gotta read your history," Marcus said, keeping his voice careful and close to white. "At least you care about finding out who's killing people in Treetown. Some people are still stuck in the old days, man: Only good nigger is a dead nigger."

"You're losing me, Marcus," Harley said. "Call me up when you find it."

"I'm looking myself."

Harley paused at the door. "Oh—I'll be looking, too. And you'll be right in my line of vision, huh?"

•   •   •

Zefi lay in the threshold of the apartment door, screaming, her long fingers like spiders scrabbling up the doorjamb. "No! Not Usher! He ain't done nothin! No! It ain't him!"

Enchantee bent to try and hold her cousin, whose lips stretched as flat as tape when she screamed again, soundless, wordless now. But Zefi rolled herself as tight as a bundle and sobbed away from any hands.

D'Junior stood in the parking lot, near the car, staring at Zefi, and Enchantee went to grab him up, hold his face to her shirt. She saw three boys come from around the corner of the building, and Zefi's son Chris broke into a run to squat beside her. "Mama! What?"

Zefi raised her face and said, "Your daddy. That was your daddy."

"What?" Chris shouted again. Enchantee stared at his thick hair in braids, his wide, sculpted face like something they'd studied at the art college. Toltec, she thought. The long eyes, broad nose and mouth, the cheekbones. Usher Price.

Chris leaned against the stucco, his face granite now. Zefi raised herself up and crouched in the doorway, her fingers deep in her hair, her face slick and shoulders shaking.

When Enchantee heard D'Junior's querulous voice ask, "Where his daddy?" she said, "Hush," and put him in the car.

Lying in bed with her face under Demetrius's jaw, she whispered, "It's only losin now. From now on. People goin down."

"I don't want to think about it like that," he said, his voice vibrating against her forehead.

She pressed harder against the muscles in his neck, pressed her lips there, but abruptly she got up and went downstairs to the living room. In the dark, she turned on the radio. Killer oldies. Tower of Power. "You're Still a Young Man." War. "All Day Music." She closed her eyes and saw them all in the parking lot of the Gardens, herself sitting in someone's car because that was all they had for furniture. Usher and Zefi nearby, leaning against a hood, kissing, his hands slipping from her waist to circle, her slapping them away. Enchantee watching . . . thinking, "No babies. Uh-uh." She wanted her back bent like that, for a moment . . .

It was love, for then, and it only meant future loss. That's what she'd whispered to herself at night, in the college dorm room. Now she cried great shuddering sobs, the passion in the singer's voice brushing over her carpet instead of ringing against the asphalt. Only more loss to come. Demetrius stalking around his father's place with a gun. Driving on deserted freeways with pissed-off tows. Demetrius Junior whirling on a palm frond in the dirt, frowning at Dylan's questions, chasing after Stevie's found bullets.

He was there, at her legs, pushing up on her chin. She could smell his nighttime warmth when he snaked tiny arms around her. Enchantee stifled her sobs. He'd seen way too much already—the cops, the drug bust, now this. She didn't want those pictures imprinted behind his eyelids forever. "Mama?" he whispered. "You all wet? You just now take a bath?"

CHAPTER SEVENTEEN

HOSEA WALKED THROUGH his trees in a dawn as dull as a tarnished knife, smelling the layers of smoke that had collected on the eucalyptus leaves and shredded bark skin. No more rain. Smoke. Smoke from the burning women. From Oscar's barbecue drums. Smoke from the Kozy Komfort fire last night, more moist ashes carried by the wind to drift and rest, sighing in the branches.

Opening the wrought-iron gate, he kept on through Oscar's trees, and felt for the derringer in his pocket. Oscar had given him one, kept Lila's for himself this morning. "Can't be strollin over there with no shotgun," Oscar had said. "And I ain't strollin nowhere without no protection."

Oscar was at the back of his place, staring at the charred, chemical-stinking scar on the trees and leaves grown tight into the chain link. Whoever Rock shot at had tossed a bottle filled with something lit on fire, thrown it just over the fence. But the tangle of leaves had caught it, letting it burn a black circle on the wire before Rock had thrown buckets of water from the irrigation tank onto the flames.

"Fool obviously didn't think nobody was back here," Oscar said when Hosea approached. "Didn't know nothin about canals, or he'd know it was water right here, too."

"Smell like somethin other than gas," Hosea said, crouching next to him, looking at his brother's cheeks, seamed from years of squinting into harsh stage lights and drinking faces.

"Somebody threw ether in a bottle. Rock smelled it, cause he remember somebody used to make that angel dust with it. Stuff Finis lost his head smokin. PCP." Oscar touched his fingers to his nose.

"Ether burn better than gas?" Hosea looked at the scorched, oily leaves lying like dark commas near his feet.

"Ether make it look like a drug lab. I know where else we gon smell it," Oscar said, standing now. "Ain't nobody thrown no fire at your place. Could be cause Rock done shot at em by then. Could be cause they don't care bout burning mine, but they ain't plannin to burn yours."

They were silent, Oscar turning the key in the thick chain locking his back gate, which no one had used in years. The gate had been covered with woven bark and wood and pepper berries; now it was skeletal dark mesh.

They walked along the canal where the water wound as dark as oil into the purple light of lowering clouds. Hosea smelled the soot still floating in the eddying wind.

"I don't know who I gotta shoot yet," Oscar said, keeping pace beside Hosea when they crossed the small stone bridge over the canal and onto the old pea field. "When I do, I ain't gon hesitate."

Hosea stared at the makeshift pens Lanier had built for the pigs at the far end of the field, near the base of the hill. The old olive-packing house loomed, weathered gray and blank-eyed near the pile of pallets Lanier had collected. Following the blurred path past the pigs, who were quiet and dusty in the cold, they came to the flood-control tunnel under the freeway.

"Bet not be nobody foolish in here," Oscar said loudly at the entrance to the tunnel. Hosea smelled the sharp damp and urine and the permanent wet. This sandy channel, cutting away steeply from the cement mouth, led through Oscar's pea field and then gathered in several pipes underneath the canal; the water spilled out into the gully through Hosea's land, went under the riverbottom road, and emptied into the river.

The tunnel was empty. They walked through quickly, the pitted cement just inches above their heads, and Hosea breathed hard through his mouth, feeling the curving walls too close, like the banks of the creeks where he'd huddled in Texas, waiting for dogs, for gunshots, for voices.

When they came out into the dim light again, they could see the Kozy Komfort's dollhouse shacks smoldering like matchstick piles on someone's plate. Only two rooms were left, closest to them, their pink paint darkened with soot.

As Hosea and Oscar walked along the fence at the back, Hosea held his breath, trying not to let the acrid carbon fall deep into his chest. After a few minutes, he turned his face toward the blank concrete overpass nearby, where cars ripped over the same crease with the sound of tearing rubber.

Oscar came close to him. "Marcus said Finis told him three boys come runnin behind here, and then they run into the tunnel like they was headin toward your place," Hosea said softly. "Said Finis told him the whole thing, but then he run away his ownself."

"Yeah," Oscar said. "They burnt this place up, come runnin by me and threw they bottle. Then they quiet. Coulda been on to yours next, but Rock hit one or scared three." He paused. "Listen. You done told me about this bridge. Remember the old bridge? Didn't nobody go over but us, headin to work. And now—all them houses over there. Look. If this Matheson live up there in the Diamondbacks, he seein this like a goddamn Monopoly game, and he want us out the way. He sent Fulton Chester to try and buy us out, and when that didn't work, he sent somebody else to burn us out." Oscar frowned. "But them two women, and the other guy—I don't know what the hell that was."

Hosea turned to stare at the charcoaled wood lying in heaps; the discarded cassette tapes near his feet, blown against the asphalt, looked like metallic brown snail trails.

Land. It always came down to the dirt and rocks and boundaries In the Texas woods, with his shins gashed by ax blades and his neck swollen with thirst, the flickering fires of tree stumps sending clouds of smoke over his eyes and coating his tongue with death—that was land that someone wanted cleared. Cleared and burned until long after dark, when they'd be marched back to the cages where rotting, withering men lay underneath the ones who hadn't yet refused to work, who hadn't broken and run or slashed out or said the wrong thing. When he'd swung the ax and run in the creek beds along someone's fields, he'd stared at the land in unclaimed tangles or neat, plowed rows. And the neat, plowed rows were far more frightening.

The smoke of Tulsa—that was land, the plotted squares of property and bricks close to the railroad tracks. It was the white businessmen who'd wanted the place for more railroads, who hated the smiling dollars of Greenwood, the lack of Greenwood interest and coin for downtown. But if it came down to his land, to a bridge or whatever was being planned, was he looking at fire or more bodies or another police set-up? "Chester didn't work out for the man," Hosea murmured to Oscar. "These three boys did they job pretty good here, look like. I guess they be back."

Natalie Larchwood said she didn't know why Whalen was playing games with her, using up all his sick time and hell, he should just retire. "A few more days, that's it," she'd added in her office.

"I'm not complaining," Marcus told her. "I'd miss it."

She shook her head. "I guess he doesn't."

When the kids were all silent, staring or scratching with pencils, he looked at the small newspaper article. The three men who died in the Kozy Komfort fire had been identified as Usher Price, thirty-one, of the Treetown area, and James Eugene and Malcolm Turner, both forty, of the Westside area. Harley was quoted as saying that the fire appeared to have been caused by a drug lab explosion, possibly in a feud. Three males had been seen fleeing west, wearing black watch caps and black jackets. One male fled separately, wearing braided hair and dark jeans.

Finis had fled all right. Marcus knew he wouldn't see him again unless he could find him, somewhere with chalky, clinging dust and skunk-eye stones. That's what they'd called the rocks when they were kids. Where had they found them?

He stared at his scribbled notes. SaRonn thought Chris, Zefi's boy, had killed the drug dealer. And Usher was Chris's father . . . who'd shot Usher? A Japanese guy that Finis gave a strange Brooklyn accent when he called "Ca-mere!"

Drugs. Everything was drugs. And history. What was he supposed to do with this paper now? Paper didn't impress his father or uncle; he couldn't show this to Harley. It didn't mean anything to anyone. Not even him.

Chris stood up suddenly and said, "I ain't in the mood for this. Shit. It's hot in here. Too many fools in here." He walked out the door, sending back a glare at Josh, then at Mortrice. The door clicked quiet.

Marcus said, "I thought today's topic was cool. Movies and music in your history. Hey, I started mine with the Floaters." He kept his voice easy and stood up, knowing he'd have to chase Chris down.

Josh nudged Mortrice. "Yo, homes, how you spell 'Terminator'?"

Mortrice shrugged, his head down, and Marcus looked at the long, elegant fingers on his mostly blank paper. Homes. Homey, doncha know me? Treetown brothers always stayed home. Home boys. Now all the white kids called each other "Homes." Now it was cool.

"You writing about *Terminator*?" he said.

"Man, that's old," someone said.

"Just like me," Marcus said. When he stepped outside, seeing Chris head across the quad, B-Real came out with him.

"Man, his dad got killed in that fire. They buryin him tomorrow. I think he's just goin home," B-Real said.

"Yeah," Marcus said as the bell rang. "I hope so." The escape began, and he saw a small square of paper fluttering in the breeze from the open door, near where Josh and Mortrice had sat, and he picked it up. "After Hours Party—Cool as Fuck," it read, with a picture of a cow wearing sunglasses and smoking a big joint. The back of the flyer was covered with cramped, tiny writing. The bell rang, and the next faces poured in through the door, rumpled and damp and bored.

Mortrice found him in the apartment, lying on the torn couch in the plywood darkness. B-Real and Teddy stood in the doorway, and Chris said, "Shut the fuckin door, man. I don't want to see the fuckin light." He put his fingers over his eyes. "I don't want to see fuckin Sketch every day."

Mortrice sat on the floor beside him. "This dude I use to know, Kenneth. One time we was on a expedition and shit, and I heard him say, 'Sometimes the nigga what pull the trigga ain't the one you gotta figure.' "

"I don't give a shit," Chris said. "I want to take him out."

Teddy said, "Take all three of em out. Shit."

"Y'all gettin in deep," B-Real said, nervous. "Way past deep."

Mortrice looked at the black squares of window, outlined in pushing, gray light. "Just let him talk first. Speedin fools always like to talk. And then we can go on a expedition for reals."

"Check this out," Teddy said. "B-Real and them havin that reggae-rap thing at the club by the bus station, right? Them wiggers always tryin to rap like Vanilla Ice and shit."

"Yeah, well, I ain't up for—" B-Real began, but Chris cut him off.
"Hell, yeah," he said, sitting up. "Cap they sorry rap."

All colors are cool, B-Real had said at the club. Mortrice saw Bebos in the crowd of Worlds. But he kept his eyes on the Casper-pale faces nodding hard. They were sketchin fast.

In the parking lot, Mortrice approached them near the Jeep. "So, loc, you like that stuff?"

Sketch twirled around and said, "Hey! That shit was down." He bent to pick up one of the flyers scattered on the ground. "You see this one? I heard this party's like the bomb. Ecstasy and whatever else you want."

"You done did your jobs?" Mortrice said. "You get bullets?"

"Fuck, yeah," Sketch said. "We got more to come. Conflagrations."

Mortrice frowned. "Who payin you?"

"Come on," Sketch said quickly, his voice proud. Mortrice nodded at Chris to warn him; Mortrice had the .9, but he'd made sure Chris wasn't strapped. They got in the Jeep.

Sketch drove past the bus station. "We got one right there. Lotta jobs to be had down here, you know where to pick em up."

"Who payin you?" Mortrice said again, and the other one, Tweak, glared.

Suddenly Sketch pulled the Jeep up a hill and they passed large, fancy houses. He cruised slowly past a dark-brown two-story hidden in pine-tree shadows. "My dad lives here. He got the jobs. He got everything everybody needs. He says rocks for blacks, speed for whites, tar for Mexicans. You know that dude got shot down in Treetown? He was workin for my dad."

"The rock man?" Chris said, his voice tight. "Vernon?"

Tweak turned in his seat, agitated. "You're just talkin, Sketch, you don't even know that rich guy, you just think he's your dad."

Sketch said, "Any fuckin cowboy in Texas could be your dad." He floored the Jeep and careened around several blocks to the poorer part of downtown, stopping by a lime-green stucco house near the school. "Yeah. This is my crib, okay? And my moms goes over to the other house and has a big fight with the guy, talkin about all he send her is enough money for a ten-year-old. She says I ain't ten no more. He

says, 'How do I know it's my kid? You been sayin that for years and
fuckin everything you see.' She says, 'Cause he's a asshole like you and
his teeth are big as fuckin refrigerators like yours.' " Sketch's voice was
rising, skating. "She says, 'Look at him,' and he says, 'I don't need to.'
I heard her on the phone. And I went over there one day. He let me
in and didn't say shit. I said, 'You got any jobs?' He said, 'I'm just a
consultant' or something. I said, 'So I need a job.' He said, 'Okay, but
you do em on your own. All I give you is cash.' "

Mortrice looked at the faded yellow grass when silence fell. The
shades on the tiny house were drawn like closed drawers. "She works
nights," Sketch said, fingers in his hair again. "So we do, too. Me and
Tweak."

"Man, shut the fuck up," Tweak said, his voice breaking. "Let's go."

Sketch drove away, laughing. "First night job was do two winos and
dump em in a car on this lot, huh, Tweaker? But you did some crank
and got horny. You wanted some girl winos."

They were back at the club. Tweak got out and walked jerkily away.
Sketch said, "All he cares about is the money. But I like the jobs. I'm
a wigger with an attitude."

B-Real had come out of the club now, medallions swinging. "You
was rappin all smart, like, about thinkin and shit," Sketch said to him.
"I like NWA better, loc."

Mortrice leaned against B-Real's van. The blacktop gleamed with
rainbow oil, and the wind blew hot. He knew Chris wouldn't wait
long.

B-Real said nervously, "That's cause we're all about intellect, man,
we got MC Brains, DJ Forehead, The Academic Rasta. We're like One
World, use your head."

Chris said, "I'm a trigga-happy nigga! I'm hollerin 187, tryin to send
your boy to heaven, and if he ain't been strong, then hell where he
belong."

Sketch smiled. "I likes that, man."

Mortrice looked at Tweak, who stood nearby now, his arms folded,
his face pinched small and tight like a leprechaun. "So maybe we can
run together one night. Homes. We got some jobs, too. But y'all might
not be down."

Sketch threw out his arms. "Shit, we down for anything! We got a
posse!"

"I ain't seen your friend," Mortrice said.

"Bodie?" Sketch asked.

Tweak said, "He's a Jap, you can't trust Orientals. Probly ratted us out."

"He gets pissed off when you call him a Jap," Sketch said impatiently.

"He don't like when you pay him off with crank, man. Says your dad got cash."

"So what other jobs you done did?" Chris said now, hard, his eyes as narrow as iron filings. Mortrice watched him.

Sketch tilted his head, and his yellow braids fell around his ear. "You know a junkyard down by the river? Some old dude?"

"Naw, man, you know I'm from L.A., I ain't from here," Mortrice lied easily. Kenneth used to tell him, "Never admit you know nobody. Not even me."

"We were supposed to dump two winos in one of them junk cars. Get paid. My dad said get em from under the bridge or somethin. But old Tweak seen these girls downtown, and we gave em some crank, and the one girl passed out."

"Shut up, Sketch!" Tweak shouted.

"See? He be tweakin, flyin too high. Always nervous." Sketch danced around on the glittering blacktop. "But he wants some pussy. The other chick, she's, like, I'll give you somethin if you give me the crank. And then we got by the riverbottom and she sees Tweak's dick is so small."

"Fuck you!" Tweak rushed for his friend, but Chris grabbed him.

Sketch shouted, "She said I won't fuck a gook, either, my brother was in Vietnam. And Tweak and Bodie were both highly pissed, man, and Tweak punched her, knocked her ass out. So Bodie cut some wires and opened up this gate. We put em in this car and lit the fire, man, cause that was the job. A termination and conflagration. That's what my dad said. He likes them big words. The one chick woke up and started yellin, so I had to cap her."

"What you had?" Chris said, his arms around Tweak's neck.

"I had a nine, man, found it in my mom's closet." He laughed. "And this old dude fired on us!"

"What he had?" Mortrice said, his head aching. The Pompey gun.

"I don't know. He hit the bumper, and my friend had to fix it. We had to dump the nine after Tweak here freaked on this dude."

Tweak jerked himself away from Chris and shouted, "I'm fuckin leavin your ass!" He walked toward the Jeep.

"I got the keys," Sketch rapped, but Tweak kept walking. "He's gonna hot-wire it." His eyes darted, as bright as flying sparks.

"What dude?" Mortrice stood close, smelling the speed sweat like acid.

"This he/she dude! Tweak seen her by the bus station, and she gets in the Jeep, and Tweak feels on her. And she's a fuckin dude! Tweak went off and bashed in his head. Since my dad said where the first dump place was, we dropped him there, too."

"But you ain't burnt nothin," Chris said.

"Yo, man, we did a good one for the nine-deuce," Sketch said, and a car roared into the parking lot. "Fucked up some comfort!" he called, starting to run for the Jeep.

Tramaine, the one who called himself MC Brains, leaned out of the Camaro. "B-Real, man, you got my jacket! What y'all doin hangin out here?"

"We gone," Mortrice said, moving away.

"Shit!" Chris shouted. "I'ma take him now! That mother—"

Mortrice lunged forward and put his arms around Chris's shoulders from behind, feeling him wrench inside the grip. "He ain't goin nowhere. Nowhere AK can't go, man. Ain't you AK-2? Ain't you down for how it gotta go? You gotta do it right. You gotta use your head, huh, B-Real?"

But B-Real was walking away. "I ain't down no more," he said.

When Marcus took off his jacket at Chile, he heard a crinkle of paper. The small flyer he'd picked up a few days ago—he'd forgotten about it. "Phone, Marcus," Kurt called before Marcus could squint at the tiny writing.

"Hey," Bent's voice said. "Marcus. I, uh, I'm lookin forward to hangin out with you again, at The Q."

"You sure?" Marcus said, distracted.

"Yeah. I've got a great idea for a story about your uncle. But look—I'm callin about another story. I keep hearing Abby's aunt, the historian for the newspaper? She's talking about some Thompson place, something historic."

Marcus tried to remember. "Oh, yeah, she wrote a book about local history. It was in there."

"The Blue Q?"

"No, uh, my father's place." Marcus hadn't wanted to tell anyone. He hesitated. "Next door."

"I'm lost now," Bent said. "Abby's aunt keeps talking about some article, and I was all confused because I couldn't see her writing about The Blue Q."

"Marcus," Kurt called. "Let's go."

"Hey, I'll talk to you later," Marcus said. "Dinnertime."

After the crowd had thinned out that night, he took out the flyer in the bar. Bending his face to the small letters, he made out "Terminations."

Terminations - $500
Regular Fire - $200
Confligrasion - $400
Oriental Predater - $100
Feed Somebody Speed - $100
Speciel Delivary - $50

Who the hell was this? Mortrice? The white kid? He stared at the words. Oriental Predater. It had to be the three from the canal—but who would pay them this kind of money? He buried his face in his fingers and moved around the tight skin of his forehead: Samana? And the two white kids? The ones who liked rap, the voices he'd heard above the water. Yeah—like he could call Harley with this, all this speculation and crazy hints that no one would believe? Finis was a more believable suspicion.

He didn't want to think about this. He wanted to bring SaRonn to his place and present her and Willa with blue-corn tortillas drizzled with honey and cinnamon. He'd been patting them into shape at Chile now and then; when Javier looked surprised, Marcus said, "Hey, I got a great-*abuela* from Mexico, man, I been watching her do this forever."

He went home to form the rounds in his kitchen, feeling the flyer crackle in his pocket, lost in the scene of his mother and *abuela* standing at the stove, their hands flying in tandem. When the phone rang, he thought it was SaRonn. "Teacher, he is come," Som said quickly, and then he hung up.

Marcus raced down Pepper, his hands gritty on the wheel. Inside the doughnut shop smelling of incense and warm sugar, he saw Samana coming around the counter with a small bag. Marcus grinned casually at him. "Hey, your hair is longer. Haven't seen you in a while."

Samana smirked and said, "I don't need history now."

"You shouldn't quit school, man. Come on, let me give you a ride somewhere." Marcus saw Som hovering in the doorway, his eyes ringed with gray, and he stepped close to Samana. The boy's frail; I'ma have to push him in the car and talk sense, he thought.

But Samana got into the VW easily, his hair falling to his ears now, dusty black, a tiny foxtail caught near his neck. "You look like you need some sleep," Marcus said. How the hell did you ask questions about terminations?

Samana smirked again. "In my country, man sleep in a tree, not the cave, so tiger can't surprise."

Bodhi. "Why you sleepin in trees?"

"I sleep where I want," Samana mumbled. "I tired of making doughnuts." He glanced up when Marcus parked. "You live expensive, huh? Downtown."

"Me? A teacher?" Marcus said, reminding him. "You kidding?"

Inside, Samana studied the figurines without putting down his bag. Marcus warmed the cast-iron griddle and waited for faint brown blisters to form on the tortillas. "You hungry?"

Samana chewed and frowned at the small table. "Weird," he said.

"New Mexican," Marcus said. "Indian and Spanish."

"Here." Samana's voice was sharp. He held a splinter of brown. "Try Cambodian." Marcus chewed the wood-dry fish, the fish he'd seen on the hill behind his father's with the *saladitos* he glimpsed now in the bag.

"Those are Mexican," Marcus said, nodding at the salted plums.

"So I look like Mexican. Or Jap. Whatever." Samana laid his hands on the table. "Oriental hard worker get five fucking dollar an hour. Fuck that. Fuck the doughnuts." From his bag, he took the assignment sheet Marcus had left for him. "You want me write essay with the asshole in that class? Everybody think they have the tough life. So they live gangster, always talk killing." He dropped the paper on the table.

"If they kill one hundred people, they don't see enough blood. I see so much blood." His eyes were surrounded with red, like he had a fever, and his fingernails were outlined with dirt. Marcus saw mica glinting on his cheek.

"You always talk history, history is important. Never forget. What they write?" He imitated his classmates. "I was born and then my mommy change my diaper. I go to school, I ride my bike, I get my car, I want to drink beer and fuck somebody, okay? My mommy so mean to me. She never give me the money."

"What you gonna write?" Marcus said. He tried to be careful. "You gon write about killing? Killing who?"

"Shit." Samana stared out the window. "I ride in the cart with the other boy to take the body. All so many body. The ox pull the cart so slow, and the blood run down the cart to my back. When we get to the field, my shirt like in the rain. And they put the body in the ditch. When I get back, my shirt dry like—" He said words in Cambodian. "The Camere—"

"The who?"

"Camere Rouge. Look." He grabbed a pencil and wrote "Khmer Rouge." Kampuchea. "This is what they call. We are Khmer. But Khmer Rouge kill all. Everyone but my aunt. And when we go to the camp, to Khao-I-Dang, we stay for year. They kill in the camp, too. My aunt, she stay with Som so nobody kill us. We sit all day. Then we come here." He stood up, swaying. "Come and make the fucking doughnuts. Hard worker."

"You okay?" Marcus said, but when he touched Samana's arm, the boy pulled away violently.

"I can use the bathroom, okay?" Samana said.

He didn't come back out, and Marcus sat at the table, looking at the salted plums and tortillas. He read the flyer, paced around the living room. Listening at the door, he heard nothing. After an hour, he called SaRonn, nearly whispering in case Samana thought he'd called the cops. "Hey," he said. "I miss you. I got a problem. Wrong person here."

She thought Samana was coming off drugs. "Sound like he's been sleepin outside," she said, her voice low, too.

When midnight passed, he listened again. Nothing. He sliced a butter knife as quietly as he could down the crack in the old door. The click sounded deafening.

Samana lay in the tub, a towel over him, his mouth open, hands folded on his chest as if he were dead. His clothes lay over the old heater; the smell of damp jeans was almost like blue cornmeal.

"Your mama say you fifteen today," Hosea said. He handed the .22 to Mortrice.

"You bought this?" Mortrice shifted it to look at the barrel.

His grandfather nodded. "Brand-new. Like I given my boys. In May we can go in the hills and practice shootin. Targets. Then maybe we can do some huntin. I'm gettin Kendrick one, a BB gun." He turned and said, "You ain't got no bullets yet. Not till May. You better keep it dry. Have to keep your gun dry."

His mother gave him a gold necklace, a snake chain with an *M* and a St. Christopher medal. "From your grandma and me," she whispered. "You goin to a party? With Zefi's boy?"

He nodded. She took out the vial of oil and daubed it on his forehead, his collarbone, his wrists. His chest, her finger poking into his T-shirt. Mortrice stood patiently, feeling the streams of cold fan out from her touch.

"We stayin here?" he asked.

She glanced around at the white plaster walls. "Here? Inside?"

Mortrice stared at his mother's eyes across from his. "On this place. This where we gon stay now? You know?"

Now she nodded. "Don't you want to? That's your blood. Your family."

He saw himself, a statue taking up half her eyes, and he turned to go.

"Cool as fuck," Chris said. "Stupid-ass name for a party."

"Stand out in a field with big speakers on a truck, get drunk and fucked up," Teddy said. "Keggers." He drove a Nissan he'd gotten on the Westside.

The black Jeep was ahead of them. Sketch had been excited when they'd said they wanted to see where the party was. Mortrice saw the field where they'd practiced shooting the first time, and he thought of the new .22 in the trailer. His grandfather's gun, the one from the man who'd walked to Texas, was gone forever with the cops. Cause Sketch made my grampa shoot it. Pompey gun.

Sketch parked the black Jeep near a stand of trees; a sea of cars stretched to the barbed-wire fence. Mortrice saw lights pulsing from the truckbed of speakers; faces of all colors bobbed up and down past the fence, and the smell of beer rose from the ground like dank fog.

"One World," Chris said. "A world a hurt."

"Samana?" Marcus said, not too loud. "You okay, man?"

The boy sat up like a zombie, his hand clean and brown on the porcelain tub rim. "Why you in here?"

"It's my damn bathroom," Marcus said, irritated. "Come on. You're clean, you got some slightly cleaner clothes. I'ma take you to your uncle's." He hesitated. "We gotta talk about a list, so get dressed."

He had the flyer in front of him when Samana came out wearing the big black barn coat again. The standard uniform. "If I write the essay, you see when I am born," Samana said. "Nineteen seventy-one."

Marcus frowned. "No, I'm talking about a list of jobs . . ."

"Yeah, so fuck class, okay? My uncle want me to learn four years, then go college four years, then get a job. I look young. Be Jap hard worker." Marcus saw the gun come out of Samana's pocket, the huge-mouthed barrel. Thirty-eight or larger. Like Salcido's police issue.

"Shit, Samana, what the—" Marcus sat still on the couch.

"I don't need fucking five dollar an hour. I need money for send back to my country. For my grandmother. She blind, from the Khmer Rouge, she want to go home sometime. I send money to the one fight Khmer Rouge."

"So you gon kill people, too? You doin these jobs for the money, and don't think about killin?" Marcus couldn't point at the list. "Usher Price, man, that was a person."

"I do that before. I don't need school for that. They teach me in the field. They try to teach my uncle, but he forget. They teach the kid better." Samana moved the gun slightly, like it was heavy. "I go on my own, okay, and tell my uncle stop fucking with me. I don't see him again. I need some money."

"All I got is twenty bucks."

"Yeah," Samana said. When he had the bill, he opened the apartment door and went down the stairs, his hands in his big square pockets.

Marcus looked out the window to see him disappear through the archway. He looked for Harley's card amid the papers on the table, staring at the list. Cool as fuck.

"We gotta piss first, man," Chris said to Sketch. Teddy idled the Nissan on the shoulder of the road.

"You ain't even been in yet," Sketch said. "You ain't drank." Tweak groaned, his pupils like pepper grains, his cheeks sunk into a sprinkling of red sores. "Too much crank, man," Sketch said.

"You get paid for another job?" Mortrice asked, watching the two faces, floating pale toward the trees with them. "The man pay you with speed?"

"Naw, loc, we got cash money for the last one. Conflagration. That motel. But Bodie lost it. Orientals can't do crank, man. He hates when people call him a Jap, and he shot some dude."

Mortrice put his hand on Chris's rising arm, saying, "Stall out, man." He ran his tongue inside his mouth so he could think. He couldn't taste ink or blood or anything but chronic-dull smoke from the weed. He kept thinking of Paco's face in the sand, the jerky-dancing figures in the parking lots, the tingling dimples in his back. My peoples. He wanted to think away from this voice that tried for black and shaded into white and then skittered along as gray and flat as cement.

"You get good dinero?" Mortrice said slowly to Sketch. "From your dad? He got any more jobs? Like the old dude?"

Tweak was facing a tree, peeing. Sketch laughed. "Don't show no girls that," he said. "No, man, I'm just playin!" He turned to Mortrice, his tongue lolling. "Shit, I'm fucked up."

"Your dad?" Mortrice said, louder.

"Man, my dad got this rich friend in them blue towers. Like a spider or somethin. They go way back when. I heard em on the phone. The way-back dude wants all kinda shit. All kinda jobs. He buys somethin. I don't know. Fuck, he ain't got no posse. We got a posse. You can be in our posse, man. Homes."

Chris was holding the .9. He shot Sketch twice in the chest, and the talking mouth flew open wider before the rest of him fell against the tree. Chris turned to Tweak, who lifted his hand like a crossing guard.

"Come on," Mortrice said, looking for Teddy's taillights like drunken eyes in the dark. The music was thumping harder than his heart.

"They could think it's a robbery and shit," Chris said, hesitating. "But they ain't got nothin I want."

"AK, man," Mortrice whispered to the nostrils raised toward the branches. "It ain't a posse." Suddenly, he saw Paco's bone face, as pale as these two, among the damp leaves, down the river. He started to run for the car.

CHAPTER EIGHTEEN

THE GRIEF COUNSELING team was on campus all week. Marcus sent Sharon and Araceli to talk with the black-haired woman whose voice was as soothing as heated milk, since every time they saw the two empty seats, their eyes spilled over and they set everyone else off.

Samana's seat was empty, and so was Chris Perry's. Marcus had asked B-Real and Mortrice, who said, "Chris ain't into school no more." Samana was in the wind, Marcus knew.

He'd called Harley, who was busy with the two shootings and didn't call back. Marcus went to the gym to find Salcido; in the free-weight corner, he'd tried to explain about the list, about Samana's gun and how he left. "Remember the canal, man?" he'd said. Salcido nodded, but no police had called.

Whalen was coming back Monday. Marcus looked at the faces, drawn and wary, in the circle. "You guys better get used to rows again," he said. "Hey, it was cool working with you. You did a great job on the essays."

"They were depressing," Sharon said. "Everything was sad, like now."

"Not everything," Marcus said. "Come on."

"I liked writing about my grandpa was a cowboy in Mexico," Rubén said.

"I liked hearing about my mom when she was a singer," Araceli said. "But now she says she just a mom."

"So's mine," Marcus said. "I like moms. My girlfriend's a beautiful mom."

Bebos rolled his eyes. "So you're a ready-made pops."

The bell rang. "Guys," Marcus called, and most of them stopped in their scramble. "Be cool out there, okay? Peaceful. Good histories, right?"

In his apartment, he stared at the newspaper articles and photos. Joshua Firola Roberts. William Reese McFall. Shot during a party in a field. Random act. No known motive. No gang ties. Average students. Victims of increasingly senseless violence.

At the funeral, the photographer had captured Josh's mother and father, standing separately near the casket. Mary Firola had brown hair in limp waves. Trevor Roberts had very blond hair that looked nearly white in the photo, sharp Ray•Bans, and his mouth was open and grim. His teeth were large and straight. He was the guy who wanted to bring vacuum cleaners to the Jungletown market.

There was no way Trevor Roberts even remembered the house where he'd sold some colored woman a Silver King, among the hundreds of houses he must have made fun of when he got into his car with a signed contract for far too much money. Marcus didn't even think Web Matheson remembered the place. They all look alike—the people, the yards, the kids, right?

He called Harley again, and he was surprised to hear the tired voice answer. "Hey, uh, this is Marcus Thompson. Finis brother?"

"Yeah?"

"Did, uh, did Tony Salcido tell you the information I had about some stuff? About the Cambodian kid?"

"Yeah, he did, Marcus. The kid had a thirty-eight, you think. But the two kids got shot by a nine-millimeter. None of the party types saw anybody, but there were definitely at least two guys around the victims. Hey, I appreciate the call, though. And I'll get back to you. I'm just really swamped right now. I got people looking out for this Asian kid, okay?"

On the weekend, he went to his father's place. His mother and his *abuela* were washing aphids from the new purple leaves on their roses. "Spring come right on, didn't it?" his mother said, looking at the apricot tree. "After all that rain, we gon have a good year."

"Maybe," he said, smiling. Maybe the shit was all over now.

. . .

Enchantee had just hung up the dishcloth when two men came in the open front door. She could still hear Abby, Dylan, and Bent talking outside with Abby's mother and aunt. Web Matheson—his hair combed back like a hundred tipped brown barbs, and another man with blond hair and deep ravines beside his mouth. Web smiled and said, "Hi! We're gonna wait for Señor Smith in the library. Can you bring us *cervezas? Dos cervezas? Muchas gracias.*"

Enchantee saw him lay a folder on the table. "The nanny, I guess, for my sister-in-law's kid," she heard Web say when the men headed down the hallway. "Connie's aunt dropped off those proofs of her story, but she wants them back tomorrow at Easter brunch. You're coming, right?" The door snapped shut.

They didn't look up when she knocked and then put the tray down on a table. Charts and maps and papers were spread near the men's knees.

She closed the door and stood listening. "Okay, you got three phases. Cedar Crest, Willow Crest, Timber Crest. The green, the lake, the whole thing." There was a long drinking pause. Then Web said, "I'm tired of Connie's aunt bugging me about this place. You see how she was just now, with this story? She's obsessed with this place in Tree-town—handed me the story like it's her top-secret lethal weapon." They both laughed. "She's sure once they see her little article, the city council and redevelopment can step in and save the day. As broke and slow as government is."

"The idea's okay, what she's proposing?" the other man asked.

"Yeah, Swede, no problem, but this building, where it is—damn, the only solution for a place like that is a nuclear bomb, okay? Level it out and start over. Build a replica. With a different population, you know."

"If it's a historic site . . ."

"Hey, goddamnit, these people aren't budging, and I've offered above market price." She heard bottles clink against gold rings. "Hey, what about those new smart bombs that take out the people and leave the structures?" Web laughed. Enchantee heard the glass clink wetly onto the tray. "The other place is worthless. A pit. She's talking petting zoo or something. I say burn it, there's nothing of value. The other obstacle was like a fucking asylum, worst eyesore around. It needed a crazy bomb. But it's gone now."

Moving her feet carefully on the Oriental runner striping the hallway, Enchantee headed for the kitchen. She heard Abby come inside and say, "Let's go celebrate your contract, babe. I'll change."

Enchantee stepped into the bathroom, leaving the door open. Bent was on the phone with someone now. "Marcus?" Enchantee frowned. "You going to work? Hey, meet me at the restaurant, I've gotta show you something."

When he'd gone, she went back to the kitchen, her hands shaking. She hoped she could remember all the words, to tell Demetrius. When Web Matheson came up behind her, she jumped. "That folder's gone," he muttered, moving papers on the table. He looked at her. "Where— uh—*como*? How do you say where?" He sighed. "Folder?"

Enchantee shrugged and turned away.

They were drinking at the outdoor tables when Marcus arrived. "Hey, Kolavic," Bent was saying to a brown-haired guy. "I've been researching this one."

"*Esquire*, man, I'm jealous as hell," Kolavic said. "What's the title?"

Bent saw Marcus then, and he motioned him over. Abby's voice was slurring a little, and Marcus couldn't tell what she was drinking. "Lost and Found—A Bluesman in Southern California," she read from a piece of paper.

"Hey, this is Marcus," Bent said, standing up. "He's . . ."

Marcus shook his head slightly, and Bent seemed to understand. Marcus didn't want to talk about The Blue Q. "Can I get you guys something else?"

Abby hadn't heard. "Well, I love you, babe," she said to Bent, "but I'm jealous, too. I've gotta find some long-lost foods, something buried in obscurity, write about it for *Gourmet* or something."

Bent rolled his eyes at Marcus. "Oscar wasn't buried," he said, his voice sharp. "He was pretty alive, Abby. That stuff's pretty strong, huh?"

Abby lifted her glass. "This is medicinal, okay, it's good for me and the baby. It's *amaro*—people drink it in Italy, it's got herbs and spices. I should get a whole bottle for tomorrow—Easter brunch with Web and Connie. All his political assets—a stupid blond wife who'll smile and a fat baby on the way. She's all freaked out over the way it's still flooded over there."

Marcus turned, but Bent came with him. "You got a clear table in the back?" Bent said.

He laid out the folder and photos. "I heard Abby's aunt talking about Thompson land, and I thought she knew some history about The Blue Q, right? I figured they'd freak if they knew I'd been there, but when I saw these pictures—it's the place where those girls were killed. I had just moved here, and I went with Kolavic to tag along for the story."

Marcus looked quickly at the photos, then closed the folder and raised his eyes to Bent's face. The man looked serious. "This is your father's house?"

"Yeah," Marcus said slowly. "This is for the paper, right? Can I borrow it for tonight?"

Bent nodded. "You know, you took all that heat for me at The Blue Q, and I owe you. I figured I'd tell Abby's aunt I got my story folder mixed up with hers. She's supposed to get this back tomorrow, at brunch. I heard Connie telling Web her aunt couldn't wait to show it to him."

Marcus breathed hard, looking at Bent's tie. "You owe me? Okay. I want to come to brunch. I'll give this back to you then." He paused, looking at the afternoon sun gleaming through Chile's window.

"Hey, it's like a gated community," Bent said, chewing on his lip. "But this is half Easter and half fund-raiser. You'd know if you knew Web."

"I don't want to know him," Marcus said. "I don't want him to know me." He raised his chin at Bent. "How bout if you call down to the guard? And I'll try to act like a fund giver."

Bent shook his head. "Not with these Republican types. Listen— it's catered. We can deliver some food from here? Chani can call down from the kitchen."

"Chani?" Marcus frowned.

"Your sister-in-law. She's bringing Dylan so Abby can help set up." Bent turned to go outside. "I'm not asking any questions right now, okay? But I'm curious as hell."

"So am I."

. . .

Sitting at his mother's kitchen table, Marcus listened while Enchantee tried to remember all the words. Nuclear bomb. Market price. Redevelopment. Petting zoo. Asylum.

"Asylum?" his mother asked, her voice vibrating.

"A place for the mentally insane," Marcus said. "And it's gone. The Kozy Komfort."

"Petting zoo?" Alma whispered.

Hosea nodded toward the story proofs and photos on the table. "In my yard?"

Marcus glanced at the headline again. "Historic Adobe Building Neglected: Crime Site Eligible for County Landmark Status." He didn't look at the words. Four large photos paraded down the page.

A dark door surrounded by pale wall, where a large hole was dug out near the cement steps. A blackish patch floated near the screen. Then Alma's veranda, where bare wisteria vines tangled like thick string and tiny baby dresses hung from a line. Junked cars on the storage lot. And the barn wall, festooned with tools and coffee cups, sawhorses and beer cans near the doorway.

"Where are we?" Demetrius shouted. "I ain't seen nobody takin pictures."

Alma's knuckles pressed her chin like she was holding it onto her face. "She say she from the city, ax can she walk round. She come when I was cookin. Come back and ax me was there problems here lately. I told her no. Then she got in her car and go. Y'all was on a job somewhere."

Marcus reached for the folder. He looked at Enchantee. "I'll meet you up there tomorrow. At his place. But I don't know what I'll say."

"I've been there once before," she said. "I'll get you inside."

"And what Sissy do when he get him?" Demetrius said. "Talk to him till he drop dead?"

"You can't take somebody like Matheson out and kick his ass, okay?" Marcus shouted.

"Asylum?" his mother was whispering. "For crazy people?"

. . .

"I thought Web hated pearls," Abby said. She and Enchantee made a nest of blankets on the nursery floor for Dylan, who'd fallen asleep in the car.

"He does," Connie replied, smoothing the baby blanket in the crib. "But Aunt Carrie's coming, and she makes a big deal when I wear them."

"It's brunch, Connie," Abby said.

"It's an opportunity for Web to talk to contributors, and Aunt Carrie is a big help," Connie said, pausing at the nursery doorway, her silk dress pleated over her belly. Enchantee watched her larger smile set itself into her face.

The nursery was all blue, since Connie knew she was having a boy. The rocking-horse theme, with wallpaper border and mobile and quilt, was cute, Enchantee thought. Abby had groaned and said, "Predictable."

They walked down the stairs, and Enchantee looked quickly out the window at the cars winding up the long driveway. She bent and unplugged the baby monitor, watching Dylan twitch and dream.

Enchantee saw a pile of brochures on the counter. "Matheson and Associates," she read. "Is this your husband's company?" she asked casually.

Connie nodded, arranging silverware. "Except there's some problem with that tract, a bird or moth or something. I don't know. He's pretty upset." She glared at Abby. "Are you going to answer the door or not?"

"I'll put these in the great room," Enchantee said. She looked at the brochure. The text read: "On the sun-drenched, oak-covered hills of southern California, a unique gated community of magnificent proportions is evolving, a place of incredible beauty and Old West charm, but devoid of modern-day problems and pressures. This hidden paradise is Heritage Oaks. Two-acre estates, five exciting floor plans. No expense has been spared in planning construction of these lovely Old-World estate homes for your family . . ."

She saw the lots laid out in puzzle formation. A crowd of people had come into the room, and Abby led them outside to the deck. She came back to peer over Enchantee's shoulder. "That's where I was trying to talk Bent into buying, if he gets a book contract. And he isn't going for it. He likes downtown."

"Where is he?" Enchantee said nervously, watching Web and another crowd of people come in.

Abby smiled. "He said he's bringing some food just for me, from Chipotle Chile."

Enchantee nodded. She watched Web greet people in the great room, on the deck, at the door. "Yeah! A boy! I can't wait to teach him to play golf! Yeah, I know, Connie'll have to try for her girl next. Dresses and all that stuff. Hey, you look great!"

He moved through the rooms like a pinball in a machine, Enchantee thought, seeing him bounce deftly from an elbow to a hand to a shoulder, touching, turning, clasping lightly, always smiling. She heard Bent's voice in the kitchen, and she saw that he and Marcus were paused in the doorway. Marcus wore his Chipotle Chile work clothes, and he raised his chin slightly to her.

Web had finally approached the two older women on the couch, their hair as puffed and insubstantial as dandelions. Enchantee walked over to Marcus, saying, "Go into the guest bathroom, hurry up. Open the door under the sink and plug in the receiver. Hurry up."

After a few minutes, she saw Carrie Smith Donohue and Bent gliding up the stairs.

When Marcus plugged in the receiver to the baby monitor, the static spat at him so loudly that he hit his head on the sink when he jumped up. Turning it down, he stared at the locked bathroom door, sweating, hearing voices eerie and liquid. Demetrius would love this, he thought, Sissyfly holdin a baby walkie-talkie. And what I'ma do? Daddy said at least listen and try to see if they got a plan. Okay.

Bent was saying, "So this is your home office, huh, Web? I'd love to have this much space."

"Abby tells me she wants to buy in Heritage Oaks," Web said. "Lots of space."

"Yeah." Bent must have moved. "So I'm sorry I took your folder by accident. This story's coming out Wednesday?"

"Yes," Carrie Smith Donohue said. Her voice was dismissing. "Thank you."

"See ya down there, Bent," Web said.

Marcus crouched near the bathtub, pushing the rug near the door crack with his shoe, hoping no one had to pee. "He picked up my folder by mistake yesterday," she said. "He's very absent-minded."

"Yeah—he's a liberal asshole who likes rap music," Web said. Marcus could hear shuffling papers. "I hadn't seen the place before, not close up. Damn—it looks like hell."

"I agree. That's why I'm bringing it to the public's attention."

"But if you do the story now, and the city goes for landmark status, the price goes up," Web said.

"You only worry about money," she said impatiently. "This place is going to be a museum attraction."

Marcus heard someone pouring a drink. "Museums are never profitable, okay?"

"The barn and outbuildings are ideal for gift shops and boutiques, and the adjacent property for parking, if nothing else. There's your profit." She paused, and Marcus heard footsteps outside the bathroom. He got up and turned on the sink tap. "What are you drinking?" she asked.

"Glenfiddich," Web said. "Classy enough?" Marcus heard him walk, a series of muffled thumps on the monitor, and then he said from a distance, "I can't believe you know everything, the history of the whole damn area, and you've been up here before, and you couldn't bother to mention the fucking lake."

"Your mouth, Web," she said.

His voice was closer again. Marcus imagined him leaving the window. "I'm serious, they tell me this lake's been here before. But not wrecking homes on the seventh tee." He paused. "What? What are you staring at?"

"Your house has no aesthetic value, really, Web. It's worthless architecturally. There are hundreds like it."

"You old bitch," Matheson said softly, and Marcus heard the consonants pop.

"There's no class in this design," she went on. "The old Mission Revivals, the old Craftsmen, they have class. Truthfully, if water ruins something over here, across the bridge, it isn't worth saving."

"There isn't any goddamn bridge yet."

She continued like he hadn't spoken. "Even the Archuleta adobe is worth more architecturally than your whole development here."

"Yeah, well," he began, but she cut him off, her voice sharp.

"The waste of that whole area, the filthy shacks and dirt, and oh, the Archuleta place breaks your heart. Wrecked cars, a sea of mud. Not a blade of grass. I'd planned a garden. My father always said, 'Where Negroes go, grass won't grow.'"

Web began to laugh, and Marcus put his own hand over his mouth. "You can't call them Negroes now." Marcus heard him set down a glass on a tabletop. "Look, the whole schedule is off now. After all that, I thought the guys would either be dead or in jail and the women would sell the place. But the pale one? With the shack? She's past unreasonable. The last time I tried her, I said, 'A good-looking woman like yourself, you'd probably rather live in the city, closer to shopping and salons, I know my wife does.' And the woman goes nutso, she says, 'Get out my kitchen,' like it's a goddamn country club."

Aintielila, Marcus thought. Matheson went on. "I wanted something acquired by February and cleaned up by May, so I could use it in the campaign. A guy who gets the job done fast, no government bullshit. rescued from blight by private enterprise. But if this historic gateway plan goes through, the city can condemn the lots and do eminent domain."

"You can still use it if you stop talking and start thinking," she said, impatient again. "The city council takes it up next week, and they can set it aside in committee for a short time, and you can go back to negotiate. I'm sure the woman would rather deal with you than with the city." Marcus heard her sigh, and then feet trod past the monitor, as light as a wary bird.

He turned off the receiver and put it back under the sink. When he pushed open the door, a woman frowned at him and turned to let him pass. Marcus's face was hot. He saw Bent in the kitchen then, holding Dylan in his arms. "Hey, Marcus," Bent said. "I had to get this little guy for Abby. Did you get to talk to Web? Or Abby's aunt? Or did you want to?"

Enchantee stood near the refrigerator, shaking her head slightly, her gaze hard. "I didn't want to," Marcus said. He looked at Bent's gray eyes, behind glasses like his own. He couldn't explain this to Bent, couldn't trust him yet. He knew what his father would say. "I didn't feel so hot."

Abby was saying, "I wish I had a sorbet, after all that great spicy stuff, Chani, you know, to clear the palate."

Marcus slipped out the kitchen door without looking at anyone. Sorbet. Sherberts. Pastel, sweet, grainy-dissolved, instantly gone. He could taste the lime in his throat. To clear the palate for the next new taste. No mingling.

Alma had craved the watery blue. She'd painted and stood back to breathe the wet. She'd raked and trimmed and touched the sea-urchin purple window frames.

"She talk about the blue in here," Hosea had said, looking at the article.

Alma had read most of it. The woman mentioned a garish shade of paint visible for miles, a color historically inaccurate. And the forlorn photos—Alma knew them with her eyes shut. "She talk about she can see them old cars on your lot for miles," Alma said, her throat heated. "How they a eyesore."

Her hands, swimming among the canning jars in the sink now, were as numb as padded oven mitts dangling from her wrists. She had pruned the roses, scrubbed the floors, oiled all the heavy wooden furniture Archuleta had left them. She couldn't feel anything below her elbows. She could pick up a hot-handled pot with no towel.

But the woman with cotton-candy hair hadn't taken photos of the roses, or the gleaming carved furniture, or the Madonna amid her candles and dried flowers in the arched plaster hollow made just for her.

The house was immaculate. It was the men's things all over the property that had attracted the attention. Their cars and tools and cups and trash. That looked so bad in the pictures. No one could see how she kept her house in that article. After living in a station wagon, in the seas of mud and overflowed outhouses, how would she keep her house anything but perfect?

Demetrius and Octavious came into the kitchen now, their boots shedding dirt onto her floor. "Take your plate and go!" Alma shouted. "Look what you doin to my floor! Always bringin in a mess." When she looked up, she saw Sofelia peering out the window.

"Look like some white men here," she said, holding the sheer curtain aside. "City car, got a picture on the side."

"Go get your father," Alma said, feeling bitter seed tears under her lids. City code enforcement, probably. "They mad about all his junk."

"Here come Marcus, too," Sofelia said, and Alma stepped outside blindly, not looking at the city men or her husband. Abuela's hand was a tiny starfish on Marcus's sleeve, and Alma helped her into the car.

"She want to see the lake again," Alma told her son. "The one she ain't seen in so long." She refused to look back.

Paz kept her eyes carefully on the moving sky while Marcus tried to find a place where they could stand near the lake. She had never gotten used to cars; the only places she let someone drive her were the market and Salcido's place. When she felt the car stop, she let herself look at the water.

Standing at the muddy, licking edge, she saw that it was still silty-brown from the violence of the canyon, of all the small ravines and arroyos and canyons that emptied here, in the low valley. At the southern edge of the lake, a stream wound its way to the river; Paz remembered that when she'd first seen the lake, it was here for four years before the water had drained.

Espíritu. She had stood near here when her daughter was small, staring out at the water, remembering the ocean near Maneadoro, the olive trees and cliffs and shifting blue. This was the closest she had ever come. In Mexico, she'd been sweeping someone else's dirt, dirt that had clung to her legs and then rubbed off on his hands when he grabbed her. Here, the first time, she'd been watching her second grandchild wither and yellow and die.

Now she looked across the lake to her olive trees, a patch of faint silver like a dew-coated spiderweb in the field. The fairy shrimp would come soon to this place and to the pools scattered farther west; the angel moth would hover over her flowers at dusk. The barn owl was already peering from the rafters of the olive shed, her small-outlined face melancholy company. Not white with death, like the bobbing image in the window that night, but pale and watching.

The boy was gone from the hills. Maybe he was a ghost, Paz thought. Maybe he had only hovered near the fence while the water was gathering here, like a movable spirit.

"Show me his house," Alma said.

Marcus drove down the clattering dirt road from the lake, near the groves of the man Hosea had always called the Hungarian. The lake lapped at the edge of a housing tract, covered a golf course, and partially submerged a construction project to its floating, golden, plywood roof. Marcus skirted the water, driving down from the groves on the old road that was now four lanes. Up a sloping street where mud had washed in reddish veils along the asphalt, the earthen berms along the road had slumped like giant toes.

"That's his house," Marcus said, pointing to the peach-stuccoed mansion on the slope, behind the gated entrance.

Alma stared at the balconies and windows. "It's beautiful. Spanish."

"Mediterranean," Marcus said. "I think."

Paz had tilted her head to peer up at the house. She said, *"Dios, Dios les da el dinero a los ricos. Porque si no lo tuvieran, se morirían de hambre."* She rubbed her belly and sucked her teeth.

"God," Marcus said, frowning. "God gives money to the rich. Because . . ."

Paz pointed to her stomach, then cut her finger across her throat.

"Morir. Muerto. Mortrice," he whispered. Alma frowned at him. Then he smiled. "Because—"

"Without it, they'd starve to death," Alma said. "Ain't nobody starvin at my house. Nobody."

When they'd reached the riverbottom road again, Alma saw a planter made of black stones, small, round rocks with white stripes, near one house. She smiled. "Finis used to love them rocks," she murmured. "Always said he was gon go down to Salcido's and get enough to build him a skunk house."

"Skunk-eye rocks," Marcus said. "That's what he called them." He stared across the river. "Damn. I know where he is."

Marcus and Demetrius greeted Rubén Salcido at the gate. "I'm glad you came, cause, you know, I couldn't keep him much longer. Tony's a cop, man, and that was hard, to hide your brother. He's in the shack."

They walked past the piles of gravel, the mounds of river rock, the stacks of brick. Those round, black stones with the white ring—they'd been piled near the door of the old shack at the very edge of the yard near the fence, along the riverbottom. "Rubén said he brings food every day," Demetrius said. "Finis! Brothaman!"

His chest wasn't hollow or thin, Marcus thought, seeing him in the doorway. But his face was more gaunt than Bob Marley's, as if the constant dust had leached out the moisture.

"Come on, man, Mama got tamales and Oscar got chitlins," he said, taking Finis's arm gently. "You didn't have to run, man."

"Damn, brother, maybe Sofelia can do somethin with your hair," Demetrius said.

"Sofelia?" Finis whispered, his brows drawing together.

When he saw her in the kitchen, leaning against the stove, he put his arms around her, and Marcus saw her plum-dark eyes fill with tears. Then his mother came flying into the kitchen like a plump pigeon to hold him tight.

"You mess with his bones?" Mortrice's mother caught him in the yard, her fingers strong now, stronger than they'd ever been at Soul Gardens. Her forehead had a straight line like a needle between her eyes. "You was only supposed to be sleepin in his place."

"I ain't messed with nothin," he said, waiting until she'd relaxed her grip. "I'ma go get my stuff. My music and books."

"You gon sleep in the house again," she said.

"The other trailer empty, cause y'all won't let Kendrick in there." Mortrice tried to move away. The gats. He had to get the gats hidden.

But she shook her head. "Sleep in the house for now. Until the trouble over."

"Shit, this trouble ain't never gon be over," he said to himself, nearly running down the path to the trailer. "Until I get Sketch and them job."

Inside the murky light of the trailer, which always sat in shade and then darkened as fast as a cough when the sun fell, Mortrice looked at the bones. He had moved them when he'd tried to make bullets for the buffalo gun. The lead had come out of the forms perfectly—the damn casings, man, he needed the gunsmith to make those. If he was going to take someone out when this job came down, he wanted to use the buffalo gun, and it wouldn't be ready. The *cinco*-six would be the right one, for the land. His mother's place. Cause the *cinco*-six wouldn't leave nothin behind.

Squatting on the narrow channel of floor, he pulled out the duffel bag with his guns and books and kits. He didn't want to go back to Olive Gardens, where Chris and Teddy were always hollering, where too many eyes were watching. He wanted to stay here and think, try to figure out how to do the job.

He saw the silver drops of lead on the table where the bones had been, and he pulled at the thin, white splinters jammed in a heap near the window, trying to arrange the hand. His own fingers shook. The skull-faced guy with wild braids who'd come to the door—this was his place. His uncle. Shit. He wanted this place. The finger bones spun, and Mortrice ran down the two metal steps, stopping near the other trailer.

He knelt near the back wheel and dug out a pile of eucalyptus bark and tiny red flowers that were falling even now, in the wind. Laying the duffel bag behind the flattened tire, he pushed leaves and bark back over it until it was only a heaped drift in the earth.

"I'ma take him out," Oscar said, sharpening his chitlin knife with a whetstone. "I know his car. Chevy Blazer. I'ma go to that damn tower and shoot him."

Hosea sat in the barn doorway, watching Demetrius work on another carburetor. Marcus squatted in the sunlit yard. "Maybe I could find out more about the deal," he said slowly. "Shit, I don't know what to do with what I already found out." Hosea waited for Demetrius to spit out something smart about his brother, but Demetrius only probed the metal.

"I say take his ass out," Demetrius murmured then.

Hosea felt the piece of paper folded into his work-shirt pocket. He hadn't shown it to anyone since Alma had handed it to him—not Oscar or Demetrius or Marcus. He said softly, "What Marcus done heard, Matheson give it to the government now. Killin him ain't gon stop it."

Oscar took a drink from his jar. "Once the government get it, like a goddamn pit bull. Gotta kill it to open that jaw." He put the empty jar near his feet. "The man scare the shit outta Lila last time he come. I don't know what he said, but he ain't sent no government. She couldn't hardly talk when I got back." Oscar rubbed his blade. "Maybe he mention them pigs. Somebody done seen em from the freeway. But they cleanin up—Lanier pigs eat paper, McDonald's, everything but cans."

Hosea saw Mortrice standing at the edge of the barn. "Why you listenin to old folks talk?" he said. "What you want?"

"Nothin," Mortrice said, raising his chin toward Marcus before he left.

"I don't see him now that I'm not at school," Marcus said, drawing in the dirt. "Seems like a long time since I had that class. I think those two kids got shot, they killed Pammy Sawicky and her friend. And Bessier. But the other one—Samana—I don't know where he is." He looked up at Hosea. "So if that was intended to get us out, and it didn't work . . ."

Hosea waited. Us. Then he said, "You takin me to lunch. Your mama been mad at me, about my junk." He thought about his son Finis, hiding in the shack. "I want to see Matheson for myself."

What was his father planning? Marcus rolled down the drive. They walked the walk, talked the talk, no extra words—his father and uncle and brothers never let a swirl of extra words and definitions rise inside their foreheads to hide the physical layout of the fight or the car or the danger. But him, he loved the vocabulary and construction of the sentences, loved talking to Kurt or the students or Brother Lobo. Because underneath, if he were challenged, words were his only escape. His father wanted to kill Matheson. But there had to be a way out with conversation. The right words.

He loved talking to SaRonn. She and Willa got into the VW, and Willa turned to her mother and said, "Bumpdragon!"

SaRonn pulled in her lips to hide her smile. "She know your car now."

"That's a good thing, right?" Marcus said easily. He wanted to try the blue-corn tortillas again. "You think she's gon like my place?"

SaRonn had a grave look on her face. "Do you have any milk?" To his puzzled frown, she added, "In case we both spend the night."

"Damn, I'll take care of that now, if you gon offer me that kinda possibility," Marcus said, pulling into the minimall. Som's window was dark. Inside the liquor store, the Korean man behind the counter was arguing with a guy who looked like a Kozy Komfort resident. Except that Marcus saw only faint black outlines of nothing across the street now.

"You give me ten! Not twenty!" the cashier said.

"Man, I given you a damn twenty, and you given me two a these!" The brother held up two bag-wrapped forty-ounce bottles. "You better give me my change, motherfucka!"

"Look! Ten!" The cashier held up a ten he'd taken from the shelf of the register.

"No-win situation," SaRonn murmured in the back, reaching for a small carton of milk. "Who knows who's tellin tales?"

"I don't want to know right now," Marcus said. They put the carton on the counter, and the cashier turned toward them. Marcus saw the brother heading out the door; he couldn't tell who had won, or lost.

"Eighty-two!" the man said loudly. When Marcus reached into his pocket, a woman came from the back of the small store, shouting, "What she get? What she get? Look!"

She was pointing at Willa, who held something tightly in her fist and came up behind SaRonn's leg to clutch her mother's skirt. Marcus said, "If she got some candy, I'll cover it, okay?"

"No! Not candy. She get something shine!" the woman said. "Jewelry!" She pointed toward the display of cheap jewelry and hair accessories nearby.

SaRonn knelt and said, "Willa, what you got, baby girl? Somethin good?"

Willa opened her hand like a tiny flower; she held a washer with faceted edges. "My ring," she murmured.

SaRonn stood up, her cheeks hollow with her pulled-in breath. "She found it in your car, Marcus." She took Willa's hand and walked out.

"I sorry for that," the man said, his voice hard. "We come here from L.A., have so many people steal every day."

"She look like a hardened criminal?" Marcus said, putting the change on the counter. "I look like a wino?"

In his kitchen, Marcus said, "Why bother wearin J. Crew and I still look like—"

But SaRonn surprised him with the softness of her voice. "You know, I used to hate it in L.A., too. The Koreans always arguing with the brothers. And when I got back here, the Super Save store was just as bad. I tried to think about all the nice store owners I knew in L.A., tried thinkin they were into a Middle Eastern bazaar type thing, you know, only respect the customer if he haggles for bargains. But then I saw those Super Save guys pull a Taser on somebody, and I saw the video of Latasha Harlins gettin shot."

Marcus nodded. Watching TV was painful, seeing that footage and the King video over and over.

"I don't know," she said, propping her chin on her fingers. "You can't go from store owner to sheriff. I guess I worry about it cause that's what I want to do, Marcus. I want to open a store, maybe in that minimall, or downtown here if I could afford the overhead."

"What kind of store?" Marcus gave Willa another tortilla.

"A boutique, with Indian incense and spices and jewelry, and African prints, and Mexican furniture, who knows what else." She smiled. "You think I'm crazy. But I've been sellin some jewelry, savin my money, gettin Bennie and Malinda to pay rent, and if I could pull this off, Willa could hang out in the store with me. I can't go off to work somewhere and let somebody else watch her. I'd miss her too much."

"I don't think you're crazy," Marcus said, looking at the golden slivers radiating from her pupils, at the deep curve over her lip. "You seen Finis?"

SaRonn shook her head. "You seen Chaka?" He laughed. "But I hope he comes by to watch videos with Willa."

After Willa had touched all the figurines one more time, after she'd jumped on the bed, she went to sleep there on his pillow. On the couch, the door shut and candles lit, SaRonn lay on top of him with her face buried in his shoulder. Then she whispered, "You gotta be careful, cause I don't want to have a baby with you."

"What?" Marcus said, his fingers in her hair.

"Cause I want to have a baby with you. Cause you'd probably give me a nice boy. Grow up to be a nice man like you. And I can't do that yet."

Marcus ran his hands over her back. "I can't either," he said. "Cause I ain't sure I'm a nice man. Got Thompson genes, remember? The Jungle Brothers? Nice wasn't what people called us."

She was silent for a long while, kissing him, touching his chest, and then she said, "Back then, when I was small, I wanted to know what

it was like to sleep with a boy. Sleep with him. I was lonely. I used to
sleep like this." She curled on her side, lifting her own shoulder so that
her cheek was pressed against the soft part. "So I would feel like
somebody was with me," she said, closing her eyes.

Someone knocked on his door just as Willa was waking up, calling,
"Mama?" He and SaRonn lay on the floor in blankets, and she scrambled
up to the bedroom while Marcus pulled on his jeans and threw the
blankets onto the couch.

Mortrice nodded in the doorway. "I need to ax you somethin from
your pops," he said.

He and B-Real stood in the living room, looking at the books. "We
goin to class like good students," B-Real said. "But Whalen's class is
past deadly, brothaman, it's like—rigor mortis."

Marcus saw Mortrice look at B-Real hard, strange, and then Mortrice
said, "Uh, Grampa say he need to borrow a jacket. For the restaurant.
Say you know what he mean."

"A jacket?" Marcus shook his head. "I guess he's right. He can't get
away with the ripped jeans and Dickies look at his age."

In the bedroom, SaRonn was dressed, and Willa was leaping, naked,
on the bed again. "I had to wash her up," SaRonn said, "and she loves
to air dry."

"My nephew and his friend are out there," Marcus said. "Just so you
know."

She lifted her chin. "You embarrassed to have me here?"

Marcus stopped moving jackets. "Embarrassed? Hell, no. Proud,
baby." When they went into the living room, SaRonn stared at Mortrice,
frowning.

Mortrice was reading the articles on the coffee table. "Who this
dude?" he asked, and Marcus bent over to see.

"Trevor Roberts," he said. "His son was Josh. Roberts sold my mom
a vacuum cleaner once." He dropped the picture. "I don't know what
he sells now, but he had it in his blood."

Mortrice nodded. "Who this dude with the big forehead?"

"Web Matheson," Marcus said. SaRonn was giving Willa cereal in
the kitchen. "Big-time developer running for office. He's the one wants
to buy Daddy's place, and Uncle Oscar's."

"What for?" B-Real said.

"I guess to build a bridge over it," Marcus said, rubbing his eyes. "I don't know. Matter of fact, Matheson sold my mom the vacuum cleaner, too." He laughed. "Big buddies. Except one's sellin the most expensive thing in California, and I never heard of the other one again."

"Yo, we gotta go, man," B-Real said. "One World, Mr. Thompson."

"Later," Mortrice said, taking the jacket.

SaRonn glanced out the window, and through the archway she must have seen B-Real's Jamaican-painted van pull away. "That boy was the one with Zefi Perry's boy," she said. "Your nephew."

Marcus, who was trying to make toast, didn't pay much attention. "Yeah?"

She came into the kitchen then and smiled wide. "That was what I was going to call the store," she said. "One World."

Hosea remembered the blow to his ear, the bitter crystalline air needling into the canal, the walking along ditch banks so that pale eyes behind windshields wouldn't gleam with the thought of him thumping off a fender—that satisfying thud they so loved, the solid connection of metal to bone however they could hear it—car to hip, pipe to skull, bullet to backbone.

Oscar could shoot this man, the one ten feet away. He'd killed the white man who'd left blood stripes across Lila's face. Oscar could shoot a man stepping over his fence line. Hosea glanced at the nails on the cellular phone, remembering the slew of bullets on the porch. Maceo's body. The sweet, floating fire. He'd taught his sons to fight so hard no one would try. He'd taught them to shoot possums.

The man who wanted his land, speaking to people on the phone, the voice spiraling through those wires as tight-curled as a pig's tail, couldn't shoot a horse, a pig, a rabbit, a quail. Couldn't remove skin or feathers or coarse hair and silken-blue inner walls to find meat. He couldn't shoot a man, or he would have shot Hosea already. And this wouldn't be done, this shooting, because now when a man wanted your land, he couldn't just hide in your pecan grove and shoot you, or walk into your shotgun shack near Greenwood and shoot you and throw your still-moving body back into the flames. He couldn't do those things knowing that your children or grandchildren or whoever you claimed as your blood would see the killing and learn and leave. Not in 1992. Not when you had five sons, three who loved to fight, who loved the barn and rocks and hubcaps and cars.

One who wandered like a ghost, a ghost who might see but never learn.

One who might not have loved a damn stone on the place, who never seemed to give a damn about the land or cars, but who hadn't given up on this yet. He sat down across from Hosea and they were the same size, thin-legged, chests tapered hard. Not swollen broad like the other sons. The blazer Marcus had lent him was the color of pine needles. "We wear the same size, huh?" Marcus said, grinning. "What you want to eat?"

Hosea shrugged, trying not to stare at the men two tables over. Matheson. Brown hair combed back as sharp as porcupine quills, mouth as thin-edged and square as a mail slot. Another man so fat, he had a second face behind his first one. Two silver-haired, seal-suited men with their backs to Hosea.

"Olive tamales for my dad," Marcus told the girl who came. "And carnitas."

Hosea sipped the lemony water and heard Matheson saying, "So let me get this right—this fairy shrimp is about an inch long. Nobody can eat it except a damn duck or bird, and we have to protect it."

"The sand moth is even more laughable," the fat man said.

"Yeah, what, nobody's ever seen this moth eat, nobody knows exactly where in the habitat it lives, and I can't use two hundred damn acres now? Not until they figure out what stick it sleeps on?"

Hosea was silent until the food came. "I don't know how this is gon help you," Marcus murmured over the steaming bowl of meat.

"I ain't said it would help." Hosea looked at the carnitas. "Salcido comin over soon with that goat meat."

"Kurt does okay," Marcus said. "How you like your tamales?"

Hosea put down the fork. "I rather eat your mama's food or Oscar's." He pulled the letter from his pocket and slid it across the table. He'd memorized the typing. Dated March 25. Requesting that Alma Thompson attend a hearing in one month at the city council chambers to consider acquiring her property through eminent domain. Rio Seco Redevelopment Agency.

"This is what he and the historian were talkin about," Marcus said softly. "Why you didn't tell me before?"

Hosea took back the letter and slid it inside his pocket. "What was you gon do till the day come? Talk? Now you gon go speak for her. You talk to them kinda people all the time."

Marcus shook his head. "I talk to kids. Customers," he whispered harshly, leaning forward. "Talk about what? Eminent domain means the city wants it, the city takes it."

"For him?" Hosea nodded toward the table of men.

"Hell, I don't know." Marcus sat back.

Hosea swallowed the taste of the too slick sauce pooled around the tamale. "Listen. I walk around the place, I look at the letter, I think about them people got killed. Oscar just as well go on up and shoot the man." His voice felt rough from the strange food and too many night walks. "I'm gon go in there and you gon talk. After that, whatever happen, I do what I have to." He stood, his head swaying with the fluorescent lights and refrigerated air, and walked outside, not looking at the upturned faces like swiveling lamps.

Alma didn't stare at the swelling fruit every day. She only walked among the fallen petals, brushing a few off her head. In a few weeks, she'd glance up at the oval nubs, as small and sharp as baby fingernails. Then she'd move her eyes slowly over the thumb-plump green fruit she had now. Each apricot was hers, to eat right off the tree with grandkids, to halve and preserve with Abuela, to spread on a biscuit for Hosea.

Everything was his, too. She couldn't touch a hubcap. Last night, she'd sat outside the coldhouse with him, back to cool stones. "I'm sorry I fuss about your cars and your junk," she'd whispered. "All that time, I didn't never think we'd grow no cars."

Summer was coming already—living through the heat and smog and dry again, waiting for night to turn ashen purple, like now. But you could survive that. You couldn't survive winter, those freezes when she was a girl, the ice that coated lemons and avocados and took not only the workers' fruit but their pay while the warped wood shacks let the air inside.

That was when Hosea had told her he would have his own land, with his jaw set so tight she knew the ache that jolted cold over his

back teeth, and wanting like she felt for her babies. And he'd told her
he'd plant so many different crops that one disaster of weather couldn't
ruin them. A freeze would hurt citrus, but not the apricots or nectarines.
A drought wouldn't bother the olives or figs.

But he ended up with the cars, too, his fingers coated with oil and
callused by metal, the worn dollars edged in black. And when she
thought of all the plants she'd tied and staked and hoed and then
harvested, her fingertips scarlet with blood or strawberry juice, her shins
aching and contracted from her thirst, her head swollen with heat, she
walked among her roses.

Now she lay in the bathtub, trying to breathe the morning light,
remembering when they'd had so little running water that the boys
were happy to take dunk-splash baths outside all summer and Alma
would be the only one in the tub, in the hot water. Back when the
soreness could be drawn from her muscles and bones by hot water, the
aching beaded up on her shoulder blades, down her spine, like moisture
gathering on the veins of broad leaves to swell and finally drop.

Now her skin was dimpled and soft, holding the pain inside her
hidden bones. She dried herself and put on her best dress, the black
church-going dress with tiny white flowers. She'd last worn it to Ocie
Mae's funeral, the last time she'd gone under the freeway, up that road
lined with beckoning ditches.

"You comin?" Hosea saw her in the doorway, her hair tightly rolled,
the soft skin at her temples as thin as tissue.

"My name on that paper," she said. "I want to—I want to see what
y'all do."

He drove slowly up Pepper so she wouldn't be frightened. He didn't
know what the hell he'd do, and he didn't want her watching him feel
helpless. Just like the hospital, when he could barely turn his mouth for
water, and that was part of this. This plan. This shit. When he parked
below Marcus's apartment, she said, "I ain't never seen his place. Too
far."

"Just seem far," Hosea said when Marcus came through the archway.
"Downtown."

"Mama?" Marcus said, sliding into the back. "You comin, too?"

The modern building had turquoise windows and beige walls. The amphitheater was half-filled, facing the ring of men behind a wooden horseshoe, nameplates and microphones at their wrists. A small blond woman spoke into a microphone at the podium. "This Wal-Mart would bring an incredible amount of traffic and noise into our neighborhood," she said. "I have a signed petition from . . ."

Alma sat in the fold-down chair, but Hosea couldn't breathe. He walked to the back, hearing a councilman say, "It's unfortunate that people are unhappy to see new enterprise coming to the area, but . . ."

"Tell her to shut up, cause we want a Wal-Mart," someone called from the audience, and a stern voice said, "You're out of order there."

He went outside. He could hear the amplified voices when the swinging doors opened and closed. The words flew out in bursts. "Micromanaging. Sure, it's doable, Mr. Pérez, but . . . The traffic commission meeting . . ." Hosea's stomach rolled like spoiled meat was inside. He went inside the door marked MEN. The bathroom's tiled walls echoed with the voices, climbing the squares, falling. He leaned over the sink and drank some water, hearing one woman's voice now rising, now falling, going on as long as a speech. Oscar said people went to clubs to learn how to talk like that, to keep people entertained. Toastmaster, Oscar had said. Hosea's mind spun when he stared into the gleaming sink. He closed his eyes and pictured The Blue Q, where people were drunk and flirting and tired. And if you could tell a story like Oscar could, and mouths left beer-bottle rims to laugh, you were a hell of a speaker. Like Oscar. Not like me.

The door opened and voices rose thicker in the air. "Daddy," Marcus said. "Come on. Only one more item before you. Us."

A suited young man was at the podium. "I know Councilman Sawicky has been highly critical of the U.S. Fish and Wildlife Service, but this area is the heartland for several rare and endangered species, and the current rate of development is devastating. For example, the fairy shrimp lives only in vernal pools, and not a single pool is left in Los Angeles or Orange counties."

Sawicky asked, "And we have them, right?" He looked at his notes.

"They're at a real risk, and we've had a severe drought for seven years, so some of them are just making a resurgence."

Sawicky said, "I love this—we lose tax dollars, piss off landowners, and prevent new development for—let's see, a few birds, and now a

moth. And a fairy." Ripples of laughter rose from the crowd. "Mr.
Olafson?"

"I'm with Matheson and Associates," another man said. "I'd just like
to say that we oppose spending tax dollars for county and city surveys
on these, species, that then harm us businesswise. Right now, we've
got one large housing project blocked, and one postponed. As you
know, Mr. Matheson is running for Congress in June, and he'd like it
known that he opposes the frivolous use of taxpayer money like this.
He had another meeting this morning and couldn't attend."

"Look, we don't have a vote on this, right?" a younger councilman
said impatiently, looking at his watch. "We need to move on, okay?"

The city clerk read off the words. Eminent domain. Alma Thompson.
Hosea saw the official who'd stood in the barn. Redevelopment.

"Well, the redevelopment agency is asking the council to acquire
the property at 2498 Pepper Avenue through eminent domain, as both
our developer, the previously mentioned Mr. Matheson, and city officials
have been unable to come to terms with Mrs. Thompson on the purchase
of her land. This property falls inside the boundaries of the proposed
historic gateway corridor project, which we just passed approval on last
week, if you recall. The project includes an off-ramp and on-ramp to
the forty-two freeway, widening of the existing street, and construction
of a bridge to replace the old Pepper Avenue bridge."

"Is the property owner present?" asked the younger councilman.

Marcus pulled Alma from her seat and walked with her to the podium
while she held herself stiff. "Yes, sir."

"You are?" said the councilman. "State your name and address, please."

"Alma Thompson, 2498 Pepper Avenue," she whispered into the
microphone. The city official stood off to the side, holding his papers.
Hosea gripped the armrest of the chair.

"You have negotiated with the developer, Mrs. Thompson?" the
younger councilman said, frowning. "Because I, for one, am opposed
to using eminent domain in a situation like this." He looked at the
other men around him. "I mean, from this map, the area to the west
of the existing street is largely empty, right? Why take the property east
if you don't have to?"

The older councilman beside him smiled. "From what I understand,
Mr. Sutter, the property in question is neglected, it's the site of recent
criminal activity, including homicides, and the city has offered slightly

above market value for it. Mrs. Thompson, you did speak with Mr. Matheson and with the gentleman to the side of you, correct?"

"I don't want to sell my place," Alma said, her voice as dull as a mourning dove through the speakers. Hosea stood up and walked down the aisle, where a man put out his arm into the space before him. "Wait," the man said. Marcus was gripping the microphone now.

"Marcus Thompson. 1563 Las Palmas. I know that my mother and another property owner never received notice in the mail of this proposed project, and it obviously affects them."

The city clerk stood and said, "Notices were mailed out in December."

The older councilman smiled and said, "Do you know what I recall about that date? This property is in Treetown, correct? If I recall correctly, wasn't that the month when there was so much shooting going on down there that the post office stopped delivering?"

Marcus said, "Look, my aunt also owns land, right next to my mother, and she hasn't received this notice about condemnation. Maybe the city council should look into why somebody really wants my mother's land."

The men behind the horseshoe frowned, and one said, "I don't understand your meaning, young man."

Hosea strode past the outstretched hand. "Hosea Thompson. Same number. That's my wife's land. It ain't neglected." Then his head roared with words and the glinting of their glasses and watches and the spotlights over them. "You gotta know the land." He heard nothing behind him but a hundred mouths stealing air. "What the city gon do with it? I got olives up on that hill. She got olives." He looked desperately out the smoky windows to the trees in the plaza. "If you was roamin around starvin, would you eat them olives outside?"

"Excuse me?" one man.

"Them black olives hangin on them trees right now," he said, sucking at his molars, shaking his head. "Already black."

"There should only be one person behind the podium, please," someone said, and Hosea stepped away to the wall.

The councilman behind number 5 said, "This isn't a racial issue, and I'm not sure why the gentleman is trying to portray it as such. This has to do with upkeep of property, with code enforcement and neglect, and with the city's desire to . . ."

The younger councilman was frowning at his notes. "Mrs. Thompson," he interrupted. She stood there alone. Hosea saw her wide-tipped fingers pale on the podium's edge. "Do you have an attorney or an appraisal of your property?"

"No."

"Why don't you get those and meet with the developer again. If the price hasn't been fair, I think those two things might help. Let's postpone the vote on this for three weeks, okay?"

"Second."

"All those in favor?" Suddenly four green buttons and two red ones lit up over their heads, and someone said, "The next item on the agenda concerns . . ."

"You did what you could, Daddy." Marcus sat at the kitchen table. "Let me try to get a lawyer downtown to look into this."

But Hosea went outside. Oscar was there, and Lanier, and Roscoe Wiley with a part for his big truck. Darnell Tucker came to take Wiley home, and Kickstand grumbled at him about his Toyota. "Man, grouchy as you are, how you get a nickname like you got?" Darnell said.

"He give it to me," Kickstand said, nodding toward Hosea. "Man, I come up from Texas, I was hangin around forever lookin for work, and the man said, 'Hell, Kickstand, I give you a job cause look like you holdin up the whole damn barn by yourself.'"

"I know they want them pigs outta there," Lanier said suddenly. Oscar had been silent, his wrists hanging loose on his knees. Hosea stared at the Miller cans lined on the stone wall.

"They want the whole thing," he said finally. "The whole damn thing."

"You know what people said," Lanier went on. "In the South, they don't care how close a nigger get, long as he ain't too big. In the North, they don't care how big he get, long as he ain't too close."

"How the hell that work out here?" Oscar said.

"Work like the Wild Wild West," Hosea said. "I'ma have to shoot."

"It ain't got nothin to do with shootin," Marcus said from near his car. "Has to do with paperwork and lawyers."

Hosea stood and bent over the ten-foot length of old irrigation pipe. "Lift me up that end," he told Oscar. "Paperwork," Marcus was saying. "They can't just grab what they want, man."

Hosea worked the old pipe cutter onto the iron, jerking it hard. The Indian guy from the riverbottom used to sharpen it. Now Oscar did. The blade sliced clean silver gashes into the dull rust. Like the engraved letters on his father's shell. He took it out nearly every night, wondering what tool the Frenchman had used during the war. ALL MY LOVE.

"They gon let them cops off," someone said, pointing to the TV.

"Naw, man, that shit is on *tape*," Darnell said.

"Hell, yeah," Kickstand said. "Tired a seein that trial every five minutes."

Marcus said, "They say the jury's seen it so many times, they don't even take it seriously now."

Hosea glanced at the screen, at the blurry boots and elbows and faces. After the riot, the newspaper had blamed it all on the men like his father, the dead bodies. What did it matter if this picture flashed over and over, slow enough to see the angle of the elbows hanging for a moment to gain swing power before chopping at the head with the baton? He'd heard the voices from the TV. Hit any home runs? Power swing. What did it matter if the faces turned to the camera and said, Hell, yeah, we're beating this nigger because he didn't do what we told him to. He had a knife. He probably had a gun. He didn't do it, what we said. And there are ten, twenty, a hundred of us in a circle, and we're right as right can get because we're standing here hard on this patch of ground in our shoes. All our shoes.

Alma always washed the white clothes on Tuesdays. She came to him in the coldhouse, holding out her hand for the T-shirt he'd worn that afternoon. "I'm gettin to it late," she said. "I'm so tired, Hosea." The lines between her eyebrows radiated into her forehead like sun rays.

"I'm tired, too," he said. "So tired I can't think."

When he went out in the dark, he saw the sheets and shirts hung on the line behind the coldhouse, and he felt a tremor. His mother's white wash, dancing ghostly between the trees. He went closer, seeing his T-shirt laid out on a stone, putting his finger to the lemon juice and salt paste she'd rubbed into the tiny rusted smiles marking the cloth.

He heard the shouts, the burst of gunfire on the porch, felt Oscar's baby foot in his back. I ain't sleepin till he come, he thought. Whoever comin next. If it's Matheson come to the house or someone else sneak round the back fence, I'ma kill him. I lived a long time. I done done what I had to. But the place . . . I leave it for the rest of em.

He didn't walk to the storage lot, like usual, but stood at the front gate watching the moon rise. From where he stood under the tallest palms, he could see their fronds shifting wild, the frayed tips glowing silver as if electricity had lit the fringes.

Bats slanted in the currents with plinking cries. Cirrus clouds moved across the moon, thin and stretched like silt wafting downstream, and he thought of how he'd looked for rain the last seven years. When he'd first come here, all the signs his grandfather had taught him—the halo around the moon, the arrangements of the stars, the thickness of bark— hadn't worked. Hosea had missed the thunderstorms, the lightning in great veins, the Oklahoma sky. He'd touched the eucalyptus trunks with disdain, the bark wrinkled like skin at the joints, splitting to reveal pink, pearly stuff like tissue. Not home, he thought. But now, home. He stared at the sky. Maybe the sixty years that had passed meant something, too. Maybe the stars had shifted imperceptibly, and no one could read the sky.

CHAPTER NINETEEN

MORTRICE WAS AT his door after school. Marcus let him in, saying, "Ain't you kinda hot in all that, man?" Mortrice wore a huge Patagonia jacket, unlaced hiking boots, and jeans bagging like elephant legs. "Hikin boots?"

"It's new school. And them boola-pocket kids wear this for skiin."

"We old school over here," Marcus said. "Remember what you guys called me in class? The eight-track brotha." Marcus looked at the jacket. Yeah, Treetown kids never saw the average white guy wearing Dockers. They saw TV and GQ. Moola-boola. Go straight for upscale leisure wear. He smiled. "Just don't let the baggy pants get mixed up with the ones I used to see—the guys who didn't have belts when they did time, and they came out in ass-draggin jeans cause they were tryin to tell us somethin."

"That's for gangsta rappers," Mortrice said. "I ain't a rapper."

"Speakin of rappers, how's B-Real? How come you didn't ride with him?"

Mortrice shrugged. "He's trippin. He ain't down." He picked up the article about the fairy shrimp and sand moths that Marcus had cut out. "You gon send all these papers to the lawyer?"

"How do you know what's goin on?"

He shrugged again. "I ain't deaf. This dude Matheson want to buy Grampa place. He work up there in them blue towers, right?" Mortrice pointed to the fairy shrimp. "Science class talked about this today. Fairy shrimp. Sandy somethin moth. Whatever." He stood up. "You gon give me a ride?"

"I'm walkin to the gym," Marcus said, pulling on his sweats. "I like to walk in Funkytown."

Mortrice followed him out the doorway. They walked in silence for a minute, and then Mortrice said, "You see how people check out the jacket?"

"Yeah," Marcus said. "That why you wear it?"

"I wear it cause I want to," Mortrice said. After another block, he said, "See, you ain't a bad nigga. You invisible. Don't nobody see you, man. I see them check you out—just bip, bap, move they eyes—they sayin he ain't no problem for me. And then *bam*. You gone. You *think* you walkin round Funkytown, but you ain't."

"You hella talkative today," Marcus said. "So I ain't here?"

"You here for yourself. For your friends. Just like me." Mortrice turned down the street.

"And you a bad nigga, so you stand out?" Marcus called softly.

"Uh-uh. Don't nobody see me neither. They try not to look."

Marcus was on the StairMaster thinking about what Mortrice had said when Bent came in. "Hey," Marcus said. "You want to cruise by my uncle's? Should be quieter this time." Bent grinned. Marcus didn't mind taking him to The Blue Q, pay him back for something he didn't have to know about; Bent wasn't part of the trouble. Uncle Oscar would probably say a few funny, bluesy things. SaRonn had told him she was going to L.A. with Bennie, to the beauty shop.

But when they pulled into the parking lot, Rock was raking trash from the dirt. "Your uncle gone to French Oaks with Mr. Lanier, lookin at a place for them pigs. They ain't comin back till late."

"We can just cruise in general," Bent said.

They drove down Grove, along the riverbottom. Samana had told Marcus that the foliage looked like Cambodia; Marcus saw a homeless man with a military duffle trudge into the cane, and he thought, That would be too dangerous, to be a vet and run into a kid like Samana sleepin in the bamboo. Wherever he sleeps.

"Let's stop at that little store," Bent said. "Abby loved that tamarind."

Shawnette was behind the counter. Marcus said, "You still starin at B-Real?" But instead of grinning, she shot Bent a look of pure hatred and slammed down his change.

"I got something on my face?" Bent asked in the car, and Marcus shrugged. They cruised slowly up Olive Avenue, near the Gardens. Bent peered out his side at the parking lot, where people were milling around. "I wish we could talk to some young rappers," he said. "Are those firecrackers right there?"

Marcus slowed, bending his head to see small flames. Flowers, a photo. "No, that's a memorial. For somebody who got killed." Starchild, he thought, wondering if Finis knew yet.

"Sounds like somebody's calling you," Bent said. Marcus stopped the car.

"Fuck you, white boy, take your ass outta here," someone shouted, and someone else threw a rock at his car. It landed in the dirt, raising a thread of dust.

"What the hell?" Marcus pulled away, looking in the rearview. "Somebody drivin a blue Bug musta messed up big-time over here." He saw two brothers walking down Olive; from the long, loping step of the tall one, he knew it was Stridin Mojo. Mojo came up hard on the car, leaning on the hood. Marcus looked out the window and said, "Hey, man, what up?"

"Sissy?" Mojo squinted at the car. "How long you had a Bug?"

"A while, brothaman, you just ain't seen me," Marcus said easily, but both men were staring mad-dog at Bent. "This is my partner Bent, man."

"I don't care if he fuckin Casper the Friendly Ghost, man, you better take his ass on outta here," Mojo said, and Bent's lips went thin.

"What's goin on?" Marcus said, feeling the familiar dread finger across his back.

"You ain't heard about the verdict? They walked, man. All four." Mojo's voice rasped sharply at Bent. "This ain't no time for sight-seein. You ain't no anthropologist, and this ain't no damn *Gorillas in the Mist,* all right?"

Near the restaurant, Bent finally said, "Mojo?" in a shaky voice. "Like the mojo hand in the blues?"

Marcus's neck tingled, and he blinked hard. "No." Stridin Mojo had money, but he wouldn't buy a car; he said his head didn't work unless he gave Moe and Joe their time on the road.

"No," Marcus said again. "His feet." He leaned his whole body over the wheel. "They fuckin walked. All four. Goddamnit."

"I'm sorry, man, I'm sorry it's so fucked up," Bent said, following him into Chile. "It's wrong. Way beyond wrong."

The bar TV was on. A minister's broad, brown face and upraised arms. A crowd throwing rocks and bottles. A line of courtroom faces crumpling in relief when the verdicts were read. Clenched fists raised at traffic.

Marcus threw back his head and stared at the rough-plastered ceiling. A dog. A fuckin dog's worth more than me. You get six months for cruelty to animals. Beat my ass and you won't do a weekend.

He heard Bent's friend Kolavic shouting suddenly. "Look at this guy! He's innocently driving through the fucking intersection and these thugs are trying to kill him! This is savage shit, now!"

"It's all savage shit!" Bent said. "None of it's right!"

"Oh, but this is justified revenge, right? His ancestors had slaves, so he gets it now? Bullshit."

Marcus held his hands on the counter to keep from hitting Kolavic in the mouth.

"Come on, Marcus," Bent said, taking his arm cautiously.

"Add up the fuckin ashes, man, you don't even have the bodies!" He leaned on the bar, hearing his father's words.

Kolavic walked away. Marcus thought tears would slide down to embarrass him, but the heat stayed swimming behind his eyes, and when he looked up at the TV and saw the blows, he swallowed his own blood where he'd bitten his lip. He went out to his car. He'd drive to his father's place, to the yard where at least they could holler and shout some of the blood away, let it fall into the gravel.

Mortrice saw B-Real stalking toward the parking lot, and he said, "What you flamin about, man? I seen you yangin with your redhead Rasta friend."

B-Real spun to face him near the VW van. "Yeah—the asshole said Rodney King shoulda just pulled over early on. Said maybe the cops thought he had jacked somebody." B-Real's pale forehead was a glowing, dark red, and Mortrice saw his little goatee shaking. "Fool pointed at my Malcolm hat and said somethin about cops don't like how young guys are all revolutionary now." B-Real started shouting. "Shit! I tried to tell him yeah, white people get jacked for they dollars sometimes!

Black people get jacked just as much! But goddamn, we don't take the X and turn it into a cross and burn it on your damn grass in front of your fuckin house! We don't paint 'Caspers Go Back to England' on the fuckin garage door! Sometimes fools jack you! It's money! Dollar signs! Somebody just want your car, they ain't gon stand in a fuckin circle and stomp your ass and then some damn jury says, 'Cool, I guess that white boy was obviously on PCP and extremely dangerous while he was eatin asphalt.'"

"Shit, man, what you hollerin about?" Mortrice frowned.

"You ain't heard yet?" B-Real opened the van door. "You ain't seen it?"

In the darkened apartment, Chris and Teddy lay on the floor watching the TV. Mortrice saw the people gathering on corners, moving like ants when the helicopter swung away. Cops cruised past and parked in store lots.

Chris mumbled, "They fucked that dude up, and it ain't about shit."

Teddy snorted. "Big surprise, nigga. Like ain't nobody knew?"

B-Real sat in the corner, his knees drawn up. Mortrice saw him wipe at his cheeks. "You sweatin, man?" he said, hard, to B-Real.

The razor lines of light around the plywood went from gold to red, and the first flames ate up the TV screen. Mortrice heard B-Real's ragged breath. The helicopter circled outside; Mortrice thought it would be like seeing through a fly's eyes, all the fools looking a lot smaller from up there, no matter who they were. The hogicopter over Olive Gardens; the TV copter following toy cars and tiny plastic people.

The camera zoomed to a pawnshop, where brothers had shattered windows and were loading stuff into car trunks. Mortrice leaned forward. A dark green Monte Carlo, gun barrels dropping like blackened matchsticks into the trunk. Two men looked up and gave the copter the finger; another man paused in the doorway, suddenly pointing a rifle at the copter. "I can't believe this!" the reporter's voice said. "This is turning into a war zone!"

Mortrice stared at Kenneth, still laughing and swinging the AK-47 around, then lifting his chin for his boys.

"You see that shit!" Chris said, sitting up. "All them gats? AKs and everything! Man, we need to go get some a that! Come on—expedition to L.A.!"

"B-Real, check out all the Mexicans goin in that store." Teddy laughed. "One World, man, everybody gettin TVs and diapers for free!"

Mortrice didn't see the screen now. Kenneth's broad, freckled face. His streets. His territory. His blood. Mortrice's blood speckling the sidewalk there, right there where people were running now. His back itched fiercely. You in the country now. Who your peoples? He your peoples? Your cousins? Your blood? Paco's white skull in the leaves—Sketch's pale face in the branches. Sketch's peoples was his daddy. He had the jobs. He looked now, at the fire blazing from the store, people running like roaches with their beer and meat and diapers. The flames filled the windows like the Kozy Komfort. The other place—Sketch and them hadn't burned the other place. His grandpa's. His uncle's.

"We could get gats for free!" Chris was shouting. "Quit trippin, man, you like lost in space and shit! Let's go!"

Mortrice stood up and faced the plywood for a long minute, breathing in the marker where Teddy had written AK-Rules everywhere. "We could finish Sketch and them job," he said slowly, turning. "We could get paid, big paid, and buy what we want. Zach got the good gats, not pawnshop stuff."

He didn't want pawnshop guns. He wanted the money to pay the gunsmith for bullets. Bullets for the buffalo gun.

"What you talkin bout gettin paid? Sketch ain't had no money. He had some speed. From his daddy." Chris folded his arms, angry now. "Shit, I'm ready to go. Check em out! They hittin up Circuit City and shit!"

Mortrice stood in front of the TV. "Sketch and them didn't do that shit out the blue, man. This dude paid em. Paid em to cap your daddy, man. I ain't playin. I know the dude wanted your daddy capped. You want him or not?"

Hosea heard the helicopter moving through the darkness. The air was warm over the gravel, the last of Alma's wisteria blossoms drying on the ground. Marcus's VW crawled up the short slope like a blue tumbleweed. He got out, rubbing his forehead, and sat on a folding chair. "Shit, Daddy. It's crazy."

"Everybody's blazin," Demetrius said. "Too much, man."

Hosea listened to their voices, deep in the shadowed barn doorway.

Sofelia had just carried combs and oil down the path to the trailers. "I'ma braid Finis's hair," she said. "I missed him."

He saw two thin figures loping up the drive now, and he stood up. "Time to lock the gate and go home," he told Demetrius. "You ain't goin on no jobs. I seen em firin on people in L.A., police and fire and maybe you."

"I heard em shootin at the Gardens a while ago," Octavious said. "Belisa worried cause Bennie and SaRonn ain't came back from L.A."

"Damn!" Marcus stood up. "I forgot she was goin to the beauty shop on Crenshaw!" He ran toward his car, and the two boys came into the light near the barn. Hosea saw Mortrice and the other one, the one he liked to call his cousin.

"Where you goin?" he called to them when they walked toward the path to the trailers.

"Hey, uh, Grampa," Mortrice said. "I left somethin back there."

"Don't be foolin around back there, not tonight," Hosea said. "I ain't in the mood for hearin no strange noise." They shook their heads and blended into the trees. He sat back down. The grandboy's new .22 was locked up in the coldhouse, in a metal box under Hosea's bed. He didn't know what else the boy would have left in Finis's place. Maybe some of the wild music.

A rattle 'of gunfire rose in tiny pops from far away. Maybe the Westside. He hoped Marcus wouldn't drive around. His other sons leaned against the flatbed tow truck for a minute, Demetrius's palm slapping the metal before he turned to go.

His sister's fingers drew the oil through his hair. Braids. SaRonn braided his hair. Last year. Last dance. Last chance.

"Who out there?" his sister whispered. "Listen."

Finis moved to the window. Two boys down by the wheels of Julius's trailer. The love machine. The boys pulled out a bag. "The Blue Q," one said.

"The Blue Q, man, Sketch and them was gon burn that place or the place by the freeway. They the only buildins from here to the Kozy Komfort, right?" Mortrice glanced at the dull gold windows of his uncle's trailer and saw him, the sprung dude with the empty face. He picked up the bag.

"This white dude ain't gon tell you nothin," Chris said.

Mortrice stared at the tarnished silver wall. Kenneth's face, his silver tooth that hardly ever flashed cause he said keep your mouth shut and you find out. "If you shut up, he will," Mortrice said. "Take him to the place by the freeway and shut up, he gon tell us."

They heard the trailer door open, and they ran for the wall, racing down the black corridor under the branches to the canal road.

"Mortrice?" Finis heard Sofelia call someone. "Mortrice?"

More trees? Finis frowned, touching his braids. He followed her outside. She stood, looking into the trunks as if she wasn't sure about the trees. Then she began to run toward the house.

He squinted at his keys, on the chain with the shining stone. In his pocket, he had the finger bones and his pocketknife. He went to the storage lot and opened the gate. Three police cars cruised down the riverbottom road. Walk slow. Walk on by. Walkin in rhythm.

Two stopped at the edge of the hills. No. Not SaRonn's; Agua Dulce. He left the fence corner, his father's land, and felt naked. More police. He walked into the riverbottom. Bamboo. Cane. He pushed into the leaves.

Demetrius's house across the river—he could stay there. He fingered the bones in his pocket. The river was pink silver when he crossed the shallow.

The walls were pink, too. The roofs red. Red house over yonder. Which house? Crosstown traffic on the road. Which house? He walked along the walls, leaping to peer over into yards. Which yard? D'Junior got toys. Which yard? He saw a blue ball on the grass and clung to this part of the wall. Then he pulled up hard and dropped over.

The house was still too warm from being shut up all day. Enchantee lay on the couch. D'Junior and Dylan had whined; D'Junior had whined more when they'd got home and Enchantee had refused to turn on the TV. "No," she'd shouted. "Go upstairs and play in your room."

She'd seen the beginnings of the fists and fires at Abby's, glanced at the TV and stopped cold, the chill of fear like liquid fanning her back. Not again. Fires, shooting, the National Guard. Abby had come into the living room behind her, and Enchantee had turned quickly to leave the room. She didn't want to talk about it. She saw Web Matheson walking down the hallway, heard the same newscaster's voice from the library TV. Enchantee heard him call, "I gotta run, Abby, I got something urgent. Tell Connie I'm working late, okay?"

Now she heard D'Junior calling from upstairs. "Mommy! Mommy!"

She wasn't turning it on just to keep him quiet. She could switch from channel to channel, and he'd see it, either the fires or the damn video, Rodney King's heavy head rising slowly like a just crawling baby unsure even of his knees. If she put in a video, D'Junior would pop it out to see the fires. He and Dylan had stood, fascinated by the flames, their mouths hanging wide.

"Mommy!" he called again. Her aunt would have slapped him, she thought drowsily, turning her cheek to the couch cushion.

Demetrius Junior stared out his bedroom window at the backyard next door. The Tin Man was out there, watering. Not really a Tin Man. The boys across the street said he was nice sometimes and mean sometimes. Their mama said he was old and lonely. But he had silver hair. Silver glasses. A big chest like the Tin Man. He went inside.

The ball was over there. Demetrius kept throwing it over by accident. He saw a man come over the back wall now. The bright lights by the wall came on. A man from Grampa's? The man picked up the ball. Then the Tin Man came back out. He yelled, "What do you want? You want the VCR?" The other man dropped the ball. The Tin Man was yelling bad words. Cussing. He said, "You're a fucking African warrior? You think this is a fucking store and you can loot me like a Korean?"

The other man didn't move. The Tin Man had his silver gun. Demetrius Junior wanted a gun like that. Silver. His mama said no. Dylan's mama said no. The other man had braids like a girl. He put his hands over his ears. The Tin Man shot his gun. The other man fell next to the wall.

Demetrius Junior heard his mother on the stairs. The Tin Man was crying. He said, "No, shit, no. Why'd you do that? I thought you . . ."

He touched the other man's back. The other man must be dead. His face was in the dirt. The Tin Man was crying. He reached in the other man's pockets. Demetrius Junior saw a toy knife. The Tin Man opened the knife and put down his silver gun and scratched his hand with the knife. It wasn't a toy. It made red blood. It was messy. The Tin Man dropped the knife next to the other man and turned around. He was crying.

When her son turned around, away from the window, he looked into the bedroom light, and Enchantee saw the spokes inside his irises, the dark lines spacing the translucent brown of his eyes.

CHAPTER TWENTY

MARCUS SAW THE lights on in her house. "SaRonn!" he called.

Her eyes were surrounded with coronas of red from crying. "It was awful, Marcus, I couldn't believe it," she said, in his arms. "The shop's gone—I saw it go up on TV just now. She put a sign in the window saying 'Black Owned,' and they didn't care."

"You weren't there? You were on the road?"

"Bennie and I saw all the fighting, and we knew we had to go, but Trudy was scared. She was afraid to stay in her shop and afraid to leave it. We took her home, and down the street, me and Bennie saw this white guy taking pictures of a burning building. And three guys started chasin him, they were gonna beat the shit out of him. He was runnin, I guess to his car, and—" She wiped at her tears. "One brother started shootin at him. I backed up the car, and Bennie opened the door and told him, 'Get your white ass in here.'"

"Sounds like Bennie," Marcus said, trying to smile.

She was trancelike now. "He was laying all across the front seat, and Willa was screamin in the back, and I heard more shots. He said, 'Silverlake, take me to Silverlake.' I was trying to calm him down, tellin him I used to live in Echo Park. He hugged me and Bennie at the hospital. Our clothes are washin right now. Blood all over. But he showed me—the bullet just went across hi—"

She was touching his arm. Marcus said, "His bicep."

SaRonn nodded. "He was so scared."

"You were hella brave," Marcus said, her head on his chest again.

"No," she whispered. "I was scared, too. Scared of brothers. Of everybody."

When someone knocked, she jerked up from his arms. "Eight was worried."

But it was B-Real. "Mr. Thompson? I saw your Bug. I gotta talk to you."

Outside, Marcus heard people talking in the yards up and down the street, sitting under the trees, cigarette embers rising and falling, voices louder and then soft. "They always talk shit about me, about One World," B-Real said. "But I ain't down for smokin brothas. I ain't down for smokin nobody, and I can't tell who they gon cap. Maybe Samana, man, maybe somebody else."

"What the hell you talkin about?" Marcus said.

B-Real told him about the AK tattoos, about the guns and Sketch. "I think my brother Finis tried to tell me Samana shot Usher," Marcus said, frowning.

"I told you, I don't really know who they goin after," B-Real said. "I didn't know who to tell, man." He paused. "When we were writin, on the walls, we were writin 'Treetown Anybody Killa $.' And Mortrice said somethin about money tonight."

"Thanks, man," Marcus said, turning to go into SaRonn's for his keys.

B-Real said, "I can go to the movies, you know, see all that cappin. But I can't watch people gettin beat down, like in the face—like the trucker dude or Rodney King. It's like—" He turned toward his van, shielding his face from Marcus, and drove away.

Marcus stood in SaRonn's living room. "Ain't no way I can stop Samana or Mortrice," he said to himself. "Not me. Shit. I gotta call Harley."

He dialed, thinking that anyone he knew from Treetown would slam the receiver out of his hand. But he spoke to the answering voice that said, "Homicide."

"Can I talk to Detective Harley?"

The voice was harrassed. "Everyone's out in the street tonight, okay? Are you calling to report a homicide?"

"No, but . . ."

"Call back if somebody's dead, okay?" The voice was cut off.

"Damn," Marcus said, seeing SaRonn peer out into the short hallway.

"I gotta go, SaRonn. I'ma be back, and I'll holler so you know it's me."

He drove slowly up to the corner of Pepper and Grove, looking at a small white truck backing out of his father's gate. The truck had gardening equipment in the back, and a logo painted on the door. Darnell Tucker, he thought. Demetrius was closing the gate in the dark, the chain link glinting, and Marcus turned up Pepper toward downtown, not having any idea except to stop at the doughnut shop.

When he approached the underpass, he saw several figures running in the vacant lot before the minimall, and then small tongues of flame rose from the edges of the last store, the liquor store. Darnell Tucker's truck veered off the road and into the parking lot, and Marcus followed.

Darnell and another man ran for the back of the store, and Marcus saw the Korean owner with a hose. When the man saw the three of them running toward him, he began to shout, "I shoot you, motherfucker, don't come over here!"

"I'ma help you with the fire!" Darnell shouted, and the small Mexican man with him grabbed the hose. Darnell went into the back doorway of the store, and he came out with a fire extinguisher.

The Korean man was sobbing, screaming at the store itself. Marcus looked beyond him to where a group of men was gathered at the back of another store, and then he heard Som's voice.

Running down the narrow parking lot, Marcus saw Som waving his arms and shouting at three men who were advancing on his doorway. Larry Cotton—Marcus saw Cotton's face, heard him say, "Get out the way, Jap, cause I ain't playin." Then he saw Cotton back away and stumble, and all three men scrambled along the cinder-block wall in the back.

Samana was holding his gun, walking slow. "Fuck a Jap," he said. "I am Khmer, motherfucker, you don't even know that is a country." He fired at the men, and the bullet sent sparks off the wall. Cotton and the others ran along the edge. Marcus shouted, "Samana! Som! It's Marcus, don't fire on me, man! Marcus!"

Samana kept the gun leveled at him, and Som pushed the barrel down. "Teacher! Come inside before somebody shoot!"

A police car hurtled down the back lot now, and Marcus heard a fire engine's siren approaching. He stayed in the doorway, letting Som go out, waving his arms. "Right here!" Som screamed when the car stopped.

Salcido peered out of the window, and Marcus saw Tommy Flair driving the patrol car. "Marcus?"

"Salcido, man, I need to talk to you!" Marcus shouted. "No, not this!" He peered into the shop, knowing Samana had run. Som was shouting wildly at Tommy Flair, who'd gotten out of the car and was walking down the lot with his gun drawn.

"This is fucked up," Flair shouted. "I gotta cover the firefighters."

Salcido was panting. "Man, they're firing on the EMTs in L.A., firing on everyone. Better not happen here."

"Darnell Tucker and some dude are over there," Marcus shouted at Tommy Flair. "They're puttin out the fire, man, don't shoot them!" He turned to Salcido. "One of my kids at school told me somethin's about to go down," he said, "and I think the other kid just booked up. Out the front." He could smell the mentholatum and incense from the small back room, and Som came from the front counter, shaking his head.

"He is go," he said. "He run again."

"How you know he drive a Blazer?" Chris said. Teddy was driving one of the Proudfoots' old cars, an ancient brown Cadillac.

"I heard my mama's uncle talk about him," Mortrice said, watching the blue towers that were purple now in the dark, except for jack-o'-lantern eyes and mouth lights. Teddy was cruising slow around the parking lot, and Mortrice was watching for The Finest or the helicopter, but so far he'd seen only the Blazer and two other cars in the spaces.

He'd told Chris to keep the music low, and Chris sang, "When I pick up my AK, every fool gon have to pay."

But Mortrice held the buffalo gun in the backseat, touching the etched stock and the brass cutouts, feeling the long, heavy barrel when he raised it toward the window. When the dude came out, he'd have to put this away and bring out the .9. But he wanted to hold this one now. Kenneth had the AKs. Black, ugly, small: He had the buffalo gun.

"That the dude?" Teddy said. Mortrice saw the suited guy striding from the doorway of the lobby, a briefcase in his hands, his gleaming forehead like a valentine. The car alarm beeped like a tiny alien.

"Yeah," Mortrice said. "The one in the paper. Drive up slow, man."

When Teddy was alongside the Blazer, Mortrice got out and pointed the .9 at Matheson, who turned quickly with keys in his hand.

"Don't holler, man, I ain't gon shoot, I just don't want you to run away," Mortrice said. He didn't want to talk so much. "The man on Lowell Street send me. Mr. Roberts. Send me for the Treetown job. The—conflagration."

He waited. The man was breathing so hard he couldn't talk. "I thought you wanted the car," he said finally.

"I want the car," Teddy said out of the open window, and Mortrice glared at him.

"Mr. Roberts already called you?" Matheson said, his shoulders slumping a little, his key hand falling to his leg. Then he looked around. "We can't stand out here and talk."

Mortrice slipped the gun into his pocket. "Get in the back," he said.

"No, I—"

"Come on," Mortrice said. "We ain't got time."

Matheson's face was tight when he slid into the backseat, putting his briefcase between his feet. "I can't believe this, I mean, I just called Roberts, and since there are so many fires anyway, he said this would be a good time. But he said he'd call me back."

"We ain't got time," Mortrice said again, and Teddy pulled slowly away from the Blazer.

"What about the money?" Matheson said, his voice shaky. "Did he pay you?"

Chris turned slantwise to stare at Matheson from the shotgun seat. "You the one always payin ducats, right?" he said. "Cappin for ducats. Niggas for dollas."

"Excuse me?" Matheson looked back at Mortrice, his eyes smaller now. "Did he pay you half?"

"Ain't no half-steppin," Chris crowed. "We all the way live."

"I don't know what your friend's talking about," Matheson said.

"Stall out," Mortrice said to Chris. He turned to Matheson. "He said you gon pay, cause we in a hurry."

"How do I know you know what you're talking about?" Matheson said, his open fingers cupping his knees hard now. "This could be a fucking robbery."

"Teddy," Mortrice said. "Go." To Matheson, he said, "Cause we gon take you by the place for the job, and then you know if we right. Huh?''

Teddy drove past the Kozy Komfort, and Mortrice heard Chris singing softly to himself, facing the window. Under the freeway, he could hear Matheson's shallow breath shuffling from his nose. Teddy slowed at the old packing house, turning onto the shoulder and sliding the Cadillac's tires into the two grooved lines cutting through the tall weeds after the crumbled stone. The headlights cut off, and the hulking wooden building was pale gray in the moonlight, the empty windows dark. Teddy nosed up around the back and turned the Cadillac around in the dusty ground near the pig fence, circling around a huge pile of pallets.

Mortrice pointed to the packing house and then to the trees past the canal curving around to the right. "This one and that one, right?'' he said.

"Yeah," Matheson said, frowning. "Both of em. Something happened last time—you guys didn't do it.''

"Wasn't us," Chris said, but Mortrice took out the .9.

"Go inside and make sure you gettin what you payin for," he said. Matheson stared at the gun. "I don't know what the hell . . .''

"Get out.'' Mortrice pushed the gun slightly forward. He felt the buffalo gun near his feet. Matheson opened his door and half-fell out onto the dirt, leaving his briefcase on the car floor when Mortrice swayed the gun over it. "You don't need that.''

They walked into the broken doorway under the splintered wood. The first room was small and completely black, smelling of piss, and then they were inside the cave of the packing house, where old broken tables had been partially burned for heat. Mortrice saw a heap of blankets in the far corner, but he didn't want to know what was in them or not. He saw Matheson trying not to breathe, holding his chest up like a pigeon, saying, "You're really screwing up now. How do you expect to get paid?''

"We gettin paid," Chris sang.

"Why you want to burn this, man?'' Mortrice asked him, and the man's face tightened to a fist.

"Because it's fucking useless," he said. "What the hell do you care? Do you want the money or not?''

"Yeah, I want the money," Mortrice said. "You want the dirt.'' He smiled. "Who's your great-grandpa, some goddamn Pilgrim or some shit like that, huh? He ain't even from round here. Indians was here first."

"You're losing me," Matheson said, his voice steady again. "If you're not the ones hired to do the job, then why don't we . . ."

"I'm a motherfuckin sand moth, man," Mortrice said, and Chris stared at him. "I'm a nectar-lovin nigga, okay?"

"Mortrice," Teddy called from the doorway of the small room, his voice muffled by wood. "Come here, man. Hurry up."

"Chris, man, you got him?" Mortrice said, seeing Chris nod over his own .9. Teddy had the little .25. Mortrice walked carefully along the edge of the room and peered out into the doorway. "What, man?"

A tall woman with skin like beige paper stepped out in front of him and said, "You Sofelia boy. Put that gun down. Cause I got two right here."

Mortrice saw the tiny derringer in her hand, only a foot from his chest. He lowered his .9, and she took it away from him, putting it into a deep square pocket in her apron. Then she backed him up into the big, echoing room.

"You Sofelia boy," she repeated. "She come and tell me what you think you doin. You ain't doin' nothin. Come here."

She walked him over to Matheson and Chris, who stared at her. "Miz Thompson?" Chris said. Mortrice saw her eyebrows, crooked black lines drawn too high over silver, puckered crescents in her forehead.

"Move, now," she whispered. "Right here by the table." Then she turned to Matheson, his mouth as wide as an envelope, his lips moving.

"Mrs. Thompson," he said. "I know . . ."

"You know you done wrong when you come on my land last time. Talkin bout 'You so pretty . . .' She looked at Mortrice. "Your mama—she coulda been my girl. She so pretty. And I never want her to get hurt. But men be . . ." She lowered the derringer a few inches. "I see only thing hurt her now is you messin up."

"Mrs. Thompson," Matheson tried again, and she swung on him quickly.

"They boys," she said, low and fast. "And you a half-grown boy try and mess up a *man's* property. No. Uh-uh, don't even speak. You ain't takin nothin from me, and you ain't messin up this boy life with you. Messin up his mind with yo dead body."

She shot him three times in the chest, and he twisted backward and fell against the damp floor near the wall. Then she stood very still, listening. Mortrice heard a trickling like rain, a whisper of feet in the tall weeds, and then a bright, glittering smash that lit the small outer room with gold.

Marcus loped slowly under the flood-control tunnel, breathing the acrid wet air. He didn't want to get too close to Samana. Shit, Samana had a gun, and Marcus only had a voice. He came out into the warm, soft air and saw Samana's black T-shirt like a flag, bobbing around the silver wood of the old packing house. Samana crouched and walked three times, then stopped to flick a lighter and throw a sparkling bottle into the building. He ran toward the canal road, and the rush of flame seared Marcus's eyes.

The gaping windows were yellow now. Marcus shielded his face with his fingers, but he heard hollering like barking dogs, smelled chemical steam lifting from the burning wood. Three figures fell from the windows, dropping to the dirt like huge ants that ran blindly toward him.

"Mortrice!" Marcus shouted, seeing the boy's face, and all three swerved off. "You can't do this AK shit!" He followed him around the side of the packing house, where he saw a ghostly, pale figure with a white square for a belly crossing the canal bridge and disappearing into the pecan trees, hovering there like a feeding night moth.

Mortrice had stopped near a car in the weeds, the tires already ringed with flames. The chemical smell was overwhelming now, and the whole building crackled and hissed with falling wood.

But it was Chris who turned to face him, holding a gun. "Who that fool?" Chris shouted, his voice high, and Marcus saw the wide, shaky reflections in his eyes. He could telll the boy didn't recognize him in the flaring light. "Back off, cause we strapped!" Marcus held up his hands to show they were empty, and the bullet pulled his palm backward before dropping him in the weeds.

He lay with his eyes open, sparks drifting overhead like red insects, approaching footsteps crushing dry stems. Mortrice bent over him. "He got the fever," Mortrice said. He touched the outstretched hand. "Shit. What you know about AK? You don't know, man." He pulled Marcus up by the other hand. "Come on, we take you downtown to the hospital."

Marcus saw Chris aiming at the fire, shooting into the flames engulfing the car. "Walkin?" Marcus gasped. "With you guys? Shit, get me killed. I'm all right. I'ma go home." He looked across the canal, but the blood drained from his head and left a black film over his eyes. The weeds were racing scarlet now, toward them.

"Home to your daddy's?" Mortrice hollered, backing away. Marcus took a few steps toward the cool, slipping water. "Marcus. Tell my mama I'ma be gone for a while. Tell her I went to Tulsa, man, okay? I'ma be back. I ain't . . ."

Marcus knelt for a minute, hearing the car's gas tank explode. His hand had disappeared, had flown off into the dry grass, he thought, but streaks and torrents of pain raced up from his wrist to his elbow, to his shoulder, and he pushed himself up with the other hand. Walk. He'd have to cross the canal behind his father's fence; he stumbled toward the path Samana had taken, the glisten of fire in the wild oats just behind him.

Hosea had gone into the coldhouse to see what he would do after they told him about Finis. Demetrius's wife had called, crying, to say that someone had shot Finis, and Demetrius and Alma had driven over the bridge. Hosea sat on his bed. He looked at the empty mouth of his fireplace. He had taken a drink of Oscar's hard whiskey. Then he let himself cry silently, not moving his shoulders or hands. Nothing but his mouth, stretching.

His face hurt. The TV screen had jerked crazily with shattering glass storefronts, people streaming from doorways like ants, racing cars. Gunfire chasing away a fire engine while someone lay on a sidewalk.

The white men had broken into the armory that night, when he stood in the doorway smelling hot bricks; they had carried guns from the hardware stores, and tools and clothes. He'd seen their arms full when he got to the mouth of the alley. The black man lay twisting and moaning under the huge sign of the blond woman, and the circle of white men held the ambulance back with pointed guns.

He heard the rapid stutter of gunfire again, heard more sirens in the distance, and the helicopter whined overhead. Then he heard shots, closer, somewhere on Pepper Avenue, and the helicopter's beam strafed his trees. He felt as if he were shrinking in the chair, back to his boy legs, his skull tight, his father's Chinese eyes.

Hosea knelt near his bed and pulled out the case with the new .22. His grandson's gun. The metal smelled of oil and bluing, cold still and too sharp. He loaded the gun. Walking toward the olive grove and the back fence, he felt it too light, not the right weight like his old gun. His grandfather's gun.

The helicopter circled and locked on to something; the noise was deafening, roaring chatter like the planes and machine guns over Greenwood. He didn't know he'd bitten his tongue until he tasted his own blood, clinging to the back of his throat when he neared the olive shed.

Marcus ran along the slope of the hill where the road rose up to the brush. His arm was fading now, too, his shoulder like an exposed joint sheared off, lonely, and his head was blurred. Finis in his trailer now. He's back. Go over the fence. We fixed the fence.

His feet slid loudly on the decomposed granite where the hill came right down steep to the canal's edge, and he crouched for a moment, looking for the plank bridge, hearing his own voice, hoarse. "Goddamnit!" His eyes dimmed and then saw the water trembling dark green, the strap of wood, the black mouth of the intake.

He saw the flash in the trees, heard the shot go past him and hiss into the tiny pebbles. Falling on his good arm, his feet went, cool and floating, away from him first, then the rest of him slid into the water that pulled him, gentle and smooth, along the slick, mossy channel.

He raised his head, his shoes scuffing along the bottom. His fingers scraped the cement, and his feet planted on a metal grate. Piece of shopping cart, he thought, his ears full of water, his eyes shedding liquid. He could see feet and knees, boots and work pants, behind the chain link. "Daddy?" he called. "Daddy?"

The shivering pressure pushed on his chest now, water working like it was supposed to, and the metal gave way in the watery grass. He fell sideways again, sliding under, seeing the lip of dark close over him in the intake.

The dank cave was only a few inches above the water. Marcus turned and swirled, his good hand hitting the side, sliding off, hitting the side and scrabbling for the chunk. He found it, but he could barely breathe through his nose, the water filling his mouth. He tried to seal his lips, peering into the stripe of light to see a white shape near the entrance, a white cloth hanging into the water. A hand dropped something in the canal, something that bumped him hard in the neck. A silvery small fish, solid and heavy, then gone clattering through the grate behind him. The cloth floated down to him now, and he felt it near his mouth. Grabbing it, he felt the cloth pulling slowly. Then a long stick came alongside it, and he pulled harder on that, sliding his feet forward for rocks or holes or debris to anchor him.

His father's hand was reaching under the last few inches of the concrete now, and he felt the bone-hard fingers grasp his shirt, then his shoulder. His father was crouched, knees digging into the earth, and AintieLila grabbed his other shoulder. Marcus screamed with pain, and they pulled him out onto the bank. He fell on the heap of shredded bark along the fence, the acrid dry scent of oil racing into his throat.

CHAPTER
TWENTY-ONE

AT DAWN, ALMA lay next to Hosea in the bed under the apricot-filled window. The fruit pressed against the screen, rubbing in the breeze.

She had waited all this time for the death of an infant, shrunken and helpless; for the death of a child, the bacteria floating into a small cut or grinning mouth; for the death of one of the fighting, hard-eyed boys, falling from a tire iron or knife or bullet fired by an angry Treetown rival.

Finis had lain in the barren backyard for hours, while Enchantee sobbed and police measured and squatted and wrote. The neighbor had sat quietly in a plastic chair next to his back door, his hand loosely bandaged, while they asked him questions.

Finis was being cut open. He was downtown.

Alma heard Hosea's harsh, steady breathing. She slid from the bed to the floor.

When Sofelia hadn't come home, all those years, Alma had kept waiting for the bad news, the good news, any news, and by then, it was too late to do what she'd always thought she would when one of them was gone. She knew she would crawl.

She lay flat on the cool hardwood floor near the bed, feeling her damp skin on the boards. Summer heat was here. She could smell the lemon oil on her floors, the waxy-citrus shine as if she were crawling under her own trees, in her own grove.

Pulling herself along by the elbows, each new section cooler until she passed over it, she slithered into the hallway. At the next doorway, she saw saw them all laid out like tamales in their sheets on the floor, where there was room for them all. Kendrick, Jawan, Jalima, D'Junior. Enchantee lay on the bed. She couldn't go back to the house across the river.

Alma slid into the front room, table legs like beams before her eyes. Sofelia lay on the couch. Her boy Mortrice was gone. Hosea had told her, when they took Marcus to the hospital, and she had only nodded, lips tight.

Julius sprawled in the big chair, his feet wide on the floor, his mouth trailing sleep-spit. She passed his shoes. He'd heard about Finis from someone already, and he'd come home until the burial. He hadn't said yet where he'd been, and Alma crawled toward the kitchen, not sure she wanted to know at all.

The candles were lit at the Madonna's feet, and she glowed in the dim archway. Alma knew her grandmother was already awake. She put her palms flat on the threshold of the kitchen, where the tile floor was porous and she could dig her nails into the ancient grouting.

Her grandmother stood at the stove, her tiny feet in the round-toed lace-up shoes she wore every day. They were close to Alma's cheek, blunt as puppy noses, and then Abuela bent and crouched near her, holding a hot tortilla, the brown lightly-burnt circles still smoking.

Alma leaned her head on her arm at the table, chewing the gritty corn with her eyes closed.

Abuela poured coffee in front of her, set out the plates of *chorizo* and *huevos* with *salsa* and then put Alma's palm around the jar of last year's apricot jam. Her grandmother sat across from her, the tiny eyes like seeds, the nose bent hard like a turtle, the fingers moving her own into a soft clasp. *"Mi hija,"* she whispered. *"Mi hijita."* My little girl. My child.

The last thing Marcus remembered before the long sleep was the waiting room, the other bleeding, coughing people, the blaring TV, and finally Paul Moyer, his voice trembling. "The rampage of looting and arson has reached the landmark Frederick's of Hollywood store. People, they are burning history in Hollywood."

"Oh, now it counts," Marcus remembered murmuring, and his father staring at him. Then he dropped off.

SaRonn came to his room on the second floor. "I heard about your brother, baby, I'm sorry. I'm sorry for me, too. All of us." She lay on the bed beside him after she'd closed the door, crying silently, her head on his chest. His bandaged hand lay useless in the channel of blankets beside him, and his good hand rested on her head.

Finis was in the newspaper she brought, as the final paragraph in a roundup of local riot news and victims.

The front page story was dominated by a large picture of Lanier's pigs. Marcus stared at the blackened heaps around their snouts.

"In an incredible photograph showing the wide swath of riot damage in southern California, pigs are shown rooting through ashes in rural Rio Seco. The city, sixty miles east of Los Angeles, suffered several incidents in the urban unrest that exploded after the Rodney King verdicts. This dilapidated building was burned to the ground, but it is believed that only transients might have been inside. Some charred evidence of habitation were found, but as in many other burned buildings in Los Angeles, no remains can be positively identified."

Marcus put down the paper for a moment. SaRonn went into the hospital bathroom, and he heard water running. He glanced at the rest of the article.

"Scattered reports of rioting came in from San Francisco, Las Vegas, and Atlanta; closer to home, Pomona, San Bernardino, Long Beach, and Rio Seco reported violence or looting.

"In the city of Rio Seco, the SuperSave market was looted and burned while owners Reza Soltani and Essey Borzog watched helplessly. Several people were injured in random shooting incidents, and one man was killed in a riot-related shooting. Finis Thompson, 32, was apparently attempting to break into a Rivercrest home hours after the unrest began; when Thompson, of the Treetown area, wounded the homeowner with a knife, he was shot and killed. Police are investigating; the homeowner has not been charged."

Harley came into the room when SaRonn was drying her face. Marcus saw Harley's mouth working hard, and he nodded. "I'm sorry about your brother," Harley said, standing uncomfortably. "I came to tell you thanks for the information about the Cambodian kid. Salcido pieced more of it together."

"There's another chair right here," Marcus said, and Harley sat down.

"Usher Price had a forty-five-caliber slug from a stolen CHP weapon in his chest," Harley said. "Same kind of slug, from the same gun, was in the wall behind the doughnut shop. Salcido told me what happened the other night. So it looks like the owner's nephew—"

"Samana," Marcus said.

"He gave his grandma a bunch of money, and then he ran away for good. He left her a piece of paper saying he was going to Texas, to join some gang called the Cold-Blooded Cambodians. I had to get most of this out of the uncle."

Marcus nodded. SaRonn said, "Was this one of your students?"

"Yeah," Marcus said. "You think he shot the other two kids."

Harley shrugged. "Different gun. It's hard to tell." He stood up. "Thanks for your help, though. I'm still working on the two kids, and I don't have conclusive evidence or proof about the two girls or the cross-dresser or the guy in the Kozy Komfort."

"The shadow man," Marcus murmured.

Harley looked at him. "Yeah. Lotta shadows out there, huh? We got Web Matheson's wife sure he got car-jacked, but it looks like he skipped town or something. That's a great one to sort out. All right. I hope you get the use of your hand back."

"The doctor said it should be stiff but usable. All I ever do is write and read and talk. It's not like I do any hard work. That's all I hear," Marcus said.

Harley raised his thick eyebrows like leaping fingers. "Hey, that's what I do, and I call it hard as hell."

The hand throbbed and ached, and Marcus tried to imagine what his father's shoulder had felt like months before. Months of the shit, he thought, dressing in his street clothes. The shit has gotta be over.

The doctor said no infection had set in, and Marcus didn't tell him about the canal water washing his blood down the grate, washing whatever organisms into the webbing of tendon and bone and skin that was puckered and raw around the two holes. "You weren't too close to the guy, huh?" the doctor had said, and Marcus shook his head. "All that gunfire we had, I'm surprised we didn't get more random bullet wounds like this."

He stared at the hand now, waiting for SaRonn to help him tie his shoes, thinking, His blood's all over Daddy's orange trees, Abuela's olive trees, and Uncle Oscar's place. Mixed in with all that choc dumped over the years.

SaRonn came into the room with a bag for his things. "You ready?" she said. "You comin to my place and rest. I won't let Willa jump on you unless you want her to."

"Only after you do," he said. But he walked over to the mirror slowly, his laces dragging, to look at his hollowed-out face. Like Finis, he thought, when I don't eat much. His eyes were clear from so much sleep, his hair was puffy-long, growing out from the fade. I can't handle braids, he thought. I gotta get a trim. Tomorrow's the funeral. Don't say good-bye. Say, I'll check, man. I'll check.

Enchantee spread the newspaper over the table at work. The voices creaked into her headset. Late paper. Stolen paper. Wet paper. She tapped the computer keys, murmured into the tiny piece of metal near her mouth.

At lunch, she and Janine read silently.

EMBATTLED DEVELOPER HAD TROUBLE CHASING HIM;
WEB MATHESON APPARENTLY ABANDONS CAMPAIGN AND LIFE

From the endangered sand moths and fairy shrimp in their natural habitat to the creditors pressing him for loan payments to the floodwaters inundating his exclusive golf-course community, Web Matheson's recent problems had mounted to the point that police feel he may have decided to disappear, leaving his numerous troubles behind for a new life elsewhere.

Matheson had withdrawn the last of his personal savings from a Rio Seco bank the afternoon of his disappearance, and his wife reported that he had called her, sounding distraught and angry, to say he would be working very late. His new Chevy Blazer was seen by a casual acquaintance that night, heading eastward on the freeway toward the desert, where he had recently purchased a large tract of land for which his payments were delinquent ...

Janine said, "I see y'all ain't gettin no bridge now," and she laid another newspaper section near Enchantee.

The City Council has decided to shelve plans for the Historic Gateway Corridor at this time. In light of the recent unrest in part of the area considered for the project, along with the disappearance of developer Web Matheson, who had supported the plan, council members voted to scrap plans for the restored bridge and freeway entrance until further studies have been made. The council voted increased funding for crime prevention and police staffing ...

"He was Abby's brother-in-law," Enchantee said, looking at the campaign photo. "His wife's having a baby any day now, and he's gone. In the wind. Like they always say about Treetown brothers."

"Hey," Janine said. "Like men in general, okay?"

After work, Enchantee had to drive to Abby's to drop off a coat she'd borrowed. A dark, Indian-featured woman she'd never seen before answered the door, frowning at her. "Abby?" Enchantee said, holding up the coat, and the woman nodded warily and let her in, pointing to the living room.

Enchantee heard several voices, one loud and professional that she didn't recognize. She stopped at the small table with the blue bowl and one floating pink camellia. "Okay, now, if you've got the gun with the safety off, and an intruder is approximately ..."

She touched the camellia petals. Carrie Smith Donohue's clear, irritated voice cut him off. "You're all being remarkably paranoid."

The professional voice said, "Hey, I'm from Utah. This place is one disaster after another—fires, floods, earthquakes. But if you want to learn how to handle riots and criminals ..."

But Carrie Smith Donohue wasn't finished. Enchantee spun the camellia in the water and heard, "Really, this is no different than any other place with a Mediterranean climate and residents of Mediterranean temperament. You have the weather, the heat, and you have people of varying southern-type bloods—Indians, Spaniards, and Africans. And I feel terrible for Connie, but even though Web was from Orange County, his grandfather was orginally from the Ozarks. White trash. Blood is—"

"Carrie, shut up for once, huh?" Abby's father cut in. "I've got things to do, if the gentleman can finish his presentation."

Enchantee put the coat on the floor in the foyer and turned to go. She was outside when Abby came around the corner of the house.

"Chani! I was checking on Dylan in the back. God, he misses you. Lourdes is Salvadoran, she's really nice, but she can't have a conversation with him."

"D'Junior misses Dylan, too," Enchantee said carefully. "You guys are having a class, huh?"

"It's so stupid," Abby said. "Some former sheriff with a security firm came over because my mom wants to hear about protection. Bent won't do it. He says he's not falling for mass mentality. He says look at guys like Marcus." Abby put her hand on Enchantee's arm. "But aren't you glad you weren't in your old neighborhood?"

"It was scary all over," Enchantee said, heading down the walkway under the roses. "I'll see you."

She drove down Pepper to the house on the corner of Olive and Grove. Ocie Mae's old house. Her granddaughter was renting it to Demetrius for a few dollars. SaRonn had fixed it up. Enchantee stood on the stone steps, looking inside. She hadn't been able to go back to her house yet. Maybe someday. D'Junior came running outside, holding a stick. "Uncle Marcus get shot, too!"

"I know," Enchantee said, taking the stick away.

Hosea handed the hubcap to Octavious. He and Kickstand and Nacho King stood around looking at the car.

"Oh, man, check him out! He got the '52 Chevy, the dual carbs . . ."

"Man, your cousin wantin a hooptie, I got a '66 Rivvy for sale at the crib, come check it out. Got them original skirts."

Hosea saw Marcus walk slowly up the gravel drive, his hand in a sling. His chest ached with a sharp, stabbing pain, and he leaned against the stones, feeling for the jar of choc he'd put on the flat rock shelf. He took a drink, seeing the sun falling behind the trees along the riverbottom in the distance. Tomorrow he would bury his walking son, his ghost-eyed son. This one came up, trying to grin, his forehead clear and unmarked, his wire-rimmed glasses hiding his eyes.

"The Rivvy," Marcus said to Octavious and the other men. "The Deuce and a Quarter. The El Dog. What you gon sell me, Eight, my brother? I'm tired of my Funkytown Bug."

"You got any money?" Kickstand said, and they all laughed.

Oscar came out of the coldhouse, motioning for Hosea to follow him to the palm-lined fence overlooking the riverbottom. "Marcus bringin back his reporter friend sometime," Oscar said. "He were okay for a sherbert. He ain't drank a drop a choc—he throw that up if I give it to him. But he ate him some chitlins."

Hosea looked at his brother. "You let them pigs out day after that fire—didn't none of em run?"

"Hell, no," Oscar said, looking at the river. "Soon as them ashes was cool, I let em look for what they want in there. And Lanier dropped a load a lettuce and strawberries somebody thrown out the market. They ain't foolish. They went on back in."

Hosea nodded. He'd heard what Marcus had said the newspaper wrote about Matheson running away, what the detective had told them. More drug chemicals—ether—just like the Kozy Komfort fire. But Oscar wasn't saying anything.

Hosea turned to walk back, and he saw his wife's grandmother sitting in a bronze-painted chair near her rose garden, watching a large moth move so fast from flower to flower that Hosea could barely see a blur. She looked up at him and pointed to the movement. *"Angel. Paloma de la luz,"* she said, but she could see that he didn't understand. "Nobody see," she whispered, her tongue hesitant.

The apricots were still green. The other fruit was just pebble-sized. The olive trees were covered with their dangling sprays of tiny florets.

In May, the only thing Paz harvested was the mirage of water. The jacaranda tree bloomed now, the fern-swayed branches turning to bursts of lavender trumpet flowers that eventually wilted and fell during the warmer days, until the trunk was circled with a pond of pale blue. All she gathered was the scent of jasmine tangled with the roses in the corner and the sight of the icy blue carpet near her feet, before the heat of summer swept in with Santa Ana gusts. When she looked across the river at the spirit lake, still trembling in the saddle of the hills the way it would for months, she felt the cool wafting across the water and through the branches, to touch her folded hands.

CHAPTER TWENTY-ONE

AT DAWN, ALMA lay next to Hosea in the bed under the apricot-filled window. The fruit pressed against the screen, rubbing in the breeze.

She had waited all this time for the death of an infant, shrunken and helpless; for the death of a child, the bacteria floating into a small cut or grinning mouth; for the death of one of the fighting, hard-eyed boys, falling from a tire iron or knife or bullet fired by an angry Treetown rival.

Finis had lain in the barren backyard for hours, while Enchantee sobbed and police measured and squatted and wrote. The neighbor had sat quietly in a plastic chair next to his back door, his hand loosely bandaged, while they asked him questions.

Finis was being cut open. He was downtown.

Alma heard Hosea's harsh, steady breathing. She slid from the bed to the floor.

When Sofelia hadn't come home, all those years, Alma had kept waiting for the bad news, the good news, any news, and by then, it was too late to do what she'd always thought she would when one of them was gone. She knew she would crawl.

She lay flat on the cool hardwood floor near the bed, feeling her damp skin on the boards. Summer heat was here. She could smell the lemon oil on her floors, the waxy-citrus shine as if she were crawling under her own trees, in her own grove.

Pulling herself along by the elbows, each new section cooler until she passed over it, she slithered into the hallway. At the next doorway, she saw saw them all laid out like tamales in their sheets on the floor, where there was room for them all. Kendrick, Jawan, Jalima, D'Junior. Enchantee lay on the bed. She couldn't go back to the house across the river.

Alma slid into the front room, table legs like beams before her eyes. Sofelia lay on the couch. Her boy Mortrice was gone. Hosea had told her, when they took Marcus to the hospital, and she had only nodded, lips tight.

Julius sprawled in the big chair, his feet wide on the floor, his mouth trailing sleep-spit. She passed his shoes. He'd heard about Finis from someone already, and he'd come home until the burial. He hadn't said yet where he'd been, and Alma crawled toward the kitchen, not sure she wanted to know at all.

The candles were lit at the Madonna's feet, and she glowed in the dim archway. Alma knew her grandmother was already awake. She put her palms flat on the threshold of the kitchen, where the tile floor was porous and she could dig her nails into the ancient grouting.

Her grandmother stood at the stove, her tiny feet in the round-toed lace-up shoes she wore every day. They were close to Alma's cheek, blunt as puppy noses, and then Abuela bent and crouched near her, holding a hot tortilla, the brown lightly-burnt circles still smoking.

Alma leaned her head on her arm at the table, chewing the gritty corn with her eyes closed.

Abuela poured coffee in front of her, set out the plates of *chorizo* and *huevos* with *salsa* and then put Alma's palm around the jar of last year's apricot jam. Her grandmother sat across from her, the tiny eyes like seeds, the nose bent hard like a turtle, the fingers moving her own into a soft clasp. *"Mi hija,"* she whispered. *"Mi hijita."* My little girl. My child.

The last thing Marcus remembered before the long sleep was the waiting room, the other bleeding, coughing people, the blaring TV, and finally Paul Moyer, his voice trembling. "The rampage of looting and arson has reached the landmark Frederick's of Hollywood store. People, they are burning history in Hollywood."

"Oh, now it counts," Marcus remembered murmuring, and his father staring at him. Then he dropped off.

SaRonn came to his room on the second floor. "I heard about your